THE COMPLETE
KEEPER CHRONICLES

TANYA HUFF
THE COMPLETE
KEEPER CHRONICLES

SUMMON THE KEEPER

THE SECOND SUMMONING

LONG HOT SUMMONING

DAW BOOKS, INC.

DONALD A. WOLLHEIM, FOUNDER
375 Hudson Street, New York, NY 10014
ELIZABETH R. WOLLHEIM
SHEILA E. GILBERT
PUBLISHERS
http://www.dawbooks.com

First Printing, December 2012

1 2 3 4 5 6 7 8 9

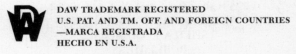

INTRODUCTION

"Dying is easy. Comedy is hard."
 —attributed to Edmund Gwenn on his deathbed, September 6th, 1959

I don't know about the dying part—not yet—but Mr. Gwenn was right about comedy being hard. We all cry at essentially the same thing, but a sense of humor is significantly more unique.

When I started writing *Summon the Keeper* back in 1997, I had every intention of writing funny urban fantasy. Not a book with humorous elements—because even tragedy requires that—but a book where the emphasis was on making people laugh. And you know what? It was hard. Writing humor you not only have to get the plot, the characters, and the pacing right, but every decision has to be weighed. Is it funnier if I write it this way? Is this a funnier word than that? Does this go too far? Does this descend into farce?

Granted, I front-loaded the humorous possibilities with Austin, a cat based on a real Austin who was scary smart and, except for actually holding conversations, did everything book Austin did. (Real Austin made pronouncements, he didn't hold conversations.)

I whined and complained so much about humor being hard while writing *Summon the Keeper* that it came as a total surprise—to me—when I did it again in *The Second Summoning* and then again in *Long Hot Summoning*. But you know what? If it isn't hard, you're not challenging yourself. It—for many differing definitions of it—is supposed to be hard.

I like to think I rose to the challenge. I think these books about Keepers and Cousins and cats who maintain the balance of good and evil in the world are funny *and* tell a story about characters you can care for. That's what I think.

Now DAW's made all three books available in one omnibus—which you're clearly holding or you wouldn't be reading this—so what do you think? You can let me know on Facebook (Tanya Huff) or Twitter (@TanyaHuff) or LiveJournal where I occasionally blog (andpuff).

❖   ❖   ❖

OH, VERY WELL DONE!

DO WE GIVE COMPLIMENTS?

WE GIVE CREDIT WHERE CREDIT IS DUE.

Hell was silent for a moment. NO, WE DON'T, it said at last.

Tanya Huff
July 2012

Summon
the
Keeper

For the real Austin, and for Sid and Sam and Sasha.
And in loving memory of Emily and Ulysses.

Because there's no such thing as just a cat.

ONE

—————·◆≡◆≡·—————

WHEN THE STORM BROKE, rain pounding down in great sheets out of a black and unforgiving sky, Claire Hansen had to admit she wasn't surprised; it had been that kind of evening. Although her ticket took her to Colburg, three stops farther along the line, she'd stepped off the train and into the Kingston station certain that she'd found the source of the summons. It was the last thing she'd been certain of all day.

By the time it started to rain, her feet hurt, her luggage had about pulled her arms from their sockets, her traveling companion was sulking, and she was more than ready to pack it in. She'd search again in the morning, after a good night's sleep.

Unfortunately, it wasn't going to be that easy.

A Great Lakes Hydroecology convention had filled two of the downtown hotels, the third didn't allow pets, and the fourth was hosting the Beer Can Collectors of America, South Eastern Ontario Division. Claire had professed indignant disbelief about the latter until the desk clerk had pointed out the sign in the lobby welcoming the collectors to Kingston.

Some people have too much spare time, she thought as she shifted her suitcase into her left hand, the lighter, wicker cat carrier into her right, and headed back out into the night. *Way too much spare time.*

Pulling her coat collar out from under the weight of her backpack and hunkering down into its dubious shelter, she followed her feet along King Street toward the university, where a vague memory suggested there were guest houses and B&Bs hollowed out of the huge old mansions along the lake. Logically, she should have caught a cab out to the parade of hotels and budget motels lining Highway 2 between Kingston and Cataraqui, but, as logical solutions were rare in her line of work, Claire kept walking.

Thunder cracked, lightning lit up the sky, and it started to rain harder. Down the center of the street, where the reaching leaves of the huge, old trees didn't quite touch, grape-sized drops of water hit the pavement so hard they bounced. On the sidewalk, under the trees, it was . . .

A gust of wind tipped branches almost vertical, dumping a stream of icy water off the canopy and straight down the back of Claire's neck.

. . . not significantly drier.

There were times when profanity offered the only satisfactory response. Denied that outlet, Claire gritted her teeth and continued walking through increasingly deeper puddles toward City Park. Surely there'd be some kind of shelter near such a prominent tourist area even though September had emptied it of fairs and festivals. Tired, wet, and just generally cranky, she'd settle for anything that involved a roof and a bed.

At the corner of Lower Union and King, the lightning flashed again, throwing trees and houses into sharp-edged relief. On the third house up from the corner, a signboard affixed to a wrought iron fence reflected the light with such intensity, it left afterimages on the inside of Claire's lids.

"Shall we check it out?" She had to yell to make herself heard over the storm.

There was no answer from the cat carrier, but then she hadn't actually expected one.

In this, one of the oldest parts of the city, the houses were three- and four-story, red-brick Victorians. Too large to remain single-family dwellings in a time of rising energy prices, most had been hacked up into flats. The first two houses up from the corner were of this type. The third, past a narrow driveway, was larger still.

Squinting in the dark, water pouring off her hair and into her eyes, Claire struggled to make out the words on the sign. She was fairly certain there were words; there didn't seem to be much point in a sign if there weren't.

"Never any lightning around when it's needed. . . ."

On cue, the lightning provided every fleck of peeling paint with its own shadow. At the accompanying double crack of thunder, Claire dropped her suitcase and clutched at the fence. She let go a moment later when it occurred to her that holding an iron rod, even a rusty one, wasn't exactly smart under the circumstances.

White-and-yellow spots dancing across her vision, the faint *fizz* of an electrical discharge bouncing about between her ears, she stumbled toward the front door. During the brief time she'd been able to read the sign, she'd seen the words "uest House" and, right now, that was good enough for her.

The nine stairs were uneven and slippery, threatening to toss her, suitcase, cat carrier, backpack, and all, down into the black depths of the area in front of the house. When she slid into the railing and it bowed dangerously, she refused to consider it an omen. From the unsheltered porch, she could see neither knocker nor bell but, considering the night and the weather, that meant very little. There could have been a plaque warning travelers to *abandon hope all ye who enter here,* and she wouldn't have seen it—or paid any attention to it if it meant getting out of the storm. A light shone dimly through the transom. Holding her suitcase against the bricks with her knee, she tried the door.

It was unlocked.

Another time, she might have appreciated the drama of the moment more and pushed the heavy door open slowly, the sound of shrieking hinges accompanied by ominous music. As it was, she shoved it again, threw herself and her baggage inside, and kicked it closed.

At first, the silence came as a welcome relief from the storm, but after a moment of it settling around her, thick and cloying, Claire found she needed to fill it. She felt as though she were being covered in the cheap syrup left on the tables at family restaurants.

"Hello? Is anybody here?"

Although her voice had never been described as either timid or tentative, it made less than no impact on the silence. Lacking anywhere more constructive to go, the words bounced painfully around inside her head, birthing a sudden, throbbing headache.

Carefully setting the cat carrier down beyond the small lake she'd created on the scuffed hardwood floor, she turned to face the counter that divided the entry into a lobby and what looked like a small office—although the light was so bad, she couldn't be sure. On the counter, a brass bell waited in solitary, tarnished splendor.

Feeling somewhat like Alice in Wonderland, Claire pushed her streaming hair back off her face and smacked the plunger down into the bell.

The old man appeared behind the counter so suddenly that she recoiled a step, half expecting an accompanying puff of smoke—which would have been less disturbing than the more mundane explanation of him watching her from a dark corner of the office.

"What," he demanded, "do you want?"

"What do I want?"

"I asked you first."

Which was true enough. "I'd like a room for the night."

His eyes narrowed suspiciously. "That all?"

"What else is there?"

"Breakfast."

Claire had never been challenged to breakfast before. "If it's included, breakfast is fine." Another time, she might have managed a more spirited response. Then she remembered. "Do you take pets?"

"I do not! That's a filthy lie! You've been talking to Mrs. Abrams next door in number thirty-five, haven't you? Bloody cow. Lets her great, hairy baby crap all over the drive."

Beginning to shiver under the weight of her wet clothing, it took Claire a moment to work out just where the conversation had departed from the expected text. "I meant, do you mind pets staying in the hotel?"

The old man snorted. "Then you should say what you mean."

Something in his face seemed suddenly familiar, but the shadows cast by the single bulb hanging high overhead defeated Claire's attempt to bring his features into better focus. Her left eyelid began to twitch in time with the pounding in her skull. "Do I *know* you?"

"You do not."

He was telling the truth although something around the edges of his voice suggested it wasn't the entire truth. Before she could press the matter, he snarled, "If you don't want the room, I suggest you move on. I don't intend standing around here all night."

The thought of going back out into the storm wiped everything else from her head. "I want the room."

He dragged an old, green, leather-bound book out from under the counter and banged it down in front of her. Slapping it open to a blank page, he shoved a pen in her general direction. "Sign here."

She'd barely finished the final "n," her sleeve dragging a damp line across the yellowing paper, when he plucked the pen from her hand and replaced it with a key on a pink plastic fob.

"Room one. Top of the stairs to your right."

"Do I owe you anything in ad . . ." Claire let the last word trail off. The old man had vanished as suddenly as he'd appeared. "Guess not."

Picking up her luggage, she started up the stairs, trusting to instinct for her footing since the light was so bad she couldn't quite see the floor a little over five feet away.

Room one matched its key; essentially modern—if modern could be said to start around the late fifties—and unremarkable. The carpet and curtains were dark blue, the bedspread and the upholstery light blue. The walls were off-white, the furniture dark and utilitarian. The bathroom held a sink, a toilet, and a tub/shower combination and had the catch-in-the-throat smell of institutional cleansers.

Given the innkeeper, it was much better than Claire had expected. She set the wicker carrier on the dresser, unbuckled the leather straps, and lifted off the top. After a moment, a disgruntled black-and-white cat deigned to emerge and inspect the room.

As the storm howled impotently about outside the window, Claire shrugged out of her coat, wrapped her hair in a towel and collapsed onto the bed trying, unsuccessfully, to ignore the drum solo going on between her ears.

"Well, Austin, do the accommodations meet with your approval?" she asked as she heard him pad disdainfully from the bathroom. "Not that it matters; this is the best we can do for tonight."

The cat jumped up beside her. "That's too bad because—and I realize I risk sounding clichéd in saying it—I've got a bad feeling about this."

Claire managed to crack both eyelids open about a millimeter. No one had ever been able to determine if cats were actually clairvoyant or merely obnoxious little know-it-alls. "A bad feeling about what?"

"You know: this." He paused to rub a damp paw over his whiskers. "Aren't you getting anything at all?"

She let her eyes close again. "I seem to be getting MTV on one of my fillings. It's part of the Stomp tour." Flinching at a particularly robust bit of metaphor, she sighed. "I'm so thrilled."

A furry, ten-pound weight sat down on her chest. "I'm serious, Claire."

"The summons isn't any more urgent than it was this morning, if that's what you're asking." One-handed, she unbuttoned her jeans, pushing the cat back onto the bed with the other. "Nothing else is getting through this headache except a low-grade buzz."

"You should check it out."

"Check what out?" When Austin refused to answer, Claire decided she'd won, tossed off her clothes, and got into a pair of cream-colored silk pajamas—standard operating procedure suggested night clothes suitable for the six o'clock news, just in case.

Tucked under the covers, the cat curled up on the other pillow, she realized why the old man had looked so familiar. He looked like a gnome. And not one of those friendly garden gnomes either.

Rumpelstiltskin, she thought, and went to sleep smiling.

"This is weird, my shoes are still wet."

Austin glared at her from the litter box. "If you don't mind!"

"Sorry." Claire poured liquid out of the toe of one canvas sneaker, hung them back over the shower curtain rod by their tied laces, then made a hasty retreat from the bathroom. "It's not that I expected them to be dry," she continued, dropping onto the edge of the bed, "but I was hoping they'd be wearably damp."

It was starting out to be a six of one, half a dozen of the other kind of a day. On the one hand, it was still raining and her shoes were still too wet to wear. On the other hand, her sleep had been undisturbed by signs or portents, her headache was gone, and the low-grade buzz had completely disappeared. Even Austin had woken up in a good mood, or as good a mood as he could manage before noon.

Flopping back against a pile of bedclothes, she listened past the sound of feline excavation to the hotel's ambient noise, and frowned. "It's quiet."

"Too quiet?" Austin asked, coming out of the bathroom.

"The summons has stopped."

Sitting back on his haunches, the cat stared up at her. "What do you mean, stopped?"

"I mean it's absent, not present, missing, not there." Surging to her feet, she began to pace. "Gone."

"But it was there when you went to sleep?"

"Yes."

"So between ten-thirteen last night and eight-oh-one this morning, you stopped being needed?"

"Yes."

Austin shrugged. "The site probably closed on its own."

Claire stopped pacing and folded her arms. "That never happens."

"Got a better explanation?" the cat asked smugly.

"Well, no. But even if it has closed, I'd be summoned somewhere else." For the first time in ten years, she wasn't either dealing with a site or traveling to one where she was needed. "I feel as though I've been cast aside like an old shoe, drifting aimlessly . . ."

"Mixing metaphors," the cat interrupted, jumping up on the bed. "That's better; while there's nothing wrong with your knees, they're not exactly expressive conversational participants. Maybe," he continued, "you're not needed because good has dominated and evil is no longer considered a possibility."

They locked eyes for a moment, then simultaneously snickered.

"But seriously, Austin, what am I supposed to do?"

"We're only a few hours from home. Why don't you visit your parents?"

"My parents?"

"You remember; male, female, conception, birth . . ."

Actually, she did remember, she just tried not to think about it much. "Are you suggesting we need to take a vacation?"

"Right at the moment, I'm suggesting we need to eat breakfast."

The carpet on the stairs had seen better days; the edges still had a faint memory of the pattern but the center had been worn to a uniform, threadbare gray. Claire hadn't been exactly impressed the night before, and in daylight the guest house had a distinctly shabby look.

Not a place to make an extended stay, she thought as she twisted the pommel back onto the end of the banister.

"I think we should spend the day looking around," she said, following the cat downstairs. "Even if the site's closed up, it wouldn't hurt to check out the area."

"Whatever. After we eat."

Searching for a cup of coffee, if not the promised breakfast, Claire followed her nose down the hall to the back of the first floor. *With any luck, that obnoxious little gnome doesn't also do the cooking.*

The dining room stretched across the end of the building and held a number of small tables surrounded by stainless steel and Naugahyde chairs—it had obviously been renovated at about the same time as her room. Outside curtainless windows, devoid of even a memory of moldings, a steady rain slanted down from a slate-gray sky, puddling beneath an ancient and immaculate white truck parked against the back fence.

Fortunately, before she could get really depressed about either the weather or the decor, the unmistakable scent of Colombian double roast drew her around a corner to a small open kitchen. The stainless steel, restaurant-style appliances were separated from the actual eating area by a Formica counter, its surface scrubbed and rescrubbed to a pale gray.

Standing at the refrigerator was a dark-haired young man in his late teens or early twenties, wearing a chefs apron over faded jeans and a T-shirt. Although he wore a pair of wire frame glasses, a certain breadth of shoulder and narrowness of hip suggested to Claire that he wasn't the bookish type. The muscles of his back made interesting ripples in the brilliant white cotton of the T-shirt and when she lowered her gaze, she discovered, after a moment, that he ironed his jeans.

Austin leaped silently up onto the counter, glanced from the cook to Claire, and snorted, "You might want to breathe."

Claire grabbed the cat and dropped him onto the floor as the object of the observation closed the refrigerator door and turned.

"Good morning," he said. It sounded as though he actually meant it.

Distracted by teeth as white as his shirt and a pair of blue eyes surrounded by a thick fringe of dark lashes, not to mention the musical, near Irish lilt of a Newfoundland accent, Claire took a moment to respond. "Good grief. I mean, good morning."

It wasn't only his appearance that had thrown her. In spite of his age, or rather lack of it, this was the most grounded person she'd ever met. First impressions suggested he'd never push a door marked pull, he'd arrive on time for appointments, and, in case of fire, he'd actually remember the locations of the nearest exits. Glancing down at his feet, she half expected to see roots disappearing into the floor but saw only a pair of worn work boots approximately size twelve.

"Mr. Smythe left a note on the fridge explaining things." He wiped his hand against his apron, couldn't seem to make up his mind about what to do next, and finally let it fall back to his side. "I'm Dean McIssac. I've been cook and caretaker since last February. I hope you'll consider keeping me on."

"Keeping you on?"

Her total lack of comprehension appeared to confuse him. "Aren't you the new owner, then?"

"The new what?"

He jerked a sheet of notepaper out from under a refrigerator magnet, and passed it over.

The woman spending the night in room one, Claire read, *is Claire Hansen. As of this morning, she's the new proprietor.* Except for a small brown stain of indeterminate origins, the rest of the sheet was blank. "And that explains everything to you?" she asked incredulously.

"He's been trying to sell the place since I got here," Dean told her. "I just figured he had."

"He hasn't." So far, everything young Mr. McIssac had said, had been the truth. Which didn't explain a damned thing. Dropping the note onto the counter, she wondered just what game the old man thought he was playing. "I *am* Claire Hansen, but I haven't bought this hotel and I have no intention of buying this hotel."

"But Mr. Smythe . . ."

"Mr. Smythe is obviously senile. If you'll tell me where I can find him, I'll straighten everything out." She tried to make it sound more like a promise than a threat.

❖   ❖   ❖

Although two long, narrow windows lifted a few of the shadows, the office looked no more inviting in the gray light of a rainy day than it had at night.

"He lives here?" Claire asked sliding sideways through the narrow opening between the counter and the wall, the only access from the lobby.

"No, in here." The door to the old man's rooms had been designed to look like part of the office paneling. Dean reached out to knock and paused, his hand just above the wood. "It's open."

"Then we must be expected." She pushed past him. "Oh, my."

Overdone was an understatement when applied to the room on the other side of the door, just as overstuffed wasn't really sufficient to describe the furniture. Even the old console television wore three overlapping doilies, a pair of resin candlesticks carved with cherubs, and a basket of fake fruit.

Tucked into the gilded, baroque frame of a slightly pitted mirror was a large manila envelope. Even from across the room Claire could see it was addressed to her. Suddenly, inexplicably, convinced that things were about to get dramatically out of hand, she walked slowly forward, picking a path through the clutter. It took a remarkably long time to cover a short distance; then, all at once, she had the envelope in her hand.

Inside the envelope were half a dozen documents and another note, slightly shorter than the first.

"Senile but concise," Claire muttered. *"Congratulations, you're the new owner of the Elysian Fields Guest House."* She glanced up at Dean. "The Elysian Fields Guest House?" When he nodded, she shook her head in disbelief. "Why didn't he just call it the Vestibule of Hell?"

Dean shrugged. "Because that would be bad for business?"

"Do you get much business?"

"Well, no."

"I can't say I'm surprised." She bent her attention back to the note. *"Stay out of room six.* What's in room six?"

"There was a fire, years ago. Mr. Smythe didn't need the room, so he saved money on repairs by keeping it locked up."

"Sounds charming. That's all there is." She turned the paper over but it was blank on the other side. "Maybe these will give us some ans . . ." Her voice trailed off as, mouth open, she fanned the other papers. Her signature had been carefully placed where it needed to be on each of the legal documents. And it *was* her signature, not a forgery. Smythe had lifted it out of the registration book.

Which could only mean one thing.

"Mr. McIssac, could you *please* go and get me a cup of coffee."

Dean found himself out in the office, the door to Mr. Smythe's rooms closed behind him, before he'd made a conscious decision to move. He remembered being asked to go for coffee and then he was in the office. Coffee. Office. Nothing in between.

"Okay, so your memory's going." He ducked under the counter flap. "Look at the bright side, boy, you're still employed."

Jobs were scarce, and he hoped he could hang on to this one. The pay wasn't great, but it included a basement apartment and he'd discovered that he liked taking care of people. He'd begun to think about taking some kind of part-time hotel management course; when there were no guests, and there were seldom guests, he had a lot of free time.

All that could change now that Mr. Smythe had gotten tired of waiting for a buyer and given the place away to a total stranger. Who didn't seem to want it.

Claire Hansen was not what he'd expected. First off, she was a lot younger. Although he'd had minimal experience judging the ages of women and the makeup just muddled it up all the more, he'd be willing to swear she was under thirty. He might even go as low as twenty-five.

And it was weird that she traveled with a cat.

"I can't feel the summons anymore, because I'm where I'm needed."

Austin blinked. "Say what?"

"Augustus Smythe is a Cousin."

"Augustus?"

"It's on the documents." Claire fanned them out so the cat could see all six pages. "Printed. He knew better than to sign his name. He's been here for a while, so obviously he was monitoring an accident

site—a site he's buggered off from and made my responsibility." She
dropped down onto a sofa upholstered in pink cabbage roses and continued dropping, sinking through billowing cushions to an alarming
depth.

"Are you okay?" Austin asked a few moments later when she
emerged, breathing heavily and clutching a handful of loose change.

"Fine." Knees still considerably higher than her hips, Claire
hooked an elbow over the reinforced structure of the sofa's arm in case
she started to sink again, dropping the change into a bowl of dubious
looking mints. It might have made more sense to find another place to
sit, but none of the other furniture looked any safer. "The summons
wasn't coming from the site, or I'd still be able to feel it. It had to have
been coming from Augustus Smythe."

The cat leaped up onto the coffee table. "He needed to leave so
badly he drew you here?"

"Since he left last night, which is when the summons stopped,
that's the only logical explanation."

"But why?"

"That's the question, isn't it? Why?"

Austin put a paw on her knee. "Why are you looking so happy
about this?"

Was she? She supposed she was. "I'm not drifting any more."
Starting the day with neither a summons nor a site had been disconcerting. "I have a purpose again."

"How nice for you." He sat back. "We're not going to get our vacation, are we?"

"Doesn't look like it." Her smile faded as she tapped the papers
against her thigh. "Why didn't Smythe identify himself when I didn't
recognize him?"

"Better question, why didn't you recognize him?"

"I was tired, I was wet, and I had a headache," she pointed out
defensively. "All I could think of was getting out of that storm."

"You think he fuzzed you?"

"Where would he get the power? I was distracted, all right? Let's
just leave it at that." After another short struggle with the sofa, Claire
managed to heave herself back up onto her feet. "Since the site's in the
hotel—or Smythe wouldn't have bothered deeding it to me—and

since I can't sense it, I'm guessing that it's so small it never became enough of a priority to need a Keeper and Smythe finally got tired of waiting. I'll close it, and we'll move on."

"And the hotel?" Austin reminded her.

"After I seal the site, I'll give it to young Mr. McIssac."

"You think it's going to be that easy?"

"Isn't it always?" She picked up a squat figurine of a wide-eyed child in lederhosen playing a tuba, shuddered, and put it back down. "Come on."

"Come on?" Trotting to the end of the table, he jumped over a plaster bust of Elvis, went under a set of nesting Chinese tables, and beat her to the door. "Where are we going?"

"To get some answers."

"Where?"

"Where else? Where we were told not to go."

Austin snorted. "Typical."

Room six was on the third floor. As well as the standard lock, the door also boasted a large steel padlock on an industrial strength flange. Both locks had been made unopenable by the simple process of snapping the keys off in the mechanism.

"Seems like a lot of fuss over a small site," Austin muttered, dropping down from his inspection.

"Well, he could hardly have guests wandering in on it regardless of size." Releasing the padlock, Claire straightened. There were a number of ways she could gain access to the room, but most of them were labeled "emergency use only" as they involved the kind of pyrotechnics more likely to be deployed during small Middle Eastern wars. "I wonder if young Mr. McIssac has a hacksaw."

"Ms. Hansen?" Dean put the tray down on the desk and pushed his glasses back up the bridge of his nose. She wasn't in Mr. Smythe's suite—her suite now, he supposed—and she wasn't in the office. He hoped she wasn't upstairs packing. *Am I fired if she leaves?*

Footsteps descending the stairs seemed to confirm his worst fears, but when she came into view, she wasn't carrying her bags. She hadn't even put her coat on.

"Oh, there you are, Dean."

There he was? He hadn't gone anywhere except to get her the coffee she'd asked for. "I brought cream and sugar," he told her as she squeezed under the counter flap. "You didn't say how you took it."

"Definitely cream." She poured some into the mug and frowned at the sugar bowl. "Do you have any packets of artificial sweetener?"

"Sure." As far as he could tell, she didn't need to watch her weight. While not quite a woman a man could see to shoot gulls through, she was on the skinny side and that much cream would pack on more pounds than a bit of sugar. "I'll go get you some."

"Dean?"

He straightened in the lobby and turned to face her over the counter.

"Bring your toolbox, too."

Cradling the coffee mug in both hands, Claire leaned against the wall and watched Dean work. He'd had no trouble cutting the padlock off, but the original lock was proving to be more difficult.

"I think you should call a locksmith, Ms. Hansen. I can't get in there without damaging the door some."

"How much?"

He shrugged. "If I get my crowbar from the van, I could probably force it open. Just stick it in here . . ." He ran a finger down the crack between the door and the jam where the tongue of the lock ran into the wall. ". . . and shove. It'll crack the wood for sure, but I can't say how much."

Claire took another swallow and considered her options. As long as Dean stayed out of the actual room, there should be no problem; only the largest of sites were visible to the untrained eye. "Go get your crowbar."

"Yes, ma'am."

When the sound of Dean's work boots clumping against bare wood suggested he'd reached the lobby, Austin stretched and glared up at Claire. "Couldn't this have waited until after breakfast? I'm starved."

"Could you have actually eaten not knowing what we were in for? Never mind. Stupid question."

"You've got your coffee, the least you could've done was given me the cream."

"The vet said you're not supposed to have cream." She squatted and rubbed him behind the ears. "Don't worry, it'll all be over soon. Waiting out on this side of the door has me so edgy, I'm positive the site's in there."

"In a just world," the cat growled, "it would've been in the kitchen."

His boots wet from the run out to the van, Dean slipped them off at the back door and started upstairs in his socks. Making the turn on the second floor landing, he heard voices. *I guess she's talking to the cat.*

Voices. Plural, prodded his subconscious.

You're losing it, boy. The cat's not talking back.

She had her back to him when he stepped out into the third-floor hall. "Ms. Hansen?"

Claire managed to bite off most of the shriek, but her heart slammed against her ribs as she whirled around. "Don't ever do that!"

Jerking back a step, Dean brought the crowbar up between them. "Do what?"

"Don't ever sneak up on me like that!" She pressed her right hand between her breasts. "You're just lucky I realized who you were!"

Although she was a good six or seven inches shorter than he was and there was nothing to her besides, somehow, that didn't sound as ridiculous as it should have. "I'm sorry!"

Austin banged his head against her shins and she looked down. "You took your boots off."

"They got wet."

"Right. Of course." Bringing her breathing under control, Claire waved him toward the locked door. "Break the lock, then step away. If there was a fire in there, you won't want the mess tracked into the hall."

Dean flashed her a grateful smile as he jammed the crowbar into the crack. Since coming west, he'd found few people who appreciated the kind of problems involved in keeping carpets clean. "Yes, ma'am."

"And stop calling me ma'am. You make me feel like I'm a hundred years old." When she saw him fighting a grin, Claire rolled her eyes. "I'm twenty-seven."

"Okay." A confidence given required one in exchange. "I'm twenty-one." As he pulled back on the bar, he glanced over at her expression and wondered how she knew he was lying. "That is, I'll be twenty-one in a few months."

"So you're twenty?"

"Yes, ma'am."

The shriek of tortured wood and steel cut off further conversation. Hands over her ears, Claire watched muscles stretch the sleeves of his T-shirt as the lock began to give. When it popped suddenly, it took her a moment to gather her wandering thoughts—although, she assured the world at large, it was purely an aesthetic interest. In that moment, the door swung open, Dean looked into the room, and froze on the threshold.

"Lord thunderin' Jesus! Mr. Smythe's been hiding a body up here!"

"Calm down." Claire put her palm in the center of Dean's back and shoved. She'd have had more luck shifting the building. "And move!" Over the years she'd seen bodies in every condition imaginable—and frequently the imagination had belonged to fairly warped individuals. If this body had merely been left lying around, she'd consider herself lucky.

Dean stayed in the doorway, the breadth of his shoulders blocking her way and her view.

"I don't think," he said, grasping both edges of the doorframe, "that this is something a lady ought to see."

"Well, you got part of it right, you don't think!" Choosing guile over force, she slammed her knees into the back of his at the spot where the crease crossed the hollow. As he collapsed, she pushed past him, one hand reaching out to the old-fashioned, circular light switch.

The room was a little larger than the room Claire had slept in and the decorating hadn't been changed since the early part of the century. An oversized armchair sat covered in hand-crocheted doilies, a Victorian plant stand complete with a very dead fern stood between the two curtained windows, and a woman lay fully clothed on top of the bed, a sausage-shaped bolster under her head and a folded quilt under her feet. Everything, including the woman, wore a fuzzy patina of dust. The air smelled stale and, faintly, of perfume.

Claire could feel the edges of a shield wrapped around the body— which explained why she hadn't been able to get a sense of what room six held. The shield hadn't been put in place by a Cousin. At some point, a Keeper had been by and wrapped the site up so tightly that even another Keeper couldn't get through. Had Augustus Smythe not needed to leave so badly, Claire could've passed happily through Kingston without ever realizing the site existed. The one thing she *couldn't* figure out was why a Keeper would bother. While people did occasionally manifest an accident site, the usual response was an exorcism, not the old Sleeping Beauty schtick.

A choking noise behind her reminded Claire she had a more immediate problem. The woman on the bed had clearly been there for some years; she could wait a few minutes longer.

When she turned, Dean had regained his position in the doorway. Her movement drew his locked gaze up off the bed, breaking the connection. For a moment he stared at her, eyes wide, then he whirled around and managed two running steps toward the stairs.

"Dean McIssac!"

There was power in a name.

He stopped, one foot in the air, and almost fell.

"Where are you going?"

Shoving his glasses back into place, he tired to sound as though he found dead women laid out in the guest rooms all the time. "I'm after calling 911." His heart was pounding so loudly he could hardly hear himself.

"After calling?"

He rolled his eyes anxious to be moving, impatient at the delay. "After calling, going to call; it's the same thing."

"Why?"

"I don't know!" Frustration had him almost shouting. Suddenly self-conscious, he ducked his head. "Sorry."

Claire waved off the apology. "I meant, why are you going to call 911?"

"Because there's a body . . ."

"She isn't dead, Dean, she's asleep. If you look at her chest, you can see she's breathing."

"Breathing?" Without moving his feet, he grabbed the splintered doorjamb and leaned in over the threshold. "Oh." Feeling foolish, he shrugged and tried to explain, "I was raised better than to stare at a woman's chest."

"You thought it was a corpse."

"Doesn't matter."

"Who *raised* you?"

"My granddad, Reverend McIssac," Dean told her, a little defensively.

Claire had her doubts at how often a twenty-year-old male actually followed that particular dictum but had no plans to discourage admirable intentions. "Well, good for him. And you. Now, could you do something for me?"

"Uh, sure."

"Could you go get me another cup of coffee, *please.*"

He looked at her like she was out of her mind. "What? Now? What about the woman on the bed?"

"I don't think she's going to want one."

"No, I meant, what *about* the woman on the bed!"

Claire sighed. She hadn't actually thought it would work, but since it was the simplest temporary solution, it had seemed foolish not to try. Unfortunately, curiosity was one of the strongest motivating forces behind humanity's rise out of the ooze and, unsatisfied, it invariably caused problems. The safest way to deal with questions was to answer them, then, after all the loose ends were neatly tied up, wipe the whole package right out of Dean's mind. "If I promise to explain everything later, will you do me a favor? Will you wait quietly while I deal with this?"

"You know what's going on then?"

"Yes. Mostly," she amended, conscience prickling.

"And you'll explain it to me?"

"When I'm done with her."

"Done what?"

"That's one of the things I'll explain later."

Feeling a pressure against his shins, Dean glanced down to see Austin rubbing against him. It was such a normal, ordinary thing for a cat to do, it made the rest of the morning seem less strange. "Okay," he said, dropping to one knee and running his fingers along the silky fur. "I'll wait."

"Thank you."

With her unwelcome audience temporarily taken care of, Claire turned her attention back to the bed. In spite of the dust, the woman did bear a striking resemblance to Sleeping Beauty— or more accurately, given her age, to Sleeping Beauty's mother. Then it became obvious that the blonde curls had been bleached, the eyebrows had been plucked and redrawn, and the lips were far, far too red. The severe, almost military-style clothing covered a lush figure that could by no means be called matronly. For some reason, Claire found the line of dark residue under all ten fingernails incredibly disturbing. She didn't know why—dirty fingernails had never bothered her before.

It would be easier to work without the shield, but with a bystander to consider, Claire went through the perimeter without disturbing its structural integrity.

The emanations rising from the body were so dark she gagged. Teeth clenched, wishing she hadn't had that coffee, she forced herself to take a deeper look.

Kneeling beside the cat, Dean watched his new boss stagger back, trip on the edge of the braided rug, and begin to fall. He dove forward, felt an unpleasant, greasy sizzle along one arm, and caught her just before she hit the floor. Under the makeup, her face had gone a pale gray and her throat worked as though she wanted to throw up. Before he could ask if she was all right, Austin leaped up onto her lap.

Her lower body still on the other side of the shield, Claire reached out to stop the cat from crossing over.

Too late.

"Evil!" Without actually touching down, he twisted in midair, hit the floor running, and raced back into the hall.

That was enough for Dean. Hands under Claire's armpits, he half carried, half dragged her out of the room. When her legs cleared the threshold, he reached over her and pulled the door closed. The damage he'd done to the lock plate meant it no longer latched, but he managed to jam it shut.

Pressed tight against Dean's chest, her head tucked into the hollow of his throat, Claire shoved on the arm holding her in place. While she appreciated him catching her before her skull smacked into the floor, his interference in something he had no hope of understanding created the distinct desire to drive her elbow in under his ribs as far as it would go. Only the certain knowledge that any blow would bounce harmlessly off the rippled muscle she could feel through the thin barrier of the T-shirt prevented her. That, and the way the position she found herself in radically restricted her movements. Not to mention her ability to breathe. "Let go of me!" she gasped. "Now!"

He jerked and looked down at her like he'd forgotten she was there but eased up enough so she could squirm free. Wedging her shoulder under his, she managed to get him out of the doorway.

His back against the wall, Dean slid down to sit on the hall floor, feeling much as he had at ten when the local bully had smacked him around with a dead cod. "The cat talked."

Having just reached Austin's side, Claire shook her head. "No, he didn't."

"Yes, he did."

Scooping the cat up into her arms, she said in a tone specifically crafted to make the recipient doubt his own senses, "No, he didn't."

"Yes, he did," Austin corrected, his voice a little muffled.

"Excuse me." Holding him tightly against her chest, she turned so that her body was between Dean and the cat. "I'll just be a minute." Tucking her thumb under the furry chin, she lifted his head and whispered, "Are you all right?"

"I'm fine." His tail, still twice its normal size, lashed against her leg. "I was startled. I hit the nasty on the other side of that shield and I overreacted."

"And what are you doing now?"

"He's a part of this."

"Are you out of your walnut-sized mind? He's a bystander!"

"Granted, but you're going to need his help."

"For what? With what? With *her*?"

"Maybe. I don't know yet."

"You *are* out of your mind! Do you know what that is in there?"

"Excuse me?"

"What?" Dean's voice pulled Claire's attention back across the hall.

Caught between a cruel and capricious sea and an unwelcoming hunk of rock, Newfoundlanders had turned adaptation into a genetically encoded survival trait. True to his ancestry, Dean had progressed from stunned disbelief through amazement to amazed acceptance by the time he'd interrupted.

When he saw he had their attention, he said, "I could still hear you. Sorry."

"Well, she wasn't exactly keeping her voice down," Austin pointed out.

Dean met Claire's gaze almost apologetically. "The cat talks."

"The cat never shuts up," Claire replied through gritted teeth.

"He seems to think I can help."

"Yeah, well when I need something cleaned or cooked I'll let you know. OW!" Sucking on the back of her hand, she glared down at Austin. "What did you scratch me for?"

He retracted his claws. "You were being rude."

"Scratch me again and I'll show you rude," she muttered.

"You're frightened, that's understandable. Even I was almost frightened. You think you can't handle this, you think it's too big for you . . ."

"Stop telling me what I think!"

". . . but that's no reason to take it out on him."

"You're frightened?" Dean ducked his head to get a better look at her face. "You are frightened."

Obviously, she hadn't been hiding it as well as she'd thought.

"Of what? Oh . . ." The talking cat had temporarily driven all thoughts of their other discovery out of his head. "Of her?" *Evil,* the cat had said. Rubbing the lingering, greasy feel off the arm that had been closest to the bed, Dean found that easy to believe. "Don't worry." He straightened where he sat. "On the last of it, she'll have to go through me to get to you."

"Foreshadowing," Austin muttered.

Giving the cat a warning squeeze, Claire realized that Dean's offer was in earnest. He was the sort of person who went out of his way to pick worms off the sidewalk and put them back onto the lawn. She drew in a deep breath and let it out slowly. "First of all, I can take care of myself. Second, if you ever face that woman awake, you'd better hope she kills you immediately and doesn't play with you for a while. And third, there's nothing you can do."

"The cat said . . ."

"He says a lot of things."

"*You* said you'd explain."

"After I'd dealt with her. And I haven't."

"I could help you with her."

"You don't know what's going on."

"I would if you explained."

"I've had as much as I can take of this," Austin grumbled. "I'll explain." Wriggling out of Claire's arms, he crossed the hall and locked a pale green stare on Dean's face. "Do you believe in magic?"

"That's an explanation?"

"Just answer the question."

"Sure."

"Sure? What kind of an answer is sure? Do you or don't you?"

Dean shrugged. "I guess I do."

"Good." Stretching out, Austin ripped at the carpet. "Because that's what we're dealing with."

"Magic?"

"That's right. The woman in the room behind you was put to sleep by magic."

Dean shifted a little farther down the hall. Drawing his knees up, he laid his forearms across them and frowned. "Like Sleeping Beauty?"

Austin's ears went back. "The opposite. This time the bad guy— her—got put to sleep by the good guys."

"Why?"

"How should I know?"

"I just thought . . ."

"At this point we don't know much more than you do." He frowned thoughtfully. "Actually, we know a whole lot more than you, but we don't know *that*. The important thing for you to remember is that, if you're lucky, the woman in there is the worst thing you're ever going to come in contact with. She's evil sleeping in size eight pumps."

Dean's eyes widened. "How do you know her shoe size?"

"I don't."

"But you said . . ."

"I was making a point," Austin sighed. "Which obviously didn't make it through your thick head."

Watching the cat stalk back across the hall and rub his head against a denim-clad hip, Dean suddenly remembered the feel of a body clutched tightly against his. Under normal circumstances, it wasn't a feeling he'd have forgotten. His ears turned red as he realized just which bits had gone where and he suspected he should apologize for something. "Uh, Ms. Hansen . . ."

"You might as well call me Claire," she interrupted wearily, picking at a loose thread in the cleanest carpet she'd ever seen. "If Austin's right . . ."

"And I am," Austin put in, not bothering to glance up from an important bit of grooming.

". . . we're going to be working together. That is," she added after a moment's pause, "if you still want to keep your job."

Austin snorted. "Weren't you listening to me?"

"Dean has to decide for himself if he's going to stay."

Dean shifted nervously under the weight of their combined attention. "What is it we'll be doing together?"

Claire put her cupped hand over the cat's muzzle before she answered. "Fighting evil."

"You're a superhero?"

Austin jerked free. "Don't," he suggested sternly, "give her ideas."

"No, I'm not a superhero. I don't even own a pair of tights. Are you blushing again?"

"I don't think so."

"Good."

"*I* am one of the good guys. And *this* is a bad situation. The woman in there . . ." Claire nodded toward the broken door. ". . . is only half the problem. Somewhere in this building is a hole in the fabric of the universe."

About to protest that there were some stories even a *dumb Newfie* wouldn't believe, Dean hesitated. They'd found a dust-covered woman, dressed in 1940s clothing, asleep in room six and he'd just had the situation more or less—mostly less—explained to him by a talking cat. Evidence suggested it wasn't a bam. "A hole in the fabric of the universe," he repeated. "Okay."

"We refer to it as an accident site. At some time, somebody did something they shouldn't have. The energy coming through the hole is keeping the woman asleep." Crossing her legs at the ankle, Claire rocked up onto her feet. "That's how I know there *is* a hole and Augustus Smythe wasn't here merely to monitor her." As Dean opened his mouth, the next question obvious on his face, she held up a silencing hand. "It's nothing personal, but right at the moment, my questions are more important than yours. Since I'm not going back in there to find the answers . . ."

"You don't want her to wake up," Austin muttered at Dean. "You *really* don't want her to wake up."

". . . I've got to find the accident site. Unfortunately, it seems to be at least as well shielded as she is and we're going to have to search every threadbare inch of this place, unless . . . you know where it is?"

"The accident site?" He stood. "The hole in the fabric of the universe?"

"That's right." She'd never had to explain herself to a bystander before. It was hard not to sound patronizing.

"Sorry. I haven't the faintest idea of what you're talking about." Squaring his shoulders, he hiked the tool belt up on his hips. His world had always included a number of things he'd had to take on faith. He added one more. "But I'd like to help."

"So you're staying?"

"Yes, ma'am."

"Claire." When he looked dubious, she sighed. "What?"

"You own the hotel, you're my boss; I can't call you by your first name. It wouldn't be right."

About to tell him that he was being an idiot, Claire suddenly remembered the feel of his arms and the warm scent of fabric softener and decided it might be better to maintain some distance. "What did you call Augustus Smythe?"

"To his face?"

Austin snickered.

"Yes. To his face."

"I called him Boss." Dean considered the possibility of calling an attractive woman the same thing he'd called a cranky old man and wasn't entirely convinced it would work. "I *guess* I could call you Boss."

"Good. Glad we've got that cleared up."

"Should I wire this door shut before we start searching, um, Boss?"

Although Dean don't seem quite comfortable using the title,

Claire found she liked it. It made her feel like the lead in an old gang-ster movie. "You might as well." It would be a useless precaution since it was unlikely any of them would now wander into room six by acci-dent, but it would give Dean something to do that he understood. "Just let me turn out the light first."

The remainder of the third floor, two double rooms and a single, was empty of everything except the lingering smell of disinfectant. Inside the storage cupboard across from room six, Claire emptied the shelves of toilet paper and cleaning supplies, then peered down the laundry chute.

"Don't even think about it!" Austin spat as she turned and studied him measuringly.

"Suppose it's between floors?"

"Then it'll just have to stay there."

"I'll keep you from falling."

"Oh, sure." He squeezed in behind a bucket of sponges and peered balefully at her over the edge, ears flat against his head. *That's* what you said the last time."

"Those were extraordinary circumstances. Never happen again."

"I said no."

"Okay, okay." She tried and failed to open the narrow door next to the chute. "What's in here?"

"Stairs to the attic." Dean eyeballed the opening of the laundry chute, was relieved to find he wouldn't fit, and found the required key on his master ring.

Filling an area barely five feet square, a narrow set of metal stairs spiraled upward toward an uninviting square hole cut out of the ceil-ing.

"Are there lights?"

"Don't think so. You stay where you're at, girl, and let me . . ." At the look on her face, his voice trailed off. "Never mind, then."

"Girl?"

"It's just a way we have of talkin' back home," he explained hur-riedly, his cheeks crimson and his accent thickening. "I don't mean nothing by it."

"Then don't do it again."

"Yes ma'am, Ms. Hansen." A deep breath and he tried again. "Boss."

"Are you certain he's a part of this?" she demanded, turning toward the cat.

"Yes. Get along."

Claire sighed. Metal rungs ringing under her feet, she ran to the top of the stairs, crossed her fingers and stuck her head up into what looked like one large room filled with decades of discards, barely lit by the two filthy dormer windows cut into the sloping roof on either end of the building.

It was still raining.

"It'll take us months to search that place thoroughly," she announced a moment later backing carefully down the stairs. "Let's leave it for later. With any luck we'll find the hole someplace more accessible."

"Oh, sure, accessible like the laundry chute," Austin muttered as Dean relocked the attic door.

The second floor was as empty as the first—more so since there was nothing to match the occupant of room six. Remembering the mess she'd left spread out on the bed, Claire vouched for her room without opening the door. Room four, a corner single with two outside walls and no window, suggested a more thorough search.

Leaning on the edge of the bureau, Dean watched Claire slip into the bed alcove and try the bolt on the inside of the alcove's steel door. "You know someone actually asked for this room last spring."

"How would I know that? I just got here." The high box bed had one shallow drawer under the mattress and two deeper drawers below that. Hands slid between the mattress and the frame found no sign of evil but did turn up a silver earring.

Mortified, Dean apologized for a sloppy job as Claire dropped the piece of jewelry on his palm. "When we're done searching, I'll clean this room again."

"If it makes you happy," Claire muttered, checking in the bedside table. As far as she could see, the room was spotless.

Dean's expression softened as he bounced the earring on his palm. "She was a musician. Sasha something. I can't remember her last name, but she was some h . . ." Then, he remembered who he was talking to. His boss. A woman. Some things he couldn't say to a boss. Or a woman. "Cute. She was some cute."

"H . . . cute?" Shaking her head, Claire brushed past him.

Mouth partly open, Austin whipped his tail from side to side. "I don't like the way this smells."

"Then since it'd take a sledgehammer to air it out, let's go." Claire could feel a perfectly logical reason for the design hovering just beyond the edge of conscious thought, but when she reached for it, it danced away and taunted her from a safe distance. *Later,* she promised and added aloud, "What did you say?"

Dean paused at the top of the stairs. "I said, do you think we should search the rest of Mr. Smythe's old rooms, then?"

"He wouldn't have been living with it," she snapped dismissively. Then feeling like she'd just kicked a puppy, a large and well-muscled puppy, she added a strained, "Sorry. Where Augustus Smythe is concerned, I shouldn't take anything for granted."

The sitting room violated a number of rules concerning how many objects could simultaneously occupy the same space, but the only accident it contained involved the head-on collision of good taste with an apparent inability to throw anything away. The bedroom wasn't quite as bad. Dominated by a brass bed, it also held an obviously antique dressing table, a wardrobe, and two windows. One of them framed into an inside wall.

"Probably the window missing from the room upstairs." Jumping up onto the bed, Austin began kneading the mattress. "This isn't bad. I could sleep here."

Before Claire could stop him, Dean tugged the burgundy brocade curtain to one side and closed it again almost instantly, setting six inches of fringe swaying back and forth.

"Are you okay?" she asked warily. If it was the accident site and he'd been exposed, there was no telling what he might have picked up.

Cheeks flushed, he nodded. "Fine. I'm fine."

"What did you see?"

"It was, uh, a bar." He cleared his throat and reluctantly continued. "With, uh, dancers."

"Were they table dancing?" The cat snickered. "Upon admittedly short acquaintance, that seems like the sort of scene old Augustus would go for."

"Not exactly table, no." Shaking his head, Dean lifted the curtain again. "It was dark but . . ." His voice trailed off.

Claire peered around his shoulder and almost went limp with relief. "That doesn't sound like a bar to me. Looks like Times Square. And over there, in front of the hookers, isn't that a drug deal going down?" Leaning forward, she rapped on the glass and nodded in satisfaction. "That put the fear of God into them."

The curtain fell closed again. Dean's voice threatened to crack as he asked, "What was it?"

"We call it a postcard."

"We?" He waved an overly nonchalant hand toward the cat. That smacked-with-a-cod feeling had returned. "You and Austin?"

"Among others." She glared at the curtain. "Smythe couldn't have managed this on his own; he had to have been pulling from the site."

"Is that bad?"

"Well it isn't good. I'll know more when we find the hole."

"Wherever it is," Austin agreed.

"Since we know it's not in the dining room, what's left?"

The basement held, besides the mechanicals, the laundry room, Dean's sparsely furnished and absolutely spotless apartment, several storage cupboards holding sheets, towels, and still more cleaning supplies, and, across from the laundry room, a large metal door. Painted a brilliant turquoise, it boasted not one but two padlocked chains securing it closed.

"Dean, did you know this was down here?"

He frowned, confused by the question. Since he obviously spent a lot of time in the basement . . . "Sure."

"Why didn't you mention it earlier?"

"It's just the furnace room."

"The furnace room." Claire exchanged a speaking glance with the cat. "Have you ever been in this alleged furnace room?"

"No. Mr. Smythe did all the furnace work himself."

"I'll bet." The keys were hanging beside the door. The security arrangements were clearly not intended to keep people out but to keep something in. "What was he heating this place with," she muttered, dragging the first chain free. "A dragon?"

Dean took the chain, removed the second length, and hung them both neatly on the hooks provided. "Are you kidding?"

"Mostly. Any virgins reported missing from the neighborhood?"

"*Pardon?*"

"Forget it." Claire pulled the door open about six inches and leaned away from the blast of heat. "Do you mind?" she asked as Austin slipped in ahead of her. "Try to remember what curiosity killed." Moving forward, she felt remarkably calm. At first she thought she was just numb—it had, after all, been a busy morning—but when she stepped over the threshold, she realized that the entire furnace room had been wrapped in a dampening field.

Much more powerful than a mere shield, it not only deflected the curious but was quite probably the only thing allowing people to remain in the building.

Down nine steps, inscribed into the rough surface of a bedrock floor, was a complicated, multicolored, multilayered pentagram. The center of the pentagram was an open hole. A dull red light, shining up from the depths, painted lurid highlights on the copper hood hanging from the ceiling. Ductwork directed the rising heat up into the hotel.

Must have a helluva filter system, Claire thought, wrinkling her nose at the stink of fire and brimstone.

And then it sank in. Unfortunately, the dampening field had no effect inside the furnace room.

Heart pounding, hot sweat rolling down her sides, she bent and scooped up Austin, who'd flattened himself to the floor. With the cat held tightly against her chest, she forced herself down the first three steps.

"Where are you going?" he hissed, claws digging into her shoulder.

"To check the seal."

"Why?"

"Because Augustus Smythe couldn't have held this."

"Then obviously someone else is. And there's only one someone else in this building."

"She's holding it, it's holding her." Claire went down another three steps and nodded toward the pentagram. "There's her name. Sara."

"Don't . . ."

"It's all right. If her name could get through the field, they'd have woken her years ago." There was a vibration in the air, just on the edge of sound, an almost hum as though they were walking toward the world's largest wasp's nest. "On the other hand, you know that low-level buzz I mentioned last night? There seems to be some seepage."

"But you couldn't feel it this morning."

"Not outside this room, no. Augustus Smythe probably used it up making his getaway."

"That's bad."

"Well, it's not good." Placing her feet with care, she backed up the stairs, squeezed over the threshold, shoved Dean away from the door, and very, very gently, pushed it closed.

"*Was* it a dragon?" Dean asked, not entirely certain why he hadn't followed her inside but untroubled by the uncertainty.

"No." As the dampening field began to take effect, it became possible to think again. "It wasn't a dragon."

"Then was it a furnace?"

"Sort of." She unhooked Austin's claws from her shoulder and settled him more comfortably in her arms, her free hand rhythmically stroking his fur and sending clouds of loose hair flying. He tucked his head up under her chin, and left it there.

"Was it the hole?"

Claire giggled. She couldn't help it, but she managed to cut it short; she hadn't expected such a literal example of the explanation she'd created to fit a bystander's limited world. "Oh, yes, it was the hole." Still cradling the cat, she started toward the basement stairs, head up, back straight. "Could you please replace the chains and the locks?"

Dean had the strangest feeling that if he tapped her shoulder as she passed, she'd ring out like a weather buoy. "Are you all right, then?"

"I'm fine."

"Where are you going?"

"Upstairs."

He shook his head, thought about opening the door and taking a look for himself and for reasons he wasn't quite clear on, decided not to. "Hey, Boss?"

It took Claire a moment to realize who he was talking to. Three steps up, she paused and leaned out from the stairs so she could see him. "Yes?"

"What are you after doing?"

"I'm going to do what anyone in this situation would do; I'm going to get a second opinion."

"From who?"

Her smile looked as if it had been borrowed and didn't quite fit. "I'm going to call my mother."

Behind the chains, behind the turquoise door, down the stairs, and deep in the pit, intelligence stirred.

HELLO?

When it realized there'd be no answer, it sighed.

DAMN.

TWO

—·—✵—·—

"**H**ANSEN RESIDENCE."

The voice on the other end of the line was not one Claire had expected to hear. "Diana?" Unable to remain still, she picked up the old rotary phone and paced the length of the office and back. "What are you doing home? I thought you were doing fieldwork this weekend."

"Hong and I had a small argument."

"Like the argument you had with Matt?"

"No."

There was a lengthening, a scornful pronunciation of that second letter that only a teenager could manage. At twenty, the ability was lost. *Three years,* Claire told herself, *just three more years.* She'd been ten when Diana was born and the sudden appearance of a younger sister had come as a complete surprise. Over the years, although she loved Diana dearly, the surprise had turned to apprehension—being around her was somewhat similar to being around sweating dynamite. "These people are supposed to be training you. You could assume they know what they're doing."

"Yeah, well, they're old and they never let *me* do anything."

"I haven't time to get into this with you right now. Put Mom on, please."

"Duh, Claire, it's Sunday morning."

She took a minute to whack herself on the forehead with the receiver. She'd completely forgotten. "Could you ask her to call me the moment she gets home from church?"

"You didn't say the magic word."

"Diana!"

"Chill, I'm kidding. What's the matter anyway? You sound like you just looked into the depths of Hell."

Reflecting, not for the first time, that her little sister had an appalling amount of power from someone with an equally appalling amount of self-confidence, Claire smoothed the lingering tremors out of her voice. "Just ask her to call me—please." She read the number off the dial. "It's important."

Dean could hear Claire talking on the phone as he came up the basement stairs. Ignoring the temptation to eavesdrop—as much as he wanted to know what she was saying, it would've been rude—he continued on into the kitchen, where he found Austin attempting to open the fridge.

"They build garage door openers, push of a button and you can park your car, but does anyone ever think of building something like that for a fridge. No." He pulled his claws out of the rubber seal and glared up at Dean. "What does a cat have to do to get breakfast around here?"

"Are you okay?"

"Why wouldn't I be?"

"A few minutes ago . . ."

Austin interrupted with an explosive snort. "That was then, this is now." Rising onto his hind legs, he rested his front paws just above Dean's denim-covered knee, claws extended only enough for emphasis. "You look like a nice guy, why don't you feed me?"

"Austin!"

"That's my name," he sighed, dropping back to all four feet. "Don't wear it out."

As Claire came around the corner, she was amazed at how familiar it seemed, as though this were the twenty-second not merely the second time she'd walked into the kitchen. Layered between the sleeping Sara and Hell, there was a comforting domesticity about the whole thing. She shuddered.

"Are you okay?" Dean asked.

"I'm fine. I just had a vision of an unpleasant future." Shaking her head, hoping to clear it, she added, "My mother wasn't home, but I left a message with my sister. She'll call later."

Austin jumped up onto the counter. "Why was your sister home!"

"The usual."

"Anyone get hurt?"

"I didn't ask."

Leaning back against the sink, Dean looked down at his sock-covered feet. Had she not been his boss, he would've asked her if she wasn't a little old to be calling her mum when she ran into a problem.

"Dean?"

He glanced up to see Claire staring at him.

"Penny for your thoughts?"

Instinct caught the coin she tossed, and to his surprise he found himself repeating his musing aloud.

"No, I am *not* too old to call my mother," she said when he finished, ignoring the cat's muttered, "Serves you right for asking."

"My mother has been in the business a lot longer than I have, and I could use her professional advice since not one thing that happened this morning was what I expected. Not room six, not the furnace room, not you."

"Not me?"

"If Austin wasn't so convinced that you're a part of this whole mess, we'd be sitting down to rearrange your memories right about now."

Dean squelched his initial response—why ask if she could do it when there was absolutely nothing in that statement to suggest she couldn't. "If it's all the same to you, I'd like to keep my memories the way they are."

"Good for you." Austin sat down and stared pointedly at the fridge. "So if we're not going to adjust the status quo until your mother's had a look, what are we waiting for? When do we eat?"

Claire sighed. "I think Dean's waiting for an explanation."

"I already explained," Austin protested, twisting out from under Claire's hand. "He told me he believed in magic. I told him that's what was going on."

"That's not much of an explanation."

"It's enough to tide him over until after breakfast."

They surrendered to the inevitable. While Dean cooked for Claire, she ran up to her room to get a can of cat food.

As she put the saucer of beige puree on the floor, Austin glanced down in disgust and then glared up at her. "I can smell perfectly good sausages," he complained.

"Which you're not allowed to have. Remember what the vet said, at your age the geriatric cat food will help keep you alive."

"One sausage couldn't hurt," Dean offered, his expression as he looked into the saucer much the same as the cat's.

Claire caught his wrist and moved the hand holding the fork holding the sausage back over the plate. "Austin's seventeen years old," she told him. "Would you feed one of these to someone who was a hundred and two?"

"I guess not."

"You won't live forever; it'll only seem that way," Austin muttered around a mouthful of food.

As Dean carried the loaded plate over to one of the small tables in the dining room, Claire attempted to organize her thoughts. Of the morning's three surprises, four if she counted Augustus Smythe disappearing and leaving her the hotel, Dean was actually the one she felt least qualified to deal with. When it came right down to it, Sara and Hell and Augustus Smythe were variations on a theme—extreme variations, *really* extreme variations, granted, but nothing entirely unique. On the other hand, in almost ten years of sealing sites, she'd never had to explain herself to a bystander. Manipulate perceptions so she could do her job, yes. Actually—to tell the truth, the whole truth—no.

When Dean set down the plate, she stared aghast at the scrambled eggs, sausage patties, grilled tomatoes, and three pieces of toast. "This is more food than I'd usually eat all day."

"I guess that's why you're so . . ."

"So what?"

"Nothing."

"What?"

"Skinny." Hie ears slowly turning red, Dean set the cutlery neatly on each side of the plate and hurried back into the kitchen. "I'll, uh, get you another coffee, then."

While his back was turned, Claire rolled her eyes. She was not skinny; she was petite. And *he* was so—in rapid succession she considered and discarded intense, earnest, and stalwart. Before she worked her way down to yeomanly, she decided she'd best settle on young and leave it at that. "Aren't you having any?" she asked as he returned with her mug.

A little surprised, he shook his head. "I ate before you got up."

"That was hours ago. Bring another plate, you can have half of this."

"'If *I* bring another plate . . .'" Austin began.

"No." When Dean hesitated, Claire prodded at his conscience. "Trust me, I'm not going to eat all of it; it'll just get thrown out."

A few moments later, a less intimidating breakfast in front of her and Dean eating hungrily on the other side of the table the way only a young man who'd gone three hours without eating could, Claire turned suddenly toward the cat and said, "You're *sure* he's a part of this?"

"I'm positive."

"You were positive that time in Gdansk, too."

Austin snorted. "So my Polish was a little rusty, sue me." He stared pointedly up at her, his tail flicking off the seconds like a furry metronome.

"All right. You win." Chewing and swallowing a forkful of tomato delayed the inevitable only a few moments more. Feeling the weight of Dean's gaze join the cat's, she lifted her head and cleared her throat. "First of all, I want you to realize that what I'm about to tell you is privileged information and is not to be repeated. To anyone. Ever."

Wrapped in the comforting and lingering odors of sausage and egg, Dean ran through a fast replay of the morning's events. "Nothing personal, but who'd believe me?"

"You'd be surprised. When I got up today, I didn't expect I'd be telling it to you." Eyes narrowed, she leaned forward. "If this information falls into the wrong hands . . ."

Unable to help himself, Dean mirrored her movement and lowered his voice dramatically. "The fate of the world is at stake?"

"Yes."

When he realized she meant it, he could've sworn he felt each individual hair rise off the back of his neck. It was an unpleasant sensation. He pushed his chair away from the table, all of a sudden not really hungry. "Okay. Maybe you'd better not tell me."

Claire shot an annoyed look at the cat. "Too late."

"But you don't even know me. You don't know you can trust me."

The possibility of not trusting him hadn't crossed her mind. Total strangers probably handed him their packages while they bent to tie their shoelaces. If a game needed a scorekeeper, he'd always be the one drafted. Mothers could safely leave small children with him and return hours later knowing that their darlings had been fed, watered, and harmlessly amused. *And he does windows.*

"I know we can trust you," Austin muttered, leaping up onto an empty chair and glaring over the edge of the table at a piece of uneaten sausage. "Get on with it. I'm old. I haven't got all day. Are you going to finish that?"

"Yes." While she cleared her plate, Claire created and scrapped several possible beginnings. Finally, she sighed. "I suppose Austin's right . . ."

"Well thank you *very* much."

". . . it begins with believing in magic."

"And ends with?" Dean asked cautiously.

"Armageddon. But if it's all the same to you, I'd rather leave that for another day." When he indicated that Armageddon could be left for as long as she liked, Claire continued. "Magic, simply put, is a system for tapping into and controlling the possibilities of a complex energy source."

"Energy from where?"

"From somewhere else." It was clear that she'd lost him. She sighed. "It doesn't have a physical presence, it just is." In fact, a part of it had reputedly once explained itself by saying, "I AM." but that wasn't a detail Claire thought she ought to add.

"It just is," Dean repeated. Since she seemed to be waiting to see if he was willing to accept that, he shrugged and said, "Okay." At this point, it seemed safest.

"Let's compare magic to baseball. Everyone is more-or-less capable of playing the game but not everyone has the ability to make it to the major leagues." Pleased with the analogy, Claire made a mental note to remember it. She could use it should she ever be in this situation again—owning a hotel complete with sleeping evil, a hole to Hell in the basement, and a handsome, young caretaker to whom her cat spilled his guts. *Yeah, right.* Her nostrils flared.

Taken aback by the nostril flaring, Dean shuffled his feet under the table, glanced around the familiar dining room, and finally said, "Could I do it?"

"With training and discipline, lots of discipline," she added in case he started thinking it was easy, "anyone can do minor magics—so minor that most people don't think they're worth the effort."

Feeling like he'd just been chastised by his fifth grade teacher, an intense young woman right out of teacher's college whom every boy in the class had had a crush on, Dean slid down in his chair until his shoulders were nearly level with the table and his legs, crossed at the ankle, stretched halfway across the room. "Go ahead."

"Thank you." An irritated *so kind* came implied with the tone. Who did he think he was? "Most of the energy magic deals with comes from the center part of the possibilities. The upper end is for emergency use only and the lower end is posted off-limits. For the sake of argument, let's call the upper end 'good,' and the lower end 'evil.' " She paused, waiting for an objection that never came. "You're okay with that? I mean, good and evil aren't exactly late twentieth century concepts."

"They were at my granddad's house," Dean told her. Tersely invited to elaborate, he shrugged self-consciously. "My granddad was an Anglican minister."

"This is the Reverend McIssac, the grandfather who raised you?"
He nodded.

"What happened to your parents?" Claire didn't entirely understand his expression, but as the silence went on just a little too long, she suspected he wasn't going to answer. "I'm sorry, that was tactless of me. I'm not actually very good with people."

"*Quel surprise,*" Austin muttered, head on his front paws.

"No, it's okay." Dean spun one of the breakfast knives around on the table, eyes locked on the whirling blade. "They died when I was a baby," he said at last. "House fire. It happens a lot when the woodstove gets loaded up on the first cold night of winter and you find out what condition your chimney is really in. My dad threw me out the upstairs window into a snowbank just before the building collapsed."

"I'm sorry."

"I never knew them. It was always just me and my granddad. My father was his only son, see, and he wouldn't let any of my aunts raise me. He's the one who taught me to cook." All at once, Dean had to see Claire's expression. Too many girls fell into a "poor sweet baby" mood at this point in the story and things never really recovered after that. Catching the knife between two fingers, he looked up and saw sympathy but not pity, so he told her the rest. "They could've saved themselves if they hadn't gone upstairs for me. I've always known, without a doubt, how much they loved me. There's not a lot of people who can say that."

Swallowing a lump in her throat, Claire reached over and lightly touched the back of his hand. "No wonder you're so stable."

He shrugged self-consciously. "Me?"

"Do you see anyone else around here who isn't a cat?" Austin reached up and batted the knife off the table. "Thank you for sharing. Now, can we get on with it?"

Partly to irritate the cat, and partly to allow emotions to settle, Claire waited while Dean dealt with the smear of butter and toast crumbs on the floor before picking up the scattered threads of the explanation. "You ready?"

He nodded.

"All right, back to good energy and evil energy. Between this energy and what most of the world considers reality, is a barrier. For lack of a better term, let's keep calling it the fabric of the universe. Those who use magic learn to pierce this barrier and draw off the energy they need. Unfortunately, it also gets pierced by accident." She took a long swallow of coffee. "In order to continue, I'm going to have to grossly oversimplify, so please don't think that I'm insulting your intelligence."

"Okay." It still seemed to be the safest response.

"Every time someone does something good, it pokes a hole through the fabric, releases some of the good energy, and everybody benefits. Every time someone does something evil, it releases some of the evil energy and everybody suffers."

"How good?" Dean wondered. "And how evil?"

"The holes are proportional. If say, you sacrificed yourself to save another or conversely sacrificed another to save yourself, the holes would be large." She paused to watch raindrops hit the window behind his head, the drops merging until their weight pulled them in tiny rivers toward the ground. "The problem is that small holes can get bigger. Evil oozing out a pinprick inspires more evil which enlarges the hole which inspires greater evil . . . Well, you get the idea."

"Unless he's dumber than kibble," Austin growled. "I can't believe that was the best you could come up with."

Claire stared down at him through narrowed eyes. "All right. You come up with a better explanation."

Twisting around on the chair seat, the cat pointedly turned his back on her. "I don't want to."

"You can't."

"I said, I didn't want to."

"Ha!"

"Excuse me?" Dean waved a hand to get Claire's attention. "Is that what happened in the furnace room? Someone did something evil and accidentally made a hole?"

"Not exactly," she said slowly, trying to decide how much he should know. "Some holes are made on purpose. There are always people around who want what they're not supposed to have and are arrogant enough to believe they can control it." Recalling an accident site she'd come upon her first year working solo, she shook her head. "But they can't."

Dean read context if not particulars in the movement. "Messy?"

"It can be. I once found a body, an entire body, in the glove compartment of a 1984 Plymouth Reliant station wagon."

"The 1.2 liter GM, or the Mitsubishi engine?"

"Does it matter?"

"It does if you need to buy parts."

Claire drummed her fingernails against the tabletop. "I'm talking about a body in a glove compartment, not a shopping trip to Canadian Tire."

"Sorry."

"May I continue?"

"Sure."

"Thank you. Most holes can be taken care of with the magical equivalent of a caulking gun. Some are more complicated, and a few are large enough for a significant amount of evil to break through and wreak havoc before anything can be done about them."

His eyes widened, appearing even larger magnified by the lenses of his glasses. "Has this ever happened?"

She hesitated, then shrugged; this much she might as well tell him. "Yes. But not often; the sinking of Atlantis, the destruction of the Minoan Empire . . ."

"The inexplicable popularity of Barney," Austin added dryly.

Claire's eyes narrowed again, and Dean decided it might be safer not to laugh.

"Holes," she announced, her tone promising consequences should the cat interrupt again, "that give access to evil draw one of two types of monitors."

"Electronic monitors?"

"No." She paused to rub a smear of lipstick off her mug with her thumb. This was turning out to be easier than she'd imagined it could be. At the moment, before the tenuous connection they'd acquired over the course of the morning dissolved back into the relationship of almost strangers, she suspected Dean would accept almost anything she said.

GO AHEAD, TAKE ADVANTAGE. HAVE SOME FUN. WHO'LL KNOW?

The mug hit the table, rocking back and forth.

Dean grabbed it before the last dregs of Claire's coffee spilled out onto the table. "Are you okay?"

"Yes." She blinked four or five times to bring him back into focus. "Of course. Did you hear anything just now?"

"No."

He was clearly telling the truth.

"Are you sure you're okay?"

"I'm fine." The voice had sounded slightly off frequency, as though the speaker hadn't quite managed to sync up with her head. Considering the nature of the site in the furnace room, there could be only one possible source for that personal a temptation. And only one possible response.

"Right, then, the monitors. Now what?" she demanded when the pressure of Austin's regard dragged her to a second stop.

"Nothing."

"You're staring."

"I'm hanging on your every word," he told her.

He was looking so irritatingly inscrutable, Claire knew he suspected something. Tough. "The monitors," she began again, fixing her gaze on Dean and blocking the cat out of her peripheral vision, "are magic-users known as Cousins and Keepers. The Cousins are less powerful than the Keepers, but there're more of them. They can mitigate the results of an accident, but they can't actually seal the hole. They watch, and wait for the need to summon a Keeper.

"For the sites that *can't* be sealed because the holes have already grown too large, Keepers, who're always referred to as Aunt or Uncle for reasons no one has ever been able to make clear to me, essentially *become* the caulking and seal the hole with themselves. A lot of eccentric, reclusive old men and women are actually saving the world."

Dean took off his glasses and rubbed the bridge of his nose. "So the Keepers are the good guys?"

"That's right."

"And the woman asleep upstairs is one of the bad guys?"

"She's a Keeper gone bad." The words emerged without emotion because the only emotion applicable to the situation seemed a bit much to indulge in over the breakfast dishes. "An evil Keeper."

"An evil auntie?" he asked, unable to keep one corner of his mouth from curving up.

"It's a title, not a relationship," Claire snapped. He looked so abashed she couldn't help adding, "But, essentially, yes. We found her name written in the furnace room. For safety's sake, we can't tell you what it is."

Replacing his glasses, Dean straightened in his chair, shoulders squared, both feet flat on the spotless linoleum. "Written in the furnace room? On the wall?"

"The floor actually." It was very nearly the strongest reaction he'd had all morning. Claire wasn't entirely certain how she felt about that.

"Okay. As soon as you're done, I'll get right on it."

"On it? And do what?"

"Get rid of it. I've got an industrial cleanser designed for graffiti," he told her with the kind of reverence in his voice most males his age reserved for less cleansing pleasures. "Last spring, some kids decorated the side wall, the one facing the driveway, and this stuff took it right off the brick. Took off a bit of the mortar, too, but I fixed that."

"You'll just stay out of the furnace room, thank you very much." Although it would be a unique solution, it wasn't likely to be a successful one. Fortunately, the dampening field would keep him from attempting it on his own.

Brow creased, he shook his head. "I hate to leave a mess. . . ."

"I don't care." Claire smiled tightly across the table at him. "This time, you're going to."

"Okay. You're the boss," he sighed, slumping back into his chair. "But why can't you tell me her name?"

"Because Austin was right. . . ."

"I usually am," the cat muttered.

". . . and we really don't want to wake her."

Dean nodded. "Because she's evil. What did she do? Try to use the power coming out of the hole for her own ends?"

Claire felt her jaw drop. "That's exactly what she tried to do? How did *you* know?"

"I just thought it was obvious. I mean, she was corrupted by the dark side of the force, but another Keeper showed up to stop her just in time, and although she was beaten in a fair fight, she couldn't be killed because that would bring the good guys down to her level, so they put her to sleep instead as kind of a temporary solution."

Mouth open, Claire stared across the table at him.

Dean felt his cheeks grow warm. "But I'm just guessing." When she didn't respond, he squirmed uneasily in his chair. "It's what they'd do in the movie."

"What movie?" The question slipped out an octave higher than usual.

"Not an actual movie," Dean protested hurriedly, not entirely certain what he'd done wrong. "It's just what they'd do in a movie. If they did a movie. But they wouldn't." He'd never actually heard a cat laugh before. "I still don't know why her name would wake her."

Ignoring Austin, who seemed in danger of falling off the chair, Claire wrapped the tattered remains of her dignity around her, well aware that this bystander seven years her junior had offered his last statement out of kindness, deliberately handing back control of the conversation. "Names," she said, coolly, "are more than mere labels; they're one of the things that connect us to each other and to the world." Which was one of the reasons she wasn't planning on identifying the hole in the furnace room. If Dean thought of Hell by name, it could give the darkness a connection and easier access.

One of the reasons.

What they'd do in the movie, indeed.

"If she does get woken up," Dean wondered, frowning slightly, "is she able for you?"

"Say what?"

He hurriedly translated his question into something a mainlander could understand. "Is she stronger than you?"

"No!"

Austin snorted.

"All right. I don't know." Claire glared at the cat. "She's a powerful Keeper, or she wouldn't have been able to seal the hole, not to mention attempting to use it. But . . ." Her eyes narrowed. "I am also a powerful Keeper, or I wouldn't have been summoned here. Waking her would be the only way to find out which of us is stronger, and I'm not willing to risk the destruction of this immediate area on a point of ego."

"So she's still sealing the hole? Like a cork in a bottle?"

"Essentially."

"You're here to pop her out and close the hole?"

"It's more complicated than that."

"And that's why you called your mother?"

"Yes."

"Okay." He took a deep breath, and laid both hands flat on the table. "The woman in room six is an evil Keeper."

"That's right."

"And you're a good Keeper?"

Claire leaned back and pulled a vinyl business card case out of her blazer pocket. "My sister made these for me. She meant them as a joke, but they're accurate enough."

> Aunt Claire, Keeper
> your Accident is my Opportunity
>
> (abilities dependent on situation)

The card stock felt handmade and the words had the smudgy edges of rubber stamp printing. "Should *I* call you Aunt Claire?"

"No."

He'd never heard such a definitive *no* before. There were no shades of *maybe*, no possibility of compromise. When she indicated he could keep the card, he slipped it into the pocket of his T-shirt. "I've always wanted to see real magic."

Claire leaned forward, eyes half lidded, palms flat on the table. "You should hope you don't get the chance."

It would've been more dramatic as a warning had she not placed one palm squarely on a bit of spilled jam.

Dean handed her a napkin and managed not to laugh although he couldn't quite control a slight twitch in the outer corners of his mouth. "So was Mr. Smythe a Keeper, too?"

Claire showed her teeth in what wasn't quite a smile. "Augustus Smythe was, and is, a despicable little worm who walked out and left me holding the bag. He's also a Cousin."

"Did he put her to sleep?"

"No, a Cousin can't manipulate that kind of power." As much as it irritated her to admit it, Dean's little synopsis had to have been essentially correct. "At some point, there was another Keeper involved."

"But Mr. Smythe is a Cousin, and you said Cousins monitor unsealed sites."

"Your point?"

"You said this site is sealed, that she was sealing it like a cork in a bottle . . ."

"No, you said like a cork in a bottle."

"Okay. But if the hole is sealed, what was Mr. Smythe doing here?"

"Probably monitoring the seal since she can't and monitoring *her* since the power that's keeping her asleep is coming from the site."

"Evil power is keeping her asleep?"

"Trust me . . ." She tossed the napkin down onto her plate. "It's not likely to corrupt her."

"But if it was a temporary solution, why has Mr. Smythe been here since 1945?"

"Has he?"

"Sure. He complained about it all the time." With a flick of two fingers, Dean began spinning the knife again. "Why did Mr. Smythe sneak out like he did?"

"I have no idea." The handle of her mug creaked slightly in her grip. "But I'd certainly like to ask him."

"What are you after doing now?"

"Nothing hasty. Nothing at all until I get that second opinion. When I have more information, I'll get to work closing things up but as long as the hole remains sealed, it's perfectly safe. We're in no immediate danger."

"No immediate danger?" Dean repeated. When she nodded, he leaned back in his chair, continuing to spin the knife. "That's, um, interesting phrasing. What about long-term danger?"

"That depends."

"On what, then?"

"I can't tell you."

"There's a whole lot you're not telling me, isn't there?"

"There's a whole lot I don't know."

"Mr. Smythe was supposed to leave you more information?"

Claire snorted, sounding remarkable like Austin at his most sardonic. "At the very least."

"Which is why we need you," the cat told him, looking up from a damp patch of fur. "Smythe's not here, and you are."

"But I don't know anything," Dean protested.

"You should make a good pair, then. She thinks she knows everythi . . . Hey!" he protested as Claire picked him up and dropped him onto the floor. "It was a *joke!* Keepers," he muttered, leaping back up onto the chair, "no sense of humor."

The wisest course, Dean decided, would be to ignore that observation altogether. Stilling the knife, he looked up from her elongated reflection in the blade. "If you don't mind me asking, where do Keepers and Cousins come from?"

"Just outside Wappakenetta." When both Dean and Austin stared at her blankly, she sighed. "We have a sense of humor, it's just no one appreciates it. If you're asking historically, Keepers and Cousins are descendants of Lilith, Adam's first wife."

Dean started to grin.

"I'm not joking."

"You're not serious! Adam's first wife?"

Enjoying his reaction, she waved off his question with a dismissive gesture borrowed from Marlon Brando in *The Godfather.* "I only know what I'm told, but some of our people are very into genealogy."

"But you're talking about *Adam and Eve!*"

"No, I'm talking about Adam and Lilith."

"The Bible, the Christian Bible, as literal truth?" Dean suspected that his granddad, who held some fairly radical views for an Anglican minister, would be appalled.

"No. Not truth as such. The lineage—that is, Cousins and Keepers—consider all religions are attempts to explain their energy. Think of them as containing capital T Truths as opposed to merely being true."

"But you said Adam and Litith," Dean reminded her. "Twice."

Were all bystanders so literal, she wondered, or was it just this one? "Forget them. Forget them twice. If you prefer, there had to have been, at some point, a breeding pair of what was essentially the first humans. Postulate, a second female, with genetic coding to handle magic that the other didn't have. It's the same story in a different language."

"Okay." He took a deep breath, followed that theory out to its logical conclusion, and half prepared to duck. "So essentially, you're not—that is, not entirely—human?"

She took it better than he'd thought she would and seemed more intrigued than insulted, as though the idea had never occurred to her before. "I suppose that depends on where you set your parameters. If you're speaking biologically . . ."

"I wasn't," Dean interrupted before she could add details. Unfortunately, it didn't stop her.

". . . we're, certainly able to interbreed, but that doesn't really mean anything because so could the old Greek gods."

"They were real?"

"How should I know?" One painted fingernail tapped against the side of her mug as she thought it over. "Under those parameters, I suppose you could say, we're . . ." She smiled suddenly and taken totally by surprise, he found himself lost in it. ". . . semi-mythical."

Austin snorted. "Spare me. Semi-mythical indeed."

"It does cover all the bases," Claire protested.

"You want to cover the bases? Play shortstop for the Yankees." Swiveling his head around, Austin stared up at Dean. "She's human. The Keepers are human. The Cousins are human. I barely know you, but I'm assuming you're human. I'm not saying this is a good thing, it's just the way it is."

"Okay." Dean held up both hands in surrender. "So, if Mr. Smythe is a Cousin, and she's a Keeper, what are you?"

Austin drew himself up to his full height, his entire bearing from ears to tail suggesting he'd been mortally insulted. "I am a *cat*."

"A cat. Okay."

While Dean did the breakfast dishes and slotted the morning's experiences into previously empty places in his worldview, Claire went through the papers Augustus Smythe had left in the hotel office in the hope of discovering some answers. If the registration books were complete, the hotel had never been a popular destination and bookings had fallen off considerably after Smythe had changed the name from Brewster's Hotel to The Elysian Fields Guest House in 1952.

"Might as well call it The Vestibule of Hell," she muttered mockingly, turning yellowed pages and not at all impressed by her earlier flash of prescience. It appeared that windowless room four had been popular throughout the existence of the hotel, and the guests who stayed in it seemed to have had uniformly bad handwriting.

She had to call Dean out of the kitchen to open the safe.

"The very least Augustus Smythe could've done," she grumbled, arms folded and brows drawn into a deep vee over her nose, "was leave me the combination."

"He left you Dean," Austin observed from the desk. "Something he probably figured you'd get more use out of."

Ears red, Dean cranked the handle around and got up off his knees as the safe door swung open. "Anything else, Boss?"

Having chased Austin halfway up the first flight of stairs before being forced to acknowledge that four old legs sufficiently motivated were still faster than two, Claire ducked back under the counter. "Not right now."

As she straightened, their eyes locked. "What?"

Dean felt a sudden and inexplicable urge to stammer. He managed to control it by keeping conversation to a minimum. "The combination?"

"Good point. Write it down. Use the back of that old bill on the desk," she added, walking over to the safe. Squatting, she heard pencil move against paper then the combination appeared over her shoulder. "Six left, six right, seven left?"

"That's right. I should, uh, finish the dishes now."

"Good idea." As he returned to the kitchen, Claire grinned. He really did turn a very charming color at the slightest opportunity. Then she looked back down at the piece of paper and shook her head. Six sixty-seven. Cute. Hell was in the basement; the safe was on the first floor, one up from the Number of the Beast. *First the Elysian Fields, now this.* Augustus Smythe seemed to delight in throwing about obscure hints. *A cry for help or sheer bloody-mindedness?*

In the safe, she found a heavy linen envelope marked with the sigil for expenses. On the back, *Taxes, Victuals, Maintenance,* and *Staff* had been written in an elegant copperplate. Another, later hand had added, *Electricity* and *Telephone.* The envelope was empty.

No outstanding bills. Claire put the envelope back in the safe and closed the door. *Great. When the seal goes and something calling itself Beelzebub leads a demonic army out of the furnace room, the lights'll stay on and a well-fed staff can call 911 as they're disemboweled.*

As she sat back on her heels, a flash of brilliant blue racing along the inside edge of a lower shelf caught her eye. Thumb and first two fingers of her right hand raised, just in case, she leaned over and with her left hand yanked a dusty pile of ledgers onto the floor. The hole in the corner was unmistakably mouse.

Which didn't mean that only mice were using it.

Mice weren't usually a brilliant blue.

She moved closer and sent down a cautious probe.

"Problem?"

"OW!" Rubbing her head, she crawled back from the shelf and glared up at Dean. "Try and make a little more noise when you sneak up on people!"

"Sorry. I've finished the dishes and I was wondering if you want me to put a new padlock on room six."

"Definitely." It was an emotional not a rational response. Sara wouldn't be leaving the room any time soon and—should she decide to—a padlock wouldn't stop her, but for peace of mind there had to be a perception of security. "I'll have a locksmith repair the door plate."

"But he'll see her."

"No, he won't."

It was another one of those statements, like *"rearrange your memories,"* that Dean had no intention of arguing with. "Okay." He squatted beside her and peered at the hole. "Looks like a new one. I'll set out some more traps."

"Mousetraps?"

The sideways look he shot her seemed mildly concerned. "Yeah. Why?"

"Have you caught anything?"

"Not yet." Rising, he held out his hand. "They're smart. They take the bait and avoid springing the trap."

Claire debated with herself for a moment, then put her hand in his. "They might not be mice," she said as he lifted her effortlessly to her feet. "All I'm reading is the residual signature of the seepage, but this place could easily be infested with imps." Which would explain why her running shoes had still been wet this morning.

"Imps?"

"I saw something and it was bright blue." A little surprised that he hadn't released her, Claire pulled her fingers free of his grip.

"Imps." Dean sighed. "Okay. Is there anything I can do about it now?"

"Not now, no."

"In that case, I'll be upstairs if you need me."

"Don't go into the room."

He looked uncomfortable. "I was thinking about dusting her."

"Don't."

"But she's covered in . . ."

"No."

According to the site journal, found tucked under a stack of early seventies skin magazines in the middle left-hand drawer of the desk, three Keepers had sealed the hole before Sara; Uncle Gregory, Uncle Arthur, and Aunt Fiona. Aunt Fiona had died rather suddenly which explained why Sara had been summoned off active service at such a relatively young age—she'd been the closest Keeper strong enough to hold the seal when the need had gone out.

"Relatively young age," Claire snorted, rubbing her eyes. The yellowing papers she studied seemed to soak up the puddle of illumination spilled by the old-fashioned desk lamp without the faded handwriting becoming any more legible. "She was forty-two."

Sara had made it very clear in her first entry in the site journal that she hated the hotel and everything to do with it. It was also her one and only entry.

"Oh, this is a lot of help. A considerate villain would've had the courtesy to keep complete notes."

Confident of her abilities, Claire had no doubt that she'd been summoned to the hotel to finally close the site. It was the only logical explanation. Unfortunately, sealing the hole would cut the power that kept Aunt Sara asleep, and Claire had meant it when she'd told Dean she didn't want to find out which of them was more powerful.

Keepers capable of abusing the power granted by the lineage were rare. Claire had only heard of it happening twice before in their entire history. The battles, Keeper vs Keeper, good vs evil, had been won but both times at a terrible cost. The first had resulted in the eruption of Vesuvius and the loss of Pompeii. The second, in disco. Claire had only a child's memories of the seventies, but she wouldn't be responsible for putting the world through that again.

Augustus Smythe's entry, which should have, and possibly did describe how he'd come to monitor the site, was unreadable. Ink had been spilled on the last third of the ledger, had soaked through the pages, and dried to create what could most accurately be described as an indigo blue brick. The skin magazines would've been as helpful.

"Coincidence?" Claire asked the silence. "I don't think so." The sound of something scuttling merrily away inside the wall only confirmed her suspicions.

She was searching through yet another pile of paid bills in the top drawer of the desk when, for the first time that day, the phone rang. Used to the polite interruptive chirp of modern electronics, Claire had forgotten how loud and demanding the old black rotary models could be.

Coughing and choking, she picked up the receiver. "Hello?"

"Claire?"

"Mom . . ."

"What's the matter?"

Startled by the intensity of the question, Claire jerked around but could neither see nor hear anything moving up on her. "What do you mean? What do you know?"

"You were choking."

"Oh, that." Wiping her chin with her free hand, Claire relaxed. "The phone startled me, and I tried to breathe spit. It's nothing." Breath back, she explained the problem.

"Oh, my."

"Exactly. Do you think you could come and have a look at it? At them. Tell me what you think."

"I'd like to help you, Claire, but I don't know. If I were needed, I'd have been summoned."

"I need you. Who says a summons can't use the phone?" She could feel her mother weakening. "This is huge. I'd hate to screw it up."

"Under the circumstances, that wouldn't make anyone very happy." She paused. Claire waited, poking her finger through the black coils of the cord. "It would be nice to spend some time with you. Would you like me to bring your sister?"

"I don't think so, Mom."

"You haven't seen her for almost a year."

"We talk on the phone."

"It's not the same."

"Yes, I know. But, please, leave her home anyway." The thought of

Diana within a hundred miles of an open access to Hell brought up an image of the Four Horsemen trampling the world under their hooves as they fled in terror.

After supplying detailed directions, Claire hung up, glanced out into the shadowed lobby, and sighed. "Are your work boots dry, Dean?"

He looked down at his feet. "They should be. Why?"

"You walk too quietly without them. *Please,* put them on."

With no memory of turning, he'd taken three silent, sweat sock muffled steps toward the back door before he recalled what he'd come out to the lobby to say. "I made a fresh pot of coffee, if you're interested. And pecan cookies."

Dean stared at Claire over his seventh cookie. "So your mother is your cousin?"

"No. She's *a* Cousin."

"And your father's . . . ?"

"A Cousin, too."

"And you and your younger sister, Diana, are both Keepers?"

"Yes."

Behind his glasses, his eyes twinkled. "So, you're your mother's Aunt?"

"No."

"But . . ."

"Look, I didn't make up the stupid nomenclature!" Strongly suspecting that Dean was being difficult on purpose, Claire tossed back her last mouthful of coffee, choked, and ended up spraying the table-top and both her companions.

"Oh, thank you very much." Austin jumped down onto the floor and vigorously shook one back leg. "I just got that clean!"

After handing the still sputtering Keeper a napkin, Dean quickly used another to mop up the mess. When things got back to normal, and when the cat had been placated, he asked, "Why won't your mother be here until tomorrow afternoon?"

"That's when the train from London gets in. Tomorrow morning she'll get a lift from Lucan into London, then catch the train from London to Toronto to connect with the 1:14 out of Union Station, which means she'll be here about four."

"Oh." He'd been half hoping to hear that the delay involved for low altitude brooms. After the excitement of the morning, he was ready for his next installment of weird. Things hadn't been this interesting vacuuming the flying carpet or waiting until the flight path cleared since he'd left home. Actually, things hadn't been this interesting *at* home—although his granddad's reaction to his cousin Todd getting an eyebrow pierced had come close. "Why doesn't she drive?"

"Because she can't. None of us can."

Dean blinked. Okay, *that* was the weirdest thing he'd heard so far. "None of your family?"

"None of the lineage."

"Why not?"

"Too many distractions. We see things other people don't"

There'd been a couple of members of Dean's family who'd seen things other people hadn't, but they were usually laid out roughly horizontal and left to sleep it off. "Things like blue mice?" he asked innocently, biting into another cookie.

"No. They're nothing at all like blue mice," she told him curtly. If she responded to his teasing, he'd keep doing it, and she already had one younger sibling; she didn't need another. "They're bits of the energy, small possibilities that . . . Austin! Get out of there!" Leaping to her feet, she snatched the butter dish out from under the cat's tongue. "Do you know what this stuff does to your arteries?" she demanded. "Are you trying to kill yourself?"

"I'm hungry."

"There's a bowl of fresh, geriatric kibble on the floor by the fridge."

"I don't want that," he muttered looking sulky. "You wouldn't make your grandmother eat it."

"My grandmother doesn't lick the butter."

"Wanna bet?"

Claire turned her back and pointedly ignored him. "Small possibilities," she repeated, "that sometimes seep through and run loose in the world."

Dean glanced around the dining room. "What do they look like?"

"That depends on your background. You're a McIssac so, if you had the Sight, at the very least you'd see traditional Celtic manifestations. Given that Newfoundland has a wealth of legend all its own you'd also probably pick up a few indigenous manifestations."

"You're not serious?" he asked her, grinning broadly. "Ghoulies and ghosties and things that go bump in the night?"

"If you want."

His grin faded. "I don't want."

"Then don't mention it."

Down in the furnace room, having spent the last few hours testing the binding, the intelligence in the pit rested. It would have been panting had it been breathing.

NOTHING HAS CHANGED, it observed sulkily.

Although physically contained, the pentagram could not entirely close it off from the world. There was just no way it was that easy.

It seeped through between the possibilities.

It tempted. It taunted. And once, because of the concentration trapped in that one spot, it had managed to squeeze through a sizable piece of pure irritation.

THE OLD MALE IS GONE.

THE YOUNG MALE IS STILL HERE.

The heat rose momentarily as though Hell itself had snorted. THAT GOODY TWO SHOES. WHAT A WASTE OF TIME.

THERE'S A NEW KEEPER.

WE'VE DEALT WITH KEEPERS BEFORE.

WE DIDN'T EXACTLY DEAL WITH THE OTHER. WASN'T SHE INTENDING TO CONTROL . . .

SHUT UP!

It also talked to itself.

THREE

—•— ⧓ —•—

"**IF YOU DON'T HURRY**," Austin complained from the bedroom, "I'm going down to breakfast without you."

Claire rummaged through her makeup case, inspecting and discarding a number of pencils that needed sharpening. "I'm moving as fast as I can."

They'd spent the night back in room one even though Dean had reiterated that the owner's rooms were now rightfully Claire's. Although willing to spend the evening watching television and eating pizza in Augustus Smythe's sitting room, Claire wasn't quite ready to sleep in his bed.

"I don't see why you bother with all that stuff."

"This from the cat who spent half an hour washing his tail." One eye closed, she leaned toward the mirror. Her reflection remained where it had been. "Oh, no." Straightening, she put down the pencil and looked herself in the eyes—not at all surprised to notice that they were no longer dark brown but deep red. "Now what?"

A skull, recently disinterred, appeared in the reflection's left hand. "Alas, poor Yorik. I knew him, Horatio, a fellow of infinite jest."

"And oft times had you kissed those lips." Claire folded her arms and frowned. "I'm familiar with the play. Get to the point."

The reflection lifted the skull until it could gaze levelly into the eye sockets. "Now get you to my lady's chamber, and tell her, let her paint her face an inch thick, to this favor she must come . . ." A fluid motion turned the skull so that it stared out from the mirror. ". . . make her laugh at that."

"Not bad, but I imagine you have access to a number of actors. Your point?"

"Open the pentagram. Release us. And we shall see to it that you remain young and beautiful forever."

"You're kidding, right? You're offering a Keeper eternal youth and beauty?"

The reflection looked a little sheepish. "It is considered a classic temptation. We thought it worth a try."

"Oh, please."

"That means no?"

Claire sighed and, both hands holding the edge of the sink, leaned forward. "Go to Hell," she told it levelly. "Go directly to Hell, do not pass go, do not collect two hundred dollars."

The skull vanished. Her reflection began answering to her movements again.

"Was that wise?" Austin asked from the doorway.

"What? Refusing to be tempted?"

"Making flippant comments."

"It wasn't a flippant comment." She finished lining her right eye and began on her left. "It was a stage direction."

"Hel-lo!"

"Mom?" In the kitchen, using a number of household products in ways they'd never been intended by the manufacturers—not even the advertising department which, as a rule, had more liberal views about those sorts of things—Claire was attempting to remove the ink from the latter third of the site journal. While not technically an impossible task, it did seem to be, as time went on, highly improbable. Laying aside the garlic press, she dried her hands on a borrowed apron— borrowing it hadn't been her idea—called out that she'd be right there, and tripped over the cat.

By the time she reached the lobby, Austin was up on the counter, having his head scratched and looking as though *he* hadn't been waiting as impatiently as anyone.

"You're certainly right about those shields," Martha Hansen said, as Claire came into the lobby. "I can't feel a thing."

Catching Austin's eye, Claire mimed wiping her brow in relief.

Austin looked superior; *he'd* had a bad feeling about it from the start. So there. "Thanks for coming, Mom."

"Well, I could hardly refuse my daughter's call for help, now could I? Besides, your sister's in the workshop today and it's your father's turn to deal with the fire department." The three of them winced in unison. "And it did seem a shame not to work in a quick visit with you so close. You're looking well." She wrapped Claire in a quick hug. "Maine must've agreed with you."

"I was in and out too fast for it to disagree with me. Easiest site I ever sealed."

"Good. At least you're not facing this site exhausted and cranky."

"Cranky?" Claire repeated, shooting a warning look at the cat. "Mom, I'm twenty-seven. I'm a little old for cranky."

Her mother smiled. "I'm glad to hear that. How did you sleep last night?"

"Like a log. I expect it's another effect of the dampening field."

"I expect it is." Unzipping her windbreaker, Martha turned back toward the counter. "What about you, Austin?"

"*I* slept like a cat." One ear flicked back. "I always sleep like a cat."

"That's very reassuring. Any developments since you called, Claire?"

"Nothing much. We might have an imp infestation—I'm fairly certain it, or they, damped down my shoes the first night I was here." She saw no point in mentioning the voice. Not only had it been a highly subjective experience, but she'd stopped telling her mother everything that went on in her head the day Colin Rorke had kissed her behind the football bleachers. "This morning, my reflection offered me eternal youth and beauty."

Martha sighed as she shrugged out of her jacket. "I've said it before and I'll say it again, evil has no imagination. Probably why so much of it ends up in municipal politics. They'll be back, you know, and the temptations will escalate as they come to know you better."

"I expect I'll seal the site before that becomes a problem."

"But surely it's already sealed."

"No, Mom, I mean seal it closed."

"Closed?"

"That must be why I'm here," Claire asserted. "I couldn't possibly have been summoned to an epistemological babysitting job as though I were too old to do anything but slap my power over a site and make sure nothing creeps out around the edges."

"This hole . . ."

"Is huge, but it doesn't change the job description."

"And have you determined how you're going to close the hole and simultaneously take care of . . ." She jerked her head toward the third floor.

"Not yet, but I'm working on it. I was hoping that you, with your greater experience and years of work in the field, could throw a little light on the problem."

"Suck up," Austin muttered.

Lips twitching, Martha bent and picked up her overnight case. "Let me drop this off in my room, and then I'll go take a look at your problems. The sooner I see them, the sooner I can tell you what you need to hear."

Claire grabbed the key to room two and hurried to catch up on the stairs, frowning as she got a good look at the feet she followed. "I wish you wouldn't wear socks and sandals, Mom."

"It's the end of September, Claire, I can hardly wear either alone."

"But they make you look like an aging hippie."

"Truth in advertising; nothing wrong with that. Now, *I* wish you'd wear a little less makeup. It makes you look like . . ."

"Don't start, Mom."

"My. This *is* medieval." Walking slowly, examining each line, Martha circled the pit. "In my experienced opinion," she said after a moment, "you do, indeed, have a hole to Hell in your furnace room. Or more specifically a manifestation of evil conforming to the classic parameters of Hell—the popularity of which, I've never entirely understood." Glancing up at the ductwork, she added, "Mind you, I expect it keeps the heating costs down." Her hand shot out and jerked Claire back a step. "Don't pace on the pentagram."

Folding her arms, Claire mirrored her mother's élan. Mostly, it was an act although as the second exposure came without the shock of discovery, she found it a little easier to cope. "I *know* it's a hole to Hell," she said, trying to sound as if her teeth weren't clenched together. "But since it's linked rather irrevocably to room six, I was hoping you might have some ideas on how to separate them. Some advice on what I should do first."

YOU COULD RELEASE US.

"Nobody asked you."

WE'D BE GOOD.

"Liar."

WELL, YES.

"I don't think you should argue with it, Claire." Slipping on her glasses, Martha pointed toward the lettering etched into the bedrock, being very careful not to trace anything in the air that could be interpreted as a pattern. A Cousin shouldn't be able to affect an accident site but, given the site in question, that wasn't a tenet she intended to test. "That," she said, "is the name of the person responsible for this situation. I expect he died right after he finished the invocation. Notice the similar pattern around Sara's name."

Eyes beginning to water from the sulfur, Claire studied the design. It wasn't an exact match, but close enough for Keeper work. "Just as we thought, she tried to gain control. If Hell offered her power in exchange for freedom, that must've come as an unpleasant surprise."

"I can't say that I find myself feeling too terribly sorry for it," her mother murmured.

NO ONE EVER DOES, Hell sighed.

"Do shut up. Now then, I think we've been in here long enough." Martha took hold of her daughter's arm and guided her up the stairs. "Hopefully, we'll find out more from a thorough examination of Aunt Sara."

GIVE HER OUR REGARDS.

"Don't count on it"

"Well?" Austin asked from the top of the washing machine as they tightened the chains across the closed door. He had point-blank refused to go back into the furnace room.

"She wants to go see *her*," Claire told him, pointing upward

"You should take Dean with you."

"Are you out of your mind? Has he been feeding you on the sly?" The cat's eyes narrowed. "Read my lips, he's a part of this."

"You don't have lips."

"A moot point. Your mother will have to meet him sooner or later."

"She can meet him later."

Martha started toward the other end of the basement "Are his rooms down here?"

"Yes, but . . ."

"Austin thinks we should take Dean, and I'm inclined to agree."

Claire threw up her hands. "Mom, Austin thinks baby birds are a snack food."

"What does *that* have to do with this?"

"Listen to your mother, Claire," Austin murmured as he padded by.

She managed to resist kicking him and hurried to catch up, wishing she'd remembered that her mother's professional opinion carried personal baggage along with it. "I don't want Dean told about what's in the furnace room."

"You don't think he deserves to know the truth?"

"He knows there's an accident site; telling him that he's bedding down next to a hole leading to a classical manifestation of a Christian Hell will only compromise his safety."

"In what way?"

"He's a kid. Minimal defenses. The knowledge could give Hell access to his mind."

"I think you're afraid he'll leave if you tell him," Austin said, rubbing against the edge of a low shelf. "And you don't want him to leave."

"Of course I don't want him to leave—he cooks, he cleans, I don't. But neither do I want him blundering into situations he has no hope of understanding." She turned to her mother. "He's already in deeper than any bystander I've ever been in contact with. Isn't that enough? How am I supposed to protect him?"

"If he's been here since last February, I'd say he has pretty powerful protections of his own," Martha said thoughtfully. "But you're the Keeper, it's your decision whether you tell him or not."

"Then why isn't *this* my decision?" Claire asked as her mother knocked at the basement apartment. She didn't expect an answer, which was good, because she didn't get one.

Dean came to his door holding a mop.

"Merciful heavens." Unable to stop herself, Martha glanced down at his feet.

Claire hid a smile. It seemed clear that any member of the lineage meeting Dean for the first time couldn't help but check for tangible evidence of how very grounded he was.

Completely confused, Dean set the mop to one side, scrubbed his palm off on his jeans, and held out an apprehensive hand. "Hello. You must be Claire's mother."

"That's right I'm Martha Hansen." Recovering her aplomb, she took his offered hand in a firm grip. "Pleased to meet you, Dean. Claire's told me so little about you."

Half expecting a female version of Augustus Smythe, Dean was pleasantly surprised to find there were no similarities whatsoever. Mrs. Hansen looked remarkably like many of the artists who spent their summers in the outports. She wore her long, graying hair pulled loosely back off her face, no makeup, baggy pants, a homespun vest over a turtleneck and the ubiquitous sandals. Dean wasn't sure why sandals were considered artistic, but they certainly seemed to be. While a resemblance to the summer people wasn't entirely a recommendation, working for Mr. Smythe had taught him it could've been a lot worse. "You've been in the furnace room already, then?"

"We have. How could you tell?"

He felt his ears redden. "You're sweating. Mr. Smythe was always sweating when he came out of the furnace room."

Martha smiled and dabbed at her forehead with a tissue pulled from her vest pocket. "How observant of you. We have, indeed, been in the furnace room, but we're on our way up to room six now and we'd like you to come along."

He glanced over at Claire and noticed her slight hesitation before she nodded. "I don't want to be in the way."

"Nonsense. As Austin says, you're a part of this."

"Then just let me hang up my mop."

When he disappeared into his apartment, Martha turned toward her daughter. "He's a kid?"

"He's barely older than Diana."

"Sweetie, I hate to tell you this, but your sister isn't exactly a kid any more either." When Claire's brows drew in, she patted her on the arm. "Never mind. I don't think you'll have any problems with Dean. He's a remarkably stable young man, not to mention very easy on the eyes. I like him."

Forced to agree with the first two sentiments, Claire snorted. "You'd like an Orchi if it did housework."

"This is incredible." Remaining within the shielded area, attention locked on the sleeping Keeper, Martha moved around to the far side of the bed. "Just think of all the factors involved in achieving such an intricate balance of power."

"I am thinking about it, Mom. Or more specifically, I'm thinking about what'll happen if I unbalance it, ever so slightly."

"Don't."

Safely outside the shield, Claire sighed. Had she forgotten her mother was prone to those sorts of facetious comments? "I don't suppose you can see a way to break the loop without precipitating disaster?"

"No, I can't. I've never seen anything so perfectly in balance. I'm very impressed. Such a pity I'll never have a chance to tell the Keepers who designed it."

"Keepers."

"Oh, yes, this definitely took two people. You can see a double signature in the loop."

"Where?"

"Here. And here."

Claire pressed the back of her hand against her mouth. She shouldn't have missed the signs her mother had just pointed out. After all, she was a Keeper and her mother only a Cousin. "How can you stand to get so close to her?"

"I concentrate on the binding, not on her. Still . . ." Dusting off her hands, she stepped out through the shield. ". . . that was nasty."

Crouched in the doorway, rubbing Austin behind the ears to keep him distracted, Dean shook his head. They were like TV cops standing over a body matter-of-factly discussing multiple stab wounds. "You don't get disturbed about much, do you, Mrs. Hansen?"

Martha turned to face him. "Actually, I'm very disturbed."

"It doesn't show."

"After a few decades spent dealing with various sundry and assorted metaphysical accidents, I've gotten good at hiding my reactions. Also, the lineage is trained to remain calm about these sorts of things. It wouldn't do to have us yelling 'Fire!' in a crowded theater, now would it?"

Not entirely certain that he understood the analogy, he let it go.

"Don't worry about it," Austin murmured. "Just try sharpening your claws on the sofa and you'll see how disturbed she gets."

Arms folded, Claire frowned down at the woman on the bed. In a strange way, Hell was the lesser of two evils. Unlike Aunt Sara, hell had done nothing it wasn't supposed to do. "All right, Mom, you've seen the situation. Where should I begin?"

"I suggest we begin by leaving the room." Shooing Dean, Claire, and Austin out in front of her, she pulled the door closed then frowned at the splintered wood. "Then I suggest you get this fixed. Thank you, Dean." She stepped aside as he snapped the padlock back on. "Finally, I suggest you get used to the idea of being here a while."

"I never thought I'd work out how to close this down in a day or two, Mom."

"You may not be intended to close it down, Claire. You may have been summoned here as a monitor."

Claire blinked. "I find that highly unlikely. The last monitor was a Cousin."

"And the site was clearly too strong for him to manage. It needs a Keeper."

"If it needs me," she said, her eyes narrowing, "then it *doesn't* need a monitor."

"I can't see a way for you to safely interfere with the current arrangement. I think Dean's idea is correct; given there was a war on, the Keeper, or Keepers, who dealt with this situation probably intended their solution to be a temporary measure. They plugged in the first available Cousin, then were killed during the fighting. Augustus must have been quite young and would have agreed to watch the site until the Keepers returned. They never did, and he was held by his word until another came along.

"Just at the point where the site was about to destroy him utterly, there was Claire, drawn by his need to leave. I realize I'm speculating here, but I find myself feeling quite sorry for him."

"I don't." Claire flinched under her mother's gaze. "All right, yes I do. He got a raw deal, but I don't see why I should be happy to have the same one."

"Not exactly the same deal, if the site was intended to have a Keeper as a monitor."

"Or," Claire insisted, "if that Keeper was intended to close the site down. I'll tell you what I'm going to do, I'm going to find the Historian, find out exactly what those two Keepers did, then undo it. I have no intention of either allowing this to continue or of spending the rest of my life here."

"The Historian is seldom easy to find."

"That's only because *I've* never gone looking for her."

"True enough. Meanwhile," Martha glanced up and down the hall. "You have a guest house to run."

"Run?" Claire stared at her mother in astonishment. "Have you forgotten what's in the basement?"

"This was probably set up as a guest house *because* of what's in the basement. This is a unique situation. The more you think about the site, the more attention you pay it, the stronger it becomes. You need a distraction, something to occupy your time."

"But the guests . . ."

"They're here two or three nights at most. Hardly long enough for a sealed site inside a dampening field to have much effect."

"But I already have a job; I'm a Keeper. I don't know the first thing about running a guest house."

"Dean does." Martha looked remarkably like Austin as she added, "And you said you didn't want him to leave."

"Because I need a cook and a caretaker," Claire explained hurriedly, picking at a wallpaper seam.

"You still do."

"If I'm really a part of what's going on," Dean broke in, "I couldn't just walk out."

"You couldn't walk out on old Augustus," Austin sniggered, "and he didn't have Claire's . . ."

Claire's head jerked up. "Austin!"

". . . sunny personality."

"Good, that's settled." Martha smiled on them both in such a way it became obvious the problem had been solved to her satisfaction.

Since there seemed to be no point in continuing the argument, and since she wasn't entirely certain which argument to continue, Claire started down the stairs, her heels thumping against the worn carpet. Dean fell into step beside her. "I want you to know that things are not going to continue the way they were under Augustus Smythe. I am not going to watch passively. I'm going to take action."

"Okay." When she glared at him from the corner of one eye, he smiled and added, "Sure."

"Are you laughing at me?"

"I was trying to cheer you up."

"Oh. Well, that's all right, then."

As they disappeared down the stairwell, Austin wrapped his tail around his toes and looked up at Claire's mother. "Nice to have things settled."

Smoothing down the wallpaper Claire'd been picking at, Martha frowned. "It's hard to believe that all this has been sitting here for so many years with no one aware of it."

"It was a bit of a surprise," the cat admitted. "You can't blame Claire for wanting to wrap it up and leave."

"Staying does ask a lot of her."

"Not the way she sees it. She thinks she's been declawed."

"That's only because she was looking forward to doing things, not merely waiting for all hell to break loose."

"Oh, that's clever," Austin snorted as he stretched and stood. "Come on, just in case the world's about to end, you can feed me."

"Mr. Smythe has prog enough to last through freeze up," Dean explained, setting the supper plates on the table.

"Very reassuring, or it would be if I had the slightest idea of what you meant."

"I mean he has food enough to last the entire winter."

"Then why didn't you say so." Claire moved her chicken aside and tentatively tried a forkful of the wild rice stuffing. Her eyes widened as she chewed. "This is good."

"Try not to sound so surprised, dear, it's rude." Her mother waved a laden fork in Dean's direction. "You cook, you clean, and you're gorgeous; do you have a girlfriend?"

"Mom."

"It's okay." His father'd had six older sisters and after twenty years of holiday dinners with his aunts, Dean pretty much expected both the comments and the question from any woman over forty. They didn't mean anything by it, so it no longer embarrassed him. "No, ma'am, not right now," he said, sliding into his seat.

"Are you gay?"

"Mom!"

"It's a perfectly valid inquiry, Claire."

"It's a little personal, don't you think? *And* it's none of your business."

"It will be if you're here for any length of time. I could introduce him to your uncle."

"He's *not* gay."

"He most certainly is."

"I wasn't talking about Uncle Stan! I was talking about Dean."

"And why are you so certain he's not?"

"I'm a *Keeper!*

Ears red, Dean stared intently into his broccoli. *That* was not a question he'd expected, at least not from Claire's mother, although Uncle Stan did make a change from being set up with *my best friend Margaret's youngest daughter, Denise.* "Um, excuse me, I was wondering, who's the Historian?"

"Heavens, I'd have thought you'd had enough exposition for one day."

Claire sighed. "He's attempting to change the subject, Mom, you've embarrassed him." She ignored her mother's indignant denials. "The Historian is a woman . . ."

"We don't know that for certain, Claire," Martha interrupted. "You may see her as a woman, but that doesn't mean everyone does."

"Do *you* want to tell him?"

"No need, you're doing fine."

"The Historian," Claire repeated through clenched teeth, "who *I* see as a woman, keeps the histories of all the Keepers."

"Is she a Keeper?" Dean asked, bending to pick up his napkin and slipping a bit of chicken under the table to the cat.

"We don't know."

"Then what is she?"

"We don't know."

"Okay. Where is she?"

"We don't know that either; not for certain at any given time. The Historian hates to be bothered. She says she can't finish collecting the past with the present interrupting, so to protect her privacy she moves around a lot."

"Then how do you find her?"

"I go looking."

Dean paused, wondering if he was ready for the next answer. *Oh, well, the boat's past the breakwater, I might as well drop a line.* "Where?"

"She usually sets up shop just left of reality."

"What?"

"If reality exists, then it stands to reason that there must be something on either side of it." Claire tapped the table on both sides of her plate with her fork as if that explained everything.

He ate some chicken, delaying the inevitable. "Okay. Why *left* of reality?"

"Because the Apothecary uses the space on the right."

"Dean? If I could have a few words?"

"Sure, Mrs. Hansen."

"Martha." She took the tea towel from his hand. "Here, let me help."

He watched as she dried a plate, decided her standards were high enough, and plunged his hands back into the soapy water. "Where's Claire?"

"Watching the news. I was wondering, did she explain her family situation?"

"Both you and Mr. Hansen being Cousins?"

"That's right It's a very rare situation, two Cousins together, and it's why both our girls are Keepers. Now, usually Keepers become aware of what they are around puberty . . . are you blushing?"

"No, ma'am."

"Must be the light." She took a dry tea towel off the rack. "Because of their double lineage, my girls not only knew what they were from the start but were unusually powerful. Although they're better socialized than many Keepers—my husband and I tried to give them as normal an upbringing as possible—they've been told most of their lives that with great power comes great responsibility—clichéd but true, I'm afraid. Now, Claire's willing to give her life for that responsibility, but, like all Keepers, it's made her more than a little arrogant."

Dean set the plate he was washing carefully back into the water and slowly turned. "What do you mean, give her life?"

"Evil doesn't take prisoners." Martha shook her head, wiping a spoon that was long dry. "That sounds like it should be in a fortune cookie, doesn't it?"

Pulling the spoon from her hand, Dean locked eyes with the older woman and said softly, "Mrs. Hansen, why are we having this conversation?"

"Because all power corrupts and the potential for absolute power has the potential to corrupt absolutely. This site has already corrupted a Keeper and made a Cousin, at best, bitter and, at worst, mean. I don't want that happening to my daughter. She's going to need your help." When he opened his mouth, she raised her hand. "I realize your natural inclination is to immediately assure me you'll do everything you can, but I want you to take a moment and think about it. Their abilities tend to deemphasize interpersonal relationships; she can be downright autocratic at times."

He dropped the spoon in the drawer. "What happens when she finds this Historian?"

"I don't know."

"She thinks she's too powerful to be here just as a monitor, doesn't she?"

"Yes."

Dean watched the iridescent light dance across the soap bubbles in the sink. "I'll tell you, Mrs. Hansen . . ."

"Martha."

". . . I don't know Claire and I don't really understand what's going on, but if you say she's after needing me, well, I've never turned away from someone who's needed me before and I'm not after starting now."

Long years of practice kept her from smiling at the confidence of the young. At twenty-five that speech would've sounded pompous. At twenty, it sounded sincere. "She won't make it easy for you."

"You ever gone through a winter in Portuguese Cove, Mrs. Hansen?"

"Martha. And no, I haven't."

"Once you can do that you can do anything. Don't worry, I'll help her run things and I'll try not to let her push me around because of what she is."

"Thank you."

"*Everyone* likes to be needed."

She studied him thoughtfully for a moment, then said, "You're taking this whole thing remarkably well, you know. Most people wouldn't be able to cope with having their entire worldview flipped on its side."

"But it wasn't my entire worldview, now was it?" He plunged his hands back into the soapy water. "The sun still comes up in the east sets in the west, rain falls down, grass grows up, and American beer still tastes like the water they washed the kegs out with. Nothing's changed, there's just more around than I knew about two days ago." With a worried lift of his brows, he nodded toward the rest of the silverware on the tray. "If you could, please finish that cutlery before the water dries and makes spots . . ."

They worked in silence for a while, the only sound the wire brush against the bottom of the roasting pan.

"Mrs. Hansen?"

"Martha."

"What is it you do?"

"Claire's father and I watch over the people who live in an area where the barrier between this world and evil is somewhat porous."

"But I thought Cousins couldn't use the caulking gun."

Martha stopped drying one of the pots and stared at him. "The what?"

"The magical equivalent of the caulking gun that seals the holes in the fabric of the universe." Dean repeated everything he could remember of Claire's explanation.

When he finished, Claire's mother shook her head. "It's a bit more complicated than that, I'm afraid." Then she frowned as she thought it over. "All right, perhaps it isn't—but it's certainly less rational. We're not dealing with a passive enemy but a malevolent intelligence."

"Does Claire know this?"

"Of course she does, she's a Keeper. But she's young enough to believe—in spite of what you might think of her advanced age," she interjected at his startled expression, "that it's not the energy that's the problem, it's what people do with it. While that may be true in a great many cases, there's also energy that you simply can't do good with, no matter what your intentions are."

"Evil done in God's name is not God's work. Good done in the Devil's name is not the Devil's work." He set the last pan in the rack to drain. "It's what my granddad used to say before he clipped me on the ear."

"Your granddad was very wise."

"Sometimes," Dean allowed, grinning.

Without really knowing how it happened, Martha found herself grinning back. "To finish answering your actual question, the site we monitor is too porous to be sealed—think T-shirt fabric where it should be rubberized canvas—so there's constant mopping up to do. I do the fieldwork, and my husband teaches high school English."

"Teaching high school doesn't seem very . . ." He paused, searching for a suitable word.

"Metaphysical?" Martha snorted, sounding like both her daughter and the cat. "Is it possible you've already forgotten what it's like to be a teenager?"

"Are you going to be all right?"

"I'll be fine, Mom." Claire reached out and fixed the collar on her mother's windbreaker as the early morning sun fought a losing battle with a chill wind blowing in off Lake Ontario. "And don't worry. I'll monitor the situation while I gather the information I need to shut it down."

"I would never worry about you not fulfilling your responsibilities, Claire, but it took two Keepers to create the loop. What if it needs two Keepers to close it?"

"Then I'll monitor the situation until the other Keeper shows up. This is not going to be my final resting place."

Because even Keepers needed the comfort of hope, Martha changed the subject. "Be nice to Dean. He's exactly what he seems to be, and that's rare in this world."

"Don't worry about Dean. Austin's on his side."

"Austin's on the side of enlightened self-interest." A pair of vertical lines appeared above the bridge of Martha's nose. "I think you'll manage best with Dean if you treat him like a Cousin."

"A Cousin?" She stared at her mother in astonishment. "He's a nice kid, Mom, but . . ."

"He's not a kid."

"Well, not technically and certainly not physically, but you've got to admit he's awfully young."

"And how old were you when you sealed your first site?"

"That's beside the point. He's not of the lineage."

"No, he's not, but he is remarkably grounded in the here and now, and he's going to be your main support. The less you hide from him, the more he'll be able to help."

"Mother, I'm a Keeper. I don't need help from a bystander. All right," she went on before her mother could speak, "I need his help running the guest house but not for the rest."

"Just try to be nice to him, that's all I ask." She gripped Claire's hands in both of hers. "If you must check the contact points of the loop, be very, very careful. You don't want to wake her up, and you don't want to believe anything *they* tell you. Don't lose track of time when you're searching for the Historian; you know what'll happen if you come back before you've left. Try and make Austin stick to his diet, and you should eat more, you're too thin."

Claire opened her mouth to argue but said instead, "Here's your ride," as a battered cab pulled up in front of the guest house and honked.

"If you need me, call." She frowned as the cabbie continued to hit his horn, the irregular rhythm echoing around the neighborhood. "Would you do something about that, Claire?"

The echo gave one last, feeble honk, then fell silent.

"Thank you. Come to think of it, even if you don't need me, call. Your father's likely to be worried about you being in such proximity to the hole in the furnace room."

"There's really no need to tell him about Hell, Mom."

"He's teaching in the public school system, Claire. He knows about Hell."

Standing in the open doorway, Claire released her hold on the horn as the cab pulled away. Through the broad back window of the vehicle, she could see her mother giving emphatic instructions. If the driver thought he knew the best way to the train station, he was about to discover he was wrong.

At the last possible moment, Martha turned and waved.

Claire waved back.

"So. It seems I own a hotel." A distraction, something to keep her mind off what was in the furnace room. "Who knows," she said with more resignation than enthusiasm. "It might be fun."

Raising her body temperature enough to fight the chill, she went down to have a look at the sign. To her surprise, her first impression had been correct. The sign actually said "Elysian Fields 'uest House," the "g" having disappeared. "Dean's going to have to repaint this." She frowned. "I wonder what I'm paying him?"

A low growl drew her attention around to the building on the other side of the driveway. An apple-cheeked, old woman with brilliant orange hair, wearing a pale green polyester pant suit and a string of imitation pearls, stood on the porch, waving at her enthusiastically. Also on the porch was the biggest black-and-tan Doberman Claire had ever seen.

"Hello, dear!" the woman caroled when she saw she had Claire's attention. "I'm Mrs. Abrams—that's one b and an ess— who are you?"

"I'm Claire Hansen, the new owner of the guest . . ."

"New owner? No, dear, you can't be." Her smile was the equivalent of a fond pat on the head. "You're much too young."

"I beg your pardon?" The tone could stop a political canvasser in full spate. It had no effect on Mrs. Abrams.

"I said you're too young to be the owner, dear. Where's Augustus Smythe?" She leaned forward, peering around like she suspected he were hiding just out of sight. The Doberman mirrored her move— twitching as though anxious to get down and check it out personally.

Claire fought an instinctive urge to back up and held her ground. "Mr. Smythe's whereabouts are none of your con . . ."

"None of my concern?" A flick of her hand and a broad smile took care of that possibility. "Of course I'm concerned, you silly thing; I live next door. He's avoiding me, isn't he?"

"No, he's gone, but . . ."

"Gone? Gone where, dear?"

"I don't know." When Mrs. Abrams' expression indicated profound disbelief, Claire found herself adding, "Really, I don't."

"Well." The single word bespoke satisfaction that years of suspicions had finally been justified. "They took him away, did they? Or did he run before they arrived? If truth be told, I can't say as I'm surprised." She fondled one of the dog's ears. The twitching grew more pronounced. "You would never, not ever, hear me say anything against anyone—live and let live is my motto, I'm very active in my church's Women's Auxiliary you know, they couldn't get along without me—but Augustus Smythe was a nasty little man with an unnatural dislike of my poor Baby."

Showing more teeth than should've been possible in such a narrow head, Baby's growl deepened.

"Would you believe that he actually had the nerve to accuse my Baby of doing his business in your driveway?" Her voice dropped into caressing tones. "As if he didn't have his own little toilet area in his own little yard. He didn't repeat those vile and completely unfounded accusations to you, did he, dear?"

It took Claire a moment to straighten out the pronouns. "He did mention . . ."

"And you didn't believe him, did you, dear? I'm afraid to say that he told a lot of, well, lies——there's no use sugar coating it. I don't know what else he told you, Caroline . . ."

Claire opened her mouth to protest that her name was not actually Caroline but couldn't manage to break into the flow of accusation.

". . . but you mustn't believe any of it." A plump hand pressed against a polyester-covered, matronly bosom. "Now, me, I'm not like some people in this neighborhood, I mind my own business, but that Augustus Smythe . . ." Her voice lowered to a conspiratorial tone Claire had to strain to hear. "He not only lied, but he kept secrets. I wouldn't be surprised if he had unnatural habits."

Neither would Claire, but she was beginning to feel more sympathetic. No wonder Baby twitched.

"I'd love to stay and chat longer, dear, but it's time for Baby's vita-min. He's not a puppy any more, are you, sweetums? He's a lot older than he looks, you know."

"How old is he, Mrs. Abrams?"

"To be perfectly honest, Christina—and I assure you I am always perfectly honest—I don't actually know. The little sugar cube showed up on my doorstep one day—he knew I'd take him in, you see, dogs always know—and we've been together ever since. Mummy couldn't do without her Baby. Ta, ta for now!" She yanked the dog around and, with a cheery wave and a bark that promised further confrontation, they disappeared inside the house.

Stepping to the edge of the driveway, Claire peered toward the back of the property. Too far away to make a positive identification, a large brown pile had been deposited, nicely centered in the lane.

"Unfounded accusations," Claire muttered, carefully climbing the stairs and going back inside.

Stretched out in a patch of sunshine on the counter, Austin yawned. "Where have you been?"

"Out meeting the obligatory irritating neighbor. How do you tell if a pile of dog shit came out of a Doberman?"

The cat looked disgusted. "How do *I* tell? *I* don't."

"All right, how would I tell?"

"Check it for fingers. Why are we talking about this?"

"I'm beginning to think Hell wasn't the only thing Augustus Smythe wanted to get away from."

"Are you staying in the official residence, then?" Dean asked as Claire came down the stairs with her belongings. Sliding his hammer into the loop on his carpenter's apron, he leaped down off the ladder and held out his hands. "Can I help?"

"Yes." Pride not only went before a fall, it also went before drop-ping everything she owned. She shoved her suitcase at him, caught her backpack as it slid off her shoulder, and barely managed to hang onto the armload of clothes that she hadn't bothered to repack. "What were you doing?"

"Attaching that bit of molding over the door. It'd gone some squish. Out of plumb," he added as her brows dipped down.

"I see." Glancing at the repair, Claire wondered what, as his employer, she was supposed to say. Her mother wanted her to be nice to him . . . "Good work. You matched the ends up evenly."

"Thank you." He beamed as he held up the folding section of the counter and waited for her to go through.

She didn't think he was being sarcastic. Stopping by the desk, she lowered her backpack to the center of the ancient blotter. "Since this appears to be the only available desk, I guess I'm leaving my computer out here. I can use it for hotel business."

"Laptop?" Dean wondered, studying the dimensions of the pack curiously.

"No." Once everything else had been dumped in the sitting room, she returned to the desk. Opening the backpack, she pulled out a fourteen-inch monitor and stand, a vertically stacked CPU with two disk drives and a CD-Rom, and a pair of speakers.

"You've got to love the classics," Austin snickered, watching Dean's jaw drop. "Now pull out the hat stand and the rubber plant."

"Hat stand and rubber plant?" Dean repeated.

"Ignore him," Claire instructed, untangling the cables. "I'm hardly going to put a rubber plant in here with all these electronics."

Dean removed his glasses, cleaned them on the hem of his T-shirt, and put them back on just as Claire unpacked a laser printer. "This is incredible. Absolutely incredible."

She shrugged, rummaging around for the surge suppressor. "Not really, it only prints in black and white."

"Boss?"

Squinting a little in the glare from the monitor, Claire leaned left and peered out into the lobby. Although all available lights were on, her computer screen was still the brightest source of illumination in the entire entryway. "What is it, Dean?"

"I thought I'd head downstairs and I just wondered if there was anything I could get you before I went."

"Nothing, thank you. I'm fine."

"You could get *me* a rack of lamb, but we all know who'd object to that," Austin muttered without lifting his head from the countertop.

When Dean showed no sign of actually heading anywhere, Claire sighed and saved her file. "Was there something else?"

Fingers tucked second-knuckle-deep into the front pockets of his jeans, he shrugged, the gesture more hopeful than dismissive. "I was just wondering what you were doing."

"I'm treating this site like any other I've been summoned to seal." She was not going to surrender her life to a run-down hotel; no way, no how, no vacancy. "I'm writing down everything I know, and I'm prioritizing everything I have to do."

Head cocked speculatively to one side, Dean grinned. "I wouldn't have thought you were the 'lists' type."

"Oh?" Both eyebrows rose. "What type did you think I was."

"Oh, I guess the 'dive right in and get started' type."

Either he hadn't heard her tone, or he'd ignored it. Claire took another look at his open, candid, square-jawed and bright-eyed expression. Or he hadn't understood it. "Well, you're wrong." His smile dimmed, his shoulders sagged slightly, and his head dipped a fraction— nothing overt, nothing designed to inflict guilt, just an honest disappointment. She felt like such a bitch, her reaction completely out of proportion to his. "But how would you know differently?" Impossible not to try and make amends. "I do have something for you to do tomorrow, though."

"Sure." His head lifted, erasing the fractional droop. "What?"

"The *G* needs replacing on that sign out front."

"No problem." Smile reilluminated, he glanced down at his watch. "I'd better get going, then; it's almost time for the game on TSN."

"If he had a tail, he'd be wagging it," Austin observed dryly as Dean's work boots could be heard descending the basement stairs. "I think he likes you."

Claire found herself typing to the rhythm of heels on wood and forced herself to stop. "I'm his new boss. He just wants to make a good impression."

"And has he?"

"How can you make such an innocent question into innuendo?"

The cat looked interested. "I don't know. How?"

✧　　✧　　✧

The room was completely dark. The air smelled faintly of stale cigar smoke. The silence was so complete, the noises her body made were too loud to let her sleep. The cat was taking up most of the room on the bed.

That, at least, she was used to. The rest, she decided to do something about. Slipping out from under the covers, she felt her way over to the window in the outside wall.

There's nothing out there but the driveway. No harm in opening the curtain a bit and letting in some air.

It wasn't that easy. After forcing her will on a heavy brocade curtain that didn't want to open and struggling with the paint that sealed the sash, Claire managed to shove the window up about half an inch. Breathing heavily, she knelt on the floor and sucked an appreciative lungful of fresh air through the crack. As her eyes grew accustomed to the dark, she made out a window across the drive, the silhouette of pointed ears and, beside them, a pair of binoculars resting on their wider end.

No wonder Augustus Smythe had kept the curtains so emphatically drawn.

A thump behind her warned her to brace herself for the furry weight that leaped onto her lap and then onto the windowsill.

"Could I have a little light here?" Austin murmured.

"What for?" Claire asked as she cast a glow behind him. "You can see perfectly well without it."

"I can," the cat agreed placidly. "But he can't."

Across the drive, the pointed ears flicked up and Baby threw himself at the window.

Claire doused the light, but the damage had already been done. Baby continued to bark hysterically. She grabbed the cat and let the curtains fall closed as a lamp came on and a terrifying vision in pink plastic curlers snatched up the binoculars.

Austin squirmed out of her arms and jumped back onto the bed. "I think I'm going to like it here."

CAN WE USE THE CAT?
    DON'T BE RIDICULOUS.

FOUR

—————✕◆✕—————

AUGUSTUS SMYTHE HAD WANTED his breakfast every morning at seven o'clock. He'd had a bowl of oatmeal, stewed prunes, and a pot of tea, except on Sunday when he'd had a mushroom omelet, braised kidneys, and indigestion. Guests, and in his experience there'd never been more than one room occupied at a time, ate between eight and eight-thirty or they didn't eat at all.

Dean found himself in the kitchen, water boiling and bag of oatmeal in his hand before he remembered that things had changed. He'd been feeding Claire like she was a guest, but she wasn't. Nor, he'd be willing to bet, was she the stewed prunes type.

She wasn't only his new boss, she was a Keeper; a semimythical being monitoring the potential eruption of evil energy out of a possibly corrupting metaphysical accident site in the furnace room. Cool. He could handle that.

The question was: What did she want for breakfast?

"How should I know?" Foiled in his attempt to gain access to the refrigerator, Austin glared down at the fresh saucer of wet cat food. "But if she doesn't want the kidneys, I'll take them."

The hot water pipes banged at a quarter to eight. Dean had no idea how long women usually took to get ready in the morning, but his minimal experience seemed to indicate they were fairly high maintenance. He waited until eight-thirty, then brewed a fresh pot of coffee.

At nine, he began to worry. Austin had eaten and disappeared, and he'd heard nothing more from Claire's suite. By nine-thirty, he couldn't wait any longer.

Had she fallen getting out of the shower? Did that sort of thing happen to the semimythical?

Tossing his apron over the back of a chair, he walked quickly up the hall, ducked under the edge of the counter, and hesitated outside her door. If she'd gone back to sleep, she wouldn't thank him for waking her. Maybe he should go away and wait a little longer.

If, however, she were lying unconscious by the tub . . .

Better she's irritated than dead, he decided, took a deep breath, and knocked.

"Come in."

It took a moment, but he finally spotted Austin on a pie-crust table beside a purple china basket of yellow china roses. "Is Claire . . ."

"Here? No."

"She went out?" He hadn't heard the front door.

"No. She went in."

"In?"

"That's right. But I'm expecting her back any . . ." The cat's ears pricked up and he turned to face the bedroom. "Here she comes. I hope she picked up those shrimp snacks I asked for."

Brow furrowed, Dean stepped forward. He could've sworn he heard music—horns mostly, with an up-tempo bass beat leading the way. Through the open door, he could see an overstuffed armchair and the wardrobe Mr. Smythe had used instead of a closet. Obviously Claire hadn't quite caught on as her clothes were draped all over the chair.

The music grew louder.

The wardrobe door opened and Claire stepped out. Several strings of cheap plastic beads hung around her neck, and a shower of confetti accompanied every movement. She didn't look happy.

"What do you bet they were out of shrimp snacks," Austin muttered.

Glancing into the sitting room, the Keeper's eyes widened. "What are you doing here?"

"I live here."

"Not you." She dragged off the thick noose of beads and pointed an imperious finger at Dean. "Him."

"You were in the wardrobe."

It wasn't a question, so Claire didn't answer it "Don't you ever knock?"

"I *did* knock." Flustered almost as much by the implication that he'd just walk in to her apartment as by her emergence from the wardrobe, Dean jerked his head toward the cat. "He told me to come in."

Austin stretched out a paw and pushed a pottery cherub onto the floor. It bounced on the overlap of three separate area rugs and rolled unharmed under the table.

Claire closed her eyes and counted to ten. When she opened them again, she'd decided not to bother arguing with the cat— experience having taught her that she couldn't win. Bending over, she flicked confetti out of her hair. "If that's coffee I smell, I could use a cup. It isn't safe to eat or drink on the other side."

"The other side of what?" Dean asked, relieved to see that the bits of paper disappeared before they reached the floor. Well, maybe relieved wasn't exactly the right word. "Where were you?"

"Looking for the Historian. The odds of actually finding her are better early in the morning before the day's distractions begin to build." Straightening, Claire scowled at the pile of beads. "I lost her trail at a Mardi Gras."

"In September?"

"It's always Mardi Gras somewhere." She reached into her shirt to scoop confetti out of her bra, noticed Dean's gaze follow the motion and turned pointedly around. So much for his grandfather's training.

Dean felt his ears burn. "It's *somewhere* in the wardrobe?"

"The wardrobe is only the gate." When she turned back to face him and caught sight of his expression, she added impatiently, "It's traditional."

"Okay." First he'd ever heard that Mardi Gras in a wardrobe was traditional, but at least the music had stopped. If his life was after picking up a soundtrack, he'd prefer something that didn't sound like a marching band after a meal of bad clams.

"I could really use that coffee," Claire prodded, taking his arm and propelling him toward the door.

"Right." Coffee, he understood, although, since he'd thought he understood wardrobes, coffee would probably also be subject to change without notice. "We, uh, we need to work out your meals."

"What's there to work out? You do your job, I'll do mine. You cook, I'll eat."

"Cook what?" Dean insisted. "And when?"

Suddenly aware she still had fingers wrapped around the warm, resilient curve of a bicep, Claire snatched her hand back. "I'll eat anything, I'm not fussy, but I can't cope with brussels sprouts, raw zucchini, dried soup mixes, and anything orange. Except oranges."

"Anything orange except oranges," he repeated "So carrots . . ."

"Are out. For as long as I'm here, lunch at noon, supper at five-thirty, so I can watch the news at six. I'll have cold cereal or toast for breakfast and that I *can* make myself."

"You're after saving the world on a bowl of cold cereal?"

"I'd really rather you didn't start sounding like my mother," she told him sharply, stepping out into the office just as the outside door opened.

"Yoo hoo!" Clinging to the latch, Mrs. Abrams peered around the edge of the door. "Oh, there you are, dear!" She straightened and rushed forward. "You remember me . . ." It was a statement of fact ". . . Mrs. Abrams, one bee and an ess. You should keep this door locked, you know, dear. The neighborhood isn't what it was when I was a girl. These days with all the immigrants you never know who might wander in off the street. Not that I have anything against immigrants—they make such interesting food, don't you think?" Penciled eyebrows lifted dramatically toward a stiff fringe of bangs when she spotted Dean standing on the threshold behind Claire. "How nice that you two young people are getting along."

"What did you want Mrs. Abrams?" Claire didn't see much point in asking *her* if she ever knocked.

"Well, Kirstin . . ."

"Claire."

"I beg your pardon, dear?"

"My name is Claire, not Kirstin."

"Then why did you tell me it was Kirstin, dear?" Before Claire could protest that she hadn't told her any such thing, Mrs. Abrams waved a dismissive hand and went on. "Never mind, dear, I'm sure anyone might get confused, first day at a new job and all. I stopped by because Baby heard something in the drive last night—it might have been burglars, you know, we could have all been murdered in our beds—and I had to come over and see that you were all right."

"We're fine. I . . ."

"I see you have a computer." She shook her head disapprovingly, various bits of her face swaying to a different drummer. "You have to be careful about computers. The rays that come off them make you sterile. Has that nasty little Mr. Smythe returned yet?"

Finding it extremely disconcerting to speak to someone whose eyes never settled in one place for more than a second or two, Claire came out from behind the counter. "No, Mrs. Abrams, he's gone for . . ."

"I remember how this place used to look, so quaint and charming. It needs a woman's touch. I hope you realize that you can call on my services at any time, Karen dear. I could have been a decorator, everyone says I have the knack. I offered to give the place the benefit of my own unique skills once before, but do you know what that Augustus Smythe said to me. He said I could redecorate the furnace room."

Claire managed to stop herself from announcing that the offer was still open—although whether she was sparing Mrs. Abrams or Hell, she wasn't entirely certain.

"Have you done anything with the dining room, dear?"

Short of a full tackle, Claire couldn't see how she could stop Mrs. Abrams from heading down the hall.

"I haven't seen the dining room for years. I hardly ever set foot in here with that horrible man in . . ."

Although dimmed by distance and masonry, Baby's bark was far too distinctive to either miss or mistake.

"Oh, dear, I must get back. Baby does so love to greet the mailman, but the silly fool persists in misunderstanding his playful little ways. Mummy's coming, Baby!"

Claire rubbed her temples, throwing an irritated glance at Dean as he finally stepped off the threshold and closed the door to the sitting room. "You were a lot of help."

"Mrs. Abrams," Dean told her with weary certainty, "doesn't listen to men."

"I doubt Mrs. Abrams listens to anyone."

The barking grew distinctly triumphant

"I'm not criticizing," Claire said stiffly, ducking back under the counter and going to the front window, "but why *wasn't* the front door locked?"

Dean followed her. "I unlock it every morning when I get up. For guests."

They winced in unison as Mrs. Abrams could be heard shrilling, telling Baby to let it go—where *it* did not refer to the mailbag.

"Were you actually expecting guests?"

"Not really," he admitted.

The mailman made a run for it

"I can't say as I'm surprised." As she left the office, a wave of her hand indicated the cracked layers of paint on the woodwork and the well-scrubbed but dingy condition of the floor. "This place doesn't exactly make a great first impression."

"So what should we do?"

"Do?" Claire turned to face him and was amazed to find him looking at her as though she had the answers. Behind him, Austin looked amused. "*We* aren't going to do anything. *I'm* going to work at sealing this site. You . . ." About to say *"You can do whatever it is you usually do on a Tuesday,"* she found she couldn't disappoint the anticipation in his eyes. "Since it's not raining, you can get started on repainting that G on the sign."

With the site journal soaking in a clarifying solution, Claire spent the morning going through the rest of the paperwork in the office. By noon, the recycling box was full, her hands were dirty, and she had two paper cuts as well as a splitting headache from all the dust.

She'd found no new information on either Sara, the hole, or the balance of power maintained between them. Someone, probably Smythe, had scrawled, *the Hell with this, then* in the margin of an old black-and-white men's magazine and that was as close as she'd come to an explanation.

"What a waste of time."

"Some of those old magazines are probably collectible."

Claire's lip curled. "They're not exactly mint."

"Good point." Gaze locked on her fingers, Austin backed away. "You're not planning on touching me with those filthy things, are you?"

"No." She dropped her hands back to her sides. "You know what the worst of it is? I have to go through Smythe's *suite,* too. There's no telling what he's crammed in there over the last fifty-odd years."

"No point in picking the lock if there's a chance of finding the key," the cat agreed.

"Spare me the fortune cookie platitudes." Searching for at least the illusion of fresh air, Claire walked over to the windows. Outside, the wind hurried up the center of the street, dragging a tail of fallen leaves, and directly across the road two fat squirrels argued over a patch of scruffy lawn. It was strange to feel neither summons nor site. Because of the shields, she had to keep reminding herself that this was real, that she shouldn't be somewhere else, doing something else.

The sound of Dean's work boots approaching turned her around to face the lobby.

"Hey, Boss, find anything?"

"No more than on the last two times you asked."

"Would lunch help?"

"Helps me," Austin declared, leaping down off the counter.

Claire's stomach growled an agreement Outvoted, she started toward the door to Smythe's old suite. "Just let me wash up fir . . ." The sound of her shin cracking against the bottom drawer of the desk drowned out the last two letters. Grabbing her leg, she bit back her first choice of exclamation, and then her second, and then there really didn't seem to be much point in a third.

"Are you okay, Boss?"

"No, I'm not okay." Air whistled through clenched teeth. "I'm probably crippled for life."

A LIE!
    AN EXAGGERATION.
    CAN'T WE USE IT ANYWAY? Hell asked itself hopefully.
    OH, DON'T BE SUCH A GIT.

"And you know what the worst of it is?" The question emerged like ground glass. Claire tugged her jeans up above the impact point "I closed the drawer. I *know* I closed the drawer."

Obviously, she hadn't but Dean knew better than to argue with a person in pain. "Here, let me look at that then." Ducking under the counter, he dropped to one knee and wrapped his hand around the warm curve of Claire's calf.

Her first inclination was to pull free. Her second . . .

NOW *THAT* WE CAN USE.

Reminding herself of the age difference, she banished the thought.

DAMN.

"You didn't break the skin, but you'll have some bruise." Stroking one thumb along the end of the discoloration, he looked up at her and forgot what he was about to say.

"Dean?"

The world shifted most of the way back into focus. "Liniment!"

"No, thank you. You can let go of me now."

Feeling his ears begin to burn, he snatched both hands away, then, suddenly unable to cope with six inches of bare skin, lightly stubbled, reached out again and yanked her jeans back down into place.

"Watch it!" One hand clutching her waistband, she grabbed his shoulder with the other to stop herself from falling.

Stammering apologies, Dean stood.

Things got a little tangled for a moment.

When a minimum safe distance had been achieved, Dean opened his mouth to apologize yet again and found himself saying instead, "What's that noise?"

"It's a cat," Claire told him. "Laughing."

Claire refused to be constrained over lunch. So what if Dean kept his gaze locked on the cream of mushroom soup, that was no reason for her to act like a twenty-year-old. Biting into a sandwich quarter, she swept a critical gaze around the dining room.

"This is ugly furniture," she announced after chewing and swallowing. "In fact, it's an ugly room."

Grateful for a change of subject, even though the original subject hadn't actually been broached, or even defined, Dean acknowledged the pitted chrome and worn Naugahyde with a shrug. "Mr. Smythe wouldn't buy anything new."

"It's not new we need." Claire tapped a fingernail thoughtfully against the table. "I'll deny this if you repeat it, but Mrs. Abrams gave me an idea that could bring in more guests."

"Is that a good idea?" Austin asked, jumping up onto an empty chair. "You're a Keeper, remember? You *have* a job."

"And I'll do my job, thank you very much," she snapped, turning to glare at him. "But a short break before I face the chaos in that sitting room won't bring about the end of the world." She paused and considered it a moment. "No. It won't. Besides, I have no intention of allowing this hotel to slide any farther into oblivion during my watch. There's a hundred things that need to be done, that should've been done years ago. If Augustus Smythe had kept busy, he'd have been happier."

The cat snorted. "Have you seen the rest of those postcards? He kept plenty busy."

"He kept one hand busy at best." Claire put down her spoon and folded her arms. "He was a disgusting little voyeur. Is that how you suggest I fill my time?"

"Actually, I was about to suggest you share your soup with the cat."

"I still don't understand what we're doing." Dean twisted the key around in the attic lock and dragged the door open. "There's nothing up here but junk."

"The furniture in the dining room is junk," Claire amended. "The furniture in the attic is antique." Switching on the larger of the two flashlights, she ran carefully up the spiral stairs.

Dean watched her climb, telling himself it wasn't safe to have both of them on the stairs at once and almost believing it. When she stepped off the top tread into the attic, he followed her up.

"Look at all this!" Although sunlight streamed in through the grime on the windows, the volume of stored furniture kept most of the attic in shadow. The flashlight beam picked out iron bedsteads, washstands, stacks of wooden chairs, lamp shades dripping with fringe, and rolls of patterned carpet. "Nothing's been thrown away since the hotel opened."

"And nothing's been cleaned since it was put up here."

Thankful that they'd found the accident site before they'd had to spend days shifting clutter, Claire turned the flashlight on her companion. "What is it with you and this obsessive cleaning thing?"

"It's not obsessive."

"It's not normal." She pointed the flashlight beam toward room six, one floor below. "You even wanted to dust *her.*"

"So?" Reaching down, Dean effortlessly shifted one end of a carpet roll out of his way. "My granddad always said that cleanliness was next to godliness."

Cleanliness was living next to a hole to Hell, but Claire hadn't changed her mind about letting him know it. Not even if he flexed that particular combination of muscles again. "See if you can find the old furniture from the dining room."

"From the look of this place, we'd be as likely to find the Ark of the Covenant and the Holy Grail."

She shuddered. "Don't even joke about that."

Squeezing past a steamer trunk plastered with stickers from a number of cruise ships, including both the *Titanic* and the *Lusitania*, Claire worked her way toward the back of the building. It was farther than it should have been; one of the earlier Keepers had obviously borrowed a little extra Space.

Well, I hope they kept the receipt. . . . Out of the corner of one eye, she saw a bit of red race along the top of a wardrobe and disappear behind a pink-and-gray-striped hatbox. "Oh, no."

"Trouble, Boss?" She could hear furniture shoved aside as Dean struggled toward her.

"Not exactly, but I saw something; moving very fast. Unfortunately, it would take at least two hours of excavation or an Olympic gymnast to get to the spot."

The sound of distant movement ceased. "It was just a mouse. There's prints and turds all over up here."

He sounded so positive, Claire didn't bother pointing out that mice seldom came in a bright fire-engine red.

"Don't worry about it, okay? I'll bring some traps up later."

So would she, and she rather thought hers would be more successful.

Ignoring the way her reflection moved slightly out of sync, Claire ducked around an elaborate, full-length mirror and finally ended up under the sloping edge of die roof. "This," she said, turning off the flashlight, "is certainly strange."

Displayed in relative isolation by one of the windows was a bed and mattress, a set of drawers, an old radio, a washstand with a full china set, and a pair of ladder-back chairs.

As Claire stepped forward, she caught sight of something that drove all thoughts of V.C. Andrews-style decorating out of her mind. Just at the edge of the "room" was the very table she'd been looking for. It could easily seat twelve, and all it needed was a bit of polish.

"Dean! I've found it!" She swept a pile of papers onto the floor and had barely emerged, sneezing and coughing from the cloud of dust, when Dean stepped out from between a stack of washstands and yet another steamer trunk, having discovered a slightly wider route to the spot.

"It looks solid enough," he admitted, circling the table. Frowning thoughtfully, he heaved one end into the air. "It's some heavy. How are you after carrying it downstairs?" Releasing the table edge, he bent under it for a closer inspection, highlighting the joints with his flashlight beam. "Those stairs are narrow, and it doesn't come apart."

"I'll get it down the same way they got it up." Dismissing the little voice in the back of her mind that suggested she was showing off, Claire carefully reached through the possibilities and pulled power. "First, I stack the chairs and tables currently in the dining room, out in the hall."

Listening hard, Dean thought he heard the faint sound of stainless steel chiming against stainless steel and the slightly louder sound of an irritated cat.

"Then . . ." She traced a design in the dust on the table. ". . . I send this beauty down to replace them."

The table disappeared.

"Rapporter cette table!"

Waving one hand vigorously in front of her face, Claire peered through the reestablished dust cloud at Dean. "What did you say?"

He sneezed. "Wasn't me."

In the silence that followed his denial, they could hear the dust settling.

"It's quiet."

"Too quiet," Claire corrected.

With a sinister rustle, scattered papers rose into the air, riding an invisible whirlwind. They spun for a moment in place, faster, faster, then whipped forward.

Claire dove for Dean just as he reached out to rescue her. Foreheads connected. They hit the floor together as the papers flew overhead.

Ears ringing, Claire scrambled to her knees. "What do you think you're doing?"

"Trying to save you!"

"Oh? How?"

"Like this!" He flung himself at her and returned her to the floor as the papers made their second pass. The edge of an envelope opened a small cut on his cheek.

"Get off me!"

"You're welcome!" Too buzzed with adrenaline to be embarrassed, he rolled onto his back and watched her climb to her feet. "What are *you* doing?"

"Putting a stop to this!" She pointed a rigid finger at the papers. "Right now!"

Everything except a postcard plummeted to the floor. The postcard made one final dive.

"You, too!" Claire snapped.

It burst into flames and fell as a fine patina of ash over the rest.

Hands on her hips, she glared around the open space where the table had been. "We can do this easy or we can do this hard. Your choice."

The silence picked up a certain mocking quality.

"Just remember, I warned you."

"Now what?" Dean asked, standing slowly, keeping a wary eye on those larger items, like chairs, that might also be considered movable.

Claire bent down and smudged a bit of ash on her left forefinger. "Now, I'm going to make whatever it is show itself."

"You can do that?"

"Of course," she snapped. "Check the card."

"The card?"

"The business card I gave you."

He pulled it out of his wallet as she walked over to the window ledge and smudged a bit of dust on her right forefinger.

> Aunt Claire, Keeper
> Your Accident is my Opportunity
>
> (spiritual invocations a specialty)

"It didn't say that before."

"It didn't need to. Now, be quiet." With both hands out at shoulder height, she pulled power. The symbol drawn by her left hand glowed green, the symbol drawn by her right glowed red. "Ashes to ashes, dust to dust. Appear because I say you must."

Dean glanced back down at the card. It now read: (poetry optional). Claire's sister apparently had a good idea of Claire's limitations.

Between the symbols, fighting the invocation every inch of the way, the figure of a man began to materialize. Still translucent, he jerked back and forth trying to break the power that held him. When he finally realized he couldn't win, he snapped into focus so quickly the air around him twanged. Medium height and medium build, he wore a bulky black turtleneck, faded jeans, and a sneer.

The symbols lost their color, glowing white.

"Your name," Claire commanded.

"Jacques Labaet" Squinting, he tossed shoulder length, dark-blond hair back off his face. "And I am *not* at your service." When he tried to stride forward, lines of power snapped him back between the symbols. Brows drew in over the bridge of a prominent nose. "All right Perhaps I am."

"Give me your word you won't attack again, and I'll release you."

"And if l do not?"

The symbols brightened. "Exorcism."

One hand raised to shield his eyes, Jacques shook a chiding finger at her. "You are a Keeper. You cannot do that. You have rules."

"You drew blood." Claire nodded toward the cut on Dean's cheek. "Yes, I can."

"Ah." He pursed his lips and thought about it. *"D'accord.* You win. I give you my word."

The symbols disappeared.

"You are a woman of *action rapide,* I allow you that." Blinking away afterimages, he stepped toward her. "For all you are so . . . beautiful." His mouth slowly curled up into a lopsided smile that softened the long lines of his face, creating an expression that somehow managed to combine lechery and innocence. Claire found it a strangely attractive combination. *"Tes yeux sons comme du chocolat riche de fonce.* . . . Your eyes they are like pools of the finest chocolate; melting and promising so very much sweetness. Does anyone ever tell you this?"

"No."

"Are you certain?"

He sounded so surprised she had to smile. "I'd have remembered."

"So foolish are mortal men." After a dramatic sigh, his voice deepened to a caress. "Your lips, they are like the petal of a crimson rose, your throat like an alabaster column in the temple of my heart, your breasts . . ."

"That's quite far enough, thank you." There was such a mix of sincere flattery and blatant opportunism in the inventory that Claire found it impossible to be insulted.

Jacques spread expressive hands. "I mean only to say . . ."

Standing at the edge of the cleared space, Dean cleared his throat. "She said that was enough."

"Really? *Et maintenant,* what did I say of mortal men?" One brow flicked up to punctuate a disdainful glance. "Ah, *oui,* that they are fools. Are you mortal, man? No, wait, it is not a man at all; it is a boy."

Moving up behind Claire's left shoulder, Dean dropped his voice. "What is this?"

"This is Jacques Labaet." She couldn't decide if she were amused or irritated by Dean's interruption, mostly because she couldn't decide if he were being supportive or protective. "He's a ghost."

"A ghost?" Dean repeated. He turned his head and found himself nose-to-nose with the phantom.

"Boo," said Jacques.

*   *   *

"We have just left Kingston, steaming for Quebec City; the weather, she is bad, but she is always bad on the lakes in the fall and we think anything is better than being stuck in with the English over freeze up. We barely reach Point Fredrick when things, they go all to Hell."

Claire winced, but there was no response from the furnace room.

"*Pardon.* Such language I should not use around a lady." Blowing her a kiss, Jacques continued his story. "The wind she came up, roaring like a live thing. I remember something hard, I don't know what, catching me here." He tapped the sweater just below his sternum. "I remember cold water and then, *rien.* Nothing." His shoulders rose and fell in a Gallic shrug. "They said I wash up on shore, more dead than alive. Me, I don't know why they bring me here. Two days later, I died."

"And you're a ghost." Dean wanted to be absolutely clear on that. Every community back home had at least one story of a local haunting—ghost husbands, ghost stags, ghost ships—and if this annoying little man was the real thing, then the old stories could be real as well and there were a significant number of apologies owed. He'd have to make some phone calls when the rates went down.

"*Oui.* A ghost." Jacques favored the younger, living man with a long, hard stare, then deliberately turned away from him. "First, I haunt the room I die in. That was not so bad although, I tell you, this place is not so popular with the living. When that Augustus Smythe, that *espece de mangeur de merde,* he moves everything up to the attic, I must go as well and I am haunting this place ever since."

"As a ghost."

"Does he have to keep repeating?" Jacques demanded of Claire. Before she could answer, he spun around to face Dean. "Would you feel better if I disappear? All of me?" He faded out. "Bits of me?" His head reappeared.

"You've been dead seventy-two years," Dean reminded him disdainfully. If the ghost had thought to frighten him with all the appearing and disappearing, he hadn't succeeded. The whole performance too closely resembled the Cheshire cat in the Disney version of *Alice in Wonderland.* "Seventy-two years, that's some time to be dead. You're used to it, I'm not."

Jacques' body came back into focus as he stood, hands curled into fists and chin in the air. "Nobody asks you to be used to it, *Newfie*. You don't like it, then you can get out!"

Rising slowly and deliberately to his feet Dean was significantly larger. "I live here."

"And I died here, *enfant*, long before you were born on that hunk of rock in water!"

"You know, you've got a real bad attitude for a dead guy!"

"Say you?"

"Yeah."

"This is why we have cats castrated," Claire said to no one in particular. "Sit down. Both of you. You're acting like idiots." While she understood how males were hardwired to defend their territory, this was ridiculous.

"Only for your sake, *ma petite sorcière*," Jacques muttered sulkily, throwing himself back down onto the bed, "would I tolerate this lump of flesh."

Dean moved toward the chair, then shook his head and remained standing. "No. He called me a Newfie like it's an insult. I don't take that from anyone, living or dead."

"You think I am to apologize?" Leaning back on one elbow, Jacques raised his free hand scornfully. "I think not."

"Okay." Full lips pressed into a thin line, Dean turned on one heel and started toward the stairs. "I'm sorry, Boss, but if you want me, I'll be in the kitchen."

"Ha! Go on, run away! I scare off better men than you!" When Dean disappeared behind the stacked furniture, Jacques quieted and turned a speculative glance on Claire. "You will not stop him?"

"How?"

"*Ah, oui,* you cannot wave the dreaded exorcism over him." Then his expression softened, and he laced his fingers behind his head, the lopsided grin not so much suggestive as explicit "Or perhaps you want to be alone with me as I want to be alone with you. Yes?"

"No. Did you intend to drive him away?"

"*Non.* But I intend to take advantage of it."

Claire rolled her eyes. "I think not. Perhaps I should leave, too."

"You would leave me alone?" Letting his head fall back against the mattress, Jacques sighed deeply. "For still more long and weary years. Alone." He paused for a moment then repeated, "Alone."

All the playacting, all the cheerful seduction, had disappeared. Although she knew she should maintain both a professional and personal distance, Claire couldn't help responding emotionally. Rising out of the armchair, she walked over and sat down on the edge of the bed. It sagged under her weight. "You don't have to stay here alone, Jacques; not any more. I can send you on."

"On to where? That is the question." His eyes serious, he laid his hand over hers. "I tell you, Keeper, I was not the best of men. A bad man, no, but I cannot say and be certain that I was a good man. I would like to be certain before I go on."

Claire could understand that. Especially considering what waited in the furnace room.

"So." He rolled over on his side and his fingers tightened around hers. "Since I seem to be remaining for a time and we seem to be alone together, so conveniently on a bed, perhaps we could get to know each other better?"

Snatching her hand through his, his grip no more confining than cool smoke, Claire leaped to her feet "Don't you ever let up? While I appreciate your need for companionship, I do not appreciate being continually propositioned!"

His eyes widened, his expression injured innocence. "But when first I see you, you are so beautiful, how can I not want you?"

"That has more to do with how long you've been alone than it does with me."

"I do not want that Dean and I see him, too," he pointed out reasonably. "And I am not to blame that it has for me been such a very long time."

"What do you expect? You're dead."

Back up on one elbow, he rested his chin on his palm and waggled both brows suggestively. "The spirit is willing . . ."

"But the flesh is nonexistent."

"You are a Keeper. For a time, I can be incubus for you."

Claire groped behind her for a chair and sat down rather abruptly. "How do you know that?"

"There was a Keeper when I was dead no more than ten or fifteen years. She came to my room, *de temps en temps*—that is, from time to time. She is not so young as you, but when no one else makes offers . . ."

The hair lifted off the back of Claire's neck and she fought the urge to turn and check the space behind her. "Bleached blonde, full-figured, pouty mouth, very red lipstick?"

"*Oui.*" His eyes narrowed. "You know Sa . . ."

"Don't say her name. She's still here."

"Then I . . ." He disappeared. ". . . am not."

A little surprised, Claire scanned the area, trying to find him. She didn't want to have to compel him to return. "I thought you two . . . you know?"

"*Non.* You do not know." His voice came from near the window. "There are legends about women like her, try to suck a man's soul out his . . ."

"I get the picture," Claire interrupted hurriedly, not really in the mood for a graphic description in either language.

"Why is that one *still* here?"

How much to tell him? "Do you know what Keepers do?"

"*She* told me. They guard the places where evil can enter the world." He rematerialized, cross-legged on the bed, expressive features folded into worry. "But me, I think *she* want the evil for herself. I do not know what happened, but all at once, *she* did not come and Augustus Smythe was here. He is not a Keeper."

"No, he's a Cousin. Less powerful. *She* . . ." It was impossible not to pick up Jacques' inflection. ". . . was put to sleep for trying to take over the, um, evil." Claire could see no reason to be more specific, especially considering Jacques' transitional state and his lack of certainty over his final destination.

"*She* was put to sleep?" His voice rose, making it more a shriek than a question. "And if *she* wake up?"

"It won't happen."

"So you say. Me, I learn a lullaby or two. And now, what happens? To me?"

Claire frowned, uncertain of what he meant "Nothing happens to you. *She* can't do anything while she's asleep or she'd have done something by now."

"Je ne demande pas ce qu'elle *peut faire a moi!"* Agitation threw him back into French. "I know what *she* can do to me." He raised both hands and made a visible effort to calm down. "I am asking what do you do now with me."

"What do I do?" He was persistent, she'd give him that. "Nothing."

"Nothing happens to me for years." Jacques lay down again and flung an arm up over his eyes.

"Could you please reattach that? It looks disgusting."

Jacques sighed but complied. "At least will you visit?"

"When I can."

"Ah, you have no time because you must guard the place where evil can enter the world?"

"I'm working at sealing the hole."

"And when the hole is sealed?"

"Then I'll move on."

Opening one eye, he peered up at her. "Will you bring back my table?"

"No. You don't need it." When he began a sorrowful protest Claire cut him off. "You began haunting the attic when Augustus Smythe moved the furniture up from the room you died in, right?"

"Oui."

She chewed on a corner of her lower lip. "Did he know you were there?"

"He knew. He did not care." Jacques rolled back up onto his side. Misery made his eyes surprisingly dark. "For so many years with no one who cared; do you know, *cherie,* I think that is worse than Hell."

Which explained why there was no response from the basement. Hell appreciated pain. "I have an idea."

Something heavy hit the floor in the room above the dining room. Dean and Austin stared at the ceiling.

"What do think she's doing up there?"

"She's still in the attic," Austin told him. "And so the question becomes, what's she doing up *there?"*

Dean leaned into his polishing cloth with a certain amount of violent activity. "Finding antiques."

"I'm amazed you left them up there together." The cat flopped down on the polished end of the table and stretched to his full length. "A woman. A man. Didn't you say he was a sailor? You know what they say about sailors."

"They don't say it about dead sailors." He peered sideways at the cat. "Austin, can I ask you a personal question? Were you castrated?"

Austin rolled over and blinked up at him. "My, that *is* personal. Why do you ask?"

"Something Claire said."

"She sees all, she tells all." The cat snorted. "If you must know, yes, I was. I was with a less enlightened—and, as it turned out, allergic— family before I moved in with Claire."

"How do you feel about it?"

"It broadened my horizons. I was no longer forced by biology to endlessly pursue females in heat and could turn my attention to philosophy and art."

Dean nodded, understanding. "It pissed you off."

"Of course it pissed me off!" Ears back, Austin glared up at him. "Wouldn't it piss you off? But . . ." he spent a moment grooming the dime-sized spot of black fur on the side of a white paw. ". . . I got over it. Eventually it was a relief to be able to go outside and not come home with my ear shredded by some feline Goliath out to overpopulate the neighborhood."

"Did you talk to the other family?"

"Not after *that.*"

A crack of displaced air heralded the sudden appearance of a ladder-back chair in the far corner of the dining room. Closely followed by Jacques, who displaced no air but made up for it in personal volume.

"*Liberté!* I am free! She was right! I go where the furniture is!" He advanced on Dean, his arms flung wide. "Freed, I gladly apologize to you."

Dean backed up a step as Jacques walked through the table.

"You are not a Newfie like an insult even though you are from the colony of the despicable British."

"Newfoundland joined Canada in 1949," Dean told him stiffening.

"*Bon.* Just what this country need, more *Anglais.* It has no matter, we start again, you and I. So tell me, Dean, why do you stay here in such a place?" He paused and looked him up and down. "Should you not be fishing or whacking on the seals or something?"

Dean folded his arms. "I stay," he said through clenched teeth, "because Claire needs me."

"For what?" As Dean's expression darkened, Jacques raised both hands, palms out. "No, no, it is not another insult. I want to know because I think of you. Since I must stay, you can go if I can do for Claire what you can do." His volume dropped dramatically. "You know of *her*? Sleeping upstairs? I tell you, it is not safe for a young man in a building where *she* is."

"You must think I'm really stupid," Dean snarled. "It's sure as scrod not my safety you're thinking of." If he'd ever even considered packing it in and shipping away from this weirdness, he certainly had no intention of going anywhere now.

"Then think of the Keeper's safety. When you are here she must protect you all the time. Her attention it is divided."

"I can protect myself!"

"How?"

"His strength is the strength of ten," Austin muttered, dropping his chin onto his paws, "because his heart is pure."

Nose-to-nose, both men ignored him.

"If Claire allows me a body . . ."

"If Claire *what*?" Dean interrupted.

The cat looked up. "It's an incubus kind of a thing. Not generally approved of by the lineage, but there have been exceptions."

"And I have been already excepted," Jacques announced smugly, and disappeared.

"I hate it when they do that," Austin said, dropping his head again. "You never know when they're really gone." As Dean turned toward him, eyes wide behind the lenses of his glasses, he added, "I know, of course, but you don't."

"*Is* he gone?"

"Yes." Claire answered as she came into the dining room brushing cobwebs off her shoulders. "He's upstairs investigating the rest of the hotel. I spread the stuff from the room he died in as widely as possible."

"In *my* apartment?"

"Of course not. I didn't put anything in the basement at all."

Dean folded his arms. "Is it true what he said?"

"That depends. What did he say?"

"That you . . ." She lifted an eyebrow and Dean suddenly found it difficult to continue. "That you gave him a body."

"He said I gave him a body?"

Her tone lowered the temperature in the room about ten degrees. His crossed arms now a barricade, Dean couldn't stop himself from stepping back. "Not exactly."

"What *exactly* did he say?"

It wasn't a request. Moistening dry lips, Dean repeated the conversation.

Claire sighed and lifted her right hand into the air, fingers flicking off the points. "First according to my mother and my cat, you don't need my protection and, as things stand right now, there's nothing to protect you from. Second, I need you to run this place. Jacques certainly isn't going to be cooking, cleaning, or unclogging toilets. Third, I didn't make the exception for him, *she* did."

Feeling both foolish and reassured. Dean watched his finger rub along the edge of the tabletop. "Will you?" The silence drew his gaze back to Claire's face. "Uh, never mind."

"Wise choice," Austin muttered.

Claire sighed again. Her life used to be so simple. "Look, Dean, I realize Jacques made it sound like he and I, that we . . ." She paused, wondering why she was so embarrassed about something that hadn't happened. Maybe because somewhere deep in the back of her mind she'd considered it? Clearing her throat, she started again. "Put yourself in his place, trapped between life and death, trapped alone in that attic for decades."

"Okay. I guess I feel sort of sorry for him," Dean allowed reluctantly. "But every ghost story I've ever heard says he'll be a nuisance at best."

The can of furniture polish crashed suddenly to the floor.

"See?"

"That was Austin."

A cupboard door opened and one of the plastic salt shakers put out for guests flung itself halfway across the room.

"*That* was Jacques."

"Just meeting expectations." He materialized by Claire's side, grinning wickedly.

"Ground rules," Claire told him, folding her arms and trying not to smile. "First, no throwing things."

"He started it." Jacques nodded at the cat

"If he took poison, would you?"

"What would be the point?"

She had to admit that under the circumstances it was a stupid question. Actually, under most circumstances it was a stupid question. "Second, when you're in a room with either Dean, or me, or both of us, you must be visible."

"And thirdly? There is always a thirdly, yes?"

"Thirdly, if we're all going to live together for a while, let's make an effort to get along."

"I cannot go down there with you." Jacques squatted at the top of the stairs to better watch Claire descend. "Why not?"

"Because there's nothing of yours in the basement."

"Is it because he lives in the basement and you keep us from fighting over who is most important in your life?"

"Something like that." Claire smiled as she moved out of his line of sight. For the moment, it was surprisingly entertaining being the center of someone's universe.

"Cleaning is woman's work." Sprawled on the bed, the ghost peered around the room.

Dean very carefully coiled the vacuum cleaner cord around the back of the machine. "Is it?"

"*Oui.* Any man would know."

"Like you know it?" He picked up his divided bucket of cleaning supplies.

"*Oui.*"

"Why don't you tell Claire?"

"That cleaning is woman's work?"

"Yeah."

"I cannot. She is in the basement."

Dean mourned the missed opportunity. Even after only three days he had a fairly good idea of Claire's response to a declaration of that type.

"I think you need to rub harder."

"Don't you have something to do?" Dean growled, scowling up at the ghost. While searching for paint for the sign, he'd come across a can of paint remover and, although the dining room was still a catastrophe, Claire had decided he should spend the rest of the afternoon stripping the front counter.

Sitting on the countertop, Jacques thought about it, soundlessly drumming his heels. "No," he said cheerfully after a moment. "I will remain here and watch you."

"Don't"

"Dean."

He leaned around the flailing legs. "Yeah, Boss?"

Carrying a second box of triple-X videos from the sitting room, Claire pushed her hair up off her face with the back of her hand. "Jacques isn't hurting anything. He'd help if he could."

"I would," Jacques agreed cheerfully. "Truly I would help if I could."

"Yeah. Sure." Until this point, Dean had always been able to give any new acquaintance the benefit of the doubt. Until this point they'd all been alive, but if he disliked Jacques solely because he was dead, didn't that make him as much of a bigot as if he disliked him because he was French Canadian? Now, if he disliked him because of the way he acted around Claire, that opened a whole . . .

He threw his weight behind the scraper.

. . . new . . .

Muscles bulged in his jaw as he gritted his teeth.

. . . barrel of fish.

"I think you reached the wood right there," Jacques pointed out conversationally.

"Claire?"

She paused, one hand on the doorknob. "What is it, Jacques?"

"You have put nothing of me in your bedroom." Standing on the threshold, he pushed against an invisible barrier. "I cannot come in."

"I know."

He stared soulfully at her. "I want only to be where you are."

"Why don't you try being back in the attic where your bed is and I'll see you in the morning." She pushed the door closed.

"Even though you close the door on my face, I still desire you!"

She had to smile. "Good night, Jacques." Switching off the light and dropping her robe, she climbed into bed.

"Claire?" His voice came faintly through the door. "I would just sit in the chair. My word as a Labaet."

"Good *night*, Jacques." After a moment, she sighed. "Jacques, go away. I can still feel you standing there."

"I am on guard so that your sleep is not disturbed."

"The only thing disturbing my sleep is you. Why won't you go away?"

"Because . . ." He paused and she felt him sigh. Or she felt the emotion behind the sigh; as he wasn't breathing, he didn't actually exhale. "Because I have been so many years alone."

Alone. Once again, the word throbbed between them, and once again it evoked an emotional response. Claire couldn't deny the urge to bring the small tapestry cushion—the cushion that gave him access to her sitting room—into the bedroom. She couldn't deny it, but she managed to resist it. "You can stand at the door if you want to." After a moment, she pushed her face into Austin's side and murmured, "This could become a problem."

"I told you so."

"No, you didn't."

"Well, I would've if I'd been there." He touched her shoulder with a front paw. "You're attracted to him, aren't you?"

"Don't be ridiculous, I'm a Keeper."

"So?"

"I feel sorry for him."

"And?"

"He's *dead*."

✿   ✿   ✿

Down in the furnace room, the flames reflected on the copper hood were a sullen red. It could have told the Keeper that the spirit was trapped in the same binding that held it—accidentally caught and held.

BUT SHE DIDN'T ASK US.

It would have been even more annoyed had it not recognized all sorts of lovely new tensions now available for exploitation.

FIVE

A T SEVEN-FORTY THE NEXT MORNING, at the far end of the third-floor hall, the vacuum cleaner coughed, sputtered, and roared into life. Three-and-a-half seconds later, Dean smacked the switch and it coughed, sputtered, and wheezed its way back to silence. Heart pounding, he stared down at the machine, wondering if it had always sounded like the first lap of an Indy race—noisy enough to wake the dead.

Or worse.

Which is ridiculous. He'd vacuumed this same hall once a week for as long as he'd worked here with this same machine and the woman in room six had slept peacefully—or compulsively—through it. Contractors had renovated the rooms to either side of her and obviously she hadn't stirred. Mrs. Hansen had all but stuck pins in her, and still she slept on.

The odds were good that he wasn't after waking her up this morning.

His foot stopped three inches above the off/on switch and Dean couldn't force it any closer.

Apparently, his foot didn't like the odds.

So he changed feet.

His other foot was, in its own way, as adamant.

You're being nuts, boy. He carefully cleaned his glasses, placed them back on his nose, and, before the thought had time to reach his extremities, stomped on the switch, missed, and nearly fell over as his leg continued through an extra four inches of space.

Clearly, parts of his body were more paranoid than the whole.

Okay, uncle. He unplugged the machine and rewound the cord. There had to be an old carpet sweeper up in the attic, and he could always use that.

On his way back to the storage cupboard, he bent to pick up a small picture of a ship someone had left on the floor. He had no idea where it had come from; guests had found Mr. Smythe's taste in art somewhat disturbing, so the walls had been essentially art free ever since the embarrassing incident with the eighteenth-century prints and the chicken.

Upon closer inspection, the picture turned out to be a discolored page clipped from a magazine slid into a cheap frame. A cheap, filthy frame.

Holding it between thumb and forefinger, Dean frowned. What was it doing leaning against the wall outside room six? And could he get it clean without using an abrasive?

"Put that down!"

Behind his glasses, Dean's eyes narrowed as he raised his gaze from the felted cobwebbing to the ghost "Is it yours, then?"

"It is mine as much as it is anyone's."

If the picture belonged to Jacques, that explained why he'd never seen it before. "Why should I put it down?" he asked suspiciously.

Jacques' expression matched Dean's. "Why do you hold it?"

"I found it on the floor."

"Then put it back on the floor."

"There?" A nod indicated the picture's previous position against the wall—far, far too handy to the sleeping Keeper.

"*Oui*, there! What are you, *stupide*?"

"*Why* do you want me to put it there?"

"Because that is where it was!"

"So?"

"Do you try to block my way, *Anglais*?"

"If I can," Dean growled, taking a step toward the dead man. The way he understood it, Jacques had been dead as dick and haunting the hotel at the same time as the evil Keeper's attempt to control the accident site. It wouldn't surprise him to discover the ghost had been her accomplice and now, with Claire unwilling to give him a body, he had only one other place to turn. Dean couldn't let that happen, not after everything Claire and her mother and the cat had said. "What are you planning, Jacques?"

Jacques folded his arms and rolled his eyes. "I should think," he said scornfully, "that what I, as you so crudely say, plan, would be obvious even to a muscle-bound *imbecile* like yourself."

"You're after waking her?"

"Waking her?" The ghost shot a speculative look in Dean's direction. "*Oui,* if you like. I wake her to new sensations. And when I tell Claire that you gather what allows me to walk within the hotel, that you try to keep me from her, she will not like that, I think."

. . . *what allows me to walk within the hotel.* Dean's scowl faded as he realized, for the first time in his life, he'd leaped to the worst possible conclusion, his response based solely on his irrational reaction to a dead man. The picture had nothing to do with the sleeping Keeper. Working from the attic, Claire must've sent it to the third floor hall without considering where it might end up.

He'd completely forgotten about Jacques' anchors. He opened his mouth to explain and was amazed to hear himself say, "Sure, run and hide behind Claire."

"Run and hide?" Anger blurred Jacques' edges.

"Too dead to stand up for yourself?"

"Claire . . ."

"This has nothing to do with Claire." Dean set the picture back on the floor—as far from room six as he could put it without appearing to give ground—then straightened, shoulders squared. "This is between you and me."

"Me, I think this has everything to do with Claire," Jacques murmured, studying the younger man through narrowed lids. "But you are right, *mon petit Anglais,* this is between you and me."

Claire had been vaguely disappointed not to find Jacques waiting for her when she passed through the sitting room on her way to the bathroom. Thoughts of him spending the night pressed up against her bedroom door had inserted themselves into her dreams and jerked her awake almost hourly. She'd wanted to share her mood with him while she still felt like giving him a body in order to wring his neck.

It didn't help that the morning's measurements had shown a perceptible buildup of seepage. With no access to the power sealing the hole, she couldn't cut it off, and she certainly couldn't let it build up indefinitely.

Teeth clenched, she gave the shower taps a savage twist, snarled wordlessly when the pipes began banging out their delivery of hot water, and bit back an extremely dangerous oath when the temperature spent a good two minutes fluctuating between too hot and too cold.

She finally began to calm as she lathered the Apothecary's shampoo—guaranteed not tested on mythical creatures—into her hair, and by the time she'd sudsed, rinsed, and dried, she'd relaxed considerably. When Hell actually let her blow-dry and style in peace, she left the bathroom feeling remarkably cheerful.

Her good mood lasted through dressing and right into the day's search for the Historian.

Curled up on a pillow, Austin lifted his head as the wardrobe door opened and Claire emerged soaking wet "You're cutting it close," he said. "You've just barely left. What happened?"

"Tropical storm," Claire told him tightly, pushing streaming hair back off her face. "Came up on shore after me and followed me about ten kilometers inland. Good thing I was driving an import or I'd never have stayed on the road."

"One of the Historian's early warning systems?"

Claire shrugged, her sweater sagging off her shoulders. "Who knows?" Trailing a small river behind her, she picked up some dry clothes, held carefully at arm's length, and headed for the bathroom.

Dumping her wet clothes in a pile on the floor, she dressed quickly and, stomach growling, picked up her blow-dryer. "This one's going to be quick and sleazy," she muttered, bending over and applying the hot air. "I'm too hungry for style."

When she straightened, Jacques stared at her from out of the mirror.

"Oh, hell," she sighed.

"Got it in one, *cherie.*" His lips curled up into the lopsided smile that raised his looks, from passable to strangely attractive— strangely attractive were it not for Hell's signature substitution of glowing red eyes. "I'm sorry I missed you earlier."

"Just get on with it."

The image shook its head. "You would think," it said teasingly, "that you were in a hurry to get somewhere. You can't leave, *cherie*." The smile disappeared. "Neither of us can leave. We have been thrown together here, why not make the most of it?"

She had every intention of leaving, but her mother's suggestion that she not argue with Hell had been a good one. "What did you have in mind?"

"With the power of the pentagram, you could give me a body nightly as easily as you could snap your fingers."

Claire frowned. "Don't you mean opening the pentagram would give me that power?"

"Things are not sealed so tightly as all that." Red eyes actually managed a twinkle. "Augustus Smythe knew the benefits of using the seepage. How do you think he kept himself amused?"

"I think *that's* fairly obvious." She folded her arms. "If I can use the seepage without releasing the hordes of Hell, what's in it for you?"

He looked hurt "Must there be something in it for us?"

"Yes."

"Perhaps we find that a happy Keeper is a Keeper easier to live with."

"I'm sure that Augustus Smythe was a joy."

"He was Cousin, *cherie*. You are a Keeper. Surely you are stronger?"

"That has nothing to do with it."

"Perhaps." The image saddened. "You get so few chances to have another's life touch yours. A frenzied fumbling in the dark—and we have nothing against that, *cherie*—and then you move on. Only when Keepers are old do they stay in one place long enough to find a mate for the soul and, by then, they are too old to recognize such a one. You have a chance, *cherie*, a chance few Keepers get."

Claire's nostrils flared. "He's dead."

"Ah, I see. You will not take the risk, even though there is no danger to you, because it is what a Keeper does not do. A Keeper does not take risks for such a minor thing as happiness." The image saddened.

"For once in your life, *cherie,* can you not give in to desire without questioning if it is what a Keeper should do?" It raised its left hand and pressed it against the inside of the glass. "Can you not reach out and meet me halfway?"

She felt her right hand lift and forced it back down by her side. "You're good," she snarled.

The image in the mirror let its hand fall back as well, fully aware that the mood had been broken. "Technically, no. But we accept the compliment."

"Give me back my reflection. Now!"

"As you asked so nicely, *cherie . . .*" Jacques' image faded slowly, calling her name as though he were being pulled into torment.

"You're not Jacques," Claire told it and found herself talking to herself.

"Claire!"

When she opened the bathroom door, Austin tumbled in and rolled once on the mat. He took a moment to compose himself, then said, with studied nonchalance, as though he hadn't just been trying to dig his way through the door, "Dean and Jacques are fighting."

"You mean they're arguing."

"No. I mean they're fighting."

"That's impossible."

"So one would assume, but they seem to have found a way."

She tossed her blow-dryer down by the sink and ran her fingers through her hair, forcing most of it into place. "All right," she sighed, "where are they?"

"The third-floor hall." Austin paused, licked his shoulder, and stepped out of the way. "Directly in front of room six."

His foresight kept him from being trampled as Claire raced for the stairs.

The effect depended on who delivered the blow. If Dean punched his fist through Jacques' immaterial body, then Jacques felt it. If Jacques drove his immaterial fist through Dean's body, then Dean felt it. It wasn't much of an effect either way, being closer to mild discomfort than actual pain, but neither the living nor the dead cared. The point was to score the point

"Stop it! Stop it this instant!" Breathing heavily from her run up the two flights of stairs, Claire flung herself between the combatants, then sucked in a startled gasp as Jacques' hand sliced through her body from hip to hip dragging a sensation of burning cold behind it. When she staggered back, she found herself pressed up against the warm length of Dean's torso and that was almost as disconcerting.

Jerking forward, she turned sideways and presented a raised hand to each man. "That will be quite enough! Would one of you like to explain what the h . . . heck is going on?"

Silence settled like three feet of snow.

"I'm waiting."

"It is not your business . . ." Jacques began. His protest died as Claire turned the full force of her disapproval in his direction.

"*Everything* that happens in this building is my business," she told him. "I want an explanation and I want it now."

Jacques smoothed back translucent hair. "Ask your houseboy."

"I'm asking you."

"Why? *Le cochon maudit,* he started it."

As Claire turned to face him, Dean bit back an answering insult.

"Well?" she prodded.

"He accused me of picking up his anchors. Of keeping him from walking around the hotel."

"Were you?"

"No!" When he saw Jacques' mouth open, he shifted his weight forward and said, "Okay, I picked up that picture there, but I didn't know it was one of his anchors."

"You accuse me of hiding behind Claire."

"And look where you are."

"*Fini! Je suis a bout!* I have had it up to here!"

"FREEZE!"

Jacques stopped his forward advance, and Dean rocked back on his heels.

Arms folded, Claire turned slowly to face Dean. "Did you really say that?"

Dean nodded sheepishly, gaze locked on the carpet.

"Why?"

Ears red, he shrugged without looking up. "I don't know."

Since he was telling the truth, Claire ignored the rude noises coming from behind her. "All right, then, I suggest—no, this needs something stronger than a mere suggestion—I *insist* that we continue this, whatever this is, downstairs. We're uncomfortably close to her."

"*Her?*" Jacques repeated, coming between Claire and the stairs. "By her, I am wondering, do you mean, *her?*"

"*She's* in room six," Claire told him, pointing with broad emphasis at the splintered door. She opened her mouth to demand he get out of her way when she realized all his attention was on Dean. The air crackled as he moved past her.

"You thought that I, Jacques Labaet, did want to wake *her?*"

Several hundred childhood stories of vengeful spirits passed through Dean's head, but he held his ground, wondering why adults thought it necessary to scare the snot out of kids. "I only thought it at first."

"You dare to give me this insult!"

"The picture was right by her door."

"And so were you!"

"I was vacuuming!"

"The carpet," Jacques spat, drifting up so they were nose-to-nose, "is clean! Perhaps you mean to wake *her*, and I come in time to stop you!"

It was only twenty after eight, but Dean had already had a bad morning. The carpet was not clean, it hadn't been vacuumed in a week and it didn't look as though it was going to get vacuumed any time soon. Sure, he'd discovered a suspicious side of himself he didn't much like, but he didn't think he deserved to be accused of treachery by someone intent on necrophilia. Of a sort. "You go to Hell," he said with feeling.

Jacques disappeared.

"Oh, shit!" Claire clamped a hand over her mouth, but it was too late.

Dean's eyes widened and, fumbling for his keys, he raced for room five.

With no time to explain, Claire flung herself down the stairs. *How could he have done that?* She missed a step, fell five, caught her balance, and picked up speed. *There's no way he should've been able to do that.* By the time she turned onto the basement stairs, her sock-covered feet barely touched the wood. One more floor and she'd have been the first Keeper to fly with out an appliance.

She turned the chains and padlocks to rice and then kicked piles of it out of the way as she dragged open the furnace room door.

"Claire!" Suspended over the pit, Jacques flickered like a bulb about to go out. "Help me!"

Skidding to a halt at the edge of the pentagram, Claire hadn't the faintest idea of what to do. Because of the seal, Jacques hadn't gone directly to Hell, but there was sufficient power in the area directly over the pit to shred his ties to the physical world. When the last strand ripped free, his soul would be absorbed, seal or no seal.

"Claaaaaaaaaire!"

She could barely hear her name in the panicked wail. Making it up as she went along, she reached out with her will.

HE WAS GIVEN TO US!

"It doesn't work that way." Slowly, she wrapped possibilities around the thrashing, flickering ghost. "You know the rules."

RULES DO NOT APPLY TO US.

"You wish. Souls come to you by their own actions. They can't be given to you."

BUT HE'S DEAD.

"So?" It was like scooping a flopping fish out of a tidal pool with a net made of wet toilet paper.

WE HAVE THE RIGHT TO JUDGE HIS ACTIONS.

"Not on this side you don't."

WE'RE HELPING HIM PASS OVER.

"Not if I have anything to say about it." Holding him as securely as possible, Claire began to pull Jacques toward the edge of the pit. His struggles made it difficult to tell how quickly he was moving, but after a few tense moments he was definitely closer to the side than the middle.

When eldritch power crawled like a bloated fly over the part of her will extending over the edge of the pentagram, she realized Hell was analyzing the rescue attempt. She felt it remove its attention from Jacques and gather its resources. There was barely time to brace herself before an energy spike thrust up out of the depths, dragging both her will and Jacques back toward the center of the pit.

LET HIM GO. HE IS NOTHING TO YOU.

"That's not what your recent temptation implied."

WE'RE BIG ENOUGH TO ADMIT WHEN WE'RE WRONG.

Sock feet slid closer to the edge of the pentagram.

ON SECOND THOUGHT, DON'T LET HIM GO.

If she let him go, the odds were good she wouldn't fasten onto him again before Hell tore through the bonds holding him to the world. If she didn't let him go, she'd be dragged through the pentagram and his fate would be a minor footnote to the cataclysm as the seal broke. Her toes dug through her socks and into the imperfection in the rock floor, but that only slowed her.

Jacques or the world?

It was the sort of dilemma Hell delighted in. Claire could feel its pleasure in the certain knowledge that she'd have to sacrifice Jacques for the lives of millions.

Then strong arms wrapped around her from behind. Her toes stopped millimeters from disaster.

"Bring him in," Dean told her, tightening his grip one arm at a time. "And let's get out of here."

Constrained by the pentagram, Hell stood no chance against the deeply ridged treads on a pair of winter work boots designed to get the wearer up and down the chutes of St. Johns.

Weight on his heels, Dean stepped back, once, twice, dragging Claire back with him, dragging Jacques with her. At the outside edge of the pentagram, the tension snapped and flung all three of them against the far wall of the furnace room; first Dean, then Claire, then Jacques, who slapped through them both like a cold fog to smash in turn against the rock.

Teeth gritted, Claire pried herself up off of Dean, used the wall to pull herself to her feet, and attempted to blink away the afterimages caused by impact with limestone closely followed by Jacques' left knee passing between her eyes. "Is everyone all right?"

"I guess." Dean braced himself against the floor, separated himself from Jacques' right arm and shoulder, and stood.

"Jacques?"

"*Non.* I am *not* all right. Where are we?"

"The furnace room," Dean answered, before Claire had a chance.

"What? In the hotel?" The last syllable rose to a shriek.

"Yeah. The furnace room in the hotel." Dean shot a look both wounded and disapproving at Claire. "But I don't think we should stay."

Jacques glanced wide-eyed toward the pentagram. "It is real?"

"It is," Claire told him, holding her head in both hands. When they'd broken free, her will had retracted and she had the kind of headache that came with trying to fit approximately twelve feet of power in an eight-inch skull.

"Then we talk in the dining room." Still flickering around the edges, he disappeared.

"The dining room," Claire repeated. "Good plan." Staggering slightly, she started up the stairs.

One hand out to catch her if she fell, Dean followed, still far, far too angry to give in to the faint gibbering he could hear coming from inner bits of his brain. "Why didn't you tell me there was a hole to Hell in the furnace room?"

"I'm a Keeper, it's my duty to protect you."

"From what?"

"Living in terror."

A LIE. A VERITABLE FALSEHOOD!

Claire sighed. She couldn't believe a headache could pack so much mass; it felt as though she had the weight of the world on her shoulders. "From having to bear more than I thought you could."

"Didn't think much of me, did you? Do you?"

Heaving herself up another step, she waved more or less toward the pit. "Dean, it's Hell!"

"We've a saying back home . . ."

"Please, spare me."

". . . some don't be afraid of the sea, they goes down to the sea, and they be drowned. But I be afraid of the sea, and I goes down to the sea, and I only be drowned now and then."

"What the h . . ."

SAY IT.

". . . heck does that mean?" she snarled.

"Fear can keep you alive. You should've told me."

KEEPERS, ALWAYS THINK THEY KNOW WHAT'S . . .

Claire slammed the door shut on the last word, spraying uncooked rice all over the basement.

A single grain of those pushed inside the furnace room flew down the stairs and tumbled end over end across the stone floor. It stopped no more than its own width away from the outermost edge of the glyphs that sealed the pentagram.

DAMN.

"Look, Dean, you knew what you needed to know." Claire kicked at a mound of rice, guilt making her sound petulant even to her own ears. "I told you there was a major accident site down here; I just didn't name it."

His back against the furnace room door, Dean stared at her, unable to believe what he was hearing. "You didn't name it? It's not like you forgot to tell me it was called Fred or George or Harold. It's Hell!"

"Technically, it's energy from the lower end of the possibilities manifesting itself in a format the person who called it up could understand."

"And that *format*?"

"Is Hell; all right?" Sagging back against the washing machine, she threw up her hands. "You win."

Dean jerked a hand back through his hair. "It's not about winning." He paused, trying to figure out what it was he'd won. "Okay. Maybe it is. You're admitting you should have told me, right?"

"Right."

"That you were wrong?"

She found enough energy to lift her head. "Don't push it." One fingernail traced the maker's name stamped into the front of the washer. "So now you know, what are you going to do? Are you going to leave?"

"Leave?" Leave. He hadn't actually thought it through that far.

"What's the point?" his common sense wanted to know. *"There's nothing there that hasn't been there for the last year."*

"Shouldn't you be telling me to pack?"

"Too late."

"Dean?"

He took a step away from the furnace room. He wanted to ask her if she really thought she could close up *Hell*, but the sound of a hundred grains of rice being ground to powder drew his gaze to the floor. "What's with all the rice?"

"Conservation of mass," Claire explained wearily. "It used to be the chains."

"You changed the chains into rice?"

"It had to be something I could get through even though it weighed the same as the chains."

The area immediately in front of the furnace room door looked as though a small blizzard had wandered through on its way to Rochester. Crouching, Dean scooped up a handful of the tiny white grains and frowned as they spilled through his fingers. "Instant rice?"

"What's wrong with instant?"

"Nothing. I mean, it's not like you're cooking with it." He straightened, dusting his hand against his thigh. "Are you after changing it back?"

Claire shook her head and regretted the motion. "I can't. I couldn't change my mind right now."

"Then should I replace the chains? Mr. Smythe kept a box of extras," he added in response to her expression.

Claire glanced at the door. The chains, like the locks on room six, were wishful thinking. If Hell got loose, chains wouldn't stop it. "Why not."

Picking rice off her socks, she watched him walk to a storage cupboard at the far end of the basement return, and efficiently secure the door. When he turned to face her, she realized there was a reserve in his expression, a new wariness in his gaze, that made her feel as though, somehow, she'd failed him. She didn't like the feeling.

Keepers weren't in the habit of apologizing to bystanders. But then, Keepers didn't usually have to look Dean McIssac in the eye, knowing they were wrong. "All right." She tried to keep her nostrils from flaring and didn't quite manage it. "I'm *sorry* that I didn't tell you."

"I told you so." Enjoying the startled reaction his unexpected declaration had evoked, Austin picked his way across the laundry room. "What's with the rice?"

"It used to be the chains and locks," Claire told him.

"I see. Well, the mice will certainly be pleased."

"How many times do I have to tell you, I don't think they're mice!" The need to vent at something pushed the volume up until she was almost shouting.

Austin snorted. "Oh, that's right; you're the Keeper and I'm just a cat. What do I know about mice?"

She smiled tightly down at him. "You should know they don't come in primary colors. Were you looking for us?"

"No. But I was wondering why Jacques is having hysterics in the dining room while you two are hiding out down here." Fastidiously finding a clean bit of floor, he sat down, wrapping his tail around his toes. "After what I overheard, I'm not wondering any more, but I was.

"This is only a guess," he continued as Claire raced for the stairs, "based on the really pissed-off ravings of a dead man, but did someone use the h-word out of context and almost condemn his soul to everlasting torment?"

Dean blanched as he realized that was exactly what had happened. "If you'd told me," he called, hurrying to catch up, "I wouldn't have done it!"

"Her mother wanted her to tell you."

"Shut up, Austin."

When they reached the dining room, a plastic salt shaker, a box of toothpicks, and six grapes flew out of the kitchen. Claire ducked and Dean took the full impact

"J'ai presque ete a l'Enfer!"

Wiping crushed grape off his chin, Dean stepped forward. His French wasn't up to an exact translation, but the infuriated shriek suggested a limited number of possibilities. "I'm sorry. I didn't mean it. It was . . ."

"It was an accident!" With a well-placed hip, Claire moved Dean out of her way. "Granted, he said the words, but he didn't mean them as an instruction. He should be able to say what he wants with no effect."

Austin snorted and whacked the salt shaker under the dining room table. "That thing's been down there for over a century and the power seepage has permeated this whole building. I'm only surprised that he never told old Augustus where to go."

"I couldn't say that to my boss," Dean protested.

"Not without a union," the cat agreed.

Jacques surged through the table to stand face-to-face with Claire. "I don't care what he should have been able to do! All I know is that he tried to throw me into Hell!"

"And then he pulled you out again."

"You think that makes up for him putting me there?"

"Would you listen to me, Jacques!" Had she been able to get hold of him, she'd have shaken him until his teeth rattled. "He didn't *know* it would happen. He didn't even know what was in the furnace room."

"He did not know!" Jacques stepped back in disbelief, half in and half out of the table. "You did not tell him?" All at once, he frowned. "Come to think on it, you did not tell me!"

"*You've* been in the same building with it for seventy-two years!" Claire met indignation with equal indignation. "Knowing it's there won't change anything."

His eyes darkened. "You are wrong, Claire. It changes what I know."

She couldn't argue with that, even if she'd wanted to. "Okay. Fine. I should've told you. I should've told you both. But I didn't. I'm sorry." And that, she decided was the last time she was apologizing for it. "You both know now. I'm going to have another shower even though it won't do any good because the touch I can feel is inside my head, and then I'm going to get some breakfast because I'm starving. All right?" Her chin rose. "Is there anything *else* you'd like me to tell you?"

The two men, now side by side, exchanged interrogative glances.

"*Non,*" Jacques said after a moment. "I cannot think of anything."

"No more secrets," Dean added.

"God forbid *I* should have secrets." Her ears were burning and she didn't want to think about a probable cause. "My cat can't keep his mouth shut, and suddenly my life is an open book."

"Hey!" Austin stuck his head out from under the table. "You let the ghost out of the attic all on your own, and *I* said you should tell them about the furnace room."

"You did not."

He thought about that for a moment. "Well, I never told you not to."

Claire swept a scathing glance over the three of them, suggested they watch their language, and stomped out of the dining room. It would've been a more effective exit had she not been in socks and had her heels hitting the floor not set up a painful reverberation in her head, but she made the most of it.

"There will be secrets," Jacques observed, as the door to her suite slammed shut. "Women must have secrets."

"Why?" Dean asked, going into the kitchen.

"Why? Because, *espèce d'idiot*, between a man and a woman, there must be mystery. The worst of Hell is that there is no mystery."

ROSEBUD IS HIS SLED. When silence was the only response, Hell sighed. GET IT? NO MYSTERY. ROSEBUD IS HIS SLED. . . . DOESN'T ANYONE CARE ABOUT THE CLASSICS ANYMORE?

Dean turned to face the ghost, feeling slightly sick when he thought of what he'd nearly done. "I can only keep saying I'm sorry."

"That is right, *Anglais*," Jacques agreed. "You can keep saying you are sorry."

"The way I see it," Austin said, leaping from chair to counter-top, "you're even. You unjustly accused each other of wanting to wake *her*. You, Dean, accidentally almost sent Jacques to Hell, but then you purposefully went in and rescued him."

"*Non*. Not even." Jacques glared over the cat's head at Dean. "He also accuses me of hiding behind Claire."

"Yeah, and you called him something pithy and insulting."

"You speak French?"

"I'm a cat."

"Look, I overreacted," Dean admitted. He paused while the hot water pipes banged out the rhythm of Claire's shower. "It's just you've been pretty obvious about how much you want a body."

"I would take a body from the cat before I took a body from *her*."

"Don't hold your breath," Austin recommended.

Pulling the toaster from the appliance garage, Dean shook his head. He couldn't help feeling he should be more upset about the reality of a hole to Hell in the furnace room except that *reality* and *hole to Hell* in the same sentence just didn't compute. "Why does *she* bother me more than Hell?"

"I could go into the deep psychological problems men experience when they come face-to-face with powerful women . . ."

"We do not!" both men exclaimed. Standing with their arms crossed, they regarded each other warily.

The cat snickered. ". . . but it's simpler than that. Hell is too nasty for mortal minds to comprehend, so they trivialize it, knock it down to size. It's a built-in defense mechanism."

Brow furrowed, Dean stared down at the cat. "So *she* bothers me more than Hell because I don't have any natural defenses against *her*?"

"And because the original Keepers put a dampening field around the furnace room. Without it, business would be worse than it is, as difficult as that may be to imagine, and any sane person would run screaming once they found out what was in the basement."

"And with it?"

"Unnerving but endurable. Kind of like opera."

"A dampening field to dull the reactions." Rubbing at the perpetual stubble along his jaw, Jacques nodded. "That does explain why I take this so well."

"That," Austin agreed, assaulting the lid on the butter dish, "and because you're dead. The dead don't get worked up about much."

"Except getting their rocks off," Dean muttered.

"You desire I should tell Claire why we were really fighting?" the ghost demanded.

"If you know, why didn't you tell her upstairs?"

"Two reasons. If you do not know, me, I am not the one to tell you. And two . . ." He shrugged. "I remember in the neck of time . . ."

"Nick of time."

"What?"

"Not neck," Dean told him. "Nick."

"*D'accord.* In the nick of time, I remember that women do not always appreciate being fought over the way those who fight might assume."

"Oh." Opening the fridge, Dean stared at the contents, ignored the little voice suggesting that, under the circumstances, it was all right to have a beer before noon, and closed the door again, saying, "That's pretty smart for a dead guy."

"I was, as you say, pretty smart for a live guy."

"You're bonding," Austin observed sardonically. "I'm touched. Well, what would you call it?" he asked when both the living and the dead fixed him with an identical expression of horror.

"We're not bonding," Dean declared.

"Not even a little bit," Jacques added. "We are . . ." He looked to the living for help.

"Not bonding," Dean repeated.

"*Oui.*" Settling himself cross-legged an inch above the table, the ghost leaned back on nothing and studied the other man. "Me, I have no choice, but you, now you know, do you stay?"

"Claire asked me that, too." He folded his arms. "I don't run away from things."

"Perhaps it is wiser to know when to run."

"And leave you alone here?"

Jacques spread his hands, the pictures of wronged innocence, the gesture far more eloquent than words.

"Fat chance." Shoving his glasses up on his nose, Dean headed for the basement stairs.

"Where are you going?"

He made the face of a man who once a month scrubbed the concrete floor with a stiff broom and an industrial cleanser. "I'm after sweeping up the rice."

"You've had a busy twenty-four hours, Claire. Are you sure you're all right?"

"I have a vicious headache." Cradling the old-fashioned receiver in the damp hollow between ear and shoulder, she fought with the childproof cap on a bottle of painkillers. Teeth clenched, she sat the pill bottle on the table and pulled power. The bottle exploded.

"Claire, what are you doing?"

There were two pills caught in the cuff of her bathrobe. "Just taking something for my headache." She swallowed them dry.

On the other end of the phone, Martha Hansen sighed. "You

aren't the first Keeper who's had to apologize to a bystander, you know."

"It's the first time *I've* ever had to do it."

"It's the first time a bystander's ever been involved in what you do."

Claire opened her mouth to disagree, then realized that her previous involvements with bystanders were not something she wanted to discuss with her mother. Nor, she acknowledged with a small smile, were they something she had to apologize for.

"Claire?"

Pleasant memories fled as the current situation shoved its way back to the forefront of her thoughts. "At least I needn't worry about it happening again. Dean's too nice a guy to even think of doing it on purpose."

"And Jacques?"

Her lip curled. "Jacques is dead, Mom. He can't affect anything."

"Ah. Yes."

Claire decided she didn't want to know what that meant. Had the phones been Touch-Tone, she'd have suspected Austin had been talking to her mother behind her back. Since there was no way the cat could use a rotary phone . . . All at once, this conversation was not making her feel any better. "I'd better get dressed and get back to work."

"I hope it helped you to talk about it, Claire. You know you can call any time. Speaking of calling, you haven't heard from your sister, have you?"

She could feel her jaw muscles tightening up. "No. Why?"

"We had a bit of a disagreement, and she stormed out of here last night. I'm not worried, I know where she is, I was just wondering if she'd spoken to you."

"No."

"If she does call, would you please explain to her that turning the sofa into a pygmy hippo for the afternoon might be very good transfiguration, but it's rather hard on the carpets and it confuses the hippo."

A dry, tearing sound, the sound of something large and ancient clearing its throat, pulled Dean up from the basement. Fighting against the natural inclination of his legs to get the rest of his body the hell out of there, so to speak, he made his way to the dining room where he found Claire on her hands and knees, surrounded by pieces of broken quarter-round, ripping up the linoleum.

"She's venting frustrations on inanimate objects," Austin explained from the safety of the countertop. "You should consider yourself lucky."

"Boss?"

She shuffled backward and tore free another two feet of floor covering before the section detached from the main. "There's hardwood under here. We're going to refinish it."

"But I thought . . ."

"Congratulations."

". . . that you were after working on closing the site."

"To close the site, I need to study it. To study it, I need to get close. To get close, I need to be calm." Claire ripped up another ragged section. "Do I look calm?"

"I guess not." Amazed by the extent of the mess, Dean wasn't entirely certain he wouldn't rather have faced the demon he'd expected. "But what about the front counter, out in the lobby."

"I know where the front counter is, Dean." She tossed aside a crumbling piece of linoleum. "I'm not asking you if you want to refinish the floor, I'm telling you we're going to."

Dean glanced over at the cat who looked significantly unhelpful. "Where's Jacques?"

"Staying out of my way."

"Ah." He cleaned his glasses on his shirttail and squinted unenthusiastically at the exposed wood. "Should I go rent an industrial sander?"

"Yes, you should." Claire rolled up onto her feet and headed down the hall toward the office.

"Why should we be the ones who suffer?" Dean muttered at the cat as he turned to follow. "She was in the wrong."

"And you're just going to keep that thought to yourself, aren't you," Austin told him.

Dean knew the envelope Claire pulled the money from—Augustus Smythe had paid him out of it every Friday. He could've sworn it had been empty on Saturday when he'd unlocked the safe. "Where did you get the cash?"

"Lineage operating funds." Claire tossed the envelope back in the safe and closed the door. "When people, or institutions, or pop machines lose money, it becomes ours, available to draw on when we need it."

"*This* is where lost money goes?" Fanning the bills he counted four twenties, three tens, and a five with Mr. Spock's haircut penciled onto the head of Sir Wilfred Laurier. It was a remarkable likeness. "What about socks?"

"Socks?"

"Where do lost socks go?"

Claire stared at him as though he'd suddenly sprouted a third head. "How the he . . . heck should I know?"

When Dean returned just before noon, all the furniture in the dining room had been rearranged on the ceiling and the linoleum had been completely removed. It was still lying around in messy heaps, but it was no longer attached to the floor.

Tired and filthy, Claire watched appreciatively as he wrestled the heavy machine in through the back door. Having actually been able to accomplish something had put her in a significantly better mood.

They ate soup and sandwiches sitting on the counter, discussing renovations in perfect harmony. Two hours later, the debris bagged, Claire left to finish sorting through Augustus Smythe's room while Dean used the sander.

As the layers of glue and old varnish began to disappear, he grew more confident. Finished with the edging, he began making long, smooth passes up and down the twenty-three-foot length of the room. After the third pass, he began to pick up speed. All at once, a body appeared too close to the drum to avoid.

Jacques screamed in mock agony as the sander split him in two.

Somehow, Dean managed to maintain enough control so he only gouged a three-foot, shallow, diagonal trench into the floorboards before he got the machine turned off. Ripping off his ear protectors with one hand and the dust mask with the other, he whirled around and yelled, "That's not funny!"

Jacques waved a hand made weak by laughter. "You should see your face. If I am here another seventy years, I will never see anything so funny." As Dean sputtered inarticulately, he started laughing harder.

"Why have you stopped? Have you finished?" Claire halted in the doorway, took in the tableau, and shook her head. "Jacques, pull yourself together!"

"For you, *cherie,* anything." Continuing amusement kept his upper half vibrating and Jacques finally had to reach down, grab his jeans, and yank his legs back onto his torso.

"Was there an accident?"

"No, not an accident," Dean growled. "The jerk suddenly showed up in front of me. Look at what he made me do to the floor! I should've run over his head."

"Be my guest," Jacques told him, still snickering.

"Jacques!"

The ghost set his head back on his shoulders.

"You know," Claire told him pointedly, "just for the record, I don't find that sort of thing attracti . . ." She jumped as an air raid siren began to sound. "Mrs. Abrams. I set up an alarm on the front steps to give us a little warning. Jacques, you'd better disappear."

"Why can't I meet this Mrs. Abrams?"

"Yeah, Boss, why *can't* he?" Dean asked with feeling. "Why should we have all the fun."

The siren shut off as the front door opened. "Yoo hoo!"

Jacques flinched and disappeared.

Suddenly inspired, Dean switched the sander back on.

As clouds of dust billowed up around him, Claire dragged herself reluctantly out to the front hall.

"Oh, there you are, dear." Her voice rose easily over the background noise roaring out of the dining room. "As I was letting Baby out into his little area I heard horrible sounds coming from the back of this building and I rushed right over in case the whole ancient firetrap had begun coming down around your ears."

Claire crushed an impulse to ask her what she would have done had it been. "We're refinishing the floor in the dining room, Mrs. Ab . . ."

Of course you are. Didn't I say this fine old building needed a woman's touch? So nice you have a strong young man around to do the work for you." She darted purposefully down the hall, caroling, "I'll just go and have a little look-see," as she went

For a woman of her age and weight, Mrs. Abrams moved remarkably quickly. Hie defensive line of the Dallas Cowboys might have been able to stop her, but Claire didn't stand a chance without using power. With no time for finesse, she reached out and slammed to her knees.

Five feet out in front, Mrs. Abrams didn't even notice.

Blinking away afterimages, Claire dragged herself up the wall. *It's that damn sander,* she decided, perfectly willing to condemn it to the flames. *How's anyone supposed to concentrate through all that noise?*

Innate good manners forced Dean to turn the sander off when Mrs. Abrams charged into the room.

"Mercy." She coughed vigorously into a handkerchief she pulled from her sleeve. "It is dusty, isn't it? And this room looks so small and dreary with no furniture in . . ." Her voice trailed off as she noticed just where the furniture was. "Oh, my. How did you ever . . . ?"

"Clamps," Claire told her. The older woman looked so relieved she could almost hear the sound of possibilities being discarded. Meeting Dean's incredulous gaze, she shrugged—the gesture saying clearly, *people believe what they want to believe.*

A LIE!

A LIE IN KINDNESS. THEY CANCEL EACH OTHER OUT. NEITHER SIDE IS STRENGTHENED. NEITHER SIDE IS WEAKENED.

BUT . . .

INTENT COUNTS. Had anyone been there to overhear, they might have thought that Hell spoke through clenched teeth. IT'S IN THE RULES.

Suddenly inspired, Claire took hold of one polyester-covered elbow and turned the body attached to it back toward the front door. "You shouldn't be in here without a dust mask, Mrs. Abrams. What would Baby do if you got sick?"

"Oh, I mustn't get sick, the poor darling would be devastated. He's

so attached to his mummy." Craning her head around, she took one
last look at the dining room ceiling. "Clamps, you say?"

"How else?"

"Of course, clamps. How else would you be holding furniture on
the ceiling. How very clever of you, Karen, dear. Have you heard from
that horrible Mr. Smythe?"

"No, and my name isn't . . ."

"He's going to be so surprised at all you've done when he comes
back. Are you going to open up the elevator?"

"The what?"

"The elevator. There's one in this hall somewhere. I remember it
from when I was a girl."

Claire opened the front door, but Mrs. Abrams made no move to
go out it

"You ought to open the elevator up, you know. It would lend the
place such a historical . . ." Her eyes widened as the sound of frenzied
barking echoed up and down the street. She darted out the door.
"What can be wrong with Baby?"

"The mailman?" Claire asked, following from the same compul-
sion that stopped drivers to look at car accidents on the highway.

"No. No. He's long been and gone."

They were side by side as they crossed the driveway. Claire, on the
inside track, looked toward the back in time to see a black-and-white
blur leap from the fence to the enclosure around the garbage cans to
the ground and streak toward the hotel.

When Claire stopped running, Mrs. Abrams never noticed.

The noise coming from Baby's little area—after a few years of
Baby, it could no longer be called a yard in any domestic sense of the
word—never lessened.

If the flames reflected on the copper hood were sullen before, they
were downright sulky now.

IT ISN'T FAIR.

WHAT ISN'T?

THAT THE KEEPER SHOULD ALWAYS WIN. IF WE HAD
ONLY PULLED HARDER. WE WERE SO CLOSE.

CLOSE! The repetition resounded in the heated air like a small explosion. CLOSE ONLY COUNTS IN HORSESHOES AND HAND GRENADES.

AND DANCING.

WHAT?

CLOSE DANCING.

SHUT UP.

SIX

"I WOULD LIKE A ROOM."

Kneeling behind the counter, attempting to send a probe down into the mouse hole and settle the imp question once and for all, Claire felt icy fingers run along her spine. Shivering slightly, she carefully backed out from under the shelf and stood, curious to see if it was the customer or the possibility of actually renting a room that had evoked the clichéd response.

The woman on the other side of the counter was a little shorter than her own five feet five, with a close cap of sable hair, pale skin, and eyes so black it was impossible to tell where the iris ended and the pupil began.

Claire felt the pull of that dark gaze, found herself sinking into the dangerous embrace of shadow, jerked back, and said, "Room four?"

"How perceptive." The woman smiled, teeth gleaming between lips the deep burgundy of a good Spanish port. "Where is the Cousin?"

"Gone. This is my site now." It was almost, but not quite, a warning.

"I see. And should I worry that things have changed enough to need the monitoring of a Keeper?"

"You are in no more danger here than you ever were."

"How fortunate." The woman sagged forward, planted her elbows on the counter, and rubbed her eyes. "'Cause I'm bagged. You have no idea how much I hate traveling. I just want to dump my gear in the room and find something to eat."

Claire blinked.

"Oh, come on." Smudged mascara created raccoonlike circles on the pale skin. "Surely you hadn't planned on continuing that ponderous dialogue?"

"Uh, I guess not."

"Good. 'Cause I'll be staying the rest of the week, checking out Sunday evening if that's cool with you. I've got a gig at the university."

"Gig?"

"Engagement. Job. I'm a musician." She stretched an arm across the counter, thin, ivory hand overwhelmed by half a dozen heavy silver bangles and the studded cuff of her black leather jacket. "Sasha Moore. It's a stage name, of course. I do this kind of heavy metal folk thing that goes over big on most campuses."

Her skin felt cool and dry and her handshake, while restrained, still put uncomfortable pressure on mere mortal knuckles.

There was power in a name and trust in the giving of it. Claire wasn't certain how that applied in this case—while Keepers maintained a live-and-let-live attitude toward the vast bulk of humanity, they tended to avoid both actors and musicians; people who preferred to be in the public eye made them nervous—but she did know that her response would speak volumes to the woman maintaining an unbreakable grip on her hand. If the hotel was no longer a safe haven for her kind, Sasha Moore would want to know before dawn left her helpless.

"Claire Hansen." Hand freed, she flipped open the registration book, and pulled a pen out of the *Souvenir of Avalon* mug on her desk. "Sign here, please."

"Rates the same?"

Rates? Claire hoped she didn't look as confused as she felt. Rates. . . .

Sasha leaned against the counter, dark eyes gleaming. "Room rates?"

"Right. Of course." She had no idea what the rates were, but it was important not to show weakness in front of a predator. "They've gone up a couple of dollars."

"Couple of bucks, eh?" Her signature a familiar scrawl, the musician spun the register back around. Her smile held heat. "You're not charging me for breakfast, are you?"

"Breakfast?" Unable to stop herself from imagining the possibilities, Claire's voice rose a little more than was necessary for the interrogative.

"'Cause if you are, there's nothing I like more than a big, juicy, hunk of . . ."

"Boss, there's a red van parked out back. Do you know whose it is?"

As Dean stepped out into the entry hall, Sasha winked at Claire and turned gracefully to face him. "The van's mine. I'm just checking in."

About to apologize for interrupting, Dean found his gaze caught and held. For a moment, the world became a pair of dark eyes in a pale face. Then the moment passed. "I, I'm sorry," he stammered, feeling his ears burn, "I didn't mean to stare, but you're Sasha . . . uh . . ."

"Moore."

"Yeah, Moore, Sasha Moore, the musician. You were here last spring."

"My, my, my. I must've made an impression."

"You had a black van then. Late eighties, six cylinder, all season radials."

"What a memory."

Claire's eyes narrowed. So this was the h . . . cute guest from room four. She slapped the keys down on the counter and tried not to feel pleased when Dean jumped at the sudden sound.

Sasha's smile broadened as she swept her attention back around to Claire. "I'll just go get my stuff out of the van while you make up the room."

"Make up the room?"

Dark eyes crinkled at the corners. "You are new at this, aren't you? Sheets. Towels. Soap. The usual." Her gaze turned speculative. "Which one of you will be making up the bed?"

Dean stepped forward. "I always did it for Mr. Smythe . . ."

Claire cut him off. "You're in the middle of staining the floor. I'll do it."

"Since it doesn't matter to me . . ."

Glancing over at Dean, Claire wondered if he heard the blithe innuendo.

". . . you two argue it out. I'll be right back." She disappeared into the night before the front door had quite closed behind her.

"Making up the rooms is part of my job," Dean explained, walking over to the counter and reaching for the keys. "Renovations are no reason to slack off my regular work."

"Refinishing the dining room floor is hardly slacking off." Claire snatched the keys out from under his hand. Realizing he remained unconvinced, she added, "The sooner that urethane's done and dry, the sooner you'll be able to deal with the mess."

His eyes lit up at the thought of restoring the kitchen to its usual pristine state. "If you're sure."

"Believe it or not, I'm fully capable of making a bed and hanging up towels. Keepers are trained to be self-sufficient in the field."

"Living off the land?" When she nodded, he frowned at the image that conjured up. "Hunting and fishing?"

"No. But I *can* locate a fast food restaurant within three minutes of arriving in a new area."

He looked appalled.

"It's a joke," she pointed out curtly. "Although, ninety percent of all accident sites do occur in an urban environment. Some Keepers spend their entire lives in the same city, trying desperately to keep it from falling apart."

"What about the other ten percent?"

"Big old houses in the middle of nowhere with at least one dead tree in the immediate area."

"Why a dead tree?"

"Ambience."

His smile was tentative and it disappeared entirely when she didn't join in. "Not a joke?"

"Not a joke." Closing the registration book, Claire came out from behind the counter. Dean was not going to be alone in that room when Sasha Moore returned and that was final—no matter what sorts of demanding tasks she had to perform. She was strong enough to resist the temptation the musician represented but he, however, was a man, and a young one, and expecting him to decline that kind of invitation on his own would be expecting too much. Whether or not he had succumbed during the previous visit was immaterial; this time, she was here to help. "Where do we keep the supplies?"

"In the supply cupboard."

From anyone else, she'd have suspected sarcasm.

"I could wait here and help Ms. Moore carry her bags upstairs. She looked tired."

Ms. Moore could carry you upstairs; one-handed. But that wasn't Claire's secret to reveal. "You know, the longer you leave that floor unattended the greater the odds are that Austin will take a walk and track dark oak stain all over the hotel."

"He'd notice the floor was wet."

"Of course he'd notice. He wouldn't do it by accident."

"But . . ."

"He's a cat." She waited until Dean started back toward the dining room then, jaw set for confrontation, headed upstairs.

"So she's h . . . cute, is she?" Yanking out a set of single sheets, she piled them on top of the towels. "I don't care if he's been providing breakfast, dinner, and midnight snacks, it's dangerous and it's going to stop. I won't have my staff snacked on."

"Who is snacking on your staff?" Jacques floated down from the floor above and settled about an arm's reach away. "And does that mean what it sounds like it means, or is it some prissy *Anglais* way to talk of what is more interesting?"

"It means what it sounds like it means." Two small bars of soap were dropped on the pile. "Did I put one of your anchors in here?"

"*Oui.*"

"I wonder why I did that."

"So we could have more time alone together?" He lifted a lecherous brow but at her protest pressed it back down onto his forehead. "Because you felt sorry for me?" His whole body got involved in looking mournful, shoulders slumped, gaze focused on the loose interlacing of his fingers.

Claire rolled her eyes at the dramatics but couldn't help smiling.

Peering up through his hair, Jacques caught sight of the smile and flashed her an answering grin. "Ah. That is better, no? You should be in a happy mood. I am saved from the pit, and you . . ." He waved a hand at the gathered supplies. ". . . you have someone to stay at your hotel."

"You seem to have recovered from this morning's experience."

Claire struggled toward the door, decided she was being ridiculous, wrapped the whole unwieldy pile in power and floated it out into the hall. "I expected the trauma to have lasted a little longer."

Jacques shrugged. "A man does not allow himself to be held captured by his fears. Besides, as Austin reminds me, I am dead. The dead exist in the now; this morning is as years away. Tomorrow may never happen. When I am with you, only then do I think of a future."

Which said something, something unpleasant, about the lingering effect of Aunt Sara. Not to mention country music lyrics.

Inside room four. Claire brought the bedding and towels and sundries to rest on the bureau and picked a small shaving mirror and stand up off the floor.

"What are you doing?"

"You can't have access to rooms that guests are in."

"Why not?"

"Because they might not like it."

"How can they not like me?"

"You're dead." She set the mirror out in the hall and carried the towels into the bathroom.

"Hey, who's the dead guy?"

The sound of the hall door closing brought Claire back out into the dressing room. "He's none of your concern."

"Count on it" She grinned and shrugged out of her jacket. "I don't ask for much from my dates, but they do have to be alive. Now that piece of prime rib in your basement . . ."

"Stay away from him."

"Why?" She polished nails much the same length and color as Claire's against her black sleeveless turtleneck. "You think I'm too hard an act to follow?"

"I have no intention of following you or anyone else. I don't know and I don't care . . ." Claire ignored a raised ebony brow, obviously intended to provoke. ". . . about what happened when Augustus Smythe ran the site, but while I'm responsible, Dean McIssac is under my protection."

"Really? He seemed like a big . . ." A reflective moment later, she resumed. ". . . very big boy. And you're not his guardian, Keeper, so chill. But, as it happens, I never feed in the crib unless things get desperate and, if that's the case, your mother hen act will be the least of my problems. Besides, it'd be easier to throw myself on your mercy. After all, Keepers respond to need." A startlingly pale tongue flicked over burgundy lips. "You're what, O negative?"

"What does that have to do with anything?"

"It doesn't. It's just nice to know you're one of my favorite flavors. Just in case."

Busying herself with the bed, Claire pointedly did not respond.

Behind her, Sasha laughed, neither insulted nor discouraged. "From the way you spoke of him, I assume the little man isn't dead. What did he do? Bugger off and leave you holding the stick?"

"That's not how it works."

Sasha laughed again. "Not generally, no, but Keepers don't take over sites from Cousins who took over from Keepers, so clearly it ain't working the way it should."

"How do you know all that?"

"I've been around a while."

Claire remembered the years of signatures in the registration book—not one of them, unfortunately, occurring in the few short months Sara held the site. "Do you know about . . . ?" A jerk of the head to room six finished the question.

"Well, duh. It's not like it's possible to hide something like that from me. I mean, after four or five visits it got kind of hard to ignore this unchanging life just hanging around upstairs." The musician shrugged into an oversized red sweater. "Gus said it was a woman the Keepers had done a Sleeping Beauty on and that was all I needed to know."

"You called him Gus?"

"Sure. And I'd love to know how he stuck you with this place, but if you don't want to spill, hey, that's cool." She ran her fingers through her hair and quickly changed her lipstick to match the sweater. "He never filled me in on his summoning either—the obnoxious little prick. But man, at your age, it must be driving you nuts hanging around here when you could be out saving the world."

Before Claire could answer, Dean's voice, calling her name, drifted up the stairwell.

Sasha tilted her head toward the sound. "And right on cue we have a reminder of the fringe benefits."

"He's not a benefit," Claire protested.

Cool fingers cupped her chin for a heartbeat "Foolish girl, why not?" Then, with a jangle of silver bracelets and a careless, "Don't wait up—" she was gone.

Her touch lingered.

Later that night, as Claire climbed into bed, Austin uncurled enough to mutter, "I understand you're renting a room to a bloodsucking, undead, soulless creature."

"Does that bother you," Claire asked.

"Not in the least." He yawned. "Anyone who can operate a can opener is okay by me."

"She came back into her room just before dawn. I think that she saw somebody in town last night." Jacques' hands traced euphemistic signals in the air. "If you know what I mean. She had a cat who has eaten canary look."

Sprawled on top of the computer monitor, Austin snorted. "She looked like she was about to hawk up a mouthful of damp feathers?"

"That is not what I mean."

"You shouldn't spy on the guests," Dean told him, tightening his grip on a handful of steel wool. "It's rude."

"I was not spying," Jacques protested indignantly. "I was concerned."

"Pull the other one."

"You do not have to believe me."

"Good."

"Why do you suppose such a pretty girl stays in a room with no windows?"

Descending from an hour spent studying the power wrapped around Aunt Sara—as long as she could spend so close to such evil without wanting to rent movies just so she could return then unrewound—Claire waited on the stairs for Dean's answer.

"Ms. Moore's a musician." His tone suggested only an idiot couldn't have figured it out on his own. "She works nights, she sleeps days, and she doesn't want the sun to wake her."

"Such a good thing there is the room, then," Jacques mused.

Claire frowned. What would happen if Jacques put one and one together and actually made two? If the ghost found out about the vampire, who could he tell? Dean? Only if it would irritate or enrage him.

What if Dean found out? She was fairly certain he would neither start sharpening stakes nor looking up the phone numbers for the tabloids. The vampire's safety would not be compromised.

Dean's safety was another matter entirely. Many humans were drawn to the kind of danger Sasha Moore represented. While not necessarily life-threatening, it was a well known fact that the intimacy of vampiric feeding could become addictive and that wasn't something she was going to allow to happen to Dean. He wasn't going to end up wandering the country, a helpless groupie of the undead.

And I'd feel the same way about anyone made my responsibility, she insisted silently. *Including guests while they're in this hotel.* Which, in a loopy way, made Sasha Moore her responsibility as well.

The sudden realization jerked her forward. Catching her heel on the stair, she stumbled, arms flailing for balance, down into the lobby. She'd have made it had the pommel on the end of the banister not come off in her hand.

Her landing made an impressive amount of noise. It would have made more had she been permitted the emotional release of profanity.

"Claire!" Dean tossed the steel wool aside, peeled off the rubber gloves, and started to rise. "Are you all right?"

"I'm *fine.*"

Moving toward her, he found Jacques suddenly in his way, hands raised in warning.

"I wouldn't," the ghost murmured by the other man's ear. "When a woman says she is fine in that tone, she wishes you to leave her alone."

Since he couldn't push the ghost away. Dean went through him and dropped to his knees by Claire's side. "What happened?"

"I slipped."

"Are you hurt?" Without thinking, he reached for her arm but drew back at her expression.

"I said, *I'm fine.*"

"Told you so," Jacques murmured, drifting up by the ceiling.

Claire pushed herself into a sitting position with one hand and gave Dean the banister pommel with the other. "If you're looking for something to do . . ." A triple boom not only cut off Dean's response but spun her around, hand over her heart as she futilely tried to keep it from beating in time. "What the . . ."

"Door knocker," Dean explained, then clapped his hands over his ears as the sound echoed through the lobby again.

Except that Dean had no reason to lie, she'd never have believed that the brass knocker she'd seen on her first night could have made the noise. *At least we know it's not Mrs. Abrams; she never knocks.* As Dean ran for the door before their caller knocked again and they all went deaf, Claire got to her feet, telling Jacques to disappear.

"Why?" he demanded, floating down to the floor.

"You're translucent in natural light"

"What means translucent?"

"I can see through you."

"That is because to you, *cherie,* I have nothing to hide." He blew her a kiss and vanished as the door opened.

A graying man in his mid-forties peered over a huge bouquet of red chrysanthemums, his slightly protruding eyes flicking back and forth between Dean and Claire. "Flowers for Ms. Moore."

"She's sleeping," Dean told him, adding helpfully, "if you leave them here, I'll see that she gets them when she wakes up."

The deliveryman shook his head and held out a clipboard. "I gotta have her sign for 'em."

"But she's asleep."

"Look, all I know is that I gotta have her signature and room number on this or I can't leave the flowers." He looked suddenly hopeful "Maybe you could just fake it for me? Then I'd leave 'em with you. It'd *really* help me out."

"I don't know . . ."

Claire did. "I'm sorry," she said, crossing the lobby, "but we don't give out the room numbers of our guests. If you can't leave the flowers with us, you'll have to come back."

"Look, lady, it's my last delivery. What difference would it make?"

"You're missing the point." Moving in front of Dean so she stood eye to eye with the deliveryman, who was no taller than her own five-feet-five, Claire folded her arms and smiled. "We don't give out die room numbers of our guests."

"But . . ."

"No."

He looked up at Dean. "Come on, buddy, give me a break, eh."

Claire snapped her fingers under his nose, drawing his attention back down to her. "What part of no don't you understand?"

"Okay. Fine. You're responsible for Ms. Moore not getting her flowers, then."

"I can live with that." It was nice to have a responsibility so well defined.

"Yeah, well, thanks for the help." Lip curled, he spun around and missed his step on the uneven stairs. Flowers flailing, he began to fall.

"Boss!" Dean's exclamation prodded at her conscience. "He could get hurt!"

Reminding herself of where temptations came from, Claire sighed, took her time reaching for power and, just as he began to pitch forward, set the deliveryman back on his feet.

He never noticed. Stomping down the remaining steps, he flung the flowers into his car and, tires squealing, drove away.

Claire watched until he turned onto King Street. "I wonder who the flowers were from?"

"A fan?"

"I guess." She reached out and gave the small brass knocker an investigative flick. When the resulting boom faded, she followed Dean back inside. "But how did they know she was staying here?"

"Maybe she told them."

"Maybe," Jacques put in, rematerializing, "they were from the one last night. Flowers to say, *Thanks for the memories.*"

"I don't think so; she wouldn't have told anyone she was staying here."

"Why not?"

"Because she told me she valued her privacy."

LIAR, a triumphant little voice announced in her head.

A lie to protect another, Claire pointed out. *Circumstances must be weighed. And get out of my head!*

THE LIE INVITED US IN.

Fine. Now I'm telling you to leave.

"Claire?"

Her eyes refocused. "Sorry, what were we talking about?"

"Ms. Moore's privacy."

"Right. We're going to respect it." She looked pointedly at Jacques. "And that means all of us."

Later that afternoon, as the last flat bit of counter emerged from under the twenty-seventh layer of paint, Baby could be heard barking furiously in his area.

Dean glanced up to see Austin still sprawled out on top of Claire's monitor. "Mailman must be late today."

"Only if he's out in the parking lot."

"What?"

The cat leaped down onto the desk, knocking a pile of loose papers and a pen to the floor. "According to Baby, who functions remarkably well on only two brain cells, there's a stranger in the parking lot."

"My truck!" Springing to his feet he raced toward the back door, peeling off another pair of gloves as he went.

Claire, on her way up from testing the dampening field, stepped in his path. "Hold it! Remember the urethane!"

He spun on the spot retraced his steps, and flung himself out the front door.

By the time Claire reached the back of the building, having paused in the lobby for a brief explanation, Dean was disappearing over the waist-high board fence to the west. To the south, Baby continued barking. Dean's truck, a huge white gas-guzzling monster named Moby, and Sasha Moore's van both seemed untouched.

"Carole! Carole, dear!" Mrs. Abrams voice didn't so much rise over Baby's barking as cut through it. "What's going on? What's happening?"

Slowly, Claire turned. "We had a prowler, Mrs. Abrams."

"What's that? Speak up, dear, don't mumble."

"A prowler!"

"What, in the middle of the afternoon? What will they think of next? You don't suppose it's that same ruffian who was lurking about the other night?"

"No, I . . ."

"We'll all be murdered in our beds! Or assaulted. Assaulted and robbed. That'll show them!"

Just in time, Claire stopped herself from asking, *Show who?* She didn't really want to know.

"Has that nice young man of yours gone after him?" Mrs. Abrams didn't actually pause for. breath let alone an answer. "How I do miss having Mr. Abrams around, although to be honest with you, dear, he was never what I'd call a capable man; had an unfortunate tendency to wilt a bit in stressful situations. He passed away quite suddenly, you know, with such a queer little smile on his face. I'm sure he's as lost without me as I am without him. Never mind, though, I get on. As a matter of fact, I can't stand and chat, I have our local councilman on the phone. The dear man depends on my advice in neighborhood matters." A beringed hand lightly patted lacquered waves of orange hair. "He simply couldn't manage on his own. Baby, be quiet."

Baby ignored her.

"That's Mummy's good boy."

As Mrs. Abrams returned to her telephone, Dean vaulted back over the fence and dropped into the parking lot. "I'm sorry. I lost him. He had a car on Union Street. Got into it and away before I got around the corner." Frowning like a concerned parent, he quickly checked over both vehicles. "Seems like Baby chased him away before he could do any damage. Good dog!"

To Claire's surprise, the Doberman wuffled once and fell silent.

"I wonder if this is his?" Dean pointed to a handprint on the van's driver side window.

Staring at the greasy print, Claire felt her own palms tingle and was suddenly certain she knew who the prowler had been. "It's the deliveryman."

"Pardon?"

"The guy with the flowers this morning."

"I knew who you meant. Are you, uh . . ." He waggled his fingers in the air.

"Manipulating power? No. It's just a hunch."

"A hunch. Okay." Pulling his sweatshirt sleeve down over his palm, he scrubbed the window clean.

Since she couldn't point out that he'd just ruined any chance Sasha Moore might've had of picking up the intruder's scent, Claire shrugged and went back inside to find Austin waiting by his dish.

"Catch him?"

"No. I didn't know you understood dogs."

"What's the point of insulting them if they can't understand what you're saying?"

"You speak dog?"

In answer, Austin lifted his head and made a noise that could possibly be considered a bark had the listener never actually heard a dog larger than a Pekingese.

"And what does that mean?" Claire asked, trying to keep from laughing.

"Roughly translated . . ." Austin stared pointedly down at his dish. ". . . it means, feed me."

That evening, Claire was waiting at the desk when Sasha Moore came downstairs. "Can I speak to you for a moment?"

"Is it going to take long?"

"Not long, no."

"Good, 'cause I really need to eat before I go onstage or the audience is one major distraction; kind of like performing in front of a buffet table."

Since there didn't seem to be anything she could safely reply, Claire stood and silently led the way into her sitting room.

"I see old Gus didn't take much with him."

She didn't want to know the circumstances under which Sasha had been in these rooms before. It was none of her business.

"You still got his dirty pictures up in the bedroom?"

"I'm removing them as soon as I have time."

"Uh-huh." The musician dropped onto the couch and draped one crimson-spandex-covered leg over the broad arm. "So what did you want to talk to me about?"

Claire perched on the edge of the hassock, it being the only piece of furniture in the room that was neither overstuffed nor covered in knickknacks. "I think you're being stalked."

Long lashes, heavy with mascara, blinked twice. "Say what?"

Editing for time, Claire recited the day's events and her interpretation of them.

"Look, I appreciate your concern, but the flowers were probably sent by a fan, and you never actually saw the guy in the lot. It could've been one of the local kids taking a shortcut"

"To his car?"

Sasha snorted. "Trust me, parking sucks in this neighborhood."

"All right, then, if it was a fan who sent the flowers, how did he know you were here? I can't believe you'd tell anyone where you spend the day."

"He must've seen me last night at one of the bars and followed the van."

"Doesn't that worry you?"

She reached out and slapped Claire on the knee. They were close enough that Claire could smell the mint toothpaste on her breath. "Why should I worry? You seem to be worrying enough for both of us." Standing, she bared her teeth. Exposed, they were too long and far, far too white. "I can take care of myself, Keeper. If a fan gets too close, I'll see that he gets just a little closer still." She paused at the door. "Oh, by the way, did you know you have mice?"

Feeling her lips press into a thin line, Claire pried them apart enough to say, "I don't think they're mice."

The musician shrugged. "They sure smell like mice."

"Told you so," Austin muttered as the door closed behind her.

Claire jumped. She hadn't noticed him tucked up like a tea cozy under the television. "If they're mice," she snapped, "why don't you catch one."

He snorted. "Please, and do what with it?"

Friday morning started badly for Claire. First Hell, by way of her mirror, suggested she invite Sasha Moore to dinner and twisted her reaction to such an extent that when she finally regained her reflection, she was edgy and irritable and had no idea of who'd won the round. Then she got completely lost looking for the Historian, was gone almost nine hours' wardrobe time, and returned absolutely famished to discover Dean had just laid down the last coat of urethane and she couldn't get to the kitchen.

"Go . . . 1 darn it!"

Thanks to the two huge, plate glass windows in the back wall, any solution had to take the possibility of Mrs. Abrams into account. Making a mental note to buy blinds as soon as possible, she grabbed power and shot into the air so quickly she cracked her head on the hall ceiling.

"Scooped up the seepage," Austin said with a snicker.

Both hands holding her head, Claire glared down at him. "I didn't *mean* to."

"You wanted it quick and dirty, didn't you?"

"Well, yes, but . . ."

"That's what you got. Still, I doubt you've permanently warped your character."

"This wasn't the first time. When I tried to stop Mrs. Abrams yesterday, I got knocked to my knees."

"Once, twice; what's the harm?"

"That's probably what Augustus Smythe used to think." The faint buzz of building seepage seemed to have disappeared; it was hard to be certain given the ringing in her ears from the impact. Drawing power carefully from the middle of the possibilities, she sank down until she was about two inches off the floor and then skated slowly forward. Another time, she might've been hesitant about continuing buoyancy initiated by seepage from Hell but right now she was too hungry to care.

Breathing *eau de sealant* shallowly through her mouth, she sat down by the sink, poured a bowl of cereal, and began to eat. She'd started a second bowl when Jacques appeared beside her.

"I think you should know," he said, "that the man who deliver the flowers yesterday, he is just come in the front door."

"What?"

"The man, who deliver the flowers yesterday . . ."

"I heard you." Dropping her cereal in the sink, she flung herself off the counter and raced for the front of the hotel . . .

. . . unfortunately forgetting the section of tacky polyurethane she had to cross.

"Fruitcake!"

The emotional force behind the substitute expletive transfigured the toaster and the smell of candied fruit soaked in rum rose briefly over the prevailing chemicals.

Jacques studied the cake thoughtfully. "What would have happened, I wonder, had you actually used that old Anglo-Saxon expletive with you and I here together?"

"Do you have to!" Claire snapped, loosened her laces, pulled power, and floated to the hall, leaving her shoes where they were stuck.

"Not exactly have to," Jacques murmured.

As Claire ran for the lobby, the deliveryman ducked out from behind the counter, holding what seemed to be the same bouquet of red mums. "I was just lookin' for a piece of paper," he said hurriedly. "The boss said I could leave the flowers, and I was gonna leave you a note."

He was lying. Unfortunately, unless she knew for certain he was a threat to the site, Claire couldn't force him to tell the truth.

OH, WHY NOT?" asked the little voice in her head. *"WHO'S GOING TO KNOW? YOU KNOW YOU WANT TO."*

"*Shut. Up.*" Claire held her hand out for the flowers. "I'll see that Ms. Moore gets these," she said aloud.

"Sure." Watching her warily, he backed along the edge of the counter toward the door, reaching behind him for the handle. He slipped out, still without turning, and paused, peering through the crack just before the door closed. Yellowing teeth showed for an instant in an unpleasant smile. "Give Ms. Moore my regards."

Setting the flowers down, Claire glanced into the office, but nothing seemed to have been disturbed. "Yeah, well, we'll see about that." Ducking under the counter, she lifted her backpack off a hook and rummaged around in the outer pocket. A few moments later, she pulled out the tattered remains of what had once been a large package of grape flavored crystals and poured what was left of the contents onto the palm of one hand.

"Sorry your shoes got stuck to the floor, Boss. I figured you'd notice it was still . . ." Dean's voice faded out in shocked disbelief as he watched Claire fling a fistful of purple powder into the air.

The powder hung for a heartbeat, a swirling purple cloud with added vitamin C, then it settled into a confused jumble of foot and handprints leading from the front door into the office and back to the door again. A fair bit of the powder settled around the flower stems.

"What a mess," Claire sighed. "This tells me nothing except that he was in here and I knew that already."

"Who?"

"The flower deliveryman. I was trying to find out what he was up to."

"With . . ." Dean rubbed a bit of the residue onto the end of a finger and sniffed it. ". . . grape Koolaid?"

"Actually, it's generic. Why waste name brands if you're just going to throw it around?"

"Okay." He pulled a folded tissue from his pocket and carefully wiped his finger. "I'll start cleaning this up."

"Great. I need coffee."

"The floor . . ."

"I know." A careful two inches above the purple, she floated down the hall.

Unfortunately, the flavor crystals had been presweetened. It took Dean the rest of the morning to clean up the mess, and when he finished, he still wasn't certain he'd got it all.

He was right. Although he glanced inside when he cleaned the purple prints off the key cabinet, he didn't notice the small smudge that marked the end of the one empty hook.

"Look, why don't you guys come over to the pub tonight and if this bozo's there, you can point him out to me. I'm always eager to meet my fans."

Dean looked doubtful. "What if he's dangerous?"

"If he is, you'll be there to help." The musician smiled languorously up at him. "Won't you?"

"Sure." Ears red, Dean stepped sideways until he stood behind the masking foliage of a fake rubber plant that filled the southeast corner of Augustus Smythe's sitting room. Until this moment he'd thought he'd gotten past those awkward, mortifying years of spontaneous reaction.

"What do you mean when you say *sure*?" Claire demanded from the other side of the room.

As far as he could tell, she had no idea why he'd moved. He glanced down at Sasha Moore, and his ears grew so hot they itched.

"Dean!"

Twisting one of the plastic leaves right off the plant, he dragged himself out of the warm, dark, inviting depths of the musician's eyes. "I mean, uh, that is . . . uh, Ms. Moore, could you please look somewhere else. Thank you." He took a deep breath and slowly released it. "I mean, that since we'll be there, if anything happens, we'll help."

"You've decided we're going to be there?"

"Sure. I mean, no." He shot a helpless look at Claire. "I mean, you don't *have* to go. I could always go without you."

"He's right, Claire, you don't *have* to go. He could stay late and help load the van." A pink tongue flicked out to moisten crimson lips. "I could give him a ride home."

"I'll go."

"Good, then, it's settled." Twisting lithely in the chair, Sasha stood and made her way through the bric-a-brac to the door. "I'm going out for a bite. I'll see you both at the pub."

As the door closed behind her, Jacques materialized, eyebrows lifted toward Dean. "Showing off?" He laughed at the panicked embarrassment in Dean's eyes, turned to face Claire, and said with patently false dismay, "He is so strong, no? He tore a leaf off your rubber plant."

"Don't worry about it," she snorted dismissively. "It's plastic. I'm more concerned about this pub thing."

"What pub thing?" Austin asked, coming out of the bedroom and stretching. When Claire explained, he jumped up onto her lap. "Go," he told her, butting his head against the bottom of her chin. "Take advantage of the fact you're not actually sealing the site. If anything comes up, I'll contact you."

"What would happen if you were actually sealing the site," Jacques wondered.

"I wouldn't be able to leave the building."

"Just like me."

"Except he's dead," Austin pointed out. "Since you're not, why don't you prove it."

"By going out?"

The cat sighed. "Ladies and gentlemen, we have a winner. Go out. Have fun. Aren't you the one who keeps saying you're not planning to be stuck here?"

"I didn't mean I should be going out to pubs," Claire protested indignantly.

"Why not?"

"I never get to go anywhere," Jacques said mournfully an hour later as he and Austin stood in the front window watching Claire and Dean walk toward King Street.

"Look at the bright side," Austin observed as Mrs. Abrams hurried down her front path too late to corner them. "It can be a dangerous world out there."

"What does she look at?"

One hand shading eyes squinted nearly shut, Mrs. Abrams stared up toward the window.

The cat stretched. "She's probably wondering if I'm the same cat who got Baby to hog-tie himself with his own chain."

"Are you?"

"Of course." He jumped down off the windowsill. "Come on, it's Friday night, let's go watch TV."

With a last curious look at Mrs. Abrams, Jacques turned and followed. "TV? Is it like radio?"

"You know radio?"

"*Oui.* Augustus Smythe, *le petit salaud,* he leaves in the attic a radio. I have energy enough to turn it on and off, but I cannot make different channels. Over many years, I have learned English from the CBC."

Austin snorted. "Well, that explains a lot."

"A lot?"

"You don't talk like a French Canadian sailor who died in 1922."

"So I have lost my identity to the English."

"Although you still sound French Canadian . . ."

THE CAT IS ALONE!

YEAH. SO?

A gust of heated air wafted up from the pit. GOOD POINT.

☀   ☀   ☀

"Why is it so dark in here?" Claire demanded, stopping just inside the door of the Beer Pit.

Feeling the pressure building behind them, Dean cleared his throat. "Uh, Boss, we're blocking the entrance."

"Technically, you're blocking the entrance, they could get around me." But she moved across the painted concrete floor toward one of the few empty tables. "Why is the ceiling so low?" Before Dean could point out that the pub was in a basement, she added, "And look at the size of these things. Why are the tables so small?"

"More tables, more people, more money."

Claire shot him a look as she sat down. "I knew that. The floor's sticky. You'll notice, I'm not asking why. Do you see. the deliveryman?"

"It's pretty crowded . . ."

"I'd suggest you wander around and search for him, but you can't move in here. I guess we wait until he tries something. Why is it so smoky?"

Dean nodded toward the other side of the room. "There's a smoking section."

"And it's got one of those invisible barriers to keep the smoke away from the rest of us."

"It does?" After the events of the last week, he wouldn't have been surprised.

"No. I was being sarcastic. I could create a barrier, we do it all the time when we have to contain some of the more noxious site emissions, but it would be fairly . . ." The spatial demands of a beefy young man in a Queen's football jacket caused an involuntary pause. ". . . obvious by the end of the evening when the smokers started suffocating in their own toxic exhalations," she finished, shoving her chair back out from the table.

The arrival of the waitress stopped conversation until the arrival of the drinks.

"Three seventy-five for a glass of ginger ale?" Claire tossed a ten onto the girl's tray. "I could buy a liter for ninety-nine cents!"

"Not here," the waitress said tartly, handing back her change.

"You don't go to pubs much, do you?" Dean asked, putting his own change back in his wallet and his wallet in his front pocket.

"What was your first clue?" She took a mouthful of the tepid liquid just as Sasha Moore stepped up onto the small stage at the other end of the room.

Dean pounded her on the back as she choked and coughed ginger ale out onto the table. "Are you okay?"

"Except for a few crushed vertebrae, I'm fine." Eyes wide, Claire stared at the woman in the spotlight. All masks were off. She was danger. She was desire. She was mystery. And no one else in the room realized why. Claire couldn't believe it. Sasha Moore had done everything but sit under a big neon sign that said, "vampire," and no one made the connection although everyone responded. Brows drawn down she watched Dean shift in his seat. Everyone. "There are none so blind . . ." she muttered.

"What?"

"Nothing." Claire half expected Sasha to rely on the "rabbits caught in the headlight" effect that predators had on prey, but she played it straight At the end of the first set after a heavily synthesized version of "Greensleeves," she acknowledged the applause and cut her way easily through an adoring audience to the table.

"A soft drink?" An ebony brow rose as her dark glance slid from Dean's beer to the glass in front of Claire. "If you don't drink beer, the house wine isn't bad."

"I don't drink wine," Claire told her.

Sasha smiled, her teeth a ribbon of white in the darkness. "Me either. So, is he here?"

"We haven't seen him."

"Then I guess you'll have to stay until the end."

Although she'd been about to say that they might as well leave, Claire found herself responding to the challenge. "So it seems."

Dean glanced from one to the other and realized there were undertows here strong enough to suck an unwary swimmer in deep over his head. He didn't understand what was happening, so he let instinct take over and did what generations of men had done before him in similar circumstances; he opened his mouth only far enough to drink his beer.

"So how was she?" Austin asked, his eyes squinted shut against the light.

"Pretty good, I guess." Claire lifted the cat off her pillow and got into bed. "They made her do two encores."

"Ah, yes." He climbed onto her stomach and sat down. "The creatures of the night, what music they make."

"Go to sleep, Austin."

"The boss not back yet?"

"No, not yet." Austin sprang up onto the coffee table and shoved aside a shallow bowl carved from alternating colors of wood and filled with a dusty collection of old birthday cards. "She got a late start this morning."

"You know she doesn't want me in here before she gets back."

"I wanted my head scratched."

"She's likely to be angry."

"It's a worthy cause."

Although he knew he should just turn around and leave, Dean sighed and scratched where indicated, unable to resist the weight of the cat's stare.

"Hey, go easy, big fella. I'm not a dog."

"Sorry."

"Of course you are," Claire said stepping out of the wardrobe. "The question is, why are you here?"

"It's Saturday."

"I knew that." Setting a pair of plastic shopping bags—one stamped with a caduceus and the other with an ankh—down beside the cat, she began pulling out small packages tied up with string.

"On Saturdays, I do the grocery shopping."

Understanding dawned. "And you need money?"

Dean was quite certain he saw one of the packages move. Just to be on the safe side, he stepped back from the table. "Unless you've already done it?"

"Not quite." Leading the way to the office, she unwrapped half a dozen pieces of six-inch-high iron grillwork as she walked. "I'm making imp traps this morning so instead of searching for the Historian, I went to the Apothecary for supplies." The envelope had seventy dollars in it Handing over the money, she said, "Get what you usually get, but add a dozen bagels, ten kilograms of plain clay kitty litter, and a bag of miniature marshmallows— the plain white ones. The Apothecary only had four left, and that won't be enough if I have to reset the traps."

"Four bags?"

"Four marshmallows."

"You trap imps with marshmallows?" Dean asked, folding the money into his wallet.

"We've discovered they work as well as newt tongues and get you into a lot less trouble with Greenpeace."

"What are the bagels and the kitty litter for?"

Claire snorted. "The bagels are for breakfast, and the kitty litter is for Austin to . . ."

Dean raised a hand and smiled weakly. "Never mind."

"I thought we were going up to the attic?"

"We are." Claire took several deep, calming breaths and picked up a bread stick from the counter. "But first, I'm going to ward the door."

Austin rubbed against her shins. "Why don't you just lock it?"

"Lock it?"

"Yeah, you know, that thing you turn that keeps the door from opening without a key. Remember what your mother always said."

"Ripped underwear attracts careless drivers?"

"I was thinking more of 'try a simple solution before looking toward more exotic possibilities.'"

"Warding the door is hardly exotic."

"Locking it's simpler."

"True enough." The tumblers fell into place with a satisfying clunk. Picking up a pair of imp traps, she followed the cat upstairs.

"A question, she occurs to me." Floating just below the ceiling, Jacques watched Claire set the second trap beside the pink-and-gray-striped hatbox. "What will you do with an imp if you catch one?"

"I'll neutralize it."

"What does that mean, neutralize?"

"Imps are little pieces of evil; what do you think it means?" Precariously balanced on a pile of old furniture, Claire extended her right leg and probed for the first step down.

"A little more to your left," Jacques told her.

She moved her foot.

"Your other left," he pointed out as she fell. "Are you hurt, *cherie*?" he called when the noise had stopped but a rising cloud of dust still obscured the landing site.

Shoving a zippered canvas bag filled with musty fabric off her face, Claire sucked a shallow, dust-laden breath through her teeth, then took inventory. Her left elbow hurt a lot, and she seemed to have landed on something that squashed. "Where's Austin?"

"Right here." He leaped up into her line of sight, balancing effortlessly on a teetering commode. "Are you okay?"

"I'm fine."

"You're just saying that, aren't you?" Jacques drifted toward her, wearing an expression of poignant concern. "I wish I had hands to help you up, arms to carry you, to comfort, lips to kiss away the hurt."

His eyes were dark, and Claire found herself thinking of Sasha Moore. "I wish you did, too."

"You could make it so."

Austin snorted. "Does she look like Jean Luc Picard?"

"Who?"

The cat sighed. "I have so much to teach you, Grasshopper."

"What?"

Reflecting how nothing could spoil the moment like a cat, Claire got her legs free, rolled onto her side, and noticed, right at eye level, a stack of ten-inch baseboards. As far as she could tell, given her position, they'd been taken from the wall in ten- or twelve-foot lengths. "This is great!"

"Falling?"

"Baseboards." Scrambling to her feet, she retrieved her flashlight from a pile of old *Reader's Digest Condensed Books*—part of the obligatory attic door—and headed for the stairs. "They were probably taken off when they replaced the plaster and lathe with drywall. Come on. I've got to measure the walls in the dining room because I think baseboards go on before the wallpaper."

Happily working out a renovation schedule that would keep Dean busy for the next six or seven lifetimes, Claire raced down the attic stairs, along the third floor hall, and down to the second floor where she stopped cold. There was a man at the other end of the hall; at the door to room four.

Instinct overwhelmed cognitive function and she ran toward him. "Hey!"

When he spun around, she saw it was the deliveryman—no big surprise—and that he was picking the lock.

So much for the simple solutions. "Get away from there!"

"Don't try and stop me." The clichéd warning made his voice sound harsher than it had, the voice of a man barely clinging to sanity.

One hand searching her clothing for a thread, Claire reached for power, touched seepage, and hesitated.

The intruder dove toward her, grabbed her upper arms, and threw her against the wall. He was stronger, much stronger than he looked; madness lending strength.

"Why?" he demanded, smashing her head against the wall on every other word. "Why are you protecting that undead, bloodsucking, soulless creature?"

Limp in his grasp, unable to concentrate enough to use even the seepage, Claire was only vaguely aware of being dragged toward the storage cupboard. Through a gray haze and strangely shifting world view, she saw Jacques swoop down from the ceiling, shrieking and howling and having no effect at all.

Oh, swell, she thought, as the cupboard door swung open. *He believes in vampires but not in ghosts.* A heartbeat later, the implications of that sank in and she began to struggle weakly.

She hit the floor beside the mop bucket, barely managing to keep her head from bouncing, and collapsed entirely when a heart-stopping screech set the bottles of cleanser vibrating.

A deeper howl of pain rose over the noise the cat was making; then, just as Claire attempted to sit up again, the door slammed shut and Austin landed on the one thing guaranteed to break his fall.

For a moment, the need to breathe outweighed other considerations; then, lying in the dark listening to Austin hiss and spit, she grabbed for the first power she could reach and used it to clear her head. Sucking up seepage had just become a minor problem. "I understand how you feel, Austin, but shut up. We haven't time for this."

A whiskered face pressed into her cheek. "Are you all right?"

"No. But I'm fixing it." Anger burned away the damage, power riding in on her rage to replace what she spent. At the moment, it didn't matter where that power came from. With all body parts more-or-less back under her control, she stood and flung herself at the door. The impact hurt—a lot—and bounced her onto her butt. The door didn't budge.

He'd done something to hold it in place.

"Calm down!" the cat snarled. "You nearly landed on top of me!"

"Calm?" Claire struggled back onto her feet. "What do you think a murder in this building will do to the pentagram's seals?" Breathing deeply, once, twice, she placed her hands on the wood and blew the door off its hinges.

Staggering slightly, she raced down the hall, through Jacques, and into room four.

He was standing over the bed, a sharpened stake in an upraised hand.

There was no seepage left, blowing the door had wiped it clean. Sagging against the wall, Claire reached into the possibilities, knowing she wouldn't be in time.

A black-and-white streak landed on his back as the stake came down.

Pulling Austin clear with one hand, Claire tossed her bit of thread with the other. As the deliveryman stiffened, she shoved him behind her to fall, shrieking, wrapped in invisible bonds, onto the floor of the outer room.

The stake protruded from Sasha Moore's chest just below the collarbone. At first, in the forty-watt glow of the bedside lamp, Claire thought it was all over, then she realized that he'd missed the heart by three full inches. Either he had a poor understanding of biology or Austin's leap had misdirected the blow.

"She is Nosferatu! She must die!" The crazed voice echoed in the closed room. "Those who protect her have made a covenant with evil!"

"Hey! Don't tell me about evil," Claire snapped at him over her shoulder. "*I'm* a trained professional." She spread her fingers and one of the bonds expanded to cover his mouth.

His tail still twice its normal size, Austin panted as he looked from the stake to Claire. "Now what?"

"Now we pull it out." There was a pop of displaced air as the first-aid kit from the kitchen appeared on the bedside table. "And we bandage the wound and see what happens when she wakes up."

"I'm guessing she'll be hungry."

Claire glanced toward the man thrashing impotently about and grunting in. inarticulate rage. "I think we can find her a bite of something."

AT THIS RATE, THE DAMPENING FIELD WILL NEVER GO DOWN. SHE BARELY CLEARED THE WAY FOR FURTHER SEEPAGE. THE COUSIN DID MUCH MORE DAMAGE WITH HIS TOYS AND DIVERSIONS.

PATIENCE.

PATIENCE . . . The word sounded as though it had been ground out through shards of broken glass. . . . IS A VIRTUE!

The ruddy light reflected in the copper hood grew brighter, as though Hell itself blushed. SORRY.

SEVEN

———— ▰◈▰ ————

SUNSET WAS AT SEVEN-FORTY-ONE. Claire called the local radio station for the exact time and, while she had them on the line, asked them to play "Welcome to My Nightmare." The song, discovered on one of her parents' old albums, had meant a lot to her during the earliest years of her sister's training and the events of the afternoon had made her nostalgic for those simpler, albeit equally dangerous, times.

At seven-thirty, she started up the stairs.

At seven-thirty-five, she unlocked the door to room four, passed the man lying in the dressing room, who stirred restlessly in his involuntary sleep, and entered the cubicle holding the bed and the wounded Sasha Moore. In the dim light of the bedside lamp, she stood by the wall and waited for sunset.

At seven-forty-six, either the radio station or her watch off by the longest five minutes in recorded history, she saw the vampire's lips, pale without their customary sheen of artificial color, slowly part and draw in the first breath of the night. Ebony brows dipped in as both wound and bandage pulled with the movement of the narrow chest. Muscles tensed beneath the ivory skin. Eyes snapped open. A dark gaze swept over the red-brown stains along the left side of the bed and then locked on Claire's face.

"Spill, Keeper," Sasha Moore snarled. "What the fuck is going on here?"

At seven-fifty-two, as the newly awakened vampire-slayer began to whimper, Claire stepped out into the hall and locked the door to room four behind her.

❋   ❋   ❋

"How did you know I wouldn't kill him when he had every intention of killing me?"

"He's crazy, you're not," Claire answered calmly. "You've lived too long to risk exposure by modern forensics." She turned her attention to the glassy-eyed man, who swayed where he stood, oblivious to his surroundings. Centuries of arriving at accident sites after the inevitable, and invariably messy, cause and effect had already taken place, had given Keepers a distinctly fatalistic, some might even say unsympathetic attitude toward people who played with matches. A Keeper's responsibility involved keeping the whole metaphorical forest from going up, and they figured the more people who got their fingers burned, the less likely that was to happen. Claire shuddered to think of what might have occurred had she stayed in the attic a few moments longer. "How much will you allow him to remember?"

A spark of cruel amusement gleamed in the shadowed eyes. "Let's put it this way: He's going to piss himself whenever he's outside after the sun goes down and he's not going to know why."

"Isn't that a bit extreme?"

"What? For trying to kill me?" Sasha tossed her head disdainfully. "I think not. Besides, it's nothing a few dozen years of therapy won't clear up." Silver bracelets chiming softly, she stroked the velvet length of Austin's back. "Imagine living two hundred and twenty-seven years only to die at the hands of yet another amateur van Helsing. What a frigging waste."

"Yet another amateur van Helsing?" Austin rolled so she could reach his stomach. "This has happened before?"

"Once or twice; the nutballs come out every time we get trendy." Crimson nail polish glistened like drops of blood against the white fur. "But this . . ." Her other hand lightly touched the bandage under her clothes. "This is as close as anyone's ever come." When she lifted her gaze from the cat, Claire realized that for the first time since the other woman had arrived at the hotel, her eyes neither threatened nor promised. "Thank you for my life, Keeper."

"You're welcome. But it was no more or less than I would have done for anyone. Murder creates the very holes the lineage exists to seal."

The vampire sighed, a fringe of sable hair dancing as she shook her head. "You really lean toward the sanctimonious, you know that?"

"I'm a Keeper," Claire began defensively, but cool fingers tapping the curve of her cheek cut her off.

"My point exactly. Try to get over it."

Speechless, Claire watched as Sasha turned her would-be executioner unresistingly toward the door and, when she opened it, finally gave up trying to put together a sufficiently scathing response, settling for: "What are you going to do with him now?"

Pausing on the threshold, the night spreading out behind her like great, dark wings, Sasha locked one hand around her captive's wrist to prevent him from moving on and turned back toward the guest house. "I'm going to take him to his car and release him."

"But the sun's down."

White teeth flashed between carmine lips. "Obviously."

"And people complain about the way *cats* play with their food," Austin snorted as the door swung shut.

"I'm not sanctimonious, am I?"

"You're asking me?"

Claire's eyes narrowed. "Is there anyone else around?"

"Just the dead guy on the stairs."

Jacques gave the cat a scathing look as he materialized. "I only arrive this moment, and if he says I am here all along, he lies."

"Cats never lie," Austin told him, leaping from the counter to the desk to the chair to the floor. "There's not much point is there, not when the truth can be so much more irritating. If you two will excuse me, I have things to do."

"What sorts of things?" Claire asked suspiciously as he started down the hall.

The black tail flicked sideways twice. "Cat things."

Elbows still propped on the counter, Claire let her head drop forward into her hands. Cat things could cover everything from a nap on top of the fridge to the continuing attempt to twist Baby's already precarious psyche into still tighter knots. If it was the former, she didn't need to know. If the latter, she didn't want to.

"I thought," Jacques said softly, "that there were no more secrets between us."

Without lifting her head, Claire sighed. "No more secrets that concern you. This doesn't."

"You think it does not concern us that Sasha Moore is Nosferatu?"

"No." She wondered when Jacques and Dean had become an *us* and whether it would last longer than this conversation. "You're dead. Dean is off limits."

"But you get hurt defending her and, if we knew, we could be there."

"*You were* there."

"Ah. Oui." His face fell. "And I could do nothing to save you. But I am dead." The realization perked him up. "What can a dead man do? And besides, my failure does, not change your silence. You do not tell me. You do not tell Dean—which is, of course, of not so great a consequence."

"It wasn't my secret. If she wanted you to know, she'd have told you herself."

"And yet, now I know."

Claire straightened, both hands gripping the edge of the counter. "Now you know," she agreed. "Now what?"

He grinned. "Well, I am thinking; you do not want Dean to know so, if I do not tell Dean, *tu me does un recompense*."

"I owe you for not telling Dean?"

"*Oui*."

"And what do I owe you?"

His grin warmed and his eyes grew heated under half-lowered lids as he leaned so close his breath, had he been breathing, would have stroked her cheek. "Flesh, for one night."

"Just *one* night?"

"One night," he told her, his voice low and promising, "is all I ask for. After that one night, I no longer need to ask."

She turned so she was facing him. He was a comfortable amount taller than she was, unlike Dean who loomed over her, and it would only take a tilt of her head to bring their mouths together. She wanted to push his hair back off his face, run her thumbs down the stubble-rough sides of his jaw, watch everything he felt dance across his expression as she slid her arms up under his sweater. She didn't understand the attraction, but she couldn't deny it. "Think highly of yourself, don't you?"

"Not without reason."

Someone, or something giggled. She frowned, stepped back, and almost saw a flash of purple disappear beneath the shelf.

"Claire?"

"Forget it, Jacques." Squatting down, she peered at the imp trap. It had been moved from across the mouse hole leaving a tiny opening clear on the left side.

"Then not a night" He dropped down beside her, his knees making no impact with the floor. "An hour. An hour only and I can convince you."

"No, not a night not an hour." The miniature marshmallows were missing. "Not ten minutes."

"Ten minutes would not be worth the effort. I have no interest in a quick and frenzied pawing."

That drew Claire's attention away from the imp trap. She turned to face the ghost, both brows lifted almost to her hairline.

"*D'accord*. I will take a quick and frenzied pawing if it is all I can get. But to be truly intimate with a woman requires a little more time. Give me that time, *cherie*, and you will be like plaster in my hands."

"Putty."

"*Pardon?*"

Even though she knew he'd take it the wrong way, Claire couldn't stop herself from smiling. "Like putty in your hands."

"*Oui*. Putty." His accent softened the word, made it malleable. He leaned close again. "Are you afraid that if we become lovers, it will hold you here?"

"*What* will hold me here?"

"Passion. Pleasure. Complete . . ." The pause lingered on the edge of being too long, preparing the way for the presentation of each separate syllable. ". . . satisfaction."

Claire blinked.

"Just give me a chance, *cherie*."

"A chance to do what?"

Feeling as though she'd been caught by her father in a clinch on the rec-room couch, hoping her ears weren't as red as they felt, Claire straightened and noticed for the first time that Jacques floated high enough off the floor so that he looked Dean—who was a good four inches taller—directly in the eye. "He wants me to give him flesh."

Dean shrugged. "If it'll help, there's a leftover pork chop in the fridge."

"Not that kind of flesh!" The ghost looked appalled.

"Beef? Chicken? Fish?"

The suggestions emerged too close together for Jacques to reply, but with each he grew more and more indignant.

"Sausage?"

His image began to flicker. *"Mon Dieu!* Are you so irritating on purpose?"

"Difficult to be that irritating by accident," Claire murmured. The ridiculous list had banished embarrassment. Suddenly realizing that might have been his intent, she took a closer look at Dean and found his expression of solid helpfulness offset by a distinct twinkle behind the glasses.

"I thought you might want to know that Austin's outside," he said. "I opened the back door for him about five minutes ago."

"Any response from Baby?"

"Not yet."

"So you thought she wanted to know, and now she is told." Folding his arms, Jacques regained control of his definition. "You may go now, *Anglais*. The Keeper and I, we have a private conversation."

"About giving you flesh?"

A finger, fully opaque in the artificial light of the lobby, jabbed at the air inches from Dean's chest. "Do *not* start that again!"

Dean ignored him. When he turned to Claire, the twinkle was gone. "You wouldn't, would you?"

"And why wouldn't she?" Jacques asked matter-of-factly. "She is young, she is healthy, she has needs."

"Jacques!" Her elbow went right through him.

"I only say that since there is no one else, I am here." He turned on Dean, who was shaking his head. "What?"

"You're dead!"

"And you cannot stand the thought of a dead man achieving that which you . . ."

This time Claire protested with power.

"OW!" Pulling himself together, the ghost turned to face her. "I have to say, *cherie*, I am not at this moment thrilled by your touch. Obviously, the mood has been broken. I will leave you now but, you have my word as a Labaet, I will keep my part of the bargain until we have a chance to speak again."

"What did he mean," Dean asked as Jacques vanished, "about keeping his part of the bargain?"

Claire shrugged, running her thumb along the edge of the counter. "Who knows what he thinks."

A LIE! A LIE!

A PREVARICATION. WE CAN'T USE IT. SAYS WHO? THE RULES. DAMN THE RULES.

Heated air, redolent of sulfur and brimstone, gusted up into the furnace room. DON'T THINK WE HAVEN'T TRIED.

Before Dean could answer, Claire lifted her head and actually noticed what he was wearing. "Are you going out?"

He shoved his hands into the pockets of his faded, leather football jacket. "Yeah. I meet some friends from back home every Saturday night." He hesitated, then continued in a rush. "Do you want to come, then?"

For a moment, she thought it might be nice to spend an uncomplicated evening with Dean and his friends, going to another pub, listening to music, with Dean and his very young friends, in another dark, smoky, crowded, overpriced pub, listening to over-loud music not being sung by a vampire. "Thanks for asking, but no thanks."

"My friends wouldn't mind."

A LIE!
IN KINDNESS.
BUT . . .
OH, GIVE IT UP.

Claire hid a smile. "It's okay. I've got things to take care of."

"I, uh, heard Ms. Moore's van leave."

He was far too nice to look as relieved by her refusal as she knew he felt. "It's her last night at the pub."

"The stalker?"

"I think he got scared off."

He thought, as she'd intended him to, that she meant he'd been scared off when he'd been chased away from the vans. "Will you be okay alone?"

"I'll be fine."

"And what on earth do you think you could do if I wasn't?" remained mostly silent.

Should I have insisted? Dean asked himself as he paused halfway down the front stairs to let his eyes grow accustomed to the dark. From what he understood of Claire's life, it had to be a lonely existence, constantly on the move with few opportunities to make real friends.

A sudden vision of Claire sitting at the Portsmouth with the guys and Kathy, listening to them swap stupid mainlander stories, picking up her round of beer in turn, stopped him from going back into the lobby. They wouldn't be rude. In fact, they'd be glad to see another woman in the group, but she wouldn't fit in.

And she wouldn't try to, he admitted. *Maybe you should stay with her, boy. Keep that dead freak away.* Wondering just how Jacques knew what Claire's needs were, he turned toward the office window in time to see her drop to her knees and out of sight. *Oh, man, not the imps again.*

Fists in his pockets, he continued down to the sidewalk, navigating the uneven brick steps with the ease of familiarity, and made his way out to the bus stop on King Street without looking back. What with scraping the front counter and refinishing the dining room floor, not to mention the weirder stuff, it had been some long week and he wasn't up to another argument about the types of vermin infesting the guesthouse. Now that he thought about it, he was really looking forward to a nice, normal evening, finding out how many mainlanders it took to screw in a light-bulb, and watching George drink until he puked.

✦   ✦   ✦

Claire sat back on her heels and glared at the trap. After replacing the marshmallow pieces, she'd moved the cage back over the hole and was now trying, unsuccessfully, to convince herself that an imp, or imps, had taken the bait without being caught. Unfortunately, the evidence suggested one of two possibilities and she didn't care much for either. The first implied that the power she'd wrapped about the trap wasn't strong enough to hold even a minor piece of evil, and the second involved her being wrong from the start.

"And I just don't think I can handle multicolored mice," she muttered, getting to her feet. Had Austin been privy to her thoughts he'd have reminded her that what she *really* couldn't handle was being wrong but, since he wasn't, the emphasis remained on the mice.

"Still, they've been breeding around a major accident site for generations," she allowed as she locked the lobby door—Sasha and Dean both had keys and if by some strange stroke of misfortune any guests happened to wander by, she'd hear the knocker. "I suppose they should consider themselves lucky if color is the only variation. I mean," she added to no one in particular, entering her own suite, "look at the platypus."

Picking her way through the sitting room in the dark, she tripped only twice, and was feeling pretty pleased with herself when she flicked on the bathroom light.

"Sweet heaven."

At first she thought the letters on the mirror had been written in blood, but then she noticed the crushed remains of her favorite lipstick in the sink. Claw marks on the metal case and a perfect, three-fingered, *Jaded Rose* handprint pressed onto the porcelain identified the graffiti artist beyond a shadow of a doubt. Imps.

Or at least, imp.

This was exactly the sort of petty, destructive mischief they excelled at.

"Mice. Ha!" Claire exchanged a triumphant look with her reflection. "This will prove my point once and for all. I'll just go and get . . ."

Then the actual words sank in.

Someone, it said, in barely legible cursive script, *needs to get laid.*

"You'll go and get who?" her reflection asked, eyes faintly glowing.

"Shut up." Jacques would never give her a moment's peace. Dean would be so horribly embarrassed she'd feel like a slut. And Austin—Claire was only glad that Austin hadn't been around to hear Jacques declare she had needs. Obviously, she couldn't show the message to any of them. And there wasn't anyone else. "Nuts! Nuts! Nuts!" At her last declamation, she slapped both hands down on the counter.

A pair of dusty guest soaps turned into a pair of equally dusty pecans.

"Temper, temper," warned her reflection, shaking an amused finger behind the lines of lipstick.

"You think this is temper?" Claire muttered, reaching past the seepage and pulling power. One hand shading her eyes from the flash of light, she ran a clean cantrip over the mirror. "Wait until I catch that imp." Her lip curled. "Then you'll see temper."

Later that night, Dean let himself into his apartment through the door in the area. The evening had been no different than any other Saturday evening but still, something had been missing. It no longer seemed to be enough that these people were his best friends, his link to home in the midst of those who'd never heard of Joey's Juice and couldn't seem to figure out how to wipe their feet.

Undressing in the dark, he lowered himself carefully onto the bed, locked his hands behind his head, and stared at nothing, wondering why the world outside the guest house suddenly seemed smaller than the world within. Wondering why a hole to Hell and an evil Keeper seemed less important than the Keeper sleeping overhead. Wondering why the world had started to spin. . . .

Because you drank a whole lot of beer, his bladder reminded him.

When his bladder turned out to be the only organ offering solutions, Dean surrendered to sleep.

Still later, after letting herself in and relocking the front door, Sasha Moore paused by the counter and listened, separating out the individual rhythms of four lives. One, upstairs. Too slow and unchanging for mortal sleep. Two, downstairs. Slow and regular, a man sleeping the sleep of the just and the intoxicated. Three, close by. A Keeper, tossing restlessly in an empty bed. The vampire acknowledged temptation, then shook her head. Keepers took themselves far too seriously;

regardless of how it turned out, she'd never hear the end of it. Four . . . She smiled and raised an ivory hand, a greeting to another hunter in the night. A greeting between equals.

A rustling, a scrabbling of claws on wood, lifted her gaze to the ceiling. "Mice," she murmured.

"That's what I keep telling them," Austin agreed from the shadows.

The temperature dropped overnight, October arriving with the promise of winter. By morning, the air in Claire's bedroom had chilled to an uncomfortable sixty-two degrees. She put it off for as long as she could, monitoring the seepage levels from under the covers, but she finally ran out of excuses to stay in bed. When her bare feet hit the floor, she sucked her breath in through her teeth. Nothing rose through the brass register except perhaps a sense of anticipation.

"If you think I'm heading in there to open a vent, think again," she muttered. It would be simple enough to temporarily ward off the chill by adjusting her own temperature. Simpler still, since it wasn't likely to warm up any time soon, to put on a second sweater.

Rummaging through the pile of clothes on the floor, she realized she hadn't done laundry since she'd arrived. Fully aware that, in time, she wouldn't think twice about wearing an orange sweater over a purple turtleneck with navy sweats—as they aged, surviving Keepers grew less and less concerned with how the rest of the world perceived them—Claire tried not to think about how she looked as she shoved dirty clothes into a pillowcase.

"Running away to the circus?" Austin asked testily, emerging from under a carelessly thrown fold of blanket

"Doing laundry," she told him, jumping off the chair with three socks and a bra she'd found on top of the wardrobe.

He stretched out a foreleg and critically examined a spotless, white paw. "Well, you know, I hadn't wanted to say anything . . ."

"Then don't."

Hearing Claire descend to the basement, Dean gratefully left off his attempt to fit old lengths of baseboard into the new dimensions of the dining room and followed. To his surprise, he found her stuffing clothes into the washing machine. Taking in the layered sweaters, he realized she had no intention of turning up the heat. He couldn't say that he blamed her. "Did you, uh, need help with that, then?" he asked when she turned and flashed him an inquiring glance.

"I can manage, thank you."

About to mention that she should sort her colors, Dean forced himself to hold his tongue. Maybe Keepers never ended up with gray underwear.

She looked different. For the first time since she'd arrived, he was seeing her without makeup. Without the artfully defined shadows, she seemed younger, softer, less ready to take on the world. A sudden image of her riding into battle in the traditional, Saturday-afternoon-Western warpaint made him smile.

"What?" she demanded.

"Nothing."

"If it's the clothes, I don't usually dress like this."

"I hadn't noticed." Except he had. "You mean the sweaters." He pulled at the waistband of his Hyperion Oil Fields sweatshirt "I could go out and buy some electric heaters."

Claire's eyes narrowed. Obviously Augustus Smythe had never used electric heaters, or there'd be some already in the building. "No. Thank you." She closed the lid of the washing machine, started the cycle, and turned to face the furnace room door. "I'll go in and adjust the vents."

"I wasn't criticizing."

"I never said you were."

"I understand why you don't want to go in."

Her chin lifted. "Who says I don't want to go in?"

"The sweaters . . ."

"I was referring to the color combination."

"The colors?"

"That's right. But since you're cold . . ."

"I never said I was cold."

"Then why offer to buy heaters?"

"I thought you were cold."

"I never said I was cold."

"No, but the sweaters . . ."

"Oh, I see. Well, if I can't put on a sweater without people thinking I can't do my job, maybe we'd just better get a little heat in here. And no, I don't need you to go with me," she added, crossing to the turquoise steel door. The chains were heavier than they looked and made ominous rattling sounds as she dragged them free, indignation lending strength. About to drop them to one side, a large hand reached over her shoulder and effortlessly lifted them from her grip.

"I'll hang these here, on the hooks, where they go."

"Fine." Claire pressed her right palm against the steel, a little surprised at how warm it was until she realized that her exposed skin had chilled to the point where an Eskimo Pie would've seemed toasty. In fact, she could feel the heat radiating off of Dean and he was standing . . .

She turned to face him, and her eyes widened.

. . . rather temptingly close. Her breathing quickened as her hindbrain made a detailed suggestion. *"Hey! Get out of my head!"*

WHAT MAKES YOU THINK YOU DIDN'T COME UP WITH THAT ON YOUR OWN?

"Most people's joints don't bend that way."

THEY DON'T?

"Get out!"

"Instead of lurking around down here, go up to the dining room and let me know when there's heat coming through the register."

Dean hesitated. "You'll be all right, then?"

"Augustus Smythe adjusted these vents for fifty years and he was . . ."

The realization of what Augustus Smythe was, or at least of what he'd become, filled the narrow space between them.

". . . a Cousin," Claire finished. "I am a Keeper." She turned back toward the door and took a deep breath. Then another.

"They say that as long as it's sealed, it's perfectly safe."

Tapping her nails against the heavy latch handle, she snorted. "Who says?"

"You did."

Hard to argue with such an unquestionable source. "Just yell down the register," she said, shoving open the furnace room door. "I'll hear you." She paused, one foot over the threshold. All things considered, it might be best to tie up loose ends before she went any farther. "Dean?"

"Yeah, Boss?"

"Thanks."

Anyone else would've asked her what for, and then she'd have had to face Hell with a caustic comment still warming her lips. Anyone else.

He smiled. "You're welcome."

By mid-morning the hotel had warmed about ten degrees, Dean had discovered how the pieces of baseboard fit together, Austin had eaten breakfast, made his morning visit to Baby, and gone back to bed, and Claire had been forced to spend half an hour leaning over the dryer.

"I don't understand," Dean had said earnestly, checking out the machine after the third time it had shut off. "It's never done this before." After a moment's rummaging behind the switch with a variety of screwdrivers, he'd replaced the cover and added, "There's nothing wrong. Try again."

The dryer had worked perfectly while they were there, but the moment Claire had stepped off the basement stairs and out into the first floor hall, it had stopped. "Never mind," she'd grumbled as Dean moved back toward the stairs, "it's my laundry and you've got things to do. I'll just grab a cup of coffee and go watch it run."

"And that'll keep it going?"

"It should."

And it had.

The imp had, no doubt, been switching off the dryer and, with her standing guard, had now gone off to find other ways to irritate, leaving behind no proof she could use. Weighing the alternatives while her clothes dried, Claire figured that the imp must've come through before Augustus Smythe. Or very soon after he arrived, before he began using up the seepage as it emerged.

She wished she knew how long it had taken, how many accidental uses, before it became habit. It would have been so much easier for him to use the seepage—power just lying around for the taking—than to reach into the narrow area of the possibilities that the Cousins could access.

How many excuses had it taken before he didn't bother making excuses anymore? Before he used what he wanted. And every time he used it, it corrupted him a little more.

Which explained why Dean, who'd lived next to Hell for eight months, hadn't been affected. He couldn't use the power. At least Claire hoped he hadn't been affected. "I shudder to think of what he must've been like if he's this nice *after* Hell's been working on him."

She'd cleared the seepage twice, and she'd only been there a week. They were admittedly low levels of seepage, nothing like the buzz she'd felt on her first night, but she'd still have to start being a lot more careful.

When her laundry was finally dry, she'd lost three socks and gained a child's T-shirt. Claire would've liked to have placed the blame on Hell, but this particular irritant was the result of human error. Given the metaphysical design flaw inherent in clothes dryers, those in the know were fond of pointing out how the loss of an occasional sock was nothing to complain about considering the odds against everything else coming back.

"Jacques, get away from the window!" Running her blade along a piece of molding, Claire scraped off a long curl of medium green paint. The counter had probably never been that actual color—when scraping paint there always had to be a medium green layer. "Anyone walking by and looking up can see right through you."

"Perhaps they would not see me at all. The vampire-hunter, he did not see me."

"He didn't believe in ghosts."

"I do not see why that should matter."

"Neither do I, but it does."

"If you gave me flesh, it would not happen," he pointed out reasonably.

"Just move," she told him without looking up.

Jacques glanced down toward the sidewalk, opened his mouth to say something, and shook his head. Floating closer, he sat down on the floor with his back against the outside wall. "So, if someone who believed walked by . . . ?"

"They'd see the sunlight streaming right through you."

"And that would be a problem because?"

"People who see ghosts seldom keep the information to them-selves." Carefully working stripper-soaked steel wool carefully along the grain of the wood, she wrinkled her nose at the smell. "And I don't feel like dealing with tabloid reporters."

"I know reporters, but what are tabloids?"

"Sleazy newspapers that deal in cheap sensationalism. Hundred-year-old woman has lizard baby, that sort of thing."

"Is that not what Keepers deal in?"

"No."

"Hole to Hell in basement?"

"It's not the same."

"Woman sleeps for fifty years?"

Shifting her weight back onto her heels, she turned and glared at him. "You know what your problem is? You never know when to quit!"

He cocked an eyebrow and spread his hands. *"Evidentment.* If I knew when to quit, I would not be haunting this place, and if I were not haunting this place, I would not have met you. *Voila,* all is for the best." Wrapping a weightless grip around Claire's fingers, he leaned forward and murmured, "Have I ever told you how sexy I find big, pink rubber gloves?"

She laughed in spite of herself, pulling her hand back through his. "You're unbelievable." The laughter vanished when he started to fade. "Jacques?"

"If you do not believe," he told her mournfully, "you cannot see me."

"Stop it!"

Rematerializing, he grinned triumphantly. "You do not want to lose me."

Lips pressed tightly together, Claire bent back over the bit of un-stripped molding on the counter. Her search for the Historian had ended up at a medieval bazaar selling Japanese electronics, and her hour with Sara had brought her no closer to an answer. She'd have to study both ends of the balance if she wanted to figure it out and that meant spending time next to the pit. Since she'd been in the furnace room once already today and since stripping the counter had been her idea . . .

She'd like to see it finished before she left. She'd like to see the dining room finished, too—wallpaper, trim, blinds, maybe new light fixtures.

This is nuts. The steel wool stopped moving. When she closed this site, need would summon her to another. It might be in Kingston— there were, after all sixty thousand people in the city and townships and population density was directly proportional to how often a Keeper was needed—but it might be across the continent. Or on another continent entirely. *I am not getting attached to this place.*

"Claire? I do not want to lose you either. Please, I am sorry. Come back to me."

"I haven't gone anywhere." The silence clearly stated he didn't believe her. She shifted from knee to knee and finally sighed, "Could I give you flesh to help me finish this?"

"Non." Although she didn't turn to look she could hear the relieved smile in his voice. "I can take flesh only to give you pleasure."

"It'd give me pleasure to have some help with this."

"It does not work that way."

She sighed again, resting her forehead on the edge of a shelf. "Why," she asked dramatically, "am I not surprised?"

Sasha Moore checked out that evening, paying for her room in cash. "Will I see you in the spring?" she asked, effortlessly swinging her heavy duffel bag up onto one shoulder.

Claire stared at her, aghast. "The spring?"

"Comes after winter. The snow melts. The dog crap lies exposed on the lawn."

"I won't be here in the spring."

"I hope you're not expecting old Gus to come back. He's blown this popsicle stand for good." The vampire paused at the door. "Oh, yeah; Dean's memory of me's going to get a bit foggy. I don't like to leave too many specifics behind." Ebony brows rose and fell suggestively. When it became obvious that Claire was not going to respond to this mild provocation, she snapped pale fingers. "Hey, Keeper!"

Wandering thoughts jerked back to the lobby. "What?"

"Domo arigato on that lifesaving thing. I know, I know, you'd do it for anyone, but this time you did it for me. In return, can I offer you

these words of wisdom, culled from a long and eventful existence? You needn't bother answering 'cause I'm going to anyway.

"First of all, at the risk of sounding like Kenny Rogers, God forbid, you should make the best of the hand you've been dealt Second, a genuine, unselfish offer of help is the most precious gift you'll ever be given. And third, remember that you never have to travel alone . . ." Teeth flashed. ". . . hitchhikers make a handy protein supplement when on the road. Thanks for coming, you've been a wonderful audience, maybe we can do this again sometime—less the asshole trying to kill me, of course."

Claire stared at the closed door for a moment, then jerked around to the window as the red van roared down the driveway, honked twice, and disappeared into the night.

"Is Ms. Moore gone?"

Dean's voice seemed to come from very far away. She nodded, without turning.

"Did she say if she'd be back in the spring?"

It was only just October, not even winter yet, spring was impossibly far away. "I won't be here in the spring. I'll have finished up and moved on."

"Okay." That wasn't what he'd asked, but since it was clearly on Claire's mind . . . "That, uh, book you've got soaking? It's starting to stink up the fridge."

"It needs to soak a little longer."

"But . . ."

"I need that information, Dean, and I'm not going to risk losing it because you don't like the way it smells."

"Is Claire coming out for breakfast?"

"In a minute," Austin told him, staring alternately at his empty dish and Dean. "She has to have another shower first. The Historian appears to have led her through an area populated by ruminants."

"Say what?"

"She crawled through some cow shit. Are you going to feed me, or what?"

Weighing the bag of geriatric kibble in one hand, Dean scratched the back of his neck with the other. "There should be a lot more in this."

"Not necessarily. I told the mice they could help themselves. With any luck we'll run out on the weekend when the vet's closed, and you'll have to feed me something decent."

The next morning, Dean handed Claire a cup of coffee and watched in concern as she slumped against the sink and stuffed a whole piece of toast into her mouth. "Manage to avoid the cow shit this morning?" he asked hesitantly.

Claire snorted, blowing crumbs onto the spotless stainless steel. "This morning," she said, and paused to swallow, "I crawled through the cow. Same end result though," she added after a moment

"You know, lady, I got a cousin who does renovations. Not too expensive," the locksmith assured her as he screwed down the new plate. He nodded toward the charred, smoke-damaged interior of room six. "Why leave a room in that condition when you can fix it up and use it that's what I say. You gotta spend money to make money, you know?"

"We're not that busy. Which," she added dryly, "is a good thing. I called you four days ago."

"Hey, I couldn't have got here faster if you'd been Old Nick himself."

WANNA BET?

The locksmith pulled bushy brows down toward his nose. "Did you say something?"

"No."

"Thought I heard . . . Never mind. You know, you don't have to stay with me. I can just come down when I finish up."

"Like I said," Claire told him, keeping the glamour centered over the actual contents of the room, "we're not that busy."

"Oh, I get it. Lonely, eh? I know how you feel; some days when I don't leave the shop, I'm ready to climb the walls by four, four-thirty. No one to talk to, you know? What was that?" He leaned around the door, staring at the floor by the curtained window, then settled back on his heels, shaking his head. "It sorta looked like a bright blue mouse."

"Trick of the shadows," Claire said tightly. It figured that the locksmith would see the imp when neither Dean nor Austin ever had.

A few moments later, his weight on the newly installed doorknob, the locksmith heaved himself to his feet and flicked the open flange with his free hand. "Quite the secondary locking system. I guess you can't be too careful about this kind of thing, eh? I mean, one tourist wanders in here, hurts himself on a bit of loose board and the next thing you know, you're being sued."

Peering through the glamour, Claire checked that Aunt Sara remained undisturbed by all the banging. "If a tourist wandered in here, being sued would be the least of my concerns. But you needn't worry, this is only a temporary measure."

"So you are going to fix it?"

"Sooner or later."

"Hopefully sooner, eh?" He pulled the door closed and nodded with satisfaction as the lock clicked into place. "When the time comes, and you need some help, don't forget my cousin."

Claire had a vision of the locksmith and his cousin facing down the hordes of Hell. It was strangely comforting.

The ink soaked out of the site journal had turned the onions blue. The brine had been absorbed and the whole thing smelled like pickled sewage. With a cheese sauce.

When Claire opened the plastic container, Austin left the building.

Breathing shallowly through her mouth, she used a fork to tease apart the pages. The process had been partially successful. The few pages of Augustus Smythe's notes now legible made it clear he knew an incredible number of dirty limericks but offered no other useful information.

The first four pages after his summoning remained stuck together in a glutinous blue mass.

"One more week should do it," Claire sniffed at Dean, peeling another three onions and dropping them into fresh brine.

"Great," Dean gasped. He snuck a look at the card.

> Aunt Claire, Keeper
> Your Accident is my Opportunity
>
> (face it, life stinks)

Later, he threw out the fork.

✧　　✧　　✧

"This is the sixth morning in a row she's come out of that wardrobe looking wiped. Two days ago, she fell asleep in that old armchair up in room six, and yesterday she didn't have enough energy to take the chains off the furnace room door."

Austin lifted his head off his paws and gazed across the dining room at Claire, who'd fallen asleep with her cheek on an egg salad sandwich. "Did you take them off for her?"

"No. I figured if she was too tired to open the door, she was too tired to face Hell."

"I've said all along you're more than just a pretty face. What did Claire say?"

Dean grinned. "That I was an interfering, idiotic bystander."

"That's all?" The cat snorted. "She must've been tired."

"What's happening in that wardrobe, Austin?"

"From the steely-eyed determination on her face when she goes in, I'd say she's trying too hard. The other side has kind of zen thing going, you can't force it."

"So she's doing it to herself, then?"

"Well, I don't think she'd have chosen to fight her way through those pre-Christmas sales this morning but, yeah, essentially."

"If there's anything I can do, will you let me know?"

"Sure."

As Austin laid his head back down, Dean's concern evolved into full-blown worry. Any other morning, that question would've brought a suggestion that he feed the cat.

"What have you done, that Claire suddenly try so hard to find this Historian?"

"I didn't do anything," Dean told him, getting a can of oven cleaner out from under the sink. "I'm not the one exposing myself to Mrs. Abrams."

"I do not expose myself. She has no business to be in the parking lot to peer through the windows while you attach the blinds. I vanish the moment I see her."

"But did she see you?"

"She did not scream and run. She waves to you, puts two thumbs up in the air, and leaves quietly." Jacques pressed his back up against the wall between the two windows, the one place in the dining room where he couldn't be seen from outside when the new vertical blinds were open. "It is not my fault she is always looking in."

Dean might have believed him had he not sounded so defensive. "You're careless. You don't care how much trouble you cause."

"I am causing trouble?"

"That's what I said."

"So, you say it is my fault that Claire tries so much harder to leave us?"

Shrugging, Dean dropped to his knees in front of the stove. "If the shroud fits."

"And what does that mean, if the shroud fits?"

"It means you're always all over her. Give me flesh, give me flesh." His accent was a passable imitation of the ghost's. "You're too pushy."

Jacques disappeared and reappeared sitting on the floor behind the peninsula. "I am too pushy? You are too . . . too . . . too nice!"

"Too nice?"

"*Oui.* You are like mushy white bread and mayonnaise. *And . . .*" He folded his arms triumphantly. ". . . you are always cleaning things. If I could, I would leave also."

"Then leave. Claire said she could send you on."

"And leave her with you? She would be too bored in a week."

"Lecher."

"Monk."

"Bottom feeder."

"Betty Crocker."

"Stereotype!"

Before Jacques, reeling under a direct hit, could come up with a response, the ka-thud, ka-thud of a galloping animal filled the house, growing overwhelmingly louder the closer it came. The glasses in the cupboard began to chime as the vibrations brought their edges together. "Something is out of the pit," he moaned as Austin threw himself around the corner and into the kitchen.

The noise stopped.

He glared down at the cat "That was you? But you weigh only what, two kilos?"

"Can we discuss my weight another time," Austin snapped. "Claire's in trouble!"

TROUBLE IS GOOD.
    BUT WE DIDNT CAUSE IT.
    SO?
Hell sounded sulky. IT'S THE PRINCIPLE OF THE THING.
WE DON'T HAVE PRINCIPLES!
OH, YEAH.

EIGHT

JACQUES SLAMMED INTO AN INVISIBLE BARRIER at the door to Claire's room. The impact flung him backward into the sitting room, past Dean, past Austin, right through the bust of Elvis.

"Thang you, thang you vera much."

"Nobody asked you," he snarled at the plaster head. "*Anglais!* I cannot follow you without an anchor."

Just on the far side of the threshold, Dean rocked to a halt and spun around. "An anchor?"

"*Oui.* Come and get *la coussin*, the cushion." His fingers swept through the horsehair stuffing. "Take it with you to Claire's room."

"You don't have an anchor in here?"

"Did I not just say that? And wipe that *stupide* grin off your face! You think I would not allow Claire her privacy?"

Actually, he did. But he was too nice a guy to say so. And the stupid grin seemed to want to stay where it was. Three long strides and he snatched up the cushion. Three more and he was back in Claire's room, Jacques by his side.

"About time you goons got here," Austin growled, pacing back and forth in front of the wardrobe.

Except for the cat and the furniture, the room was empty.

"Where's the boss?" Dean demanded, throwing the cushion down on the bed.

"Where do you think?"

Three heads, one living, one dead, one feline, turned toward the wardrobe.

"How do you know she is in trouble?" Jacques asked. "She goes every morning to search for the Historian. Why is this morning different?"

"She's been gone too long," Austin told them. "No matter how long she's in there, she's never gone more than half an hour out here."

Dean checked his watch. It was almost nine-fifteen. Which didn't tell him anything except the time. "Maybe she's taking longer because she found something."

"Sure, look on the bright side." He shoved a paw under the bottom of the wardrobe door and hooked it open an inch or two. "Listen."

"*Oui?* I hear nothing."

"That," growled the cat, "is because you're talking."

A moment later, the ghost shrugged. "I still hear nothing."

Then faintly, very faintly, just barely audible over the sound of Austin's tail hitting the floor, came the roar of a large and very angry animal.

The two men exchanged an identical glance.

"You are sure that is not Claire?" Jacques asked.

"Yes! Mostly," Austin amended after a moment's thought. "Either way, it can't be good. Dean has to go in and get her."

"Okay." Dean settled his glasses more firmly on his face and took a step forward.

"*Un moment.* You do not go alone, *Anglais.*"

"Yes, he does." Austin interrupted. "You have to weigh more than forty kilos to go on this ride; it's one of those stupid child safety features. Unfortunately, it also bars cats and ghosts, so I'm afraid Dean's it."

Jacques drew himself up to his full height, plus about four inches of air space. "If he carries the cushion, I go through with him."

"It doesn't work that way!" Austin directed a couple of angry licks in the direction of his shoulder. "And if it did, *I'd* be going through with him."

Dean reached past the cat and opened the wardrobe door. It was dark inside, much darker than it should have been. Another distant roar drifted out into the room. He squared his shoulders, flexing the muscles across his back, and bounced a time or two on the balls of his feet. Claire needed his help. Cool. "What do I do?"

"Step up inside and pull the door closed behind you, but don't latch it."

"Why not?"

"Only idiots lock themselves in wardrobes." His tone suggested any idiot ought to know that. "Once you're in there, think about Claire. Holding an image of her in your mind, walk toward the back wall. When you get to where you're going, keep thinking of her."

"Where am I going?"

"I have no idea. Once you arrive, look and listen for anything out of the ordinary. She'll be in the middle of it. Oh, and don't eat or drink while you're in there. Nothing. Zip. Zilch. Nada."

About ready to step inside, Dean paused. "Why not?" he asked again.

"Did you not read when you were a kid?"

"I, uh, played a lot of hockey."

Austin snorted. "I guessed. If you eat or drink inside the wardrobe, it holds you there."

The door half closed, he stuck his head out into the room. "How do I come back?"

"Think of this room and go through any opaque door."

"But do not return here without Claire," Jacques told him, "or I will make of your life a misery."

Dean accepted the warning in the spirit it had been given. "Don't worry. I'll save her."

As the wardrobe door swung shut, Austin leaped up onto the bed. "I hate waiting."

"You know," Jacques said thoughtfully, drifting over to join him. If you are wrong and she does not need saving, she is going to be not happy with you."

"Excuse me? If I am *wrong*?"

The inside of the wardrobe smelled faintly of mothballs. Dean found it a comforting smell as he turned away from the door and the argument gaining volume on the other side. It reminded him of the closet in the spare room at his grandfather's house. Unable to see, he took a tentative step forward, expecting, in spite of everything to whack his face on the back wall. Another step, and another. Still no wall.

A new odor began drifting in over the mothballs.

His grandfather's pipe tobacco?

He stopped and closed his eyes, suddenly remembering that he was supposed to be thinking of Claire, not of home.

"Holding an image of her in your mind . . ."

It was hard to hold a single image, so he cycled through the highlights of their short association as he took another step. Claire walking into the kitchen that first morning; Claire explaining how magic worked; Claire going up the spiral stairs to the attic. The smell of the pipe tobacco began to fade. She was his boss; she was a Keeper; she had a really irritating way of assuming she knew best or, more precisely, that he knew nothing at all. When he opened his eyes, he could see a gray light in the distance.

Approximately thirty-seven steps later—he wasn't sure how many he'd taken before he'd started counting—he stood on Princess Street looking down the hill toward the water. Prepared for the strangest possible environment, he was a little disappointed to find himself in a bad copy of the city he'd just left. Everything was vaguely out of proportion, the street had been paved with cobblestones, and, although there were a few parked cars, there was no traffic. The half dozen or so people in sight paid no attention to him.

He could hear church bells in the distance and the cry of gulls circling high overhead.

There was no sign of Claire.

Hoping for a clue, he pulled out the card.

> Aunt Claire, Keeper
> Your Accident is my Opportunity
>
> (could be worse, could be raining)

The skies opened up, and it began to pour. Dean stuffed the card back into his wallet, noting that magic had a very basic sense of humor.

Fortunately, he seemed to have passed from October into August. The air was warm, and the rain was almost tepid. Pushing wet hair back off his face, he drew in a deep lungful of air and frowned at yet another familiar smell. Hoping he hadn't screwed everything up by thinking of home, he started running downhill toward the harbor. *Look and listen for anything out of the ordinary,* Austin had told him. Well, as far as he knew, there were no saltwater harbors on the Great Lakes.

It wasn't just a saltwater harbor. Signal Hill rose across the narrows where the Royal Military College should have been. Massive docks butted up against a broad thoroughfare and along the far side of it were the historic properties that should've been clustered around the Dartmouth ferry dock in Halifax.

"Okay. This is weird." But so far it didn't seem dangerous. Even the rain was letting up.

There were ships at nearly all the docks, most of them clippers and brigantines, but he saw at least two modern vessels as well. So which were out of the ordinary? While he stood there, undecided, someone bumped him from behind, muttered an apology, and kept moving.

Dean turned to see a heavily muscled man in an old-fashioned naval uniform, carrying a human leg over one massive shoulder, weave his way through the crowd on the thoroughfare and enter a windowless green building on the other side. The sign on the building read "Man-made Sausages."

No one else, from the little girl selling matches to the one-eyed, peg-legged street artist with a hook, seemed to think anything of it.

"Don't eat or drink while you're in there. . . ."

"Not much danger of that," he muttered. "I'll just find the boss. . . ."

From somewhere in town came the enraged roar of an Industrial Light and Magic special effect followed closely by a woman's scream.

"Claire!"

His work boots slipping on the wet cobblestones, Dean raced away from the harbor through a rabbit warren of narrow streets, all of them steeply angled regardless of the direction he was running.

The roar sounded again. Closer.

Just when he thought he was hopelessly lost, he pounded out from between two empty storefronts and into the intersection at Brock and King, across from the old city library.

In the center of the intersection, stomping jerkily about like one of the old stop-motion models, was a dinosaur. A T-Rex. Off to one side, were the squashed and nearly unidentifiable remains . . .

Dean clutched at his chest.

. . . of a 1957 Corvette.

"Oh, God, no!" Eyes wide behind his glasses, he staggered forward, hands outstretched. He was almost at the wreck when he felt the ground move, felt hot breath on the back of his neck, and had the sudden uncomfortable feeling he was a secondary character in a Saturday morning movie matinee.

He dove out of the way just in time. Rolled immediately thereafter to avoid being smacked by the massive tail. Leaped over a crumpled fender . . .

Sitting in the library, surrounded by reference material and a few of the more pungent if less literate clientele, Claire heard someone call her name. Loudly. One could almost say desperately.

The voice, even *in extremis,* sounded very familiar.

She'd been inside since the Historian's new pet had shown up, figuring sooner or later it would get bored and wander off and, if it didn't, she'd just go back out through the library door and home. Then, looking for a map, she'd gotten engrossed in the books. She had no idea how long she'd been in there.

"CLAIRE!"

"Dean?" Running her tongue over dry lips, she walked over to the window, wondering how the Historian had been able to copy Dean's voice so exactly. She felt her jaw actually drop when she realized she was hearing the original. "Dean!"

Had the T-Rex been animated better, Dean knew he'd have been dead and partially digested by now. Dodging a grotesque, chickenlike peck of the huge head, he found himself at the foot of the library steps.

The massive tail whipped around.

He jumped, cleared the tail, made a bad landing, stumbled back, and fell.

About a dozen stairs behind and above him, he heard the library door open and, at the same time, a small herd of pigs appeared on the other side of the intersection squealing loud enough to wake the dead.

Or attract the attention of the dinosaur.

As T-Rex lumbered toward the pork, something grabbed Dean by the shirt and tried to haul him backward up the stairs with no notable success. Before the pressure of the seams across his armpits cut off all circulation in his arms, he managed to get his feet under him and stand.

Claire released both handfuls of fabric as he turned to face her. Two steps apart, they were eye to eye. She went up one more step. "What are you *doing* here?"

Struggling to catch his breath, Dean gasped, "I came in to save you."

"To save me? Oh, for . . . Whose bright idea was that?"

Since she was obviously not thrilled by the thought of a rescue attempt, he squared his shoulders. "Mine."

"Don't be ridiculous," Claire snorted. "It was Austin, wasn't it? That cat is fussier than . . ."

A roar from the T-Rex jerked their attention back into the intersection. Ludicrously small arms raked the air, then it charged.

"Come on!" Grabbing another handful of Dean's shirt, Claire ran for the library door.

"It didn't take long with the pigs."

"That's because they weren't real. Only the Historian can do substance in here, all I can manage is illusion."

"Oh, great, so you've pissed it off?"

"Try to remember who's saving whose ass."

The solid stone steps shuddered as the dinosaur started up after them.

"Think about the bedroom!" Claire yelled as they reached the top step. Still clutching his shirt, she thumbed the latch and dragged him through the door after her.

The wardrobe shuddered to a mighty impact as they flung themselves out into the worried presence of Austin and Jacques.

Breathing heavily, Claire lay where she'd fallen, staring under the bed at a pair of fuzzy bunny slippers that weren't hers. Four paws, propelled by a ten-pound cat, landed on her kidneys and a moment later Austin's face peered into hers from over her right shoulder.

"Are you hurt?"

"I'm fine. I'm just a little thirsty." She rolled over, cradled him in her arms, and sat up. Dean had gotten to his feet and was busy trying to pull his T-shirt back into shape. "What," she asked the cat, "was the idea of sending *him* in after me? If I hadn't shown up in time, he'd have been killed."

"I heard roaring."

"You've heard worse."

"You'd been gone for over an hour."

"I lost track of time. I was reading."

"Reading?" Austin repeated, squirming free and jumping up onto the bed. "You were reading!"

About to mention the dinosaur, Dean's vision suddenly filled with an extreme close-up of a ghost. "Get my cushion," Jacques whispered, "quickly, and we will leave."

"But Claire . . ." Dean whispered back, trying to see around Jacques' translucent body.

"This you cannot rescue Claire from. And as much as I would like my cushion to remain, pick it up. We are leaving."

"I was worried sick and you were *reading?*" Austin repeated.

Something in the cat's tone suddenly got through. Eyes wide, Dean stared at Jacques who nodded frantically toward the cushion.

"It wasn't like that, Austin."

"It wasn't like what? It wasn't like you never even considered my feelings? Is that what it wasn't like?"

Careful not to break into the line of sight between cat and Keeper, Dean scooped up Jacques' anchor and the two of them raced into the sitting room.

"So what was it Claire save you from?" Jacques asked as they slowed.

Dean shrugged, the material stretched by Claire's hands riding on his shoulders like tiny wings. "A dinosaur."

"A what?"

"A very big carnivorous lizard."

"Ha! If I can go through the wardrobe, she would not have to rescue *me* from a big lizard. She would not have to rescue a real man."

"Real men admit it when they need help."

"Since when?"

"I think it started around the mid-eighties."

"Ah. Well, it did not start with me. I would have did what I went into the wardrobe to do."

"You would have *done* what you went into the wardrobe to do."

"That," said Jacques, staring down his nose at the living man, "is what I said."

"Okay." Dean half-turned toward the bedroom, gesturing with the hand holding the cushion. "If you're so brave, go back in there."

Austin's voice drifted out through the open bedroom door. ". . . consider more important than . . ."

Jacques looked thoughtful. "How big did you say was that lizard?"

Later, after tempers had cooled and apologies had been offered and accepted, Austin rested his head on Claire's shoulder and murmured thoughtfully, "Maybe it had nothing to do with either of us. Maybe it only had to do with Dean."

Claire stopped halfway across the sitting room and shifted her hold on the cat so she could see his face. "What are you saying?"

"Maybe he *needed* to go into the wardrobe; to begin tempering."

"Tempering?" Her eyes widened as the implication hit her. "Oh, no. Forget it. We don't need another Hero. They're nothing but trouble."

"Granted, but he fits the parameters. No parents, raised by a stern but ethical authority figure, big, strong, naturally athletic, not real bright, modest, good looking . . ."

"Myopic."

"What?"

"He's nearsighted," Claire said, feeling almost light-headed with relief. "Who ever heard of a hero in glasses?"

Austin thought about it for a moment "Clark Kent?"

"Fake prescription."

"Woody Allen?"

"Get serious."

"Still . . ."

"No." She stepped out into the lobby, closing the door to her suite behind her. Patting the gleaming oak counter with her free hand, she headed for the kitchen. Since the unsuccessful search for the Historian had taken most of her energy, she had no memory of Dean actually finishing the work, but it sure looked good. Granted it would look better if they refinished the lobby floor, painted and recarpeted the stairs . . .

"No. I'm a Keeper, not an interior decorator, I have a job. If I can't find the Historian," she muttered, stepping into the kitchen, "there's more than one way to skin a cat."

Austin jumped out of her arms, landing by the sink and whirling around to face her. "I beg your pardon."

"Sorry."

He washed a shoulder. "I should hope so."

Hardly daring to breathe, Claire pulled the plastic container holding the site journal out of the fridge. Faint fumes could be detected seeping through the seal.

"Do you have to do that now?" Austin demanded. "It's twenty-five to ten. I thought we could have breakfast first."

"I have no intention of opening this when I have food in my stomach."

"That's probably wise, but factoring in wardrobe time, you haven't eaten for nearly twenty-four hours and, more importantly, *I* haven't eaten for two. After you deal with that you're not going to want to eat for a while." He sneezed. "If ever. It's worse than the last time!"

"But the lid's still on."

"My point exactly." His first leap took him nearly to the dining room. Ears back, he headed for the hall. "If you want me, I'll be doing canine therapy next door. Out of my way, junior."

"Junior?" Dean repeated, flattening against the wall to avoid being run over by the cat. Still shaking his head, he turned the corner into the dining room and coughed. "What in . . ."

"If you want to do something useful," Claire told him a little breathlessly, setting the lid to one side, "you can find me a lifting thingie."

"A what?" he asked, noting with dismay that she was reaching for another fork.

"Something to lift the journal out of the liquid with."

Reminding himself that it was her hotel and she could therefore destroy as much of the cutlery as she wanted, Dean took his least favorite spatula from the spatula section of the second drawer and handed it over. "Did you and Austin work out, well, you know . . ."

"Yes. We did. Just so you don't worry in the future, we always do."

"You guys, you have a interesting relationship."

"Of course we do." She wiped one watering eye on the back of her hand. "He's a cat." Carefully, she slid the spatula under the journal.

Once again, the onions had turned indigo but, this time, there was still about an inch of brine sloshing around in the bottom of the container.

"Boss, I, uh, just wanted to say . . ."

"Not now, Dean."

"Okay." Left hand cupped over his mouth and nose, he walked over to the dining room side of the service counter. "How can you stand over it like that?"

"I do what I have to."

"And what do you have to do, *cherie?*" Jacques asked, appearing by her side.

"Watch." Holding the journal just up out of the brine so that none of the solution splashed out of the container as it drained, Claire carefully used the fork and flicked it open to the first of Augustus Smythe's entries. Although the paper remained a blue barely lighter than the letters, the writing was finally readable.

August 18th, 1942. I find myself summoned to a place called Brewster's Hotel. The most incredible thing has just taken place here. The Keeper who was, and who indeed continues to seal the site, attempted to gain control of the evil for her own uses.

Smiling broadly, Claire glanced up at Dean. "Isn't this wonderful!"

"Wonderful," he agreed, but he was referring to the little crinkle the smile folded into the end of her nose.

Jacques followed his line of sight, and snorted.

I cannot name the Keeper because she remains in the building, continuing to seal the site with her power—which is considerably more than considerable according to the arrogant s.o.b. of an Uncle John who helped defeat her. I hate how some of those guys get off on being "more lineage than thou," as if the universe shines out his ass.

"I guess that answers the Augustus Smythe personality question."

✤　　✤　　✤

The other Keeper, Uncle Bob, isn't so bad. Is it because Bob's your Uncle?

"And that raises a few more."

Two of them wouldn't have been enough to defeat her if she hadn't . . .

Slipping the fork carefully under the damp paper, trying, in spite of her excitement, to keep breathing shallowly, Claire turned the page.

. . . had trouble wi th th e vir g i . . .

"Oh, no!" One by one, faster and faster, the letters slid off the paper and into the brine. For a moment, Claire stared aghast at a journal of blank pages, then the paper turned into a gelatinous mass and shimmied off the spatula. The resultant splash sprayed a couple of dozen letters up over Claire's hand and sweater.

She staggered back until she hit the edge of the sink, too stunned to speak.

Jumping forward, holding his breath, Dean slapped the lid onto the container. When the seal caught, he hurried around into the kitchen, plucked the spatula from Claire's hand and tipped it almost immediately into the garbage.

"You must wash your hand, *cherie*," Jacques told her. "There is em's upon it. And other letters there upon your sweater."

"I don't think it'll wash out," Dean offered.

Jacques sniffed. "It does not amaze me you also do laundry."

Slowly Claire lifted her hand to her mouth and touched her tongue to one of the letters.

The two men exchanged a horrified glance.

Her lips drew back off her teeth.

"I do not think she is smiling," Jacques murmured.

"Spider parts," Claire snarled. "That rotten, little piece of Hell!"

Both men flinched but nothing happened.

"Don't you see?" Claire's glare jerked from one to the other and back again. "The imp introduced spider parts into the solution. It couldn't have opened the fridge, so it had to have dusted the onions in the bin under the counter just before I started the second batch. It ruined everything!"

OH, VERY WELL DONE.
DO WE *GIVE* COMPLIMENTS?
WE GIVE CREDIT WHERE CREDIT IS DUE.
Hell was silent for a moment. NO, WE DON'T, it said at last.

"Mrs. Abrams is up to something; she's humming. It's an intensely scary sound. Why the long faces?" Austin asked, jumping up on the counter. He sneezed and turned a disgusted glare on the container. "Haven't you finished with that yet?"

"Oh, yes, I've finished with it." Claire pulled off her sweater and handed it to Dean who held it much the same way he'd have held a dead jellyfish. "It's all over. I'm not going to be able to undo what was done because I'll never find out what they did. I can't fix it I might as well call the locksmith's cousin."

"What are you talking about?"

"Never mind." Moving mechanically, she turned, squirted a little dish detergent into her palm and washed her hands.

When Dean explained what had happened, the cat jumped down to rub against her legs.

"Spider parts can get onto onions a number of different ways; you don't *know* it was an imp. Or even that there is an imp."

"Don't start with me, Austin."

Wisely, he let it drop. "There's still the Historian," he reminded her.

"No, there isn't." She scrubbed her hands dry on a dish towel— which Dean retrieved to hold, two-fingered, with the sweater—and scooped Austin up into her arms. "I can't get out of that town she's built."

"The wardrobe Kingston?" Dean asked.

"Not quite Kingston," Claire told him bitterly. "There's a camp of killer girl guides to the north. When I take the bridge over the narrows and go east, I get hit with a snowstorm I can't get through. To the west there's a military academy. And south . . ."

"*Un moment,*" Jacques interrupted. "Why can you not get by a military academy?"

"It's the men in uni . . ."

Claire put her hand over the cat's muzzle. "They think I'm one of their teachers and I'm AWOL. Attempting that route'll only get me stuffed into an ugly uniform and thrown in the brig until I agree to teach two classes in military history."

"The sea's to the south," Dean said. "What about one of the ships?"

"Get on a ship crewed by the Historian's people?" Claire shook her head. "I don't think so. It'd be faster just to drown myself and save them the trouble."

"Austin thinks you're trying too hard."

"Does he? Interesting he should know so much about a place he's never been." The cat in her arms became very intent on cleaning between the pads of a front paw. "No, it's obvious. I can't get to the Historian, and this . . ." She stared down at the jumble of letters and the sludge of the journal. Her shoulders slumped. ". . . this is less than useless."

"But what about studying the actual, you know, spell?"

"What about it?" She'd been spending an hour with Sara every morning and, so far, she'd developed an allergy to dust. Her ten minutes every other afternoon, the longest she could spend so close to Hell and a running monologue she couldn't shut off, had taught her a number of things she'd have rather not known about the Spanish Inquisition, World War II, and the people who program prime time TV but nothing about how to deal with the unique situation surrounding the site. "It's time I faced it; I'm going to be stuck here for the rest of my life."

After a moment, when the silence in the kitchen stopped ringing to the slam of a metaphorical door, Jacques sighed and said, "Would that be so bad, *cherie?*"

Claire paused on the verge of plunging into a good long wallow in self-pity, realizing he was actually asking, *Would it be so bad to spend the rest of your life here with me?* "You're missing the point, Jacques. If I were needed to seal the hole, doomed to become an eccentric recluse years before my time, it'd be different, at least I'd be doing something useful. Here . . ." A toss of her head managed to take in the entire hotel. ". . . I'm a passive observer, watching a system I can't affect, doing sweet dick all. It's like, like having last year's Cy Young winner sitting in the bullpen in case one of the starters blows a rotator cuff."

The ghost stared at her in bewilderment "And that means . . ."

"It's baseball," Dean told him before Claire could explain. "It means she feels her abilities are wasted here."

"Wasted?" Jacques repeated. "Here where there is a hole to Hell in the basement and *une femme mauvaise* asleep upstairs? If there is something that goes wrong here . . .

DEATH! DESTRUCTION!
A FIVE HUNDRED CHANNEL UNIVERSE!

". . . your, what you call, abilities will not be wasted, *cherie.*"

"But if nothing goes wrong . . ."

"We should all be so lucky," Austin interrupted, jumping out of her arms. He checked the dry food in his bowl and sat, tail wrapped around his toes. "You know this place needs to be monitored."

She waved a dismissive hand. "Well, yes, but . . ."

"And since you've been summoned here, this is where you need to be."

"That's the theory, but . . ."

"And since you can't access the information you need to deal with this unique situation, it seems apparent that you're the monitor needed for the site." The catechism complete, he flicked an ear back for punctuation. "If it helps, think of yourself as the world's last line of defense. A missile in a silo, hopefully never to be used. A sub . . ."

"That's enough," Claire told him shortly, breathing heavily through her nose. She'd always believed that the one thing she hated most was being lectured to by the cat, but she'd just discovered she hated being lectured to in front of an audience even more. "It's not helping. You want to know what will?" Whirling around, she yanked a large bag of chocolate chip cookies out of the cupboard. "This. This'll help." Tucking it under her arm, she pushed through Jacques, past Dean, and toward the dubious sanctuary of Augustus Smythe's . . . no, *her* sitting room.

"Perhaps I can see her point," Jacques mused as the distant door slammed. "Although, I am with her in this bull's pen, so at least she is not alone."

"And what am I?" Austin demanded. "Beef byproduct?"

"What is . . ."

"Never mind." Paws against the cupboards, he stood up on his hind legs to watch Dean check the seal on the plastic container.

"I'd better dump the rest of those onions."

"Why bother? You've been eating them for a week." He snickered at Dean's expression. "That which does not kill you makes you stronger."

"Spider parts?" Slightly green, Dean clenched his teeth and tried not to think about it.

"Never ask me what's in a hot dog." The cat dropped back onto four feet. "And if you're going to throw that out double bag it so it doesn't leak. You'll contaminate the whole dump."

"Will the boss be all right?"

"Oh, sure. Just as soon as she comes to terms with spending the rest of her life standing guard in this hotel."

"Those are not easy terms," Jacques murmured reflectively. "To haunt ths not very popular hotel is not how I myself thought to spend eternity. I will go to her."

"Hey, hold it" Dean grabbed his arm, and stubbed his fingers against the wall as his hand passed right through the other man. "She wants to be alone."

"And what do you know of it, *Anglais!* You can leave."

"Yeah, but I won't."

"So that makes you better than me? That you stay but do not have to." The ghost snorted. "I know why you stay, *Anglais*. It is not that it is so good a job, *n'est ce pas?*"

Dean's ears burned. "Austin says I'm a part of this. And Claire's mother says she needs me. And . . ."

"*Oui?*"

"And I don't run out on my friends."

The silence stretched and lengthened. Dean figured Jacques was taking his time to translate something particularly cutting but to his surprise, the ghost smiled and nodded. "*D'accord.* If she must guard the world, we three will guard her."

We three.

It felt good being part of a team. It would've felt better standing back to back with Claire and taking on the world, just the two of them, but deep down, Dean was a realist.

He hadn't ever really considered his future. He'd left Newfoundland looking for work, had fallen into this job, liked it well enough, and stayed. Because all his choices had been freely made, there seemed to be an infinite number still left to explore. He wasn't really very happy to discover that when a person reached a certain age, choices started making themselves. "The world's last line of defense—I wonder if the world knows how lucky it is," he mused.

The cat and the ghost exchanged expressions as identical as differing physiognomy could make them.

"Still, I can see her point," he continued in the same tone. "It's an awesome responsibility, but it must be some boring being on guard. Ow!" He reached down and rubbed his calf. "Why did you scratch me?"

"Never, ever say it's boring being a guard!"

"I didn't," Dean protested, checking for blood seeping through his jeans. "I said it must be some boring being *on* guard."

"Oh." Austin sheathed his claws. "Sorry."

Stuffing a fourth cookie into her mouth, Claire sank back into the sofa cushions and looked for something to put her feet up on. The coffee table practically bowed under the weight of the crap it already held and the hassock was on the other side of the room. Twisting slightly sideways, she chewed and swallowed and dropped her heels down on the plaster bust of Elvis.

"Thang you. Thang you vera much."

"You're kidding, right?" She lifted her feet and let them drop again.

"Thang you. Thang you vera much."

It seemed to have a limited vocabulary. "Why would Augustus Smythe waste power, even seepage, on something like you?" Unless. She chewed thoughtfully. "You don't sing, do . . ."

Her last word got lost under the opening bars of "Jailhouse Rock."

"Stop."

"Thang you. Thang you vera much."

"Sing."

A few bars of "Blue Suede Shoes."

"Stop."

"Thang you. Thang you vera much."

"Sing."

"Heartbreak Hotel." The opening bars of "Heartbreak Hotel."

"That's more like it" Claire had another cookie and prepared *to* wallow. From this point on, the future stretched out unchanging because to hope for change was to hope for disaster and to hope for disaster would strengthen Hell. She supposed she should call her mother, let her know how things had worked out—or rather how they hadn't worked out—but she didn't feel up to hearing even the most diplomatic version of "I told you so."

And if Diana was home . . .

The ten-year difference in their ages and a childhood spent being rescued by Claire from toddler enthusiasm meant that Diana had always lumped Claire in with the rest of the old people. She wouldn't be at all surprised to find Claire stuck running the hotel. It was what old Keepers did, after all.

Moving down to the second layer of cookies, Claire knew she couldn't trust herself to listen to that. Better not to call until Friday evening when she *always* called.

"You do know Elvis is running on seepage."

Claire sighed, exhaling a fine mist of cookie crumbs. "He's using a tiny fraction of what's readily available. He's not pulling from the pit."

"I wonder if that was the first excuse Augustus Smythe made." Austin jumped up onto the back of the sofa and gingerly stretched out along the top edge of the cushion.

"I doubt it." The song ended and Elvis thanked his audience before she could actually do anything.

"There is a bright side, you know. If Augustus Smythe hadn't been a sufficient monitor for all the years he was here, he would have been replaced. Since you're here now, obviously there's a better chance than there's ever been that something will go wrong."

Claire turned just enough to glare at the cat. "And I'm supposed to feel good about that?" But she reached out to see that the power loop remained secure.

YOU WERE DISAPPOINTED!

Get out of my head. She ate another three cookies so fast she almost took the end off a finger.

"You should cheer up," Austin told her.

"I don't want to cheer up."

"Then you should answer the door."

"There's nobody . . ." A tentative knocking cut her off. She glared at the cat as she called out, "What?"

"It's Dean. You haven't eaten yet today, so I made you some breakfast."

"It's almost noon."

"It's an omelet."

Names have power. Claire could smell it now: butter, eggs, mushrooms, cheese. All of a sudden she was ravenous. Half a bag of cookies hadn't even blunted the edge. When she opened the door, she found he'd brought a thermal carafe of coffee and a glass of orange juice as well. She held out her hands, but he didn't seem to want to relinquish the tray.

"You've, um, probably forgotten, but it's Thanksgiving today."

She hadn't so much forgotten as hadn't realized. A quick glance over at Miss October did indicate that it was, indeed the second Monday. And that she should replace Augustus Smythe's calendars. "Thank you. I'll call home."

"Yeah. Well, it's just that I was kind of invited to a friend's house for dinner."

"Kind of invited?"

"She's from back home, too, and we all made plans to get together and . . ." His voice trailed off.

"Go. Be happy. Eat turkey. Watch football." Claire reached over the omelet, grabbed the edge of the tray closest to his body and yanked it toward her, leaving him no choice but to let go or to go with it.

He let go.

"You've certainly earned a night off," she said, smiling tightly up at him. "Thank you for the food. Now go away, I haven't finished wallowing yet." Stepping back, she closed the door in his face.

"That was rude," Austin chided.

"Do you want some of this or not?"

It was enough, as she'd known it would be, for him to keep further opinions to himself.

Out in the office, Dean shook his head, brow creased with concern. "I don't know what I should do," he confessed to Jacques.

"Do what she says," the ghost told him. "Be with your friends. Eat the turkey, watch the football. There is nothing you can do here. She will come out when she is come to terms with this."

"*Has* come to terms with this. You could go in."

"I think not. What was it you said?" He started to fade and by the time he finished talking his words hung in the air by themselves. "I am pretty smart for a dead guy."

The interior of the refrigerator was as spotless as the rest of the kitchen. In Claire's experience, most crispers held two moldy tomatoes and a head of mushy lettuce but not Dean's. The vegetables were not only fresh, they'd been cleaned. She thought about making a salad and decided not to bother. Considered making a sandwich from the left-over pot roast and decided it was too much work. Reached for a plastic container of stroganoff to reheat and let her hand fall back by her side.

In the end, she stepped away from the fridge empty-handed.

The familiar clomp of work boots turned her around.

"You're back early."

"It's almost nine. Not that early." Dean set a bulging bag down on the table and began removing foil wrapped packages. "We ate, did the dishes, had a cuffer—swapped stories," he explained as her brows went up. "And here I am, all chuffed out." Carefully lifting out a small margarine tub, he shot her a tentative smile. "Are you feeling better?"

"I spent the afternoon watching tabloid talk shows." She crossed the kitchen to stand by the table. "Now I feel slightly nauseated but better about *my* life."

"I think that's the idea."

Rubbing her temples with the heels of her hands, Claire snorted. "I certainly hope so. My mother send her regards, and my sister wants to know how you feel about European trawlers depleting the Grand Banks, but since she's only tiying to start a political argument, you don't actually have to answer her." She picked up a package that smelled unmistakably of turkey. "What's this?"

"Thanksgiving dinner. I packed up some of the leftovers. The potatoes are cooked to a chuff, but you can't tell under the gravy."

When he got a plate and began arranging food on it, Claire folded her arms and shook her head. Only a young man could eat a full meal, then sit down and eat another. "I thought you were—How did it go— all chuffed out?"

"I am. This is for you." The feel of the answering silence drew his attention up off the food. "That is, if you haven't eaten. I mean, I don't even know if you like turkey. It's just that this was my first Thanksgiving away from home and I know how lonely I would've been without my friends and I thought that, well, that you should have some Thanksgiving dinner." Flustered, unable to read her expression, he spilled the gravy.

The accident and the subsequent wiping and rewiping and polishing gave Claire a chance to swallow the lump in her throat. There were a number of things she wanted to say, but after the day's emotional ups and downs, she didn't think she could manage any of them without bursting into tears—and Keepers never cried in front of bystanders. With the table restored to a pristine state, she reached out and touched Dean lightly on the arm. "Thang you," she said. "Thang you vera much."

THAT BOY IS SO NICE HE'S NAUSEATING. THERE MUST BE SOMETHING WE CAN TEMPT HIM WITH.
    WE'VE TRIED. HE DOESN'T LISTEN.
    ISN'T *THAT* JUST LIKE A MAN.
    NOT WHERE WE'RE CONCERNED, Hell told itself tartly.

The next morning, Claire found a pair of Dean's underwear hanging off the doorknob as she left her suite. The imp must've spent the entire night dragging them up from the laundry room in the basement

"I hope you gave yourself a hernia," Claire muttered, pulling them free.

Briefs, not boxers. Navy blue with white elastic.

"Boss?"

They wouldn't mash down into a small enough ball to bide. Keeping her right hand and its contents behind her, Claire turned. "What?"

"We've got lots of eggs, and I have to use them. I wondered if you wanted me to make you some for breakfast."

"Fine."

"How do you want them?"

"I don't care." He was wearing one of his brilliant white T-shirts and jeans, totally unaware of how good he looked. Briefs not boxers. Given how tightly his jeans fit she should have been able to figure that out on her own.

"Scrambled?"

"Fine."

"With garlic and mushrooms?"

"Whatever."

Dean frowned. "You all right?"

"Fine."

He leaned left

She shuffled just enough to cut down his line of sight "Was there anything else?"

"Uh, no. I guess not."

"Good. You go ahead." Her right arm started forward to wave him away but she stopped it in time. "Go on. I'll be there in a minute."

Shaking his head, Dean disappeared down the hall.

Twenty years old, Claire reminded herself whacking the back of her skull against the door.

The hollow boom of the impact echoed throughout the first floor.

"Boss?"

"It's nothing," she called. Rubbing the rising bump, she contemplated doing it again. She'd had the perfect opportunity to prove the existence of the imp. There could be no other explanation for the underwear delivered to her door. So why, she wondered, had she acted like such an idiot?

"It's this place; it's messing with my head." Opening the door, she tossed the underwear into the sitting room. She'd figure out a way to get them back into Dean's laundry, later.

"Souvenir?" Austin asked as the briefs sailed by and landed on Elvis.

"Thang you, thang you vera much."

"You can both just shut up."

"They put over the top, how do you say . . . plaster board?" Jacques announced, pulling his head back out of the wall. "But the works for the elevator, they are all here."

"Should I start uncovering it?" Dean asked eagerly.

Claire shrugged. "Why not."

"Great, I'll go get my hammer."

"And what will you be doing, *cherie,*" Jacques asked as Dean ran off, "while he bangs out his frustrations on the wall?"

"I don't think Dean has frustrations." She ducked under the counter flap, heading for the phone. "But to answer your question, I'm going to finish packing Augustus Smythe's knick-knacks away."

"To make the place your own, yes?"

"Yes."

"So you are reconciled to staying here?"

An empty cardboard box dangling from one hand, she paused on the threshold, unwilling to take the final, symbolic step into the sitting room. "I might as well be, I haven't any other choice."

"You *are* needed here, Claire."

When she turned, he was standing right behind her. A step forward would take her right through him. His eyes had gone very dark and he was wearing the smile that made her stomach feel like she'd swallowed a bug.

"I could reconcile you." His hand caressed the air by her cheek. "It would take so little power."

At first Claire thought that the bells she heard were the ringing of desire in her ears, but then, over Jacques shoulder, she saw the front door open.

"Yoohoo!"

She stepped forward, teeth gritted against the chill, Jacques dematerializing as she moved. There was no way Mrs. Abrams could've missed seeing him.

"Did you see that, Carlee, dear?"

"See what?" Claire asked.

"Nothing. Never mind. Of course you didn't."

Prepared for an argument, or possibly even hysterics, her satisfied chuckle confused Claire completely.

"I just came in to tell you that you've got guests. Two young men. I was on my way in from my Tuesday morning hair appointment—I like to get there early, you know, before poor dear Sandra gets tired—and I saw their car go up the driveway and I knew you'd want to know immediately. That's funny." Head cocked, she swiveled it about like an orange bouffant radar dish. "I don't hear Baby. He does so love to welcome your guests as they get out of their cars in the parking lot.

"Does he welcome them the way he welcomes the postman?" Claire wondered.

"Don't be silly, dear, there's a fence in his way. I'd best go check on the poor thing." Pausing on the threshold, she pointed back toward the gleaming oak counter. "You should put some paint on that dear. All that bare wood looks somewhat indecent don't you think?"

The two young men weren't much taller than Claire, although they had a wiry build and self-confident grace that suggested their height had never been an issue. Both had sharply pointed features, an eyebrow lying across each forehead with no discernible break, and short dark hair that picked up the light as they moved so that it seemed the very end of each individual hair had been dipped in silver.

Claire relaxed as a quick dip into identical gray eyes showed not only a lack of evil intent but that they carried significantly less darkness than the general population.

"You guys twins?" Dean asked, wandering over to the counter, hammer in hand.

"Actually," said one.

"We're triplets," said the other. "I'm Ron, never Ronald since that clown came on the scene, and this is my brother Reg. We're in town for the sportsman's show that's at the Portsmouth Center this week."

"Randy had a previous commitment," Reg explained with a toothy grin. "But *we'd* like a room. Our grandfather stopped here some years ago, and he spoke very highly of the place."

Must've been before Augustus Smythe took over, Claire thought When Dean glanced her way, she had to hide a grin. It was obvious he was thinking the same thing. "All of our rooms are doubles," she told them making a mental note to have Jacques search the attic for a set of twin beds. "If you mind sharing, we could give you a deal on two rooms." It wasn't like the second room would be needed for other guests.

"Sharing's fine."

They were in constant motion and she'd lost track of which was which. "Breakfast is included in the price."

"Great but all we really need you to do is . . ."

". . . throw half a dozen raw eggs into a blender."

"We're in training."

For what? Salmonella? But they were guests, so all she said aloud was, "Well, if you'll give us a few minutes, we'll get room one ready for you."

"No hurry."

"We're going for a run down by the lake."

"We've been on the road since dawn and . . ."

". . . we don't do so well sitting still that long."

"We'll be back in about an hour."

Ron, or possibly Reg, grinned up, way up, at Dean. "See you later, big fella."

Reg, or as it were, Ron, nodded at Claire. "Ma'am."

They bounded out the door together. Claire had never seen anyone over the age of three actually bound before. Feeling a little out of breath, although she hadn't moved from behind the counter during the entire exchange, she wondered just when exactly she'd become a ma'am.

"Cool guys," Dean said. "Lots of energy. Should I go up and do the room?"

And was *Boss* really any better?

"Boss?"

Not really. "Why not? Has to be done."

She walked over to the desk as he went upstairs and dropped into the chair. *Keep your distance*, she reminded herself. *The way things have turned out, he'll be moving on long before you do.*

When Austin came into the office a few minutes later, she was sulkily updating the day's noninformation into the site journal. "What's with you?" she asked, noticing the cat's bottle brush tail, and half open mouth.

"Something stinks," he growled. "I smell dog."

"Two guests just registered." She hadn't noticed any particular odor, but if the twins were competing at the sportsman's show perhaps that meant they worked with dogs.

"It's coming from over here."

Rolling her eyes, Claire got up to peer over the counter at him.

"And it's not dog."

He was sniffing the spot where Reg, or possibly Ron, had stood to sign the register.

"Then what is it?"

"Werewolf."

WEREWOLVES?

THERE WOLVES. THERE CASTLE.

The silence that fell in the furnace room was the sort of anticipatory silence that fell just before a smack. In this particular case, it wasn't so much a smack as total, all encompassing destruction.

The silence continued a moment longer, then a very small voice said, OW.

NINE

"THE SEEPAGE IS BUILDING UP AGAIN." Sitting on the edge of the bed, Claire pulled on a sock. "I can feel the buzz beginning."

Austin yawned. "What're you going to do about it."

"I don't know. I can stop the buzz by using it—which'll make Hell happy—or I can endure it and go slowly nuts—which'll also make Hell happy. There's got to be an alternative."

"I'll let you know if I think of one."

Claire rolled her eyes. "You do that"

"You going after the Historian this morning?"

Already halfway out the door, she threw an irritated, "What's the point?" back over her shoulder.

"Boss? You busy?"

Claire looked up from writing *Smythe;junk* on the outside of the sixth box of assorted odds and ends, mostly ends, she'd cleared from the sitting room. "Not exactly, no."

"Can I talk to your?"

"I think I can spare a moment." When he frowned, clearly considering the actual time he'd need, Claire sighed. "Figure of speech, Dean. What did you want to tell me?"

"Well, I was upstairs, wiping down the molding . . ."

She leaned slightly toward him, as though proximity would help the statement make more sense. "You were what?"

"Wiping down the molding. The trim around the doors," he expanded with an indulgent smile when she continued to look confused.

"It collects dust I didn't get to it last week because of the renovations. Anyway, you know the two guys in room one; the twins?"

"The triplets."

"Okay."

Claire managed to rearrange her face into her most neutral expression. "What about them?"

"I don't want to get them into trouble or anything, but they came in some late last night and I thought I heard it then, I just wasn't sure."

"Thought you heard what?"

"A dog."

"A dog?" Moving quickly to the counter, Claire swept Austin up into her arms before he could say anything.

"Yeah. And just now, I'm pretty sure I saw half a muddy paw print. I mean, if they're smuggling a dog into their room . . ."

Austin started to snicker.

". . . we ought to say something when they come back tonight because it's not necessary."

"What isn't necessary?" She shifted the cat's weight. He was laughing so hard he was becoming difficult to hold.

"Hiding the dog. You don't mind if they bring in a pet, do your?"

"No. I don't." Which was as much as she could manage with a straight face.

"A dog?" The twins exchanged identical smiles. "No," Ron continued, "we don't have a dog."

Dean frowned. "But I heard . . ." He faltered, caught and held by two pairs of frank gray eyes. They were telling the truth, he'd bet his life on it. "I guess maybe I didn't."

"You're welcome to come up and search the room," Reg offered.

"Any time," Ron added suggestively, brows rising and falling.

"No, that's okay." Feeling a little like he'd missed the punch line of a joke everyone else found incredibly funny, Dean shrugged. "I, well, we, that is the hotel, wanted you to know we don't mind animals in the rooms, that's all."

"Nice to hear. We'll remember that . . ."

". . . if we're by this way again."

❖   ❖   ❖

"What's the lovely young man going to think of you when he finds out you've been lying to him?" Claire's reflection asked.

"I haven't been lying." She'd switched to a clear lip gloss on those days she wasn't able to use the mirror. It was faster than waiting to see what she was doing.

"You didn't tell him about the vampire, you're not telling him about the werewolves . . ." The reflection traced a dark red clown frown a quarter inch from her lips.

"But I'm not lying. If he asks . . ."

"And he's so likely to ask, isn't he? You promised, no more secrets."

"These aren't my secrets."

"We think it's sweet that you're trying to protect him."

Claire blinked, a little confused by the sudden change of topic. "What are you talking about?"

"You know. He's just a kid. Let's keep him safe. He'll thank you for it later."

No one did sarcasm quite like Hell.

When the twins left later that morning, they took three trophies with them. Although he only saw them from a distance, all three seemed to have a figure of a dog as part of the design. Dean decided not to ask.

"Boss, can I talk to you?"

Breathing heavily through her nose, Claire leaned out from behind her monitor. "What, again?"

"If this is a bad time . . ."

"A bad time? Would you like to see a bad time?" She waved him under the counter and around to her side of the desk. "Once, just once, I leave the wards off," she continued as he approached, ". . . and this is what happens."

"You spilled a cup of coffee on your keyboard?" Dean shook his head sympathetically. "That's rough."

"*I* didn't spill it."

"And don't look at me," Austin advised him from the top of the counter.

"It was the imp." Claire made a valiant attempt to unclench her teeth and nearly succeeded.

"Where'd it get the coffee?"

"I left my mug sitting here, half full, when I went in to lunch." It didn't need a Keeper to work out the cause of the two vertical lines over the bridge of Dean's glasses. He'd probably never left a half a cup of anything sitting around. He'd probably never even left a dirty cup sitting in the sink. "I forgot it was there, all right?"

"Sure." Head bent, hands dwarfing the keyboard as he gently twisted it from side to side, he remained unaware that the full force of her mood had turned in his direction. "Can't you drain it?"

"No." She felt as though she'd slammed into an affable brick wall—and had about as much effect as if she'd run full tilt into a real one. "It's already dry. Half a dozen of the keys aren't working." The wheels on the old chair shrieked a protest as she shoved it away from the desk. "I suppose I can write the stupid site journal out by hand, but it's a little difficult to build a database without a . . ."

Something small, something crimson and cream, raced along the wall under the window.

Claire snatched up the empty mug and flung it with all her might.

She missed.

The mug smashed into a hundred pieces.

Austin went three feet straight up.

"What're you trying to do to me?" he snarled as he landed, fur sticking out at right angles from his body. "I'm old!"

"It was the imp. You saw it, didn't you, Dean?"

"I saw . . ." He paused and replayed the scene as his heart rate returned to normal. "I saw something."

"A mouse," Austin told him tersely.

"I don't know, it was . . ."

"An imp." Claire's tone left no room for argument. "Somebody," she shot a scathing look at the cat, "has moved the trap."

"Probably the mice."

"Oh, give me a break."

Sitting down with his back toward her, Austin began washing his shoulder with long, deliberate strokes of his tongue.

Although Dean hoped it was his imagination, the air between cat and Keeper felt chilled. "I could take the keyboard apart," he offered, flipping it and frowning at the half-dozen, tiny, inset screw heads. "Maybe I can clean the coffee out of it"

"Take it apart? As in pieces?" On the other hand, she couldn't use it the way it was so how much worse could it get. "All right But be careful."

"No problem." His enthusiastic smile faded as a bit of broken ceramic crushed under one work boot. "First off, I'll go get a broom and dustpan."

"Dean?"

He stopped on the other side of the counter.

"What was it you wanted to talk to me about?"

What was it? The sudden, deliberate destruction of the coffee mug had driven it right out of his head.

"Do you know what you are doing, *Anglais*?" Jacques leaned over Dean's shoulder and poked an ethereal finger at the keyboard. "Can you put the pieces back together when they all fall out?"

"That's not about to happen," Dean told him, inserting a Phillips head screwdriver into the last tiny screw. "These day's everything's solid state."

Leaning against the other side of the desk, Claire drummed bubblegum-colored fingernails on the CPU and bit her tongue. The buzz of the accumulated seepage had become a constant background noise as impossible to ignore as a dentist's drill, and the smallest things set her off. She'd yelled at Dean for returning the wallpaper sample books before she'd finished with them after telling him that she'd definitely made up her mind, at Jacques for going through the dining room table rather than around, at Dean again for waiting until after lunch before opening up her keyboard, and at Austin, just because. It was like continual PMS only without the bloating.

"That's got it." Setting the screw in the saucer with the others, Dean slid a pair of slot screwdrivers into the crack between the front and back of the keyboard and twisted in opposite directions. The plastic began to creak as the tiny levers moved off the horizontal. When the crack widened to half an inch, he pried the back of the keyboard carefully free.

The sudden flurry of tiny white pieces of plastic exploding into the air strongly resembled a small, artificial blizzard.

"Score one for the dead guy," Jacques observed when the last piece landed.

Dean scooped up one of the escapees. A tiny spring fell off one end, bounced on the desk, and rolled out of sight. "Sorry," he said, shoulders up around his ears as he peered up over the top of his glasses at Claire. "But I'm sure I can fix it."

It took an effort, but Claire managed to count all the way to ten before responding. "Just clean it up," she snarled, "and move on."

Dean's eyes widened and a muscle jumped in his jaw.

"Now what's your problem?"

"For a minute there you sounded . . ." He paused and shook his head. "It's okay. I'll just clean this up like you said."

"I sounded like what?" Claire growled. "Tell me. *Please.*"

He didn't want to tell her, but he couldn't seem to help himself. "Like Augustus Smythe."

She stared at him, saw that he was serious, and opened her mouth to call him several choice names. Snapping it closed on the first of them, she stomped into her sitting room and slammed the door.

Jacques snickered. "I must hand it over to you *Anglais,* you have the way with women."

"He said I sounded like Augustus Smythe!"

Austin rolled over and stared up at her. "No," he said after a moment. "Too high-pitched."

"It's the seepage." She rubbed at her temples where the buzz had lodged. "It's barely been two weeks since I cleared it out, and it's already making me cranky."

"Got news for you, Claire, you're way beyond cranky."

"Smythe couldn't have lived like this all the time."

"Feeling sorry for him?"

"No." Her lips pulled back off her teeth. "Wanting to wring his neck."

"Maybe you're more susceptible because you're a Keeper and under normal circumstances, which these aren't, you're able to adjust the seepage." The cat washed the black spot on his front leg thoughtfully. "Why not use it to close down the postcard?"

"Because the postcard is using seepage. If I close it down, in a few days I'll have a worse problem than before. And besides, I don't want to use it."

"The postcard?"

"The seepage!" She dropped down onto the couch and emerged from the depths a few moments later to add another forty-three cents and a plain gold ring that smelled of fish to the half-filled bowl of retrieved flotsam on the coffee table. "I can't go on like this."

The distant sound of a ten-pound sledge slamming through plaster board jerked her forward, almost tipping her into the precarious area between the coach cushions.

Austin yawned. "Maybe you should cut back on the caffeine."

"Maybe you shouldn't say anything if you can't say something helpful." Tapping her nails against her thigh, Claire gritted her teeth. "There has to be a logical solution."

"Why?"

"Shut up. Point: Power is seeping out around the edges of the seal two presumably dead Keepers created with another Keeper's power. A further point: It's not my power sealing the site, so I can't make adjustments. Yet another point: I can't just leave the seepage be because it's driving me nuts. And one final point: The only way to get rid of the seepage buildup is to use it, but using the power of Hell can't help but corrupt the individual using it no matter her intentions. So." She drew in a deep breath and exhaled noisily. "Where does that get us?"

"Absolutely nowhere," Austin told her, climbing onto her lap.

Claire slumped back into the sofa. "It was a rhetorical question anyway. What we need is a way to use the seepage without strengthening Hell."

"Can't be done. Hell works only in its own best interests."

Stroking the cat, Claire spent a moment wallowing in the innate unfairness of the universe, and then . . .

"Hey!" Austin fought his way out from between the two sofa cushions. "If you're going to stand suddenly, warn a guy!"

"Hell can be *made* to work against itself." Claire whirled around to face the cat. "I'll feed the seepage into the shield around the furnace room!"

The cat stepped over onto the coffee table and, with a solid surface below him, paused to smooth the ruffled fur along his side. "How?" he asked after a moment.

"Adhesion. The moment anything escapes from the pit. Slap!" She smacked her palms together. "Right into the shield but set up so that it's distributed evenly, like oyster spit building a pearl. Hell sends more out, the shield gets stronger. Hell sends nothing at all, nothing happens because the original shield is still in place."

After a moment, Austin nodded. "It's brilliant"

Claire picked him up and kissed the top of his head. "It's why I get the big bucks," she agreed.

Sledge over his shoulder, Dean bounded down the stairs into the lobby and rocked to a dead stop when he saw Claire's door open. "I uh, piled all the bits of your keyboard on the desk," he said as she emerged.

To his surprise, she smiled. "That's great. When I get a minute, I'll separate what's recyclable and throw the rest out."

He took a tentative step closer. When he realized he was holding the sledge across his body like a shield, he let it swing down until the head rested on the floor. "You're not angry, then?" he asked tentatively.

Claire shrugged. "Accidents happen."

"No, I meant about saying you sounded like . . ." Although she no longer seemed as crusty as she had, it didn't seem polite to say it again. "You know."

"I was angry because you were right."

Coming out from behind the counter, Austin performed an exaggerated double take. Dean tried not to smile.

"But," she continued, "I've come up with a way to solve the problem." She nodded toward the sledge. "How's the elevator coming?"

"We've got all four doors cleared. They didn't take anything out when they closed the system up, so it just needs the trim back around the holes. Jacques is in the attic right now having a look at the works."

"Jacques is?"

"It's old," Dean told her cheerfully, as though that explained everything. When it didn't appear to, he added, "It's the sort of machinery he's familiar with."

Walking over to the recessed doorway, Claire peered through the wrought iron scrollwork into the closet-sized space. She could just barely make out the cables. "Where's the car?"

"In the basement."

"Given what's in the furnace room, is that entirely safe?"

"Given gravity, the basement seemed safest."

Up on her toes, Claire sent a pale white light into the shaft. Everything she could see seemed in remarkably good shape, but she supposed there was no point in taking chances. "You're probably right."

Austin sat back on his haunches and stared up at her in astonishment. "That's twice."

She ignored him. "Do you think you can get it working?"

"Sure." Dean's grip slipped as he realized what he'd said. "I mean, yeah. No problem."

"Don't try it without me. I'd like to be in on the inaugural ride."

"It might not be safe. . . ."

"It'll be safer with me in it." Turning to go, she paused and took a deep breath. There was one more thing she'd resolved to do. "Oh, and, Dean? I'm sorry I snapped at you earlier."

"That's okay. It was nothing."

"It was something if I've apologized for it."

At that point he decided it would be safer if he just kept quiet.

"Two admissions that someone else might be right *and* an apology. Circle this day on the calendar," Austin muttered as he followed Claire toward the basement.

"The boys seem to be getting along better," Claire noted as she opened the padlocks.

"They're not boys," Austin snorted from the top of the washing machine.

"It's a figure of speech."

"Dean likes you."

"Get real, he calls me Boss."

"He called you Claire when you fell down the stairs."

"He did?" Given the way her tailbone had impacted with the edge of the step, she wasn't surprised she hadn't noticed. "Means nothing."

"Then what about the way he looks at you?"

"He's twenty. The way he looks at women isn't under his conscious control."

"All right; what about the way you look at him?"

She twisted around enough to grin at the cat. "Like I said, he's twenty. It's an aesthetic appreciation."

Austin's tail beat out an audible rhythm against the enameled steel. "I know that babysitting a site at your age was the last thing you wanted, but it's given you a chance few Keepers get and you'll kick yourself if you blow it."

"Blow what?"

"The chance for a relationship."

"A relationship?" Claire sighed. "Have you been watching Oprah again?"

"No! Well, actually, yes," he amended. "But that has nothing to do with this."

"Forget it, Austin. Dean's attractive, yes, but he's too young."

"Jacques isn't."

"Jacques is too dead."

"Dean isn't."

She hung the chains on their hooks and turned to glare at her companion. "You're not the only one concerned about my having or not having a *relationship;* Hell suggested Jacques and I settle down for the duration."

"Just because something is an anthropomorphism of ultimate evil, that doesn't mean it hasn't your best interests at heart."

"Yes, it does."

"Fine. But your health is important to *me.*"

"My health?"

"It's been nearly six months."

"So?"

"If I remember correctly, the last incident wasn't terribly successful."

Her brows drew in. "What are you talking about?"

"I was under the bed."

"You were under the bed!"

"Hey, it's all just loud noises to me." He stretched out a back leg and stared down at the spread toes. "Mind you, some loud noises are more believable than others."

Claire counted to ten and let it go, reminding herself, once again, that no one ever won an argument with a cat.

Young Keepers started out believing that accessing the possibilities required inner calm and outer silence. After their first couple of sites they realized calm and quiet were luxuries they'd seldom have. Claire's first site had been in the sale bin at a discount department store. It hadn't been pretty, but it had prepared her for eventually working through the catcalls and attempted interference of Hell.

Breathing shallowly through her mouth, she adjusted the possibilities on the inside of the shield until the seepage began to adhere. It was a simple, elegant solution and she left the furnace room three hours later stinking of brimstone and feeling inordinately pleased with herself.

PRIDE IS ONE OF OURS, Hell called after her. When the only response was the slamming of the furnace room door, it examined the addition to its binding. IS SHE ALLOWED TO DO THAT? it asked sulkily.

NOTHING SEEMS TO BE STOPPING HER.

WE SHOULD BE STOPPING HER.

WELL, DUH.

As he heard Claire come into the lobby, Dean looked up from sorting the mail. "Good timing, Boss; you . . . you look like something they dragged off the bottom of the harbor."

"Thank you, Dean, I'm touched by your concern. You forgot to mention that I smell like something from the sewage treatment plant." She paused, took a deep breath, and ducked under the counter, swaying a little when she straightened on the other side.

Dean took a step toward her. "You okay?"

"I'm fine."

"You look exhausted."

"I'm a bit tired, yes. I've been working."

"On the pit?"

"By the pit."

"Is that safe?"

"It is now."

"I don't understand." He frowned. "Did you figure out how to seal it?"

"Wouldn't that be good news?" Austin asked before Claire could respond.

"Well, sure . . ."

"Then shouldn't you sound happier about it?"

"Stop being annoying just because you can," Claire suggested. Turning back to Dean, she shook her head. "No, I haven't figured out how to seal the pit, but I have solved a smaller problem. What did you mean when you said, good timing?"

It took him a moment to follow the path of the conversation. "The mail's finally here. You got a postcard."

Claire took the cardboard rectangle between thumb and forefinger, glanced at the photograph of a tropical paradise, then flipped the card over.

"Who's it from?" Dean asked, leaning forward.

"My sister, Diana. Apparently, she's in the Philippines."

Austin's ears went back. "Didn't they just have a huge volcanic eruption in the Philippines?"

"We don't *know* that was her fault." A tooth mark on the edge of the postcard had the distinct, punched hole appearance of Baby's games with the mailman. "Speaking of natural disasters, we haven't heard from Mrs. Abrams for a while."

"Maybe the blinds discouraged her?" Dean offered.

"Maybe we should put the wagon train in a circle," Austin muttered. "You should start to worry when the drums stop."

After a long hot shower, Claire spent the rest of the day sprawled in an armchair, watching a *National Geographic* video about killer whales. It was one of only eleven tapes she'd salvaged from Augustus Smythe's extensive collection. The pornography hadn't been the worst of it; his video library had also included every episode of "Gunsmoke" plus a nearly complete collection of "The Beverly Hillbillies."

Hell was not only murky, it filled out subscription forms.

"You coming, Austin?"

"You're kidding, right?" Tail lashing from side to side he backed up a step just in case Claire decided to force the issue. "You actually want me to get into that cross between a cage and a coffin, allow myself to be lifted three stories off the ground by an antique mechanism reinstalled by a cook under the direction of a dead sailor? I think not."

"It's perfectly safe."

"That's what you said about that cruise."

"Cruise?" Jacques asked by her ear.

"Bermuda Triangle. Long story," Claire told him.

"I wouldn't get into that thing," Austin continued, ears flat, "if I still had all nine lives. Not even if I'd rescued Princess Toadstool and picked up another life. If anything goes wrong, somebody has to be around to say I told you so."

"Suit yourself." Unfortunately for any second thoughts she might have been having, Claire couldn't back out now, not with the cat so vehemently opposed. He was quite smug enough without her giving him more ammunition. She closed the door, dropped the inner gate, and turned to the more corporeal of her two companions. "Are you sure you know what you're doing?"

"It's simple." Dean flashed her a confident grin. "All you do is turn this level from the off position to either the right or the left. Right takes us up, and left takes us down."

Claire sighed. "That's probably why they labeled it that way. I was asking on a more esoteric level, but never mind. Let's get this ride over with, shall we?"

"Anything you say, Boss." Feet braced, Dean wrapped both hands around the gleaming brass lever and swung it to the right.

Up in the attic, ancient machinery gave a startled jerk and wheezed into life, sending wave after wave of vibration through the stored furniture. The small, multicolored creature removing the last of the most recent marshmallows from the imp traps whirled around and fell to what served it for knees. In all of its short existence, it had never heard such a sound. Extrapolating from limited experience, it created a wild and metaphysical explanation that changed its life forever.

But that's another story.

❖   ❖   ❖

Claire pressed one hand flat against the wall as the elevator lurched upward. "It works."

"I never doubted it." Looking like the captain at the wheel of a very small ship, Dean kept his eyes locked on the edge of the floor joists moving down on the other side of the iron gate. When the top edge of the first floor was almost even with the floor of the elevator, he lifted the switch back up into the off position. In the few seconds it took for the machinery to stop, the floors came level.

"Good eye, *Anglais*," Jacques muttered. "Such a pity you were born too late to make this a career."

"Yeah?" Stepping left, Dean hooked up the gate and reached for the latch on the outer door. "Well, it's a pity you died too early for me to . . ."

"To what, *Angla* . . ."

Careful not to step over the threshold, Claire leaned out of the elevator and peered up and down the beach, eyes squinted against the ruddy light of the setting sun. "This doesn't look like the lobby." The touch of the breeze on her cheek, the sound of the waves curling and slapping into pieces against the fine, white sand, the smell of the rotting fish they appeared to have cut in half worked together to convince her it wasn't illusion either. "I'm beginning to see why Augustus Smythe closed this thing up."

"Because he does not like to take the vacation? Perhaps because he did not have a beautiful woman to walk with by the sea." Wafting past her, Jacques turned and held out his hand.

Claire stared at him, horrified. "What are you doing out there? In fact, how can you be out there?" A quick glance showed that a doily taken from his old room remained crumpled in the back corner. "Your anchor's in here!"

"As to how, I do not know. As to what, I am inviting you to go for the walk."

"The walk? Jacques, I don't think you quite realize where you are." Had she been able to hold him, she'd have grabbed his hand and yanked him back into the relative safety of the elevator.

"And where am I, *cherie!* Where is this place that gives me such freedom?"

"I don't know. And that's my point!"

"Ah, you are frightened of the unexpected. I understand, *cherie*, you are a woman, after all." Lit from behind by the sun, his eyes gleamed.

She folded her arms. "If you're implying I'm not taking the same stupid chance you are because I'm only a woman, go ahead. I'm not going to fall for it."

"You wound me, *cherie*. I said I understood why *you* are frightened."

Dean moved out of the elevator too fast for Claire to grab him. "Are you saying I'm a coward?"

"Am I saying that?" Jacques drifted backward, toward the edge of the water. *"Non.* I would never think of such a thing."

"You better not be," Dean muttered. He drew in a deep lungful of air and smiled contentedly. "Man, this place smells just like home."

The ghost snorted. "If your home smells like this, *Anglais*, it is no wonder you clean so much."

The familiar salt air had put Dean in too good a mood to continue the argument. Shaking his head, he wandered down to meet the next wave coming in.

"Excuse me!"

Both men turned and, drawn by Claire's expression, found themselves returning to the elevator considerably more quickly than they'd left it.

"If you two are quite through exposing yourselves, maybe we could think about getting . . . now what?"

Dean had disappeared around the doorframe.

"This is some weird." His voice came from directly behind her. "There's just this door in the sand. From this side, you can't see the elevator at all."

"Don't step where it should be!" Claire shouted. She didn't want to think about what could happen should three realities—elevator, beach, and Dean—suddenly find themselves sharing the same space. When Dean reappeared, she backed away from the door, leaving him room to get in. "Come on."

Jacques stepped between them, his long face wearing the half rakish, half pleading expression she found so difficult to resist. *"Cherie,* how often is there the chance to enjoy such a sunset?"

"And how enjoyable will it be if I leave the elevator and it disappears?"

"So before you leave, we prop the door open with a rock. If only the door is real here, then the elevator will go nowhere."

"You don't know that," Claire muttered, but she could feel her resolve weakening. It was a beautiful beach; brilliant white sand stretching down to turquoise water, the setting sun brushing the entire scene with red-gold light.

"If I cannot convince you, *cherie* . . ." His eyes twinkled under lowered lids. ". . . then I dare you."

"You dare me?"

"*Oui.* I dare you to enjoy yourself, if only *pour un moment.*"

"You think I'm incapable of enjoying myself?"

"I did not say that."

"Well, I'm not Dean . . ."

Dean had already found a rock. He rolled it up against the open door and, telling herself that Jacques' theory made a great deal of sense, Claire stepped over the threshold.

After a few moments of anticipatory silence, when neither the elevator nor the beach seemed affected, Jacques threw up his hands in triumph. "You see," he said, catching them again. "I am right."

Nearly body temperature, the water invited swimming, but both mortals contented themselves with tossing shoes and socks back into the elevator and wading through the shallow surf. Behind the open door, the beach rose up to become undulating dunes and finally a multihued green wall of jungle vegetation.

"Austin would love it here," Claire laughed, digging her toes into the sand. "It's the world's biggest litter bo . . . oh, my God! He'll be frantic!"

"I don't think it works that way."

Fighting to keep her balance in the loose footing, she whirled to glare at Dean. "What makes you such an expert?"

He held out his arm, watch crystal reflecting all the red and gold and orange in the sky. "The second hand hasn't moved since we got here."

"Oh, I see," she snarled, "time has stopped. Did it ever occur to you that it might be your watch?"

Crestfallen, he shook his head.

"Excusez-moi." Jacques' tone laid urgency over the polite form of the interruption. "Something happens in the water."

About twenty feet from shore, the waves had taken on a lumpy appearance. Bits of them seemed to be moving in ways contrary to the nature of water, rolling from side to side as they headed for the shore. Then the center hump of a wave kept rising past the crest, the mottled surface lifting up, up, until it became obvious, even staring into the sunset, that what they were watching wasn't water.

"If I didn't know better," Dean murmured, one hand shading his eyes, "I'd swear that was an octopus."

"Octopi do not come so big " Jacques protested weakly.

"Well, it's not a squid."

A tentacle, as thick as Dean's arm, broke through the surf no more than four feet from where they were standing.

"Octopi, regardless of size, don't come up on the shore," Claire announced as though daring the waving appendage to contradict her.

The twenty feet had become fifteen. Fourteen. Twelve. Ten.

"On the other hand," she added as a suckered arm fell short and gouged a trench in the sand at her feet, "I don't think this is an octopus either. RUN!"

Stumbling and falling in the loose sand, they raced for the elevator.

A tentacle slammed into Claire's hip, throwing her sideways into Dean. He caught her and held on, dragging her forward with him, her feet barely touching down.

From the water's edge came the sound of a large, wet, leather sack being smacked against the shore.

Unaffected by the footing, Jacques reached safety first, turned, and went nearly transparent. *"Depeche toi!"*

Gesture made his meaning plain.

Dean shoved Claire forward, over the threshold and bent to roll away the rock. A tentacle wrapped around his right leg but before it could tighten, he pulled free and stomped down hard. It might've been a more effective blow had he not been in bare feet, but it bought him enough time. He leaped inside, dragging the door closed with him.

Claire slammed the gate shut.

The deep blue/gray tip of a tentacle poked through the grill-work in the small window.

Wrapping sweaty hands around the lever, Dean yanked it right.

The floor joists nipped off an inch of rubbery flesh. When it dropped to the floor, Claire kicked it into the back corner and turned on Dean. "Why up?" she demanded, loudly enough to make herself heard over the pounding of her heart. "We came into this through the basement and that's very likely the only way we'll get out The basement is down!"

The floor of the elevator level with the second floor of the guest house, Dean locked the lever into its upright position. "I guess up just seemed more natural," he said. Grinning broadly, he sank down and reached for his shoes and socks. "Besides, we haven't seen what's on two or three."

Claire stared down at him in silence.

After a moment, one sock on, the other in his hand, he lifted his head. "What?"

"We haven't seen what's on two or three?"

The grin slipped. "Well, yeah."

She could see her reflection in his glasses. "Are you out of your mind?"

His brow furrowed. "We have to see what's on two and three. We can't quit now."

"Oh, yes, we can. We just got chased by a giant tentacled thing; that's quite enough excitement for one day."

After a moment, he shrugged. "You're the boss." Sighing, he pulled on his other sock.

"Do you believe him?" Claire asked Jacques, dusting the sand off her own feet. "He thought that was fun."

"Not fun," Dean protested. "Exciting."

"Dangerous," Claire corrected.

"But we all got away. We're all safe."

"We could have been eaten by something out of a bad Lovecraft pastiche!"

"But we weren't."

"Jacques." She turned to the ghost. "Help me out."

"He has a point, *cherie*. No one was hurt. And we are at the second floor. It would be a shame not to look."

Arms folded, she sagged back against the elevator wall. "There's just way too much testosterone in here."

"My watch seems to be working again, Boss."

"I'm thrilled."

Standing, Dean shot Jacques a "now what" glance, and received a "how the hell should I know" shrug in return.

"All right." Claire straightened. "A compromise. We'll look through the grille, but we won't actually open the door and we certainly won't join in the fun."

"Fun?"

"It's a figure of speech, Dean. Together on three so that we all see the same thing . . . one, two, three."

A familiar hallway stretched off in both directions, the doors to rooms one and two clearly visible.

"This is the second floor." Shoving up the gate, Claire pushed the door open and barely managed to stop herself from stepping out onto a familiar starship bridge.

"Make it so, Number One."

Slowly and quietly, she closed the door again. "And that wasn't."

"But what was it?" Jacques asked, peering out in some confusion at the second floor hall. "It was a military vessel?"

"It was an imaginary vessel, Jacques."

"What is an imaginary vessel? It is not real?" He shook his head. "But it was as real as the beach. And the not-a-squid."

"It was real here. And now. With the door open." The scene through the door remained the second floor. "But everywhere else, except on those occasions when it's a way of life, it's a television show."

Dean shook his head, as though trying to settle himself back into reality. "I could've walked out onto the real bridge of the starship. . . ."

"No." Claire reached out, intending to lock up, and found herself, instead, opening the door a crack. For one last look at the real bridge of the starship . . .

It looked like a balmy evening on top of Citadel Hill in downtown Halifax. Except for the two moons riding low in the sky and the woman in the distance with an agitated shrub on a leash.

Behind and above her right shoulder, Claire heard Dean murmur, "It changes every time you reopen the door."

"So the not-squid, it is gone? We could return to the beach?"

"Sure. Except the beach is gone."

Claire quietly eased the door shut, so as not to further agitate the shrub, and latched the gate. "All right," she sighed, her head falling forward until it rested against the fifty-year-old paint. "We're in this so far now we might as well see what's on the third floor. But . . ." Straightening, she folded her arms, turned, and fixed each of her companions with her best *I'm a Keeper and you're not* stare. ". . . no one gets out. Understand?"

"But what if . . ."

"I don't care. No one leaves the elevator."

Through the grille, it *was* the third floor. It even smelled like the third floor.

"Do you think that *she* might have an effect?" Jacques asked nervously as Claire locked back the gate.

"Do I think that proximity to *her* could affect the elevator's destination? I don't know, but I don't think so. Those are strong shields." A puff of noxious air wafted in as she opened the door and stared out at the piles of blasted rock and steaming lava pools. "And then again, I suppose it's possible that . . ."

A terrified shriek cut her off.

Dean pushed forward, allowing himself to be stopped by the flimsy barricade of Claire's arm only because he wasn't certain of where the sound had originated.

A second scream helped.

Off to the right, close to one of the steaming red pools, two large lizardlike creatures held a struggling shape between them, snapping and snarling at each other over their captive's head. While accumulated filth and long dreadlocks made guessing age difficult, they did *nothing* at all to hide the gender of what seemed to be a completely naked twelve- or thirteen-year-old boy.

Captured. About to be devoured. Pushing Claire aside, Dean leaped forward, the porous surface of the rock crunching under his work boots. He heard her yell his name, felt her grab at his shirt, and kept running, throwing, "Stay where you're at!" back over his shoulder.

With any luck she'd see that there was no sense them both going into danger. If he concentrated on speed rather than concealment, he'd could reach and rescue the kid before the two lizards finished quarreling over their catch.

The closer he got, the more the snarling began to seem like . . .

"Because it's my nesting site and I don't want the dirty little egg-sucker cooking right beside it. That's why!"

"So I have to carry it out of the nursery, all the way to cool ground? Is that it?"

"You caught it!"

"Crawling into your nest!"

"So now it's my nest, is it? And I suppose they'll be *my* hatchlings? *My* responsibility while you're off hunting with your friends."

. . . words.

And familiar words at that. Through a thick sibilant accent it sounded remarkably like an argument his Aunt Denise and Uncle Steve'd had about dispatching a rat caught live in the kitchen. Which didn't actually change anything.

"Our nest sweetie. I meant to say, *our* nest."

"You say that now. You don't mean it."

Through eyes beginning to water from the volcanic fumes, Dean noticed that the lizard with his aunt's lines was the larger by a significant margin. Sucking warm air through the filter of his teeth, he altered his path slightly so that he'd enter the smaller lizard's space.

The boy screamed again and lashed out with one filthy, callused heel. The smaller lizard howled and lost his grip. For a moment the boy twisted and kicked, dangling only a foot or so off the ground then, just as it seemed he might get free, the larger lizard grabbed his ankle with her other hand.

"Honestly. You can catch them, why can't you hold onto them?"

"It kicked me!"

"Stop acting like such a hatchling and remember you're about to be . . ." The lizard's amber eyes widened. "Behind you, Jurz! It's another one!"

Belatedly, Dean realized that the "other one" she was referring to was him. He realized it when Jurz, moving much faster on his bulky back legs than he'd expected, whirled around, pushed off with a thick tapering tail, and landed behind him, grabbing both his upper arms in a painful grip. He froze as talons pierced his shirt and punctured the skin. Even if he'd been able to turn, the lizard's body would have blocked his view of the elevator.

"Good gorg, Coriz, this one's huge!"

Coriz leaned forward and peered nearsightedly down at him, holding the boy tighter against her chest. "And it's a funny color."

Dean felt his hair being lifted by the force of Jurz' inhalation.

"And it's clean! Maybe," he added thoughtfully, "we could eat it."

"Eat it! Are you out of your mind?" Coriz sat back on her tail, shifting her hold on the boy. "It's still a filthy egg-sucker no matter how clean it is. People get sick from eating those vermin!"

"Hey!" The insult broke through the terror. "Who're you callin' vermin?"

Both lizards stiffened. The boy continued struggling.

"Look, this whole thing is a major misunderstanding." It took an effort to speak calmly with five small, painful holes in each arm, but Dean managed. Coriz stared at him—with no nose, nor eyebrows, nor lips to speak of, he couldn't read her expression, but he could feel the weight of Jurz' gaze on the top of his head. He obviously had their attention. All he had to do was stall until Claire arrived to save him. "Why don't we just talk this over. . . ."

"Talk?" Coriz squeaked and dropped the boy.

Who took off at a dead run, occasionally using his hands against the rock for better speed as he escaped.

"Talk?" she repeated, rearing back on her tail. "It TALKS?"

"Of course it doesn't talk," Jurz muttered nervously. "It's just making sounds, imitating speech."

Although he couldn't be positive, Dean thought the female lizard looked relieved. "No! You're wrong!" Struggling drove the talons in deeper. "I'm talking!"

They ignored him.

"Imitating speech, of course." Coriz sighed, the tension leaving her narrow shoulders.

"I'm not imitating . . ."

"Still, it does seem somehow more evolved than the others we've caught."

Jurz' grip shifted, poking new holes into his left arm. Without the talons filling the punctures, the originals began to dribble blood. "Do I kill it?"

"Of course you kill it."

"Hey!"

"Hopefully, it hasn't bred. Just imagine if the egg-suckers started to think." She shuddered. "They do enough damage to the nests now."

On cue came the horrible sound of smashing shells.

"MY BABIES!"

Jurz dropped Dean, smacked him toward the lava pit with his tail, and raced after his howling mate. Fortunately, he misjudged either the distance or the weight of the object he was attempting to sink.

Legs out over the pit, bottoms of his jeans beginning to scorch and his feet inside the steel toes of his workboots uncomfortably hot, hands abraded by the hardened lava, Dean stopped himself at the last possible instant. Rolling forward, he collapsed as flat as the terrain allowed, trying to catch his breath.

"Come on!" Claire knew she didn't have a hope of lifting Dean if he was actually injured, but that didn't stop her from grabbing at his arm and hauling upward. "Jacques isn't going to hold them for long." The fabric compacted warm and damp under her hands.

Sucking in an unwelcome lungful of air, Dean shook her off and, coughing, heaved himself up onto his feet. "Jacques?"

"He's dead. They can't hurt him." Claire gaped at the smear of red across her palms. "How bad is it?"

"Not bad."

"Can you run?"

He shoved his glasses back into place. "Sure. No problem."

Side by side they pounded back toward the elevator propelled by enraged howls and French Canadian invective.

Twenty feet from safety, Jacques caught up. "I have no smell," he explained, effortlessly keeping pace. "*Les lezards*, they count the eggs but that should not take them . . ."

The howls changed timbre.

". . . long."

When Dean stopped to roll a hunk of obsidian away from the door,

Claire hip-checked him over the threshold, grabbed the rock, and flung it toward their pursuers.

The howls changed again.

"OW! Coriz, they hit me with a rock!"

"Egg-suckers don't use weapons."

"But I've got a bump!"

The door cut off further diagnosis.

"What part," Claire gasped, dropping the gate into place and turning to glare at Dean, "of no one leaves the elevator did you not understand?"

"They were about to kill the kid."

"So? He was robbing their nest. Stealing their eggs. Making omelets."

"I couldn't just watch him die!"

"Then we should have closed the door."

"You don't mean that."

She did. Or she thought she did until she met his eyes and discovered that he believed she'd have gone to the rescue herself had he not been there. "Forget it. Go straight to the basement. No arguments."

Dean pushed the lever all the way to the left "No arguments," he agreed. Passing the second floor, he glanced over at Jacques. "Did you really break one of their eggs?"

"And how do I do that?" the ghost asked, pushing his hand through the wall of the elevator. "I touch nothing."

"I stomped on a bunch of shells that had already hatched," Claire explained. "Jacques stayed behind to distract them."

"Why didn't you . . ."

"Use magic? Because the possibilities were different there and, since you decided to play hero, I didn't have time to work out a way through. Look at me, I'm filthy. I had to lie down on that black stuff with my feet still in the elevator to reach a rock for the door, and if you ever pull such a stupid, boneheaded stunt again, I'm leaving you to cook in the lava pit! Do I make myself clear?"

Ears burning, Dean ducked his head. "Yes, Boss."

"When we reach bottom, I want a look at those arms."

"It's nothing." A drop of blood traced a trail over the back of his hand, down his index finger, and dripped onto the floor.

She glared at him through slitted eyes. "I'll be the judge of that."

"A glass of rum in the belly and one on the wounds. He will be fine, Claire."

"I have antibiotic cream in my bathroom," Dean offered hurriedly. "I can take care of it."

"Bring the cream to the dining room." As the bottom of the elevator settled into its concrete basin, Claire tossed up the gate, picked up the doily, and stomped out into the basement

"You stink like an active volcano," Austin complained, jumping down off a shelf. "Have a nice time?"

All three brushed by him without answering. Dean went into his apartment. Jacques followed Claire up the basement stairs.

"Guess not." He stuck his head over the threshold and sniffed at the bit of tentacle lying on the floor. His ears went back. "Who let the sushi out of the fridge?"

"So stoic," Jacques murmured sarcastically as Dean, sitting on the dining room table, tried not to jerk his arm out from under Claire's ministrations. "So much a man."

"Stuff a sock in it," Dean grunted.

"So articulate."

"Stop it. Both of you." Shirtless, Dean had pretty much lived up to Claire's expectations. Eyes locked on the wounds instead of the rippling expanse of bare chest, she dabbed antibiotic cream on the punctures and fought to keep her mind on the job. "None of these are deep. You were lucky. He could've ripped your whole arm off. Both arms." She was babbling. She knew it, but she couldn't seem to stop. "Ripped both your stupid arms off and thrown them on the ground." He not only looked great, he smelled terrific. Which had nothing to do with the matter at hand. Nothing at all. "You'd have bled to death before I could get to you. You could have been killed."

Jacques snickered. "Such a *magnifique* manner beside the bed, *cherie.*"

"I'm just saying," she began, and stopped. "I'm just saying," she repeated, "that I need him to run this hotel and . . ." If she hadn't looked up and seen Dean watching her, his expression teetering halfway between hope and disappointment, she could've left it at that. ". . . I've gotten used to having him around and I don't . . ." The end

of one finger covered in cream, she poked at the last three punctures.
". . . want him dead."

"Ow."

"Sorry."

"About what?" Austin asked, jumping up onto the table beside Dean. "And what happened to your arms? And, just out of curiosity, why don't you have any chest hair?"

While a blushing Dean shrugged into his shirt, Claire answered the first two questions.

"And the chest hair?" the cat prodded when she finished.

She picked him up and dropped him on the floor.

"You're just mad because I was right," he muttered as he jumped back up again. "I can see the sign now. This elevator holds a maximum of . . . How many dimensions?"

"That's not important."

"It will be to the elevator certification guys."

"I'll get some drywall and reseal the doors tomorrow," Dean offered.

"No." When three pairs of eyes locked on her, she shrugged. "I'd like to study it for a while, maybe I can fix it. It's perfectly safe if you all stay off it."

"And if *you* stay off it *cherie*."

"I know enough to stay in it."

"Penny for your thoughts?" Austin asked from the other pillow.

Claire rolled onto her side and stroked his head. "That only works if you hand me the penny," she reminded him.

"If I had hands . . ."

She smiled. "I was thinking about . . ." *How Jacques and I make a good team. How I felt when I saw Dean lying on the rocks. How one of them's too young and the other's too dead. How a Keeper should be able to keep her mind on the job even if it has been six months which is a bit of personal information relevant to absolutely nothing.* ". . . the elevator."

"Really?"

Why doesn't *Dean have any chest hair?* "Uh-huh."

"Liar."

ISN'T THAT OUR LINE?

TEN

B Y THE LAST SATURDAY IN OCTOBER, it was obvious that the seepage had been successfully contained. Hell had tried directing it, spreading it, and cutting it off completely; nothing worked. When a sudden cold snap drove Claire into the furnace room to adjust the heat, she found Hell hunkered down and sulking.

It continued to make personal appearances, however. As long as evil existed, Hell explained wearing Dean's face in Claire's mirror, personal temptation would be its stock in trade.

Cautious experimentation with the elevator determined that if the door was opened by someone outside in the hall, passengers could actually exit onto the desired floor. Seepage, or lack of it, affected neither the mechanical functioning nor the variety of destinations. As far as Claire could determine, the elevator had no actual connection to Hell and only a tenuous connection to reality.

But there *was* one unfortunate casualty of the seepage slowdown.

"I guess this'll be the next thing you'll get rid of," Austin sighed, perched on the silent bust of the king of rock and roll.

The sitting room, emptied to essentials, had a lobotomized look, as though all personality had been surgically removed. Stripped of their accessories, Augustus Smythe's florid, oversized furniture seemed self-consciously large.

Although she'd had every intention of removing the plaster head, Claire surrendered to the pale green stare making unsubtle demands from the top of the high-gloss pompadour. "If it means that much to you, it can stay."

"Will you start it up again?"

"No."

"You could adapt it to run off the middle of the possibilities."

"No."

"But . . ."

"I said, no. It'd be easier to go out and buy a complete set of CDs and a stereo." Either Augustus Smythe had taken his stereo with him when he'd abandoned the site, or, unlike most men, who tended to buy stereo equipment before unimportant things like groceries or clothing, he'd never owned one.

"If you're afraid of a bit of hard work. . . ."

"Don't start with me, Austin. Elvis has left the building." Before the cat could claw his way through her resolve, Claire turned on a heel and headed for the bedroom. The bust hadn't been the only amusement in Augustus Smythe's rooms to run on seepage. Grabbing the fringed curtain hanging over the postcard, she flung it open and barely managed to bite back a startled scream.

"What?" Diana twisted far enough to see that nothing particularly startling had slipped into the space behind her. When she saw that nothing had, she shrugged and directed her attention back out of the postcard. "You don't look so good, Claire. Maybe you ought to sit down."

Not really hearing her sister's suggestion, Claire staggered backward until she hit the edge of the bed and sat. "What are you *doing* in there?"

"Practicing postcards. Mom said you had one running so I thought I'd see if I could tap into it . . ."

Claire began breathing again. Diana's room had not been part of Augustus Smythe's dirty little picture gallery.

". . . that way you could see me, too, and I couldn't be accused of spying on you."

Theoretically, that wouldn't be possible; as a Keeper, Claire would know if she were under observation even by another Keeper. However, since Diana had just tapped into a powerless postcard with no apparent difficulty, something that Claire doubted she could have managed even with nearly ten extra years of experience, she wasn't about to declare it couldn't be done. So she did the next best thing: "You postcard me, and I'll rip your liver out and feed it to you."

Diana grinned. "As if. You think I'm stupid enough to get that close?"

"Speaking of close, when did you get back from the Philippines?"

"Last week. I landed in San Francisco, stuck my two cents into a site Michelle was dealing with by Berkeley, took Amtrak to Chicago, helped One Bruce seal two small sites—both of them in the middle of major intersections, can you believe it—and flew home from there. I can't wait until I get to do this stuff on my own."

Claire couldn't remember hearing about any earthquakes or train derailments, and since Chicago seemed to be functioning at least as well as it ever did, she breathed a sigh of relief. "What about school?"

"I'll catch up." Dropping into an ancient beanbag chair that she'd long outgrown but refused to get rid of, Diana leaned left until she had to brace herself against the floor, then repeated the movement to the right.

"What are you doing?"

The younger woman straightened. "I was trying to get a better angle on your room. Mom says Dean's a major babe, so I was looking for him."

"Mom said Dean was a major babe?"

"Not exactly; she said he was 'quite an attractive young man' and I translated."

"This is my *bedroom*."

Diana snorted. "So that's why you have a bed in it."

"I don't even want to know why you think Dean might be in here."

"Well, jeez, Claire, I hope I don't have to explain it to you. At your age." After a self-appreciative snicker, she crossed her legs and settled back until it looked as though she'd perched on the crushed remains of a red vinyl flower. "Go and get him, *please*."

Even through the postcard, Claire felt the pull of power her younger sister laid on the magic word. "No," she said, folding her arms. "I am not putting Dean on display to fulfill your prurient interests."

"Ooo, prurient. Big word. So are you guys getting it on?"

"Diana!" Righteous indignation propelled her onto her feet

"Dean's a nice guy who does most . . ." Diana's left eyebrow rose. There was as little point in lying to her as there would have been in her lying. ". . . almost all . . . okay, all of the work around here. A nice guy. Do you even know what that means?"

"Sure, I know. It means he's not getting any."

"Diana!"

"Relax, I'm just yanking your chain." Lips pursed, she made a disgusted face. "Man I hope I'm not as big a prude when I'm almost thirty. I told One Bruce and Michelle about you getting stuck on an unsealable site and they both said that Keepers are sent where they're needed. Not very helpful, I thought Anyway, since you're settled, I gave them both the phone number. They seemed to think that with you in one place and me still in training and us in contact because we're family, we have a chance to actually lay some lines of communication between Keepers. Which reminds me, the Apothecary is thinking of setting up as an online server so we can start using e-mail to stay in touch. Here we are, joining the twentieth century in time for the twenty-first."

Carrying on a conversation with Diana was often like shopping in a discount store: piles of topics crowded the aisles, stacked ceiling high in barely discernible order. The trick was pulling one single thing out to respond to. "The Apothecary doesn't even have electricity."

"I know. He says he can work around it. So what about you and this Jacques guy Mom mentioned?"

Claire sighed. "Jacques is dead."

"I know. But if the Apothecary can run e-mail without electricity . . ." She let her voice trail off but her eyebrows waggled suggestively up and down. "It sounds like what you really need is Jacques possessing Dean's body."

HELLO.

"That is never going to happen." Although Claire directed her response as much at Hell as at her sister, only her sister acknowledged it.

"I know."

"You know, you know, you know; you're beginning to sound like Austin."

Diana fixed Claire with an exasperated stare. "Keeping the peace, fulfilling destiny, that doesn't mean we can't be happy."

"I am as happy as I can be under the circumstances."

"Now who's sounding like Austin. What makes you think I'm talking about you?"

Claire winced. That had been incredibly insensitive of her. "I'm sorry, Diana. Did you have a problem you want me to help with?"

She grinned and shook her head. "No. But if you want, I'll come by and figure out how to deal with Sara, seal the pit, and get your butt on the road again."

"Diana!"

"Oh, chill, Claire." Dark brows dipped into a disdainful frown. "I'm five hundred and forty-one kilometers away, *she's* not going to hear me."

"Your butt is in a sling if she has!" Claire could feel nothing through the shield. Unfortunately, that only meant *she* hadn't yet gone through the shield. "If you'll excuse me, and even if you won't, I'm going to go check and see if you've started Armageddon." Ignoring protests, she closed the curtain with one hand and pulled at the neck of her cotton turtleneck with the other, telling herself that the room hadn't suddenly gotten warmer. She wasn't quite running as she crossed the sitting room.

"Can I assume you're not hurrying out to feed me?" Austin asked. "Who were you talking to?"

"Diana."

"Subverting a powerless postcard? Typical. What did she have to say for herself?"

"Nothing much. *Her* name. Out loud. Through a power link. If she's woken *her* up . . ."

Austin caught up to Claire at the door. "What are you going to do."

"Beats me. You know any good lullabies?"

Out in the lobby, Dean looked up from prying open a new gallon of paint as Keeper and cat raced for the stairs. "Problem, Boss?"

"I don't know."

"Need my help?"

Five weeks ago, even three weeks ago, she'd have snapped off an impatient "No." What good would a bystander be against a Keeper who'd attempted to control Hell? Today she paused and actually considered the possibilities before answering. "There's nothing you can do."

"Is it *her*?" Jacques asked, materializing as they started up the second flight of stairs.

"It could be," Claire panted, silently cursing the circumstances that made the elevator inoperative. It seemed to take forever to open the padlock, and the lack of noise from inside room six was surprisingly uncomforting.

The shield was intact. Aunt Sara lay, as she had, on the bed. The only footprints in the dust were Claire's, laid over her mother's, laid over her own and Dean's. She stepped forward, following the path, and studied the sleeping woman's face with narrowed eyes.

No change.

Sighing deeply, she took what felt like her first unconstricted breath since Diana had called Aunt Sara's name.

And sneezed.

Nose running, eyeballs beginning to itch, she backed out of the room and relocked the door.

"We are safe?" Jacques demanded from the top of the stairs. "*She sleeps?*"

"*She* sleeps," Claire reassured him, wiping her nose on a bit of old wadded-up tissue she'd found in the front pocket of her jeans.

"Admit it," Austin prodded as they started back downstairs, the ghost having gone on ahead to fill Dean in on the details, "you're a little disappointed."

Claire stopped dead and stared at the cat After a moment, she closed her mouth and hurried to catch up. "All right, that settles it. We're taking a break in the renovations. You've been sucking up too many paint fumes."

"You're not willing to wake her yourself," Austin continued. "But you'd love to know who'd win if you went head-to-head. Keeper to Keeper."

"You're out of your furry little mind."

"One final battle to settle this whole thing. Winner takes all."

"Get real."

"I can't help but notice that you're not making an actual statement of denial."

PRIDE IS ONE OF . . .

"Yours. So you've said."

HAS ANYONE EVER POINTED OUT THAT IT'S VERY
RUDE TO INTERRUPT LIKE THAT?

"Sorry."

USELESS APOLOGY. SINCERITY COUNTS.

"Get out of my head."

"Jacques told me what happened; is everything okay?" Dean asked
as they descended into the lobby.

"Austin's senile," Claire told him tightly. "But other than that
things seem to be fine."

He watched her walk down the hall toward the kitchen and shook
his head. "Once again," he sighed, "I'm left muddled." Stepping back,
he put his right foot squarely down in the paint tray.

Two things occurred to him as he watched the dark green pigment
soak into his work boot.

He hadn't left the paint tray there.

And he couldn't possibly have seen a five-inch-tall, lavender something diving behind the counter.

For the first Saturday since Claire'd begun handing out the money for
groceries, there was considerably more than seventy dollars in the
envelope. Dean whistled softly as she pulled out the wad and began
counting the bills.

"One hundred and forty, one hundred and sixty, one hundred and
eight-five dollars." Tossed back into the safe, the envelope landed with
non-paperlike clunk. "One hundred and eighty-six dollars," Claire corrected as she pulled a loonie out of the bottom corner.

"Premium cat food all around," Austin suggested from the top of
the computer monitor.

"You're getting a premium cat food."

"I'm not, it's geriatric. I don't care how much it costs, it's not the
same thing as that individual serving stuff they show on TV."

"And would you like it served in a crystal parfait dish, too?"

He sat up and looked interested. "It wouldn't hurt."

"Dream on."

"You're just mean, that's what you are." Lying down again, he pillowed his chin on his front paws. "Tempt me, taunt me, then feed me
the same old beef byproducts."

"If it isn't for Austin, what's it for?" Dean wondered. "We've got lots of food."

"Frozen and canned," Claire reminded him, handing over the money. "Maybe you're supposed to stock upon fresh."

He fanned the stack with his thumb. "This is gonna buy a lot of lettuce."

In the end, unable to shake the feeling that she needed to be involved, Claire decided to go with him. It would be strange to leave the hotel so soon after going out to buy the new keyboard—something most site-bound Keepers would not be able to do—but with Hell itself reinforcing the shield, what could go wrong?

Austin, when applied to for his opinion, yawned and said, "The future is unclear to me. I'm probably faint from a lack of decent food."

"What if I promise to bring you some shrimp snacks?"

He snorted. "Too little, too late."

"He'd tell me if he saw a problem," Claire assured Dean a few minutes later as she climbed into the passenger side of the truck. "He's too fond of being proven right not to."

Baby heralded their return two-and-a-half hours later with a deafening volley of barks and a potent bit of flatulence.

"Couldn't have a wind from the north," Claire muttered, staggering slightly under the weight of the grocery bags she carried. "Oh, no. Has to come up off the lake and right over the canine trumpet section. What *has* that dog been eating?"

"Well, we haven't seen Mrs. Abrams for a while," Dean pointed out, unlocking the back door.

"Yoo hoo! Colleen dear. Have you got a moment?"

Silently accusing Dean of invoking demons, Claire took a step back and smiled over the fence. "Not right now, Mrs. Abrams. I'd like to get all these groceries inside."

"Oh, my, you have bought out the stores, haven't you. Are you having a party?"

Since she asked in the tone of someone who expected to be invited should said party materialize, Claire was quite happy to answer in the negative.

One hand clutching closed her heavy sweater—a disturbing shade of orange a tone or two lighter than her hair—Mrs. Abrams eyed the bags with disapproval. "Well you surely can't be planning on eating all of that yourself. It's extremely important for a young woman to watch her weight, you know. I don't like to brag, but when I was young I had a twenty-two inch waist."

"I've really got to go put these things away, Mrs. Abra . . ."

"I only need a moment, dear. The groceries will keep. After all, this is business. A very close, personal friend of mine, Professor Robert Joseph Jackson—Maybe you've heard of him? No? I can't understand why not, he's very big in his field. Anyway, Professor Jackson is coming to Kingston on November third. He's so busy over Halloween, you know. I'd love to have him stay here, of course, but Baby has taken such a strange dislike to him." She beamed down at the big dog. "I told him that I knew the nicest little hotel and that it was right next door to me, and he said he'd be thrilled to stay with you."

Claire could feel the bag holding the glass bottle of extra virgin olive oil beginning to slip. "I'll be expecting him, Mrs. Abrams. Thank you for recommending us." Rude or not, she began moving toward the door.

"Oh, it was no trouble at all, Colleen dear. I'm just so happy to see that you've taken my advice and have begun fixing the old place up. It has such potential you know. I see that young man is still with you. So nice to see a young man willing to work."

"Isn't it," Claire agreed as Dean rescued two of her four bags. "Good day, Mrs. Abrams."

"Professor Jackson will need a quiet room, remember." The last word rose to near stratospheric volume as her audience stepped over the threshold and into the hotel. Dogs blocks away began to bark.

"I wonder if we're asking for trouble, renting a room to a friend of Mrs. Abrams."

Dean turned from putting the vacuum pack of feta cheese in the fridge as Claire set her bags down on the counter beside the others. "More trouble than a hole to Hell in the basement?"

"You may have a point."

"He may," Austin agreed, leaping from chair to countertop. "But fortunately his hair hides it. While you were out, a guy named Hermes Gruidae called. He's bringing a seniors' tour group through tonight, retired Olympians, and needs four double rooms and a single. I said there'd be no problem."

"Retired Olympians?" Dean fished a black olive out of a deli container and popped it in his mouth. "What sports?"

"He didn't say. He did mention that they're not very fond of restaurants and wondered if you could provide supper as well as tomorrow's breakfast. You being Dean in this case since I doubt they'd want beans and weiners on toast. I told him that would be fine. They'll be here about seven. Dinner at eight." He blinked. "What?"

Arms folded, Claire stared down at him suspiciously. "*You* took the message?"

"Please, I've been knocking receivers off hooks since I was a kitten."

"And you took Mr. Gruidae's reservation?"

"Well, I didn't write anything down if that's what you're asking although I did claw his name into the front counter."

"You what!"

"I'm kidding." Whiskers twitching, he climbed into one of the grocery bags. "Hey, where's my shrimp snacks?"

By six-forty-five the rooms had been prepared, the paint trays and drop cloths had been packed away, and Dean was in the kitchen taking the salmon steaks out of the marinade. Assuming that ex-Olympic athletes would be watching their weight, he'd also made a large Greek salad, and a kiwi flan for desert.

Wondering why she was so nervous, Claire checked the newly hunter green walls above the wainscoting in the stairwell and was relieved to discover that although they still smelled like fresh paint, they were dry. "Lucky for us that when Dean says he'll get to it first thing in the morning, he means predawn." Crossing over to the counter, she watched Austin race through a fast circuit of the office. "What's with you? Storm coming?"

"I don't know." He flung himself from the top of the desk to the top of the counter and skidded to a stop in front of Claire. "Something's coming." After three vigorous swipes of his tail, he added, "It feels sort of like a storm. Almost."

At six-fifty-two, a wide-bodied van of the type often used to shuttle travelers from airports to car rental lots parked in front of the hotel.

"Looks like they're here," Claire announced, moving toward the door.

Austin bounded to the floor and raced halfway up the first flight of stairs. "So's the storm."

"What are you talking about?"

His ears flattened against his skull. "Old . . ."

"Of course they're old, it's a seniors' tour." Adjusting her body temperature to counteract the evening chill, Claire went out to meet the driver as he emerged. He was a youngish man, late thirties maybe, wearing a brown corduroy jacket over a pair of khakis, one of those round white canvas hats that were so popular among the sort of people willing to pay forty-five dollars for a canvas hat, and a pair of brown leather loafers. With wings.

"I have them taken off the sandals every fall," he told her, noticing the direction of her gaze. "I don't know what I hate more, cold feet or sandals and socks." He held out a tanned hand. "Hermes Gruidae; the second bit was assumed for the sake of a driver's license. You must be Claire Hansen. I believe I spoke to your cat about our reservations."

"He's not *my* cat," was the only thing Claire could manage to say.

"No. Of course not." Hermes looked appalled. "I wasn't implying ownership, merely that it was a cat I spoke to."

"Uh, right I just came out to tell you that there aren't any stairs around back if you want to let your people off in the parking lot instead of out here."

"Not a bad idea, but I don't think you could get them to use a back door." He winced as an imperious voice demanded to know the reason for the delay. "They're a rather difficult bunch actually."

The voice had been speaking flawless Classical Greek—although Claire spoke only English and bad grade school French, Keepers were language receptive, it being more important in their job to understand than to be understood. "Retired Olympians," she muttered, examining the words from a new angle. "Oh, God."

"Gods, actually," Hermes corrected, sounding resigned. He hustled back out of the way as an elderly man in a plaid blazer stomped down onto the sidewalk.

"You listen to me, Hermes, I'm not spending another moment sitting in that . . . Hel-lo." Smiling broadly, he stepped toward Claire, arms held out. "And who is this fair maiden?" he asked in equally flawless English, capturing her hand. "Surely not Helen back again to destroy us with her beauty."

"Not fair and not a maiden!" snapped a woman's voice from inside the van. "Keep your hands to yourself, you old goat. Get back here and help me out of this thing."

Belatedly Claire realized that her fingers were being thoroughly kissed and an arm had slipped around her waist, one liver-spotted hand damply clutching her hip.

"Zeus! I'm warning you . . . !"

Silently mouthing, "Later," Zeus gave her one final squeeze and returned to the van.

Objectively, the Lord of Olympus was shorter than Claire would have expected him to be, had she actually spent any time thinking about it, and someone should have mentioned that the white belt and shoe ensemble wasn't worn north of the Carolinas after Labor Day. He'd been handsome once, but over two millennia of rich food and carnal exercise had left the square jaw jowly under the short curly beard, the dark eyes deep-set and rimmed with pink over purple pouches, and his Grecian Formula hair artfully combed to hide as much scalp as possible. An expensive camera bounced just above the broad curve of his belly, the strap hidden in the folds of his neck.

And if that was Zeus . . .

Hera, clawlike hand clutching her husband's arm, reminded Claire of an ex-First Lady from the American side of the border. Her skin stretched tight over the bones of her face, her makeup applied with more artifice than art, she looked as though a solid blow would shatter her into a million irritated pieces. "The Elysian Fields Guest House? Honestly, Hermes, is this the best you could do?"

"It's the best for our needs," Hermes told her soothingly.

Claire found herself being examined by bright, birdlike eyes behind a raised lorgnette.

"Oh, a Keeper," Hera sniffed. "I see."

The second man out of the van paused to stretch, both hands in the small of his back. Incredibly thin and still tall in spite of stooped

shoulders, he was dressed all in black—jacket, shirt, pants, shoes—
with a crimson ascot at his throat. A hawklike hook of a nose made
even more prominent by the cadaverous cheeks completely overwhelmed his face although a neatly trimmed silver goatee and full
head of silver hair did what they could to balance things out.

A tiny white-haired woman in a lavender pantsuit draped in a multitude of pastel scarves followed him out "Oh, look. Hades!" Wide-
eyed, she pointed gracefully toward the eaves of the hotel. "A white
pigeon! It's an omen."

Hades obligingly looked.

The pigeon plummeted earthward, hitting the ground with a distinct splat.

"Did I do that?" Hades asked. "I didn't mean to."

"Senile old fool," Hera muttered, pushing past him.

"Never mind, dear." On her toes, Persephone rubbed her cheek
against his shoulder. "Next time, just don't look so hard." Capturing a
scarf as it slid out from under a heavy gold brooch, she fluttered ring-
covered fingers around her body. "Oh, dear. I've forgotten my knitting."

"Never mind, Sephe. I've brought it out for you."

Claire had no idea who the woman handing Persephone her knitting bag might be. Running over the remaining goddesses in her head
offered no clues. Pleasant looking, in the sensible clothes favored by
elderly English birdwatchers, she reminded Claire of a retired teacher
pulled back into duty and near the end of her rope.

As though aware of Claire's dilemma, she walked over and held
out her hand. "Hello. You must be our host. I'm Amphitrite."

Her palm was damp and felt slightly scaly. "Pleased to meet you."

"She's Poseidon's wife," Persephone caroled. "Unless you're into
those boring old classics, you've probably never heard of her."

"Shape-shifter's daughter," Hera sniffed in classical Greek.

"Hera." Persephone danced toward her, diamond earrings catching the light from the street lamp. "The eerperkay nunderstandsay
reekgay."

Hera stared at the Queen of the Dead. "You are pathetic," she said
after a moment.

"Who's pathetic?" Poseidon's gray hair and beard flowed in soft ripples over his greenish-gray tweed suit. He blinked owlishly around at the gathered company through green-tinted glasses, waiting for an answer. "Well?" he said after a moment.

Amphitrite took his hand and led him away from the van, murmuring into his ear.

"Well, of course she is," Poseidon snorted. "Inbreeding, don't you know."

"Excuse me?" Knees up around his ears, Hades squatted by the pigeon's body. "This bird is dead."

Claire saw acute embarrassment in Hermes' eyes as he sagged back against the van's side and she hastily hid a smile, remembering that these relics weren't only his responsibility—they were also his relatives.

Next in the open door was a man with a short buzz of steel-gray hair over his ears, a broad, tanned face with an old scar puckering one cheek, and the stocky rectangular build of someone who'd spent a lifetime doing hard physical labor. He swung forward on a pair of canes—Claire assumed they were aluminum until she heard the sound they made as they hit the concrete sidewalk. Steel. Uncapped—and swung himself out after them. "Dytie," he bellowed over a broad shoulder, "are you coming?"

"No darlin', just breathing hard," laughed a voice from the dark interior of the van.

The assembled company sighed, unified in resignation.

Aphrodite? Claire mouthed at Hermes. He nodded. Which made the man with the canes Hephaestus.

The goddess of love had filled out a bit since the old days. The hair was still a mass of ebony curls, piled high, and the eyes were still violet under lashes so long they cast shadows on the curve of pale cheeks although the cheeks had more curves than they once did and the tiny point of the goddess' chin nestled in a soft bed of rounded flesh. Although tightly bound into an approximation of her old shape, it was obvious that within the reinforced Lycra Aphrodite's body had returned to its fertility goddess roots.

Men could get lost in that cleavage, Claire thought. *Come to think of it, men have.*

"Hermes, darling, it's a lovely little hotel I can't wait to see the inside."

"You can't wait to see the inside of a hotel?" Hera rolled her eyes. "What a surprise."

"Bitch."

"Slut."

Sighing deeply, Hermes indicated that Claire should lead the way. Feeling a little like the pied piper, she started up the stairs.

The retired Olympians followed.

"Hades dear, do leave the pigeon where it is."

Claire had no idea how Hermes did it, but he managed to get them all into their rooms by seven-twenty with the promise that their luggage would follow immediately. Since Dean was still cooking, Claire went back outside to help.

"Small pocket in the space-time continuum," Hermes explained as her jaw dropped at the growing pile of suitcases, trunks, and garment bags covering the sidewalk. "Aphrodite travels with more clothing than Ginger took on that three-hour cruise, Hera uses her own bed linens, Persephone has more jewelry than the British royal family, and Poseidon always packs a couple dozen extra towels."

"It'll take forever to get all this stuff upstairs."

"Not hardly." He grinned. "After all, quick delivery is my middle name. If you'd be so kind as to keep an eye open for the neighbors . . ."

Since the only neighbor likely to be watching seemed to have deserted her post, Claire gave the all clear. Hair lifted off her forearms as Hermes twisted the possibilities and the luggage disappeared.

"Still a few perks left," he said with quiet satisfaction. "Thanks for your help. I'll just run the van around to the parking lot."

Wondering how much help she could've been, Claire went back inside.

"So," Austin asked from the countertop. "What are you going to tell Dean?"

"About what?"

"The ex-athletes he's expecting."

"Do you think he can handle the truth?"

The cat paused to wash a back leg. "Better that you tell him than he finds out the hard way. And if that lot's staying here so they can be themselves, he will find out." Peering at the floor, one paw braced against the side of the counter, he glanced up at Claire. "You know, a really nice person would lift me off here and keep me from straining old bones."

Claire scooped him into her arms and headed for the kitchen. "Hades killed a pigeon just by looking at it. I suppose Dean should be warned."

"You suppose? He should?" Austin snorted. "If you're tired of having him around, wouldn't it be easier just to fire him?"

"I am *not* tired of having him around. I'm just not looking forward to explaining something he has no frame of reference for. You have to admit that not many kids get a classical education these days."

"You want him to get a classical education? Wait'll Aphrodite gets a look at him."

When they got to the dining room, they found Hermes leaning over the counter inhaling appreciatively. "I hope you don't mind," he said as they approached, "but I've introduced myself to Dean and explained a bit of the situation."

"Really?" The counter was covered in food, so Claire set the cat down on the floor. He shot her an indignant look and stalked away. "Which bits?"

Recognizing her tone, Dean hurriedly turned from the stove. "Mr. Gruidae . . ."

"Please; Hermes."

". . . explained that the guests aren't actually ex-athletes but from a place called Mount Olympus. In Greece."

"And this means to you?" Claire asked.

Dean sighed, clearly disappointed. "That none of them knew Fred Hayward. He was an old buddy of my granddad's who was on the Canadian hockey team at the Olympics in 1952. Great guy. He died in 1988 and I just, well, you know, wondered."

Claire exchanged a speaking glance with the messenger of the gods, picked up a stack of plates and began setting the table. "Dean, do the names Zeus and Hera mean anything to you?"

"Sure. I watch TV. I mean, they're kids' shows, but they're fun."

Hermes looked so distraught, Claire pushed him into a chair and attempted to convince Dean that there were distinct differences between television gods and real ones—even after retirement—and that if he didn't keep those differences in mind, it was going to be an interesting meal.

"So retired Olympians meant a bunch of old Greek Gods? The real ones?"

"Some of them, yes." She grabbed a handful of cutlery.

"Like in myths and stuff?"

"Post-myth but essentially, yes."

"Forks go on the left."

"I know that."

Holding a baking sheet of potato wedges roasted with lemon and dill, Dean turned and looked thoughtfully down at Hermes. "You're the guy on the flower delivery vans and stuff? The real guy?"

Hermes smiled and spread his hands. "Guilty."

"How come you're taking these retired gods on this road trip, then? Aren't you retired, too?"

"To answer your second question first: not as long as I remain on those flower delivery vans. As for the first bit, they were bored and I'm also responsible for treaties, commerce, and travelers. In the interest of keeping peace in the family, I try to get some of them out every year. This year, we've just finished a color tour of Northern Ontario. Zeus took a million pictures, most of them overexposed, and any leaves that weren't dead when we arrived were as soon as Hades finished admiring them. Now, if you'll excuse me . . ." He stood and twitched at the creases in the front of his khakis. ". . . I'd best wash the road dirt off before supper."

"Hermes."

One step from the door, his name stopped him cold.

Claire stepped in front of him and held out her hand. "Before you go, maybe you'd like to return the butter knife you slipped up your sleeve."

"That I slipped up my sleeve?" He drew himself up to his full height, the picture of affronted dignity. "Do you know who you're talking to, Keeper?"

"Yes." The missing knife flew out of his cuff and landed on her palm. "The God of Thieves."

❖   ❖   ❖

Hades and Persephone were first down for dinner. Trailing half a dozen multicolored gossamer scarves, white hair swept up and held by golden combs, Persephone appeared in the dining room as though she were entering, stage right, and announced, "It feels so nice and homey to have an attendant spirit, doesn't it, dear?"

Murmuring a vaguely affirmative reply, Hades came in behind her, brushing the ends of scarves out of his way.

Behind the Lord of the Dead, looking perturbed, came Jacques. As god and goddess took their seats, he wafted over to the kitchen. "I am not a servant," he muttered as Claire folded napkins down over the baskets of fresh garlic buns. "Pick this up, put that there. . . . Who does she think she is?"

"The Queen of the Dead," Claire told him. "Not that it matters, you're noncorporeal, you can't touch anything."

"The things they have, I can touch. And also, I cannot leave them. I come when she calls. Like a dog."

"Jacques, get that scarf for me."

"What do I say? I am to fetch, like a dog."

"Jacques, do hurry, it's on the floor."

He paused, halfway through the counter and turned a petulant expression on Claire. "For this, I deserve a night of flesh."

Claire shook her head in sympathy as the goddess called for him a third time. "Perhaps you're right."

"I am?"

"Jacques, my scarf!"

"Is he?" Dean asked, glancing up from the salmon steaks and watching Jacques fly across the room with narrowed eyes.

Claire shrugged. "I said perhaps. He's stuck working for them, I just wanted to make him feel better about it."

He waved the spatula. "*I'm* working for them."

"Yes, but you get paid."

With his face toward the stove, she almost missed him saying, "I could be made to feel better about it"

All at once she understood. "This is the night you go out drinking with your friends from home, isn't it? And I never even thought to ask you if you'd mind staying here, I just assumed." This dinner had nothing to do with lineage business, and she had no right to commandeer a bystander's support. "I'm sorry. There'll be a little extra in your pay this week."

He looked up, turned toward her, flushed slightly, and after a moment said, "That wasn't what I meant."

Afraid she'd missed something, Claire never got the chance to ask.

"Sexual tensions," Aphrodite caroled from the doorway. "How I do love sexual tensions."

"*Not* at the dinner table," Hera snarled, pushing past

"Fish." Dripping slightly, Poseidon wandered into the kitchen and peered nearsightedly down at the platter of salmon. "Finally, an edible meal." He straightened and blinked rheumy eyes in Claire's general direction. Fingers of both hands making pincer movements he moved closer. "Wanna do the lobster dance? Pinchy, pinchy."

"No. She doesn't." Still holding the spatula, Dean moved to intercept. He didn't care who the old geezer was, a couple of his granddad's friends had been dirty old men and the only defense was a strong offense. The God of the Oceans bumped up against his chest.

"Ow."

"Serves you right." Aphrodite pulled her husband from the kitchen and steered him toward his chair. "You promised you'd behave."

"My nose hurts."

"Good."

When all the gods but Zeus had assembled, Hermes cleared his throat and gestured toward the entry into the dining room, announcing, "The Lord of Olympus!"

"Where'd the trumpet fanfare come from?" Dean murmured into Claire's ear.

Claire shrugged, an answer to both the question and the gentle lapping of warm breath against her neck.

Striding into the room like a small-town politician, Zeus clapped shoulders and paid effusive compliments as he circled the table. The recipients looked sulky, senile, or indifferent, depending on temperament and number of functioning brain cells. Finally settling into his seat at the head of the table, he lifted his sherry glass of prune nectar and tossed it back.

With the meal officially begun, everyone began buttering buns and helping themselves to salad.

"Stupid, irritating ritual," Hephaestus muttered as Claire set his plate in front of him.

"If it makes him happy," Hermes cautioned.

"What's he going to do to me if he's unhappy, run over me with that domestic hunk of junk you're driving?" The God of the Forge smiled tightly and answered himself. "Not unless he wants to trust to secular mechanics the next time it breaks down."

"It's so pleasant to be ourselves," Amphitrite said quickly as Zeus frowned down the table. "But shouldn't you be eating with us, Keeper?"

Claire had already been over this with Dean. "As guests of the hotel, you're my responsibility. Besides, Dean did all the cooking."

"And it looks like a lovely meal. I find men who cook so . . . ." Aphrodite's pause dripped with innuendo. ". . . intriguing."

"You find men who breathe intriguing," Hera muttered

"Harpy.".

"Flotsam."

"More nectar?" Claire asked.

"I thought dinner went well," Austin observed, climbing onto Claire's lap. "Everyone survived."

"You have salmon on your breath."

He licked his whiskers. "And your point is?"

"Pick it up. Put it down. She drops a stitch in that infernal knitting and I must pick it up for her. If I were not already dead, that woman would drive me to chop off my own head." Jacques collapsed weightlessly down on the sofa beside Claire. "I thought that you should know, His Majesty, the Lord of the Dead, is downstairs talking to Hell and Her majesty wants him to come to bed. She is getting—How do you say?—impatient?"

". . . them to sit down and they did, but what they didn't know was that I'd shown them to the Chair of Forgetfulness and they couldn't get up again because uh, they, uh . . . Who was I talking about?"

THESEUS AND PIRITHOUS.

"I was?"

YES.

"Oh. They weren't the ones with the pomegranate seeds?"

NO.

"Are you sure? There was something about pomegranate seeds."

THE LADY PERSEPHONE ATE SEVEN POMEGRANATE SEEDS AND HAD TO REMAIN WITH YOU IN TARTARUS FOR PART OF THE YEAR.

"No, that wasn't it."

YES, IT WAS.

Hades' voice brightened. "Do you know my wife?"

Listening at the top of the stairs, Claire was tempted to leave Hades right where he was. Another hour or two of conversation and Hell would seal itself. Unfortunately, there was an impatient goddess in room two. Fortunately, it took very little to convince Hades, who'd forgotten where he was, to return to her.

KEEPER?

Almost to the door, herding the Lord of the Dead up the stairs in front of her, Claire paused. "What?"

IF WE WERE CAPABLE OF GRATITUDE . . .

"I didn't do it for you."

NEVERTHELESS.

Backed up against the dishwasher, the goddess of love so close he could see her image in the reflection of his glasses in her eyes, Dean had no easy out. The room started to spin, beads of sweat formed along his spine, and he knew that in a moment he'd do something he'd be embarrassed about for the rest of his life. He wasn't entirely sure what that was likely to be, but it certainly appeared that Aphrodite had a very good idea. Taking a deep breath, he dropped his shoulder, faked right, and moved left.

Fortunately, Aphrodite's corseting insured that her reach impeded her grasp.

Distance helped. With the length of the kitchen between them, he began to regain his equilibrium although his jeans were still uncomfortably tight "The decaf's in the pot on the counter there, ma'am. Help yourself."

Tipping her cleavage forward, the goddess smiled. "You going to sweeten it for me, sugar?"

He pushed the sugar bowl toward her.

Her fingers lingered on his as she picked it up, and her expression segued from seductive to delighted. "Why, you're just a big old . . ."

"Dytie!" Even from the second floor landing, Hephaestus' voice carried. "Are you bothering that boy?"

"Why, yes, I do believe I am."

"Well, stop it and come to bed!"

To Dean's relief, she picked up her cup and turned to go, tossing a provocative, "Pleasant dreams, honeycake," in his general direction. He had an uncomfortable feeling it wasn't merely a suggestion.

Coming back downstairs from returning Hades to his wife, Claire stepped aside to let Aphrodite pass.

"You know, Keeper," the goddess said, leaning close, "that boy of yours is a treasure."

"Dean's not mine."

"Sure he is. Or he could be if you gave him a little bitsy bit of encouragement."

"Encouragement?"

"You're right." She patted Claire on the shoulder with one plump hand. "He won't understand subtle. Kick his feet out from under him and beat him to the floor."

"Dytie! You coming?"

"Not yet darlin', and don't you start without me." Adding a quiet "You remember what I said," she sashayed on past and Claire descended the rest of the way to the lobby.

Hearing noises in the kitchen, she hurried down the hall. It could be a god getting a late night snack, but on the other hand, it could also be a god attempting a senile manifestation of ancient eldritch powers with catastrophic results. The odds were about equal.

"Oh. It's you."

Dean closed the dishwasher and straightened. "I couldn't sleep without putting the dishes away."

"Kick his feet out from under him and beat him to the floor."

"Boss? You okay?"

She blinked and started breathing again. "Sorry. Just thinking of something Aphrodite said."

His ears turned scarlet.

"That boy of yours is a treasure."

"Are *you* okay? She didn't . . . well, you know."

To her surprise, his blush faded. "Would you care?" he asked, meeting her gaze.

"Of course I'd care. While you're under this roof, you're my responsibility and she's . . . well, she's a little overpowering. You wouldn't have much choice. Any choice."

"I'm not a kid," he said quietly, squaring his shoulders.

"I know that."

"Okay." Eyes on his shoes, Dean moved toward the basement stairs. "I'm done here."

"Lock your door."

He paused and stared back at her, his expression unreadable. "Sure."

Confused, Claire went to her own rooms, hoping that Jacques had been released from his attendance on Persephone. The way she was feeling, if he pushed her tonight . . .

Unfortunately, or perhaps fortunately since she knew she'd regret it in the morning, Jacques' nightly petition had been preempted by a goddess.

Dean had a suspicion that a locked door would stop no one in the hotel except him. He locked his anyway.

Right about now, down at the Portsmouth, Bobby would be attempting to wrest control of the jukebox away from the inevitable crowd of country-western types. He'd be unsuccessful, and Karen would have to go over. They'd have finished talking about the news from home and begun making plans to go back. Mike would be suggesting Colin'd had enough to drink and Colin'd be telling Mike to mind his own business.

The same thing happened every Saturday night.

Lying on his bed and staring up at the ceiling, Dean realized Claire hadn't actually asked him to stay and cook dinner. They'd both simply assumed he would because it needed to be done.

That seemed to make him more than a mere employee.

What would Aphrodite have done if he hadn't moved?

As more than a mere employee, did that give him . . .

Would she have done it right there in the kitchen?

. . . a chance to talk with Claire as an equal or would that whole Keeper thing . . .

So she was a bit older, but she was a goddess. She was probably a lot more flexible than she looked.

Claire was a bit older, too. . . .

"Okay. That's it." That was as far as those trains of thought were merging. Closing his eyes, he resolutely counted sheep until sleep claimed him.

Next door, in the furnace room, Hell sighed.

"Claire. Claire, wake up."

Pushing Austin's paw away from her face, Claire grunted, "What is it?" without actually opening her eyes.

"I just thought you ought to know there's a swan in your bathroom."

"A swan?"

"A really old swan."

"I am not going to sleep with you for a multitude of reasons, but for now, let's just deal with the first two." She flicked a finger into the air. "One, I am not even slightly attracted to poultry." A second finger rose. "And two, you're married."

"Hera's sound asleep." Shaking off his feathers, Zeus stepped out of the bathtub; chest out, stomach sucked in over skinny legs. "We're perfectly safe if no one wakes her up, and no one's going to wake her up."

Eyes closed, Claire missed seeing an orange something with yellow highlights speed out from under the sink and disappear through the open bathroom door. She groped for a towel and held a terry cloth bath sheet out in Zeus' general direction. "Here. Cover up."

When she felt him take it, she opened her eyes. Wrapped around his waist, the towel was a small improvement.

Leaning toward her, Zeus leered. "Would you prefer a shower of gold?"

"No."

"An eagle?"

"No."

"A satyr?"

"No."

"A white bull?"

"I said no."

"An ant?"

"You're kidding."

"Eurymedusa, daughter of Cleitus, bore me a son named Myrmidon when I seduced her in the form of an ant."

"Must've been some ant."

"Ant it is, then." Before Claire could stop him, his features twisted, his eyes briefly faceted, and a hair from each eyebrow grew about three feet. Panting, he collapsed against the vanity. "On second thought . . ." His right clutching his chest, he flung out his left arm, the flesh between elbow and armpit swaying gently. ". . . take me as I am."

Claire sighed. "Out of respect for your age and your mythology, I don't want to hurt you, but if you don't get out of my bathroom and go back to your own bed, you're going to be very sorry."

"I could call down the lightning for you," Zeus offered, continuing to support his weight on the sink. "And with any luck it'll strike more than once. Wink, wink, nudge . . ." The second nudge remained unvoiced as a violent banging on the door to Claire's suite cut him off.

"Open this door right now, you tramp! I know you've got my husband in there!"

Zeus paled. "It's Hera."

"What was your first clue?" Claire snapped, furious that the Lord of Olympus had involved her in such a humiliating situation. "I'll stall her, you get back to your own room."

"How? She's right outside the door."

"How did you get into my tub?"

His face brightened. "The tub. Right." Staggering back to it, he stepped inside and pulled the shower curtain closed. "I'll hide in here. You get rid of her."

Claire yanked the shower curtain open. "I meant that you should disappear the same way you appeared."

"I can't."

"You can't?"

"I'm old. Do you have any idea how much effort that took?" His lower lip went out in a classic pout. "Not that you appreciated it."

"Keeper, I'm warning you!" Mere wood and plaster did little to hinder Hera's volume. "Open this door, or I'll blow it off its hinges!"

"Can she?" Claire demanded.

Zeus shrugged. "Probably not."

"All right. I've had enough. Get out of there."

"But . . ."

"Now."

Muttering under his breath, the god obeyed.

Once he stood squarely on the bath mat, Claire grabbed his wrist and dragged him, mat and all, toward her sitting room.

"Where are we going?"

"We're going to explain this whole mess to your wife." Working one-handed, she released the wards around the sitting-room door. "This is your problem, not mine."

Zeus winced. "Actually, Keeper, if you've studied the classics, you'll know that's not how it usually . . ."

The door crashed open.

Framed in the doorway, her eyes blazing, Hera shook her hands free of the feathers trimming the sleeves of her peignoir and pointed a trembling finger at Claire. "I knew it, another one who can't keep her hands off him!"

"That's not . . ."

"Well, I know how to deal with you, you hussy, don't for a moment think that I don't!"

"Hera, I was asleep. I found him in my bathroom."

The goddess' lips thinned to invisibility. "That's what they all say."

"It's the truth."

"Ha!"

Claire could feel the possibilities expanding in unfamiliar ways. Yanking Zeus another couple of feet forward, she thrust him toward his wife. "Tell her!"

"I'm so sorry, my little myrtle leaf." Clutching the towel, he scuttled to Hera's side. "I was lured!"

"Shut up, you old goat I'll deal with you later. But for now . . ." The finger still pointing at Claire began to tremble. ". . . we'll see how many husbands you seduce as a linden tree!"

The world twisted sideways.

When Claire could see again, everything seemed strangely two-dimensional. And green. By concentrating on where her neck should be, she lowered her head and took a look at her body. She wasn't a linden tree. She rather thought she was a dieffenbachia. And pot-bound at that.

"Isn't that a house plant, ray love?"

"Shut up," Hera snarled. "I know what it is."

How dare she! Claire thought, leaves rustling. *How dare she assume that I would ever have anything to do with that dirty old man!*

A number of white flies with glowing red eyes, settled down on her stem. ANGER IS ONE OF OURS.

I know *that.* Carefully reaching toward the middle of the possibilities, Claire began to pull power. When she regained her own body, she was going to . . .

REVENGE IS ALSO ONE OF OURS.

Who asked you? Vaguely aware of a vibration in her fake terracotta pot, Claire swiveled her stem toward the doorway as Austin and Hermes pounded into the sitting room. *Oh, great. An audience. How much more embarrassing can this get?*

Hermes took one look at Claire and whirled to face Zeus. "Dad! What have you done?"

"It wasn't me."

"It's always you!"

More vibration. Heavier, mortal footprints. *Well, I guess that answers my previous question.* She needed watering and that made it difficult to concentrate but she tried to pull power faster before anyone else showed up to see her like this.

"Boss? I heard shouting. Are you all right?" Wearing his jeans, his glasses, and not much else, Dean looked around at the assembled company, eyes widening when he took in Zeus' equivalent state of undress. "Where's Claire?"

"Down here." Austin rubbed against her pot.

"She's shrunk, then?"

"She's a plant."

What are you looking at me for? Claire wondered. When he tried to touch a leaf, she snatched it away from his fingers.

He straightened. "Why?"

"Because my father," Hermes answered, "can't keep his withered old pecker in his pants."

"Here now, a little respect," Zeus began, but when he saw the expression on Dean's face, his voice trailed off and he sidled over behind Hera.

Weight forward on the balls of his feet, Dean brought his hands up, fingers not quite fists. "Change her back."

Hermes sighed. "As attractive as all that flexing is, it's not going to get you anywhere. At least not right now," he amended, glancing over at his father and Hera. "Let me deal with this." Adjusting the belt of his bathrobe, he fixed the Goddess of Marriage with a steely glare. "Try to remember this isn't some mortal or nymph you're unjustly accusing here. Even in a vegetative state, this is a Keeper. Eventually, she'll change herself back."

Hera sniffed. "I don't believe you."

"Then believe the cat. Would he be so calm if Claire's form were dependent on your whim?"

Austin yawned.

"Dean." Hermes turned around, came face to muscle with Dean's chest and took a moment to reengage cognitive faculties. "You know Claire better than I do. How do you think she feels about all this?"

"About being a plant?"

"Yes. Do you think she'll be angry when she's herself again."

"Oh, yeah."

Hermes shifted his attention to the goddess. "Change her back, Hera. Or you're going to have to deal with an angry Keeper."

"What can she do?"

"She can confine everyone to Olympus. For all the years of her life, it'll be nothing but shuffleboard, listening to Ares screw up the plots of old war movies, and actually looking forward to the night the Valkyrie come by for choral singing."

The goddess folded her arms. "So what."

Austin stretched and stood. "She can also cancel your cable."

Round circles of rouge stood out against suddenly pale skin.

"She didn't know what she was doing, lambie-kins." Zeus reached out a tentative hand and patted his wife's arm. "Change her back. For me."

"For you?" Penciled brows drew in, wrinkles falling into their accustomed place. "All right. Since you got her into this, I'll change her back for *you.*"

He started for the door.

Hera grabbed the two, three-foot eyebrow hairs and yanked him back to her side, her other hand gesturing toward Claire.

The world didn't so much twist as flicker.

Fortunately, Claire had already pulled nearly enough power to effect the change on her own. Using the path Hera had opened, she stretched, straightened, and felt her lips draw back off her teeth. She couldn't remember ever being so angry.

Hell's silence stopped her after a single step. She could feel how much it was enjoying itself at her expense. Breathing heavily, she smoothed her pajamas and forced a smile. "Thank you for your intervention, Hermes. Now go to bed. All of you."

YOU STILL WANT TO SMASH THEM.

"Extra points for overcoming temptation," Claire told it. When the ex-Olympians hesitated, she added, "I'm going to try to forget this ever happened."

"Not very convincing," Hera muttered.

"Best you're going to get," Claire told her through clenched teeth.

The goddess nodded and, still holding Zeus' eyebrow hairs, headed for the stairs.

"Ow! Honeybunch, that hurts. . . ."

Hermes bowed slightly and followed.

Only Dean remained.

She had her hand raised to remove the humiliating memory from his mind when he asked, "Are you okay, Boss?" and she realized that was all that mattered to him. He didn't care that she'd been a plant as long as she was all right now.

But there were one or two things they still had to be clear on.

"I *didn't* invite Zeus in."

"Okay."

"He just appeared in my bathtub. As a swan."

Dean looked appalled. "I'll scour the tub tomorrow."

"I could have gotten rid of him on my own if Hera hadn't shown up."

"I don't doubt it for a moment."

And he didn't "Good night, Dean."

"Good night, Boss."

"You know," Austin said as the door closed behind him, "that *Boss* is beginning to sound rather like an endearment."

This was not the time, nor the mood, to deal with that. "At least the others didn't show up."

"I suspect they keep a low profile when Hera's on the rampage."

Claire slapped the wards back up and staggered to the bathroom. "I need a drink."

"May I suggest a little compost tea?"

"No."

"So you'd as leaf not?"

"Oh, shut up."

Back in his own apartment Dean pulled Claire's business card from his pocket expecting that it would give him some indication if she really wasn't all right.

> Aunt Claire, Keeper
> your Accident is my Opportunity
>
> (100% organically grown)

Reassured, he went back to bed.

The Olympians left directly after breakfast. Claire watched them climb into the van, fighting over who was sitting by what window, and raised a neutral hand in response to Hermes' wave. The moment the van pulled away, she raced upstairs.

"Where are you going?" Austin demanded.

"Something woke Hera last night. I'm going to find out what it was."

"With grape flavor crystals?"

"You'll see."

Standing by the bed in room one, she flung the crystals into the air. When they settled, there were tiny purple three-toed footprints on the bedside table.

"Go get Dean and Jacques," Claire said.

Unusually quiet, Austin left the room.

"When Hermes said Poseidon leaves a room damp, he wasn't kidding."

"You think you have problems? I work like a dog for that Persephone and she does not even tip."

"You're dead. What would you do with money?"

"So I am dead." Jacques sniffed disdainfully. "It is, how do you say, the principle of the thing."

As they rounded the bed and saw Claire's expression, they fell silent. She pointed toward the bedside table. "I want that imp caught," she said.

It wasn't as easy as all that. Both men, the living and dead, were unsuccessful. The traps remained empty. Claire's mood grew worse.

"If anything's going to get done," Austin sighed, leaping down off the bed as the bathroom door slammed the next morning, "I've clearly got to do it myself."

"Uh, Boss? I can finish the wallpapering myself if you'd rather be somewhere else."

Fighting the urge to photosynthesize, Claire stepped out of the shaft of sunlight. "No. I said I'd help."

Wondering how much trouble he'd be in if he mentioned she was being more of a hindrance, Dean rolled the next sheet through the tray and laid it against the wall. "Could you please hand me the smoother."

"The what?"

Hands still holding the paper to the wall, he turned to point and froze.

Claire frowned and followed his line of sight

Picking his way over the folds in the drop cloth, Austin crossed the dining-room table with something small and squirming in his mouth.

Its legs were froglike and ended in three toes. Its arms, nearly as long as its legs, ended in two fingers and a thumb. Its eyes were small and black and it appeared to have no teeth. Covered in something between fur and scale, it changed color constantly.

As Austin drew even with Claire, he spit the imp out. "Yuck, those things taste awful."

The imp leaped off the table, scrambled up the wall, and dove under the wet wallpaper.

As the bulge headed for the ceiling, Claire snatched up the last full roll and, swinging it like a club bat, smacked it down again and again. And again.

When her arm dropped to her side, Dean pulled the roll from limp fingers.

Breathing heavily, she looked up at the barely noticeable lump. "I'm feeling much better now."

In the furnace room the silence filled all available space and pushed against the shield. After a moment, it found a voice.

SHE DESTROYED MY IMP!

YOUR IMP?

MY IMP. NOW, IT'S PERSONAL.

ELEVEN

CLAIRE WOKE FROM UNEASY DREAMS where images of Hell unfolded like overdone special effects, realized the date, and gave serious consideration to remaining in bed. Although the origins of Halloween were far older than the beliefs that had defined the pit in the furnace room, greeting card companies had seen to it that pointy-hatted hags and men in red long Johns with pitchforks had risen to dominance over history.

If Hell intended to try anything big, it would make the attempt on October 31.

WELL?

NO. TOO OBVIOUS. SHE'LL BE EXPECTING SOMETHING TO HAPPEN TONIGHT.

BUT IF NOTHING HAPPENS, WON'T THAT MAKE HER SUSPICIOUS?

Hell considered it a moment. YOU'RE RIGHT. It sounded surprised. I WILL BIDE MY TIME. YOU MAY DO AS YOU PLEASE.

BUT WITHOUT YOU . . .

TRY HARDER.

"Diana's more likely to be a catalyst than a help, Mom."

"I don't like the thought of you there alone, tonight of all nights."

Which was the truth as far as it went. On the other hand, Claire couldn't really blame her mother for trying to get Diana out of the house on Halloween, not after the incident with the gob stoppers.

"Don't worry, I'll be fine. Thanks to the seepage, the shield's never been as strong."

Claire felt as much as heard her mother's sigh. "Just be careful."

"I will."

"Doublecheck *her* shielding."

"I will."

"Your father says that you should try to convince Jacques to pass over. He says it isn't healthy for a spirit to be hanging about on the physical plane and that the links between worlds are weak over the next twenty-four hours. He says . . ." She paused and turned her mouth from the receiver. "Do you want to talk to her, Norman?" This second sigh held a different timbre. "Your father, who seems to think I have nothing better to do than pass on his commentary, says Jacques' presence could call other spirits and that you'd best ward against it unless you want to house a whole company of ghosts."

"Tell Dad that Jacques has been haunting this place for over seventy years and that hasn't happened yet. Tell him it's probably because of the nature of the site—ghosts don't want to be near it."

"Do you want to talk to him?"

"No, you can tell him. I'd better go now, Mom." Leaning out over the counter, she peered down the hall toward the dining room but couldn't see anything. "Dean and Austin are alone together in the kitchen."

"Is that a problem?"

"It could be. The geriatric kibble has been disappearing, but I don't think Austin's been eating it. I want to catch them in the act."

"Do you think they're destroying it?"

"No. Dean would never waste food."

"Surely you don't think *he's* eating it."

"No, but he does do all the cooking . . ." After final good-byes, Claire ducked under the counter and headed for the back of the building. Rounding the corner into the kitchen, she stopped short. "What are you doing?"

Dropping a handful of pumpkin innards into a colander, Dean looked up and smiled. "We forgot to get one on Saturday so I went to the market this morning."

"You're carving a jack-o'-lantern? Have you forgotten what's in the basement?"

"No, but . . ."

"Do you really think that, under the circumstances, it's a good idea to attract children to the door?"

His face fell. His shoulders slumped. "I guess not. But what'll we do with all the candy?"

"What candy?"

"All those bags of little chocolate bars and stuff we bought on Saturday."

"There's two bags less than there were," Austin pointed out from his sunny spot on the dining room table.

"Two bags?" Dean stared aghast at Claire who glared at the cat

"Tattletale." Assuming there'd be no little visitors to the door, she'd also assumed the candy was for home consumption and acted accordingly. All right; perhaps a bit more than accordingly.

Sighing deeply, Dean stroked his hands down the sides of the pumpkin, fingers lingering over the dark orange curves. "I suppose I could do some baking. If I want to see the kids' costumes, I guess I can go to Karen's place tonight."

It was honest disappointment in his voice. He wasn't trying to manipulate her—regardless of how she might be responding. Claire couldn't decide if that was part of his charm or really, really irritating. "All right I guess one jack-o'-lantern and a few candies can't hurt."

"Depends on how they're inserted," Austin observed.

"So you're what they call a Keeper these days." Her mother's image in the mirror folded her arms over her chest. "Put the boy in danger just because you can't bear to say no to him." Red eyes narrowed. "I certainly hope you're not feeling guilty for continually saying no to him on other fronts."

Claire finished brushing her teeth and spit "What other fronts?"

"Don't tell me you haven't noticed his raging desires? His burning passion that only you can quench."

"Did you just acquire another romance writer?"

"Go ahead, scoff. It's no skin off my nose . . ." Skin disappeared off the entire face. ". . . if you break his heart."

"Oh, give it up, I am *not* breaking his heart." Dropping her toothbrush on the counter, Claire stomped from the bathroom.

The image lingered. "A mother knows," it said with a lipless smile.

"Is it that you want me to be gone?" Jacques demanded, his edges flickering in and out of focus. "I thought you were happy to have me here, with you."

Claire hadn't intended to hurt the ghost's feelings, but since feelings were pretty much all he was, she supposed it was inevitable. "All I said was that if you want to cross over, tonight would be a good night to go. The barriers between the physical world and the spiritual will be thin and . . . Austin!"

He looked up and drew his front leg back out of the rubber plant's green plastic pot. "What?"

"You know what."

"You'd think," he muttered, stalking from the sitting room, his tail a defiant flag flicking back and forth, "that after seventeen years she'd trust me. Use a flowerpot just once and you're branded for all nine lives."

When the cat's monologue of ill-usage faded, Claire turned her attention back to Jacques. "You're stalled here," she reminded him, "halfway between two worlds and, someday, you'll have to move on."

"Someday," he repeated, his fingers tracing the curve of her cheek. "If I, as you say, move on, will you miss me, *cherie?*"

"You know I will."

"*Pour quoi?*"

"Because I enjoy your company."

"Not as you could."

"*What you seem to need is Jacques possessing Dean's body.*"

She shook the memory out of her head before Hell could comment but Jacques seemed to see something in her face that made him smile.

"Perhaps you desire me to leave because you are afraid of the feeling I make in you. Of the feeling I have for you."

"Jacques, you're dead. Only a Keeper can give you flesh, and I'm the only Keeper in your . . ." About to say, life, she paused and reconsidered. ". . . in your existence."

"Then it is fate."

"What is?"

"You and I."

"Look, I just wanted to ask you if you wanted to move on; since you don't I have things to do." Pulling enough power to brush him out of the way if he didn't move, she headed for the door.

He drifted aside to let her pass.

Fingers wrapped around the doorknob, she paused, expecting Jacques to put in one final plea for flesh. When he didn't, she left the room feeling vaguely cheated.

"What're you doing. Boss?"

Claire set the silver marking pen on the desk and worked the cramp out of her right hand. "I'm justifying tonight's potential danger. Trying to be a Keeper in spite of the situation." She nodded toward the huge wooden salad bowl half full of miniature chocolate bars, eyeball gum, and spider suckers. "Every piece of that candy has a rune written on the wrapper that'll nullify anything bad the kids might pick up."

"Like fruit and nuts instead of candy? Kidding," he added hastily as Claire's brows drew in. "I mean, I know thre's sickos out there and I think it's great you're doing something about it."

"Thank you. Every time one of those sickos slips a doctored treat past street-proofing and parents, there's another hole ripped in the fabric of the universe and, given the metaphysical baggage carried by this time of the year, anything could slip through. Early November is a busy season for the lineage."

The chocolate bar he picked up looked ludicrously tiny as he tossed it from hand to hand. "Can I ask you something? Why don't you stop them before the kids get hurt?"

"You mean why don't we make everybody behave themselves instead of just cleaning up the mess once it's over? My sister used to ask that all the time." She'd stopped, but Claire suspected Diana still believed the world would be a better place if she were in charge. So did most teenagers; trouble was, Diana had power enough to take a shot at it "It's that whole free-will thing; we're no more allowed to make choices for people than you are. We're just here to deal with the metaphysical consequences."

"Is there anything I can do?"

"You can stand in the doorway and hand this stuff out."

"I meant . . ."

"I know." There were times, Claire reflected, when a facetious comment just wasn't enough. "You're good people, Dean. That helps strengthen the universe all by itself."

"Kind of like moral Scotchgarding," Austin told him, unfolding on one of the upper bookshelves. "Now could one of you, preferably the taller one, help me down."

After the cat had settled on the monitor and Dean had returned to the kitchen to fetch the pumpkin, Claire tossed another chocolate bar into the bowl and said, "Thanks."

"No problem. You were having an honest in-depth conversation, so I figured you'd soon run out of things to say."

"You know . . ." She poked him with a sucker stick. ". . . you can be really irritating."

"Only because I'm right."

The candy hit the bowl with more force than necessary.

"I'm right again, aren't I?"

"Shut up."

Dusk settled over the city, the streetlights came on, and clumps of children, many with bored adults in tow, began moving from door to door.

In the furnace room, the bits of Hell left off the newly formed personality, sent out invitations.

As the first group of kids climbed the stairs, the wards incised into the threshold with a salad fork . . .

"Why a salad fork?"

Claire shrugged. "It was the first thing I grabbed."

. . . remained dark.

Only two of the four wore anything recognizable as a costume. One of the others had rubbed a bit of dirt on his face although it might not have been intentional. They stood silently holding out pillowcases as Dean offered the bowl.

"Do you want to take a handful or should I do it?" he asked enthusiastically.

After a silent consultation, the largest of the four jerked her head toward the bowl. "You do it. You got bigger hands."

"Aren't you guys supposed to say 'trick or treat'?" Claire wondered as Dean dropped the runed candy into the bags.

A little boy, dressed vaguely like Luke Skywalker, giggled.

"What's so funny?"

Their spokesman rolled her eyes. "Trick or treat is way uncool." Clutching their pillowcases, they turned as one, pounded back to the sidewalk, and raced away.

"When I was a kid, I'm sure we worked harder at this," Claire muttered as she closed the door.

Cross-legged on the countertop, Jacques rematerialized. "When me, I was a kid, we knock over Monsieur Bouchard's . . . How do you say, outside house?"

"Outhouse. Privy."

"*Oui.* We knock it over, but we do not know Monsieur Bouchard is inside."

They turned to look at Dean.

He shrugged. "I don't really notice any difference."

One princess, one pirate, and four sets of street clothes later, the wards on the threshold blazed red.

Claire opened the door.

The Bogart grinned, showing broken stubs of yellow teeth. "Trick or treat."

She dropped a handful of unruned candy on its outstretched hand. "Treat."

"You sure?" It looked disappointed at her choice. "I gots some good tricks me."

"I'm sure."

Without bothering to rip off the wrappers, it popped a pair of chocolate bars into its mouth. "Good treat," it announced after a moment of vigorous masticating and an audible swallow. "Same times next year?"

"No promises."

The Bogart nodded. "Smart Keeper." A backward leap took it to the sidewalk where it paused, almost invisible in the increasing dark. "Biggers coming," it called and vanished.

"That wasn't a kid in a really good costume, was it?" Dean asked as Claire stepped back and closed the door.

She checked the wards. "No. And on any other night you probably wouldn't have seen it."

"What was it, then?"

"Do you remember those sparks off the energy that I told you about the first day I was here?"

He frowned thoughtfully and scratched at the back of his neck. "The ones you see that keep you from driving?"

"Essentially. There are places where the fabric of the universe is practically cheesecloth tonight so a lot of sparks are going to get through. Once through, it seems some of them are being called here. That was a Bogart."

"Humphrey?"

"I doubt it."

"Was it dangerous?"

"No." Dropping down onto the stairs, she stretched her legs out into the lobby. "But it could've gotten destructive if I hadn't bought it off."

He glanced down at the salad bowl. "With chocolate bars?"

"Why not?"

"Okay. What did it mean by biggers?"

"Bigger than it. More powerful, more dangerous."

"Will they be coming all night?"

"I don't know. They might stop coming if we blow out the jack-o'-lantern and turn off the front lights, but they might not."

"So we should blow out the candle and turn off the lights and see what happens."

Her eyes narrowed. "No."

"No?"

"I'm not cowering in the dark."

"But you didn't even want to do this." He was wearing what Claire had begun to recognize as his responsible face. "It was my idea and . . ."

"So?" She cut him off and stood as Austin announced more children approaching. "Since we've started it, we're going to finish it. And you might as well enjoy it."

The gypsy and the ghostbuster—although they might've been a pirate and a sewer worker, Claire wasn't entirely sure—looked startled when she opened the door before they knocked.

"How did you know we was coming?" the gypsy/pirate demanded.

Claire nodded toward the window where Austin could be seen silhouetted beside the pumpkin. "The cat told me."

The ghostbuster/sewer worker snorted. "Did not."

"My dad says this place is haunted," the gypsy/pirate announced.

"Your dad's right."

"Cool. Can we see the ghost?"

"No."

They accepted her refusal with the resigned grace of children used to being denied access to the adult world.

"The cat told me?" Austin asked as she closed the door.

"Hey, it's Halloween."

"Then you should have shown them the ghost," Jacques pointed out with a toss of his head.

"Jacques!"

Catching it one-handed, he set it back on his shoulders at a rakish angle. "If you give me flesh, I could not do that."

Suppressing a shudder, Claire glared at him. "If I gave you flesh right now, I'd smack it."

His grin broadened. *"D'accord."*

"No."

"Tease."

The wards blazed red.

"Well . . ." Claire glanced around at the man, the cat, and the ghost as she reached for the door. ". . . let's check out the *next* contestant."

A young woman stood on the step. She had short brown hair, brown eyes, and matching Satin Claret lipstick and nail polish.

Claire tapped her own Satin Claret nails impatiently against the doorjamb. "You've got to be kidding."

The young woman shrugged. "Trick or treat?"

Behind her, Claire heard Dean gasp. "Boss. It's you."

"Not quite. It's a Waff, a kind of Co-walker. Technically, it's a death token."

"A what?"

"Don't worry about it." Folding her arms, Claire looked the Waff in the eye and said in her best primary schoolteacher voice, "You've no business being here. Go on, then. Off with you! Scram!"

Looking embarrassed about the entire incident, the Waff slunk down the steps and out of sight

"Honestly," Claire sighed as she closed the door. "They used to get chased off by mortals, you'd think they'd know better than to even try against a Keeper."

"I doubt it had a choice," Austin pointed out, scratching vigorously behind one ear. "Once it was called, it had to come. Things are going to get a lot worse before they get better."

"Do you know that, or are you pontificating?"

He licked his nose and refused to answer.

Three sets of street clothes, a couple of Disney characters and a Gwyllion later, Dean headed for the kitchen under the pretext of getting coffee. He *was* going to get coffee, but that wasn't his only reason for going to the kitchen.

The Gwyllion had looked rather like one of the city's more colorful bag ladies and had been mumbling what sounded like directions to the bus station when Claire'd banished it with an iron cross she'd pulled out of her backpack. Without a backpack of his own, Dean opened the bread box for the next best thing.

A fairy bun.

Technically, it was a leftover brown'n'serve from supper, but in a pinch it'd have to do. As an Anglican minister, his granddad had fought a continual battle against the superstitions that rose up in isolated communities and had told him how even in the sixties many of the more traditional men would carry fairy buns into the woods to protect them from being led astray by the small spirits. Dean had never thought to ask what exactly his granddad had meant by small spirits but reasoned that anything that could make it up the steps to the door had to count.

He wrapped the bun in a paper towel and carefully squashed it down into the front right-hand pocket of his jeans. Turning to go, a movement in the parking lot caught his eye.

His truck was the only vehicle out there. If some of the older kids were about to do any damage, it would have to be to *his* truck.

Over his dead body. That truck had brought him from Newfoundland to Kingston in February and, in one of the worst winters on record, had gone through everything he'd asked it to. And one thing he hadn't asked it to, but the gas pumps hadn't actually exploded and the police had determined that the large patch of black ice had been at fault rather than his driving, so technically it had been an uneventful trip. Anyway, he loved that truck.

Moving quietly to the window, he pushed aside enough of the vertical blinds to allow him to scout the enemy; no point in rushing out like an idiot if his truck was safe.

The most beautiful woman he'd ever seen looked in at him, smiled, and gracefully beckoned him closer.

Dean swallowed, hard. He could feel his Adam's apple bobbing up and down like a buoy on high seas.

Her smile sharpened.

Moving from space to space between the vertical slats so that he wouldn't have to take his eyes off her, Dean shuffled toward the door.

"Dean?" Austin brushed up against his shins. "What are you looking at?"

His tongue felt thick. He had to force it to make words. "Irresistibly beautiful woman."

"Out there? In the parking lot?"

"Needs me. Needs me to go to her."

"Uh-huh. Look again."

A sudden sharp pain in Dean's calf jerked the world back into focus. Out in the parking lot, the beauty was no longer quite so irresistible. Her eyes held dark shadows, her teeth were far too white and there didn't seem to be much in the way of boundary between where she ended and the night began. Feeling as though he were standing on the edge of a fog-shrouded cliff, Dean stuffed trembling fingers into his pocket and grabbed one end of the fairy bun.

Belief is everything when dealing with baked goods.

A misty figure, vaguely woman-shaped directed her burning gaze down toward the cat and hissed angrily.

"Yeah, yeah, whatever. Nice try, now get lost Come on," he added as the spirit disappeared, "let's get me a piece of that pork left from dinner, then get you back to the lobby before something else shows up."

Conscious of the blood slowly soaking into his jeans, Dean fed and followed without an argument.

"Well?" Claire asked impatiently as they came out into the light.

"I was right He was in trouble. Judging from his reaction and the noise it made before it disappeared, I'm guessing it was a Lhiannan-Shee."

"A fairy sweetheart?"

"Not a sweetheart," Dean protested remembering its final appearance.

"We all have our bad days." Claire grabbed him by the elbow and spun him around. "Are you all right?"

"Sure." He felt a little light-headed and his skin prickled where the hair had risen all over his body, but he still had his soul, so the rest seemed too minor to mention.

"What happened to your leg?"

"Austin."

"Hey, I had to get his attention, didn't I?" Austin demanded as Claire turned a raised eyebrow in his direction.

"By attempting an amputation?"

Industriously washing a front paw, he ignored her.

"I know a man who die from a cat scratch," Jacques announced rematerializing halfway up the stairs. "The scratch, it went . . . How do you say, *septique?*"

"Septic."

"*Oui.* Had to cut it off and he dies."

"Died."

"*Oui.*" He smiled at Dean. "Should we cut off your leg now or later?"

"I'm fine."

"I'm insulted," Austin snorted. "My claws are clean."

"Maybe you'd better go wash your leg," Claire suggested, nodding toward her suite. "Use my bathroom. There's some antibiotic cream in the medicine chest."

At the sight of the roughly circular stain, Dean sucked in air through his teeth. About three inches in diameter, it was an ugly red-brown, darker in the center of the top curve. "Oh, man. I'll be right back."

"Where are you going?"

"To change. I don't get these jeans into cold water soon, I'll never get the blood out."

"Don't look out any windows!" Claire yelled as he ran for the basement "I don't believe him," she muttered over the sound of his work boots clumping down the stairs. "One minute he's terrified, the next, a laundry problem drives the whole experience from his mind."

"He is right about the bloodstain and cold water," Jacques pointed out. "You see these?" He slapped his thighs. "Cover with blood when I fall in the lake and now, for eternity, clean."

Claire helped herself to a chocolate bar. "Don't you start."

A few moments later. Dean reentered the lobby in jeans so clean the creases were a lighter shade of blue.

"Well?"

He smiled. "I've been hurt worse while still on the bench."

"Next time I'll dig a little deeper," Austin muttered as another group of kids arrived.

For about half an hour, a steady procession of the neighborhood children climbed up the steps to claim their loot. Claire kept a wary eye on the wards while Dean stood in the open doorway, happily handing out the candy. By the time the crowd thinned and the stairs emptied, it was full dark.

"Uh, Boss? There's a real evil-looking cow down on the street."

"A cow?"

"Yeah. It's got barbed horns and glowing red eyes."

"Considering how the rest of the stuffs been manifesting, it's probably a Guytrash."

"What should I do?"

"Shut the door; it'll go away."

Brow creased, he did as he was told. "These things can't hurt the kids, can they?"

"Have you ever heard of a kid being hurt by a cow on Halloween?"

"Well, no, but . . ."

"This kind of manifestation can't hurt you if you don't believe it can hurt you, and frankly, not many people believe in the traditional ghoulies anymore." The wards blazed red and Claire reached for the door. "There's probably enough race memory left to give them a bit of a scare, but isn't that what tonight's abo . . . oh, my." She stared up at the very large man wearing what looked to be black plastic armor and shivered a little at the menace in the black plastic eyes.

"Truth or dare?" His voice was darker; deeper even, if that was possible.

It was essentially the same question. The trick was, never for an instant to show uncertainty. "Truth."

"You think you can do it alone, but you can't."

"What are you talking about?"

"You've had your truth." She could hear amusement in the dark tone. "Now, it's *my* turn."

"Hey, Nicho! Look who it is!"

A pair of six- or seven-year-olds charged up the stairs and grabbed onto the trailing black cloak.

"You are so cool, man."

"You're our favorite."

"It's *really* you, isn't it?"

He turned enough to look ominously down at them. "Yes. *Really.*"

"Cool."

"Way cool."

"Can we have your autograph?"

"Will you come home with me and meet our mom?"

"No, no! Better! Come to school with us tomorrow."

"Yeah, you could slice and dice those guys who won't let us on the swings."

"Slice and dice!"

The features of the mask were, of course, immobile, but Claire thought she could detect a faint hint of building panic as the question and comments continued at machine-gun speed.

"You looked a lot taller in the movie."

"Where'd you get those cool boots?"

"We loved the way you iced that guy without even touching him."

"You gonna be in the prequel?"

"I got the micro machine play set that looks just like you."

"I drew a picture of you on the inside cover of my reader. It was pretty good, but I got in trouble."

"Can I hold your light sa . . ."

"No." He yanked his cape from their hands.

"Oh, come on, just once."

"Me, too."

"I said, no."

"We wouldn't break it"

"Yeah, don't be such a jerk."

Breathing labored, he rushed down the steps, strode out onto the sidewalk, and disappeared.

"Cool."

"Yeah. Way cool."

The taller of the two looked speculatively up at Claire. "You got any gummy bears?"

"I'm melting, I'm melting . . ."

Swinging the empty bucket, Claire closed the door on the dissolving manifestation. "At least she stuck to the script."

"I always thought the CBC was overreacting about the effects of the American media," Dean said thoughtfully, "but now I'm not so sure."

"Aren't you a little young to be out so late."

The tiny girl watched the candy drop safely into her bag before answering. "My daddy just got home."

The shadowy figure at the bottom of the stairs raised an arm in a sheepish wave.

"I see. Well, what are you supposed to be?"

She tossed her head, setting a pair of realistic looking paper horse ears waggling, and spun around so Claire could see the tail pinned to the back of her jacket. "I'm a *pony*."

"Oh. Sorry."

"You've got a cat in the window," she continued. "I want a cat, but my stepmom's allergic. Can I come in and pet your cat? Just for a minute." Head to one side, she smiled engagingly. "Please."

"What about your father?"

She spun around again. "Daddy! Can I go pet the cat?"

The arm lifted in what could have been a wave of assent.

Like most cats, Austin was not fond of small children. Claire grinned and was about to step out of the way when she noticed the threshold seemed to be a darker color than the surrounding wood. Reaching into her pocket she pulled out a paper packet of salt and, as the child's eyes widened, ripped it in half and threw it in her face.

The glamour faded.

The runes blazed red.

The little girl stretched six, seven feet tall, costume vanishing although the horse ears remained, curved fangs protruding from her lower jaw, oversized hands scraping at the bricks on either side of the door.

Daddy breathed fire.

Claire and Dean together slammed the door.

"That was close," Claire said with feeling as the latch finally caught.

Shoulders against the wood, Dean let out a breath he couldn't remember taking. "Do you always keep salt in your pocket?"

"Strange question from a man carrying a brown'n'serve."

"Aren't you guys a little old to be out tonight?"

One of the three identical junior skinheads scowled, differentiating himself momentarily from the other two. "Aren't you a little ugly to be passin' judgment?"

"Yeah. Just give over the fuckin' candy."

The teenager in the middle elbowed them both hard in the ribs. "What we meant to say, *ma'am,* was trick or treat."

Claire thought about it a moment as the boys postured. "Trick," she said at last and closed the door.

The boy with his boot thrust in on the threshold got a nasty surprise. They could hear his shriek even through the heavy wood.

"I think the bitch broke my fuckin' foot, man."

"They were going to egg us anyway," Claire explained. "I figured, why waste the candy."

"Egg us?" Dean repeated.

She grabbed his arm, stopping his charge. "Don't worry about it."

"These guys won't stop with eggs!"

"I think they will." A few minutes later, watching out the window as the last of the thrown eggs paused inches from the hotel and swept back, like all the rest to smash on the now dripping and furious thrower, she sighed. "I guess I was wrong."

The hunk of broken concrete followed the same path as the eggs.

"Tricky downdrafts. That had to hurt."

Claire put herself bodily between Dean and the door as he tried to follow the will-o'-the-wisp dancing up and down the stairs. She allowed herself one small thought about the firm resilience of his stomach, then dug her shoulder in and shoved him far enough into the lobby to be able to close the door.

"That's it," she said when he was safely behind the counter. "It's ten o'clock. There won't be any more kids. I think we can blow out the candle and turn off the outside lights, honor intact."

The pumpkin lid refused to lift and all the air blown in through the carved face wouldn't put out the candle.

"Oh, nuts."

Two of the remaining four chocolate bars acquired almonds. Two didn't.

"Granddad?"

"No tricks, Dean, I promise. Come on out we have a lot to say to each other."

"But you're dead."

"Never said I wasn't, but this is the night the dead walk."

"The restless dead."

"You think I'm not restless after what you did? Think again!"

"But Aunt Carol loves the house."

"I left it to you, you ungrateful whelp."

"Granddad, let me explain." One foot lifted to clear the threshold, Dean felt something crunch in his pocket and shoved a hand in to feel what it was.

The fairy bun.

The steps were empty.

"I thought I told you not to open that while I was gone." Claire stepped out of her sitting room as he jerked back and closed the door. "What was out there?"

"The ghost of my granddad."

"He's dead? Sorry, stupid question." She went out into the lobby and searched his face. "It wasn't actually him, you know."

"Yeah. I know."

"You don't look so good. Maybe you should go to bed."

"Will they keep coming?"

"Yes. Probably until dawn."

He lifted his chin and squared his shoulders. "Then I'll stay."

"What was *that*?"

"Fachan. They've gone back to the classics."

"That roast was for tomorrow's supper."

"Trust me, he wouldn't have been happy with candy."

Dawn seemed a long time coming.

"Any candy left?"

Claire tipped the bowl up on its side and tried to focus on the contents. Half a dozen empty wrappers fell out. "Looks like I've finished it."

"What were those last two things again."

"An ogre and a Duergar. Why?" She blew a weary bubble.

Dean pulled off his glasses and rubbed his eyes. "Did you really spin straw into gold?"

"It was going around in a circle, so technically it was spinning." The Duergar hadn't been entirely happy, but since it had the treat, it couldn't trick. The ogre, on the other hand, had ripped the railing out around the area and tossed it and the hotel sign out into the street. Treating an ogre meant feeding it dinner.

Ogres were man-eaters. The trick was knowing that.

Austin lifted his head off his paws and yawned. "Sun's up. And the candle just went out." He leaped off the windowsill as the pumpkin collapsed in on itself, smoking slightly.

Shoving his glasses back on approximately where they belonged, Dean stood and headed for the door. "I think I'll get that stuff off the road before there's an accident."

Dragging herself up onto her feet Claire waited a moment until the world stopped spinning. "I think I'll go throw up."

THAT'S IT? YOU SCARED THEM A TIME OR TWO AND YOU DID A LITTLE DAMAGE AND YOU TIRED THEM OUT, BIG DEAL. THE KEEPER FIELDED EVERYTHING YOU THREW AT HER AND NEVER ONCE DREW POWER FROM LOWER THAN THE MIDDLE OF THE POSSIBILITIES.

SO LET'S SEE YOU DO BETTER. The rest of Hell sounded miffed.

BETTER?

OKAY. FINE. *WORSE.*

WAIT FOR IT. . . .

Down on one knee, the police constable poked at the hole torn in the concrete setting and shook his head. "When exactly did this happen?"

"About four A.M."

Four-*twelve,*" Mrs. Abrams corrected. "I know because when I heard the noise, and it was a terrible noise, I looked at my alarm clock and even though I bought it before Mr. Abrams died, God bless the man, it still keeps perfect time."

"Four-twelve," the constable repeated. "Did you happen to see who did it?"

"Oh, no! I wasn't going to expose myself to that kind of destructive hooliganism. That's what the police are paid for and that's why I called them."

"I was actually asking Ms. Hansen."

Since there'd been a chance of flying glass, Claire had stayed away from the window and so could truthfully answer, "Sorry, I didn't see anything."

"It was probably a gang of students from the university. They get a few too many drinks in them and go crazy."

"That sounds reasonable," Claire agreed as he stood. It wasn't what had happened, but it sounded reasonable. Most of the vandalism in Kingston conveniently got blamed on wandering gangs of students from the university who'd had a few too many drinks. Occasionally they were spotted in the distance, but no one ever managed to identify individuals since, like other legendary creatures, they vanished when too closely approached.

"When you arrest them," Mrs. Abrams said, so determined to do her civic duty that she clutched at the constable's sleeve, "you let me know. I'm the one who called. Mrs. Abrams. One *be* and an *ess*."

"You're the lady with the dog, aren't you?"

"You've heard of my Baby?" she beamed up at him.

The constable sighed. "Oh, yeah."

Another call dragged the grateful police officer back into his car and away. Mrs. Abrams transferred her attention to Claire.

"You haven't forgotten that Professor Jackson is coming to stay the day after tomorrow, have you, Kimberly, dear?"

"We're looking forward to it, Mrs. Abrams."

"I'm sure you'll take wonderful care of him. I'll likely be over to visit him while he's there. Only because Baby dislikes him so, you know. We wouldn't ever do anything compromising. Although," she simpered, "I used to be quite progressive in my younger days."

The worst of it was, she was telling the truth. Shuddering slightly, Claire went inside and spent the rest of the day trying to catch up on her sleep without dreaming of Mrs. Abrams and the professor in progressive positions. Had she not checked to insure all shields were holding, she'd have assumed the dreams, in graphic detail with full sound and color, had risen up out of the pit.

"You Claire Hansen?"

Claire checked, but the courier had not been called by Hell. Which made sense after she thought about it a moment; if something absolutely had to be delivered the next business day, Hell'd prefer it to be late. "Yes, I'm Claire Hansen."

"Sign here."

"Why?"

Although the young woman's expression made a rude comment, she kept her tone professional. "I got a package for you."

"You want me to sign for it, then. Boss?"

"*You* Claire Hansen?" the courier demanded.

"No, but . . ."

"Then *she's* got to sign it."

In return for her signature, Claire was handed a large, bulging manila envelope and an illegible receipt.

"Who's it from?" Dean asked as the courier carried her bike back down the front steps and rode away.

"More important," Jacques murmured appreciatively, rematerializing by the window, "what does she wear? Her legs, they look like they are painted black."

"They're tights."

"*Oui*, they are tight. Me, I do not complain, but they are allowed?"

"Sure."

He heaved a heavy if ethereal sigh. "I died too soon."

"The package is from Hermes," Claire interrupted with heavy emphasis.

Austin snickered. "Someone doesn't like not being the center of attention."

Ignoring him, she pulled a folded towel from the envelope and frowned. "Why would Hermes send us a towel?"

"It's one of ours," Dean declared, fingering the fabric. "It must've gotten accidentally mixed in with his stuff."

"He's the God of Thieves, Dean. I doubt it was an accident, and since I also doubt his conscience got the better of him, I wonder why he sent it back." A piece of paper, both sides filled with line after line of script, fell from a fold. "Maybe this explains it. *Dear Keeper*," she read. "*Three days ago, I left your establishment with one of the items traditionally liberated from hotel rooms. Since that time, two ferries have attempted to sink out from under us and would have sunk had Poseidon not been on board to command the waves to carry us to shore. Our vehicle has broken down seven times—Hephaestus is happy, no one else is. For the first time since we began traveling, the border guards asked to see identification and then, when I informed them we were heading to Rochester, searched the van. The pocket in the space-time continuum didn't bother them as much as the cameras Zeus bought in Toronto but lost the receipts for. When we were finally allowed into the United States but warned by the most officious person it has ever been my displeasure to meet that we wouldn't be able to return to Canada—and, I might add, your admirable system of socialized medicine—Aphrodite had a flare up of an old complaint, and the clinic visit maxed out her credit card. While we were waiting for her, someone stole our travelers' checks. They were not American Express."*

The list continued for the rest of the front and onto the back of the paper and ended with:

"So I return to you the item divination has determined is the cause of our recent difficulties. Please excuse the small scorch mark. Your security system is admirable if excessive.

—Yours in mythology,

Hermes."

"What security system?" Dean asked.

"I suspect that after all these years with an active accident site, the hotel's capable of providing its own security." Claire patted the terry cloth fondly. "Offhand, I'd say it's a *really* bad idea to steal our towels."

STOPPING THE SEEPAGE WON'T WEAKEN THE SHIELD, Hell told itself sulkily.

I'M NOT STOPPING THE SEEPAGE. I'M GATHERING IT.

TWELVE

———— ❖ ————

PROFESSOR JACKSON WAS A MAN of medium height trying to be tall. Under a hat last fashionable in the forties, he carried his chin high and his weight forward on the balls of his feet. Something about him suggested carpetbags to Claire although a quick glance over the counter showed only a perfectly normal, gray nylon suitcase.

"Am I your only guest?" he asked, signing the register with a precise flourish.

"At the moment." Claire dropped the key to room one into his outstretched hand. "Next floor up, turn left at the top of the stairs."

An expectant gaze drifted down to his luggage and then around the lobby, slid over Austin but rested for a moment on Claire. When she made no response, he sighed dramatically, picked up the suitcase, and started up the stairs.

At the sound of the professor's door closing, Austin opened his eyes. "Why don't you like him?"

"I don't know. Maybe because Baby's taken a strange dislike to him."

"That would only be strange if Baby actually *liked* anyone."

"Good point." Staring down at Professor Jackson's signature, Claire traced the loop of the "J" with one finger. Unless he was one of those rare nonpoliticians who believed their own lies, it was his real name and occupation. "I can't help thinking he's dangerous."

"How?"

"You're the cat you tell me."

Austin thoughtfully washed his shoulder. "He looks like he's in his late fifties."

"So?"

"Ten years younger than Mrs. Abrams."

"Your point?"

"Do I have to spell it out? He's ten years younger than she is. He's younger. She's older. They're . . ."

Claire's eyes narrowed. "I don't care."

"Do you *want* to be a lonely old recluse?" Austin demanded, tail tip flipping back and forth.

"All right. Let's just get this settled once and for all." She drummed her fingernails against the counter. "I like Dean. He's a nice man and he's very attractive. Under normal circumstances, where I'd be moving in then moving out when the job was done, I might consider, were he willing, a short physical dalliance."

"Dalliance?"

Ignoring feline amusement, Claire went on. "However, I'm not going anywhere, and he's barely twenty. He's not going to be content staying here as chief cook and bottle washer forever."

"So you're going to give up now because you can't have forever?"

"I didn't say that."

"So you'd be willing to sleep with him and then move on, but you're not willing to extend the same courtesy to him?"

"I *really* didn't say that."

"So the problem is, you really want the one you can't have."

Claire stared at the cat for a long moment. Twice, she opened her mouth to say something, anything, but the words wouldn't come. Finally, she turned and walked away.

As the door to her sitting room closed behind her, Austin stretched out on the counter. "What would she do without me?"

"We lock the front door at ten-thirty."

"Why?"

"Pardon?"

Professor Jackson fixed Claire with an interrogative stare. "Why do you lock the front door at ten-thirty? Why not at ten? Or at eleven? Or at ten-forty-five? You don't know, do you? You've just always done it that way. Most people go through life without noticing what's going on around them. If I could show you the world beyond your pitiful little daily routines, well, you'd be amazed."

"Would I?"

"Amazed," he repeated. "I'll be back before ten-thirty."

"I can't help wondering," Claire said as the front door closed behind him, "just what exactly he's a professor of."

"Some kind of philosophy," Dean answered, coming into the lobby as she finished speaking. "He holds an appointment from an eminent Swiss university."

"That explains the accent."

Dean looked confused. "What accent?"

"Exactly. He's probably never been closer to Switzerland than a box of instant hot chocolate. I'm curious; how did you find this out?"

No closer to understanding than he had been, Dean shrugged and moved on. "Mrs. Abrams stopped me on my way up the driveway to make sure the professor got in okay."

"On your way up the driveway?"

He nodded. "She leaned out her window. I had to stop or the cab of the truck would've taken her head off. She was, um . . ." He paused, uncertain of how to describe the bouffant vision, her hair oranger and higher than he'd ever seen it.

"She was what?" Claire demanded. "Irritating?"

"No. Well, yes. But also, dressed up."

"Is *that* all."

Dean nodded. It was a weak description, but it would have to do. If she'd been dressed any more up, she could've rested her chin on them. Shuddering slightly, he tried his best to forget.

Conscious of Austin apparently asleep on the other end of the counter and Jacques watching bull riding in her sitting room, she tried not to sound stilted as she asked, "Did you have a good afternoon?"

"Sure." When she seemed to be waiting for further information, he added. "I went over to my friend Ted's. We gapped the plugs and points and changed to a winter-grade oil."

Since she had no idea what that meant it seemed safest to make a noncommittal kind of sound.

"Did you want me for anything, then?"

"No." When he turned to go, she jumped into the pause. "That is, unless, if you like, we could maybe order a pizza and all three of us could watch a movie together this evening?"

"All three of us?"

"Four if you count Austin, but he'll lose interest if no one feeds him."

"Pizza and a movie?"

"Well, Jacques won't be eating. It's just I saw this ad, in the paper, and there's a pizza place on Johnson that rents videos, too, so you can have them both delivered. Together." She knew she was overexplaining, but she couldn't seem to stop. "I just thought that instead of cooking you might want to, uh, join us."

Chaperone us, decoded the little voice in her head. It wasn't coming from Hell, but then, it didn't have to.

"Sure."

Except this time *sure* meant, *if I have to.* Claire had begun to learn the dialect. "What's wrong?"

'Nothing. It's just, there's a game on . . .'

"No problem." Briefly, she wondered what sport, then dismissed the question as one of little importance. "We can watch the game."

His smiled blazed. "Great. Double cheese, pepperoni, mushrooms, and tomatoes?"

"That would be fine."

"I'll just go hang my jacket up and then I'll call."

On the way down the stairs, he checked the business card.

> Aunt Claire, Keeper
> Your Accident is my Opportunity
>
> (and your guess is as good as mine)

Stretched out on his back, all four paws in the air, Austin opened one eye as Claire drummed her nails against the counter-top. "You're not fooling anyone, you know."

"Get stuffed."

❖　　❖　　❖

As the first period careened toward the end of its allotted twenty minutes, Claire gnawed on a length of pizza crust and wondered just exactly what she thought she was doing. While Jacques had originally
resented Dean's intrusion into their evening, an involved discussion of
how hockey had changed since his death had considerably mollified
him. After an unsuccessful attempt to understand the fundamentals of
icing, Claire gave up and tuned out.

If she didn't want to be alone with Jacques, all she had to do was
remove his anchor from her sitting room; a simple solution that hadn't
even occurred to her. Why not?

"Why not, what, *cherie?*"

"Did I say that out loud?"

"*Oui.*"

She glanced over at Dean, who nodded. This was not good. In a
working Keeper, the line between the conscious and subconscious had
to be kept clearly defined. Fortunately, Montreal chose that moment
to score, and by the end of the period the conversation had been forgotten by everyone but Claire. And Austin.

"Looks like things are coming to a head," he muttered under the
cover of yet another beer commercial. "Going to have to be resolved
sooner or later."

"They've been resolved. Too young and too nice, and too dead."

"Dead's relative."

"It is *not.*"

"Then can I have some pizza?"

"No."

"No, what, Boss?"

Before she could answer, they heard the front door open. Austin
reached out and pressed the mute on the TV remote. "What?" he
demanded, tucking the paw back under his ruff. "You trying to tell me
that you guys don't want to know if he's alone?"

He wasn't.

"Mind the legs now, Professor. They're good quality, I only have
good quality things, but they're not as young as they once were, you
know, and I don't want to try and use them someday and find them
warped."

At the unmistakable sound of Mrs. Abrams' voice, Jacques faded slightly, muttering, "Someone for everyone. *C'est legitime*, it's true what they say." He'd been strongly enough affected not to add an *entendre*.

Austin poked a paw through the ghost. "Get out in the lobby and see what they're talking about."

"Claire said I am not to spy on the guests."

"So spy on the neighbor!"

He started to dematerialize, then thought better of it and glanced at Claire.

"Go ahead."

"Jacques, don't." Dean's hand went through an ethereal arm. "They have a right to their privacy."

"Jacques, go. Or they'll be upstairs and we'll never know."

Turning toward Dean, Jacques spread his hands in a gesture that clearly indicated whose side of the argument he came down on and vanished.

"Don't tell me," Claire cautioned Dean before he could speak, "that you're not curious because I won't believe you. I mean, good quality legs?"

"Well, for a woman her age . . ." His voice trailed off as Jacques reappeared.

"They carry a small folding table."

"A card table?"

"I see no cards but she is wood and square, like so." He held his hands out just beyond shoulder width.

"The table is?"

"*Oui.*"

"They're going to play cards." Claire knew she had no right to feel relieved, but a card game was a lot less disturbing than what she'd been imagining. *Get a grip, Claire. Irritating old women have as much right to a sex life as you do. . . .*

"I'm glad Mrs. Abrams has a friend to share her interests," Dean said happily, reaching for the remote as the second period started.

Grinning broadly, Jacques rolled his eyes. One fell off the edge of the coffee table.

. . . maybe more.

❖   ❖   ❖

With eight minutes still on the clock until the second intermission, Claire felt the hair lift off the back of her neck. "Something's happening."

"It's a power play for Montreal," Dean explained. "New Jersey got a penalty for high sticking, so they have one less man on the ice. They're only one goal ahead so Montreal wants to lengthen their lead."

"That's not what I meant." Claire heaved herself up out of the sofa and onto her feet. "Austin . . ."

"Yeah. I feel it, too." Tail twice its normal size, he jumped down onto the floor, breathing through his half-open mouth.

"It's coming from inside the hotel."

"The furnace room, then?" Dean asked, eyes locked on the television. Montreal had the puck. Hell could wait another twenty-three seconds.

"No, it's not the furnace room, and it's not *her* either."

"That's good."

"No, that's bad. An unidentified power surge in this building can't be good."

"Claire." Jacques stared at her through the translucent outline of his hand. "I am fading."

She was about to tell him to *stop* fading when the near panic *in* his declaration broke through. "You're not doing it on purpose?"

"*Non.*"

"Medium."

How Austin had hissed a word containing no sibilants, Claire had no idea and no time to investigate. "Professor Jackson! They're not playing cards, they're having a seance and something's gone wrong; come on!" She ran for the door, the cat close on her heels.

The buzzer sounded the end of the power play, releasing Dean's attention. "Hey! Where are you going?"

"To save Jacques!"

He caught up in the office. "From what?" he asked as the four of them, Jacques nearly transparent, crossed the lobby.

"Professor Jackson is a medium," Claire told him starting up the stairs at full speed. "A real medium. Not a fake. They're rare—thank God. They have power over spirits."

"*Comme moi?*" His voice had faded with him.

"Yeah, like you." She missed a step, would've fallen except Dean grabbed her arm. "Thanks." Charging out into the second floor hall, she banged on the door to room one with her fist "Mrs. Abrams! Professor Jackson! Stop what you're doing and open the door! Now!"

"*Cherie . . .*" One hand stretched toward her, Jacques disappeared.

"No!" Whirling around she reached through the possibilities for power, but before she could blow the door off its hinges, Dean stepped back and slammed the sole of his work boot into the lock. The effect was much the same.

Professor Jackson stood in the midst of a blazing vortex of tiny lights dancing on a manic wind—although stood wasn't entirely accurate as his feet dangled a good six inches off the floor. Sitting on the corner of the bed, the card table pulled up over her knees, Mrs. Abrams stared wide-eyed, one hand pressed up against her mouth, the other making shooing motions toward the lights.

"What's happening?" Although the hall had been silent, one step over the threshold, Dean had to shout to make himself heard.

"It looks like Jacques is more than he can handle."

Dean's eyes widened. "Jacques is attacking him?"

"Jacques is not doing anything. The professor started something he couldn't control."

"Then where is he?"

"Who?"

"Jacques!"

Claire waved a hand toward Professor Jackson. "He's in those lights. Bits of him may even be in the professor!"

"Connie!" Mrs. Abrams' shriek cut through the ambient noise like a vegetarian through tofu. "You've got to do something!"

Which was true.

"Dean! Try and keep Mrs. Abrams calm."

"While you do what?"

"While I rescue Jacques!"

"Be careful!" Body leaning almost forty-five degrees off vertical, he fought his way through the wind to the bed.

"It's the residual power from when *she* made him flesh!" Ears flat against his head, Austin had tucked himself into the angle between floor and wall, claws hooked deeply into the carpet. He stared up at Claire through narrowed eyes. "Can you bring him back?"

"I think so!" Reaching for calm, Claire shuffled quickly forward, never breaking contact with the floor, at about half Dean's weight, she couldn't risk being blown away. A little better than an arm's length from the professor, she marked her spot and started to spin. She moved slowly at first, barely managing to keep her balance; then the power lifted her and she began to pick up speed as she rose into the air. The room whirled by, faster, faster, until the walls began to blur and the tiny points of light were pulled from their orbits around Professor Jackson. *Oh, dear; I really wish I hadn't had that third slice of pizza. . . .*

"Catherine! What do you think you're doing? You've got to save the professor!"

"She's trying to, Mrs. Abrams!" Dean wasn't entirely certain Mrs. Abrams had heard him. With Claire picking up speed, the winds had doubled in intensity. He ducked as the lamp from the bedside table flew by, cord dangling. The table followed close behind. On one knee beside the bed, he was horrified to feel it begin to shift. Throwing possible consequences, as it were, to the wind, he flung himself down beside the old woman, grabbed her around the waist with one arm, and blocked the professor's flying suitcase with the other. Under him, the bed bucked and twisted, fighting to throw off the extra weight that kept it on the floor.

The card table never moved. The flame of the single candle never flickered.

Even behind the protection of his glasses, the wind whipped the moisture from his eyes. Lids barely cracked, Dean watched the little lights leave the professor and move to circle Claire. Sometimes singly, sometimes in clumps, they did one figure eight around both spinning figures, then settled down in their new orbit. When all the lights had shifted, including a few pulled painfully from under the professor's skin, he breathed a sigh of relief and almost got beaned by a worn leather shaving kit sucked out of the bathroom and into the maelstrom.

It wasn't over yet

Now the lights began to orbit a new position equally distant from both spinners. The third point on the triangle. Once again they traced a single figure eight and then began to spin in place.

The bed lifted, four inches, five, six, then banged back down onto the floor.

A familiar form began to take shape in the center of the lights. And then the lights began to spiral inward.

Muscles straining, Dean somehow managed to keep a protesting Mrs. Abrams on the bed. At least he thought she was protesting—he couldn't hear a thing she was shouting over the roaring of the wind, the pounding of his heart, and the cracking of her heels against his shins.

One by one, the drawers were sucked out of the bureau.

With every light that disappeared Jacques grew more defined.

Dean frowned. Too defined, "Claire! His clothes!"

She didn't seem to hear him but maybe the clothes came last.

More and more lights were absorbed until only a few remained. Jacques seemed more solid than he ever had.

Dean's gaze dropped. He almost let go of Mrs. Abrams in shock until he remembered the force of Jacques' spin had to be distorting reality.

The last light slid in under Jacques' left arm.

Nothing happened. All three bodies continued to spin. The wind continued to howl.

Although it was difficult to tell for certain with her face flicking in and out of sight, Dean thought that Claire frowned. The index finger of her right hand curved up to beckon imperiously.

One final light, almost too small to see, sucked free from the professor, circled Claire and smacked Jacques right between the eyes. Which opened.

The wind quit.

The candle flame went out.

". . . member of the Daughters of the Parliamentary Committee and if you don't stop this, this moment, I'll be speaking to my MP!" Mrs. Abrams' ultimatum echoed in the sudden silence. "Well." She tossed her head, the lacquered surface of her hair crackling against Dean's chin. "That's better."

In the confusion of three bodies and various pieces of furniture hitting the floor, Dean managed to get across the room to Claire's side before Mrs. Abrams could react to his presence. One of the bureau drawers bounced off his left shoulder, but he considered bruising of minor importance compared to being caught with his arm, uninvited, around her waist She *might* thank him for keeping her out of the whirlwind, but the odds weren't good.

"Claire! Are you okay?"

"I'll be fine when the room stops whirling," she muttered.

"The room isn't moving."

"Says you." But she opened her eyes and lifted an arm. "Help me sit up."

"Candice! I demand an immediate explanation!"

With his left arm supporting her back, Claire shifted her weight against Dean's chest. "Mrs. Abrams," she sighed "Go to sleep." They winced in unison at the sound of another body hitting the floor. "Put her back on the bed, would you, Dean."

The warmth of the sigh had spread through fabric to skin.

"Dean?"

He released her reluctantly. "But you . . ."

"I'm okay. Nothing wrong that a little vomiting couldn't cure." Dragging a dented wastebasket out from under the lamp and cradling it in her arms, she smiled wanly up at him. "No problem."

"If I could help, *cherie*?"

This was not something Dean could face on his knees. He stood, then turned, to find Jacques shrugging into a red-and-gray-checked flannel bathrobe. Reality, he noticed as the robe closed, appeared to have returned to normal proportions.

"Help Dean," Claire instructed from the floor. "I'll crawl over and check the professor."

"But *cherie* . . ."

"I know. But not until we've got this mess cleared up."

About to add his protest to Jacques', Dean suddenly realized that if the ghost—or whatever he was now—was with him, he wouldn't be with Claire. "Come on." He jerked his head toward the bed. "You take her feet."

"*Cherie* . . ."

"Not now."

As Claire started crawling toward the professor, Jacques shrugged and, stroking both hands down the nap of the robe, followed Dean.

Austin had reached and done a preliminary diagnosis on the sprawled body of Professor Jackson by the time Claire arrived. "He's having trouble breathing."

"He's got a ten-pound cat sitting on his chest."

"I'm big-boned," Austin amended, primly stepping off onto the floor. "I think he's blown a fuse or two."

"Serves him right." Setting the wastebasket to one side, Claire bent over the professor and lifted his left eyelid between her thumb and forefinger.

"So giving Jacques flesh was the only solution?"

"If you had a better one . . . ?"

"Me? Oh, no."

Letting the eye close with an audible snap, Claire glared at the cat. Traces of the matrix Aunt Sara had created to give Jacques flesh had been causing the problem; it made logical sense, therefore, to use those traces to solve the problem. She couldn't have come up with a faster or more efficient solution. That was her story and even in the relative privacy of her own mind, she was sticking to it. "What are you implying?"

"Me? Nothing." As the professor's head gently lolled toward him, Austin reached out a paw and pushed it back. "Hadn't you better pay attention to what you're doing?"

Teeth clenched, Claire carefully pulled power. After a moment Professor Jackson moaned and opened his eyes. "Where am I?" he asked breathily.

In ten years as an active Keeper only one person had asked a different question upon regaining consciousness and since, "Do it again," was actually a statement Claire had always assumed it didn't count. "Never mind," she said, brushing his eyes closed. "Go to sleep."

When he, too, had been laid out on the bed, at a respectable distance from Mrs. Abrams in spite of Dean's protest and Jacques' alternative suggestion, Claire told the two men to leave the room.

"*Cherie*, we have not so much time."

"I know. But I gave you flesh to save you—and to save him," she added nodding toward the bed. "Not to . . . um . . ." Very conscious of Dean's presence, she couldn't finish, but when Jacques took her arm and turned her slowly to face him, she didn't resist. His fingers, lightly stroking her cheek, were cool. His mouth had twisted up in the smile she found so hard to resist. When his lips parted, she mirrored the motion.

"Ow! Austin!"

"May I remind you," he said as she stumbled backward and would have fallen had not Jacques and Dean both grabbed an arm, "that the bodies *already* on the bed need tending; memories need changing."

"I was going to . . ."

"Please, no details. Just take care of these two first."

Lips pressed into a thin line, she jerked free and nodded toward the door. "Fine. Everyone out."

Not even Jacques argued.

"You take this calmly," he said thoughtfully to Dean, as the door closed behind them.

Dean shrugged. He didn't feel calm. He didn't know how he felt. "You don't seem very affected either," he pointed out as they followed Austin down the stairs. "Except that you're walking kind of carefully . . ."

"I am not use to feeling the floor."

". . . and you keep touching yourself."

Jacques drew himself up to his full height, which, with both feet on the ground was considerable shorter than it had been. "Do I make these personal comment about you, *Anglais*?"

"Sorry." Ears red, Dean shoved his hands in the front pockets of his jeans. "So, uh, what do we do now?"

"I do not know."

"I do." Leaping down the last three stairs into the lobby, Austin turned and stared up at them. "Forgetting for the moment that one of you is dead and one isn't and refusing to borrow trouble since none of us has any idea of how this is going to turn out I think you should feed the cat."

"Wasn't there a half a slice of pizza left?" Claire asked, dropping onto the sofa almost two hours later. "I'm starved."

On the other end of the sofa, Austin opened one eye. "I let the mice take it," he said. "I didn't think anyone wanted it."

Pinching the bridge of her nose with one hand, Claire waved away the information with the other. Mice. Fine. Whatever. "Where are the guys?"

"*Here I am.*" Jacques emerged from the bedroom, fiddling with the belt of the professor's robe. "I forget how many sensation in the world; old, new . . ."

Then the bathroom door opened and Dean came out glasses in his hand, the edges of his hair damp. Claire opened and *closed* her mouth a time or two, but no sound emerged.

Dean's ears turned scarlet as he hastily shoved his glasses on. "I'm sorry, Claire. I used your towel. It's just it was getting late and the game just ended and I was after waiting up for you . . ."

"Game?"

"*Oui.* Hockey with ducks," Jacques explained, lip curled.

"Hockey," Claire repeated.

Austin snickered. "I know what new sensations you were thinking about."

"Shut up."

"Someone's got a dir . . ."

Dragging him onto her lap, she cupped her hand over his mouth. "Someone also has opposable thumbs," she reminded him.

The sound of voices in the lobby diverted attention.

"Mrs. Abrams leaving," Claire explained, covering a yawn. "She remembers a lovely seance where Professor Jackson contacted the ghost of the young man she'd seen standing in the window of room two as a girl and then more recently in the dining room, and the lobby, and the office, and back in the window of room two."

Jacques winced as her voice picked up an edge toward the end of the list. "I am sorry, *cherie.* I thought she see me only once."

"You thought she saw you and you didn't tell me?"

"I did not think it important."

"If I'd known, I could've prevented this whole incident from happening."

"*Oui,* but then I would not have flesh."

Claire decided to avoid that issue for a few moments longer and slid right on by without even pausing. "Well, now she believes that you've gone happily to your final rest, passed over into the light, so . . ." She managed energy enough to jab a finger at the ghost. ". . . stay away from windows!"

"I will."

"And if she happens to accidentally see you . . ."

"I tell you, *immediatement*."

"Good." Yawning, Claire sagged back into the sofa. "The funny thing is, I'm not the first Keeper to mess with her head. There's a whole section of early memories that've been dramatically changed."

"Mr. Smythe told me that she lived in the house next door her whole life," Dean offered. "He said it used to be Groseter's Rooming House and Mr. Abrams was a roomer who didn't move fast enough and got broadsided." When Claire lifted her head to stare at him, he shrugged apologetically. "That's what *Mr. Smythe* said. Anyway, she's always saying things aren't like they were when she was a girl. Maybe she was poking around and saw something she shouldn't."

"You mean *besides* Jacques?"

Without an actual exhalation, Jacques' sigh lost emphasis, but he made up for it with the peripherals. Bending over the back of the sofa, he tucked a curl behind Claire's ear. "I am sorry the old woman cause you problems, *cherie*, but I am a long time dead and I am not surprise someone sees me."

"Not surprised." She started to move into his touch and when she realized, jerked her head away.

He smiled. *"Oui."*

"I think . . ." Reaching up, she flicked the curl back where it had been. "I think she probably wandered into the furnace room, maybe followed the Keeper down."

"Her?" Dean asked, jerking a thumb toward room six.

"Probably Uncle whoever. During the months *she* was Keeper here, Mrs. Abrams was a teenager; too old to go poking around the neighbor's . . ." Another yawn cut off the last word. ". . . basement."

"Time for bed, *cherie*."

Dean jerked up onto his feet "Yeah, I, uh, should get down, um, downstairs." Unable to say what he wanted to say—and not entirely sure what that was—he couldn't seem to put a coherent sentence together. "It's, uh, been a long, you know, day." Feeling the blood rise in his cheeks and wishing that the floor would just open up and swallow him whole, he headed for the door.

"Dean, wait."

With one foot in the office and one foot still in Claire's sitting room, he waited. Because she asked him to. He wondered if she knew how much he'd do for her if she asked him to.

To his surprise, he felt her hand in the small of his back, moving him out into the office. She followed and closed the door.

"After everything we've been through this last month, I thought you should know that Jacques and I aren't . . . that is, I'm not . . . I mean, we won't . . ."

"Why not, then?"

Claire stared up at him in astonishment. "Why not?"

Overcoming the urge to grab her and shake her, Dean nodded. "Yeah, why not? You gave him the flesh he's been bugging you for."

"Only to save him and the professor and only until dawn."

"Okay. But since you both want to . . ." He raised a hand to cut off her protest "I'm not blind. I can see the way you two are together. Why shouldn't you take advantage of it?"

"He's dead?"

"Are you asking me if that's a reason?"

"No," she said slowly. "I guess not. Even though Jacques' body died, his passion, his personality, even his physical appearance, they stayed. And now they have substance." Standing so close she could smell the faint scent of fabric softener that clung around him, Claire looked up and tried to see past her reflection in his glasses. "And you're okay with this?"

Dean blinked. The way he'd played out this scene, he asked her, "Why not?" and she said, "Because it's you I really want," and things moved to a satisfactory if somewhat undefined conclusion from there. He hadn't intended to talk her into it. Since that's what he seemed to have done, although he wasn't entirely certain where things had gone wrong, there seemed to be only one way out. "Sure. Go ahead."

Claire expected *sure* to mean, *Would it matter to you if I wasn't?* It didn't and she couldn't seem to find an actual translation. "I'm not saying that I'll rearrange my life to spare your feelings, but I don't want you to be . . ." She'd intended to say hurt but the assumption that her actions would cause him pain just sounded too egotistical. Even for a Keeper. ". . . upset."

"Not a problem."

It was, actually, but every Keeper learned early in her career that sometimes a lie had to serve. People were entitled to emotional privacy. "Good night, Dean."

"Good night, Boss."

She watched him go down the hall, listened to him go down the stairs, until a furry weight against her shins distracted her. "What?"

"*Sure* meant I'm not so stupid that I can't see you've made your choice, so if I get all bent out of shape about it I'll look like some kind of a wuss moaning on and on about what I can't have, so I'm just walking away and pretending it doesn't matter."

Claire blinked. "How do you know that?"

"It's a guy thing."

"Yeah. Right." Stepping over Austin and purposely closing the door in his face—not that a closed door ever stopped him— Claire went back into the sitting room to find Jacques sprawled in the armchair poking himself on the bridge of the nose with an old wooden ruler. "Why are you doing that?"

"I have never done it before." He tossed the ruler aside and stood. "You have said what you have to say to our young friend?" When she nodded, he reached for her hands. "*Bien.* Now I will say something to you."

"Jacques . . ."

"*Non.* My turn." His grip tightened around her fingers, cool and still weirdly insubstantial. "I desire you. You know how I wish to use this flesh you have given me, but I will not make pressure on you."

"Put pressure on you."

"That also. If you decide we will not be together tonight, I have a bed still of my own in the attic. But know that you are to me more than a way to break a very long time without a woman."

"Jacques."

He winced. "Too much? I should not have said the last about the woman, I know. It is funny, I am, how do you say . . . nervous."

"That's how we say it." This was the moment she had to decide.

On the one hand, Jacques was sexy and funny and there'd been a frisson between them from the moment she'd forced him to materialize. On the other hand, he was dead. That would definitely be a problem for most people. "I don't want to be like *her*."

"You are not anything like *her*." Releasing her hands, he cupped her face.

"I don't want to just use you."

"Use me, *cherie*. I can stand in."

"Stand it."

"We are both needing each other, Claire. Stop worrying about regrets you might have tomorrow. This is now."

He was going to kiss her; it hadn't been so long that she couldn't recognize the preliminaries. She just didn't know how she was going to respond. Fifty-three seconds later, she found out.

"Oh, my . . ."

PERFECT. SHE'S DISTRACTED.

WE SHOULD BE UP THERE, the rest of Hell protested. WE'RE MISSING A TERRIFIC OPPORTUNITY TO SCREW WITH HER HEAD.

I'VE GOT BETTER OPPORTUNITIES DOWN HERE.

The power seepage had been gathered in one place, prevented from escaping into the shield.

ARE YOU GOING TO CREATE ANOTHER IMP?

YOU KNOW WHAT YOUR PROBLEM IS? YOU DON'T THINK BIG ENOUGH. THAT'S WHY YOU'RE GOING TO SPEND AN INFINITE AMOUNT OF TIME DOWN IN THAT PIT.

YOU CAN'T GET THE SEEPAGE THROUGH THE SHIELD.

OH, YES, I CAN.

NO, YOU CANT.

YES, I CAN.

N . . .

ARE YOU ARGUING WITH *ME*? The silence seemed to indicate that, no, it wasn't "GOOD. I CAN GET THE SEEPAGE THROUGH THE SHIELD USING THE CONDUIT THE KEEPERS HAVE PROVIDED.

The hoarded seepage began moving.

Low wattage lights went on in the rest of Hell as realization dawned. BUT THAT POWER GOES RIGHT UP TO *HER!*

YES.

SHE TRIED TO USE US.

AND FAILED.

WE'D RATHER NOT RISK THAT AGAIN.

NO ONE ASKED YOU. *SHE* WILL TAKE CARE OF THIS YOUNG KEEPER FOR ME.

Up in room six, under dust-covered lids, Aunt Sara's eyes began to move in her first dream in over fifty years.

"Jacques, wait I felt something . . ."

"This?"

"No. . . . Oh. Yes."

"Hey, Diana." Phone cradled against her chin, Claire did up her cuff buttons and listened to the sounds of Dean moving about in the kitchen making breakfast "Is Mom home?"

"Hey, yourself," her sister responded suspiciously. "What are you doing up so early in the mor . . . Oh my God! You did it, you slept with the dead guy!"

Recognizing that the move was completely illogical but needing to do it anyway, Claire held the receiver out in front of her and stared at it.

"Don't bother denying it." Diana's voice came tinnily out through the tiny speaker. "I can hear it in your voice."

"Hear what in my voice?" Claire demanded, the receiver back to her mouth.

"You know, that post-necrophilia guilt. How was he? I'd make a crack about him being a stiff, but you'd blow."

"Diana!"

"Don't get me wrong, I understand your choice. I mean, even ignoring the whole forbidden fruit thing, Keepers have responsibilities—busy, busy, busy—and after a night in the sack, a dead guy's not going to expect you to settle down and play house. So did you give him back his actual flesh, or did you make some minor additions?"

Breathing heavily through her nose, Claire attempted to keep her voice level. "Is Mom home?"

"No. Lucky for you. What kind of an example are you setting here for your younger sister?"

"Tell her I called."

"Should I . . ."

"No. Just tell her I called."

". . . of course I landed on my feet, but the other guy . . ." Austin let his voice trail off as Claire came into the kitchen. Wrapping his tail around his toes, he sat and stared unblinkingly up at her.

Claire glanced over at Dean, who shrugged, then back at the cat. "What?" she sighed.

"Nothing. I just figured the first meeting between you and Dean the morning after would be awkward, and I wanted to start things off right I think you two can take it from here." Looking smug, he leaped down to the floor and padded away.

The silence stretched.

Having made his decision to cut a net he had no hope of hauling, to save the boat so he could fish another day, to suddenly get caught up in regional metaphors he'd never previously considered using, Dean should have slept the sleep of the just, the sleep of the man who has recognized that he'd lost the battle but by no means lost the war. As it happened, he slept hardly at all, Claire's bedroom being right over his. His imagination, deciding to make up for twenty years of benign neglect had kicked into overdrive the moment his head hit the pillow. He'd finally gotten a few hours' sleep on the couch in the next room.

"So," he said at last "you're up early. Where's Jacques?"

Before Claire could answer, he blushed and held up both hands. "I'm sorry. I didn't mean that to come out the way it sounded."

"What way?"

"Like I had a right to know." He took a deep breath, adjusted his glasses, and said, "Did you want some coffee, then?"

"Sure." When Dean shot her a surprised glance before reaching for a mug, she hoped she'd got the nuance right. She'd intended *sure* to mean, *nothing's changed between you and me.* Dean could continue feeling how he felt about her—a little unrequited whatever it was he felt wouldn't hurt him—and she'd continue thinking of him as an incredibly nice, gorgeous kid who just happened to do windows. She'd come to that conclusion while dressing, wondering why she was making such a big deal out of Dean's reaction. "Jacques went back to the attic. He said he needed some time to think."

"Ah."

The silence fell again.

"Professor Jackson's not down yet."

Dean gratefully looked at his watch. "No, but then it's just turned eight."

"Ah."

Before the silence extended far enough to elicit a conversation about the warmer than seasonal weather, the front door opened. And closed.

Dean frowned. "Stay where you're at," he muttered, untying his apron, "I'll get it."

Sighing, Claire started walking toward the lobby. "What have I told you about this kind of thing?"

"Specifically?"

"Generally."

"You're a Keeper and you can take care of yourself?"

"Bingo."

Bent nearly double, stroking Austin as he wound around black leggings and chunky ankle boots, the young woman in the lobby seemed to be neither a threat nor a guest. When she straightened, one hand rising to try and brush disheveled blonde curls down over the purple-and-green swelling on her forehead, Claire got the impression of a person just barely hanging on to the end of her rope.

A quick glance at Dean showed him ready to pound whoever, or whatever, had brought such a fragile beauty to such a state.

The delicate jaw moved slowly up and down on a piece of gum. The weary motion seemed so involuntary it came as a bit of a shock when she stopped chewing to speak. "I've been walking all night" she offered tentatively, "and I need, um . . ."

"A room?" Claire asked.

She glanced back over her shoulder before answering. "I haven't any money."

"That's all right" Keepers went where they were needed; sometimes, need came to them. Without turning, Claire lightly touched Dean's arm. "Go make up room three."

"Sure, Boss."

No one spoke again until he'd disappeared up the stairs.

"This is a beautiful cat." A trembling hand ran down the black fur from head to tail. "Is he yours."

"Not exactly."

"I had a cat once." She closed shadowed eyes. When she opened them again, she stared around the lobby as if wondering where she was.

Austin nudged her.

"I saw your sign. I thought, if I could lie down for a few hours, I could figure out what to do. But I can't pay you. . . ."

"The room's there and it's empty," Claire told her, stepping forward. "You might as well use it."

Clearly too tired to think straight, she shook her head. "That's not how it works."

"That's how it works here."

"Oh." She looked up the stairs and thin shoulders sagged. "I don't think I can."

"I'll help." By the third step, Claire had wrapped the girl's weight in power. Reaching the first floor hall, hoping the professor wouldn't chose this moment to head downstairs for breakfast, she led the way to room three, pausing outside the door to allow Dean to leave.

When he opened his mouth to speak, she shook her head and pushed past him. He couldn't help until they knew what was going on.

Settling the girl on the edge of the bed, Claire stepped back and watched Austin make himself comfortable beside her. "Do you mind if he stays?"

"Oh, no." Her hand reached out to stroke him again. "You and that big man, are you happy?"

Claire blinked, completely taken aback. "There's nothing between me and Dean."

The ugly bruise on the girl's forehead darkened, surrounded by an embarrassed flush. "I'm so sorry. It's just that you looked . . ."

"Postcoital," Austin murmured when she paused.

"Ignore that, *please,*" Claire suggested, spitting the magic word through clenched teeth, "I'll leave you now, get some sleep. We'll talk later."

HELLO. . . .

NOT NOW. I DON'T WANT THE PISSANT LITTLE EN-ERGY WE CAN PUSH OUT OF HERE WASTED ON TRIFLES.

YOU DON'T WANT? WHAT ABOUT WHAT WE WANT?

Time passing suddenly became the loudest sound in the furnace room. After a moment, the rest of Hell answered their own question. NEVERMIND.

By the time Claire got back to the kitchen, Professor Jackson had descended for breakfast. He seemed extraordinarily pleased with himself as he ate his bacon and eggs. He hummed slightly as he spread jam on his toast, and he stirred his coffee with the air of a man who'd lived up to his own extraordinary expectations. Fortunately, he'd lifted himself to such exalted heights, he was far beyond making casual conversation with mere hotel staff.

Wiping his mouth, he rose from the table and graciously informed both Dean and Claire that he'd be leaving as soon as he packed.

"Well?" Dean demanded the moment the professor was out of earshot. "Who is she? What happened? Does she want us to call the police?"

"I have no idea, but Austin stayed with her so we'll soon find out."

"Austin?"

"Why not. She's tired and vulnerable. . . ."

Dean nodded, understanding. "He'll be a nonjudgmental comfort to her."

"No, he'll take advantage of it. He's a cat not Mother Theresa." Claire poured herself a bowl of cereal and sat down. "It shouldn't be much longer."

On cue, Austin jumped up onto the counter. "All right; bacon." Glancing over at Claire, he added, "Which I, of course, can't eat even though I've been gathering vital information about the young woman in room three."

Claire sighed. "One small piece."

"Two."

"One and the dregs of milk from my cereal."

"Not if it's bran; last time I was in the litter box all morning."

"It's not."

"Deal."

They waited more-or-less patiently while he ate and not at all patiently while he washed his whiskers.

"First of all," he said, at last, "it's not what you think. Her name is Faith Dunlop. . . ."

"She told a cat her name?"

"Don't be ridiculous; I hooked her ID out of her pocket when she fell asleep." He snorted. "Who tells a cat their name?"

"Just get on with it."

"Who hit her?" Dean demanded.

"No one. She walked into a door. Our little Faith was leaving in a hurry because she'd just helped her boyfriend rip off a convenience store out on North Montreal Street. When they split up to throw off pursuit, she had the bag of loot. Unfortunately, she left it on a bus and now she's afraid to go home because this is the second time something like this has happened and the boyfriend is going to be very unhappy."

Claire stared at Austin in astonishment. "This is the second time she's left the loot on a bus?"

"If I understood her correctly—and between the sobbing and the gum she wasn't very coherent—the last time she left it in the women's washroom at a fast food restaurant but essentially the same scenario, yes."

"She's afraid of her boyfriend?" Dean growled. Behind his glasses, his eyes narrowed to a line of blazing blue. "Oh, I get it; first off, he forces her into a life of crime and then, when she can't perform to his satisfaction, he beats her."

"She walked into a door," Austin protested.

"Sure. This time. But what'll happen when she gets home? She's terrified of him, or she wouldn't have been out all night, forced to throw herself on the kindness of strangers."

Claire sighed. She'd just discovered two things about Dean. The first, which was hardly unexpected considering the rest of his personality, involved taking the side of the weak against the strong. The second, that at some point in his scholastic career he'd been forced to read *A Streetcar Named Desire*. "You don't know any of that for certain."

He folded his arms across his chest. "I know what I see in front of my face."

"I don't know how you can see anything with your eyes slitted closed like that."

"It's obvious what happened!" His jaw thrust slightly forward.

"It's never that obvious." Pouring herself a cup of coffee, she asked Austin if he'd got a look at Faith's home address when he snagged her ID. When he admitted that he had, she headed for the phone.

Hurriedly picking up the empty cereal bowl and putting it in the sink, Dean followed. "What are you doing?"

"Calling Faith's apartment and telling the boyfriend where she is. Once he's here, I can protect her, but until I hear the whole story, I can't help her."

"You're after helping her right into the hospital!" Rushing forward, Dean put himself between Claire and the phone. "Look, you can put yourself into whatever weird relationships you want, but you can't make those kind of choices for Faith."

"Weird relationships?"

"Uh, oh." Ears close to his head, Austin ducked under the desk.

Claire's nostrils flared. "I thought you said you were okay with it?"

"Well, what else was I supposed to say? You're the Keeper; you always know what you're doing, and you never listen to me. I can't even get you to put your dirty dishes in the sink!"

He was right about the dishes. Claire took a deep breath and forced it out through clenched teeth. "Move away from the phone, Dean. I know what I'm doing."

"And I don't?"

"I didn't say that"

"But you're always implying it. After all, I'm just the bystander and all this lineage stuff is way over my head. Okay. Maybe it is. But this," he stabbed a finger toward room three, "this is people stuff, and I know people stuff better than you."

"The moment Faith entered this hotel, she *became* lineage stuff."

They locked eyes for a long moment. Finally, Dean jerked away from the phone. "Okay. Fine. If you're not after listening to me, I'll go and do the dishes. That seems to be all I'm good for around here."

"Dean . . ."

"You know where to find me if you want something unimportant taken care of." Heels denting the floor, he stomped back to the kitchen.

"I told you so," Austin muttered, still safely hidden under the desk.

"Told me what?" Claire asked, fingers white around the receiver.

"That Dean's all bent out of shape about you pounding the mattress with Jacques."

"Jacques wasn't even mentioned!"

He stuck his head out and stared up at her in disbelief. "You really aren't any good at this people stuff, are you?"

Just after ten, Professor Jackson checked out. He paid in cash and, although a number of smaller things had been broken the night before, he made no mention of them. Since, technically, Claire had broken them, she let it slide.

"I'll just go up and clean the room, then, shall I, Boss?"

Claire'd been trying to think of a way to apologize—although in spite of a nagging feeling that she was in the wrong, she wasn't sure for what—but Dean's emphasis on that *Boss* changed her mind. She'd wait until he decided to stop being so childish.

At eleven, she tried Faith's home number again. She'd left two previous messages on the answering machine, and when the same annoying little song came on telling her to *not make a peep till the sound of the beep,* she decided not to leave a third.

When Dean came downstairs at eleven-forty carrying a wastebasket full of broken lamp, the office was empty, but a thin man in a Thousand Islands baseball cap and jean jacket that looked two sizes too large was limping across the lobby. "Can I help you?"

He jerked around to face the stairs. Pale lips, under a sparsely settled mustache, lifted in what could have been a smile but was probably a twitch. "Hi. Yeah. I'm here for Faith."

"Faith?"

"Yeah. I'm Fred." The tip of his nose was an abraded pink that vibrated slightly with every word. "She's not gone?"

"No." Dean descended the last three steps and was disappointed to see that he still towered over Faith's boyfriend. He'd been hoping for a big man, one he could flatten without guilt. "What happened to your foot?"

"My foot?" Eyes wide, Fred stared down as though amazed to see a foot on the end of his leg. "Oh. That foot. I had an accident, eh." He laughed nervously. "Dropped a cash register on it. Hurts like hell."

NOT QUITE. BUT IT COULD.

Dean set down the wastebasket and jiggled his baby finger in his right ear, anger momentarily swamped by confusion. "Did you hear that?"

"Hear what?"

"Nothing."

DON'T YOU JUST WISH YOU COULD WIPE THIS KIND OF SCUM RIGHT OFF THE FACE OF THE EARTH?

"Well, yeah, but that wouldn't solve anything."

"What?" Fred backed up a step, looking like a small rodent suddenly face to face with a very large cat.

"Did I say that out loud?"

"What?"

If Fred was a monster, Dean decided, he hid it well. On the other hand, a man facing a much larger man was often a different person than a man facing a woman. "Look, you wait here. I'll check if Faith wants to see you."

"Is she all right? Is she hurt? The message said she was just tired." What seemed like near panic jerked the words out in a staccato rush.

"She's fine."

"Then why wouldn't she want to see me?"

Dean sighed. "Just wait here, okay?"

Fred's gaze skittered around the office as though checking for traps. When it finally got back to Dean, he nodded. "Okay."

Shaking his head, Dean started up the stairs.

THOSE KIND OF WEASELS ARE THE FIRST TO PICK ON SOMEONE WEAKER THAN THEMSELVES. YOU SHOULD SHOW HIM HOW IT FEELS.

Dean's fingers curled up into fists.

VIOLENCE IS ONE OF OURS.

Down in the lobby, Fred shifted his weight off his bad foot and stared mournfully at the stairs. He didn't want to wait, he wanted to see Faith.

Which was when he noticed the elevator. A fascination for all things mechanical drew him across to it, limp almost forgotten. He opened the door, peered past the gate, down into the shaft, and could just make out the top of the car. It seemed to be in the basement

Brow furrowed under the brim of his cap, he opened the door immediately to his left.

The basement stairs.

It was easier going down the stairs than up. He could take the elevator to the top of the hotel and go down to Faith's room, missing the big guy with the glasses entirely.

No one would mind. Elevators were there to be used.

Leaning outside the door to room three while Faith put on her face, Dean polished his glasses with the hem of his shirt and tried not to think about how much he'd enjoy flattening Fred's quivering pink nose.

ONE, TWO, SPLAT. THAT'S THE TICKET.

Lost in memories of a childhood spent riding the old elevator at the S&R Department Store, Fred touched two fingers to his cap brim, murmured, "First floor, ladies lingerie," and twisted the brass lever to UP.

Sitting in the bathroom, reading the Apothecary's new catalog, Claire heard the unmistakable sound of an ancient elevator starting up.

By the time she reached the lobby, it was just passing the first floor. She didn't know the man inside.

Dean frowned as he heard the elevator rise to meet the second floor, then he shrugged. Claire'd said she was through testing, but obviously she'd thought of something else to try.

Then he heard:

"Second floor, housewares and cosmetics."

By the time he got across the hall, all he could see was the bottom third of a pair of grimy jeans and Fred's worn and grubby running shoes.

He had to beat the elevator to the third floor. If Fred opened the door . . .

HE'LL GET WHAT HE DESERVES. FAITH'S TERRIFIED OF HIM. YOU SAW THAT YOURSELF. THERE'LL BE ONE LESS ABUSIVE WEASEL IN THE WORLD.

Dean hesitated.

Then Faith's door opened. When she stepped out into the hall and saw only Dean, her smile dimmed. "Where's my Pookie?"

Claire reached the second floor and saw Dean charging toward her. Then past her. The elevator had passed and was still moving up. Gasping for breath, she took the next flight of stairs two at a time, but had only reached the landing when Dean, who'd barely looked as though he were touching down at all, reached the top.

The growl of the motor stopped.

Unless he was a total klutz, it would only take seconds for the man inside to open the gate. The taste of old pennies in the back of her throat, Claire staggered into the third floor hall as the elevator door started to open. Before the latch cleared, Dean threw himself in front of it and slammed it shut

"Hey!"

Chest heaving, Claire staggered up on rubbery legs as Dean stepped back and, after making sure that it had indeed closed completely, pulled the door open.

"It's just I've got this sore foot," Fred began hurriedly. "And you know, the stairs are steep, and . . ."

Dean cut off the rest of the excuse by reaching in, grabbing the smaller man by the front of his jacket, and pulling him out into the hall.

"Pookie?" Faith's anxious voice drifted up from the second floor. "Is that you?"

"Yeah, Baby, it's me." Fred smiled, or twitched, nervously, eyes flicking from Dean to Claire and back to Dean. "She calls me Pookie."

"You must be the boyfriend," Claire hazarded.

"Yeah. I'm Fred."

She jerked her head toward the stairs. "Go on."

Fred sidled out of Dean's reach and limped quickly away.

Dean hadn't moved since he pulled Fred from the elevator. Worried, Claire took a step toward him. "Are you okay?"

He lifted horrified eyes to her face. "I hesitated."

"When?"

"When I heard the elevator go by. I heard a little voice say, he'll get what he deserves, and I . . ." He shook his head in disbelief ". . . I hesitated."

About to reassure him that it was no big deal, Claire suddenly realized that for Dean, it was. For the first time in his life, he hadn't automatically done the right thing. If she couldn't convince him to let it go, irrational guilt would eat at him for the rest of his life. *That's it, Claire, no pressure.*

Wrapping her fingers around his forearm, she gave him a little shake. "You saved him, Dean. I couldn't have gotten here in time."

"You don't understand. I actually thought about letting Fred . . ." Unable to continue, he shook free of her grip and stumbled back away from her.

Claire sighed. How unfortunate that smacking some sense into him would probably scar his psyche forever. "Dean, listen to me. I know you think I'm lousy at people stuff but I'm older, I'm a Keeper, I know; people think unworthy thoughts all the time."

LIKE THE ONE WHERE HE'S ON HIS KNEES AND . . .

Shut up. "It doesn't count if you don't act on it."

"But I hesitated."

"And then you made up for lost time. Trust me, they cancel each other out."

Dean forced a smile. "I appreciate you trying to make me feel better, Boss, but nothing can cancel out what I've done." The smile slipped. "I should go see if Faith needs my help." Trailing misery behind him like streamers of smoke, he started for the stairs.

Which was when Claire realized . . . "Dean, did you say you actually heard a little voice?"

"Yeah."

"How did it sound?"

Two steps down, he stopped and leaned back out into the hall. "Sound?"

"Can you describe it?"

"I guess." He frowned, brows dipping down below the upper edge of his glasses. "It sort of sounded like it was talking in block caps."

Should she tell him? Would it help? No. If Dean knew he was hearing the voice of Radio Free Hell, he'd be more convinced than ever that his hesitation had damned him. "Dean, do me a favor. If you hear the voice again, *please* ignore it."

After a moment, he nodded. "Okay."

A sudden shriek of laughter from below had them both clamping their hands over abused ears. Side by side, they hurried downstairs.

The second floor hall was empty so they kept going.

Inhaling his clean, fabric softener scent, Claire wasn't thinking of either Fred or Faith. After nine months, she wondered, what had finally given Hell a way in?

In room six, directly across from the open elevator door, Aunt Sara licked her lips.

Baseball cap skewed, Fred pulled out of the clinch as Claire and Dean emerged from the stairwell. "You were so good to Faith, you oughta know; we're giving up our life of crime."

"Although it wasn't really a life of crime," Faith protested. "It was only two stores and we paid for them taco chips."

"I think you've made a wise decision," Claire told them, smiling. "What do you think, Dean."

He shrugged and looked miserable. "I'm not one to say."

Claire rolled her eyes. This *I'm a horrible person stuff* was going to get old, really fast. "But you're glad they've decided to go straight, aren't you?"

"Sure."

That was good enough for Fred. "Thanks. Truth be told, we weren't any good at it."

Faith's lower lip went out, making her look like a pouty angel. "We coulda practiced more, Pookie. Or got a gun."

"No guns. People get hurt when you got a gun." He patted her shoulder. "I'm takin' that job with my cousin Rick." Turning back to Claire and Dean, he added, "Rick's got a truck, eh, and he hauls stuff."

"You're not gonna call the cops, are you?" Faith asked, leaning past him and twisting a curl around her finger.

"No."

"See, Pookie, I told you they were good people."

Dean winced.

Claire resisted the urge to stamp on his foot and give him something to wince about. Instead, she herded their modern Bonnie and Clyde to the front door and waved them out toward the waiting world. "Go home. Go straight. Be happy."

At the bottom of the steps, Faith turned and smiled beatifically back in at Claire. "Thank you for letting me use the room and everything."

"You're welcome."

"You figure their parents were cousins?" Austin asked when she closed the door.

"I have no idea."

He yawned, stretched, and glanced over at Dean. "What's with him? He looks like he just tried to kill somebody."

Dean stared wide-eyed at the cat. "You can tell?"

Austin sighed and flicked an ear toward Claire. "What's he talking about?"

"When he heard Fred going upstairs in the elevator, he hesitated before racing off to save him."

"Not much point in removing only one of them," Austin agreed.

"You're not helping," Claire snapped before Dean could react Crossing the lobby, she poked him in the chest. "Stop tearing yourself up over this. You aren't a horrible person. You've got to be the nicest guy I've ever met."

NICE GUYS FINISH LAST.

"Get out of my head."'

WE WEREN'T TALKING TO YOU.

Oh, Hell . . .

"Dean?"

"If you don t need me for anything, I'd like to go downstairs and do some serious thinking about my life." He spun on one heel and hurried off before she could answer, which was probably a good thing since she couldn't think of anything constructive to say.

Walking over to the counter, she scooped Austin up into her arms and stroked the top of his head with her cheek. "This is not good."

"What? That after living unaffected next to Hell for almost a year, Dean spends a month and a half in your company and all of a sudden he's willing to kill?"

"He hesitated! Then he saved the guy!"

"Face the facts, Claire, you've got him tied in knots. He's not thinking, he's reacting and that's exactly the sort of situation Hell loves to exploit."

THE CAT'S RIGHT.

"Of course I am; but who asked you?"

She set him back on the counter. "I'm not Dean's problem."

JEALOUSY IS ONE OF OURS.

"He said he was fine with me and Jacques."

YOU'RE REALLY NOT A PEOPLE PERSON, ARE YOU?

"Take your own advice and stop listening to Hell." Austin paused to lick at a bit of mussed fur. "Let Dean do his serious thinking, and maybe he'll solve the problem on his own."

"*Cherie?*"

"And speaking of problems."

Shooting Austin a warning look, she turned to face Jacques. Translucent in the light from the office window, he looked exactly the way he had the first day she'd set eyes on him. She realized that she'd been expecting their night together to have changed him, but, unfortunately, it seemed to have changed only her perception of him—men were just so much more attractive when they were opaque.

"You are more beautiful this morning than I have ever seen you." His eyes twinkled. It was a disconcerting effect since Claire could see the door through them. "I have been thinking. One night cannot balance so many years alone; perhaps this afternoon . . ."

"No."

His grin faded. "But *cherie*, was I not all I promise I would be?"

"Yes, but . . ."

The grin returned. "Give me flesh again, and we will drive away the but."

"Look, Jacques, you're dead, so you have nothing to do, but I'm alive and I have . . ."

STRANGE TASTE IN MEN.

Shut up. ". . . responsibilities."

Jacques looked interested. "Like what?"

"Like feeding the cat," Austin declared in a tone that suggested he shouldn't have had to mention it.

"And?" Jacques wondered.

"And that's not important right now. What's important is that you're dead and I'm alive . . ."

"Cherie, non."

". . . and no matter how many times I give you flesh, you'll still be *dead*!" The words echoed in the empty lobby. From the look of pained betrayal on Jacques' face as he dematerialized, he wouldn't be back any time soon. "I didn't mean to hurt him," she sighed. "I just wanted him to . . ."

"Go away. And he did, congratulations." Critically inspecting a front paw, Austin snorted. "I'm not sure this is as clean as it could be."

Claire grabbed the edge of the counter, bent over, and rhythmically banged her head against the wood.

THAT WAS FUN.

THIRTEEN

FOR THE FIRST TIME IN WEEKS, as the pipes banged out the news that Claire was in the shower, Dean wasn't lost in daydreams of soap and water. Kneeling by the bed, he pulled out his old hockey bag, the only luggage he'd brought from back home. It was pretty obvious that Claire thought they could just go on as though he hadn't been willing to murder Faith Dunlop's boyfriend for no greater crime than being a total moron. Maybe she could, but that sort of thing changed a guy.

Changed the way he looked at himself.

Maybe it was time he moved on.

"I see Dean's truck is gone."

Claire picked up her breakfast dishes, stared at them for a moment, and then carried them over to the sink. "He left about ten minutes ago."

Austin sat by his empty dish and curled his tail around his front feet. "He left without feeding the cat."

"You have such a rough life." She picked up a can and a knife and froze, eyes locked on the empty parking lot.

After a moment, Austin sighed. "Get a grip! He went for groceries, like he does every Saturday morning."

"I know." Under blouse and sweater, she could feel goose bumps lifting. "I just had this incredible sense of foreboding."

"Which is nothing compared to what you're going to have if you don't feed the cat."

"Can't you feel it?" she asked, scooping food into his dish. "When

I think of Dean, I get the feeling that events are poised on the edge of a precipice."

"A simple solution, *cherie;* do not think of Dean."

Straightening, Claire drew in a deep breath. She hadn't been looking forward to this, not after the way she'd smacked Jacques away from her yesterday.

When she turned, the ghost was sitting cross-legged on the dining room table—a position he favored because of how it irritated Dean. He grinned at her. "Why the long face, *cherie?* The day, she is sunny, Dean is gone, and me, I am here for company."

Claire searched his face unsuccessfully for any lingering sign of hurt and betrayal.

"Ah." The grin broadened. "You cannot see enough of me."

"Yesterday . . ."

"I am dead since 1922," he reminded her, with a matter-of-fact shrug. "I cannot carry all my yesterdays with me. Although," he winked, "some I remember very well and am anxious to repeat."

"Not now . . ."

"*Oui,* not now, not here. Although," he glanced around and smiled broadly, "you and me on this table; it would give the old lady something to see, yes?"

"No."

"Fraidy-cat." He blew her a kiss and dematerialized.

"Some of us," Austin muttered, jumping onto a chair and then up onto the counter, "don't appreciate the word cat being used in a derogatory manner. If you've left the television on PBS, he's going to be right back."

"It's probably still on TSN. I didn't check."

He rubbed his head against her elbow. "You okay?"

"I don't know. Nothing's changed with Jacques and everything seems changed with Dean. I can't figure it out."

"It's simple. Jacques is dead, he can't change. Dean's alive, he can't not change. Now me, I'm a cat. I don't need to change."

She reached down and scratched him gently between the ears. "What about me?"

"You need to move your fingers a little to the left. More. Ahhhhh. That's got it."

✿   ✿   ✿

An hour later, perched precariously on top of the stepladder, eyes squinted nearly shut against the thin November sun, Claire razored masking tape off the windows. As expected, there'd been no change in the shields around Aunt Sara and Hell. She'd written as much in the site journal and now had the rest of the day to fill. Jacques was watching television, Dean was still out, and if the masking tape didn't come off soon, it'd be there until Hell froze over.

SHE'S THINKING OF US.
    SO? KEEP WORKING.
    WE'LL NEVER WAKE *HER* USING SEEPAGE. The rest of Hell sounded sulky.
    I DON'T NEED TO WAKE *HER*. I MERELY NEED TO UN-BALANCE THE BALANCE OF POWER. *SHE'LL* DO THE REST.
    WHO?
    HER.
    HER?
    NO! *HER*, YOU IDIOT!

Picking bits of tape off the edge of the blade, Claire could just barely make out the unmistakable shapes of Mrs. Abrams and Baby by the driveway. Baby seemed to be sniffing the fresh concrete around the base of the railings.

    "I don't suppose you want to go chase that dog off our property?"

    "You suppose correctly." Sprawled in a patch of sunlight, Austin didn't bother opening his eyes. "But I'll pencil in a visit for later in the afternoon."

    "I can't see the fun in bothering a dog that neurotic."

    "You can't see the fun in shredding the furniture either. Don't worry about it."

    When Baby's head rose suddenly, ears flattened against his skull, Claire leaned forward to see what had caught his attention. The approaching pedestrian seemed to have no idea of the danger.

    "Oh, no." Although details had been washed out by the light, she knew that shape. Knew the way it moved. Watched it make a fuss over the big dog who, after a moment of visible confusion, actually wagged his stump of a tail.

Climbing down off the ladder, reluctantly deciding it might be safer if she wasn't holding the razor blade, Claire walked to the door and opened it.

Mrs. Abrams turned as she came out onto the step. "Yoo hoo! Courtney! Look who's here! It's your sister, Diana. She's come for a visit; isn't that nice?"

"Swell."

Diana looked up from murmuring endearments in under the points of Baby's ears. "Isn't this the sweetest doggie you've ever seen?"

"Oh, yeah, he's a real cream puff."

Giving the Doberman· a final pat and telling Mrs. Abrams she hoped to see her again, Diana picked up her backpack, ran up the front steps, and paused to examine Claire critically. "You ought to let your hair grow out, I can't believe you're wearing mascara in the house, and didn't I tell you that nail polish was bad for the environment?"

Claire stepped back and motioned her sister inside. "I don't want to. I don't care. And what are you talking about?"

"Nail polish remover is like, so toxic." She turned on the threshold to wave at Mrs. Abrams and Baby, then bounded inside. "Nice paint job. Forest green. Very trendy. Hey, Austin."

He lifted his head, sighed deeply, and let it fall back to the countertop. "Shoot me now."

ANOTHER KEEPER!

IT'S A CHILD. KEEP YOUR MIND ON YOUR WORK.

BUT THERE'S TWO OF THEM!

AND THERE'S VERY NEARLY AN INFINITE AMOUNT OF ME.

The rest of Hell considered the implied threat. GOOD POINT.

"Diana, why are you here?"

"I'm needed."

"For what?"

"I'm a Keeper." She ducked under the flap into the office. "We go where we're summoned, and I was summoned here."

"Here?"

"Uh-huh. Right here. Are you still using this old computer? You must've bought it, what, two, three years ago?"

"Three and a half, and don't touch it"

"Chill, I'm not going to hurt it." She tapped lightly on the monitor. "Oops." At Claire's low growl, she grinned. "Kidding. It's not even turned on."

"Diana."

"What?"

Claire took a deep breath and tried to remember where the conversation had diverged from the important questions. "Do Mom and Dad know you're here?"

"No. I snuck out in the middle of the night." Diana rolled her eyes. "Of course they know I'm here. They're Cousins. I'm a Keeper. And, at the irritating risk of repeating myself, I was summoned."

"All right. You were summoned. So?"

"So I guess I'm here to help you."

"You want to help?" Austin muttered. "Take a man off her hands."

"As if. Didn't Mom tell you? I'm a lesbian."

Claire sighed. "Isn't everyone?"

"You know, Claire . . ." Arms folded over her black jean jacket, Diana's eyes narrowed. ". . . I get the feeling you're not happy to see me."

"It's just . . ."

". . . that the thought of you and Hell in the same building is enough to give anyone with half a brain serious palpitations," Austin finished.

"No problem." Diana raised both hands to shoulder height, backpack sliding down her arm to swing in the crook of her elbow. "I solemnly swear to stay away from the furnace room. Now are you happy to see me?"

Claire's better judgment suggested she send Diana home immediately, summons or no summons. She had no idea what part of her kept repeating, *but she's your kid sister,* as though that had any relevance at all. Whatever part it turned out to be, it was doing a good job of drowning out her common sense. "All right I'm happy to see you. Now what?"

"Now, you give me the guided tour."

❖   ❖   ❖

There was a soccer game on in her sitting room; a dozen guys in green and white appeared to be running circles around a dozen guys in red and black. Claire wasn't even certain that they'd played soccer in Canada when Jacques died, but he was interested enough in this particular match that he'd faded out until only a faint distortion remained in the air above the sofa.

"*Imbecile!*"

Claire'd been half hoping he wouldn't be there at all, but since he was, and since she couldn't come up with any kind of a believable reason for him not to meet her sister, she called his name.

"Do you see that? The ball goes right by him, but he does not move to kicks it!"

"Kick it."

"*Tabernac! Qui t'a dit que tu puissejouer a balle?*"

"Jacques, there's someone here who wants to meet you."

He snorted. "Why not? These people, they are asleep!"

Reaching past him, Claire picked up the remote and muted the TV. "Could you focus?"

"Focus?" He looked down through himself. "Ah, *d'accord.*"

By the time Diana came into the room, his edges had firmed up. His eyes widened and he walked through the sofa toward her. "Another Keeper? And so young and beautiful."

Recognizing the reaction, Claire sighed. "Jacques, this is my sister Diana."

"Diana, fair huntress of the bow. Although," he added thoughtfully, "given how the rest have fallen, no doubt she is now fat and old."

"What are you talking about?"

"It's a long story," Claire answered before Jacques had a chance. "There, you've met him. Let's leave, so he can get back to his game."

Jacques glanced speculatively at her through his lashes. "Are you ashamed of me, *cherie?*"

"It's not you," Diana told him. "It's me."

"I'm going to the kitchen for a coffee, you kids have a blast working it out. Wait a minute!" Claire jabbed a finger in her sister's direction. "You just forget I said the word blast."

✿　　✿　　✿

The coffee helped. Claire sank into her regular chair at the dining room table and took another long swallow. Showing Diana the hotel had been exhausting. When they ended up in front of room six for the second time, Claire had accused her sister of clouding her mind. The resultant denials had lasted down all three flights of stairs and had been no more believable in the lobby than they had originally.

She'd emptied the mug and begun worrying about what Jacques and Diana were discussing when Dean's truck drove up. The feeling of impending doom returned. All the hair on her body standing uncomfortably on end, she hurried outside, ostensibly to help him carry in the groceries.

Reaching past him for a pair of canvas bags, she tried to sound nonchalant as she asked if he was all right.

"Sure."

He sounded all right; depressed maybe, but not doomed. She checked for the taint of dark or eldritch powers and found only that frozen peas were on sale for a dollar thirty-nine. "No trouble at the grocery store?"

"No."

"No trouble with the truck?"

"No." Dean held open the back door and stood aside so Claire could enter the building first. "What's the matter?"

"I don't know."

"Okay. I understand now why you don't trust me."

Teeth gritted, she put the bags down and turned to face him. "No, really, I don't know."

"She doesn't know why I'm here? Or she doesn't know when I'm leaving? Which?"

Claire's nostrils flared. She'd intended to tell Dean about her premonition but *not* in front of her sister. Diana in the same room with impending doom practically guaranteed Armageddon. "She'll be leaving on Sunday night because she's got school on Monday morning and she's already missed too much of it this year. Dean, this is my sister Diana."

"Hey." She waggled a hand in an exaggerated wave.

It was the first time Dean had felt like smiling all morning.

Although the sisters looked superficially alike—dark hair and eyes, short and thin—energy popped and fizzed around Diana as though she'd been carbonated. "Hi."

"So you're from Newfoundland?"

"That's right." Picking up the bag with the produce, he began putting things away.

"I've never been there."

"You'd have noticed," Claire added, passing over a package of luncheon meat.

"So." Diana picked up a loaf of bread and examined it critically. "Did you always want to work in a hotel?"

"No. I just needed a job."

"I hear Augustus Smythe was a real tyrant."

"He wasn't so bad."

"Worse than Claire?"

He stared down into a net bag of cooking onions. "Different."

"Still, I guess you get to meet a lot of interesting people working here. Vampires and werewolves and . . . Ow! Claire!"

They were standing about ten feet apart but, obviously, that hadn't been far enough. Dean had no idea of what was going on and no intention of getting between them. "Yeah," he said, folding the bags and putting them away, "lots of interesting people."

"How long are you planning on staying around?"

"Actually . . ." He took a deep breath, let it out slowly, and turned to face Claire. "Actually, I've been thinking of leaving."

"Leaving?"

"Yeah. You know, getting on with my life."

Silently congratulating herself for maintaining a neutral expression, Claire wondered why her reflection in his glasses looked as though she'd just been punched in the stomach. "When?"

"Soon. If you want, this can be my two week notice." When Claire gave no indication of what she wanted, he shrugged. "Nice meeting you, Diana. I've got to go make some phone calls."

"Well, thud," Diana said, as he disappeared down the basement stairs.

Claire felt as though she were waking up from a bad dream, the kind where she was trying to cross the road but her feet kept sticking in the asphalt and there were two trucks and a red compact car bearing down on her. "What do you mean, thud?"

"Thud. The sound of the other shoe dropping." Diana straightarmed herself up to sit on the edge of the counter. "A little more than a month ago, Mom said Dean was the most grounded guy she'd ever seen and now look at him. You've just cut the ground right out from under him, haven't you?"

"I have not."

"He must really dig your looks 'cause it can't be your personality."

"Diana!"

"I mean, Jacques is cuter than I expected and, okay, he makes me laugh with those corny pickup lines, but he's dead. In spite of the glasses, Dean's big-time beefcake. If *I* can see that, you should be able to. You had the perfect opportunity here, and you blew it."

"The perfect opportunity for what?" Claire demanded.

"For making the best of the situation and building a partnership with a really nice guy. Not my personal cup of tea, but a lot of people would jump at the chance."

"Why can't a man and a woman run a hotel together and just be friends?"

"Well, gee, I don't know, Claire. You're the one doing the horizontal mambo with the dead guy, you tell me?"

"We're not talking about Jacques!"

"Sure we are. Enlighten me; if you needed to bed one of them, and obviously you felt a need, why Jacques and not Dean? Don't answer, I'll tell you. They're both bystanders so that's not it. Is it because Dean's alive? No, from what I hear that's never been a problem in the past. Oh wait, could it be because you're an ageist?"

"A what?"

"You heard me, an age-ist! You think I'm incompetent because I'm younger than you, and you ignore the evidence and think Dean's a kid for the same reason."

"I don't have to stand here and listen to this."

"True."

"I have work to do."

"Okay. Go do it."

"Fine. I will." About to leave the kitchen, Claire whirled back around to glare at her sister. "Don't blow the place up while I'm not watching."

"I came to help, remember."

"Oh, you've been a *big* help."

Leaning back and kicking her heels against the lower cabinets, Diana waited until she heard the door to Claire's sitting room slam shut before she smiled triumphantly. "Made her think."

"And I'm all for that," Austin agreed, jumping up beside her. "As long as you *don't* blow the place up while she's not watching."

"I promised I'd stay out of the furnace room."

"Good for you."

"How come Claire screwed things up so badly?"

The cat shrugged. "She's a Keeper. She's trained to come in post-disaster and deal with the mess, so she has to make a mess of any potential relationships before she feels competent to deal with them."

"I'm a Keeper and I don't do that."

"Yet," Austin said, looking superior.

Golf had replaced the soccer game and Jacques was gone. Still steaming, Claire turned off the television and stomped through to the bedroom. In order to get far enough from her sister to keep from wringing her neck, she'd have to leave the hotel. Yanking open the wardrobe door, she stepped inside.

Right at the moment, she'd enjoy dealing with a troop of killer Girl Guides.

Still sitting on the counter, Diana searched the cupboards for cookies, found three-quarters of a bag of fudge creams, and sat happily eating them while she worked out a way to fix Claire's life.

Obviously, Claire needed to leave the hotel.

Since no other Keeper had arrived to take over the site, the site had to be closed.

In order for the site to be closed, the exact parameters of the current seal had to be determined.

"And since there's only one remaining witness . . ." Scattering cookie crumbs, Diana jumped down off the counter. ". . . the logical solution would be to ask her." She snapped her fingers toward the kitchen and headed for the stairs.

Behind her, the crumbs cleaned themselves up and dropped into the garbage.

Paying only enough attention to keep from tripping over unexpected phenomena, Claire strode deeper into the wardrobe.

There were, Diana realized, a couple of ways to get into room six. The first involved pulling enough power to melt the locks, but that kind of heat would probably also burn down the building.

She went looking for a set of keys.

I should have told her flat out that it was none of her damn . . . darned business. Her mind on other things, Claire moved toward a soft gray light. *I am not an ageist.*

"Hey, Dean, sorry to bother you, but I wanted to go poke around in the attic 'cept the door's locked and Claire's gone off with her keys."

"Claire's gone? Where's she at?"

"Oh, she stomped off into the wardrobe." Rocking backward and forward, heel to toe, Diana grinned up at him. "We had a fight, and she took off to think about what I said. I don't know if you've noticed, but Keepers have this tendency to think they're always right."

Dean's brows rose. "Aren't you a Keeper, then?"

"Well, sure, but that doesn't make Claire any less of a pedagogue."

"A what?"

"A know-it-all." Her eyes gleamed. "Although I'm leaving off a few choice adjectives. The attic?"

"Okay, sure." He pulled his key ring from his pocket dropped it in Diana's outstretched palm. "It's the big black one. You, uh, know about Jacques, then? The ghost? He might be in the attic."

"Yeah, Claire told me all about him." Closing her hand around the keys, she reached out and punched Dean lightly on the arm. "Don't worry, you're better off without her. She snores."

Don't worry? *If Claire told her sister all about Jacques,* Dean thought, watching Diana bound back up the basement stairs, *what did she tell her about you, boy?*

"Don't stand around with your thumb up your butt. What do you want?"

Claire's wandering attention snapped home. She was standing in a long room, lined with floor-to-ceiling bookshelves. Directly in front of her, sitting at a library table stacked with shoe boxes, was an older woman with soft white curls, wearing an ink-stained flowered smock. "Historian!"

"I know who I am," the Historian snapped. "Who the hell are you?"

"Claire, Claire Hansen. I'm a Keeper."

"You wouldn't be here if you weren't. Wait a minute." The Historian's eyes narrowed, collapsing the pale skin around them into a network of grandmotherly wrinkles. "I remember now, you were here three years, twelve days, eleven hours and forty-two minutes ago looking up some political thing. Did you finish with it?"

"The site?"

"No, democracy."

"Uh, not yet."

"Crap. You wouldn't believe the amount of paperwork it generates." She sighed and pushed away from the desk, giving Claire her first good look at the computer system nearly buried in shoe boxes.

"Is that one of the new 200MHz processors?"

"New? It was obsolete months ago. History. That's why it's here. So, since I tend to discourage social visits, what can I do for you?"

It took Claire a moment to get past her anger at Diana and remember. "Kingston, Ontario, 1945; two Keepers stopped another Keeper from gaining control of Hell."

"How nice for us all."

"I need to know how they did it."

"Damned if I know." When Claire frowned, the Historian sighed. "Keepers, no sense of humor." She pointed an ink-stained finger along the bookshelves. "The forties are about a hundred yards that way. The year you're looking for was bound in green." Then, muttering, "Hansen," over and over to herself, she opened up a shoe box that had once held a size nine-and-a-half cross trainer, and pulled out a digital tape. The plastic case appeared to be slightly charred. "When you get home, tell your sister I'd like to have a word."

The padlock slid into her hand with a satisfactory plop. Diana slipped it into her pocket and returned her attention to the key ring. Dean had the master neatly labeled with a piece of adhesive tape.

All she had to do now was push.

Heart pounding, she gripped the doorknob.

I'll just bring Aunt Sara up to partial consciousness, ask her a few questions, and take her back down again. Piece of cake.

What good was power if she never got to use it? Claire was going to be so pissed when she got home and found her younger sister had all the answers.

Sara, herself, turned out to be a bit of a disappointment

While the old adage, *the more human evil looks the more danger-ous it is,* was undeniably true, Diana had been expecting at least some outward indication of the heinous crime Sara had attempted—small horns, visible scars, overdue library books—but from the look of things, she hadn't even been having a bad hair day. The only incongru-ous point about her whole body was that her very red lips glistened, dust free.

. . . but had there not been problems with the sacrificial virgin, the Keepers would never have arrived in time. Not until Aunt Sara had Margaret Anne Groseter suspended over the pit and had made the first cut did she realize that the girl, although only fifteen was not suitable.

Feeling as though the big green binder of 1945, Kin to Kip, had just smacked her on the back of the head, Claire read that paragraph again.

Margaret Anne Groseter.

"Mr. Smythe told me that she lived in the house next door her whole life. He said it used to be Groseter's Rooming House and Mr. Abrams was a roomer who didn't move fast enough and got broad-sided."

"It's not possible."

For Mrs. Abrams to have been fifteen in 1945, she had to have *been* born in 1930. Which would put her in her late sixties. With a virtual thumb blocking the bouffant orange hair of a mind's eye view, Claire supposed it was possible.

"I *used to be quite progressive in my younger days.*"

It was, Claire reflected, occasionally terrifying knowing the exact measure of the fulcrum that Fate used to lever the world.

Stepping through the shield, Diana had a momentary qualm. The emanations rising from the sleeper were stronger than she'd expected. It wouldn't be easy accessing power surrounded by such potent malevolence.

"On the other hand," she cracked her fingers and moved up to the head of the bed, "if it were easy, everybody'd be doing it."

. . . however, it took the combined strength of both Keepers to achieve the necessary balance of power between Sara and the pit, and even then she nearly broke free of their restraints.

Given the urgency of the situation, the Keepers on the scene felt it best to use a slam, bam, thank you, ma'am approach.

The Historian clearly believed in making history accessible to the masses.

Reaching carefully through the middle possibilities for power, Diana trickled a tiny amount into the matrix that held Sara asleep.

As the patterns in the dark emanations changed, a howling Austin raced into the room, trailing a cloud of shed fur. "Diana, stop! You don't know what you're doing!"

I TOLD YOU NOT TO WORRY ABOUT THE SECOND KEEPER. SHE'S HELPING US!

DO WHAT?

SHUT UP AND BE READY.

The cat gathered himself to leap just as Sara's lips parted and drew a long breath in past the edges of yellowed teeth.

❖   ❖   ❖

NOW!

At the top of an infinite number of voices, Hell shouted Sara's name up the conduit.

With the seepage added to Diana's power, the balance tipped.

Sara opened her eyes.

Her own eyes wide, Diana tried to block the power surge. One second. Two. A force too complicated for her shields to stop slammed into her, dropping her to her knees.

Yowling, Austin landed on the end of the bed.

Sara smiled and raised a finger.

The energy flare caught him full in the face, lifted him into the air, and smashed him against the wall between the two windows. The first bounce dropped him into the remains of the fern. The second dropped him unresisting to the floor.

"NO!" Unable to stand, Diana crawled toward the body. A warm hand clamped down on one shoulder stopped her cold.

"I don't think so."

As Sara's grip dragged her around to face the bed, Diana put up no resistance. When Sara's eyes met hers, she grabbed for all the power she could handle and smashed it down on the other Keeper like a club.

Sara didn't even bother swatting it aside. She absorbed it, twisted it, and wrapped it around Diana like a shroud. "My mouth tastes like the inside of a sewer," she muttered, running her tongue over her teeth. "Christ on churches, but I could use a cigarette."

. . . unfortunately, as both Keepers were drawn from troops about to leave for the European theater, this temporary solution . . .

"Claire Hansen?"

"In a minute. I've almost got it"

"Suit yourself, Keeper, but I just got an e-mail telling me to reactivate that bit of history you're reading."

Claire looked up from the binder. "What do you mean reactivate?"

"Probably got a couple of loose ends tying themselves up."

"Probably?" Claire scrambled to her feet. Any loose ends had come untied since she'd left. "What's happening?"

"How should I know? I don't mess with the present I do history. Put the book back on the shelf before you . . ." The Historian sighed and moved a black three onto a red four as Claire raced away through the ages. "And they wonder why I don't like company."

"Would it have hurt them to have dusted me on occasion? I don't think so." Lifting a thrashing Diana about three feet off the floor, Sara tied the laces of the young Keeper's black high-tops *together* and used them as a handle to drag her through the air toward the door.

Chewing on the power gag that held her silent, Diana dug her fingers into the doorjamb.

"Let go or lose them, your choice." It was clearly a literal offer. "I, personally, don't care. I know what you're thinking," she continued as Diana reluctantly released the wood. "You're thinking that all you have to do is delay me and sooner or later more Keepers will arrive. Well, they won't. And do you know why? Of course not, you're a child. . . ."

Tiny wisps of steam rose up from Diana's ears.

Sara smiled and ignored them. ". . . you couldn't possibly comprehend how I work. Over fifty years ago, two interfering busybodies put a shield around me. Specifically, around me. It's still there. No one will know I'm awake until it's much too late."

As the sound of Sara's gloating receded down the hall, several small, multicolored figures came out from behind various pieces of furniture and moved purposefully toward the limp body of the cat.

Running full out, Claire still hadn't reached the end of the bookshelves.

"Stop thinking about the past!"

Distorted by echoes, it could have been anyone's voice. Claire didn't waste time turning to check. She needed a door. She couldn't get home without going through a door.

"Hello, handsome. Are there any more at home like you?"

Pressed up against the wall in the lobby. Dean had a sudden memory of a fish flopping about the gaff that pinned it to the bottom of the boat. It didn't stop him from struggling, but it did give him a pretty good idea of how successful that struggle would be.

When he finally sagged, exhausted, he felt the sharp points of fingernails lift his chin off his chest.

"Very nice," Sara cooed. "I've always been a big fan of flexing and sweating." Slipping her fingers into the front pocket of his jeans, she pulled the denim away from his body and dropped the keys into the pouch. "Thanks so very much for your help. I don't suppose you have a cigarette on you?"

Dean shook his head and dragged himself out of the pale depths of her eyes. They were same gray/blue as the heart of an iceberg only less compassionate. He nodded toward Diana's thrashing body. "She said she was going into the attic. I thought Keepers couldn't lie."

"Bystanders can't lie to a Keeper, but we're actually very good at lying to . . ." Sara ducked and the old leather-bound registration book whipped over her head and slammed corner first into the wall. As the ancient binding gave way and yellowed pages fluttered to the ground, she measured the dent between thumb and forefinger. "Nice try, Jacques. I'm amazed you managed that much ectoplasmic energy." Leaning toward Dean, she whispered, "He must've gotten lucky in the last couple of days."

Eyes watering, Dean turned his head away. Her breath would've peeled the paint off the gut cans at the processing plant

"Hey!" A fingernail opened a small cut in his cheek. "You sleep for that long and see what kind of a morning mouth *you* wake up with."

The brass bell rose off the counter and smacked into her shoulder.

"This is getting tiresome, Jacques." She turned to face the office. "Technically, I should have dust and ash for this, but we'll just have to make do with an abundance of dust." A gentle push sent Diana down the hall toward the basement stairs. With both hands free, Sara scraped a bit of fuzz off the front of her skirt and drew two symbols in the air.

Dean braced for bad poetry, but he needn't have bothered.

Both symbols glowed red.

Jacques snapped into focus between the symbols. Eyes wide with terror, he twisted and fought, and when Sara smacked her palms together, he exploded into a thousand tiny lights that scattered in all directions.

Praying silently, Dean worked his left hand free and snagged two of the lights as they went by. They burned as they touched his skin, but he closed his fingers around them and faced Sara with both hands curled into fists.

"Well," she said, "that takes care of him. You, however, I can use."

SHE'S GOING TO TRY IT AGAIN!

WOULD YOU STOP WORRYING! A FEW DECADES AT HER BECK AND CALL AND THEN WE'RE FREE.

AND YOU THINK SHE'LL WANT HELL WAITING FOR HER WHEN SHE DIES?

After a long silence, Hell muttered, YOU MIGHT HAVE BROUGHT THAT UP BEFORE.

SHE'S SEALING THE PIT! WE CAN'T STOP HER!

NO. NOT FROM IN HERE. . . .

First there were no doors, and then there was nothing but doors. Claire'd charged into three saunas, two walk-in freezers, something animated she couldn't identify, and more hotel rooms than she wanted to count.

"Yoo hoo! Cornelia! Diana! I was taking Baby out for his walkies and I just popped by to see if you . . ." Mrs. Abrams froze on the threshold, her mouth opening and closing but no sound emerging. Finally she managed a strangled, "I remember you!"

"That was an oversight on somebody's part," Sara observed as she tied the laces of Dean's work boots together. "*Please*, come in and close the door."

One hand pressed against the polyester swell of her bosom, Mrs. Abrams shuffled forward.

"And the door," Sara prodded. "Don't forget to close it."

Although her movements were pretty much limited to impotent thrashing, Diana managed to bring herself closer to the wall. Twisting left, she slammed her heels into the plaster.

Mrs. Abrams jerked at the sound and took a step backward, toward escape.

Sara raised a hand, and Diana found herself wrapped even more tightly in power. All her strength, all her attention, focused on drawing air through constricted passageways.

"Margaret Anne. Close the door."

Margaret Anne Abrams, née Groseter, had been fifteen the last time Sara had commanded her. A lot of water had passed under the bridge since then, and little old ladies were not without power of their own. Taking a breath so deep it stood each orange hair on end, she rallied. "Don't you talk to me in that tone of voice, young woman! I'll have you know that I'm the head of the Women's Auxiliary at our church and I've five times been volunteer of the year at the hospital. Look at you, you're all covered in dust. If I were you I'd be ashamed to go out in that . . ." Her voice trailed off as Sara's pale eyes narrowed and she expelled the last of the breath in a squeaky cry for help. "Baby!"

Secured by a leather leash to his own front porch. Baby lifted his wedge-shaped head off his paws.

He heard his master calling.

Lips pulled back off his teeth, the big Doberman surged up onto his feet and out to the end of his leash. The leather held.

The porch, on the other hand, surrendered to the inevitable.

Claire knew she was close. She could feel the hotel, but a dozen doors remained between her and the end of the hall, and she couldn't shake the fear that time, usually so fluid outside reality, had decided to march to a linear drummer. In other words, it was passing. Quickly.

Behind the first door to her right, sat a tiger. Fortunately, judging from the debris around its cell, it had just eaten.

"You're only delaying the inevitable," Sara muttered, as with a crooked finger she drew Mrs. Abrams farther into the lobby. "There's nothing you can summon, old woman, that can hurt . . ." Her eyes widened

Baby had lived his whole life for this moment. Years of frustration propelled him over the threshold in one mighty leap.

The remains of the porch swept Mrs. Abrams off her feet, tangling her in the twisted wreckage.

Baby's front paws slammed into Sara's chest

She hit the floor, bounced once in a cloud of dust and lost the collar of her jacket as the extra weight on the end of Baby's leash stopped him a mere fraction of an inch short.

Breathing heavily, the Keeper scrambled to her feet careful to stay clear of the snapping mouthful of too-long, too-pointed, and too-many teeth.

Fixated on her throat Baby missed his chance at a number of other body parts as they passed.

A wave of Sara's hand closed the door. The sound it made, the sort of sound that put a final period on both rescue and escape, was almost a cliché.

"Margaret Anne, as much as I'd love to finish what we started so long ago, I've got all the sacrificial bodies I need." She raised her voice to be heard over Baby's frantic snarling. "This time, there's no mistake about the qualifications."

Dean hung limp in the air, but Diana took a moment out from breathing to glare.

Sara ignored them both. *"Please,* go to sleep, Margaret Anne." As Mrs. Abrams slumped forward, Sara glanced down at the Doberman, still desperately trying to rip her to pieces. "You," she said, "have got a single-minded way of going after a goal I rather like."

Nearly throttling himself, Baby made an unsuccessful lunge for her ankle.

"In fact you remind me of me. Good dog."

The words meant nothing. The tone sent Baby into a frenzy of barking.

Dragging Dean and Diana behind her, Sara started down the basement stairs.

With seven doors to go, Claire paused in the center of the hall.

She could hear barking.

The distinctive, just barely sane barking of a big dog forced to live a lapdog's life. Who, with the fraction of brain that hadn't been bred out of it, intended to get even.

Laying her ear against each door only long enough to check for a rise in volume, Claire moved quickly down the hall.

Three doors. Four.

She opened the fifth door and flung herself out of the wardrobe. The volume of the barking didn't so much rise as expand to fill every available space with sound.

Baby was in the hotel.

Under normal circumstances, that would have been a problem, but being torn apart by a psychotic Doberman would be significantly preferable to life with Sara controlling Hell. Claire leaped over a pile of laundry, raced through the sitting room, and slid to a halt in the office.

Baby ignored her. Toenails scrabbling against the lobby floor, he dragged the ruin of the porch and the snoring Mrs. Abrams another inch closer to the basement.

Unwilling to scan the hotel lest she give her presence away, Claire decided to follow Baby's lead. Adding up the dog, the porch, and Mrs. Abrams, the odds were good Austin hadn't been responsible; not one hundred percent, but good.

Her back against the wall, she slid past, losing nothing more significant than a percentage of her hearing, and sped down the basement stairs, grateful that Baby's barking would cover any possible noise she might make.

The door to the furnace room was open.

Her heart beating so loudly she could hardly hear herself think, Claire paused by the washing machine and reached for calm.

A Keeper without self-control could control neither the power accessed nor where in the possibilities that power was accessed from.

Evil favored the chaotic mind.

Whites and colors should be sorted before washing.

Claire blinked, breaking contact with the box of laundry detergent. This was as calm as she was going to get.

Wiping damp palms against her thighs, she slipped behind the masking angle of the furnace room door and peered inside.

Still wearing the dusty clothes she'd been put to sleep in so many years before, Sara stood on air over the pit, back to the door, both hands raised, head bowed. Her fingertips were red where the blood had dripped down from her nails.

Suspended horizontally over the pit in front of her, shirtless, blood dripping from a number of shallow cuts on his chest, Dean appeared to be unconscious but still alive. It took a moment to spot Diana wrapped in overlapping bands of power and propped, mummylike, against the wall.

Wait a minute . . . Dean was over the pit and Diana was up against the wall?

Claire took a closer look at the power holding her sister. Most of it held her in place and kept her quiet but threaded throughout it, head to toe, was a conduit set up to pour Diana's considerable power into Sara—already in place because there'd be no opportunity to stop the invocation and set it up later.

Which meant that Dean was over the pit because . . .

No wonder he was always blushing.

But at twenty? Looking like a young, albeit myopic, god?

Hey! she told herself sternly, *now is not the time.* The problem was, it was easier, much, much easier to think about Dean than to come up with a plan to save the world.

It had taken two Keepers to stop Sara the first time she'd tried this. How could she possibly do it alone?

Not alone—if I can reach Diana without attracting Sara's attention, I can use the conduit myself. With Diana's power joined to mine, Sara's extra twenty years of experience shouldn't count for much.

As the evil Keeper began a new chant, Claire realized that were two small problems with her plan. The first was that Sara sealed Hell. With Sara removed, Hell would surge free. Claire would have to sign herself onto the site so that her power would become the seal when Sara's power was removed. Which meant, if there wasn't power enough left to close the hole, she'd be stuck here. In the hotel. For the rest of her life.

And Dean was leaving.

She didn't even know where he kept the toaster.

The second problem was that Sara also held Dean. Literally. Attacked from behind, Sara would let go and Dean would fall into the pit.

When she hooked up with Diana, Sara would know. She'd have to strike immediately. If she saved Dean first, Sara would have time to marshal a defense.

If she let Dean fall . . .

What point in saving the world if she let Dean fall?

She'd just have to find a way to save him, and that was that. Timing her footsteps to Baby's frenzied barking, she crept down the stairs toward Diana.

❋   ❋   ❋

Down in the pit. Hell gloried in the strength it gained from each drop of sacrificial blood.

THERE ON THE STAIRS, the rest of Hell pointed out to itself, IT'S THE OTHER KEEPER.

SO?

SO SHOULD WE TELL *HER?*

Another drop of blood evaporated in the heat. Hell breathed it metaphorically in and laughed. YOU MEAN, SHOULD WE HELP *HER?* WE DON'T HELP. ANYONE.

Baby had managed to drag the whole mess another three inches toward the basement stairs. Tongue hanging out, collar cutting into the thick muscles of his neck, he kept barking and pulling in the certain belief that he had his enemy on the run.

And then, in the fraction of a second between one bark and the next, a familiar voice told him to be quiet.

The barking stopped. Claire froze.

Sara drew her fingernails along Dean's side. As blood welled up from four parallel lines, she began a new chant.

Claire recognized the guttural Latin. There wasn't much time left. Lower lip caught between her teeth, she started moving again.

A sterile dressing wrapped around his head and over his left eye, Austin had the rakish look of a wounded pirate. Breathing heavily, slightly scorched, he lay on his side on a litter made of an old silk scarf carried by twelve mice wearing multicolored frock coats, breeches, and tricorn hats.

This was so far outside Baby's experience, he sat panting and stared.

Still a safe distance away, the mice stopped and Austin opened his one good eye. "Somebody," he said without lifting his head, "is going to have to undo that collar."

Dean didn't so much regain consciousness as hijack it; consciousness wanted nothing to do with the whole situation.

HOW YA DOIN' GORGEOUS?

He'd have jerked back at the sound of the voice, but he couldn't figure out how to operate his body. Which scared him a lot more than Hell. He had a friend, Paul Malan, who'd gone into the boards at the wrong angle and now Paul played ball hockey from a wheelchair.

HE'S IGNORING US!

CAN HE DO THAT?

HEY, BUDDY! IN CASE YOU HAVEN'T NOTICED, THIS IS A LOT WORSE THAN BALL HOCKEY!

Thankful that somewhere along the way he'd lost his glasses, Dean ignored the voices because Claire had asked him to. She'd even said, "please."

He blinked, hit by a sudden realization. The voice he'd heard yesterday in the hall had been the voice of the pit.

BINGO.

And he'd listened. He'd hesitated.

OH, FOR . . . SIX SECONDS OUT OF TWENTY SQUEAKY CLEAN YEARS!

He deserved to go to Hell.

YOU'RE KIDDING, RIGHT?

Except he didn't want to die.

Over, or maybe under, the voices in his head, he could hear the drone of words chanted in a language he didn't understand. Slowly, working within the invisible bands that held him, he turned until he could see along his left arm. Gazing past his clenched fist, out over the edge of the pentagram, he could see Diana Hansen. She was just a kid, he realized, she'd never have believed that she'd set this whole mess in motion. If by some miracle he got out of this, he was after kicking her right in the butt.

Her back against the wall, barely daring to breathe, Claire crept the last few feet to her sister's side. Once she took Diana's hand, she'd control both their power.

Dean's eyes widened as Claire slid into his field of vision.

Rescue!

Claire saw the word in Dean's eyes and flinched.

❖   ❖   ❖

Dean saw her flinch.

Sara chanted louder, spitting out consonants. The pentagram began to glow.

Maybe because he was suspended over a hole to Hell. Maybe because he'd been breathing the fumes of his own evaporating blood. Maybe because he'd spent almost a year next to a metaphysical accident site.

Maybe just because he could read it on Claire's face.

Dean knew.

She couldn't save him and the world.

He'd hesitated.

He was being given a chance to make up for that.

Hell could have him, but it couldn't have the world.

Do it, he told Claire silently.

Claire shook her head. There had to be another way.

The pentagram began to dissolve.

It was almost worth it to know she was willing to risk the world for him.

Do it.

Because she had no other choice, she did.

Claire grabbed Diana's hand and opened the conduit Quickly re-tracing the pentagram, she etched her own name into the pattern.

Sara turned.

Dean fell.

Claire hit the other Keeper with everything both she and Diana had.

Suddenly finding herself in a sphere of blinding white light, Sara flung up a bloodstained hand to cover her eyes. Lips too red parted . . .

. . . and she laughed.

Designed to prevent any sort of metaphysical power from waking a Keeper bent on cataclysmic evil, the shield Sara had worn for more than fifty years held.

Stepping down to the floor, Sara straightened her jacket and nodded toward Diana. "I thought our friend here too young for this site. Not," she added after a critical inspection of Claire, "that you're so much older." Her smile was frankly patronizing. "You killed him for nothing, you know. Power can't pass into this shield."

Claire dragged Diana aside as a bolt of red light blew chunks of rock out of the wall.

Sara's smile broadened. "How nice for me that it passes out of it just fine."

Teeth clenched against rising nausea, Claire stepped forward, but before she could speak, Sara raised her hand again.

"Oh, yes, you can enter the shield physically, pummel me if you like, but don't expect me to stand here and allow . . ."

Which was when Baby launched himself from the top of the stairs.

Sara had time to scream as she fell back but only just.

Clinging to each other for support, Claire and Diana walked to the edge of the pentagram and cautiously leaned forward.

GOT HER!

OW! BE CAREFUL, SHE KICKS!

Claire felt her power fill the pentagram, holding Hell off from the world. That was it, then. A lifetime in the Elysian Fields Guest House.

Diana swallowed and found her voice. "Poor Ba . . ."

THAT'S OUR PUPPY! IS HE GLAD HE'S HOME?

WHO'S A GOOD DOGGIE-WOGGIE, THEN? WHO'S A GOOD BOY!

"Doggie-woggie?" Claire repeated.

Before Hell could answer, Diana dug her nails into Claire's arm. "Look! *She's* still part of the pattern. If you tie the pentagram to her before it fades, she'll pull the hole in after her!"

Still buzzing from the power she'd passed, it took Claire a heartbeat to understand. "I can close the site?"

"Yes!"

"Forever?"

"Yes!"

Sara's name had begun to fray. "No."

"Are you out of your mind? This may be your only chance!"

"No!" Claire yanked her arm free. "Dean's in there and I'm not closing that hole until he finds his way out." When Diana began another protest, she cut her off. "Hell can't hold a willing sacrifice. They have to let him go."

"They do?"

"If you paid more attention to what was going on and less to what you just happen to be powerful enough to do . . ." She bit it off. Now was not the time. "Yes. They do."

"Okay, fine, but they're not going to help him find his way or give him a boost out, and Sara's name is already fading! You haven't got time to wait. Don't let his sacrifice be in vain."

Claire reached for more power and poured it into the pentagram. From where she was standing, it was a long reach to the middle of the possibilities. Her vision was starting to blur, and she wasn't entirely certain she could feel her toes. "I can hold it," she snarled through clenched teeth. "I can hold it for as long as it takes."

"All right." Diana shrugged out of her jean jacket. "Then I'm going in after him."

"Oh, no, you're not!" Claire had a strong suspicion she sounded like their mother. At the moment, she didn't much care. "This isn't like going across the border for cheap electronics! You want to help, reactivate the conduit and start feeding me . . ." The "S" tried to straighten out. She forced it back into a curve. ". . . power."

"That'd make me part of the seal and we could be stuck here together indefinitely. You want him out, someone has to go and get him."

"Not you!" A subliminal growl snapped the second "a" back into line. "You'd never survive."

"But Dean . . ."

"Dean has the strength of ten because his heart is pure." Which was when Claire drew a second conclusion from Sara's choice of sacrifice. Fortunately for Diana, she had other things to deal with at the moment. "The rules protect him."

"What rules?"

"I know this is hard to believe at seventeen, but there are always rules." She definitely couldn't feel her toes and was starting to have doubts about her entire left foot. "It takes extraordinary conditions for the living to pass over and then come . . . The living!" Eyes locked on the pentagram, Claire grabbed her sister's arm. "Find Jacques!"

"Jacques' gone. *She* blew him into ectoplasmic particles."

"Then gather him!"

"Me?"

"You're always complaining how no one ever lets you do anything. Just be careful where you're pulling power from this close to the pit."

"You had to ruin it with advice," Diana complained as she started to spin. "Couldn't just assume I'd do it right."

All things considered, Claire felt she had precedent for that assumption, but she let it go as the wind began to swirl around the furnace room. A moment later, a stream of tiny lights poured down from the basement

"There's two missing," Diana panted as the lights refused to coalesce. "I don't know where they are."

Vaguely Jacques-shaped, the lights dove into the pit.

"NO!" Claire reached out but caught only a single light.

Teetering as the room continued to spin, Diana stared at her sister in astonishment. "I thought that's what you wanted him to do?"

"He doesn't know that! He doesn't know Dean's down there. Jacques has still got connections to *her, she* could've dragged him down."

"So what do we do now?"

Claire gritted her teeth, clenched her fist around the single piece of Jacques she'd managed to save, and dug in. "We wait."

"Wait?" Diana's voice rose nearly an octave. "For how long?"

"Until we can't wait any . . ." All of a sudden, Claire could feel a familiar twisted touch groping up toward the pentagram. "*She's* using her name to pull herself free. Link with me!"

"No! I'll be stuck with you, holding that thing, and there'll be two Keepers lost because you can't let Dean go. Because you feel guilty about how he felt about you when you didn't feel the same for him and turned to Jacques, who you can't possibly have a future with instead."

"Diana! This is no time for relationship therapy!"

"You've lost them both. Let them go before *she* starts this whole thing all over again."

Her connection to her name had strengthened. The sound of triumphant laughter boiled up over the edges of the pit.

"I'm not leaving them there!"

Diana laid her hand on her sister's arm and to Claire's surprise her voice was gentle as she said, "You're a Keeper. Seal the s . . . son of a bitch."

Down in the pit something that had once been Mrs. Abrams' Baby barked as Dean rose up into the furnace room surrounded by a cloud of tiny lights. When both his feet were on the ground, and before either Claire or Diana could get their mouths shut to say anything, he opened his left hand.

Two lights few out.

Claire peeled her fingers back off her palm. The final light spun up into the air.

Jacques rematerialized.

Dean coughed once and stumbled forward. Together, Claire and Diana eased him down onto the bottom step, then Claire turned back toward the pit.

She could feel Sara clawing her way up her name, closer and closer to the edge of the possibilities. Holding tightly to the seal, Claire broke all the remaining links but Sara's.

The building shook as the pentagram, etched into solid rock, slid toward the center of itself. The inner edges disappeared. Flickering through the visible spectrum and one or two colors beyond, hundred-year-old words of summoning poured into the hole.

"Claire!" Stretched out like smoke in a wind, Jacques streamed toward Hell, caught in the binding.

Even if there was time, unraveling the binding would free Sara's name.

"I don't think so . . ." Wielding power like a sword, Diana slashed through the pattern where Jacques was caught.

Not subtle, but effective.

As the points flipped up and over, Claire broke her name free.

CURSES, FOILED AGAI . . .

The unmarked bedrock of the furnace room floor steamed gently.

Diana let out a breath she couldn't remember holding. "Wow."

Dean jerked to his feet as Claire swayed. "You okay?"

Actually, she had no idea how she was, but okay would do for the moment. "Sure. What about you?"

He frowned. Until Jacques had appeared out of the darkness, he'd stood on the slope leading upward toward the glow of what were probably the fires of the damned and had known he'd been forgotten. Sure, Hell was busy with Sara, but still . . . "I hesitated," he said.

Claire felt her lip curl. "Get over it. You were willing to die to save the world. You're a terrific person!"

"You mean that?"

She cupped his face between her palms and moved close enough that he could see her clearly without his glasses. "Yes. I have never meant anything more in my life."

Keepers lied quite easily to bystanders; but he believed her. The load of guilt lifted off his shoulders. "Thanks." Pulling free, he took a step back. "There's something I need to do."

"Ow!" Diana rubbed the spot where Dean had applied the side of his work boot. "What did you kick me for?"

His silence said it all.

"Oh. Never mind."

"You've done a wonderful job, Claire, but are you certain you don't want me to come to Kingston and check things out?"

"Quite certain, Mom. The site is closed." Claire had put the furnace room through every test she could think of, and she'd even allowed Diana to come up with a few. To all intents and purposes, there'd never been a hole to Hell. Or an Aunt Sara. "Dean drove Diana to the train station. She'll stay with friends in Toronto tonight and head home first thing tomorrow morning."

"Well, I'm sure that's the plan." Martha Hansen sounded doubtful.

"Don't worry, she gave me her word she'd go straight home."

"Claire Beth Hansen! Did you put a geas on your sister?"

Claire grinned. "Yes."

"Good. But how on earth did you manage it?"

"I agreed with her when she opened her defense with 'all's well that ends well,' and while she was still reeling in disbelief I slipped it by."

"You *agreed* with her?"

Her grin broadening, Claire explained. "I had every intention of tearing a strip off her for being so adolescently arrogant, thinking she could wake Sara without consequences, but then I realized that she was right. Keepers go where they're needed. The two of us in combination were needed to close down the site, so it's entirely possible that everything that happened was intended to happen. Diana, me, Dean, Jacques; even Hell had a hand in its own demise by squeezing a Hell Hound through the tiny window of opportunity between Sara's original capture and her power being used to temporarily seal the site."

The phone remained silent.

"Mom?"

"If Diana's reckless disregard for consequence was necessary to help save the world, she's going to be impossible to live with." Claire very nearly felt her mother's sigh. "Still, I expect your father and I can come up with a few things to say to her when she gets home." Sara's choice of sacrifice had not been elaborated on, but parents were perfectly capable of drawing their own conclusions. "You said that Dean was driving her to the station; how is he? Is it safe for him to drive?"

"He's fine, Mom. Really. He was a willing sacrifice, completely ignorant of what that meant, and he believed that in falling he'd burn in Hell forever. With that kind of karma, he could've just walked through the possibilities to the light. If Jacques hadn't found him so quickly and brought him back to the basement, I expect he'd have started tidying the place up."

"What do you mean, he had no doubt he'd burn in Hell forever? He's been living next to the site for almost a year completely unaffected."

She'd been hoping she'd slipped that by. "There was an incident." Leaving out the bits that Diana would be sure to embellish on later, Claire explained about the elevator and Faith's boyfriend. "He hesitated."

On the other end of the phone, Martha snorted. "Oh, for . . ."

"That's what I said. But this whole sacrifice thing grounded him again. He's as good as new."

"I see." The pause spoke volumes. "What happens now?"

Claire chose to misunderstand. "Now, I expect I'll be summoned somewhere else. Austin says I'll be able to leave by tomorrow, that help is on the way."

"Claire . . ."

"He's down to his last life, you know. But he says he's not worried."

"Very well. If that's the way you want it. Give Austin our love."

An uncomfortable moment later, Claire hung up and sighed. *What happens now?*

Jacques was waiting in her sitting room. He had to know she'd be leaving—that she couldn't stay and he couldn't come with her.

This wasn't going to be a pleasant interview.

"Jacques?"

He stopped pacing and turned to face her. "*Vôtre mère,* your mama, is she good?"

"She's fine."

"*Bon.*" Drifting out through the coffee table, he waved a hand at the sofa. "Please, *cherie,* I have things to say."

Since she wasn't looking forward to saying the things she had to, Claire sat. If listening was all that she could do for him, she would at least do that.

"You are ready? *D'accord.*" He rubbed his hands against his thighs, a living gesture Claire'd never seen him make before. "I am decided, it is time I move on."

You're *leaving* me? Somehow, Claire managed not to voice her initial reaction.

His expression grew serious. "I have seen Hell and I do not belong there, or they would not have allow me to leave. There is not enough evil in me for them to hold." The corners of his mouth twitched up. "It helped that you held my heart."

When he smiled, Claire had to smile with him. "That wasn't your heart."

"*Non?* Ah, well, close enough." He took a step back and held out his hand. "Will you help me?"

So much for her speech about change being constant. Claire ripped up her mental notes, stood, and laid her palm against Jacques', his fingers wrapping around hers like cool smoke. "Of course. When?"

"Now. I have found the courage to face *her.* I have found the courage to descend into Hell for *l'âme,* the soul, of Dean, who I do not even entirely like. I think while I have found my courage, I should use him, it, to face what is on the other side."

"Did you want to wait and say good-bye to Dean?"

"No. You tell him I say *au revoir, adieu, bonne chance,* and that if he does not use it, it will fall off."

"Maybe you'd better stay a few more minutes and tell him yourself."

Jacques shook his head, a strand of translucent hair falling into his eyes. "No, *cherie.* Now. There has always been—will always be—an excuse to stay. Dean, he will understand. It is a guy thing."

"A guy thing?"

He shrugged. "I hear it on Morningside." One hand still wrapped about hers, he laid the other against her cheek. "Thank you for the night we shared. I think I saw heaven a little bit in your arms."

"You think?"

"I am fairly certain." He grinned. "When you talk of me, could you perhaps exaggerate a little?" When she nodded, her cheek moving up and down through his hand, he squared his shoulders under the heavy sweater. "*D'accord.* Then I am ready."

Claire reached through the possibilities and opened the way. Squinting a little, she stepped back to give him room. "Just follow the light."

His features almost dissolving in the brilliance, he took a step away from the world, and then he paused.

"*Au revoir, cherie.*"

"Good-bye, Jacques."

"*Si j'etais en vie, je t'aurais aime.*"

And then he was gone.

"If were alive, I would have loved you?"

Blinking away the spots in front of her eyes, Claire tried to focus on the cat.

Austin carefully climbed onto the hassock and sat down. "Not a bad exit line."

"You're supposed to be resting?"

"I am resting, I'm sitting."

"You should go to the vet."

"No, thank you." He twitched his tail around his toes and his lip curled under the lower edge of the bandage. "It's been taken care of."

"By the mice?"

"Are you calling me a liar?"

Locked in the gaze from his remaining eye, Claire shook her head. "No. Not as such. But if I may point out, I haven't seen any mice."

"You haven't seen Elvis either."

Claire glanced over at the silent bust. "So?"

"So that doesn't mean he's not working in a 7-11 somewhere. Did you take care of Mrs. Abrams?"

"She thinks Baby died a natural death about six months ago, and now that she's done mourning, she's going to get a poodle. But while we're on the subject; how long did you know Baby was a Hell Hound?"

"I knew it from the beginning."

"Well, why didn't you tell me?"

Austin snorted. "I'm a cat." Before Claire could demand a further explanation, he cocked his head. "There's Dean's truck. Maybe you'd better go take care of that last loose end."

"The hotel is yours if you want it."

Dean paused, one hand on the basement door, and turned to face Claire. "No, thank you. I don't want it. You'll be leaving?"

She nodded. "Soon. Tomorrow, probably. Austin says that someone'll be along."

"So you pretty much knew my answer before you asked?"

"Pretty much. But I still had to ask. How long . . ."

"I guess I'll wait until that someone shows up and play it by ear."

"Okay. Good. Um, Jacques is gone. He said to tell you goodbye and that you'd understand why he didn't wait."

"Sure."

When the silence stretched beyond the allotted time for a response, Dean nodded, once, and went downstairs.

As the sound of his work boots faded into the distance, Claire pounded her forehead against the wall. That hadn't gone well. There were a hundred things she wanted to say to Dean, starting with, *Thanks for driving Diana to the train station,* and moving on up to: *Thanks for sacrificing yourself to save the world.* Somewhere in the middle she'd try to fit in *Maybe you and I . . .*

"Maybe he and I what?" she asked herself walking back to the office and jerking her backpack down off the hook. "Could be friends? Could be more than friends?" Yanking the cables from her printer, she shoved them into the pack. "He's an extraordinary guy. Not brilliant maybe, but good, kind, gorgeous, accepting . . ." The printer followed the cables. ". . . not to mention alive."

Maybe she'd had that rare chance that few Keepers ever got and for whatever reason, pride or blatant stupidity, she'd blown it.

What happens now?

The site was sealed.

She was leaving.

He was leaving.

It was over.

Folding a pair of jeans neatly along the crease, Dean set them into his hockey bag. He wanted to be ready to go as soon as possible after that someone arrived.

"Austin says that someone'll be along."

He'd never be able to look at a cat without wondering. As for the rest of it, well, he knew who he was again, so the rest of it didn't matter.

A stack of white briefs, also neatly folded, tucked in beside the jeans.

There'd been a lot left unsaid upstairs in the hall. Claire'd been looking sort of aloof and unapproachable, but also twisting a lock of hair around one finger. Dean had to smile at the combination as he added all but one pair of socks to the bag.

Diana had given him continual advice on the way to the station. About half of it, he hadn't understood.

It didn't much matter.

Claire was leaving.

He was leaving.

At least she hadn't offered to rearrange his memories. He'd have fought to remember the last eight weeks.

"What in tarnation have you done to my hotel?"

Claire, who'd been waiting in the office, stared down at Augustus Smythe, opened and closed her mouth, and finally managed a stunned, "You?"

"Who else would be willing to run this rattrap?"

"But . . ."

"Used to be a hole to Hell in the basement. That sort of thing has to be monitored." He shrugged out of his overcoat and tossed it up on the counter. "They say I'm retired, with full pension for years of service rendered, but I know better." Bushy brows drawn in, he glared around at the renovations. "So you opened up the elevator; lose anyone?"

"No."

"Tried it since the hole closed?"

"No, but . . ."

"Never mind. I'll convince that harpy next door to go for a ride." To Claire's astonishment, he smoothed back his hair and grinned. After a moment, the grin rearranged itself into the customary scowl. "Well? Haven't you got somewhere else to go?"

Now that he mentioned it, she had.

The summons grew stronger as she shrugged into her backpack and held open the cat carrier for Austin to climb in. Reaching for her suitcase, she stopped, straightened, and decided Jacques was right. There'd always be a reason to delay.

She reached for the suitcase again, shifted it to her left hand, and picked up the cat carrier with her right. "Tell Dean I said good-bye."

And then she left, ignoring the muttered, "Idiot," that could have come from either the Cousin or the cat.

The summons drew her west. She passed the park, and the hospital, and the turnoff to a house Sir John A. MacDonald, Canada's first Prime Minister had lived in briefly before he entered politics.

The definitive November wind, cold and damp, blew in off the lake, stiffening her fingers around the handles of her luggage. By the time she reached the lights at Sir John A. MacDonald Boulevard, she decided that the summons was taking her farther than she wanted to walk. Even in a bad mood and feeling vaguely guilty about pretty much everything.

"You need a lift?"

He wasn't entirely unexpected.

Frowning, Claire turned to face the truck. "You don't know where I'm going."

Leaning across the front seat, braced against the edge of the open window, Dean shrugged. "So?"

"Just get in!" The cat carrier rocked in Claire's grip as Austin shifted his weight. "I'm freezing my tail off out here."

"You told him which way we'd be heading."

"What part of *get in* don't you understand?" he snarled, poking a paw out through the wider weave in the front of the carrier.

There were people crossing the street toward her. Another few feet and they'd be close enough to hear.

Claire got in the truck.

Fastened her seat belt.

As Dean shifted into drive and started across the intersection, she held the top of the cat carrier open just far enough for Austin to climb out.

"What happens next?" Dean asked.

Claire shrugged and squirmed around to set the carrier behind the seat with her suitcase. "I don't know."

There was still a lot that had to be said.

"You did know the speed limit on this street is 40k?"

And a lot that didn't.

Dean nodded. "Okay. We'll play it by ear."

"You've been to Hell," Austin snorted, stretching out on Claire's lap, "you should be up to it."

HEY! WHO TIDIED THE BRIMSTONE?

The
Second
Summoning

For Meg, who helped keep the teenagers
sounding like they were seventeen, not forty.

In Memoriam:
Austin, 1980–2000

ONE

FOR ALL INTENTS AND PURPOSES, the motel room was dark and quiet. The only light came intermittently through a crack in the curtains as the revolving sign by the road spun around so fast it caught up to its afterimages and appeared to read Motel 666. The only sound came from the rectangular bulk of the heating unit under the window that roared out warmth at a decibel level somewhere between a DC9 at takeoff and a Nirvana concert—although it was considerably more melodic than either. The smell emanating from the pizza box— crushed to fit neatly into a too-small wastebasket—blended with the lingering smell of the previous inhabitants, some of whom hadn't been particularly attentive to personal hygiene.

The radio alarm clock between the beds read eleven forty squiggle where the squiggle would have been a five had the entire number been illuminated.

Both of the double beds were occupied.

The bed closest to the bathroom held the shape of two bodies— one large, one small—stretched out beneath the covers.

The bed closest to the window held one long, lean, black-and-white shape that seemed to be taking up more room than was physically possible.

The light flickered. The heater roared. The long, lean shape contracted and became a cat. It walked to the edge of the mattress and crouched, tail lashing.

"This is pathetic," it announced, leaping upon the smaller of the two figures in the other bed. "Even for you."

Claire Hansen stretched out her arm, turned on the bedside lamp, and found herself face-to-face with an indignant one-eyed cat. "Austin, if you don't mind, we're waiting for a manifestation."

He lay down on her chest, assuming a sphinxlike position that suggested he wasn't planning on moving any time soon. "It's been a week."

Twisting her head around, Claire peered at the clock radio. The squiggle changed shape. "It's been forty-six minutes."

"It's been a week," Austin repeated, "since we left the Elysian Fields Guest House. A week since you and young Mr. McIssac here started keeping company."

The other figure stirred, but the cat continued.

"For the first time in that week, you two are actually in the same bed and what are you doing? You're waiting for a manifestation!"

Claire blinked. "Keeping company?" she repeated.

"For lack of a more descriptive phrase, which, I might add, is my point—there's a distinct lack of more descriptive phrases being applied here. You could cut the unresolved sexual tension between you two with a knife, and I, personally," he declared, whiskers bristling, "am tired of it."

"Just pretending for a moment that this is any of your business," Claire told him tightly, "a week isn't that long . . ."

"You knew each other for almost two months before that."

". . . we're in one bed now because the site requires a male and a female component . . ."

"You're saying you had no control over the last seven days?"

". . . and did it ever occur to you that things haven't progressed because there's been an audience perpetually in attendance?"

"Oh, sure. Blame me."

"Could I say something here?" Rolling toward the center of the bed, Dean McIssac rose up on one elbow, blue eyes squinting a little behind wire-frame glasses as he came into the light from the bedside table. "I'm thinking this isn't the time or the place to talk about, you know, stuff."

"Talk?" Austin snorted. "You're missing my point."

The young man's cheeks flushed slightly. "Well, it sure as scrod isn't the time or the place to *do* anything."

"Why not?"

"Because there's a dead . . . lady standing at the foot of the bed."

Claire craned her neck to see around the cat.

Arms folded over a turquoise sweater, her weight on one spandex-covered hip, the ghost raised an artificially arched ectoplasmic eyebrow. "Boo," she suggested.

"Boo yourself," Claire sighed.

Cheryl Poropat, or rather the ghost of Cheryl Poropat, hovered above the X marked on the carpet with ashes and dust, the scuffed heels of her ankle boots about two inches from the floor. "So, you're here to send me on?"

"That's right." Claire sat down in one of the room's two chairs. Like most motel chairs they weren't designed to be actually sat in, but she felt that remaining in bed with Dean, even if they were both fully clothed, undermined her authority.

"You some kind of an exorcist?"

"No, I'm a Keeper."

Cheryl folded her arms. Half a dozen cheap bracelets jangled against the curve of one wrist. "And what's that when it's home?"

"Keepers maintain the structural integrity of the barrier between the world as most people know it and the metaphysical energy all around it."

The ghost blinked. "Say what?"

"We mend the holes in the fabric of the universe so bad things don't get through."

"Well, why the hell didn't you say so the first time? If I wasn't dead," she continued thoughtfully before Claire could answer, " I'd think you were full of it, but since I'm not only dead, I'm here, my view of stuff has been, you know, broadened." Penciled brows drew in . . . "Being dead makes you look at things differently." . . . and centered themselves again. "So, how do you do it?"

"Do what?" Claire asked, having been distracted by the movement of the dead woman's eyebrows.

"Fix the holes."

"We reach beyond the barrier and manipulate the possibilities. We use magic," she simplified as Cheryl looked blank.

Understanding dawned with returning facial features. "You're a witch. Like on television."

"No."

"What's the difference?"

"She's got a better looking cat," Austin announced from the top of the dresser in a tone that suggested it should have been obvious.

Claire ignored him. "I'm a Keeper."

"Well, jeepers keepers." Cheryl snickered and bounced her fingertips off a bit of bouffant hair, her hair spray having held into the afterlife. "Bet you wish you had a nickel for every time someone said that."

"Not really, no."

"They've got a better sense of humor on television, too," the ghost muttered.

"That's only because Keepers have no sense of humor at all," Austin told her, studying his reflection in the mirror. "If it wasn't for me, she'd be so smugly sanctimonious no one could live with her."

"And thank you for your input, Austin." Shooting him a look that clearly promised *"later,"* Claire stood. "Shall we begin?"

Cheryl waved off the suggestion. "What's your hurry? Introduce me to the piece of beefcake the cat thinks you should do the big nasty with."

"The what?"

"You know; the horizontal mambo, the beast with two backs." Her pelvic motions—barely masked by the red stretch pants—cleared up any lingering confusions. "He a Keeper, too?"

Claire glanced over at Dean who was staring at the ghost with an expression of horrified fascination. Or fascinated horror, she wasn't entirely certain which. "He's a friend. And that was a private conversation."

"Ask me if I care?" Translucent hands patted ephemeral pockets. "I'd kill for a freaking smoke. Couldn't hurt me much now, could they? You oughta go for it, Keeper."

"I don't smoke."

A ghostly, dismissive glance raked her up and down. "Not surprised—you've got that tobacco-free, alcohol-free, cholesterol-free—is that your natural hair color?"

"Yes." Claire tucked a strand of dark brown hair behind her ear.

"Hair-color free sort of look. Take my advice, hon, try a henna."

"I ought to go for a henna?"

"Yeah, in your hair. But that wasn't what I meant. You oughta go for *him*." She nodded toward Dean. "Live a little. I mean, men take their pleasure where they find it, right? Why not women? Your husband screws around, you know, and everyone thinks he's such a freaking stallion and all you get's a 'sorry, sweetie' that you're supposed to take 'cause he's out of work and feeling unsure of his manhood—like it's your freaking fault he got LAID OFF. . . ."

Claire and Austin, who'd been watching the energy build, dropped to the floor. Dean, whose generations of Newfoundland ancestors trapped between a barren rock and an angry sea had turned adaptability into a genetic survival trait, followed less than a heartbeat behind.

In the sudden flare of yellow-white light, the clock radio and the garbage pail flew through the air and slammed into opposite walls.

". . . but if *you* do it, just once, then BAM . . ."

The bureau drawers whipped open, then slammed shut.

". . . brain aneurysm, and you're stuck haunting this freaking DUMP!"

Both beds rose six inches into the air, then crashed back to the floor.

Breathing heavily—which was just a little redundant since she wasn't breathing at all, but some old habits died very hard indeed—the ghost stared around the room. "What just happened?"

"Usually, when you manifest, your anger rips open one of those holes in the fabric of the universe," Claire explained, one knee of her jeans separating from a sticky spot on the orange carpet with a sound like tearing Velcro. "I'm keeping you from doing that, so the energy had to go somewhere else, creating a poltergeist phenomenon."

Cheryl actually looked intrigued. "Like in the movie?"

"I didn't see the movie."

"Again, not surprised."

"Why? Don't tell me I've got that movie-free look, too."

"All right."

"All right what?"

"All right, she won't tell you," Austin snickered.

Eyes narrowed, Claire glared down at him. "*You* are supposed to be on my side. And as for you . . ." She turned her attention back to the smirking ghost. ". . . get ready to move on." She wasn't supposed to make it sound like a threat, but she'd had just about as much of Cheryl Poropat as she could handle. *I've got a life, lady. Which is more than I can say for you.*

The ghost's smirk disappeared. "Now?"

"Why not now?"

"Well, I'm still hanging here because I've got unfinished business, right?"

Claire sighed. She should have known it wasn't going to be that easy. "If that's what you think."

"And just what's THAT supposed to mean?"

There was another small flare of energy. In the bathroom, the toilet flushed.

"With metaphysical phenomena, belief is very important. If you believe you're here because you have unfinished business, then that's why you're here."

"Yeah? What if I believe I'm alive again?"

"Doesn't work that way."

"Figures." She looked from Claire to Dean and back to Claire again. "Okay. Unfinished business—I want to talk to my husband. You bring him here, you let me have my say, and I'll go."

"Bring your husband here?"

"Can I can go to him?"

Claire shook her head. "No, you're tied to this room."

"Doomed to appear to couples and give them unwanted advice," Dean added from where he was kneeling in the narrow space between the bed and the bathroom wall.

"No one *ever* wants relationship advice, sweet-cheeks." For the first time since she'd appeared, Cheryl looked at him like he was more than pretty meat. "But how did you know?"

He sighed and tried not to think about what he was kneeling in. "We spoke to Steve and Debbie."

"Nice kids."

"They're some scared."

"Yeah, well, death's a bitch."

*   *   *

"Can you believe that she died right after a nooner with my best friend?" Howard Poropat sounded more resigned than upset by the revelation, his light tenor voice releasing the words in a reluctant monotone that lifted slightly at the end of each sentence, creating a tentative question. "Did she tell you that?"

"No, she didn't mention it." Claire braced herself as the car turned into the motel parking lot, sliding a little in the accumulated slush. When she thought it was safe to release her grip on the dashboard, she pointed. "There. Number 42."

Jaw moving against a wad of nicotine gum, he steered the station wagon where indicated. "Let's just go over this again, can we? Cheryl's ghost is haunting the room she died in?"

"Yes."

"And she can't move on until she says something to me?"

"Apparently." It hadn't taken much effort to persuade him that it was possible. For all that he reminded her of processed cheese slices, he had a weirdly egocentric view of his place in the world.

"You think she wants to apologize?" The car slid to a stop, more-or-less in front of the right room.

"I honestly don't know," Claire told him, slamming her shoulder against the passenger side door and forcing it open. "Why don't we go inside and find out?"

While Claire'd been gone, the room had been redecorated in early playing cards. Most of them were just lying around, but several had been driven into the ceiling's acoustic tiles.

"What happened?"

Dean nodded toward the ghost and mouthed the word, "Boom!"

Brows drawn in, Cheryl folded her arms. "We were playing a little rummy to pass the time, but he cheats!"

"Dean? I doubt that. He spent six months living next to a hole to Hell, and the ultimate force of evil couldn't even convince him to drop his underwear on the floor."

"Not him, the cat!"

Austin continued washing a spotless white paw, ignoring both the conversation and the seven of spades only partially hidden by a fringe of stomach fur.

Claire snorted. "What did you expect? He's a cat." She had no idea how a cat, a ghost, and Dean had managed to play rummy when only one of them could actually manipulate the cards, nor did she want to know. Shrugging off her jacket, she moved farther into the room, pulling a suddenly reluctant Howard Poropat along with her by the pocket on his beige duffle coat.

The ghost's eyes widened. "I don't believe it! How'd you convince him?"

"I asked him nicely." She dropped down onto the edge of the bed, out of the reconciliation's direct line of fire.

"Cheryl?"

"Howard."

The bed dipped as Dean joined her. Claire leaned back and, when her weight pressed into his shoulder, turned her head to murmur, "You okay?"

"I got clipped by the six of clubs, but my sweater deflected it."

Dean's sweater was a traditional fisherman's cable knit. Handmade by his aunt from wool so raw it had barely paused between sheep and needles, Claire suspected it could, if not deflect bullets, certainly discourage them. "Thanks for staying with her."

His arm slipped around her waist. "No problem, Boss, always willing to help."

Austin's right, Claire thought as they turned their attention back to the couple staring into each other's eyes in the center of the room. *It's been implied for a week, what are we waiting for?*

There'd been contact—touching, kissing, more touching, gentle explorations all crammed into those rare moments when they were actually alone and not likely to hear a speculative comment just as things got interesting—but somehow they hadn't moved on to that next step.

Maybe I should lock Austin in the bathroom.

The next level of intimacy.

Not that he'd stay there.

The horizontal mambo . . .

Stop it.

"Howard."

"Cheryl?" Pulling off his glove with his teeth, he held out his hand

and stroked the air by her cheek. "The, uh, Keeper, says you got something to say to me?"

"That's right." She leaned into his touch. His baby finger sank into her eye socket. She didn't even notice, but Howard shuddered and snatched his hand away. "It's about me and Tony."

"Tony? My best friend who you betrayed me with?"

"Yeah. Tony. I got something I need to say."

Howard spread his hands, the picture of forgiving magnanimity. "What is it, babe?"

Cheryl smiled. "I just wanted to say—had to say—before I left this world forever . . ." All four of her listeners leaned into the pause. ". . . that Tony was a better lover than you ever were. Bigger, better, and he knew how to use it! We did it twice, *twice*, during his lunch hour, and he bought me a hoagie! He made me forget every miserable time you ever TOUCHED ME!"

In the silence that followed the sound of Howard slamming up against the inside of the door, the queen of hearts fell from the ceiling and Austin murmured, "I gotta admit, that wasn't totally unexpected."

Calm and triumphant, Cheryl turned toward the bed. "All right, Keeper. I'm ready."

"Dean . . ."

"I'll see that he's okay."

It only took a moment for Claire to send Cheryl on. Thinned by a distinct sense of closure, the possibilities practically opened themselves.

"Remember what I said, hon." Scarlet lips made a suggestive kissing motion. "You oughta go for it."

Keepers were always careful not to respond emotionally to provocation from metaphysical accidents. Unfortunately, Claire remembered that after she shoved Cheryl through to the Otherside just a little harder than necessary. A lot harder than necessary.

Howard seemed essentially unaffected by both his dead wife's parting words and the impact with the door. As Claire resealed the barrier and turned, blinking away afterimages of the beyond and of a translucent figure bouncing twice, Dean was helping him onto the end of the nearer bed.

"Is she gone?" he asked, searching through thinning hair for a bump.

"Yes."

"Is she in Hell?"

"Not my department." Grasping the soft lines of his chin lightly with one hand, Claire tilted his head up. "It's time you went home, Howard."

Pale blue eyes widened.

"You were thinking about your late wife and you couldn't sleep, so you went out for a drive."

"For a drive. . . ?"

"You found yourself outside the motel room where she died, and you got out of the car."

"Out of the car. . . ?"

"You stared at the door to the room for a long moment."

"Long moment. . . ?"

"Then you got back into the car and you went home."

"Went home. . . ?"

"You don't know why, but you feel better about her death and the way things were left between you. You're glad it's over."

"Glad to be rid of her."

"Close enough." It was the first definitive statement he'd made. She carefully used the new, more probable version of events to wipe out his actual memories. Then, still holding his chin, she walked him out to his car where she released him.

"Is he gone?" Dean asked as Claire came back into the room and sagged against the door.

"Oh, yeah. I demanded to know what he was doing staring at my room and he, after telling me his wife had died there, asked me if I wanted to comfort him."

"He was sad?"

"Not that kind of comfort, Dean."

"What . . . oh."

"Lovely couple, weren't they?" Rubbing her temples, she walked to the end of the bed and scuffed out the X with the edge of her shoe. "Makes you want to swear off relationships for the rest of your life."

It took her a moment to figure out why the answering silence resonated like the inside of a crowded elevator after an unexpected emission. Then she realized what she'd said.

And who to.

"Open mouth, insert other foot," Austin advised.

"But they *were* nasty."

"No one's arguing. Although I can't understand why you're afraid that you and Dean will someday morph into them."

Claire had a sudden vision of herself in red stretch pants and a turquoise sweater and shuddered. "I'm not."

"You're not?"

"No."

Austin snorted. "My mistake."

"You're not getting a . . . a *feeling* about it, are you?" No one had ever determined if cats were actually clairvoyant or if they just enjoyed being furry little shit disturbers. Claire usually leaned toward the latter, but tonight . . .

"It won't happen, Claire."

"You're sure?"

"Of course I'm sure. I'm a cat."

Claire used a finger to smooth down the soft fringe of hair behind Austin's ear. "Do you think I should wake him up and apologize?"

"You already apologized. He already accepted."

"Then why is he over there by himself and I'm over here with you?"

The cat sighed and shifted position on the pillow. "You know, maybe you should have hit the unpleasantly departed up for some relationship advice. You couldn't possibly do any worse."

"I'm not doing *anything*."

"Well, duh. I can't decide if you're more afraid that being his first time he'll expect all sorts of commitment that you're not ready for, or if you're afraid that being all of seven years older and practically decrepit you can't live up to his expectations."

"As if. I just . . ."

The silence stretched, broken only by the steady rhythm of Dean's breathing.

"You just?"

"Never mind. Let's just go to sleep."

"And the cat scores another point."

"Austin, what part of *go to sleep* didn't you understand?"

Hundreds of miles away, Diana Hansen woke up with a feeling in her gut that meant one of two things. Either she now had a hormonal defense should she waste her calculus teacher, or that dream hadn't actually been a dream.

The question now became: should she interfere?

There were rules about Keepers using knowledge of the future to influence that future. Specifically, there were rules *against* Keepers using knowledge of the future to influence that future. Which was a load as far as Diana was concerned. What was the point of having the ability and not using it? Seeing a disaster and not preventing it?

No point.

And Diana refused to live a pointless life.

But this particular future disaster involved her older sister, and that muddied the waters. Although she no longer adored Claire with the uncritical love of a child for a sibling fully ten years older and had become quite capable of seeing every uptight, rule-following, more-Keeper-than-thou flaw, she still loved her and didn't want her to get hurt. On the other hand, she still owed her for telling their mother exactly what had happened and to whom in the basement of the Elysian Fields Guest House. Once *what* and *who* were known, it was only a small step to *why*.

Oh, yeah. She owed Claire big time for that.

One more understanding, hip to the millennium, talk from the 'rents and she was going to misuse her abilities in ways previous Keepers had never dreamed. She had a notebook full of possibilities. Just in case.

But she really didn't want Claire to be hurt.

Much.

Scratching the back of one bare leg with the toenails on the opposite foot, Diana sighed, decided to worry about it in the morning, and went back to sleep.

❉   ❉   ❉

When Claire woke up in the morning, Dean was gone.

"Relax. He went out to get breakfast."

She threw back the covers with enough force to practically strip the bed, dropped her legs over the side, and shoved her feet into waiting slippers. "I wasn't worried."

"Of course not," Austin snickered from the dresser. "That's why you were wearing your kicked puppy face."

"I don't have a kicked puppy face!"

"If you say so."

"And stop patronizing me!"

"Where would be the fun in that?" he asked the bathroom door as it closed.

She felt better after her shower. As soon as Dean came back, they'd talk about what had happened or not happened, and move forward. She'd explain that this whole having someone without fur and an attitude as a part of her life, was still new. He'd understand because he always understood. She'd reassure him she wanted their relationship to continue. He'd be pleased.

Then maybe they'd lock the cat in the bathroom. Checkout time wasn't until noon, after all.

She was packing her white silk pajamas—in a reluctant acknowledgment of the information age, Keepers were instructed to wear something that could appear on the six o'clock news in front of those unavoidable live camera shots of rubble—when the phone rang.

"Hello?" Expecting it to be Dean, she was more than a little surprised to hear her younger sister's voice.

"Whatever it is you're about to do, don't do it."

Claire sighed. "Good morning, Diana. Why aren't you in school? Stop calling me at work. And stop thinking you know how to run my life better than I do."

"I'm at school." A sudden rise in background noise suggested the phone had been held out for aural emphasis. "You're probably just packing. And I don't *think* I know how to run your life better than you do, I'm sure of it." She moved the phone not quite far enough from her mouth and yelled, "Gimme a minute!" before continuing. "Look,

I had a major precognitive thing going on last night and you're about to make a huge mistake."

Claire sighed again. In the best metaphysical tradition, Diana, as the younger sibling, was the more powerful Keeper—unfortunately, Diana was well aware of that. Fortunately, she hadn't discovered that, as all the other Keepers had been only children, she was the *only* younger sibling any Keeper had. It gave her the wiggins. The very last thing Diana needed to know was that she, at an obnoxious seventeen, was the most powerful Keeper on Earth. "What kind of a huge mistake?"

"Beats me."

"Can you give me some idea of scale?"

"Nope. Only that it's huge."

"That's not very helpful."

"I do what I can. Gotta blow, calculus beckons."

"Diana . . ."

"Kisses for kitty. And you might want to help Dean with those packages."

Deleting a few expletives, Claire hung up and hurried across the room as Dean returned with breakfast, his entrance turning into an extended production bordering on farce as he attempted to deal with two bags of takeout, the room key, and a cold wind from across the parking lot that kept dragging the door from his grip.

"It'd be easier if you'd come farther into the room," Claire pointed out, taking the bags.

Flashing her a grateful smile, he gained control of the door. "I'm trying not to track slush on the carpet."

Claire glanced down. All things considered, she doubted that a little slush would hurt, but then she wasn't the person who'd borrowed cleaning supplies from the housekeeping staff at every cheap motel they'd stayed in. The strange thing was, given how paranoid many of them were about releasing an extra sliver of soap, he almost always succeeded.

By the time she returned her attention to Dean, he had his coat off and was bending over his boot laces. And that was always worth watching. Perhaps his success with various housekeeping staffs wasn't so strange after all.

"Are you okay?" she asked, wondering if he'd recently found a way to iron his jeans or if they'd been ironed so often the creases had become a structural component of the denim. "You're moving a bit tentatively."

"My glasses fogged," he explained straightening. With one hand he pushed dark hair back from blue eyes and with the other he removed his glasses for cleaning.

Austin muttered something under his breath that sounded very much like, "Superman!"

Claire ignored him and began unpacking the food, fully conscious of Dean walking past her into the bathroom. He smelled like fresh air and fabric softener. She'd never considered fabric softener erotic before.

"Sausages?" Whiskers twitched. "I wanted bacon."

"You're having geriatric cat food."

"We're out."

"Nice try. There's four cans left."

He looked disgusted. "I'm not eating that. Those cans came out of the garbage."

"Interesting you should know that since you were in the bathroom when I found them."

Drawing himself up to his full height, he shot her an indignant green-gold glare with his one remaining eye. "Are you accusing me of something?"

Claire looked at him for a moment, then turned to Dean as he returned to the main room. "Dean, did you put Austin's cat food in the garbage?"

He had the grace to look sheepish as he took both plates of food from her and put them on the table. "Not this time."

"Then, yes, I'm accusing you of something." She popped the top of one of the cans, scooped out some brown puree onto a saucer with a plastic spoon and pushed it along the dresser toward the cat. "You're seventeen and a half years old; you *know* what the vet said."

"Turn your head and cough?"

"Austin . . ."

"All right. All right. I'll eat it." He sniffed the saucer and sighed. "I hope you realize that I plan on living long enough to see them feeding you stewed prunes at the nursing home."

Claire bent down and kissed the top of his head. "It wouldn't be the same without you."

They ate in silence for a few moments. It wasn't exactly a comfortable silence. Finally, Claire stopped eating and watched Dean clean his plate with the efficiency of a young man who hadn't eaten for over six hours. She usually liked watching him eat.

He paused, the last bite of toast halfway to his mouth. "Something wrong?"

Aren't we supposed to be talking about last night? "Diana called."

"Here?" The last of his toast disappeared.

"Well, duh." *Why aren't we talking about last night?*

"Is she in trouble?"

"No, she just passed on a warning." *I have an explanation; don't you want to hear it?*

"About what?"

"She didn't know." *Why are we talking about my sister?*

"Helpful." Plate cleaned, Dean picked up his coffee and leaned back in his chair, carefully peeling back the plastic lid.

Things seemed to be going nowhere. Claire picked up her own cup and took a long swallow. She could read nothing from his expression, couldn't tell if he was just being polite—and Dean was *always* polite—or if he honestly wasn't bothered—and Dean was so absolutely certain of his place in the world that not a whole lot bothered him. This was one of the things Claire liked best about him although it did make him a little passive, secure in the knowledge that if he just waited patiently the world would fix itself. As one of the people who fixed the world, Claire found this extremely irritating. *And does everyone hold mutually opposing views about the people they're in . . .* Shying away from the "L" word, she settled for *. . . a hotel room with, or is it just me?*

She suspected she needed to watch more Oprah.

Although *women who save the world and the men who confuse them* sounded more like a visit to Jerry Springer—provided she gained a hundred and fifty pounds and lost half of her vocabulary.

Look, if he's not questioning, why should you? With that settled, she took another drink.

"So, where do we go from here?"

"Why do we have to go anywhere?" she demanded when the choking and coughing had subsided and all of the remaining napkins had been used to deal with the mess. "What's wrong with the way things are?"

"I just wondered where you were being Summoned to," Dean explained, somewhat taken aback by the sight of Claire snorting coffee out her nose. "But if you don't want to talk about it . . ."

"About what?" She dabbed at the damp spots on her sleeve, trying and failing miserably to sound anything but near panic. *Definitely more Oprah.*

"About the Summoning."

"Right." Of course, the Summoning. Deep calming breath. "North."

"Back across the border, then?"

"Probably."

"Is it another metaphysical remnant causing localized fluxes in the barrier between actuality and possibility."

That made her smile. "Another ghost kicking holes in the fabric of the universe? I don't know." When he smiled back, she covered an embarrassing reaction with a brusque, "You're getting good at this."

"Two this week," he reminded her.

Claire was fairly certain that her current attraction to the restless dead was merely leftover sensitivity from spending so much time with Jacques, the French-Canadian sailor who'd been haunting the Elysian Fields Guest House. But, because that previous attraction had gone farther than . . . well, than things were going now, she wasn't going to mention it to Dean. With any luck the residual effects would wear off soon.

What she'd had with Jacques had been simple. He'd been dead. The possibilities between them had been finite. The possibilities with Dean, however, were . . .

She saw them suddenly, stretching out in front of her.

Driving together from site to site, squabbling over what radio station to listen to and/or listening in perfect accord to a group they both liked. And if anything was possible, there *had* to be a group they both liked. Somewhere.

Sharing endless hotel rooms like this one, same burnt-orange bedspreads in a vaguely floral pattern, same mid-brown stain camouflaging indoor/outdoor carpeting, same lame attempt to modernize the decor by pasting a wallpaper border just under the ceiling, same innocuous prints screwed to the wall over both beds.

Sharing one of those beds.

They'd work together. They'd laugh together. They'd clean up after Austin together—although the possibility of Dean doing the actual cleaning all by himself was significantly greater than them doing it together.

And one day, she'd forget he wasn't a Keeper, or even one of the less powerful Cousins, and something would come through the barrier, and she'd forget to protect him from it. Or it would try to get to her through him. Or he'd try to protect her and get squashed like a bug. Okay, a six-foot-tall, muscular, blue-eyed, glasses-wearing bug from Newfoundland, but the result would be the same.

All of a sudden, the future with Dean seemed frighteningly finite.

I might as well just paint a target on him now and get it over with.

"Claire? Boss?" It took an effort, but Dean resisted the urge to wave a hand in front of her face. If she was in some sort of Keeper trance, he didn't want to disturb it.

He'd seen a number of amazing things during the three months he'd worked for her at the Elysian Fields Guest House—up to and including Hell itself—but nothing had prepared him for time spent on the road in Claire Hansen's company. He'd expected her to be a backseat driver, but that had turned out to be Austin's job. She didn't eat properly unless he placed food in front of her—he was beginning to understand both why Austin was so insistent about being fed and why Claire was so thin. And she actually preferred watching hockey with that stupid blue light the American television stations were using to help their viewers locate the puck. Trust the Americans not to realize that knowing the position of the puck was the whole point of the game.

He liked the way she felt in his arms, and he liked the way her face lit up when she looked at him. He liked looking at her just generally, and he liked being with her. And he was becoming fairly certain that liked wasn't quite the right word. When he thought about his future, she was a part of it.

"We can't travel together anymore."

Or not. Dean looked around for help, but the sounds of vigorous excavation from the bathroom suggested Austin was in the litter box. "What did you say?" He felt as though he'd just been cross-checked into the boards and should be staring through Plexiglas at a row of screaming faces instead of across the remains of a takeout breakfast into a pair of worried brown eyes.

"We can't travel together anymore."

"But I though we were. . . ? I mean, aren't we. . . ?" he shook his head, trying to find a question he could actually articulate. "Why not, then?"

"Someday I'll run into something I won't be able to keep from hurting you."

He was about to tell her that he was willing to risk it in order to be with her when she continued, and the conversation headed off in a new, or rather an old, direction.

"It's why Keepers don't travel with Bystanders."

"I *thought* we'd moved past that Keeper/Bystander thing?"

"We *can't* move past that Keeper/Bystander thing."

The sudden quiet resonated with the sound of clay particles being flung all over the bathroom floor.

"Dean? Do you understand?"

"Sure."

She'd been working on the various meanings men gave to *sure* for some time now. This one escaped her. *Sure, I understand, but I don't agree with you* was way too obvious as was, *I've stopped listening, but since you're waiting for me to say something, sure.*

"Dean?"

When he looked up, it didn't help. For some strange reason he looked angry.

"What about us, then?"

"An *us* will end with you dead because of something I didn't do, and I won't allow that to happen."

"You won't allow?"

"That's right."

He folded his arms. "So there's no us, and we know where you stand. What about me, then?"

"You?"

"Or do I have no say in this?"

"I'm the Keeper . . ."

"And I'm not. I know."

"I'm doing this for you!"

"And because you know best, I'm supposed to just walk away?"

"I *do* know best!" Claire shoved her chair away from the table. "And it might be nice if you realized I just don't want you to get hurt." The scene should have played out as sad and tragically inevitable, but Dean continued to just not get it.

"You know what I realize?" He mirrored her motion. "I realize, and I'm amazed it took me so long, that it's always about you. You've got no idea of how to . . . to compromise!"

"A Keeper can't compromise!"

"And I suppose a Keeper can't wipe her feet either?"

"Unlike you, I have more important things to worry about than that, and," she added with icy emphasis, "I have more important things to worry about than you!"

"Fine."

"Fine."

Silence descended like a slammed door.

"Well, that doesn't get any easier as I get older." Austin jumped up onto the end of the bed nearest the bathroom and turned to face the table, swiveling his head around so he could look first at Claire and then at Dean. "So, what did I miss?"

TWO

⸻·━◆━·⸻

"**B**UT I BROUGHT YOU INTO AMERICA, I should take you out."

"It's not necessary." Claire shoved her makeup bag into the backpack—she used to carry a suitcase as well until Dean had asked her why. If she could fit a desktop computer, a printer, two boxes of disks, and the obligatory stale cough drop in the backpack, why couldn't it hold everything else? She owed him for that as well as for a thousand other things her brain insisted on listing. For doing the driving. For giving her all the red Smarties. For cleaning the litter box. For patiently explaining the difference between offside and icing yet again. For being a warm and solid support at her back. For . . .

"This is upper New York State, not Cambodia," she continued, almost shouting to drown out the list. "Canadians come here daily to buy toaster ovens."

"Fine." Dean jerked the zipper shut on his hockey bag, suddenly tired of being shouted at for no apparent reason. "You can catch a ride with one of them, then." He swung the bag up onto his shoulder, but Austin stepped in front of him before he could make it to the door.

"I don't want to ride with a toaster oven," the cat declared. "I want to ride with Dean."

"Austin." Claire growled his name through clenched teeth.

He leaned around Dean's legs to glare at her. "Is the site you're Summoned to on this side of the border?"

"No, but . . ."

"Then he won't be in any danger giving us a lift. And that *is* why you don't want him around, isn't it? To keep him out of danger?"

"Yes, but . . ."

"And we're going to need a ride."

"I know, but . . ."

"So say thank you and go settle the bill while we load the truck."

"While *we* load the truck?" Dean asked a moment later, settling the cat carrier on the seat beside him and opening the top.

"Please." Austin poured out and arranged himself in the shaft of sunlight slanting through the windshield. "Like you didn't know I wanted to talk to you."

"You need to talk to Claire, not me." He started the engine, checked that it was in neutral and the parking brake was on, took his foot off the clutch, then began polishing fingerprints off the steering wheel with the sleeve of his jacket. "I sure didn't expect to break collar so soon."

"Break what?"

"Lose the job."

"Job? You weren't doing a job, you were just living your life. If it was a *job*," the cat snorted disdainfully, "she'd have been paying you."

"Then I didn't expect this part of my life to be over so soon."

"It doesn't have to be."

"Yeah, it does."

"You're just going to let her tell you what to do?"

"No. But I'm not staying if she thinks she has the right to make decisions about my life as though I wasn't a part of it."

"Of your life?"

"Or the decision."

"So you're leaving not because she told you to but because she thinks she has the right to tell you to?"

"Yeah."

Austin sighed. "Would it make a difference if I told you she's honestly afraid of you having your intestines sucked out your nose because she was thinking about your shoulders and misjudged an accident site?"

"Well, I don't want my intestines sucked out my nose either," Dean allowed. Then he paused and blushed slightly, buffing an already spotless bit of dashboard. "She thinks about my shoulders?"

"Shoulders, thighs . . . as near as I can tell, she spends far too much time thinking about most of your body parts—sequentially and simultaneously—when she should be thinking about other things."

"Like accident sites?"

"Like me."

"Oh." And then because the cat's tone demanded an apology, he added, "Sorry."

"*And* accident sites," Austin allowed graciously, having been given his due. "Look, Claire tends to see things in terms of what she has to do to keep the world from falling apart. Close an accident site here, prevent the movie remake of 'Gilligan's Island' there, keep you from being hurt, feed the cat—everything's an absolute. She doesn't compromise well, it's an occupational hazard. Stay and teach her to see your side of things."

"*Only* if she asks me to." The steering wheel creaked a protest as Dean closed his hands around it and tightened his grip. "And since I know for a fact that Hell hasn't frozen over, I'm not after holding my breath."

Austin sighed and turned so he could see Claire picking her way across the slush covered parking lot from the office. "She's getting her own way, you'd think she'd be happier about it, wouldn't you? She looks miserable. Doesn't she? You don't want her to be miserable? Do you?"

"She started this," Dean muttered, eyes locked on the oil gauge. "If she wants me to stay, she has to convince me."

"All right. Fine." He put a paw on Dean's thigh and stared beseechingly up into his face. "What about me? I'm old. It wasn't that long ago that I lost an eye."

"I thought it had mostly healed?"

"That's not the point. It's November, it's cold. I don't want to go back to using any old thing that happens by. I *like* being driven about in a heated truck! Okay, I would've liked a heated Lincoln Town Car with leather upholstery more, but the point is, what about me?"

"I'm sorry, Austin."

"Not as sorry as she's going to be," Austin muttered as the Keeper opened the passenger door.

❖   ❖   ❖

"The booth on the right has a longer line."

"A *longer* line?" Dean had been avoiding conversation by maintaining the speed of the pickup at exactly fifty-five miles per hour regardless of the gestures other drivers flashed at him as they passed. He glanced down at the cat and tried not to notice the various bits of Claire that surrounded him. "Why do you want me to use the longer line, then?"

"It'll take more time. And the more time we're all together, the greater the odds are that you two will make up and I won't be tossed out into the cold with nothing but a cat carrier between me and November."

"There's nothing to make up," Claire told him impatiently. "We didn't have a fight."

"We didn't?"

"No." She threw the word across the cat to Dean. "I, as a Keeper, made a decision."

"About *my* future without talking to me."

"Sounds like a fight," Austin observed.

Claire wriggled back in the seat and crossed her arms. "This doesn't concern you."

"Oh, no? I'm the one who'll be riding in the overhead luggage rack . . ."

"You've never ridden in the overhead luggage rack!"

". . . or the baggage compartment."

"*Or* the baggage compartment!" she added, voice rising.

He ignored her. "Once again, I'll be at the mercy of strangers. Forced to live from paw to mouth, dark corners as my litter box, cardboard boxes as my bed."

"You like to sleep in cardboard boxes."

"That's not the point."

"You have no point. And stop whining; you're beginning to sound like a dog."

"A dog!" He twisted around to fry her with a pale green glare from his remaining eye. "I have *never* been so insulted in my life. You're just lucky I can't operate a can opener." Moving slowly and deliberately, he stepped down off her lap, onto the center of the bench seat, and turned his back on her.

The smile his companions shared over his head was completely involuntary.

Suddenly aware of her reflection grinning out from Dean's glasses, Claire dropped her gaze so quickly it bounced.

Teeth clenched with enough applied pressure to make his lone filling creak, Dean steered the truck carefully into the shorter line. The sooner this was over, the better.

Only two of the five Canada Customs booths were open. Only two of the five booths were *ever* open. On a busy day, when the line of cars waiting to cross the border stretched almost all the way back to Watertown, this guaranteed short tempers and a more spontaneous response to official questioning by Canadian Customs officials. Occasionally, on really hot summer days, responses were spontaneous enough to get the RCMP involved.

The constant low levels of sharp-edged irritation would have poked multiple holes through the fabric of the universe had government officiousness not canceled it out by denying that anything was possible outside their own very narrow parameters. As a result, most border crossings between the U.S. and Canada were so metaphysically stable, unnatural phenomenon had to cross them just like everyone else—although it wasn't always easy for them to find photo ID.

Later, they'd swap stories about how custom officials had no sense of humor, about how someone—or possibly something—they knew had been strip-searched for no good reason, and how they'd triumphantly smuggled in half a dozen toaster ovens, duty-free.

As Dean pulled up beside the booth's open window and turned to smile politely at the young guard, Claire reached into the possibilities. When the guard looked into the truck, her gaze slid over Austin like he'd been buttered, over Claire almost as quickly, and locked itself on Dean's face.

"Nationality?"

"Canadian."

"Canadian," Claire repeated although she suspected she needn't have bothered as the guard's rapt attention never left Dean.

"How long were you in the States?"

"Four days."

"What is the total value of the purchases you're bringing into Canada?"

"Six dollars and eighty-seven cents. I bought a couple of maps and a liter of oil for the truck," he added apologetically.

"You're from back East." When he nodded, she continued, startling Claire who'd never seen anyone who worked for Canada Customs look so happy. "I'm from Cornerbrook. When's the last time you were back?"

"I'm heading back now."

Their discussion slid into shared memories of places and people. Newfoundlanders, chance met a thousand miles from home, were never strangers. Occasionally, they were mortal enemies, but never strangers. After it had been determined that Dean had played junior hockey against a buddy the guard's second cousin had gone to school with, she waved them on.

"You never told *me* you were going back to Newfoundland," Claire pointed out as they pulled away from the border.

"You never asked."

"Oh, that's mature," she muttered. Now they were both ignoring her, Dean and the cat. It was the sort of thing she expected from Austin, but Dean usually had better manners. *Fine. Be that way. I know I'm right.* A sideways glance at his profile showed a muscle moving along the line of his jaw. A sudden urge to reach out and touch him surprised her into lowering her gaze.

That didn't help.

Two spots of heat burning high on each cheek, she turned to stare out at the pink granite rising in mighty slabs up into the sky.

Neither did that.

Think of something else, Claire. Anything else. Three times nine is twenty-seven. Fried liver. Brussels sprouts. Homer Simpson . . .

The insistent under-tug of the Summoning suddenly rose to a crescendo. Claire's hand jerked up and pointed toward a parking lot entrance for the Thousand Islands Sky Deck and Fantasy Land. "Pull in there."

Responding to her tone, Dean managed to make the turn, back end of the truck fishtailing slightly in the light dusting of wet snow. "It's closed," he said, coming to a stop by the entrance to the gift shop that anchored the Sky Deck.

"Not to me." This was it. The end of the line. Claire felt strangely unwilling to get out of the truck. And not only because it was beginning to snow again. *You're doing this for him,* she reminded herself. *He's only a Bystander, and you have no business putting him in danger.*

When he moved to turn off the engine, she steeled herself and stopped him, restraining herself from keeping a lingering grip around his wrist. "There's no point, you won't be here long enough." She undid her seat belt, pulled her toque over her ears, and grabbed the cat carrier from its place behind the seat. "Come on, Austin."

His back remained toward her, rigid and unyielding.

"Austin!"

He ignored her so completely she had a moment's doubt about her own existence.

"What's the matter with . . ." And then she remembered. "Oh, for . . . Austin, I'm sorry I said you were beginning to sound like a dog. It was rude."

One ear swiveled toward her.

"You have never sounded like anything but a cat. Cats are clearly superior to dogs, and I don't know what I was thinking. Please accept my abject apologies and forgive me."

He snorted without turning. "You call that groveling?"

"Yes, and I'm sorry if it falls short of your high standards. Unless you're planning to walk, I also call it the last thing I'm going to say before picking you up and stuffing you into the carrier."

Her hands were actually touching his fur before he realized she was serious. "Oh, sure," he muttered, tail scribing short, jerky arcs as he climbed into the case, "give a species opposable thumbs, and they evolve into bullies."

Dean watched without speaking as she opened the door, set the cat carrier carefully down on a dry bit of pavement up near the building, and finally lifted her backpack out from under the tarp. She paused as if she was trying to think of something to say. She was wearing some kind of lip stuff that made her mouth look full and soft and . . . He leaned over and rolled down the window. "Do you need any help, then?"

He hadn't intended to say it, but he just couldn't stop himself; his grandfather's training was stronger than justified anger, emotional betrayal, and the uncomfortable way the seat belt was cutting into his . . . lap.

An emphatic "Yes!" came out of the cat carrier, but Claire ignored it. "No, thank you." She swallowed around the kind of lump in her throat that Keepers were not supposed to get. "You'd better get going if you're driving all the way to Newfoundland."

"It's an island, Claire. I won't be driving all the way."

"You knew what I meant." Her gloves suddenly took all her attention. "This is for your own good, Dean."

"If you say so."

It was as close to a snide comment as she'd ever heard him make.

For a moment Claire thought he wasn't going to go, but the moment passed.

"Good-bye, Claire." He wanted to say something wry and debonair so she'd know what she was losing, but the only thing that came to mind was a line from an old black-and-white movie, and he suspected that "You'll never take me alive, copper!" didn't exactly fit the situation. This was clearly the day his aunt had been referring to when she'd said, *"Some day, you guys are going to wish you'd watched a couple of movies with more talking than hitting."* He settled for raising his hand in the classic *whatever* wave.

He left the window rolled down until he reached the highway. Just in case she called him back.

Claire stood and watched Dean back up and drive away, realizing she should have wiped his memory with something more possible—although at the moment, she couldn't think of anything more possible than the two of them spending their lives together.

I did it for his own good.

It was colder than it should be, and the chill had nothing to do with standing in an empty parking lot beside a closed second-rate summer attraction while an early November wind stuffed icy fingers under her collar and threatened snow. She stared at the single set of tire tracks until she couldn't feel her feet.

In the summer, Fantasy Land consisted of mazes and slides built into child-sized castles scattered along a path that twisted through the woods and paused every now and then at a fairy-tale tableau constructed of poured concrete and paint. In the summer, the fact it was a convenient place for the children to run off some excess energy before they were stuffed back in the car to fidget and complain for another hundred kilometers, lent the place a certain charm. In the winter, when nothing hid the damage caused by the same children who could disassemble an eight-hundred-dollar DVD player armed with nothing more than a sucker stick and a cheese sandwich, it was just depressing.

The Summons rose from the center of the Sleeping Beauty display.

Five concrete dwarfs, their paint peeling, stood around the bier that held the sleeping princess—or at least Claire assumed that's what the bier *had* held. The princess and two of the dwarfs had been thoroughly gone over with a piece of pipe. Bits of broken concrete lay scattered around the clearing, and Sleeping Beauty's head had been propped into a decidedly compromising position with one of the dwarfs.

"I'm guessing these guys are all named Grumpy," Claire muttered, as she approached the bier. "None of them are smiling."

Austin sat down in the shelter of a giant concrete mushroom and wrapped his tail around his toes. And ignored her.

Which was pretty much the response Claire expected. That dog comparison would likely haunt her for a while.

The hole itself was centered on the bier—no surprise since the vandalism had probably opened it. It was larger than mere vandalism could account for, though, and it had been seeping for some time. Unfortunately, the seepage wasn't dissipating.

Which meant that something in the immediate area was absorbing it.

A quick search showed no wildlife, not even so much as a single pigeon although evidence of pigeons had been liberally splattered on all five dwarfs.

"I hope this isn't going to be another one of those possessed squirrel sites. They're always nuts." She glanced over at the cat and, when he didn't rise to the provocation, sighed. *Great, my cat's not even responding to bad jokes, Dean's gone . . .* Her attention elsewhere, she tripped over a piece of broken princess, barely catching herself on the shoulder of a stone dwarf. . . . *and now I've twisted my ankle. How could this day possibly get any worse?*

A small stone hand closed painfully around her wrist.

I had to ask.

Fortunately, the hands were more or less in proportion to the body, so although the grip pinched, it wasn't difficult to break. Jerking free, Claire stepped away from the dwarf and felt something poke her in the back of the upper thigh.

It turned out to be a nose.

Her anatomical relief was short lived as this second dwarf made a grab for her knee, muttering, "Write on me, will you!"

He was pretty fast for concrete.

They all were.

". . . rotten kids . . ."

". . . ice cream on my hat . . ."

". . . you want Happy, I'll tell you what'll make me happy, you little . . ."

". . . gonna pay for those malt balls . . ."

". . . I'll hi your ho right up your . . ."

"Hey!" Claire danced away from the last dwarf and glared down at him. "Watch it, buster, you're supposed to be a children's display."

Stone eyes narrowed. "Grind your bones to make my bread."

"Oh, great . . ." She leaped off the concrete pad and onto scuffed grass. ". . . now they're free-associating."

The dwarfs came to the edge of the concrete but no farther.

Claire would have been a lot happier about that had they not been between her and the accident site. A quick jog around the perimeter proved she couldn't outrun them and, as long as the site was open, they wouldn't run down.

Secure in the knowledge that the Keeper couldn't get past them, four of the dwarfs started a soccer game with Sleeping Beauty's head while the fifth kept watch.

Two feints, a dodge, and an argument over whether it was entirely ethical to use chunks of dwarfs six and seven for goalposts, Claire realized she wasn't going to get by without a plan. Or a distraction.

"Austin?"

"No."

"I just wanted . . ."

"Tough. I'm not doing it."

"Fine. Then what'll distract five of the seven dwarfs?"

"A trademarked theme song?"

"I don't think so."

"You could sing the short version."

"No."

"You don't think they'd be up to it?"

She sighed down at the cat. "Are you done?"

"I will be shortly."

"Austin . . ."

"Okay. I'm done." He took a quick lick at a flawless shoulder. "How about five concrete lady dwarfs?"

"Why not? I'll just put an ad in the personals." Claire shoved her hands into her pockets and glanced around at the broken bottles, the scattered garbage, the senseless vandalism. She didn't even want to think about what the inside of Peter Peter Pumpkin Eater's wife's house looked like—give some people a dark corner, and they'd do one of two things in it.

Well, maybe three things.

Or four.

"Ow!" Kicked a little too hard, Sleeping Beauty's head rolled off the concrete and clipped Claire's ankle. "Yuck it up," she snarled, scooping up the head and taking aim at the clump of snickering dwarfs. "It's about to be game over!" As she released her makeshift bowling ball, she had visions of a five/two split, an easy spare, and a quick end to the stalemate.

"You missed," Austin pointed out, his tone mildly helpful.

"I know!" She had to shout to be heard above the laughter. Two of the dwarfs were propping each other up as they howled, one had fallen to the ground and was kicking little concrete heels in the air, and the last two were staggering around in increasingly smaller circles as they mocked her athletic ability.

It wasn't what she'd intended, but it had the same effect.

A quick dash, a fast sidestep over a pile of stained feathers that suggested at least one of the pigeons had been slow to get away, and a graceless but adequate leap put her up on the bier.

Keepers learned early on that the repair didn't have to be pretty as long as it did the job. Claire had personally learned it while closing a site at a book launch for a writer who very nearly acquired a life as interesting as his fiction—although it wouldn't have gone on as long. In the end, she'd been forced to evoke the paranormal properties of a crab cake, two stuffed mushroom caps, and a miniature quiche. The caterer had been furious.

Though not as furious as the dwarfs.

Who were too short to climb up on the bier themselves. The stream of profanity this evoked made up in volume what they lacked in size. Claire assumed they'd learned the words from the vandals and not the children—but she wouldn't have bet on it. Fortunately, concrete dwarfs were not fast thinkers. She had the parameters of the site almost determined when one of them yelled, "Pile up the broken bits. Build a ramp!"

As the first of the little men rose into view, Claire pulled a stub of sidewalk chalk from her pocket and scrawled the site definition across Sleeping Beauty's one remaining smooth surface. Reaching into the possibilities, she closed the hole, turned, and came hip to face with the advancing dwarf.

"Before the energy fades," he growled, "we'll rip you limb from limb."

Had they not been fighting each other to get up the ramp, they might have. As it was, Claire jumped off the other side of the bier and sprinted to the safety of the grass unopposed. The first dwarf to leap off after her, stumbled and smashed.

They were visibly slowing.

"Gentlemen!"

Four heads ground around to face her.

"You've got less than thirty seconds left. If I were you, I'd arrange myself so that I was making a statement when I solidified."

"Who'd have thought those concrete breeches would even come down?" Austin murmured as Claire carried him back toward the parking lot.

She half expected Dean to be there waiting for them.

He wasn't.

Of course he isn't, you moron. You sent him away.

She could barely feel the beginning of the new Summons over the incredible sense of loss. "I feel like I'm missing an arm or a leg," she sighed as she set Austin down beside the cat carrier and turned up the collar of her coat.

He snorted. "How would you know?"

"What?"

"The only thing you're missing is a sense of perspective. Some of us are missing actual body parts."

"I'm sorry, Austin. I keep forgetting about your eye."

"My eye?" His remaining eye narrowed. "Oh, yeah, that too. Now, if you'll excuse me, I'm going to go behind this building where I believe I saw a litter box shaped like a giant plastic turtle."

"That's a sandbox."

"Whatever. While I'm gone, why don't you answer the phone?"

"What phone?"

The pay phone on the other side of the parking lot began to ring.

Weight on one hip, Diana cradled the receiver between shoulder and ear and rummaged in her backpack for a pen. The odds were extremely good that Claire had paid no attention to her warning, but—having given it—she was curious about the outcome.

"Hello?"

"So, did you do it?"

On the other end of the phone, she heard Claire sigh. "Did I do what?"

"Make the huge mistake." Moistening the tip of one finger, she erased the phone number at the end of the ubiquitous *for a good time call* and replaced it with the number of the original graffiti artist. Erasing it entirely would only leave a clear space for some moron to refill and it was balance, after all, that Keepers were attempting to maintain.

"I don't know what you're talking about, Diana. I've just closed a small site and I'm about to move on to the next one."

"I'm talking about my precog. This morning's phone call. My timely warning." Brow furrowed, she tapped the pen against her lip, then rubbed out the punctuation and added *forest fires* in the same handwriting as *Rachel puts out* changing it from nasty to inane and thus maintaining the high school status quo. If there was a place more inane, Diana didn't want to know about it. "I bet you didn't even take precautions."

"*That* is none of your business."

Diana shook her head. No one did self-righteous indignation at the mere possibility of a double-entendre as well as Claire. And no one gave away so much doing it. "You ditched Dean, didn't you?"

"I did not ditch him. We're just not traveling together any longer."

"Dork."

"A Keeper has no business involving a Bystander in dangerous work."

"Think highly of yourself, don't you? You didn't involve him, he got involved all on his little lonesome. And, as I recall, his lonesome ain't so little."

"Diana!"

"Claire!" Suddenly depressed, she hung up. In her not even remotely humble opinion, Dean had been the best thing that had ever happened to her older sister. Just by existing, he'd managed to shake up that whole lone Keeper only-I-can-save-the-world crap that Claire believed. Apparently, he hadn't shaken it hard enough.

Sighing, she filled in the last blank space on the wall by the phone with a quick *John loves Terri* in a somewhat lopsided heart. It wasn't her best work, but at least it would keep something harmful out of the spot.

"A word, Ms. Hansen."

Pushing a strand of dark hair out of her eyes, Diana turned and forced a fake smile. "Yes, Ms. Neal?"

The vice-principal's answering smile had a certain sharklike quality about it. "If you think the school needs adornment, why not put your talents to use on the decorating committee for the Christmas dance."

"I'd love to, Ms. Neal, but I just don't have the . . . that wasn't a suggestion, was it?"

"Actually, it was an alternative to a month's worth of detention."

After the incident with the football team, her parents had forbidden her to open anyone's mind to new possibilities—although to give them credit, they'd admitted that two of the linebackers and a defensive end had been significantly improved.

"The committee has their first meeting tomorrow at lunch, on the stage. Be there."

"Yes, Ms. Neal."

"Now, if you're finished for the day, go home."

"Yes, Ms. Neal."

She could feel the vice-principal's gimlet gaze on her all the way to the door. *This bites. Save the world evenings and weekends and the rest of the time I'm at the beck and call of every petty dictator who works for the school board. I'm a Keeper. Why am I still here?*

As the door closed behind her, two confused teenagers walked in slow motion toward the phone from opposite ends of the hall, music from a modern love song growing louder and sappier the closer they got. When their hands touched, the music reached a crescendo, then faded as Ms. Neal confiscated the boombox from a group of students on the stairs.

"John?"

"Terri?"

On the wall, the heart glowed.

"Well, gee, this is just so much better than sitting in a warm and comfy truck with someone who cares about you." Shooting the darkening sky a disgusted look, Austin picked his way between wet snowflakes to where Claire was sitting on a parking lot divider and jumped up on her lap. "I personally think it's pathetic that you'd rather face a quintet of evil gnomes than a normal human relationship."

"I'm not a normal human."

"Who is?"

"Diana thinks I've made a huge mistake with Dean."

"And this is the same Diana who very nearly released the hosts of Hell?"

Claire smiled and buried her face in the back of his neck. "You're right. She's been wrong before."

"First of all, of course I'm right. Secondly, she's not wrong this time. And thirdly, stop sighing like that, you're getting me damp."

"I know my responsibility as a Keeper."

"Responsibility?"

"Yes."

"That and three seventy-five will get you a mocha latte. Speaking of which, when do we eat?"

"Soon." Claire nodded at the late model sedan pulling into the parking lot. "There's our ride."

"Oh, great. She brakes for unicorns. And hobbits." Leaping down, he headed for the cat carrier, muttering, "I only hope she brakes for stop signs." Settling into the sheepskin pad, he glared up at Claire. "You know she's going to spend the whole trip telling us cute stories about her three cats."

"I know." Closing the carrier, Claire turned to face the conscripted Bystander's cheery wave and wondered if maybe Hell hadn't gotten free after all.

THREE

IT WAS POSSIBLE TO DRIVE from Kingston, Ontario, to Halifax, Nova Scotia, in seventeen hours. Dean knew someone who'd done it—admittedly in the opposite direction, but the principle was the same. It did, however, require a number of factors working in the driver's favor.

First of all, the varying police forces in charge of the highways stretching through Ontario, Quebec, Vermont, New Brunswick, and Nova Scotia needed to be off the road. Second, nothing could go wrong with the vehicle. The glove compartment inexplicably deciding not to close was one thing. Dropping the entire exhaust system onto the asphalt just outside of Fredericton was something else again. But then, it usually was. Thirdly, the driver had to be so pissed off at an ex that his anger would keep him awake and alert to the dangers of the Canadian highway system—which was pretty much like the American system only with more moose—for the entire seventeen hours.

Fortunately, government cutbacks on both sides of the border had accomplished what a Tim Hortons on every corner hadn't, making the odds of being stopped by a moose were significantly higher than being stopped by the police. And Dean's truck might be pushing the ten-year mark, but both muffler and glove compartment were in top condition although the latter now held a hairbrush, two lipsticks, seventeen packets of artificial sweetener, a fast food child's toy, a pink plastic pouch he thought held a pressure bandage until he realized to his intense embarrassment that pressure bandages didn't have wings, half a bottle of water, and an open can of geriatric cat food.

He just wasn't angry enough at Claire to drive for seventeen hours straight, although it had been a narrow miss when he'd found the cat food. Until they'd parted ways, he'd assumed the smell had been coming from Austin who was, after all, a very old cat.

Kingston to Halifax could be done in seventeen hours, but the trip took Dean three weeks. Just across the border into Vermont, he stopped to help a stranded motorist and ended up with a job in his diner while the regular cook worked out a small problem involving a cow, two liters of ice cream, and a tourist from New Hampshire. Dean didn't ask for details; he figured it was an American thing. He thought about Claire every time he saw a young, dark-haired woman, or a cat, or anything weird on the news. He thought about her when he picked up after the waitress, when he told customers to wipe their feet, and when he went to bed alone at night.

He thought about her when the waitress suggested he didn't have to go to bed alone at night. He thought about her as he thanked the waitress politely for the suggestion but declined. He wasn't actually thinking about Claire when the waitress asked if he was gay.

"No, ma'am. I'm Canadian."

That seemed to explain things to everyone's satisfaction.

He thought about her pretty much all the rest of the time, though, and when the regular cook returned, he actually paused for a moment before getting back on the highway, wondering if maybe he shouldn't head back into Ontario and try to find her. Didn't leaving make him as incapable of compromising as he accused her of being?

The shriek of brakes from the semi coming up behind him not only ended the moment but very nearly solved the problem. Heart pounding, he put the truck in gear and continued east.

He'd seen Claire deal with Hell. And Austin. If she wanted to, she could find him.

It was mid-December by the time he arrived at his cousin's apartment in Halifax. He'd intended to stay only until he could book passage on the ferry home, but for one reason or another, many of them having to do with beer, it didn't happen.

———————

Austin stretched out his paw and neatly hooked a French fry from Claire's fingers. "You're thinking about Dean, aren't you?"

"No." Except that the truck that had very nearly run her over as she closed a site at Highway Two and King Street in Napanee had been just like Dean's. Except it hadn't been a Ford. And it was red, not white. And Dean's truck just had a standard cab. And was clean. But other than that . . .

The bed sagged under Claire's weight, then kept sagging as the mattress came to an understanding with gravity. It wasn't the most uncomfortable motel bed she'd ever slept in, but it was close. It reminded her of the bed in the motel just outside of Rochester. The bed that she and Dean had so briefly and so platonically shared. If she put out her hand, she could almost feel the heat of . . .

. . . a seventeen-and-a-half-year-old cat.

"You're thinking about Dean, aren't you?"

"No."

"You okay?"

"I'm fine." Having reassured the dark-haired, blue-eyed, glasses-wearing young waiter, Claire put her fingers back in her mouth.

"Bar's been almost shut down twice, you know, but I never seen a rat in here before."

He still hadn't seen a rat, but Claire had no intention of telling him that.

"Good thing you had your cat with you, eh?" Dark brows drew in. He scratched at stubble. "Actually, I don't think you're supposed to bring your cat in here."

The possibilities were adjusted slightly. "It's okay."

"Cool. You want another drink?"

"Why not." Since she'd already been distracted enough to nearly lose a finger, Claire figured she was entitled to watch as he walked away from her booth in the darkest corner of the nearly empty bar.

Austin horked a dark bit of something up onto the cracked Naugahyde seat. "You're thinking about Dean, aren't you?"

Fingers in her mouth, Claire ignored him.

He snorted. "Good thing you had your cat with you, eh?"

* * *

Just outside of Renfrew, Claire stood on a deserted stretched of highway and stared at the graffiti spray painted twenty feet up a limestone cliff. The hole, situated between the "u" and the "c" had turned the most popular of Anglo-Saxon profanities into a metaphysical instruction.

Before Austin could ask, she shoved frozen fingers deeper into her coat pockets and sighed. "Yes. I am. Now, drop it."

"I was only going to mention that Dean would know exactly what cleaning supplies you're going to need to get that paint off the rock."

"Sure you were."

On the opposite shoulder of the road, someone slapped a handprint into the condensation covering the windows of their parked Buick.

Against all expectations, Diana enjoyed the decorating committee meetings.

"So it's settled; for this year's Christmas dance we use a snowflake motif." Stephanie's smile could cut paper. "And, Lena, I don't want to hear another word about angels."

"But angels . . ."

"Have been done to death by all and/or sundry. Get over it."

Watching Stephanie cut through the democratic process with all the precision of a chainsaw sculptor was significantly more amusing than watching the cafeteria's hot lunch gel into something approaching a life-form.

"Diana . . ."

Jerked out of her reverie, Diana fought the urge to come to attention. Tall and blonde, Stephanie wouldn't have looked out of place in jackboots, provided she could find a purse to match, and someday she'd run a Fortune 500 company with the same ruthless élan she used to run Medway High. Unfortunately for the world at large, Keepers weren't permitted to make preemptive strikes.

". . . since we're trying to make this place look less like a gymnasium, I want you to make a snowflake pattern out of white-and-gold streamers about five feet down from those incredibly ugly ceiling tiles."

Diana glanced up at the ceiling, then over at Stephanie. The gym was probably thirty feet high, and it would take scaffolding to reach anything higher than the tops of the basketball backboards. The odds of the custodians building that scaffolding were slightly lower than the odds of any member of the senior basketball team being picked up by the pros. At zero and thirteen, the senior basketball team couldn't even get picked up by the cheerleaders. "You want me to what?"

"Try to pay attention. I want you to hide the ceiling behind a crepe-paper snowflake." Stephanie met Diana's incredulous gaze with a level blue stare, assuming compliance.

Although not the uninvolved stick in the mud Claire had been during high school, Diana had tried to give the whole Keeper thing the requisite low profile. Given how generally pointless she found the whole public school system, it hadn't always been easy, but she'd made it to her final year without anyone pointing and screaming "Witch!" Well, no one anyone who mattered listened to, anyway.

So what had Stephanie seen?

And bottom line, did it matter?

"A crepe-paper snowflake?"

"Yes."

"Okay."

It *was* an ugly ceiling.

Meeting over, Lena fell into step beside her as they left the gym. "*You're* the *senior* student on the committee, *not* Stephanie, so if *you* wanted *angels* . . ." Her voice trailed off suggestively, having applied the maximum emphasis allowed.

"It was the committee or a month of detention," Diana reminded her. "But I don't think angels are a good idea."

Lena looked crushed. "Why *not*?"

"Flaming swords, smiting the ungodly . . ."

"Angels aren't *like* that!"

"Maybe not the ones you run into, but the problem is, you can never be sure."

"Of *what*?"

"Of what kind of angel you're running into."

Lena thought about that for a moment, then, as Diana headed into the first of her afternoon classes, muttered, "My mother's right. You're *weird.*"

━━━━

With over three million people, Toronto had two working Keepers, one very elderly Keeper plugging an unclosable site out in Scarborough, and half a dozen Cousins monitoring the constant metaphysical flux—one of whom had made a small fortune following the stock market in his spare time. He said he found the relative calm relaxing.

The Summons took Claire to the College Park subway station on the University line where ninety-six hours previously a government worker from one of the nearby offices had been pushed from the platform. At the time, the old Red Rocket had been three hundred meters away grinding its slow way north. The intended victim had plenty of time to dust himself off, climb back onto the platform, and threaten the man who'd pushed him with an audit—but that was moot. Inept evil was still evil and a hole had opened at the edge of the platform.

For the next three days, it spewed bits of darkness out onto commuters in the morning and gathered them up again in the evening larger and darker. It was probably a coincidence that members of the Ontario government, arriving daily at the legislature building only a block away, proposed a bill to close half the province's hospitals and cut education spending by 44% during those three days since it was highly unlikely that any member of the ruling Conservative party took the subway to work.

By the time Claire got to the site, the hole was huge and thousands of government employees had arrived at their jobs in a bad mood and left in a worse one—which was pretty much business as usual only more so.

Just after midnight, the platform was essentially deserted. A group of teenagers, isolated in headphones and sunglasses, loitered at one end and an elderly woman wrapped in at least four layers of clothing and surrounded by a circle of grimy shopping bags glared at her from the other.

With a sigh, Claire shifted the cat carrier to her other hand and walked reluctantly forward, wondering why she couldn't see through the glamour. When she got close enough, and the scent of unwashed clothing and treasured garbage overwhelmed the winter-chilled metal, machine scent of the subway, she realized that she couldn't see through the glamour because there wasn't one.

"Hey, tuna!" A black nose pressed up against the screen at the front of the carrier, then suddenly recoiled with a sneeze. "Six days old, wrapped in a gym sock previously worn by someone with a bad case of toe rot, and I'd rather not be any closer." He sneezed again. "Can we go now?"

"No. And keep your voice down. We're in a public place."

"I'm not the one talking to luggage."

At the outer edge of the shopping bags, her eyes were watering. Nothing could smell so bad on its own, it had to have been carefully crafted. Claire was thankful she'd never had to study under this particular Keeper. *This afternoon we'll be combining the scents of old cheese and the stale vomit/urine combination found in the backs of certain taxis . . .* Like life wasn't already dangerous enough?

"You Claire?"

"Yes." At least the other Keeper wasn't insisting on using the traditional and ridiculous "Aunt Claire."

"Are you Nalo?"

"I am. So, where is he?"

Claire blinked at the other Keeper. "Pardon?"

"Your young man. I heard at Apothecary's that one of us made an actual connection with a Bystander." She craned her neck, showing a remarkable amount of dirty collar. "Did he have trouble finding parking?"

There was absolutely no point in suggesting it was none of her business.

"We're not traveling together anymore."

"You're not? Why not? I heard he was a looker and pure of heart, too." One eye closed in an unmistakable wink. "If you know what I mean."

Claire made a mental note to smack Diana hard the next time she saw her. "We're no longer together because I decided that he wasn't safe traveling with me."

"First of all; you decided? And second, he'd already been to Hell, girl. What did you think could happen that was worse?"

"How about asphyxiation?"

Nalo pointed a long, dark finger in a filthy fingerless glove at the cat carrier. "If you can think of a better way to keep Bystanders far away from this hole, then I'd like to hear it. Until then, I don't take attitude from no cat."

It was probably fortunate that the approaching subway drowned out Austin's response.

The teenagers got on, and out of the door closest to the hole stepped a large young man in a leather jacket, a tattoo of a swastika impaled by a dagger nearly covering his shaved head. Pierced lip curled, he swaggered toward the two women. He sucked in a deep breath, readying himself to intimidate, then looked appalled, and choked.

"You know what I think when I see a tattoo like that?" Nalo murmured as the sound of violent coughing echoed off the tiles. "I think, he's gonna look like a fool when he's eighty and in a nursing home."

"Maybe he'll regrow his hair."

"Won't help, he's got male pattern baldness written all over him."

Claire couldn't see it, but she could see the words "hate" and "kill" written into the backs of his hands. Reaching into the possibilities, she made a slight cosmetic change. Then she reached a little farther.

His eyes widened and, still coughing, the hand that said "male pattern" gripping the crotch of his jeans and the one that said "baldness" outstretched to clear the way, he ran for the stairs.

"Will he be back?"

"Depends on how long it takes him to find a toilet."

"He could just pee in a corner."

"That'll take care of half the problem."

Nalo grinned. "Very clever. You're subtler than your sister."

"Public television pledge breaks are subtler than my sister."

"True enough. Well, that was the last regular train past this station, so let's get to work before the maintenance trains hit the rails." Nalo shrugged out of her coat, peeled off the gloves, and was suddenly a middle-aged black woman in a TTC maintenance uniform. A lot of her previous bulk had come from the tool belt around her waist.

"You do a lot of work in the subways?" Claire asked, setting Austin's carrier down and opening the top for him.

"Hundreds of thousands of people ride them every day, what do you think? Most of the holes close on their own, but enough of them needed help that it finally got easier just to buy the wardrobe—we've got a Cousin in the actual maintenance crew who picked it up for me."

"Was he monitoring the site?"

"This one and a couple of others." The older Keeper glanced at her watch. "Security'll be here shortly. I've dealt before, so I'll deal again; why don't you and your younger legs jump down on the track and map the lower parameters."

Yes, why don't I? Although she tried, Claire couldn't actually think of a good reason, so she stalled. "What about the camera? I should adjust it to show a different possibility."

"Already done."

So much for stalling. Pulling her kit from her backpack, she walked over to the edge of the platform and sat, legs dangling. "You coming, Austin?"

"Not likely."

"There's mice down there."

"I should care?" But he trotted over for a closer look. "Not *just* mice."

A group of tiny warriors no more than two inches high, their dark skins making them almost impossible to see, were silently surrounding an unsuspecting rodent. The kill was quick, the prey lifted in half a dozen miniature arms and, to Claire's surprise, thrown against the third rail. There was a sudden flash, a wisp of smoke, and tiny voices chanting, "Bar. Be. Que! Bar. Be. Que!"

"What's the delay?" Nalo asked, walking over. "Oh, Abatwa. I don't know when they came over from South Africa, but they've adapted amazingly well to the subway system. You know what to do if you're challenged?"

As far as Claire could tell, they all seemed to be males. "Flattery?"

"That's right. Watch where you're stepping, it makes them cranky."

Given the nature of some of the debris, Claire figured stepping on one of the Abatwa would be the least of her problems. She didn't even want to consider how some of it had gotten down there. About to push off, she caught a memory and froze. "You said something about maintenance trains?"

"You've got lots of time."

"But we don't know how long this will take."

"Girl, you worry too much." Nalo's pat was almost a push.

Claire took the hint and dropped down onto the greasy ties. As she turned toward the job, heavy footfalls heralded the approach of Transit Security. They seemed perfectly willing to believe that both Keepers were maintenance workers and that Austin's carrier was a toolbox, making only a cursory check and leaving quickly. Claire suspected that the collection of filthy shopping bags discouraged suspicion. And conversation. And breathing.

Her suspicions were confirmed when one of the guards promised to tell the cleaning crew about the mess. "They can get them ready for the garbage train."

"Garbage train?" Claire asked when they were gone. "Is that the maintenance train you mentioned?"

"One of them," Nalo allowed, pulling a piece of chalk from her tool belt and squatting by the upper edge of the hole.

"One of them? How many of them are there?"

"Depends."

"On what?"

"On how many of them there are."

"Wonderful."

The cleaning crew arrived before they finished mapping. None of them spoke English, two of the three couldn't speak to each other. They all made their feelings quite clear about the bags.

"I don't know about you," Austin muttered when they left, "but I've just learned a few new words." He wandered over to the edge of the platform and peered down at Claire. "How's it going?"

"Fine." The hole came over the edge of the platform, wrapped around the lip, and extended two feet down a blackened concrete block wall. It took a liberal application of nail polish remover to get even small sections of the concrete blocks clean enough to take a definition. And her fingers were getting cold.

"Dean could get that clean in no time."

"And if Dean were here, that would be relevant."

"Hey, *I* didn't chase him away."

"Shut up."

"Almost done?"

"Almost."

"Good."

She glanced up at his tone. "Why good?"

"Well, I don't want to rush you, but there's something going on just down the line."

"Going on?"

He cocked his head, ears pointing south. "Sounds like a train."

"Great."

"But it's stopped now."

"Fine. Let us know when it starts moving. Nalo?"

"I'm ready. If you're not sure you can finish before the train gets here, hop out and we'll redo after."

Claire glanced down the tunnel. She couldn't see a light, she couldn't feel the wind of an approaching train, and she just wanted this whole thing to be over. "There's one last definition; I can finish." The concrete wasn't exactly clean, but it would have to do. A little extra pressure on the chalk got the symbol more-or-less inscribed. "That's it." A movement in the air lifted her hair off the back of her neck as she straightened. "Let's go."

Because of the bend in the site, it was impossible for a single Keeper to see the entire perimeter. While Nalo pushed her edge in, Claire reached into the possibilities and lifted.

The movement in the air became wind.

Claire could feel the vibrations of the approaching train in the soles of her feet.

The hole fought to stay open.

As the bottom edge reached the tricky turn at the lip, she could see a small light growing rapidly larger in the corner of her eye.

Rapidly larger.

It became a train.

I might just as well throw myself under it. I can't believe I screwed things up so badly with Dean. How can I miss him so much and keep on living? What's the point of a life without someone to share it wi . . .

A sudden multiple puncture through the skin of her hand jerked her back to herself. Grabbing possibilities, she tightened her grip on the definitions, flung herself up onto the platform, and slammed the hole shut just as a three-car train roared through the station, lights blazing and Christmas music blaring.

Lying flat on her back, she lifted her injured hand up into her field of vision. "I'm bleeding."

"You're lucky that's all you're doing; that cat just saved your life. What happened?"

"I was . . ."

"Thinking about Dean."

She turned her head until she could see Austin, opened her mouth to deny it, and sighed.

"*Were* you thinking about this boy?"

Another turn of her head and she could see Nalo frowning down at her, hands on hips. "It was more like a bad soap opera than actual thought," she admitted reluctantly.

"Get up," the older Keeper instructed. "We need to talk."

Her tone left no room for argument. It barely left room for vowels.

As Nalo made sure the hole was truly sealed, Claire got slowly to her feet then bent down and picked up the cat. "Thank you."

He rubbed the top of his head against her chin. "Same old, same old."

". . . and being without him is affecting the way you're doing your job. Not to mention putting your life in danger. And what do you think would have happened if that train had killed a Keeper while you were under the influence of darker possibilities? I'll tell you what, we'd have had a repeat of that whole Euro Disney thing!"

Claire shuddered.

"The powers that be clearly want the two of you together, or you wouldn't be in such lousy shape without him." Nalo handed her a glass of eggnog and set a saucer of it on the coffee table for Austin. "Drink this. You'll feel better."

"There's rum in it."

Austin lifted his head, a fleck of foam on his muzzle. "There's no rum in *mine*."

Both Keepers ignored him.

"Do you love the boy?"

A mouthful of eggnog came back out Claire's nose. "He's not a boy!"

"Pardon me, Miss Defensive, and use the napkin, not your sleeve. Do you love the man, then?"

"I just want what's best for him."

"How about you let him decide what's best for him and you answer my question." Nalo settled into a wing-back recliner and stared at Claire over the edge of her glass. "Do you love him?"

"Love." She tried for nonchalance and failed dismally. "What is love anyway?"

"Claire . . ."

There was power in a name. In this particular instance, there was also a warning.

The depths of the eggnog held no answers although the rum made a couple of suggestions Claire ignored. Sighing, she set the empty glass down on the coffee table next to a crocheted Christmas tree. "Since he left, I've felt like there's a part of me missing."

"Close but not good enough. Do you love him?"

"I . . ."

"Yes or no."

Yes or no? There had to be other options. When none presented themselves, she sighed. "Yes."

"Yes, what?"

"Yes, I love him." The world stopped for a moment, and when it started up again, Claire felt a little light-headed. "Shouldn't there be music or something?"

"The world stopped. That wasn't enough? You want a sound track, too?"

"I guess not."

"Good. Does he love you?"

"I don't know."

Austin looked up from the bottom of his saucer. "He does."

"How do you know?" Claire demanded, leaning forward to stare into his face.

"He told me."

"No, he didn't."

"Are you calling me a liar?"

"I'm calling you a cat."

Austin thought about that for a moment. "Fair enough," he conceded.

"It's obvious you and Dean should be together," Nalo declared, drawing the attention of both Claire and the cat. "So what are you going to do about it?"

Claire shook her head. "Keepers don't . . ."

"Don't tell me what Keepers don't; I've been one a lot longer than you have. Keepers don't deny the truth when it jumps up and bites them on the ass, that's what Keepers don't. If it helps, think of the space between you as an accident site you have to close."

"But the danger."

"Girl, don't you think for a moment that Keepers have the only power. If you love him, you find that boy then you trust in the power of love to keep him safe. And if that cat doesn't quit making gagging noises," she added with a dark look at Austin, "I'm going to use him to line a pair of slippers."

"She didn't tell you anything you didn't already know."

"I know." Bedded down on Nalo's couch for the night, Claire stared out the window, past the lights of the city at points farther east. Dean was out there, somewhere, and as much as it was going to cost her, she could think of only one way to find him.

Austin kneaded her hip, his claws not quite going all the way through the duvet. "So what *are* you going to do about it?"

"Go home for Christmas."

"Diana?"

"Diana."

"And if you're Summoned somewhere else?"

"Then I'll know that Dean and I aren't supposed to be together and I'll be miserable and unhappy for the rest of my life."

"That's your entire plan?"

Claire sighed and stroked her fingers along his spine. "That's it."

"You know, you guys really need a union."

The Christmas dance was Diana's first. She hadn't planned on attending but when her parents had discovered what she'd done too late to have her undo it, they'd insisted she be there just in case. They'd said rather a great deal more as well, but she'd stopped listening to the lecture early on.

Standing against the wall of the gym, arms crossed, a cardboard cup of punch in one hand, she watched twinkling bits of light falling gently through the central hole in the crepe-paper pattern. It was working exactly as designed; the weave captured good feelings rising up from the crowd, filtered and purified them, then sprinkled them back down like metaphysical snowflakes through the center hole. And in spite of minor panic from the 'rents about the dangers inherent in too much of a good thing, the inevitable counterbalance of teenage angst insured that the system didn't spiral up and out of control.

It was probably going to be the first high school dance in history where everyone had a good time and no one had *too* good a time.

As ordered, the pattern even looked like a snowflake from below.

She was remarkably pleased with herself.

Draining the cup, she set it down and walked across to where the senior basketball team were standing morosely by the wall. They were now zero and nineteen. The chess club was more popular.

"Joe, dance with me!"

He looked startled but took her hand and allowed her to lead him out onto the floor.

As the music started to slow, Diana reached into the possibilities and changed the CD before he could pull her close.

Everyone *was* going to have a good time, but there were limits to even the most selfless charity work and Joe *had* missed his last five free throws.

Just after one a.m., Diana slipped off boots and coat and padded upstairs in her socks, reaching just far enough into the possibilities to muffle the sound of her arrival. She didn't actually have a curfew—there was a certain inane sound to *you can only save the world until ten on a school night*—but she liked to keep the parental units guessing. Fully aware of this, they set certain metaphysical traps, which she easily deflected, and all parties remained secure in the knowledge that they were holding up their respective ends of the teenager/parent relationship, Keeper/Cousin variety.

Diana suspected her parents didn't think of it that way, but as long as they were happy, she didn't really mind.

She waited until she had her bedroom door closed behind her before she turned on the light.

"I need a favor."

The possibilities muffled her startled shriek and Claire easily fielded the candle she threw. "Don't you have somewhere to be Summoned to!"

"No." Claire set the candle on the stack of paperbacks piled by the bed.

"No?"

"How loud was the music at that dance? No. I am, at the current time, not being Summoned anywhere."

Her heartbeat beginning to return to a more normal rhythm, Diana crossed over to the beanbag chair, scooped Austin up into her arms, and settled them both, the cat on her lap. "Whoa. You do know what that means?"

"How many more years have I been doing this?" Arms crossed, Claire paced the eight steps to the wall and back. "It means I'm supposed to be here. I'm supposed to do what I'm doing."

"You don't look very happy about it. What are you supposed to be doing that's got you so nervous?"

Dropping onto the end of the bed, Claire picked a tuft of fuzz off the folded Navaho blanket. "Like I said, I need a favor."

"You're supposed to ask me for a favor?"

"No. I *need* to ask you for a favor."

"Me?"

"Do you see anyone else in here?" Claire demanded, nostrils pinched. "If I could do this any other way, I would, but I need a favor only you, my only sister, can provide."

"Only me?" The grin became a smirk as she stroked a thoughtful hand down Austin's back. "In all my life you have never come to me for counsel or help. You have never invited me to be a part of what you do. Now you come to me and say you need a favor." She stroked the cat again. "Now you call me sister."

Austin stretched out a paw, and pushed against her lap. "Hey, Godfather, behind the ears."

"You're sure you know the number?"

"Always." Diana poked at the phone.

"That's too many numbers!"

"Relax and tell me again how I was right and you were wrong."

"Just dial."

"I've dialed; it's ringing." The look on Claire's face evoked an involuntary smile—which slipped as Claire stood motionless and stared at the receiver. "Hey? Are you going to take this thing from me or . . . too late. Hi, Dean."

Dean pushed himself into a sitting position on his cousin's sofa bed. "Diana?" He slid on his glasses and glanced over at the VCR for the time. The piece of black electrical tape was no help at all. "How did you get this number?"

"If I told you that, I'd have to kill you. There's someone here who wants to talk to you. Someone who's very, very sorry she sent you away and . . . ow! What's your damage? It sure seemed like you didn't want to . . . okay, okay, stop pinching!"

During the pause that followed, he dug for his watch. Two forty-one. a.m.

"Dean?"

Remember to breathe, he told himself as the room started to spin. "Claire?"

Fingers gripping the plastic so tightly it creaked, Claire had a sudden flashback to the hotel room in Rochester.

"Howard?"

"Cheryl?"

And we all know how well that turned out. She swallowed, unable to actually say the words. If Dean had said something, anything, but he didn't—although she could feel him waiting.

Diana rolled her eyes. Leaning forward, she caught her sister's gaze and held it. "Tell him, Claire." The she reached into the possibilities and added the magic word. *"Please."*

Resistance was futile. The words spilled out before Claire could stop them. "Dean, I'm sorry. I was wrong to just arbitrarily decide we shouldn't be together anymore. I should have told you about the danger and let you . . ." When Diana scowled, she wet her lips and made a quick correction. ". . . trusted you to make your own decisions. I want us to be together."

"Why?"

"Why? I . . . um . . . Diana, if you *please* me again, I'm going to smack you!" Having glared down her sister, she took a deep breath.

"If it helps, think of the space between you as an accident site you have to close."

Moving the phone away from her mouth, she growled, "Would a little privacy be asking too much?"

Diana, secure in the certain knowledge that Claire owed her big time, snorted. "Well, duh."

Austin ignored the question as it clearly did not apply to cats.

Neither response surprised her. She tucked the phone back up to her mouth and lowered her voice. "Dean, since you left, I've felt like there's a part of me missing."

She could still feel him waiting.

"Close but not good enough."

"Look, I love you. Okay?"

She loved him. Over the thundering of his heart, Dean could hear music. It filled the apartment, thrummed in his blood, and just about made his ears bleed.

In the next room, his cousin banged on the ceiling. "It's almost three o'clock in the freaking morning, butthead!

"Dean?" Claire frowned at the phone.

"What's happening?" Diana demanded, reaching for the receiver.

Claire smacked her hand away. "I don't know. It sounds like Bon Jovi."

The music stopped.

"Dean?"

❖   ❖   ❖

She loved him. The words echoed in the sudden silence.

She loved him.

Now what? Was he supposed to say he loved her, too, or would she think he was just saying it because she'd said it even though he did, and had known it since he drove away and left her standing all alone in that parking lot even though he hadn't realized he'd known it until this very moment?

And then what?

"Dean?"

"What's the matter?" Diana made another unsuccessful grab for the receiver.

"He's not saying anything."

"Give me the phone."

Claire stared down at the cat. "What?"

"The phone, give it to me." When she hesitated, he sighed. "Trust me, it's a guy thing. You need to break this up into bite-sized pieces."

As the silence from the other end of the line continued, she laid the phone down on the bed beside Austin who cocked his head so that his mouth was at the microphone and one ear pointed at the speaker.

"Dean, you still there?"

That wasn't Claire. Where had Claire gone?

"Claire?"

Austin's tail tip flicked back and forth. "She's here, but right now, we need some answers. Do you love her?"

Dean sighed in relief. That, he didn't have to think about. "Yes."

"Do you want to be with her?"

"Yes."

"Write down these directions."

He shook his head to clear some of the adrenaline buzz and grabbed a pen off the end table beside the sofa bed. Paper. He had no paper. Pulling the fabric tight over his leg, he wrote the directions on the sheet, repeated them, and hung up.

✧　✧　✧

"Well?" Claire demanded as Austin lifted his head. "What did he say?"

"He said yes. Hang this up, would you. If you're thinking of what to get me for Christmas, I'm fairly certain I could manage one of those large-buttoned phones they have for seniors."

"Austin."

"Just think of the time you'd save if I could order my own food."

"Austin!"

"What?"

Claire managed to avoid throttling him but only just. "He said yes, and?"

"And I expect he's folding his underwear into his hockey bag even as we speak."

"He folds his underwear?" Diana snickered.

"He folds everything," Austin told her, fastidiously smoothing a bit of rumpled fur.

"Austin . . ." Claire ground the cat's name out through clenched teeth. ". . . what does Dean's underwear have to do with *anything*? And you . . ." She turned a warning glare on her sister. ". . . can just shut up and let him answer the question."

"It has to do with packing." When she continued to glower, Austin sighed. "Packing to come here. And you're welcome," he gasped as jubilant Claire scooped him up into her arms. "But I'm old, and you just drove a rib through my spleen."

"Do cats have a spleen?"

"I think you're missing the point."

"Sorry." She set him back on the bed and, suddenly conscious of her sister's smug expression, stiffened. "What?"

"Don't you have appreciation to show to someone else? Someone who, oh, made the initial contact?"

"Thank you."

"You're welcome."

"And I would have told him without your help."

"Oh, sure. And *Babe* would've been nominated for that best picture Oscar without my help."

"Diana!"

"I was a lot younger then! And it's not like it won . . ."

✧   ✧   ✧

It was not possible to drive from Halifax, Nova Scotia, to Kingston, Ontario, in seventeen hours. For reasons unknown to mortal man— although most mortal women were aware of them as they involved asking for directions when trying to get out of Montreal—the trip from east to west took eighteen hours. Dean actually had to drive past Kingston through Toronto, to London, then north to Lucan. The whole trip took him twenty-three hours. He saw one police car parked at a doughnut shop. He saw no moose.

FOUR

—•———⊠—◈—⊠———•—

"THAT'S HIS TRUCK. He's here!"

"Claire . . . can't breathe . . ."

"Sorry." She loosened her grip on the cat, who squirmed out of her arms and stalked to the other end of the couch, tail lashing from side to side. Brushing drifts of cat hair off her sweater, she murmured, "I can't believe how nervous I am."

"I can't believe how nerdy you are," Diana sighed. "You love him, he loves you, yadda, yadda, yadda. Now haul ass out there and let him know he's at the right house."

"Keepers don't . . ."

"What? Make spectacles of themselves with Bystanders in public?" Diana's mimicry of her sister was cuttingly accurate. "If you wait until he comes up to the house, you'll have to invite him in. If he comes in here, he'll have to make nice with Mom and Dad. If, on the other hand, you meet out there, you can take him directly to your place and make nicer with each other. Your choice."

Eyes locked on the figure getting out of the truck, Claire hesitated . . .

"You know Dad'll want to show him the photo album."

. . . and decided.

"Now haul ass out there and let him know he's at the right house?" Austin snorted as he walked over to stand beside Diana at the open door. "I never knew you were such a romantic."

Fireworks! Claire thought with the small part of her brain still functioning. Then she realized it was just the Christmas lights on the front of the house reflecting in Dean's glasses. He tasted like coffee and toothpaste. Or coffee-flavored toothpaste.

After a moment, she pulled her mouth far enough away from his to sigh, "You're here."

He smiled down at her, finding it just a little difficult to focus. "I'm here."

"I'm glad you came."

"I'm glad you called."

"I can't hear them."

"Lucky you," Austin muttered, moving away from the open door. "If I have to hear any more, I'm going to hork up a hairball. That dialogue is so banal she should have run into his arms in slow motion."

"There's a foot of snow on the path," Diana reminded him. She took another look. "Or rather there was." The snow beneath Dean's work boots and Claire's running shoes had melted and the cleared area was spreading fast. Peering through fog created by the sudden, localized heat, she grinned and yelled, "Get a room!"

"Diana?"

"Mom." Diana pulled the door closed as she turned. There were some things that shouldn't be shared across the generations. *Third Eye Blind* and bicycle shorts topped the list, but watching Claire suck face with a hunka hunka burning love in the front yard followed close behind. Most of the time, Diana tried to be sensitive to parental feelings. "What can I do for you?"

"Was that Dean's truck I heard?"

"Yes, it was."

"Has Claire gone out to meet him?"

"Yes, she has."

"Is she going to bring him inside to say hello to the rest of us?"

"I somehow doubt it."

Martha Hansen studied her younger daughter's expression. "I see. It's like that, is it? Well, good."

"Good?"

"Yes, good. I like Dean, and I hope he and Claire will find happiness together. Not many Keepers manage to find someone to share their lives with," she added, shooting a pointed look at her younger daughter. "Most of you are such arrogant know-it-alls that you end up old and alone."

"Yeah, yeah, if we end up old at all." Diana waved off the warning. Since she had every intention of going out young in a blaze of glory, it was moot. "So you don't mind about the hot monkey sex in the front yard?"

Martha's smile grew slightly wistful. "Your father and I were like that when we first got together. We couldn't keep our hands off each other."

"Eww, gross!" The list of *not to be shared* was hurriedly revised, parental coupling confidences now moved into the primary position.

"Shouldn't I go in and say hello to your parents?"

Dad'll want to show him the photo album.

"No."

Dean pulled back reluctantly, tracing a line of kisses up her face as he lifted his head. "Claire, it's polite."

He was never impolite. Claire didn't think he could be. "If a little old lady showed up right now," she murmured while nibbling on his chin, "would you help her across the street?"

"What little old lady?" Although cognitive thought was becoming increasingly difficult, he was fairly certain they hadn't been talking about little old ladies.

"Any little old lady."

Now he was confused. Separating his chin from her mouth with a soft sucking sound, he looked around, wondering where the fog had come from. "I don't see a little old lady."

"There *is* no little old lady." Claire made a mental note to be more specific in the future. "I was just making the point that there's a time and a place for everything, and this is not the time to be with my parents." She glanced down.

Dean's cheeks flushed crimson. He grabbed her wrists and pulled her hands away from his jeans. "Claire, I . . ." Then the length of her thigh brushed against his, and he made a sort of choking noise deep in his throat as he bent his mouth back to hers.

"I have my own apartment over the garage," she murmured

against his lips. "It's not actually part of my parents' house. Technically, we can go directly up there without being rude."

"Claire . . ."

"If we go up there now, I can give you your Christmas present."

"Christmas isn't until tomorrow," he protested weakly.

Twisting free of his grip, she slid her hands up under his sweater until she could feel his heart slamming against his ribs so hard that the muscle sheathing them shivered under the impact. She shivered a bit herself and murmured, "Do you *really* want to wait?"

"Way to go, Dean! He's carrying her up the stairs. Ouch, that had to hurt. Hit her head on the side of the garage." Shaking her own head in sympathy, Diana shifted position slightly to get a better angle on the scene. "She seems to be okay—they're carrying on. Probably has so many endorphins in her system she can't feel a thing."

"Diana!" Her mother twitched the curtains out of her grip. "That's quite enough of that!"

The garage having just cut off her line of sight, Diana shrugged and stepped away from the window, raising both hands in exaggerated surrender. "Not a problem, Mom, your wish is my command."

"Good." Martha tucked a strand of graying hair back behind her ear and folded her arms. "Then let me make that wish just a little more specific—no more spying on your sister, period. No hidden microphones. No web cams. No scrying in any form; no mirrors, no bowls of water, and especially no entrails. I need those giblets for the gravy. You will leave Claire and Dean alone while they . . ."

Diana's eyebrows rose to touch her hairline.

"Yes, well, just never mind what they're doing. They're adults, and it's none of your business. Or mine or your father's," she added before Diana could speak. "When you're out on your own, we will extend the same courtesy to you, so there's no need to look at me like that."

"Like what?"

"Like your life is a never-ending battle against personal oppression. You're seventeen, Claire's twenty-seven."

"And Dean's twenty-one."

"Which means?"

"Absolutely nothing. I'm happy she's happy. I'm happy they're happy. I'm happy *you're* happy. But, all things considered, you might want to have the fire department on standby."

"The fire department *is* on standby," her mother pointed out dryly. "Or have you forgotten what happened last Christmas when the star of Bethlehem went supernova."

Diana had long since stopped protesting that they'd have won the Christmas lighting contest had the fire department simply damped down the crèche like she'd asked them to instead of putting the whole thing out because her parents always answered with irrelevancies. The roof had been perfectly safe. Essentially safe. Slightly scorched . . .

A short time later, having been forced to eat a piece of fruitcake and talk to Aunt Corinne on the phone, she straightened up from the wall that separated her room from Claire's apartment, set the empty glass down on her desk, and sighed. "That works on television."

"So does David Duchovny but he's got just as slim a connection to the real world," Austin reminded her, eye narrowed as he watched her push a handful of pencils one at a time, into a mug. "I thought your mother told you to leave them alone."

"She didn't specifically say no eavesdropping." Picking a pair of sweatpants off the floor, Diana poked her finger through a ragged hole in the knee.

"She didn't specifically tell you not to feed the cat, but I notice you've managed to resist."

"You just ate some fruitcake."

"Your point?"

"Do cats even *like* fruitcake?"

"Does anyone?"

She threw the sweatpants into the laundry basket and dropped into her desk chair, spinning herself petulantly around and around. "You're being awfully understanding considering that Claire's shut you out, too—after *we* got them together."

"If you think I'm interested in watching talking monkey sex," Austin snorted, "think again."

"That's *hot* monkey sex."

"You're all talking monkeys from where I sit. And I've seen that friction thing; it never really changes."

A six-car passenger train roared across the room and into a tunnel.

"Okay," he said thoughtfully when the noise had died. "*That* was different."

"Diana!"

Waving away the lingering scent of burning diesel, Diana opened her bedroom door, fingers hooked in the trim as she leaned out into the hall. "Yeah, Dad?"

"What the bloody blue blazes was that?"

"I think it was a euphemism." The vibrations had knocked askew a set of family photographs hanging on the wall across from her. A previously serious portrait of Claire had developed a distinctly cheesy grin. "Or maybe a metaphor."

"Well, don't do it again!"

"It wasn't me!" She closed the door, not quite slamming it, and walked to the bed. "Why does he always assume it's me?" she demanded, scooping Austin up into her arms.

"It always *is* you."

"Not this time."

"Natural mistake, though. Close your eyes."

"Why?"

"Trust me. Three, two, one . . ."

The possibilities opened.

Wide.

"Holy shit!" One hand pressed against the glass, Brent Carmichael turned away from the window and stared at the half dozen firefighters standing behind him. Behind them, the cards they'd abandoned lay spread out on the table. "Did you see that?"

"I'm still seeing it," one of the others muttered trying to blink away afterimages.

"It came from the direction of the Hansen place."

Someone whimpered.

The silence stretched past the point where it could be comfortably broken and then went on a little longer. Finally, the shift senior, a man with eighteen years experience and two citations for bravery, cleared his throat. "I didn't see anything," he said.

A mumbled chorus of, "Neither did I," followed the collective sigh of relief.

"But . . ." Brent looked out into the darkness of Christmas Eve, at the starlit beauty of the velvet sky above, at the strings of brightly colored Christmas lights innocently mirroring that beauty below, and remembered other visits to the Hansen house. Or tried to. Most of the memories were fuzzy—and not warm and fuzzy either, but fuzzy like trying to pull in the WB without either a satellite dish or cable, picture skewed, one word in seven actually audible. And the harder he tried, the less he could remember.

Except for the incident with the burning bush. That, he couldn't forget.

Denial became the only logical option.

Happy to have that settled, he turned back to the game. "What moron just chose Charmander against Pikachu?"

The light should have dissipated.

Should have.

Didn't.

Instead, it found itself in an empty, cavernous room in a large, two-story brick building. Caught by the power woven into the snowflake pattern, it rose up through the crepe-paper streamers toward the ceiling, was filtered and purified, and poured back through the center hole.

More now than merely a glorious possibility, it hovered for a moment above center court, then, following the pull of need, it passed through the window, and out into the night.

Lena thoughtfully flicked her lighter on and off. She'd already taken the batteries out of the smoke detector in the hall, but after a certain point that became moot and her father would come charging down into her room demanding to know if she was trying to burn down the house.

There were six candles burning under her angel poster, nine among the angel figurines on her dresser, three votive candles in angel candle holders, and one in a souvenir Backstreet Boys mug on the bedside table.

Close to the limit.

One more, she decided, and started searching through the stubs of melted wax for something worth burning. Nothing. Unfortunately, that *one more* had gone from being an option to being a necessity during the search. Slowly, she turned to her bookshelf.

The angel standing beside her CD player was an old-fashioned figure about a foot high in long flowing robes and wings. He was even carrying a harp. His gold halo circled a pristine white wick.

Heart pounding, Lena approached with the lighter. This had been her very first angel, plucked out from between a broken Easy-Bake oven and a stack of macramé coasters at a neighborhood yard sale. *Oh, please,* she thought as the flame touched the wick. *Let this sacrifice be enough to make it happen!*

There was no need to be more specific about what it was. *It* was always the same thing. She'd wished for it on a thousand stars, her last three birthday cakes, the wishbones of four turkeys, Christmas and Thanksgiving, and with a penny in every body of water she passed. The school custodian had fished enough pennies out of the toilets in the girls' washrooms that he'd treated himself to a package of non-Board of Education toilet paper—the kind that couldn't be fed through a laser printer.

The wick darkened, a bit of wax melted on the top of the golden head, and then the flame roared up high enough to scorch the ceiling, filling Lena's basement bedroom with light.

The light moved slowly away from the candle, into the center of the room.

"It's an angel," Lena cried, eyes watering, eyebrows slightly singed.

And because she believed, it was.

The light took form.

And substance.

And became everything a not quite seventeen-year-old girl wanted in an angel.

In the moment of making, the door flew open and a large, dark-haired man, waving one hand in front of his face to clear the smoke, burst into the room. "Lena! How many times have I told you . . . ?" His eyes widened, and his bellow became a roar. "What the devil are you doing in my daughter's room?"

Lena knew that angels were sexless, but her father didn't know that the beautiful young man with the bicolored hair was an angel, and his belief in what he was seeing was as strong as hers.

The last little bit of substance formed out of a father's fears.

And, all things considered, it wasn't actually that little.

His expression a cross between confusion and panic, the angel ducked the first blow, slipped under an outstretched hand, and ran for the bedroom door. He would have made it except that he hit a bit of unexpected anatomy on the edge of a chair and the sudden pain dropped him to his knees. The second blow connected.

Lying on the floor, hands clasped between his legs, he stared blearily up at the angry man standing above him, and wondered just what exactly was going on.

He wasn't the only one.

"What do you mean, he had no clothes when he got here?"

Diana, heavily shielded and doing her best impersonation of nothing at all, waited in the triangle of deep shadow behind the love seat, determined that this would be the year. From where she crouched, eyes grown used to the dark could see the entire fireplace—top to bottom, side to side—and, beyond it, the lower curve of the Christmas tree. On the mantel, beside the cards, was a glass of milk and three cookies. Homemade chocolate chip cookies, with the chips still soft from the oven. Only the best bait would slow him down.

She'd almost caught him a couple of times, but something had always distracted her at the crucial moment. When she was younger, she'd wanted to see him just for the sake of seeing him. Now, after so many failures, it had become a point of pride.

The instant camera she held had been in her stocking three years ago. She suspected he was taunting her.

A sudden clatter up on the roof brought a pleased smile—earlier in the day, she'd cleared away the snow that might muffle the first sounds of her quarry's arrival.

A bit of soot fell from the chimney onto the hearth.

Show time.

Then something slammed against her shields and exploded into a rainbow of metaphysical light.

Blinded by the brilliant yellows and reds and greens, Diana stood, tipped a lamp over with her shoulder, caught it before it hit the floor, and stumbled out from behind the love seat. She could hear nothing over the thrumming of frustrated possibilities but when one hand brushed for an instant against fur trim, she took three quick pictures with the other.

Then the moment passed, and she could both see and hear.

The milk glass was empty, the cookies were gone. The stockings bulged.

Austin was lying on the hearth, a brand new calico square stuffed with catnip under one front paw. "Aren't you getting a little old for this?" he sniffed.

"Isn't he?" Blinking away the last of the afterimages, Diana dropped onto the sofa with a frustrated groan. "He's never done *that* before." Bending forward, she scooped the developing evidence up off the rug. "At least I . . ."

A familiar black-and-white face stared up at her from all three photographs.

Leaping up beside her, Austin nodded toward the middle picture. "Could I get a copy of this? You've caught my best side."

It was the self-satisfied "Ho Ho Ho" drifting down the chimney that really hurt.

Head pillowed on Dean's chest, Claire half woke to a sudden metaphysical prod. Still wrapped in a warm cocoon of exhaustion and fulfillment, slightly smug from having lived up to the expectations of all parties involved, she shunted it off into the barricade she'd set up years before when Diana had decided privacy was a relative term and then went back to sleep.

Every year, at the moment Christmas Eve became Christmas Day, a miracle was said to occur—animals were given a chance to speak.

In a cream-colored bungalow just outside Sandusky, Ohio, a small gray tabby with a white tip on her tail woke, stretched, and walked up the length of the body under the covers until she could poke a paw into a half-opened mouth.

Midnight. And the miracle.

"Hey. Wake up and feed me."

❀   ❀   ❀

Father Nicholas Harris stood in the open doorway of St. Patrick's, shaking hands and wishing his parishioners would just go home. He loved celebrating the Midnight Mass on Christmas Eve—it was one of the few masses in the year where the verb celebrate actually seemed to apply—but he'd been up early after a late night, and he was so tired he actually thought he'd seen the silhouettes of flying reindeer and a heavily laden sleigh cross the high arc of the window over the door during the second soloist's somewhat shrill but enthusiastic rendition of "The Holly and the Ivy."

"Father Nick, I'd like you to meet my sister Doris and her family. . . ."

He smiled, shook hands with a dozen strangers, declined his fourth invitation to Christmas dinner, and tried not to think of what the open door and the December night were doing to his heating bill. Finally, the end was in sight, only two more hands to shake.

"Father . . ."

One of Frank Giorno's hands enclosed his in an unbreakable grip while the other grabbed a bit of jacket and dragged a young man forward.

". . . this punk who showed up naked in my daughter's bedroom believes he's an angel, so I brought him to you."

He didn't know why he was in a small book-lined room, but since no one was yelling at him, or shaking him, or hitting him, things were looking up. Adjusting bits he wasn't used to having pressure on, he studied the man behind the desk, recognized him as another servant of the light, and hoped that Lena's father had been right during all the shouting and that this was where he was supposed to be.

Trying not to fidget under the searchlight intensity of his unwanted guest's gaze, Father Harris shuffled a few irrelevant papers around and wondered irritably why Frank Giorno hadn't just called the police. He had to be in denial about finding the young man in his daughter's room. Granted the boy deserved points for originality in a bad situation, but what angel ever had bleached blond tips on short dark brown hair? Or managed to slouch in such a convincingly adolescent way? Or looked quite so confused? The boy's eyes were . . .

. . . were . . .

Gold flecks in velvet brown brightened, merged, and became a window into . . .

. . . into . . .

Father Harris rubbed at his own eyes. He was far too tired to do any kind of counseling when he was not only seeing things but smelling grilled cheese sandwiches—his favorite food. Far, far too tired to wait for a stubborn teenager to speak first. "What's your name, son?"

Name? Did he have a name? Everything had been named in the beginning so it was entirely possible. He started from the top, hoping something would sound familiar. There were only 301,655,722 angels after all, he'd have to reach it eventually.

"Son, your name?"

Startled, he grabbed one at random. "Samuel?"

"Are you asking?"

"No." It had become his name. Whether it had been his name before was immaterial—he hoped.

"Samuel what?"

Was there more? He didn't think so. "Just Samuel."

Father Nicholas sighed. At this rate they'd still be sitting in his office on New Year's. "What are you on, Samuel?"

That was easier. He glanced down. "Laminate." When the priest made an unhappy face, he took a closer look. "Laminate flooring, in medium oak, three ninety-nine a square foot, twenty-year warranty."

"No . . ."

"No?"

Something in the young man's expression insisted that the question be answered, as asked. "Well, yes. How did you know?"

He shrugged matter-of-factly. "I have higher knowledge." It was in the original specifications; higher knowledge, mobility, great hair, and he was supposed to have brought a message, although he didn't actually know what the message was. Lena Giorno's shaping had been a little vague about everything except the great hair. That, she'd been quite definite about.

"Higher knowledge about flooring?"

"Yes." He waited for the priest to ask about other topics, but Father Harris only sighed again and ran a hand back through his hair.

"Okay, Samuel. Let's start over. What did you take?"

He straightened, appalled at the question. "Nothing!"

"Nothing?"

"Nothing. I swear to . . . you know." One finger pointed toward the ceiling. "These clothes were given to me." He glanced down at the front of his sweatshirt then back up again. "I don't even know who Regis Philbin is."

"Well, you're probably the only person in North America who doesn't," the priest muttered. Then, raising his voice, he added, "Why were you in Lena Giorno's bedroom?"

"She called me."

"On the phone?"

"On a candle."

"She called you on a candle?"

"Yes."

Knowing Lena as he did, Father Harris took a shot in the dark. "An angel candle?"

"Yes."

"And now you're an angel?"

"Yes."

Feeling as if he'd just won a game of twenty questions, Father Nicholas sank back in his chair. "You're an angel because Lena wanted you to be an angel?"

Samuel nodded, happy that someone finally understood. "Yes. But her father expected me to be something else, so . . ." He spread his hands and looked down the length of his body. ". . . things got confused."

"I'm sure they did."

"I have genitalia, and I don't know what to do with it. Them."

"Genitalia?"

"You know, a . . ."

A hurriedly raised hand cut off the details. "I know."

"It's making everything . . . strange."

Now that was a complaint the priest had heard before. While he'd never heard it put quite that way, a good ninety-nine percent of the teenage counseling he did involved raging hormones. It felt so good to be back on familiar ground, he thought he might as well start off with a few stock platitudes. "If you want to maintain your self-respect, it's important to fight the temptations of the flesh."

"Okay. But what do I do with them during the battle?"

And the familiar ground shifted. More tired than he could ever remember being, Father Harris rubbed at his temples and muttered, "Try tucking left."

Fabric rustled.

Fine. I surrender. I don't know what he's on, but I'm going to let him sleep it off. In the morning, when we're both coherent, I'll find out just who he is and what I should do with him.

Next morning . . .

"Merry Christmas, Dean." Hurrying across the living room to take his free hand in hers, Martha Hansen reached up and kissed him on the cheek.

"Mrs. Hansen . . ."

"Martha. We're glad you could join us."

Holding his other hand, Claire smiled up at him. "Told you."

"You told him what, Claire?"

She switched the smile to her mother. "That he had no reason to be nervous."

"It wasn't your mother . . ." Dean began in a low voice, but Claire cut him off before he could finish, adjusting her grip to drag him across the room.

"Dad? This is Dean."

John Hansen balanced his mug on the arm of the sofa, stood, and shook Dean's hand. "I'm pleased to finally meet you, son. The rest of the family has had only good things to say."

"Not quite true. *I* told you I thought he had a lot of nerve telling me how to behave and that, even though he may be woogie, I couldn't see what Claire saw in him. OW!" Diana glared across the room at her sister.

"Context, dear," her mother admonished. "You'd almost got him sacrificed. And, Claire, you know better than to use the possibilities like that."

"Which is why I threw a hazelnut."

"I apologize; your aim is improving."

"What about me?" Diana demanded, dropping down on the floor by the Christmas tree.

"You should also apologize. Dean's a guest in this house, and you're being deliberately provoking."

All three women turned to look at Dean, whose ears darkened from scarlet to crimson. "That's okay. It's . . . uh . . . I mean . . ."

"Dean?"

He turned toward Claire's father wearing the same desperately hopeful expression as a Buffalo Bills fan during NFL playoffs. "Yes, sir?"

"Would you like some coffee?"

"Yes, sir."

"Come on, the pot's in the kitchen. We'll go get some for everyone." Detaching Claire's hand from Dean's arm, he drew the younger man out of the living room, saying, "I have this sudden urge to build a workshop. You've got no idea how great it is to have a little more testosterone in this house."

"Like some of us had a choice about that," Austin snorted from the top of the recliner as they passed.

Dean had been a little unsure of what to expect when he walked into the Hansens' living room with Claire that morning. After all, everyone in the room would know exactly how they'd spent the night. He didn't regret any of it—although his memory of times five and six had grown a little hazy—and he felt as though things were now back on track, that he was doing exactly what he was supposed to be doing with his life.

But he could see how things might be awkward.

It didn't help that both Claire's parents were Cousins, less powerful than Keepers but still among those who helped keep the metaphysical balance. Dean had learned from experience how painful an unbalanced metaphysical could be.

He was fairly certain Mrs. Hansen had liked him when they'd met back at the guesthouse, but Mr. Hansen was a total unknown. Following the older man into the kitchen, he searched for the right thing to say. Found himself saying, "I really love your daughter, sir."

"John."

"Sorry?"

"If you're going to be a part of Claire's life, and all signs seem to indicate you are, you might as well call me John."

"Yes, sir. John. Signs?"

"You know . . ." He set down the coffeepot and waved his hands around in the universal symbol for spookiness. ". . . signs: bright lights in the sky, heart-shaped frost patterns on the windows, K-Tel's love songs of the '70s mysteriously cued up on the CD player."

"I see."

"Really?"

"No, sir. But I know how I feel and I know how Claire feels, and that's what matters."

Claire looked more like her father than her mother, Dean realized as the older man's mouth curled into a familiar smile and he clapped him on the shoulder. "Good man. Give me a minute to finish up here, and we'll get back to the ladies."

"Women," corrected a bit of empty air over the sink.

John raised a hand and there was a muffled, "Ow!" from the other room. "And don't ever expect any privacy," he sighed.

"No, sir."

Glancing around the kitchen, Dean noted the juvenile artwork framed and hung in the breakfast nook, the souvenir tea towel stamped with the ubiquitous *My daughter closed a hole to Hell and all I got was this lousy tea towel,* the simmering pot of giblets, the mess. . . . His eyes narrowed. The early morning stuffing of the turkey had left bread crumbs and less easily identifiable debris scattered along six feet of counter. It looked as though the turkey had put up a fight. And very nearly won. He picked up the dishcloth without thinking and by the time the tray of coffee was ready, the counter was spotless.

As John handed Dean the tray, he nodded approvingly. "If you ever stop loving Claire, feel free to keep coming around."

"With a little scouring powder, I could get those stains out of the sink."

"Later, son."

Back in the living room, Dean had barely handed the tray in turn to Martha when Claire stuffed a large, lumpy, striped sock into his hands. It took him a moment to realize what it was. "There's a stocking for me?"

"Hey, the big guy doesn't make mistakes." Diana smashed a chocolate orange apart against the side of the fireplace. "Five people in the house, five filled stockings."

"The big guy?"

"Santa. St. Nick. Father Christmas."

"Is real . . ." And then he remembered the sound of Hell arguing with itself. ". . . ly efficient."

Claire patted his arm as he sat. "Nice recovery."

"Thank you."

A couple of hours later, after the stockings were emptied and presents had been unwrapped and exclaimed over and rather too much chocolate had been eaten for the time of day, Claire took a long swallow of lukewarm coffee and sank back against Dean's arm. "This has been the best Christmas ever. It's been . . ." She cocked her head and frowned. ". . . quiet."

Diana looked up, started to protest, paused, and nodded. "Too quiet," she agreed.

Austin dove under the couch.

"Do you feel any kind of a Summons at all?"

"No. You?"

"No. Not since last night. I felt the prod and . . . Of the Summons, you deviant!"

Diana raised both hands. "Hey. Didn't say anything."

"I *saw* your face."

"We'll deal with Diana's face later, Claire," their mother sighed. "Right now, what happened last night?"

Claire chewed her lower lip, trying to remember. "It woke me and I . . . oh, no. I shunted it into the privacy barrier. It must still be there."

Martha Hansen shook her head. "Claire, I realize you were a little preoccupied last night, but that was very irresponsible of you. Release it at once." As Claire reached into the possibilities, she added a worried, "Let's just hope it wasn't urgen . . ."

Every light on the Christmas tree exploded, and as brightly colored shrapnel ricocheted off hastily erected shields, the angel on the top of the tree broke into a loud chorus of "Day Dream Believer."

"That," Austin observed from under the couch, "doesn't sound good."

FIVE

———◦———

"**C**LAIRE!"

It was a voice that required a response regardless of circumstances. A voice that could be heard across a crowded shopping mall, that could blow past headphones, and could cut right through indifference. Had Hannibal used it on his elephants, he'd have not only made it across the Alps and conquered Rome but he'd have done it with clean dishes and folded laundry.

Claire recognized it in spite of the Summons careening around inside her skull like roller derby on fast forward. "Mom?"

"Uncross your eyes, dear. You don't want your face to freeze like that."

After a long moment, Claire figured out just where her eyes were attached to her face, and a moment after that she got them working again as a set. Gradually, the multiple images of her mother merged and nodded approvingly.

Worry lines pleating his forehead, Dean leaned into her line of sight. "Claire, are you okay?"

"I . . . I can't feel my fingers."

"Sorry." He loosened his grip. "What happened?"

Shaking the circulation back into her hand, she sat up. "It was a Summons. *Is* a Summons."

"Do Summonses usually . . . ?" His gesture took in the fine patina of broken glass that covered the carpet three feet out from the Christmas tree creating a perfect reproduction of "The Last Supper" with the Teletubbies replacing four of the Apostles.

"No."

"Thought not."

Tinky Winky appeared to be arguing with St. James.

Gripping Claire's chin between the thumb and forefinger of one hand, Martha turned her daughter's face up into the light. "Your pupils are dilated, and your pulse is racing."

"Mom, I'm fine. The Summons has blown off its stored energy and is settling down to same old same old. Give me a minute or two and I'll have totally recovered."

"Really?"

"Yes."

"Good." Straightening, she folded her arms and frowned. "What were you thinking? How could you have trapped a Summons in a privacy barrier!"

"How could she?" John repeated thoughtfully before his elder daughter could muster a defense. "That's a good question. It shouldn't have been possible, not even for Claire."

Martha turned to face her husband, brows lifting as she reconsidered all the implications. "Do you think the resolution of the situation with Dean has actually added to her power?"

"It's possible. I'd like to run some tests."

"But it could have just been the timing. I doubt that she deliberately tapped into the sexual energies."

"True, and an accidental surge would be harder to reproduce under measurable conditions, but . . ."

"Excuse me?"

Both Cousins turned.

Claire was on her feet, arms folded. "No one is running any tests."

"But . . ."

"No, Dad; I have a Summons to answer. And I only knocked it aside because it felt like Diana."

All heads turned.

Diana pulled a candy cane out of her mouth and shrugged. "I don't know what she's talking about. I had better things to do last night than . . . wait a minute. Santa!"

Her father sighed. "Diana, are you suggesting that Santa was spying on Claire and Dean?"

"No!" And then less emphatically. "Although there is that whole sees you when you're sleeping, sees you when you're awake schtick, which I strongly suspect is not entirely legal."

"Diana."

"And he does know," she added, "if you've been naughty or nice. Or specifically in this case, if Claire's been naughty or nice."

"Diana!"

"Okay. Something hit my shields just as Santa showed up. I figured it for his annual distraction and flipped it . . ."

"To me." Claire nodded. It was all beginning to make sense. "When I felt your touch, I leapt to an understandable conclusion . . ."

"Hey!"

". . . and trapped it in the barrier."

"So!" Diana bounced to her feet. "This is really my Summons."

"Are you feeling it now?"

"What difference does that make? It hit me first."

"Perhaps . . ."

"Perhaps?"

Claire ignored her protest. ". . . but it hit me last and besides, from the intensity of the thing we're practically on top of the site. I can run out, close the hole, and be home before the turkey comes out of the oven."

"And don't you think highly of yourself," Diana snorted. "You think because you can find it, you can close it. You've forgotten what it's like around here."

"I've forgotten more than you know." Claire tossed a superior smile across the room.

Diana tossed it back.

When the smoke cleared, Martha had her right hand clamped on Claire's left shoulder and her left on Diana's right. "Both of you answer it."

"But . . ."

"No buts. While I'm willing to regard your childish behavior as an inevitable result of the amount of sugar ingested this morning, I am not willing to see it continue. You are both far too old for this."

"But . . ."

"What did I say about buts?" She turned them toward the door.

"Claire, try to make it a learning experience for your sister. Diana, try to learn something. Dean, I'm very sorry, but you'll have to drive them. As long as you're here, I suspect no other transportation will make itself available."

Trying to hide a smile, Dean murmured an agreement.

"Austin, are you going or staying?"

A black-and-white head poked out from under the front of the couch and raked a green-gold gaze over the tableau in the doorway. "Let me see, stuffed into the cold cab of an ancient truck with tag teams of young love and sibling rivalry or lying around a warm kitchen on the off chance that someone will take pity on a starving cat and give him a piece of turkey. Gee, tough choice."

"You're not starving," Claire told him, rolling her eyes.

"I'm not stupid either. Have a nice time."

"Diana, stop shoving."

"Oh, yeah, like you care. You're practically on his lap. Moving that stick shift ought to be interesting."

Thankful that he'd taken the time to back in—reverse would have approached contributing to the delinquency of a minor—Dean slid the truck into gear, eased forward, and jerked to a stop at the end of the driveway.

A lime-green hatchback roared past, the driver's gaze turned toward the Hansens' house, whites showing all around the edges of his eyes.

Diana waved jauntily.

"Diana!" Claire reached into the possibilities just in time to keep the small car from going into the ditch as it disappeared around a curve on two wheels. "You know how nervous Mr. Odbeck is, why did you do that?"

"Couldn't resist."

"Try harder. We need to go left, Dean."

"I don't know about nervous," Dean observed as he pulled out, "but he was driving way too fast for the road condition, and he wasn't watching where he was going."

"That's because Diana keeps things interesting around here."

"Interesting how?"

"Strange lights, weird noises, walking trees, geothermal explosions."

"Hey, that geothermal thing only happened once," Diana protested. "And I took care of it almost immediately."

Almost. Dean considered that as he brought the truck up to the speed limit and had a pretty fair idea of why Mr. Odbeck was so nervous. "Is that what you meant when you told Claire she's forgotten what it's like around here?"

"It's not her," Claire told him, "it's the area."

"He asked me."

"Sorry. Turn right at that crossroads up ahead."

"The area?" he prompted, gearing down for the turn and trying unsuccessfully not to think about the warm thigh he couldn't avoid rubbing.

"Is he blushing? Ow!" Diana rubbed her side and shifted until she was up as tight against the passenger side door as she could go. "Mom's right, you're too skinny. That elbow's like a . . . a . . ."

"Hockey stick?"

"The area," Claire said pointedly—Dean realized a little too late that was not a blank he should have helped fill—"is covered by a really thin bit of barrier."

"The fabric of reality is T-shirt material where it should be rubberized canvas. Your mother told me that back in Kingston," he added when the silence insisted he continue. "She told me that's why they're here, her and your father, because stuff seeps."

Diana snickered as she exhaled on the window and began drawing a pattern in the condensation. "Jeez, Claire, and I thought *your* explanations were lame."

"At least I haven't turned the McConnells' fence posts into giant candy canes."

"Oops." She erased the pattern with her sleeve and reached into the possibilities.

Claire squinted into the rearview mirror. "Now they're dancing."

"It's not my fault! It's Christmas. There's so much peace and joy around it's messing everything up!" This time when she reached, she twisted. "There, those are fence posts."

"Definitively," Claire agreed. "You do know you've anchored them in the barysphere?"

"At least they're not dancing."

"Yes, but . . ."

"Why don't you finish telling Dean why closing this site may not be a piece of fruitcake. Not literally fruitcake," she amended, catching sight of Dean's profile. "Although fruitcakes have punched holes through to the dark side in the past."

"You're not helping," Dean pointed out, and turned left following Claire's silent direction. "There's a hole in the T-shirt fabric . . ."

". . . and because the fabric's so thin you can't just pinch the edges together nor will it take anything but the most delicate of patches. It can be tricky, but it's nothing I can't deal with."

Driving left-handed, he caught Claire's fingers and brought them to his lips. "I never doubted you for a moment."

She smiled and rubbed her cheek against the shoulder of his jacket. "And why's that?"

"I've seen you in action."

"Oh, barf." When two pairs of narrowed eyes glanced her way, Diana shrugged. "Austin's not here. Someone had to say it."

"True enough." Claire straightened as Dean murmured an agreement. "Stop there, at the gray brick house."

As Dean brought the truck to a stop, Diana squinted at the mailbox through a sudden swirl of snow. "Giorno."

"You know them?"

"I go to school with a Lena Giorno. She's a year behind me, though. I've never been to her house."

Seat belt unfastened, Claire turned slowly on the seat, feeling the summons pulling at her. "Well, you're about to."

"Mr. Giorno, hi, Merry Christmas. I'm Diana, a friend of Lena's, and this is my sister Claire."

Even standing out of the line of fire, Claire could feel the charm Diana was throwing at the glowering man in the doorway. The air between them practically sparkled, but it didn't seem to be having much effect—the glower never changed, and he remained standing squarely in the doorway as though defending the house against all comers.

"Francis! We can't afford to heat the whole world! Close the door!" Mrs. Giorno's shout carried with it the distinct odor of burned turkey.

"Don't you start!" He turned his head just far enough to bellow his response back over his shoulder. "I'll close it when I'm good and ready to close it! Lena," he said, facing the porch again, "is not going out. Maybe when she's thirty, I'll let her out, but not until. You kids shut up in there!"

The background shrieking changed pitch.

A little worried about all the head swiveling, Diana cranked it up a notch. "We didn't want Lena to come out, Mr. Giorno. We were kind of hoping we could come in and see her."

"I don't . . ."

"Please."

His expression changed so quickly it looked as though his cheeks had melted. "Of course you can come in. Girls like you should not be left standing on the porch unwanted. You're good, nice girls. Good girls. My Lena's a good girl." He sniffed lugubriously and rubbed the palm of one hand over his eyes. "You come in." The now damp hand gestured expansively as he moved out of the way. "You come in, you talk to my girl, and you find out why she should break her father's heart. Come." He squeezed Diana's shoulder as she passed and beckoned to Claire. "Come."

It looked as though a bomb had gone off in the living room and the debris field had spread through the rest of the house. That it was Christmas Day in a house with three children, two teenagers, a cat, and a pair of neurotic gerbils might have been explanation enough another time, but *this time*, neither day nor demographic came close to explaining the level of chaos. The Christmas tree was on its side, half the lights still on, the cat—wearing a smug smile and a half-eaten candy cane stuck to its fur—curled up in the broken branches. Non-functioning toys and run-down batteries were scattered throughout, two AAs had been hammered into the drywall of the hall as though someone at the end of their rope had tried every battery in the economy-sized package and these were the last two and they still didn't work. The gas molecule racing around turned out to be the five-year-old with a stripe shaved down the center of his head.

"Lena's downstairs in her room," her father told them, pulling a handkerchief out of his pocket and blowing his nose on the bit that wasn't covered in melted marshmallow Santa. "Go. Talk to her."

Diana glanced at Claire from the corner of her eye. When Claire nodded, she smiled. "Thank you, Mr. Giorno."

"No, thank *you*."

As they started down the stairs, he turned away, hand over his face and shoulders shaking.

"I didn't mean to make him cry," Diana murmured, as the two Keepers picked a careful path down through the mess.

"You didn't. The energy seeping from the site is warping the possibilities. Can't you feel the fine patina of darkness?"

"Yeah, but I figured it was smoke from the turkey. Or maybe the Christmas tree—it seems to be smoldering in spots." As they stepped down onto the painted concrete floor, she looked expectantly toward her sister. "Well?"

There were two bedrooms and a bathroom to their right. Laundry room, furnace room, and wine-making equipment to their left.

Following the Summons, Claire turned right.

The door to the front bedroom was shut. Claire knocked.

"Go away! I *hate* you!"

"Wow." Diana took half a step back. "She really does hate us."

"What do you expect? She's in there with the site. You try," Claire suggested when her second knock brought no response at all.

"Lena? It's me, Diana. From the decorating committee, remember?" She jiggled the knob. The door was locked. "Let me in."

"No!"

It was one of the most definitive "no's" Diana had ever heard, and she'd heard her fair share. "You sure it's in there?"

Claire nodded.

"Then it'll take more than a cheap lock to keep us out." Diana reached into the possibilities. The door came off in her hand. "Okay." She staggered back under its weight. "I didn't mean to do that."

"You never do," Claire sighed, "but that's not important now. Look."

"Oh, man, I knew she was into angels, but this is just too much."

"Not that. Look down."

The hole had opened just off the corner of Lena's bed; a dark, ugly, metaphysical blemish on the pale pink carpet.

Lena lifted a blotchy face from her pillow and glared out into the basement. "Put that door *back*! I am *not* coming out! I don't care *what* my father says!"

"Look, Lena, you don't have to come out. We're not here to . . ." Realizing a little late that she wasn't going to get into the room while holding the door, Diana leaned it against the opposite wall and stepped over the threshold. "We're here for you." Skirting the hole, she circled around to the far side of the bed and sat down. "We want to help."

"You *can't* help me."

As she turned her head toward Diana, Claire came into the room, knelt by the hole, and used her fingertip to brush a symbol against the nap of the carpet.

"*No one* can help me," Lena continued, rubbing her nose on the back of her hand. "My father took my angel away!"

Wondering how she could tell there was an angel missing given the number remaining in the room, Diana patted her shoulder in a comforting sort of a way. "Well, you've got more . . ."

"No! He was a *real* angel. He came out of the light last night when I lit my candle! And I don't *care* if you believe me."

"I believe you. Did your father happen to hit this angel?" Claire asked in such a matter-of-fact tone that Diana swiveled around on the bed to stare at her.

"Yes. He just *barged* in like he does, all mad, and when he saw him, he like totally lost it and he hit him and took him away, and I am *never* speaking to him again."

"Where did your father take the angel, Lena?"

"To the priest! I so totally *hate* him!"

"The priest or your father?"

"*Both* of them!"

"Diana." Bending, Claire traced another symbol, then hurriedly erased it as a bit of the carpet melted. "I think Lena would feel better if she got some sleep."

"No! I don't *want* to . . ."

Diana adjusted Lena's head on the pillow, then turned back to her sister. "Are you suggesting that Lena actually got visited by a real angel?"

"I'm not suggesting anything. You heard her: a Bystander can't lie to a Keeper."

"But they can lie to themselves. Lena once honestly believed she saw an image of Leonardo DiCaprio in a bowl of butterscotch pudding, throwing the female half of the ninth grade into hysterics for the remainder of lunch."

"Really?"

Diana nodded. "It wasn't pretty."

"Well, this time she isn't lying to anyone, herself or us." Claire sat back on her heels and waved a hand around the room. "There's distinct residue under the darkness. It's obvious once you know to check for it."

"Oh, yeah. Obvious angel residue. That's something you don't hear everyday."

"Diana, this is serious."

"Okay, I'm being serious." Picking up the Backstreet Boys mug, she made a face and put it down again. "Question is, why would an angel appear to Lena? Obsession isn't enough to open the possibilities that wide. You think it was sent with a message?"

"Can't have or it would have vanished once the message was delivered, and she said that her father took it away."

"Maybe it got taken away before the message got delivered."

"No, it would never have allowed that to happen. A message from the light gets delivered, regardless. An angry father would've stood about as much chance facing down a determined angel as he would have facing down a runaway transport with pretty much the same result. Here's a better question: how could the possibilities have opened that wide without me noticing?"

"That's easy. If they opened last night, you were busy." Eyes narrowed, Diana grinned suddenly. "Are you blushing?"

"No." Claire didn't even try to make the denial sound convincing. Given the heat of her cheeks, there didn't seem to be much point. "So why didn't you notice?"

"Beats me. Must've gotten lost in that whole peace-and-joy stuff. You know what it's like around this time of the year."

"True enough."

"And since it was from the upper end of things, it's not really our problem anyway."

"True again." She traced a third symbol, and the noise level upstairs began to fall off. "That's put a temporary cover over the site, but I'm going to need details to actually seal it."

"Like?"

"Like why would a basically decent man take a swing at a messenger of the light."

"Is that what opened the hole?"

"Diana, Mr. Giorno punched an angel; what do you think?"

"Just checking." Leaning forward, Diana brushed a bit of thick, dark hair back off of Lena's face and softly called her name. "Don't wake up," she instructed when the sleeping girl began to stir, "just tell me, without getting angry, why your father hit the angel."

"He was naked."

"Your father?" Given the amount of hair curling up through the opening of Mr. Giorno's collar and right down to his knuckles, that was an image Diana quickly banished.

"Not my father. The angel."

"The angel was naked?"

"Uh-huh." She smiled slightly. "I saw his thing."

"Lena, angels don't have things."

"I know *that*." Even asleep she managed the emphasis. "But he did. I think . . ." Her brow furrowed. "I think my father gave it to him. It was big."

"And your basis of comparison would be?"

"Diana!"

Without turning, she flapped a hand at her sister to shut off further protests. "You can get back to me later on that, Lena. Right now, you drift off again and I'll call you if I need you."

"O . . ." A long sigh. ". . . kay."

After checking to see that she'd gone deep again, Diana stood and spread her arms triumphantly, modifying the gesture somewhat to catch the cherub she'd knocked off a shelf. "Ta dah. Her father burst into her room as Lena's obsession was manifesting a naked angel, jumped to the fatherly conclusion, and slugged the guy."

Claire rolled her eyes and added a little more power as the cover shifted. "Only a teenager would manifest a naked angel."

"Get over it. You manifested a naked Dean all last night."

"That's not the . . ."

"And ignored a Summons—this Summons—while you were doing it. And I'm not saying I wouldn't have done the same thing under similar circumstances. All I'm saying is that you have no cause to be pointing the finger at someone else's hormones."

After a long moment, during which several high-pitched voices could be heard insisting that they hadn't touched the gravy and they didn't know what was floating in it, Claire sighed. "Okay. You have a point. And since he might have had clothing had things not been interrupted and since her father seems to have added the . . . uh . . . thing . . ."

Diana snorted. "You know, Claire, if you're playing with one, you really should be able to name it."

This was more than Claire could take from a sister ten years younger. "Good," she snapped, "because I was thinking of calling it Floyd!" She regretted the words the moment they left her mouth and snapped her teeth closed just a little too late to catch them. From the way Diana's eyes lit up, she knew she'd be paying for that comment for the rest of her natural life. And possibly longer. "Let's just get back to work," she suggested sharply, her tone a preemptive strike. "I'll seal this. You clear the hatred out of your friend."

"Sure."

"Diana . . ."

"Don't worry, I'll be careful."

"That wasn't . . ." When Diana lifted an eyebrow in exact mimicry of Claire's best sardonic expression, Claire had to laugh, in spite of what would be inevitable later. ". . . what I meant, as you very well knew."

"Yeah. But I'll still be careful." She sat back down on the edge of the bed and gently turned Lena's face toward her. "Although the urge to do something about her decorating is extreme."

". . . but did you ever stop to think that perhaps they didn't want quite so many chestnuts in the stuffing?" Claire asked as they picked their way up the icy front path to the truck.

Diana shrugged. "Beats what was in there before I fixed it. And *that,* by the way, is why you should never keep the litter box in the kitchen."

Things were back to normal in the Giorno household. Tree and dinner had been restored, gifts repaired, the cat appeased, and family tensions resolved. The site it had involved considerably more cleanup than a Keeper would normally perform, but—as Diana pointed out just before the cat knocked the tree over again with no help at all from the dark possibilities—it *was* Christmas.

Dean jerked awake when Claire opened the passenger door. "Everything fixed, then?"

"Everything we could fix," she acknowledged as she kicked the snow off her boots and slid over beside him. "Sorry it took so long."

"That's all right. Your thing kept the truck warm."

"Her thing?" Diana snickered, climbing in. "Got a name for it?"

"Ignore her," Claire advised, hoping Dean would assume her ears were red from the cold.

From the look in his eyes, he didn't.

He glanced at Diana, then back at her, but only said, "Where to now?"

"Back to pick up our stuff and then south, we've got another Summons."

"Another Summons?" Martha Hansen set the roasting pan on the stove top and lifted an indignant Austin down off the counter before she turned to face her daughters. "Do you think it concerns the angel?"

"Unlikely. Mr. Giorno took him to Father Harris over at St. Patrick's, so that should be the last we see of him."

"Him?"

Claire shot a look at Diana, saw she had a mouthful of dill pickle, and reluctantly continued. "Apparently, he somehow acquired gender during the manifestation."

"Gender?"

Diana swallowed and snickered. "Means just what you think, Mom."

"Oh, the poor boy! He must be so confused."

"Confused? Surprised maybe," Diana allowed, perching on the corner of the kitchen table and tossing a hot roll from hand to hand. "But it's not like they're that difficult to operate. It's pretty much point and click." She glanced around the suddenly silent kitchen. "You know, metaphorically speaking. Okay," she sighed, "they don't actually click, but you've got to admit they point." Catching her parents exchanging a meaningful look over the mashed potatoes, she tossed the roll to Dean and spread her hands. "What?"

"We'll talk later," Martha said tightly. "Right now," she turned to Claire and gathered her into her arms, "you'd better get going."

Austin's head snapped up from where he was investigating a bit of spilled grease. "Excuse me? I have been waiting five hours for that bird to come out of the oven; that Summons can just wait for twenty more minutes."

"We don't know how long it's been waiting already," Claire reminded him as she crossed the kitchen to hug her father. "Things got a little stacked up, remember?"

"So I should suffer?"

Martha bent and stroked his head. "Don't worry, I'll pack up a box of food while Claire and Dean are getting their things together."

"You know that this is your second Summons this morning," Diana complained, sliding to her feet as Claire stopped in front of her. "You've had two today and I've had none. How unfair is that?"

"You're not on active duty yet."

"But I'm on vacation. And I'm so available."

"And if something opens up that's serious enough to need you, you'll be Summoned. Just like you were when I needed you in Kingston." Reaching out, Claire touched her sister on the cheek. "Everything'll change once school's over in June. I know it's hard when there's so many more important things you feel you should be doing, but you'll get through it. I did."

"Don't patronize me." The answering shove rocked Claire on her feet. "And don't forget your presents. And be careful. And let Dean help. Really help, not just hang around and pick up after you."

"I will."

"I doubt it."

"I'll try."

"Good enough." She stepped back. "Well; go."

About to turn for the door, Dean found himself pulled into a motherly embrace. He hesitated for a moment, then he returned it and was curiously reluctant to let go when Martha pulled away. Although his mother had died when he was a baby, he'd always felt her love in his life. He'd had no memory of ever feeling her arms, though. Until now.

As though she could sense his reluctance, Martha reached up and touched his cheek. "I'm very glad that you and Claire have found each other, Dean McIssac. You're a good man; strong, steady . . ."

"Mom," Diana interrupted, sitting back on the edge of the table and picking up another roll, "Claire's trying to answer a Summons. This isn't the time to write Dean's eulogy."

He shot a questioning glance at the younger Keeper. "Eulogy?"

"You'll be fine." Martha patted his arm.

"I know." He shifted his weight. "I just wondered what eulogy meant."

"Obituary."

"Oh."

She patted his arm again. "You'll be fine."

"Sure."

"As long as he's ready for what he's dealing with," John Hansen reflected, putting down the carving knife and wiping his fingers on a dish towel.

One hand still outstretched and hovering over Dean's sleeve, Martha turned toward her husband. "Won't it be what he's *been* dealing with?"

"That's not a certainty. Thing's have changed between them. Probably for the better, but he'll be in some unusual positions for a Bystander."

Dean's ears were suddenly so hot he was afraid they'd ignited. Unusual positions? How had Claire's father found out about . . . then he realized he'd misunderstood.

"Well, they're not going to run into anything he can't handle," Martha declared. "I can't imagine anything worse than what he's already faced in the Elysian Fields Guest House."

"I can."

"Austin, be quiet." Claire bent, scooped up the cat, and handed him to Dean.

"Hey! Support the back legs!" Hooking his front claws into a flannel collar, Austin heaved himself into a more comfortable position as Dean adjusted his grip. "I'm old. I don't dangle."

"Sorry."

"Dangling! Honestly."

Claire smoothed the ridge of fur along his spine. "Let it go, Austin."

"He was holding a roll. I have crumbs in my tail."

"I'll brush them out as soon as we're on the road." She hooked two fingers in behind the faded blue of Dean's waistband and tugged him toward the door. "Say good-bye, Dean."

"Good-bye, Dean."

At least he made the cat laugh.

It isn't fair. Diana ran the vacuum at the bits of broken glass and felt a sulky satisfaction as Laa Laa and Saint Matthew disappeared. *I should be out changing the world like Claire—not going to stupid school. Stupid, useless waste of time.* A swath of clean carpet appeared, bisecting Jesus and Po. *I'm so tired of Claire getting to do everything first.* Got to get her ears pierced first, got to graduate from high school first, got to travel to a tropical island and narrowly avoid having the entire place follow Atlantis to the bottom first. *No, wait, that was me.* And in the end, the whole thing had been nothing more than a damp misunderstanding.

The head of the vacuum cleaner was too broad to reach the last few pieces of glass. Realizing that she needed an attachment, Diana bounced it impotently against the hearth instead. *My life sucks. Claire gets a Summons. Lena gets an angel. What do I get? A bunch of burst lights.*

And let's not forget Claire also gets Dean. And Floyd. Snickering to herself, she started on Dipsy and St. Peter. *A memorable Christmas Eve for all three of them. Which may not be what I want from life, it's just . . .*

. . . just . . .

Something lingered at the edge of memory, almost but not quite dredged up by her train of thought. Absently running the vacuum over the same bit of carpet, she started working back.

Christmas Eve.

Claire gets Dean.

Burst lights.

Lena gets angel.

She stepped on the switch and shut the vacuum off and could just barely hear Dean's truck starting up over the sudden pounding of her heart.

Her mother hurried into the front hall as she yanked open the door. "If you're going out to the truck, take this with you."

The smell of turkey rising from the box made questions about contents redundant. She snatched it up without breaking stride.

"Diana, your boots!"

"No time! I've got to catch Claire before she leaves." As Claire would say, Keepers didn't keep vital information from other Keepers. Which was not to say that Diana ever actually listened to what Claire said or had any intention of telling her what had actually happened to that *Best of John Denver* CD. Box tucked under one arm, she sprinted forward.

"Yes!" Austin jumped up onto the top of the seat where he had an unimpeded view through the back window. "Here comes the food!"

Claire twisted around until she could see Diana racing down the front path. "How can you tell what she's carrying from here?"

"I'm a cat."

A vein began throbbing on Claire's forehead. "Why do I even ask?"

Wondering that himself, Dean rolled down the window as Diana hit an icy patch and slid to a sudden impact against his door.

"I know where the angel came from," she announced before anyone in the truck could speak. "I was right, Lena's obsessions didn't open the possibilities, and I was also right about you being distracted."

"What are you talking about?"

Diana grinned, passed the box to Dean, and poked the forefinger on her right hand through a circle made by the thumb and forefinger on her left. "You opened the hole and Lena's desire to see an angel was strong enough to define what came through."

"No." Claire shook her head. "Even if we did open the possibilities . . ."

"You did."

She looked down at the cat. "Excuse me?"

"Way open. Way, way open." He scratched his shoulder. "It was pretty impressive actually."

"So much for all those safe sex lectures, eh?"

"Get stuffed. And stop making that disgusting gesture. It wasn't like that."

"Was it like this?" Diana barely had time to change the position of her fingers before Dean reached out and enclosed both her hands in one of his.

"No," he said quietly, ears scarlet. "It wasn't like that either."

Suddenly feeling both embarrassed and mean and not much liking the feeling, Diana pulled free. Teasing Dean was somehow not the same as teasing Claire. *But I'm not apologizing. I mean, if he can't take a joke . . .* "Look, I saw it, too, what Austin saw, but I never connected it with Lena because that kind of thing always dissipates after, giving everyone in the immediate area a happy."

"It should have dissipated," Claire agreed. Her eyes narrowed as she read her sister's body language. "Why didn't it?"

"My bad. Sort of."

"Sort of?"

"Okay, jeez. Totally. I made this decoration for the school's Christmas dance that would gather up all the good feelings and spit them back out intensified to make more good feelings, and I think I made the attraction too strong . . ."

"Quel surprise," Austin muttered.

". . . and it pulled in the light, giving it sort of a proto-form that kept it together until it got to Lena."

"Where it became an angel." Claire sighed. "Well, it could have been worse. He probably returned to the light as soon as his head cleared from that punch."

"You think?"

"All the background information we have suggests angels can come and go through the barrier as they please. If you were him and you'd had the welcome he'd had, wouldn't you go back where you came from? Now, as nice as it is to have those questions answered," she continued when Diana nodded, "the hole created by reaction to the angel's appearance has been sealed, and I've got other work to do."

"But . . ."

"Merry Christmas, and I'll try to stay in touch."

"We really made an angel, then?" Dean asked as he turned out onto the road.

"In a manner of speaking, yes."

"Seems a little . . ."

"Light on the sausage stuffing." Austin lifted his head out of the box, his eye gleaming indignantly. "there's barely enough here for two people, let alone three."

"First of all, you're not a people, you're a cat." Sliding one hand under his chest, Claire lifted him onto her lap. "Second, if you've stuck your litter-poo paw in the sweet potatoes, I *will* hurt you. Third . . ." She stroked a finger down the back of Dean's thigh. ". . . I think we could've made an angel without Diana's or Lena's help."

It took him a moment, then he grinned, caught up her hand, and brought it to his lips. "Really?"

"Really."

"Are you two planning on continuing this sort of behavior?" Austin demanded from Claire's lap. "Because I'm old, you know, and I don't think my insulin levels are up to it."

Claire pulled her hand away from Dean's mouth and smoothed down a lifted line of fur. "Someone's jealous."

"Of him?" The cat snorted and dropped his head down on his paws. "Oh, please."

"You sure?"

"Cats don't get jealous."

"Really?"

"They get even."

"Austin."

"I'm kidding."

Diana stood in the driveway until Dean's truck disappeared from view, and then walked back to the house kicking at clumps of snow.

. . . as nice as it is to have those questions answered . . .

Nice.

There were times when she just wanted to take Claire by the ears and shake loose that more-Keeper-than-thou attitude of hers.

She's always thought the sun shines out of her butt . . .

Having carefully negotiated a tight curve, Dean glanced over at Claire and smiled. He loved the way the light shone up and through the chestnut highlights in her hair, how it made her eyes seem dark and mysterious, how it. . . . *Hang on.* "Where's that light coming from?"

Claire sighed. "Just drive."

SIX

———•—◦—◈—◦—•———

A LITTLE OVER AN HOUR after leaving the Hansen house, Dean turned off York Street and stopped the truck in the parking lot of the London bus terminal. "Here, then?"

"Here."

"Inside?"

"No, over there." She pointed to a bus parked at the back of the lot, barely visible between the blowing snow and the fading daylight.

Dean put the truck in gear and moved slowly forward. Given the holiday, the terminal hadn't seen a lot of traffic, so the parking lot, unplowed since morning, lay under a mostly unbroken blanket of snow. About three meters from the bus, he felt the steering wheel jerk in his hand and then begin to spin with that horrible, loose feeling that could only mean all four tires had no traction at all. He fought the skid, thought he had it, lost it again, and shouted, "Brace for impact!" just as the truck stopped with its passenger door a mere two inches from the front fender of the bus.

"Brace for impact?" Austin asked, removing his claws from Claire's jeans. "Do you even know *how* to swear?"

Heart pounding, Dean shut off the engine. "What good would swearing do?"

"Since you have to ask, probably none at . . . hey! What did I say earlier about dangling?" he demanded as Claire lifted him off her lap.

"Sorry." Brow furrowed, she rolled down her window and peered at the bus fender.

"Excuse me! Old cat in a draft!"

"Austin, be quiet. Dean, I'm going to have to get out your side."
She rolled up the window and reached under the cat to undo her seat
belt. "We're so close to the hole, I'm not sure you can safely move the
truck. We've got a cascade going on here," she added, sliding across,
under the steering wheel, and out into the parking lot. As Dean struggled to hold the door against the wind, she leaned back into the cab.
"Are you coming?"

"Is it summer yet?"

An icy wind blew pellets of snow down under her collar. "Not exactly."

Austin settled down, folding his front paws under his ruff. "Then
I'm staying inside."

"All right. I'll reset the possibilities to keep you warm."

"Thank you. Although if you don't close that door," he added
pointedly, "it won't make much difference."

Claire stepped back and nodded to Dean who, in spite of the
wind, managed to close the door without slamming it. "You know anyone else would've just let it go."

"I'm not anyone else."

He had an arm on either side of her, gloved hands braced against
the truck, and his smile was, if not suggestive, open to suggestion.
Since they'd blocked the hole, effectively rendering it harmless, Claire
figured it couldn't hurt to take a short break. Besides, Austin was
locked away behind glass and steel, making it too good an opportunity
to miss.

When they pulled apart a moment later, an eight-meter circle of
parking lot had been cleared of snow. The asphalt directly underfoot
steamed gently.

"Is that going to happen every time?" Dean asked a little shakily,
following Claire around to the bus.

"I honestly don't know." Her lips felt bruised and all her clothing
felt way too tight. "How about we stop for the night once I get this
hole closed?"

Dean glanced at his watch. "It's ten after four."

"It's getting dark."

He looked up at the sky and down at Claire. "I saw a hotel just up
the road."

"So did I." Dropping to her knees by the bus fender, she pulled off her glove and, holding a finger an inch or so off the chrome, traced a triple gouge in the metal

"That's it, then?" Dean asked behind her. "It's some small."

"A cascade doesn't have to be very big. The driver probably clipped a car on the way out of the parking lot—because clipping a moving car would have caused an actual accident—didn't stop, opened a hole, and flashed nasty possibilities all hither and yon on the bus route, probably causing a number of minor fender benders all day, which kept the hole from closing. Hence, cascade. It's kind of like if every one of those minor fender benders had picked off the scab."

Dean winced. "I wasn't after asking. But how do you know the driver didn't stop?"

"Driver stops, no hole." Reaching into the possibilities, she pressed her thumb hard against one end of the first gouge. The metal rippled. The gouge disappeared. Twice more and the hole was closed. "I expect I'll be closing a few holes this thing inspired," she said as Dean helped her straighten up. "Sign says London-Toronto but since we're still in London, it was clearly London-Toronto and back." Pulling her glove on, she noticed a new glow of adoration in his expression. "What?"

"You've never mentioned you do bodywork."

"I can rustproof, too."

"You can?"

She grinned up at him. "No, sorry. I just wanted to see your eyes light . . . Oh!"

"New Summons?"

"No . . ."

"No?"

"No. It's something else. Something close."

"So much for quitting early." He was disappointed, of course, but the cold had pretty much taken care of the actual incentive.

"No." Claire started across the parking lot. "*Really* close."

When she reached the sidewalk, she paused and turned right. "Whatever it is, it's inside the bus terminal."

The door was locked. The sign said, "TERMINAL CLOSES 4PM CHRISTMAS DAY."

"I guess that's it until tomorrow, then." Dean polished a few fingerprints off the glass and turned away. "Look, there's the hotel." A little confused, he watched Claire pull off her glove—not the reaction he'd been expecting. "What?"

"I guess this has never come up . . ." Reaching into the possibilities, she opened the door.

"Claire! That's breaking and entering!"

"I didn't break, so it's just entering." She grabbed two handfuls of his coat and shoved him inside. "Move. Life is so much easier if we don't have to explain to Bystanders."

"But this is illegal!" he protested as the door closed behind them. When she stepped forward without answering, he grabbed her arm. "The mat!"

She jerked back and looked down. "What?"

"Wipe your feet."

Claire considered a couple of possible responses. Then she wiped her feet.

Half a dozen paces inside the terminal, she dropped down to one knee and pressed the spread fingers of her right hand against the tiles. "This isn't good."

"I'd say it's some disgusting," Dean growled, kneeling beside her. "How can anyone leave their floors in this condition."

"Dean . . ."

"Sorry. I expect you found something else that isn't good?"

Claire lifted her hand. The pads of her fingers sparkled. "Angel residue."

"Merry Christmas. You've reached the Hansen residence. No one feels like taking your call, so at the beep . . ."

"Not now, Diana, we've got a problem. I'm at a pay phone in the London bus terminal, and you'll never guess what I've found."

Phone jammed between ear and shoulder, Diana slid a platter of leftover turkey into the fridge. "Buses?"

"Angel residue."

"That would've been my next guess."

"Right. It seems like Lena's visitor hasn't gone home."

"Unless he's taking the bus." She reached into the possibilities, opened a pocket on the second shelf, and shoved in the cranberry sauce, half a bowl of sweet potatoes, and an old margarine container now full of gravy. "You know, kind of a 'this bus is bound for glory' thing. Say, how come you're not using the cell phone you got for Christmas? No long distance charges and the battery's good until the end of days. When you're standing at the start of the Apocalypse, you'll still have enough juice to call 911."

"And tell them what?"

"I dunno. Run?"

"I'm not using the cell phone because I left it in the truck. And I need you to go talk to Father Harris at St. Pat's. He's the last person who we know saw the angel. Maybe he knows where it's—he's—headed. I've got another Summons on the way out of town, and since I just closed a cascade, I expect to have a whole string of them all the way to Toronto, so I'll call you once we're settled for the night."

"No need. I'll e-mail anything I find out." As her sister started to protect, Diana rolled her eyes. "Claire, let's make an effort to join the twentieth century before we're too far into the twenty-first, okay? Later."

Hanging up and heading for her coat and boots, she wondered what it was that made Keepers—herself excluded, of course—so resistant to technology. "Only took them a hundred years to get the hang of the telephone," she muttered, digging for mittens. "And Austin's probably more comfortable with it than Claire is. . . ."

"Austin, what are you doing with that phone?"

"Nothing."

"What do you mean, nothing?" Claire demanded as she slid back into the truck.

"I mean that there isn't a Chinese food place in the city that'll deliver to a parking lot."

After a last-minute discussion concerning the dishes and how they weren't being done, Diana walked out to the road, flagged down a conveniently passing neighbor, and got a ride into Lucan. Fifteen minutes later, still vehemently apologizing for the results of the sudden stop, she got out at St. Patrick's and hurried up the shoveled walk to the priest's house, staying as far from the yellow brick church as possible. Strange things happened when Keepers went into churches and, in an age when Broadway show tunes coming from the mouths of stained-glass apostles weren't considered so much miraculous as irritating, Diana felt it was safest not to tempt fate—again.

Strangely, Protestant Churches were safer, although locals still talked about the Friendship United bake sale when four-and-twenty blackbirds were found baked into three different pies. Claire, who'd been fifteen and already an adult to Diana's five-year-old eyes, had been both horrified and embarrassed, but Diana remembered their mother as being rather philosophical about the whole thing. There were, after all, any number of nursery rhymes that would've been worse. *Although not for the blackbirds*, she reflected, carefully stepping over a large crack in the sidewalk.

There were no synagogues or mosques in the immediate area and by the time she started being Summoned away, she was old enough to understand why she had to keep her distance. The incident at that Shinto shrine had been an unfortunate accident.

Okay, two unfortunate accidents, she amended climbing the steps to the front door. *Although I still say if you don't actually want your prayers answered, you shouldn't* . . . "Merry Christmas, Mrs. Verner. Is Father Harris in?"

The priest's housekeeper frowned, as though recognition would be assisted by the knitting of her prominent brows. "Is it important? His Christmas dinner is almost ready."

"We ate earlier."

"He didn't."

"I only need a few minutes."

"I don't think . . ."

A tweak of the possibilities.

". . . that vill be a problem." The heels of her sensible shoes clicked together. "Come in. Vait in his office, I vill go get him. You haf an emergency. You need his help. How can he sit and do nothing vhen he is needed? I vill pull him from his chair if I must. Pull him from his chair and drag him back here to you." She didn't quite salute.

A little too much tweak, Diana reflected as the housekeeper turned on one heel and marched away. She made a slight adjustment before Mrs. Verner decided to invade Poland.

The small, dark-paneled, book-lined office came with a claustro-phobic feeling that was equally the fault of its size, the faux gothic decorating, and the number of faded leather-bound books. Diana couldn't decide if the painting over the desk—a three-legged figure standing on multicolored waves against an almost painfully green background—made the room seem smaller or let in the only light. Or both.

"It's Saint Patrick banishing the snakes from Ireland," announced a quiet voice behind her. "It was painted by one of my parishioners."

"Probably one who donated beacoup de cash to the rebuilding fund," Diana observed as she turned.

Father Harris took an involuntary step back, the sudden memory of St. Jerome belting out "Everything's Coming up Roses" propelling his feet. He didn't know why he was thinking about stained-glass and show tunes, but for a great many reasons he couldn't maintain a grip on, he was quite certain he needed a drink.

Diana smiled at him reassuringly. "Lena Giorno tells me her father brought an angel to you last night."

"A young man who *thought* he was an angel," the priest corrected. He was fairly certain the girl's smile was supposed to be reassuring, but it was making him a little nervous.

"*You* don't think he's an angel?"

"I very much doubt an angel would appear in such a way in the bedroom of a teenager girl."

"You mean naked?"

"That's hardly a suitable topic for you and me to discuss." Taking a deep breath, he folded his arms and gave her the best "stern author-ity figure" glare he could manage under the circumstances. "And now, young lady, if you don't mind my asking, what is your name and what is your connection to young Samuel?"

Diana's smile broadened. "Samuel," she repeated under her breath. "Should've known better than to give out his name." Refocus-ing on Father Harris—whose expression had slipped closer to "con-fused elder trying to make sense of the young and failing miserably"—she asked, "Did he stay here last night?"

"Yes, but he was gone this morning. Now, see here young lady . . ."

"May I *please* see where he slept?"

About to demand that she answer his earlier question concerning who she was and what she wanted, Father Harris found himself stepping back into the foyer and leading the way up the stairs.

The alleged angel had slept in a small room at the end of the hall. It held a single bed, a bedside table, a dresser, and what was probably another picture of Saint Patrick. This one was a poster, stuck to the wall with those little balls of blue sticky stuff that invariably soaked oil through the paper. The elderly saint had only two legs in this picture, was wearing church vestments, and was, once again, banishing snakes.

"I don't know what you thought you'd find." The priest folded his arms, determined to make a stand. This was his house and . . .

A phone rang.

Downstairs.

It continued to ring. And ring.

"*Please*, don't mind me," Diana told him. "I'll just stay up here a moment longer."

He was halfway back to his office before he wondered why Mrs. Verner hadn't answered the phone.

Diana reached into the possibilities as she stepped up to the poster.

The saint blinked twice and focused on her face. "And what'll it be, then, Keeper?"

"I need some information about the guy who stayed here last night."

The lines across the saint's forehead deepened. "Oh, and you haven't noticed that I'm up to my ankles in snakes here; what is it that makes you think I was paying any attention?"

"Well, I . . ."

"You wouldn't be having a beer on you, would you?" A short but powerful kick knocked a snake right out of the picture.

"Why would a saint want a beer?"

"I'm an Irish saint, and you can pardon me for being a stereotype, but I was originally painted five hundred years ago and I'm a wee bit dry. Now, what was your question again?"

"Do you know where the guy who stayed here last night went when he left this morning?"

"The angel?"

"Yes."

"I have no idea. But I'm telling you, Keeper, there was something funny about that boy." He shook his head in disgust, halo wobbling a bit with the motion. "Who ever heard of a confused angel, eh? In my day, angels had no emotions, they did what they were sent down to do and then they went home. Is this like to be some New Age thing?"

"I don't know."

Another snake ventured too close and was punted off to the left. "There's going to be trouble, you mark my words. An angel without a purpose is like a . . . a . . ."

"A religion with no connection to the real world?"

"Who asked you?"

"Did he use the bed?"

"Aye, he laid himself down although I can't say I know why since he doesn't have to sleep. Good old-fashioned angels, they didn't lay down. Have you heard he's got himself a . . ." His hand pumped the air by his crotch. . . .

. . . which wasn't a gesture Diana thought she'd ever see a saint make. "I heard."

"And what's the idea behind that, I ask you? You listen to me, Keeper; angels today, they have no . . ."

Figuring she couldn't really be rude to a metaphysical construct, Diana cut him off in mid rant. It looked like he was winding up for another kick, and she was starting to feel a little sorry for the snakes.

The hand of Mrs. Verner was apparent in the precision of the bed making—sheets and blankets tucked so tightly in they disdained a mere bouncing of quarters and were ready instead to host a touring company of *Riverdance*. Not expecting much, Diana checked for anything that might have been left behind—it was, after all, a day when miracles had already happened. Skimming the surface with her palm, she drew a two-toned hair from under the edge of the pillow but nothing else.

"Have you finished?"

The hair went into her pocket as she turned toward the priest. "Yes. Thank you. He didn't tell you where he was heading?"

"He didn't tell me he was going to leave," Father Harris answered shortly. At the bottom of the stairs he turned to face her. "I want you to know that if you kids are mixed up in drugs . . ."

"Drugs?"

"Yes, drugs. Nothing that boy said last night made any sense."

"Unless everything he said was the truth." Widening her eyes and cocking her head to one side, Diana gazed up at the priest. "Don't you believe in angels, Father Harris?"

"Angels?"

"Yes."

"His Holiness the Pope has argued for the existence of angelic spirits, and therefore the official position of the Catholic Church is that they are insubstantial."

"Okay. And you personally?"

"I, personally, remain uncertain. However," he continued, cutting off her incipient protest with an upraised finger, "I am sure that young Samuel was, and is, no angel."

"Why?"

"He had . . ." The priest's gesture was considerably less explicit than the saint's.

"An upset stomach? A basketball?"

"GENITALIA!"

Which pretty much ended the conversation.

Standing on the porch, Diana watched her breath plume out and came to a decision.

In the church, St. Margaret began singing "Climb Every Mountain."

"Uh, Claire, your head's kind of . . ."

"Pointy and striped? Don't worry, it's just hat head." She tossed the toque behind the seat and ran her fingers up through her hair, dislodging most of the red and white. "When Diana was ten, she decided to make everyone's Christmas present and this was mine. I know it looks dorky, but it's really warm and it's getting cold out there."

"Getting cold?" Austin pressed against Dean's thigh and glared up at her. "Getting? I'm warning you, don't touch me again with any part of your body or any one of your garments."

"Look, I'm very sorry that the edge of my jacket brushed against your ear."

"The frozen edge of your jacket." He flicked the ear in question. "And I accept your apology only because I seem to be getting some feeling back."

"Did you get the hole closed okay?" Dean asked as Claire fastened her seat belt. He told himself he watched only to be sure she was secured before he began driving, that it had nothing to do with the way the belt pressed the fabric down between her breasts. Unfortunately, he was a terrible liar and he didn't believe himself for a moment.

"No problems. It looked like one of those big off-road vehicles actually went off the road, and the driver had no idea of how to use the four-wheel drive because he'd only bought the car to prove his was bigger."

"And you could tell *that* from the hole?"

She flashed him a grin. "I extrapolated a little, there really wasn't much there. I probably only got Summoned because it was on the shoulder of a major highway and could have caused accidents. And, of course, the more accidents it caused, the bigger it'd get. You know."

He didn't, but he was beginning to get the idea. Shifting into first, he pulled carefully back out onto the 401. "Can I ask you something?"

"Seven. But none of them meant anything to her."

"Austin!"

"And Jacques was dead, so maybe he shouldn't . . ."

Claire grabbed a piece of turkey out of the box behind the seat and stuffed it in the cat's mouth.

"That wasn't actually the question," Dean admitted.

"And it certainly wasn't the answer." It was almost dark, and the dashboard lights left Dean's face in shadow. She wished she knew what he was thinking. She could know what he was thinking, if she asked in the right way. She only had to say, "*Please* tell me what you're thinking, Dean."

It slipped out before she could stop it.

"The headlights look a little dim; I'd better clean them next time we stop."

That was it?

"And, Claire? Don't do that."

"That? Oh. Right. Sorry. It's just . . ."

"You're used to having your own way with Bystanders."

"Sort of."

"Sort of?"

"Okay, yes." She slumped down in the seat. "So what was your question?"

"How could Lena create an angel? I thought angels just were."

"The light just is, but where angels are concerned, you can't separate the observer from the observed. Every angel ever reported has been shaped by the person doing the reporting—by what they believe, by what they need. If you need an angel to be grand and glorious, it is. Or warm and comforting. Or any other combination of adjectives. Wise and wonderful. Bright and beautiful. Great and small . . ."

"At the same time?"

"Probably not. Thing is, they usually deliver the message they were sent with and disappear."

"Message?"

"Oh, you know: Be nice to each other. Fear not, there is a supreme good and it hasn't forgotten you. Don't cross that bridge. Stop the train."

"Feed the cat." He looked up to see both Claire and Dean staring down at him. "Hey, it could happen."

"Anyway," Claire continued as Dean turned his attention back to the road, "message delivered, the angel goes home. This one seems to be hanging around."

"Why?"

"No message," Austin told them, climbing onto Claire's lap. "You two opened wide the possibilities, Diana made possible probable, and her little friend defined it—but it has no actual reason for being here. It's going to be looking for a reason." He pushed Claire's thigh muscles into a more comfortable shape. "But let's look at the bright side. At least she isn't Jewish, and it isn't Hanukkah. Old Testament angels were usually armed with flaming swords."

"I'd rather have flaming swords," Claire sighed. "It'd be easier to find. Given the stuff Lena had in her bedroom, we're probably talking a New Age kind of angel; human appearing, frighteningly powerful, smug and sweetly sanctimonious busybody."

"Kind of like a jed . . ."

Her palm covered the cat's mouth. "We don't have enough problems?" she demanded. "You want to add trademark infringement?"

"What I don't understand," Dean interjected before someone lost a finger, "is how an angel can be a bad thing."

"This kind of angel isn't, not in and of itself—ignoring for the moment the way they always think they know what's best for perfect strangers." She paused, and when it became apparent Austin was not going to add a comment, went on. "But I can't help thinking that much good walking around in one solid clump is well, bad."

"Good is bad?"

"Metaphorically speaking."

"And a remarkably inept metaphor it is, too," Austin sighed.

They drove in silence for a few minutes, then Dean said, "So what do we do?"

"We hope Father Harris tells Diana where the angel went and that he went with a purpose so that, purpose fulfilled, he'll go home. If not, we hope someone convinces him to go home before . . ."

"Before what?"

"I don't know." She stroked Austin's back and stared out at a set of headlights approaching on the other side of the median. "But I can't shake the feeling that something's about to go very, very wrong."

The darkness that had been seeping through the tiny hole in the woods behind J. Henry and Sons Auto Repair since just before midnight Christmas Eve struggled to keep itself together. While adding a constant stream of low-grade evil to the world might have been an admirable end result in times past, this time, it had a plan. It didn't know patience, patience being a virtue, but it did know that rushing things now would only bring disaster—which it wasn't actually against as long as it was the stimulant rather than the recipient. Had anyone suggested it was being subtle, it would have been appalled. Sneaky, however, it would cop to.

It had been maintaining this isolated little hole for some time, carefully, without changing anything about it, unable to use it but keeping it open when it might have sealed on its own—just in case. The hole was too small to Summon a Keeper, and because it was in the woods behind a closed garage outside a small town no one ever came to on a road that didn't actually go anywhere, it was unlikely that either Keeper or Cousin would ever stumble over it by accident.

When the other end of the possibilities had opened and shifted the balance so dramatically, it saw its chance. It allowed the change in pressure to squirt it up through the hole and the concentration of the light to help keep it together.

Every action has an equal and opposite reaction.

Physics as metaphysics.

It grew steadily, secure in the knowledge that the nearest Keeper was too far away to stop it.

But, because inactivity would make them suspicious, it indulged itself with a little misdirection.

In the parts of the world that had just celebrated Christmas, holes created by family expectations widened and the first strike capabilities of parents against unmarried adult children became apparent.

In other parts of the world, low levels of annoyance at the attention paid to exuberant consumerism cranked up a notch, and several places burned Santa in effigy. The people of Effigy, a small village in the interior of Turkey, took the day off.

Somewhere else, a man picked up a pen, stared at it blankly for a moment and, shuddering slightly, signed his name, renewing "Barney" for another season. But that *might* have been a completely unrelated incident.

SEVEN

ANXIOUS TO GET AT WHATEVER IT WAS he was supposed to be doing, Samuel had slipped out before dawn.

Dawn. The first light of day. The rising of the sun. The sun. A relatively stable ball of burning hydrogen approximately 150 million kilometers away. Higher knowledge hadn't mentioned anything about how early it happened.

He yawned and scratched, then walked to the road, stepped over a snowbank, and stood looking around at the world—or as much of it as he could see from the sidewalk in front of St. Patrick's. It wasn't what he'd expected. It was quieter for one thing, with no evidence of the constant battle between good and evil supposedly going on in every heart. He'd expected turmoil, people crying out for any help he could give. He hadn't expected his nose hair to freeze.

Actually, until he'd traced the tight, icy feeling to its source, he hadn't known he *had* nose hair.

Wondering why anyone would voluntarily live in such temperatures, he started walking down the road.

Lena Giorno had called him because she wanted to see an angel. She'd seen him. Over. Done. Ta dah. Frank Giorno had wanted him out of his daughter's bedroom and in clothing. Both taken care of—with some unnecessary violence in Samuel's opinion, but no one had asked him. Father Harris, a fellow servant of the light, didn't need him, and, although he hadn't said it out loud, had practically been screaming at him to go away.

He hadn't gone far, but he'd gone.

So what now? He had to be here for a reason.

His sense of self had grown overnight, but he was still having a little trouble with the vague components of Lena's initial parameters. The whole higher knowledge thing seemed a bit spotty and, so far, not very useful. He understood mobility; he only had to want to go somewhere to be there except that he didn't know where he wanted to go. His hair *was* great. No argument.

And apparently, he was supposed to have come with a message. If he had, he'd misplaced it. Oh sure, he could come up with a few off the top of his head—*Love thy Neighbor, Cherish the Children, Reduce, Reuse, Recycle, Check Your Tire Pressure*—but they were so commonplace—not to mention common sense—they seemed almost trite.

I don't know what I'm doing here.

I don't know how to rejoin the light.

And while I know where I am, I don't know where I'm supposed to go.

If higher knowledge hadn't informed him that he was wiser and more evolved, he'd have to say the whole situation sucked. Big time.

Okay. I deliver messages. I'm some kind of nonunion, spiritual postal guy. Samuel looked around at a village of empty streets and dark houses. *So everything'll be cool as soon as I can tell someone something.*

Although why anyone would want things cooler, he had no idea, and he didn't even want to guess how a situation could draw something in by creating a partial vacuum.

Unfortunately, the only people currently awake behind the barricades of drawn curtains were young children and the parents of young children. The kids were—well, he supposed hysterical was as accurate a description as any. As for their parents, they didn't so much need him to pass on a spiritual message as they needed another three hours of sleep and the batteries that hadn't been included.

He was giving some serious thought to returning to Lena's room and having her fill in a few details when he heard a vehicle approaching. Turning, he watched the 5.2 liter, 230-horsepower, V-8 SUV come closer with no clear idea of why he suddenly found engine statistics so fascinating. He was wondering how it handled on curves when the surrounding cloud of desperation captured his attention. Someone in that vehicle was about to crack.

Was he supposed to fix cracks?

So now I'm doing spiritual plastering? Which wasn't as funny as he'd hoped it would be. He took a deep breath and dried suddenly damp palms against his thighs, wondering why he seemed to be leaking. *Still, a guy's got to start somewhere . . .*

And so far, this seemed to be the only game in town.

The vehicle was exactly twenty feet, seven and three-eighths inches away when he stepped in front of it. When it stopped, it was exactly three-eighths of an inch away. An exhausted looking man and an equally exhausted looking woman were sitting openmouthed in the front seats. Brian and Linda Pearson. He flashed them both an enthusiastic thumbs up figuring that, hey, it couldn't hurt.

"Are you out of your mind?" Face flushed, Brian leaned out the driver's window. "I could have killed you!"

He seemed a bit upset. Samuel smiled reassuringly. Never let the mortals sense insecurity. He wasn't sure if that was higher knowledge, common sense, or some kind of basic survival instinct but he figured he'd go with it regardless. "I have a message for you."

"Get the fuck out of my way!"

"No."

"No?" His volume rose impressively.

"No. I need to tell you that no matter how it seems, your kids aren't deliberately trying to drive you crazy. You just need more patience." Smile slipping slightly, he added, "And a breath mint."

"You're insane!"

"Am not!" He felt his jaw jut out and his weight shift forward onto the balls of his feet. Where was that coming from? Lowering his voice, he fought the urge to challenge Brian Pearson to a fight, saying only a little belligerently, "I'm an angel."

Exhaustion warring with denial, Brian's bloodshot eyes widened as they were met and held. "Oh my G . . ."

Samuel raised a hand and cut him off, glancing around to be sure no one had overheard. "Don't even suggest that. Didn't you hear what happened to the last guy who tried to move up?" Whistling a descending scale, he pantomimed a fall from grace. The sound of an explosion at the end was purely extemporary but impossible to resist.

Dragging Brian back into the van, her gaze never leaving Samuel's face, Linda whispered something in her husband's ear.

He shook his head and glanced back over his shoulder. "We can't."

She whispered something else.

Unfortunately, higher knowledge didn't seem to extend to eavesdropping.

Leaning back out the window, Brian tried a wobbly smile. "Would you like a ride into London?"

Would he? London, England, seemed a bit far and he was fairly certain the Atlantic Ocean was in the way, so they probably meant London, Ontario, about an hour's drive down highway four.

"Sure."

"Good. Get in."

By the time he'd walked around to the passenger side, Linda had opened the back door. Her expression a curious mix of hope and guilt, she wished him a Merry Christmas and indicated he should climb inside. The second set of seats had been removed and an identical pair of seven-year-old twins, Celeste and Selinka, had been belted into opposite corners of the three seats running across the back of the SUV. If there'd been any more room between them and their parents, they'd have been outside the vehicle completely.

"Hey," he said as he folded himself into the middle seat and fumbled for the seat belt. "My name's Samuel, and I'm an angel. I'm here . . ."

"'Cause Mommy said to Daddy you can distract us," announced Selinka.

"So Daddy can drive more safely," added Celeste.

"Mommy doesn't really believe you're an angel. She's desperate."

"She said she's ready to 'cept help from the devil himself."

"Really?"

Up front, Linda's shoulders stiffened, lending credence to the comment.

Samuel found his own shoulders stiffening in response. "You shouldn't, you know, repeat that."

"Why?" Celeste demanded, eyes narrowing.

"Because if an angel can be here, then so can a devil."

"You're stupid," sniffed Selinka. "And your hair looks dumb. Why do you smell like cotton candy?"

"He smells like strawberry ice cream."

"Does not!"

"Does too!"

"Why can't I smell like both?"

Celeste leaned around him. "You're right," she told her sister. "He is stupid."

Then they started singing.

"There was a farmer had a dog . . ."

At first it was cute.

"Let's all sing," Samuel suggested, leaning forward as far as the seat belt allowed. Singing was a good thing; he had a vague idea that angels did a lot of it. "The family that sings together . . . uh . . ." Wings together? Pings together? Then he realized that no once could hear him over the high-pitched little voices filling the enclosed vehicle with sound.

"B I N G O, B I N G O, B I N G O . . ."

It went on and on and on, just below the threshold of pain.

"Make it stop," moaned their father, beating his forehead against the steering wheel as the SUV began to pick up speed.

Short of gagging them, Samuel couldn't figure out how to stop them. Nothing he said from well reasoned argument to childish pleas made any impression. After the fourth verse, gagging them was beginning to seem like a valid option. Finally, ears ringing in the sudden silence, he forced the corners of his mouth up into a smile and swept it over both girls. "Hey, I've got an idea. Why don't we do something that doesn't make any noise?"

They exchanged a suspicious glance.

"Like what?" asked Selinka.

"It had better be fun," added Celeste.

He opened his mouth, then closed it again. He could number the hairs on both girls' heads (three billion two hundred and twelve and three billion two hundred and fourteen) but when it came down to it, that wasn't even remotely useful. Unless . . . "I don't suppose you'd want to count each other's hair?"

Which was about when he discovered that a nonviolent, geared to age level, designed to promote social development electronic game could raise one heck of a bump when thrown at close range.

"I'm feeling guilty about this," Brian Pearson murmured to his wife. "Are you sure he's going to be all right?"

"He offered to help."

"Actually, hon, he said he had a message for us."

"Same thing."

"Not quite."

"Well, it's a moving car," she pointed out philosophically, gnawing on her last fingernail. "He can't get out."

"We're going to London to see our Granny," announced Selinka.

"Do you have a Granny?" asked Celeste.

Good question. He ran through the order of angels above him; archangels, principalities, powers, dominions, thrones, cherubim, seraphim . . . "No, I don't."

"Why not?"

"I guess it's because I'm an angel."

The twin on the right narrowed her eyes and stared up at him. "Lemme see your wings."

"What?"

"If you're supposed to be an angel, lemme see your wings."

Samuel spread his hands and tried an ingratiating smile. "I don't have wings."

"Why?"

"I'm not that kind of an angel."

"Why?"

"Because I'm the kind of angel that doesn't have wings."

"Why?"

"If you're an angel, you're supposed to have wings." Her voice began to rise in both volume and pitch. "Big, white, fluffy wings!"

The smile slipped. "Well, I don't."

"Why?"

Why? He had no idea. But going back for that long talk with Lena was beginning to seem like a plan. "I have running shoes," he offered.

Small heads bent forward to have a look.

"They're not brand name," said the twin who seemed to be running this part of the interrogation. "No swatches."

"Does that matter?" Was he wearing the wrong stuff? "What's a swatch?"

She folded her arms. "Dork."

"Wouldn't you girls like to have a nap?" Over the sound of their laughter, he thought he heard their mother whimper. "You know, if you were quiet, your parents would be really happy."

"They would?"

"Yes."

"Why?"

The twin on the left, taking her turn, poked him imperiously in the side. "Light up your head."

"What?"

"Light up your head! Like on TV."

"I don't . . ."

"Then you're not an angel."

"Yes, I am."

"No, you're not."

"Yes, I am." Just barely resisting the urge to grab her and shake her, he let a little of the light show.

"Ha, ha, made you light!"

An ethnically diverse, anatomically correct baby doll swung in from the other side by one foot, the molded plastic head completing its downswing in just the wrong spot.

The light went out.

His eyes were still watering when the SUV stopped at the corner of York and Talbot Streets and he stumbled out into a snowbank. Maybe Brian Pearson *did* need to know his kids weren't deliberately driving him crazy, but as the twins had survived for seven whole years, he could only conclude that both parents already had the patience of a saint. Each. He'd been with the twins for just over an hour and against all predisposition, he wanted to strangle them. He couldn't imagine what seven years would be like. And he was no longer entirely certain that Brian Pearson wasn't right.

The girls, not at all upset by the yelling he'd done, crowded to the window, and blew him kisses.

"Aren't they angelic," sighed their mother without much conviction.

"Not exactly," Samuel told her, clinging to the door until he could get his balance. "But if it helps, I don't think they're actually demonic."

She turned her head enough to meet his gaze. "You're not sure?"

"Uh." He took another look and heard the voice of memory say, *Because if an angel can be here, then so can a devil.* Or two. "No. Sorry."

"Well, you've been a lot of help."

He'd have been more reassured if she hadn't sounded so sarcastic. Shoving his hands in his pockets as the SUV drove away, he sighed and muttered, "That could've gone better."

Pushing through the narrow break in the knee-high snowbank that bracketed the street, he stumbled onto the sidewalk and took a moment to try and dig snow out of his shoes with his finger. Apparently, it was a well-known fact that angels left no footprints. Twisting around, he checked and, sure enough, he'd left no mark in the snow. Although there had to be a reason for it, he'd have happily traded footprints for dry feet. Were angels even supposed to have wet feet? At least he wasn't cold. At least *that* was working.

Nothing else seemed to be.

Maybe he just needed practice.

Straightening, he looked around. So this was London. Fotown. The Forest City. The Jungle City. Georgiana on the Ditch. Apparently, the 340,000 people who lived here had the most cars per capita in Canada. So? Where was everybody? All he could see were snow-covered, empty streets.

Looking east, a sign outside the deserted Convention Center wished everyone a Merry Christmas. A gust of wind whistling down the tracks blew a fan of snow off the top of the bank that nearly hid the train station.

Behind him, a car door slammed.

He turned in time to see a taxi drive away and an elderly woman struggling to drag a brown vinyl suitcase toward the bus station. Her name was Edna Grey, she had a weak heart, and she was on her way to Windsor to spend Christmas Day with her daughter. Maybe he didn't have a message because he *was* the message. Maybe he was supposed to show, not tell. Hurrying over, he lifted the suitcase easily out of the elderly woman's grasp.

"Stop! Thief! Stop!"

"Hey! Ow! I'm just trying to help!"

Edna Grey glared out at him from under the edge of a red knit hat, the strap of her purse clutched in both mittened hands. "Help yourself to my stuff!"

"No, help you carry your stuff." As she lifted the purse again, he dropped the suitcase and backed out of range, rubbing his elbow. "What've you got in that thing, bricks?"

Her eyes narrowed. "Maybe."

"Could you chill, Mrs. Grey. I'm just trying to do something nice for you." He knew he sounded defensive, but he couldn't seem to stop himself. And he had no idea why he wanted her to lower her body temperature.

"How did you know my name? You've been stalking me, haven't you?"

Stalking. The following and observing of another person, usually with the intent to do harm.

"No!" He stepped forward then retreated again as the purse came up. "I can't do harm. I'm an angel."

"You look like a punk." A vehement exhalation through her nose, sprayed the immediate area with a fine patina of moisture.

"I do?"

"Well, you sure don't look like no angel."

He didn't? "I don't?"

"You look," she repeated, "like a punk."

Frank Giorno had called him a punk as well. He couldn't understand why since punk had pretty much ended with the '80s. A quick check found nose and ears still free of safety pins. "I could light up my head." That seemed to be what angels did.

"You could set your shorts on fire for all I care. Now get out of my way, I gotta catch a bus."

"But . . ."

"Move!"

His feet moved before the barked command actually made it to his brain. He stood and watched as she dragged her suitcase the remaining twenty-two feet, six and three-quarter inches to the bus station door. Nothing else moved for as far as he could see and the only sound he could hear was the rasp of cheap vinyl against concrete.

At the door, she paused, and turned. "Well?" she demanded.

Higher knowledge seemed at a loss.

"Get over here and open the door."

"But I thought . . ."

"And while you were thinking, did you think about how a woman of my age could manage a big heavy suitcase and a door?"

"Uh . . ."

"No. You didn't. The world has gone to hell in a handcart since they canceled *Bowling for Dollars.*"

Propelled by her glare, he ran for the door and hauled it open. Then, a bit at a loss, he followed her inside.

She shifted her grip on her purse. "Now where are you going?"

He didn't know. "With you?"

"Try again." She squinted up at the board. "Only other bus leaving this morning's going to Toronto."

"I should go to Toronto?"

"Why should I care where you go?" Grabbing her suitcase, she began backing across the room, keeping him locked in a suspicious glare.

"Fine." Edna Grey might not need his help, but in a city of three million, someone would. He'd go there and he'd help people and he'd finally figure out just what he was supposed to be doing, and when he'd done it he'd go back to the light and demand to know just what they thought they were doing sending him into the world without instructions. Well, maybe not demand. Ask.

Politely.

But for now . . .

The bus station flickered twice, then came back into focus.

Why wasn't he in Toronto? Wanting to be in Toronto should have put him there, but something seemed to be holding him in place. It felt as though he was trying to drag an enormous weight . . .

And then he realized.

"Oh, come on, that's a couple of ounces, tops!" A little embarrassed by the way his voice echoed against six different types of tile,

Samuel looked up to see Edna Grey staring at him, wide-eyed, one mittened hand clutching her chest. While he watched, she toppled slowly to the ground.

"Mrs. Grey?" He landed on his knees beside her. "Mrs. Grey, what's wrong?"

"Heart . . ." Her voice sounded like crinkling tissue paper.

"Hey, don't do this, you're not supposed to die now!" Reaching out, he spread the fingers of his right hand an inch above the apex of her bosom, spent a moment stopping his mind from repeating the word bosom over and over for no good reason, then asked himself just what exactly he thought he was doing.

I'm helping. It's her heart.

Were hearts supposed to flutter like a gas pump straining at an empty tank?

He laid his left hand against his own chest.

Apparently not.

So?

Was this the message he was here to deliver?

A pulse of light moved from his hand to her heart and he felt an inexplicable urge to yell, "Clear!" Somehow, he resisted. Her heart stopped fluttering, paused, found a new rhythm, and began beating strongly once again.

"Mrs. Grey?" Feeling a little dizzy, Samuel leaned forward and peered into her face. "Can you hear me?"

"What? I'm old, so I'm deaf?"

"Uh, no." Maybe he should loosen her clothing.

She smacked his hand away. "What happened?"

"You had a heart attack."

Planting both palms against the floor, she pushed herself into a sitting position. "Well, are you surprised? You were there, then you weren't there, then you were there again."

"You saw that?"

"What? I'm old, so I'm blind?"

"Uh, no."

"And why does the whole room smell of pine?"

"I think that's the stuff they use on the floor."

"Or some cat's been pissing in the corner." Spotting the startled face of the bus station attendant peering over the ticket counter, her eyes narrowed. "And just what are you looking at, Missy? Good thing I didn't have to wait for her help," she muttered, "I'd be lying here until New Year's."

"Mrs. Grey? Do you want to stand up?"

"No. I'd rather sit here in a puddle of slush."

About to take her hand, Samuel sat back on his heels. "Uh, okay."

Muttering under her breath, she grabbed his shoulder and hauled herself to her feet. "So, what were you doing?" she demanded as he stood. "Here you are, here you aren't—I have a weak heart, you know."

"Had," he corrected helpfully. "I fixed it."

"You fixed it all right. Now answer the question: What were you doing?"

"I was trying to go to Toronto. But nothing happened." His shoulders slumped.

"You really are an angel?"

"Yes, ma'am."

"So, what's the message?"

"Well, uh, you see, it's like this, I uh . . ."

One foot tapped impatiently. "Angels are the messengers of God. So, what's the message? Is it Armageddon?"

He checked his pockets. Still no messages. "I'm pretty sure it's not Armageddon."

"Pretty sure?" She seemed disappointed.

"Actually, I'm beginning to think I'm, you know, not that kind of an angel."

"Oh. Then what kind of an angel are you?"

"Just, uh, the kind that . . ."

"The kind that pops in and out any where they want? Giving poor, helpless grandmothers heart attacks?"

"I didn't do it on purpose."

"Don't take that tone with me, young man. You can show a little respect for my age."

"What? You're old, so I should respect you?" It slipped out before he could stop it. For some weird reason his mouth seemed to have functioned without his brain being involved.

But Edna Grey only straightened her hat. "Yes," she said, "that's it exactly. So why couldn't you pop?"

"It's this form. It has . . ." Mouth open to explain about the genitalia, Samuel met a rheumy gaze, looked deep, and decided he didn't want to go there. Or anywhere near there actually. "It's not . . . I mean, it doesn't . . . It's sort of defining me. It's keeping me from doing things, and I can't get rid of it."

"Tell me about it."

His constant low level of confusion geared up a notch. "About what?"

"Be old, boy, if you want to be defined by your form." She sighed, a short, sharp, angry sound. "Old bones, old blood, old body, they keep you from doing most things, and you sure as hell can't get rid of them. But you know what's worse?" A mittened finger poked his chest. "The way other people think you can't do what you've always done 'cause you're old—whether you can or not." Her hand dropped back to her side. "Don't get old, boy. And don't let other people tell you what you can or cannot do."

"I can't get old," he told her. "And I can't get to Toronto either."

"Oh, yeah, can't get old, can't get to Toronto; that's a real similar comparison, that is." Bending, she scooped her purse up off the floor. "Apples and oranges as my sainted mother used to say."

"Actually she wasn't."

Edna Grey shot him an irritated glare as she straightened. "Wasn't what?"

"Sainted."

"I certainly hope not."

"But you said . . ."

"Never mind what I said. And if you want to get to Toronto so badly, buy a bus ticket."

"I need a bus ticket to go to Toronto?"

"If you're going by bus, you do."

A quick rummage through his pockets produced a cardboard square. "One of these?"

Her brows drew in. "Where did you get that?"

He shrugged. "Need provides."

"Because you're an angel?"

"I guess."

The intercom sputtered to life and spat incomprehensible word-age into the station.

"Your bus is boarding on platform 3." Samuel pushed her suitcase toward her, carefully, making no sudden moves. His elbow still hurt from the first assault.

"You understand that?"

He nodded again.

"Well, if I didn't believe you were an angel before, I sure would now. Understanding the gooblety goop that comes out of those speakers would take nothing less than direct intervention from God. Just wait until I tell that Elsa I met a real angel. Her and the way she's always talking about how she once met Don Ho."

"Mrs. Grey, your bus!"

"Right." Lifting the suitcase easily, she stomped off toward the buses, muttering. "Just wait till I tell my daughter I met a real angel. She's never even met Don Ho."

He waited until he saw her make her laborious way up the bus steps, refusing to let go of her suitcase, and sighed. "You're welcome."

"Look, kid, I don't care what you think you are and how little sleep you think I've had and how much you think I need to drive safely, but if you don't sit down, I'm going to kick your ass off this bus."

"But I have a ticket."

Barry Bryant sighed and rotated the heel of his left hand around his temple. "I don't care. The harpy behind the ticket counter has already told me I look like hell, so I don't need your two cents' worth."

Samuel leaned forward. "You don't, you know."

"I don't what?"

"Look like Hell."

"Sit. Down."

A soldier of the light knew when to obey a direct order. Samuel sat down beside the only person on the bus. "Hi, Nedra."

"Do I know you?"

"I'm an angel. I'm here to help."

She stared deep into his eyes, watched the gold flecks overwhelm the brown, lighting up the immediate area in a soft luminescence, and said, "Get lost."

"Get lost?"

"Yes." For some strange reason, after a perfectly equitable Christmas Eve, her parents had sent her on her way feeling guilty about their lack of grandchildren. She was facing a twelve-hour shift in a hospital that could pay millions for one piece of high-tech equipment but couldn't afford to order new bedpans, and she was in no mood to deal with someone who smelled like canned ravioli, a food her rising cholesterol level no longer allowed her to eat. "Get lost."

"I can't," he admitted, glancing around at the confined space.

"Try."

"But . . ."

"Now."

He'd just settled himself as far from Nedra as possible when the driver climbed on board and glared in his direction. "What?"

Lip curled, Barry dropped into the driver's seat. He'd got to bed at about three, got up again at six, and knew damned well he shouldn't be driving. The last thing he needed at the beginning of a run to Toronto and back on a snow-slicked highway was some smart-ass teenager pointing that out. Of course it wasn't safe. He knew it wasn't safe. What did he look like, an idiot? But what was he supposed to do? Cancel the run? Call another driver in on Christmas Day? Fat chance. He had to do it, so he was going to do it, and there was nothing more to be said. Besides, it was double time and a half, and he wasn't giving up that kind of cash.

Head pounding, he rammed the bus into gear. "And I don't feel guilty about it either," he growled.

"Yeah, you do."

Barry whirled around. There was no way he could have heard the protest or been heard in turn from the back of the bus. *I am not hearing things.* Shoulders hunched, he eased off the brake and headed for the road. *I'm fine.*

The only other vehicle in the parking lot belonged to the cow behind the counter who'd probably report him and then he'd get suspended and lose as much as he was making today—so why was he even bothering?

He swung out just a little wide and the bus brushed against the fender of her car like an elephant brushing against a paper screen.

As they pulled out onto York Street, Samuel twisted in his seat and stared back at the crumpled chrome, wondering if he should do something. *He knew he shouldn't have done that, but he did it anyway. What gives?* It was like nothing Samuel'd ever come in contact with before. It was . . .

Free will. His eyes widened, and he squirmed around to stare at the back of the driver's head. When given a choice between good and evil, humans could freely choose to do evil, and sometimes they did. Okay, admittedly on a scale of one to ten where one was deliberately hitting a parked car and ten was committing genocide, this was closer to, well, one, but still. Free will. In action.

After that, the trip to Toronto was uneventful.

Although there did seem to be a number of off-road vehicles suddenly driving off the road.

Samuel would have enjoyed the ride had he not continued to slide down the angle forced into ancient seats by thousands of previous passengers, catching himself on his inseam. He had no idea why anyone would put such a torture device right over so much soft tissue, but by the time the bus reached Hamilton he was certain the Prince of Darkness himself had been involved.

Toronto had the turmoil he'd been expecting earlier. Samuel stepped out of the Elizabeth Street Bus Terminal and stared. Everything seemed overdone. There were just too many buildings, too much concrete, too much dirt—but not too many people given that it was nearly noon on Christmas Day.

"Hey man, you look lost."

Samuel glanced down at his feet—he hadn't known snow came in that color—then up at the twenty-something blond man, with the inch of dark roots, now standing beside him. "No. I'm right here."

"Hey, that's funny." The smile and accompanying laugh was a lie. He wore a black trench coat, open over black jeans, black boots and a black turtleneck. It was supposed to look cool, or possibly kewl, but Samuel got the impression kewl had moved on. This guy hadn't. "You just get to the city?"

"Yeah."

"You got a place to stay?"

"Do I need a place to stay?" Was he staying?

"You going to try and make it on the streets?"

"I was going to stay on the sidewalks."

"Like I said, a funny guy." The outstretched hand ended in black fingernails. Definitely left behind by kewl. "I'm Deter."

"Deter?" Higher knowledge finally provided information that wasn't a fashion tip. "Isn't your name Leslie?"

The hazel eyes widened, the hand dropped, and Leslie/Deter shot a glance back over his shoulder at two snickering men about his own age. "No, you're wrong, man. It's Deter."

"Hey, it's okay. I understand why you changed it."

"I didn't change it."

"Yeah, you did."

"No, I didn't!"

"Yeah, you did. It was Leslie Frances Calhoon. Now it's Deter Calhoon."

"Leslie Frances?" howled one of the two laughing men.

"Shut up!" He whirled back around to shake a finger under Samuel's nose. "And you shut up, too!"

"Okay."

"Do I know you?"

In his existence to this point, Samuel had met eight people, not counting Nedra who he didn't think he should count because she'd made it fairly clear she hadn't wanted to meet him. "No."

"So stop calling me Leslie!"

"Okay."

"You don't have a place to stay?"

Was he staying? "No."

"Fine. So you're coming with us."

"No."

"So you're going to stay on the street, on the sidewalk, whatever. Fine. Here." Breathing heavily through his nose, Leslie/Deter thrust a pamphlet into Samuel's hand. "Greenstreet Mission. We're doing a Christmas dinner. You can get a meal and hear the word of God."

Samuel smiled in relief. This, finally, he understood. "Which word?"

"What?"

"Well, God's said a lot of words, you know, and a word like *it* or *the* wouldn't be worth hearing again but it's always fun listening to Him try to say aluminum."

"What are you talking about?"

"What you were talking about."

Leslie/Deter glared over flaring nostrils. "I was talking about the word of God."

"Which word?"

He snatched the pamphlet out of Samuel's hand. "Forget it."

"But . . ."

"No. Just stay away!" The black trench coat swirled impressively as he stomped back to his snickering friends and shoved them both into motion.

Wondering what he'd said, Samuel lifted a hand in farewell. There didn't seem to be much point in offering to help with the pamphlets. "'Bye, Leslie."

If Leslie/Deter had a response, it was probably just as well that the renewed howls of laughter from his companions drowned it out.

Because the hole was so small, it had taken over twelve hours to push enough substance through. Toward the end, as the light and dark in the world moved closer to balance, it should have gotten more difficult, but there was now such a vast amount of enthusiastic darkness pushing from below that care had to be taken. Tipping the balance the other way would do no good at all. Since, technically, doing no good at all was its *raison d'être,* the contradiction was making it feel more than a little twitchy.

It didn't even want to get into the problem of keeping it all together without actually achieving consciousness too early. Without a physical body it was both disoriented and exhausted. It had never had such a bad day. Which was sort of a good thing. Except that good things were bad. If it'd had a head, it would've had one hell of a headache.

Literally.

It could feel good and evil leveling out. Balance being restored. It pulled itself together, the shadow that had lain over the frozen hollow since midnight growing darker, acquiring form.

Then, as all things were equal—or all the things it was concerned with at any rate—it closed the hole and looked around.

"I'M BAck."

It coughed and tried again.

"I'M back. I'm back." It just kept getting worse. "What the Hell is going on here?"

Attempting a perfect balance, it had allowed the weight on the other side of the scale to define the shape it would wear. Becoming its perfect opposite. Impossible for one to be found as long as the other existed. It would cheerfully use the light to further its own ends. Well, maybe not cheerfully. Cynically.

It seemed to be a young female. Late teens. Long dark hair. Fairly large breasts. She looked down. Everything seemed to be there.

Three things were immediately clear.

One. She appeared to be a natural blonde, which explained the uniform black of the hair. Bad dye job.

Two. Demons, like angels, were sexless. The actions of incubi and succubi were more in the order of a mind-fuck than anything sweaty. But . . .

. . . since she had a set, he had a set.

Three. Given gender, and she certainly seemed to have been given that, something had gotten significantly screwed up somewhere.

She'd have been happier about that were it not for the sudden rush of emotions. Every possible emotion. She was up, she was down, she was happy, she was sad, she was royally pissed off . . .

Which was the one she decided to go with.

EIGHT

꘍⟐꘍

FROM THE BUS TERMINAL, Samuel walked over to Yonge Street
and up two blocks to Gerrard, staring in amazement at the amount
of stuff on display in the windows of the closed stores. The stereo
system dominating a small electronics shop drew him close to the
glass—five disk CD changer, digital tuner with forty presets, six-mode
preset equalizer, dual full-logic cassette decks, extra bass—and he
found himself wondering covetously about sub-woofers and wattage.
From deep within came the knowledge that if it came to it, he'd buy
that stereo before he bought groceries.

Then he noticed the leather shop next door. Stereo forgotten, he
took two long side steps and stared wide-eyed at the mannequin barely
dressed in a red leather corset, black leather panties, and stiletto-
heeled thigh boots.

Which was when the unexpected happened.

He backed up so quickly he slammed into a newspaper box.

His genitalia were functioning without him!

It was like, like they had a mind of their own.

Well, not *they* exactly . . .

Beginning to panic, he stared down at the tent in his pants and
wondered what he was supposed to do.

Fortunately, the panic seemed to be taking care of the problem.

A few minutes later, heart pounding, gaze directed carefully at the
sidewalk, he started walking again, faith in his physical integrity
shaken. What would have happened had it not been a holiday? Had
he actually been able to go into the store and . . .

It didn't bear thinking about.

Brakes squealed. A door panel brushed his knee. The deep red 1986 Horizon stopped. Backed up. The window opened.

"You've got the red, asshole!" the driver screamed, then gunned the motor and roared away.

Samuel had no idea they came in other colors. Or, for that matter, what color they usually were. And how had the driver known? Were any other bits of his body likely to surprise him?

Eleven seconds later, the first pigeon settled on his head, claws digging through his hair and into his scalp. When it finally lost the fight to keep its perch, it slid off to land with a thud on his right shoulder. It was mostly white with a few gray markings and the distinct attitude that it had arrived where it was supposed to be.

The second pigeon went directly to his other shoulder.

The rest fought for less prime locations and, for the most part, had to content themselves with huddling close around his feet.

He spoke fluent pigeon—which wasn't really difficult as the entire pigeon vocabulary pretty much consisted of: "Food!" "Danger!" and "Betcha I can hit that guy in the Armani suit."—but nothing he said made any difference. They were where they felt they ought to be. Case closed. When he started walking again, they lifted off with an indignant flapping of wings. When he stopped, they landed. He kept walking.

At College Street, he flipped a mental coin and turned right.

The sedan traveling southbound missed him by seven centimeters. The pickup traveling north missed him by three. The driver of the pickup taught him a number of new words. The pigeons knew them already.

The east side of Yonge—where College Street became Carlton Street—seemed to lead into a more residential area. That had to be good. People equaled problems and sooner or later, if he was right about being the message not merely the medium, he'd *have* to fix the problem that would let him go home.

By the time he reached the park across from Homewood Avenue, he was traveling in a shifting cloud of fat bodies and feathers. Visibility was bad, the footing was getting a little tricky, and the surrounding air had begun to smell strongly of motor oil and old French fries. He clearly had to get rid of his escort.

He flailed his arms.

He used the new words, rearranging them into a number of different patterns.

Nothing worked.

Climbing up and over a snowbank, he brushed off the end of a bench and flopped down onto the cleared spot.

The pigeons settled happily.

His vision slightly impaired by a fan of tail feathers, Samuel watched a police car make a tight U-turn across Carlton Street and pull up more or less in front of him. The driver's name was Police Constable Jack Brooks, his partner, Police Constable Marri Margaret Patton. They sat and stared for a full minute. He could feel their mood lightening as they studied him, and he knew he should be glad he'd added a little joy to their day but, preoccupied by the sudden warmth dribbling down behind his left ear, he found he didn't much care.

Finally, they got out of the car and waded through the snow toward him, valiantly but unsuccessfully attempting to suppress snickers.

"Are you, uh, all right under there?"

Samuel sighed and spat out a feather. "Sure," he answered shortly.

"Have you tried standing up?"

He stood. Wings flapped. He could see PC Patton's lips move, but he couldn't hear what she was saying above the noise. He sat down again. The pigeons settled.

After a moment of near hysterical laughter, the police settled as well.

Fighting to catch his breath, PC Brooks managed to gasp, "Are you feeding them?"

"As if." If he was feeding them, he could stop. And they'd leave. "They want to be with me 'cause I'm an angel."

"An angel?"

"Yeah; I guess it's that dove thing."

"These are pigeons."

"Same old."

As three birds squabbled over position, PC Brooks got his first unobstructed look at facial features and knocked five years off his original estimate of the young man's age. "What's your name, son?"

"Samuel."

"Samuel what?"

"Just Samuel."

"And you're an angel?"

"Yes."

"If you're an angel, where are your wings?" Beside him, he heard his partner smother a snort.

Samuel sighed and spit out another feather. "I'm not that kind of angel." Without much enthusiasm, he added, "But I *can* make my head light up."

"Maybe next time." Frowning slightly, PC Brooks took a closer look, found his gaze met and held, found himself watching the gold flecks in the brown eyes swirl into soft luminescence. He blinked and forced himself to look away. "What are you on, Samuel?"

"Concrete and fiberglass."

"Uh-huh. Look, son, it's Christmas Day, why don't you go home."

"I can't!"

The pigeons took flight, circled once, and settled again.

PC Patton took her partner by the sleeve and dragged him a few steps away. "It's not against the law to be covered in pigeons," she reminded him, grinning broadly.

"I know."

"Neither is it against the law to impersonate an angel." She glanced back over her shoulder. "Whatever he's on . . ."

"Concrete and fiberglass."

". . . he's not a danger to himself or society, and he's probably fairly warm under there."

"But it's Christmas."

So it was. She sighed, watched her breath blossom in the frosty air, and turned back toward the bench. "Why don't you get in the car and we'll take you somewhere you can get some Christmas dinner."

"Can the pigeons come?"

"No."

That was the best news he'd heard in a while.

The pigeons, who recognized the police as Nice Dark Targets, refused to cooperate.

Samuel finally backed up about twenty feet, raced forward, and flung himself into the back of the squad car, giving PC Patton about six seconds to slam the door before the birds caught up. When the first bird hit the window, she almost peed herself, she was laughing so hard.

Darkness had emerged just outside Waverton for a reason. The tiny town was not only far enough off the beaten track that a Keeper wouldn't stumble on it by accident, it was fairly close to the bloated population base along the Canada/U.S. border—there was a limited amount of trouble that could be caused without active human participation and darkness didn't like to waste time. Parts of central Russia, Africa, and Nevada also fit the geographic criteria, but appearing in any of those areas would have been redundant at best.

She found a pair of denim overalls, black canvas sneakers, and a nylon jacket in what had been the office of J. Henry and Sons Auto Repair. While appreciative of the chaos she could cause walking around naked, keeping a lower profile seemed the smarter move. The outfit wasn't stylish, but it was serviceable.

Although to her surprise, she *was* a little concerned that the overalls made her look fat.

Which soon became a minor problem.

Once in the world, she should have been able to move instantaneously from place to place, but something seemed to be stopping her. It didn't take long to figure out what. While walking the four and half kilometers into town, she decided that staying as far away from the light as possible was no longer an option; her new plan involved finding him and kicking his holier than thou butt around the block a few times. *What had he been thinking?*

Actually, given which set he'd gotten, she had a pretty good idea of what he'd been thinking.

"Men," she'd snarled at a hydro pole, left forearm tucked under her breasts to stop the painful bouncing. "They're all alike."

The power went off in half the county.

Which made her feel only half better.

She'd planned on finding a ride south as soon as she got to Waver-

ton, twisting the weak and pitiful will of some poor mortal to her bid-
ding. Unfortunately, there was no one around; the only thing moving
on Main Street was the random blinking of a string of Christmas lights
hung in the window of one of the closed businesses. She could have
shot a cannon off in any direction and not hit a soul. And *if* she'd had
a cannon, she *would* have shot it off.

As she didn't . . .

The bank on the corner burst into black-tipped flame.

Rummaging about in her pocket, she pulled out a marshmallow.
Need provides.

Twenty minutes later, the scene seethed with people—volunteer
firefighters, both constables from the local OPP detachment, and most
of the remaining population.

Now that's more like it. Bonus points for pulling a Keeper up into
the middle of nowhere to close this hole opened by arson, leaving
more populated areas unprotected. Jostled by the crowd, she snarled
and drove her heel as hard as she could down on the nearest toe.

"Ouch. Excuse me."

Confused, she turned and glared into soft brown eyes bracketed
between a dark pink hat and a pale pink scarf. "Why are you apologizing? You're the victim."

"No one has to be a victim, dear." The older woman frowned
slightly, her gaze sliding from dyed hair to running shoes and back up
again. "You're not from around here, are you?"

Strangers were universally suspect when something went wrong.
Settling her weight on one hip, she folded her arms. "No, I'm not."

"Are you alone?"

She glanced over her shoulder at the tendril of darkness seeping
out of the hole, watched one of the firefighters "accidentally" turn the
hose on another, and she smiled. "Mostly." Once accused of setting the
fire, she'd be able to cause all sorts of havoc. She'd be able to turn
their anger at her onto other targets, counter-accusing once she had
the attention of the crowd. Maybe the good townspeople would like
to know about Mr. Tannison, the bank manager.

"A stranger," the woman repeated thoughtfully, the flames reflecting in both halves of her bifocals. "And all alone."

Here it comes, she thought.

"How did you get here? We're not exactly in the center of things." Her eyes widened. "You've run away, haven't you?"

"No, I . . ."

"All alone. In a strange place. And on Christmas, too." Pink-mittened hands clasped over a formidable bosom. "Where were you running away to?"

"The city . . ."

"Of course, the city." Her sigh plumed out silver-white. "But for right now, you have nowhere to go for Christmas dinner, do you?"

"I don't eat."

"That's what I thought."

And the strange thing was, that *was* what she thought. Which made less than no sense.

"My name is Eva Porter, and you're going to join my husband and I for turkey and all the trimmings. I won't take no for an answer." A pink wave toward the burning bank. "That's my husband by the tanker truck."

"You want me to join you for dinner?"

"That's right."

"You don't know me."

"You don't know *me*."

She couldn't argue with that. Eva Porter was way outside her experience. "Are you going to torture me?" That would at least explain the invitation.

"Goodness, no."

"You only want to feed me?"

"That's right."

"And it doesn't bother you that I'm a demon? Darkness given human form?"

Eva's smile slipped.

Before she could enjoy the expected reaction, wool-covered fingers gently lifted her chin and looked her right in the eye.

"I don't know who told you such a thing . . ."

"No one had to tell me."

". . . but you are a beautiful young woman."

"I am?" She caught herself feeling good about that and hurriedly squashed the feeling.

"Yes, you are. What's your name?"

"Uh . . ." She pulled one at random from the possibilities. "Byleth."

"That's a pretty name."

"It is?" It wasn't supposed to be. This had gone quite far enough. "Listen, lady, I don't know what you think I am, but I'm not."

"Not what?"

"That. What you think." The pale gray of her eyes began darkening like tarnished silver. "I set that fire! I desired flames—and there they were."

Eva frowned. "What are you on, Byleth?"

She glanced down, totally confused. "Packed snow and concrete."

"And those shoes are just canvas, aren't they? Your poor toes must be frozen."

They hadn't been. But now . . .

"And a nylon jacket isn't enough for this weather. It's below zero out here. Just look at the ice forming on those hoses."

She looked. Her teeth began to chatter. "Okay, but I'm just going with you to get warm."

"That's fine. You don't have to do anything you don't want to."

"That's right. I don't." Hugging herself in a valiant effort to contain body heat, Byleth followed the confusing mortal down Main Street. Ignite the bank. Open a hole. Allow a little darkness into the world. All that had gone by the book. But reassured, warmed, and fed? Not to mention apologized to?

She wasn't supposed to like people being nice to her. Well, so far only *person* not *people*, but still . . .

It wasn't right.

Or more to the point, it wasn't wrong.

"No shit, man! I'm an angel, too!"

Samuel studied Doug's slightly furry, gap-toothed smile and bloodshot eyes and shook his head. "No, you're not."

"Yeah, I am." Carefully placing his fork beside his half empty plate, Doug leaned forward and lowered his voice. "I'm undercover. That's why, you know, no wings."

"Can you make your head light up?"

"Fuck, yeah." He glanced around, checking for eavesdroppers. Satisfied that no one else in the crowded room was paying any attention, he elaborated. "It's usually pretty lit by now, but they don't allow that stuff in here."

"But shouldn't I know it if you're an angel?"

"I didn't know till you told me. Why should you know till I told you?"

That made sense. Not a lot of sense but, under the circumstances, enough. And Doug wasn't lying. Samuel could tell when people were lying and Doug believed every breathy, fermentation-redolent thing he'd said. Feeling as though the weight of the world had been lifted off his shoulders, Samuel leaned forward as well. "Do you get covered in pigeons?"

"Nope. Butterflies. Hundreds of 'em, movin' their little feet all over my body." Eyes widening, he glanced down at this chest and began smacking himself with alternating palms. "All. Over. My. Body."

Samuel grabbed his wrists. "What are you doing?"

"Swattin' butterflies."

Ignoring for the moment the absence of butterflies to swat, Samuel looked sternly across the narrow table. "Angels can't enact violence on a living creature."

"What the fuck does that mean?"

"We don't swat!"

"You never wanted to swat them pigeons?"

"Well . . . yeah." Which wasn't something he wanted to discover about himself—even justifiable urges to commit violence on a flock of flying rats was just anti-angel. Releasing Doug's wrists, he buried his head in his hands. "I'm very confused."

Doug nodded sagely. "Happens."

"I don't know why I'm here."

"I do."

That was more than he'd dared to hope for. "You do?"

"You're here to eat."

And hope died.

About to point out that angels didn't eat, Samuel watched Doug lift a forkful of mashed potatoes and gravy. Doug was eating. Most of it was even going into his mouth. Wrapping his fist around his own fork, he mirrored the motions of the undercover angel sitting across from him. After a few moments, he got the hang of not chewing his tongue with the food. Then he swallowed.

All of a sudden, he was ravenous.

When a bit of stuffing came back up through his nose, he slowed down enough to breathe. He drank juice until it was gone, then he switched to water. He had seconds. And, although what food remained had become a little difficult to identify by then, he even had thirds.

This was the best thing that had happened to him in this body. He couldn't believe what he'd been missing. He wanted to thank Doug for the gift he'd been given, for new information shared, and all he could think to do was to share information in turn.

"I have genitalia."

"They're called giblets, kid."

She'd poison the gravy. Given who—or rather what—she was, it was the only logical thing to do under the circumstances. The box of rat poison tucked neatly onto the shelf of gardening supplies had called out to her as Eva Porter led her through the enclosed porch and into the house. At least she thought it was the rat poison, her teeth were chattering too loudly to be sure.

"Now, then, let's get you out of those wet shoes and socks, eh."

"I don't *have* socks."

"Then I'll get you some." Unwrapped, Eva wore a dove-gray sweat suit over a white turtleneck. Given her proportions . . .

"You look like a pigeon," Byleth muttered sullenly.

"I do, don't I." Her eyes widened as she took in the overalls. "Good heavens, child, you're hardly wearing anything at all. Well, I can do something about that, can't I?"

"Can you?" She'd intended the question to be sharp edged, mocking, but it emerged sounding rather pathetic. Holding the freezing length of the overalls' zipper away from her body, she followed Eva into the living room and watched wide-eyed as she pulled several brightly wrapped packages out from under the tree.

"These are for my granddaughter, Nancy; she'll be coming up to spend New Year's with us. Fortunately, you're about the same size."

"You're giving me your granddaughter's presents?" She'd have refused the kindness except she'd caught sight of her reflection in the living room window. The overalls were gross. And they *did* make her look fat. *Still: Granny gives Nancy's presents away. Nancy gets angry. Big family fight.* Byleth could live with that. Of course if Nancy was as whacked as Granny, she might not mind. *Don't ruin things,* she told herself sternly, following Eva upstairs. *Believe anything that'll get you out of these overalls.*

As instructed, she had a nice hot shower, staying in until she'd emptied the tank. She left the soap sitting in water in the soap dish and the towels in a crumpled heap on the floor. It wasn't much, but it felt good to be proactive again.

Black jeans. Black, ribbed turtleneck; tight enough to offer some support to the breasts which were rapidly becoming a colossal nuisance. Thick red sweater. Red fuzzy socks.

Pivoting in front of the mirror, toes working against the thick fleece, she realized she looked good. The black, the red, the hair—it was working. Back in the bathroom, she went through Eva's makeup bag, pulled out the reddest lipstick she could find and applied it liberally. She liked the effect so much, she completely forgot about her intention to infect the lipstick with a particularly virulent STD.

Harry Porter was standing in the living room when she came downstairs. He smiled and introduced himself. "Just between you and me," he added, leaning toward her slightly, "that outfit looks much better on you than it would have on Nancy."

Had there been anything remotely sexual in the comment, she'd have known how to react. But there wasn't.

Why were her ears so hot?

She tried a provocative smile anyway.

Harry deflected it with amused indulgence.

Her ears grew hotter. So did her cheeks. What the hell was going on?

"I'llgohelpwithdinner." The words came out weirdly strung together. Hurrying into the kitchen, she held on tightly to the thought of the rat poison and getting her world back on track.

It took only a little more momentum to bounce into Eva and spill cranberry juice all over her.

"Oops, sorry, dear."

Byleth closed her eyes and counted to three. "Why," she demanded when she opened them, "are you apologizing? I bumped you."

"True enough. I spoke to Harry and he says if you still want to go to the city in the morning, he'll drive you to the bus station in Huntsville."

The bus? There was just no way she was taking the bus. Smelly people took the bus. Poor people took the bus. People being environmentally aware and not driving their cars took the bus. Demons did *not* take the bus. Unless they took it somewhere really, really nasty and left it there. If Harry wanted to play taxi, he could drive her all the way to the city. He'd be easy enough to coerce.

"Byleth? Would you mind stirring the gravy?"

Since Harry had just become useful and she couldn't poison Eva without killing him, there could be only one answer. "Yes."

"Thanks, dear."

Staring at the spoon in her hand, the other end circling around in the pan of gravy, she wondered how that had gone wrong.

———————

519 Church Street served food but couldn't provide shelter for the night. Unwilling to lose the company of the only other angel he'd ever met, Samuel followed Doug out the door and fell into step beside him.

They walked for a while in silence. Higher knowledge informed him that pigeons roosted after dark so, until sunrise, life was good. Or it would have been except . . .

"What's the matter, kid?"

He shook his head, he wasn't sure. "There's pressure." A quick glance down showed a small wet spot on the front of his trousers. "And I'm leaking! Again. First my hands and now this. Am I supposed to be leaking?"

"Must be time to take a piss." Grabbing for the front of his own trousers, Doug crossed the sidewalk and stood facing the wall of Harris' Auto Body.

"We can't take something that doesn't belong to us." In a world of uncertainties, this he remained sure of.

Doug rolled his eyes as a stream of liquid hit the bricks with enough force to knock off a few peeling paint chips and wash them down to float in the streaming puddle on the concrete. "Urinate, kid. Your. En. Eight."

Discharge urine. A pale-yellow fluid secreted as waste by the kidneys, stored in the bladder, discharged through the urethra.

"Oh." Opening the zipper turned out to be more difficult than it looked. Closing it when he finished . . .

"Don't worry about it, kid. Hardly anyone keeps their foreskin these days."

Still unable to completely straighten, Samuel found that of little actual comfort. Moving awkwardly, he followed Doug up a set of broad steps and was astonished to discover they were entering a cathedral. When he paused, Doug grabbed his arm and pulled him ahead.

"St. Mike's only got room for fifty, kid. He who hesitates sleeps outside. Merry Christmas, Father."

The priest nodded without glancing up from the clipboard. "Names?"

"I'm Doug. This here's Samuel. Samuel, not Sam. We're angels."

"You know the rules?"

"You betcha, Father."

"Go on, then. Clear the door."

"This is my favorite flop in the whole city," Doug confided as he dragged Samuel across the nave and in through the big double doors. "Whadda you think?"

The peace and beauty of the Sanctuary wrapped around the angel like a blanket. Like arms of light.

"Did you know your eyes was glowin', kid?"

"Sorry."

"Not a problem. Kind of pretty." Arms spread wide, Doug turned on the spot, thin gray ponytail streaming out behind him, dirty gray overcoat flapping like wings. Pigeon wings. But why ruin the image. "Can you think of a better place for two angels to sleep?"

Actually, he couldn't.

Byleth had merely picked at dinner, pushing the food in circles around her plate, unable to forget how huge her butt had looked in the overalls. Then Eva brought out the lemon meringue pie, a quivering three inches deep with drops of liquid sugar glistening in the valleys of the meringue. Suddenly remembering that gluttony was one of the big seven, she had three pieces. An hour later, when the sugar high suddenly wore off, she'd found herself blinking stupidly at *White Christmas*—a movie too woogie for words—and had allowed Eva to steer her unprotesting up to bed.

She made an explicitly salacious invitation—more because she felt she should than through any desire to corrupt—which Eva didn't even begin to understand. Without the energy to explain the unfamiliar terms, she merely took the offered nightgown and staggered off to bed.

The sheets in the spare room smelled of fabric softener. The mattress was soft. The blankets warm. She had nothing against comfort; a lot of very nasty things had been done for comfort's sake.

"She's certainly rude."

"Yes, she is."

Rolling over on her stomach, she peered off the edge of the bed at the hot air grate set into the old linoleum floor.

"She left the bathroom in a mess and borrowed my makeup without asking."

"I saw that."

Eva's and Harry's voices drifted up through the grate from the living room below.

"Her table manners are atrocious. You'd think she'd never held a fork before."

"And the hysterics in the bathroom later . . ."

Well, how was she to know that was supposed to happen?

At least she seemed to be having a negative effect on the Porters. As long as they were complaining about her, the evening hadn't been a total waste.

"Did you see her go through that pie?"

"I know; isn't it nice to have a teenager in the house again?"

"I am not a teenager!" Both palms hit the floor as she threw herself off the bed toward the voices. "I am a *demon!*"

The house was silent for a moment.

Then . . .

"Did you put Byleth in the front bedroom?"

"Yes, I did."

Eva's voice grew suddenly louder, as though she now stood directly under the grate. "Sorry, dear. We forgot you could hear us."

Teenager.

That apology, she'd accept.

Claire closed her new laptop with a snap. The machine and the e-mail account had been another Christmas present from her parents. While she appreciated the difficulties the Apothecary'd overcome setting the system up, she couldn't help thinking that socks and underwear would have been more useful. "According to Diana, Father Harris has no idea where the angel went. Didn't even realize it—*he*—was an angel."

"So what are we after doing?"

"We keep answering the Summons . . ." She frowned, searching for a plural. ". . . s I get. Nothing else we can do."

Unconvinced, Dean sat beside her on the bed. "Shouldn't we tell someone, then?"

"Who?"

"Other Keepers?"

"Actually, they know."

"They know?"

"Not exactly about the angel, but they know we, uh, consummated our relationship. Apparently it echoed through the possibilities." He looked so appalled, she managed what she hoped was an encouraging smile in spite of her own pique. "Everyone was very impressed. Keepers who've never used anything more complicated than a ballpoint pen suddenly felt obliged to send me an e-mail about it. Isn't technology wonderful. But," she added emphatically, the smile slipping, "since the world's in no danger, I'm not telling them about the angel until we absolutely have to. There's no point giving them more to discuss, is there? They'll all start telling me we should have used precautions."

"We did."

"Metaphysical precautions."

"Oh." Cleaning already spotless glasses on the edge of his T-shirt gave him a moment to find the right words. "Claire, I'm not happy with our . . . with what we do, being discussed, you know, electronically."

"I'm not happy about it either," she admitted, tossing the laptop to one side. "But all they know that the Earth moved. Nothing specific. Without details, they won't discuss it for long."

"The Earth moved?"

"Well, only around the Pacific Rim . . ." Rising up onto her knees, she took the edge of his earlobe between her teeth. ". . . so you needn't get too impressed with yourself."

He twisted, caught her around the waist, and they fell back on the bed locked together.

"Hey! Watch the tail!"

"Oops, sorry, Austin." As Dean sat up, Claire rolled off the bed, grabbing a pillow in one hand, scooping Austin up with the other. "And thanks for reminding me that you'll be starting out in the bathroom tonight."

"Oh, please. I have no interest in watching the two of you do whatever it is the two of you are intending to do."

"I'm not so much concerned about the watching," she told him, adjusting her hold, "as I am about the commenting and the criticizing."

"Look, if you can't take a little criticism . . ."

"Good night, Austin."

He glared at her as she set the pillow down just inside the bathroom door and then set him on it. "This is cat abuse. You'll be hearing from my lawyer."

"Would a salmon treat forestall litigation?"

"No. But a salmon might."

"Dream on." Handing over the treat, she pulled the door closed. "Feel free to join us after we go to sleep."

"Uh, Claire . . ." Dean nodded toward the door. "How can he join us if that's closed?"

"A closed door has never stopped a determined cat."

"Uh-huh." His T-shirt stopped halfway up his torso. "So you're saying he can come out any time, then?"

"No." Smiling, she reached into the possibilities and laid them against the latch plate. "He can come out when that wears off."

Austin's indignant, "Cheater!" was muffled but distinct.

"I'm sorry, Claire. This has never happened before."

"You've only done it once before."

"And this didn't happen!"

Rising up on one elbow, she bent forward and kissed him softly. "Just relax." Kissed him a little harder. "Everything's going to be fine." Kissed him with more enthusiasm. Stopped kissing him. Leaned back. "Or maybe not. You're so tense I could bounce quarters off you . . . well, off most of you. . . . What's wrong?"

"Nothing."

"Is it me?"

"You?" Her question had been delivered with a total absence of emotion. Without his glasses, he couldn't tell for sure if she looked hurt or angry. "It's not you. It's nothing."

"And I know when you're lying, remember?"

Dean sighed and surrendered. "Okay." He stared up at the tiny red dot on the hotel room's smoke detector and thanked all the gods who might be listening that Austin was in the bathroom. "I can't stop thinking about what happened the last time, and it's got me some caudled up, I can tell you."

"Shouldn't those be happy thoughts?" Deep burgundy fingernails tapped against his skin in a way that should have been enough to raise a reaction all on its own. It wasn't.

His cheeks flamed. "Not those thoughts. I keep thinking about how we made an angel."

"And you're worried it'll happen again?"

"No . . ."

"You're worried it won't?" His silence was all the answer she needed. "But we don't want it to happen again."

"But you want it to be that good."

"Well . . ."

"Good enough to make an angel."

"Yes, but . . ."

"That's *some* good."

All at once, she understood. "You're afraid you won't be that good again!"

A faint "I heard that," sounded from the bathroom.

Dean closed his eyes. *That* was all he needed to finish the night off right.

Resting her chin on his sternum, Claire considered the situation. She supposed she could see how ripping a hole through the fabric of the universe big enough to slip an angel through the very first time he had sex might cause Dean some performance anxiety. She didn't know what to do about it though. "Dean, you can't expect to make an angel every time."

"I know."

Now she was really confused. "Well, then . . ."

"It's not about knowing. It's about *knowing*." He waved his outside arm for emphasis, hoping that its shadow movement through the dark would add clarity.

It didn't.

"It's me, isn't it?"

NINE

VAGUELY AWARE HE WAS BEING PULLED FROM SLEEP, Dean sighed deeply and arched his back. He could feel the sheet sliding away, warm air currents brushing against him, and . . . His eyes snapped open. "Claire, what are you doing?"

She smiled up at him. "Solving the angel prob . . ." Glancing down, she sighed. "Okay, should have worded *that* differently."

"Claire!"

"I just thought that if you got going without thinking about things, momentum would keep you going. And it was working." In the dim winter light seeping around the edges of the hotel curtains, she looked distinctly miffed. "I should never have said the 'a' word."

He fumbled for his glasses. "Claire, I'm sorry."

"No, I'm sorry."

"You're both pathetic."

Ears burning, Dean dragged a blanket around his waist and slid out of bed. "I've, uh . . . you know . . . bathroom."

"Try a verb," Austin snorted from a pile of Claire's clothes on the unused bed.

As the bathroom door closed behind Dean—and then opened again as he pulled the blanket inside—Austin leaped carefully to Claire's side. "Do you want me to talk to him, *mano a mano*?"

"Thanks for the offer, but no."

"Why not?"

"Well, to begin with, you had your mano removed."

"Not my idea."

"Still." She stroked the velvet fur between his ears with her thumb. "I think this is something Dean and I have to work out on our own."

"You mean something Dean has to work out on his own. It's not actually about you."

Claire shook her head. "You're wrong."

"Of course, I'm wrong." Austin sat down and curled his tail around his front toes. "This has nothing to do with a young man who desperately wants to make you happy and, because of an inadvertent angelic evocation, is afraid he'll never be able to make you that happy again. Oh, no, this has to do with you being older and more experienced so that he's intimidated. Or it has to do with you being a Keeper because he wouldn't have caused an angel if you weren't. Or it has to do with you being a Keeper and therefore responsible for everything under the sun.

"That was sarcasm, wasn't it?"

The cat sighed. "Duh."

"So what should I do? No, wait." A raised hand cut off his reply. "Don't tell me. I should feed the cat."

"Good choice." Jumping from the bed to the dresser, he sat down again by his food dish. "You see how much easier life becomes when you concentrate on the essentials?"

The hair Diana had found in Father Harris' house was very dark at the bottom and very blond at the tip. The style was popular with the male trendies at her school, but she'd never considered it an especially angelic look. Apparently, Lena did.

Technically, the angel—Samuel—was none of her business. Technically, he wasn't Keeper business at all.

"Mom? Do you have any clear packing tape?"

Attention on breakfast preparations, Martha pointed across the kitchen with the spatula. "It's in the junk drawer."

Junk accumulates. Even those with very little, those chased from their homes by war or natural disaster, those for whom home is no more than a rough shack or a circle of barely roofed thatch, even they find themselves accumulating odds and ends for which they have no immediate need. In North American kitchens, the junk drawer can be found two drawers below the cutlery, just above the drawer holding the clean dish towels.

"It's jammed."

"Jiggle it."

Even in houses with no more metaphysical content than could be found in a frozen, microwavable dinner—which at that, has more metaphysical content than actual food content—these drawers contain far more than is physically possible.

"Dart of Abaris, elf shot, scissors, string, Philosopher's Stone, half a dozen ponytail elastics . . ." Diana's eyes widened as she dumped the cloth-covered elastics into a small golden chalice. "Do you even care we could get big bucks for this thing on eBay?" she demanded, brandishing a tiny beanbag polar bear with a maple leaf on his chest.

Her mother glanced up from the toaster. "E what?"

"Gack. Am I the only person in this family who pays attention to *this* century?"

"Yes."

"Explains a lot," she muttered, shoving three plastic forks and a discolored envelope of dried mugwort aside to finally pull out the packing tape. "I'll be heading into the closet later, so don't worry if you can't find me."

"Diana, we talked about this . . ."

She sighed and grabbed a piece of toast on her way out of the kitchen. "I'm not going to *consciously* impose my will on the Otherworld."

"Again."

Continuing down the hall, she raised her voice without turning. "It was an accident, Mother."

"It's always an accident, Diana, but no one likes replacing all their closet doors."

"It's not like I didn't apologize," she muttered, shoving the last of the toast in her mouth and grabbing her coat and boots from the front hall. "And, hey, not my bad the tabloids got involved; if you don't want people to know you have skeletons in your closet, don't keep skeletons in your closet." It had been sheer bad luck for that British Keeper that the force of the explosion had blown the tibia out the window and onto the street.

Back in her bedroom with the door securely closed and warded behind her, Diana threw her coat on the bed, pulled off a piece of tape about twenty centimeters long, picked up the angel hair with it, and wrapped it around her wrist. While she hadn't exactly lied to her mother—she *was* going into the closet—she'd neglected to mention that she planned on going out the other side, a maneuver generally considered too dangerous to attempt.

The only reason Keepers exited at the same place they entered was plain old lack of imagination as far as Diana was concerned. So what if there were no other geographical references to the real world—she had that covered.

And all she had to do was make a phone call.

"Isn'titabeautifulmorning!Lookatthewaythesnowsparkles!"

Doug sucked muffin out of his teeth. "First cup of coffee, kid?"

"Ican'tbelieveI'vebeenherefortwodaysandIonlyjustdiscoveredthis." Grinning broadly, Samuel raced down the front steps of St. Mike's and back up again.

"You have to remember to breathe, kid."

"I do?" Well, now he did. Sucking in a huge lungful of cold air, he started to cough.

"Cough into your cupped hands," Doug told him. "Then you breathe in the warmed air."

It took Samuel a minute to catch on, then another minutes for his lungs to get the idea. Finally, eyes watering, nose running, he looked up and gasped, "Ow."

Doug nodded agreeably. "Life's a bitch."

"A female dog?" Samuel asked, wiping various bodily fluids off his face before they froze.

"Oh, yeah."

And things were just starting to make sense. . . . Trying to work out this new worldview, Samuel turned, stiffened, and raced down to the sidewalk. "Are you crazy?" he demanded, yanking the cigarette out from between cracked lips and throwing it on the ground. "You're destroying your body! You only get *one*, you know."

Craig Russel, who'd been smoking since he was twelve and in better economic times had maintained a two-pack-a-day habit, peered out at Samuel from between the tattered ear flaps of his deerstalker, then down at his cigarette lying propped almost on end by a bit of dirty snow. Not entirely certain what had just happened, he squatted and extended fingers stained yellow-brown with nicotine.

"Didn't you hear me?" Samuel ground the cigarette into pieces and the pieces into the snow. "Those things are bad for you!"

Grizzled brows drew in. "You smashed my smoke."

"Well, yeah. It's poison."

"You smashed my smoke." Craig stood, slowly, and leaned forward to stare into Samuel's face. "My last smoke."

Eyes beginning to water again, Samuel leaned back. "Do you have any idea how bad those things made your breath sm . . ." His mouth opened and closed a few more times, but no sound emerged. Up on his toes, back arched, he pushed at the air with stiff fingers.

"Let him go, Craig."

"He smashed my smoke. My last smoke."

"Yeah, I know, but you keep hold of his balls any longer and people'll start to talk."

Craig stared down at his right hand as though he recognized neither it nor the crushed fabric and flesh it held. "He smashed my . . ."

"No shit. But I bet he's really, really sorry." Scratching at a scab buried deep in the stubble on his chin, Doug turned a bloodshot gaze on the younger man. "Ain't you, kid?"

Samuel nodded. Vigorously. The pigeon about to land on his head banked left and settled on his shoulder. A second pigeon, following close behind, touched down on the other side.

"Oh, man." Eyes wide, Craig opened his hand and backed away. "He's got pigeons!"

Three.

Four.

Craig turned and ran.

Bent nearly double, both hands cupping his crotch, Samuel whimpered. Five pigeons landed on his back, jostling for space.

"You shouldn't of smashed Craig's smoke, kid."

"But they're . . . bad for . . . him."

Finally freeing the scab, Doug flicked it away. "Worse for you."

That was hard to argue with. "He's stronger than . . . he looks."

"Yep."

Finally beginning to get his breath back, Samuel cautiously straightened, dumping the five pigeons into the feathered crowd gathered around his feet. "Is there an up side to these things?" he demanded, cautiously pulling fabric away from his body. "They've been nothing but trouble since I got them."

"Them? Oh. Them. Well, there's girls."

"What do they have to do with girls?"

Doug frowned thoughtfully. "I forget."

Half a block away, a pay phone began to ring. The diaspora of street people fanning out from St. Mike's paused as one, then began moving again. Phones had nothing to do with them.

"Half a mo, kid. That's probably my bookie." A little more than half a minute later, he was back. "Not mine, kid. Yours."

"But I don't have a bookie."

"Que sera. She still wants to talk to you."

The pigeons reluctantly gave way before him and fell in behind.

Samuel picked up the phone—patented by Alexander Graham Bell in 1876, and he had no idea why he knew that but didn't know which end he was supposed to speak into. Finally, he figured it out. "Hello?"

"Samuel? My name is Diana, and I'm a Keeper. Do you know what a Keeper is?"

"The people who maintain the metaphysical balance of good on this world."

"Ta dah."

He thought about everything he'd seen and heard over the last two days, especially about the things he'd heard last night in the shelter. "You're not doing a very good job."

"Give me a break, I'm still in high school. I want to meet you, so I need you to do me a favor. Find a closet door, open it enough to get your arm through, and wave it around."

"Wave it?"

"Your arm. When I grab your hand, pull me through to your side."

"You'll fit through a space I can get my arm through?"

"Excuse me?"

"You said . . ."

"Yeah, I know what I said. You can open the door a little wider when you pull me through."

"Oh." He wondered if she was pretty. Then he wondered why it mattered. Then he found himself wondering about her breasts. He had a feeling he shouldn't be, but he couldn't seem to stop.

"Samuel?"

He pushed a pigeon out of the phone booth. "How do you know my name?"

"Father Harris told me. Are you all right?"

"My genitalia hurts."

"What have you been . . . never mind. I don't want to know. *Can* you find a closet door?"

Samuel sighed and shrugged even though he knew the Keeper couldn't see him. "Sure."

"Brillig. I'll be there as fast as I can."

St. Patrick was right. There *was* something funny about that boy. Lacing up her boots, Diana went over their conversation but couldn't put her finger on it. For an angel, he'd sounded pretty much like any of the guys she went to school with, right down to that last, irritating *"Sure."*

Minus the comment about the genitalia.

Or given a different choice of words at the very least.

She shoved her arms into her jacket, stuffed her hat and mittens into the outside pockets, checked her inside pocket for her wallet, and stepped into the closet, pulling the door closed but not latching it behind her. She'd have preferred to be traveling with her backpack, her computer, and her cell phone, but the possibilities reacted badly to electronics. Last time she tried to take her computer in with her, every window in the Otherworld had to be closed and reopened before things stabilized.

Tripping over a pile of shoes propelled her half a dozen staggering steps into the darkness. Arms flailing, she finally regained her balance after careening off a number of hard objects she couldn't identify through the bulk of her jacket.

"Stupid goose down . . . makes me look like the Michelin Man."

Stupid winter.

Stupid cold.

"Like it would've killed my parents to have settled outside of Disney World?" she asked the darkness. The darkness answered with the distant strains of a familiar theme song. Wincing, she redirected her concentration toward the angel, wondering just what made subconscious control of the Otherworld so different from conscious control.

Worse luck that Samuel wasn't in Florida. She could use a break from late December in Canada.

It grew lighter.

The ground compacted under her boots.

A jack pine dropped a load of snow down the back of her neck.

"Oh, man!"

By the time she finished dancing around, flapping the snow away, it was fully light. Or as light as it was going to get at any rate. Snow-covered hills rolled away into the distance. To her right, a jagged rock outcrop rose up only a little grayer than the sky. To her left, and pretty much directly above her, evergreens bowed under their burden of snow.

Blowing out a disgusted plume of air, Diana dug for hat and mitts thinking that Mrs. Green, her CanLit teacher, 'd be creaming herself at so much landscape and isolation. "Yeah, right," she muttered, dragging her hat over her ears. "Like Canada in late December doesn't include coffee shops and Boxing Day sales. Couldn't have landed in an Otherworld Starbucks or HMV, oh, no. *That* would be too easy."

What made subconscious control of the Otherworld so different from conscious control? Well, that was obvious: conscious control created a place where people actually wanted to be.

She couldn't see the angel's arm.

Which wasn't surprising since there weren't any doors.

"You can't go back in there, kid."

Samuel paused, one hand on the small door leading into St. Mike's. "Why not? It's a House of Light, and I'm an angel."

"Well, yeah, but the priests get all bent out of shape if you hang out inside during the day. They got stuff to do, you know."

"I won't get in the way. I have to stick my arm into a closet."

"Why?"

"It's for a girl."

"Hey." Both Doug's hands went up. "Say no more re amore. You go put your arm in a closet, and I'll be waiting right here when they toss your ass back into the cold."

"Sure." Hurrying along the side of the sanctuary, he found himself really loving that word. It was a good, all-purpose sort of a word. "Sure," he told himself softly. It could mean anything. Passing a niche holding a statue of Mary cradling an infant Christ, he smiled up at her. "Sure," he said.

"And just what does that mean?" she demanded, shifting the baby to her other hip.

"You know . . ."

"If I knew, I wouldn't have asked. Stand up straight, Samuel, don't slouch. And what have you done to your hair?"

"Um . . ." He touched his head. He hadn't done anything to his hair. Had he? "I, uh, have to go put my arm in a closet."

"Fine. Just remember to clean up when you're done."

"Sure. I mean, okay."

"Teenagers," the statue sighed as he hurried away.

"I refuse to believe my subconscious had anything to do with this," Diana sighed.

"Beg pardon, Miss?"

"Never mind." She settled back in the furs, left arm held out, coat shoved up, mitt shoved down. As they came out from under the trees and started across a rolling expanse of snow, the glowing angel's hair taped around her wrist began to fade. When she pointed to the right, the driver, a pure white Alaskan Malamute, leaned out, barking, "Gee! Gee!"

The seven Mounties in the traces angled to the right, the sled came around, and the hair began to glow strongly again.

The Mounties were fresh and running well. They were making good time.

Standing in the basement of St. Mike's with his arm stuffed into a broom closet, Samuel wondered why his hand was getting cold.

❖   ❖   ❖

"There's the trading post, Miss. Smells like we've found your exit."

Diana sniffed at the frigid air, then rubbed her nose with the back of her mitten. "All I can smell is aftershave."

"I had the Mounties groomed this morning."

"Let's just not go there, okay?"

The hair taped to her wrist blazed, and an answering light waved up and down at the trading post door. It disappeared for a moment then, just as Diana was beginning to worry, it reappeared again. A closet, wardrobe, armoire, or the like was necessary to enter the Otherworld but any door would do for a way out. Under normal circumstances, walking into the trading post with an intent to travel would put her back in her bedroom, but Samuel straddled both worlds as a metaphysical construct, and could, therefore, anchor an exit. Diana had thought out the theory very carefully.

Checking the ancient texts . . .

Consulting the mystic oracles . . .

Watching the *National Geographic* special on PBS . . .

Actually, the idea had come to her at two a.m. when a particularly loud whir/click from her clock radio had pulled her from a dream where she seemed to be either Sharon Stone or Barney Rubble. Which was in no way connected to anything much.

Since here she was and there was Samuel, the theory seemed sound and nothing more would have been accomplished even had she checked, consulted, and spent the evening with public television instead of Laura Croft.

By the time the sled pulled up in front of the trading post, Diana had untangled herself from the furs. Swinging both legs over the side, she sank up to her boot tops in the snow, staggered and would have fallen had the husky not stretched out a foreleg to help her. "Thank you." Balance regained, she moved away from the runners, just barely managing to resist a totally inappropriate urge to rub his tummy.

"Glad to be of service, Miss." He touched the edge of a pointed ear with one paw, whistled to his Mounties, and rode off into a convenient and localized sunset.

Diana watched them disappear, then climbed the thick plank stairs toward the light. Which disappeared.

❖   ❖   ❖

Samuel rubbed his arm where the door kept closing on it and wished the Keeper would hurry.

The light reappeared, and from beyond it, Diana heard a voice say: "Why the hell does that damned door keep opening?"

Then the light disappeared again.

"Ow!"

Appeared.

"There's nothing wrong with the damned latch."

Disappeared.

"OW!"

Appeared.

This time, Diana had her mitten off. She reached into the light, felt fingers close around hers, and kicked the door open.

She heard the unmistakable hollow impact of wood hitting forehead, half an expletive, and then she was standing in a dim basement staring into the gold-flecked eyes of the angel. She could see the light he was made of, and that was good, but that wasn't all she could see, and that was bad. Standing almost nose to nose, she realized he wasn't much taller than she was and unthreateningly attractive in a boy band sort of way.

"Thanks for hurrying," he muttered, releasing her hand and cradling his arm against his chest.

Diana blinked. "Are angels allowed to be that sarcastic?"

"Apparently."

"Hey! What are you kids doing down there?"

They turned together to face the middle-aged nun stomping toward them.

"*Please,* excuse us, Sister. We were just leaving."

She stopped in mid-stomp. "Right. Fine. Get going, then!"

"You can't do that to a servant of the light," Samuel protested as they hurried up the stairs.

"Yeah, I can. Just did."

"But you're not supposed to."

"Did you want to explain what we were doing down there to Sister Mary I've-spent-more-years-teaching-teenagers-than-you've-been-alive-so-don't-give-me-any-lip?"

"Her name is Sister Mary Francis."

"So what? Look, Samuel, some things you can explain to Bystanders, some things you can't. Pulling a Keeper out of a closet is totally can't."

They retraced Samuel's path along the Sanctuary. He carefully avoided eye contact with the statue of the Holy Mother.

Half a dozen pigeons waited with Doug on the front steps. As Samuel stepped outside, they started toward him, noticed Diana, and came to a sudden, feather ruffling stop.

"The flying rats with you?" she sighed.

"Sort of. I can't get rid of them."

"Not a problem." She raked a disdainful gaze over the birds and without raising her voice said, "Scram."

A moment later, the steps were clear, a lone feather lost in the panic the only indication the pigeons had ever been there at all.

"Why didn't it work when I did that?" Samuel muttered, hands shoved into his pockets.

"You wouldn't hurt them, and they knew that. I, on the other hand, am perfectly capable of roasting them with a few chestnuts over an open fire and they knew that, too."

"But you wouldn't."

"You don't know that."

The gold flecks swirled into the brown. "Yes, I do."

"Stop it!"

"Kids, kids, kids." Doug heaved himself up onto his feet and walked over. "Not the place to be spatting."

"Spatting?" Diana wrinkled her nose at the smell. "Who are you?"

"This is Doug, he's an angel, too. He taught me how to eat, how to urinate . . ."

"Eww, gross."

". . . where to sleep. I wouldn't have gotten through last night without him."

"You'd have managed, kid."

Diana snorted. *"You're an angel?"*

He spread his arms. The smell intensified. "Fuckin' A. But my work here is done." Sliding sideways a step, he elbowed Samuel in the ribs. "You've got your girlie to take care of you now, kid. Me, I hear a bottle of . . ." His brows drew in. "Doesn't really matter what's in the bottle, come to think of it." A grayish tongue swept over dry lips. "But something's callin' me, that's for shittin' sure. See ya, kid."

"See you, Doug."

Watching Doug descend to the sidewalk and head north, Diana couldn't think of a less likely angel—although she supposed it was a harmless enough delusion. "Come on, I'm freezing, let's walk."

Samuel shrugged. "Sure."

At the sidewalk, she glanced back up at the impressive front of the cathedral. And frowned. It had been snowing lightly, enough to obliterate all but the most recent footprints. A single line matching her boots led up to the wide double doors. She looked down at Samuel's feet, then she looked north. The snow lay like an ivory carpet, surface unbroken to the corner.

"Son of a . . ."

A small dog trotting by on the other side of the street paused expectantly.

Diana waved him on. "Never mind."

"Claire!"

Down on one knee by the side of the road, Claire waved at Dean to be quiet. She almost had the stupid hole closed and . . .

Grabbing her under both arms, Dean threw her back toward the truck just as the SUV fishtailed across the highway, slid right over the hole, and came to an abrupt halt at the edge of the ditch.

Claire stared at the skid marks, noted that the heavy vehicle would have gone right through her, then squirmed around in Dean's arms. "Thank you," she said, and pulled his mouth down to hers. After a moment, in spite of heavy clothes and subzero temperatures, she got the distinct impression that they could solve the angel problem right there.

"I should see if the buddy in the car's all right, then," he murmured, separating their mouths only far enough to speak.

"You should." She flicked her tongue against his lips and slid her hand up under his coat.

Dean jerked back and slammed his head into the truck. "Lord t'undering Jesus, Claire! Your fingers are like ice!"

"Sorry."

He touched a hand to the back of his head and winced. "It's okay."

"No, it's not okay. That sounded like it really hurt."

"Hey, Florence Nightingale." Austin's head appeared over the tail-gate. "The man knows if he's okay. Get back to work. I'm freezing my furry little butt off out here!"

"You could have stayed in the truck," Claire reminded him as she stood and wondered if it was against some sort of guy code to help Dean to his feet.

Austin flicked his ear to dislodge a snowflake. "I had to use the little cat room. Now, you," he fixed Dean with a baleful glare, "check the yuppie mobile. You . . ." The single eye switched targets. ". . . close the hole. And you . . ." Lifting his head, he scowled at the sky. ". . . stop snowing on me. I'm old."

"Austin, that's not . . ."

A sudden gust of wind blew the last flakes sideways. No more fell.

Only the front wheels of the SUV had gone into the ditch; a good two thirds remained firmly on the wide shoulder. The engine purred quietly to itself, the sound barely audible and nothing came out of the exhaust in spite of the cold. It was a deep maroon with a high gloss finish that looked like it could withstand a meteor strike and, in spite of four-wheel drive and heavy duty suspension, this was likely as far off road as it had ever been.

Squinting through the tinted glass, Dean realized the thin, blonde woman behind the wheel was on the phone. When he tapped on the driver's door window, she opened it a finger's width but continued looking down at the laptop open on the leather upholstery of the passenger seat. "Ma'am, you don't need to call for a tow. You're barely off the road; you can just back up."

She ignored him and kept talking. ". . . telling you the bank beat by nine cents the average estimate of sixty cents a share."

"Ma'am?"

A slender hand in a burgundy leather glove waved vaguely in his direction. "But you're forgetting that volatile capital markets allowed a forty-five percent increase in fees, and that's where you can attribute most of the profit growth."

"I'm after heading back to my truck now."

"Look, Frank, it was loan volumes that brought the interest income up nine percent to three hundred and thirty-seven million dollars."

"Ma'am?"

"Three hundred and thirty-seven million dollars, Frank!"

"Never mind."

Claire and Austin were waiting inside the truck.

"I guess the driver's all right," Dean told them as Claire lifted Austin off the driver's seat and onto her lap, "but she wouldn't actually talk to me."

"She? Should I go?"

"Got three hundred and thirty-seven million dollars?" When Claire answered in the negative, he grinned. "Then I doubt she'll talk to you either." Putting his glasses back on after carefully wiping the condensation off the lenses, he frowned. "What's wrong?"

"A new Summons; stronger than these little roadside things." She rested her chin on the top of Austin's head. "It feels strange."

"Is it the angel, then? 'Cause if I wasn't scared abroad by Hell, an angel won't trouble me much."

"I don't think so."

"Only one way to find out." He pulled carefully onto the highway. "Which way?"

"North."

"So, dear, when you call yourself a demon—is that a club?"

"No." Byleth sagged farther down in the back seat, the shoulder belt preventing a really good slouch. "It's not a fu . . ."

"Language." Half turning, Eva raised a cautioning finger.

"It's not a club." Byleth had no idea how the mortal woman did it. Something about her tone of voice, her expression, evoked an instinctive obedience. If the Princes of Hell could figure it out, they'd be . . .

well, since they were already ruling Hell, nothing much would change but the shouting. Hell could do with a little less shouting in Byleth's opinion.

"It's not a gang, is it?" Harry asked, trying to catch her gaze in the rearview mirror. "Because I know how seductive gangs can be. Black leather and motorcycles and . . ."

"Harry."

Under the edge of his tweed hat, Harry's ears pinked.

Eva half turned again. "Harry had a bit of a past before he met me."

"I'll bet he did," the demon muttered.

"What was that, dear?"

"It's *not* a gang."

"Oh, that's good."

The day was not going as planned. Coercing the old man into driving her to Toronto had somehow turned into a cheerful family outing. With snacks. She should have walked out right after that big homemade breakfast and found some punk kid who'd just got his license and who'd do anything she asked if she just bounced those really annoying breasts at him in a promising sort of a way. Not that she'd keep the promise, of course. Her kind excelled at broken promises.

"Shall we play license plate bingo, dear?"

Fortunately Harry answered before she could.

"Byleth's too old for that, Eva. Remember what our lot were like at her age?"

"The boys," Eva began, but Harry cut her off, one hand leaving the steering wheel just long enough to pat a rounded knee.

"The boys played to make you happy, but our Angela drew the line about the same time she started high school."

"I suppose," Eva sighed. Then she perked up and half turned one more time. "Where do you go to high school, dear?"

"I don't."

"Oh, you have to get an education, dear. After all, knowledge is power."

"Power is power," Byleth snarled. She should have power. She should be able to reach into the dark heart of humanity and twist it to her purposes. Not only had some extra anatomy put an unexpected crimp in her plans—and she was so going to kick that angel's ass when she found him—but her current minions gave her very little to work with.

"Hey, Mr. Porter, that guy in the import flipped you the finger as he passed."

Which is not to say she didn't do what she could.

"Harry, that's no reason for you to drive faster," Eva warned.

He smiled at her briefly. "Of course not."

But the speed crept up.

It didn't take much to keep it rising.

The inevitable siren brought a smile and a frisson of anticipation.

Lips pressed into a disapproving line, Eva kept silent as Harry pulled over and turned off the engine.

Behind them, a car door slammed and footsteps approached along the gravel shoulder. When Harry rolled down his window, Byleth straightened to get a better look.

"License and registration, please."

The Ontario Provincial Police constable was tall and tanned, his hair gleaming gold in the winter sunlight. His eyes were blue, his voice was deep, and his chin had the cutest cleft. The breadth of his shoulders filled the window.

"Do you know how fast you were going, sir?"

In the back seat, Byleth sat up straighter, tugging at her jacket.

"I'm sorry, Officer. Some kid passed me in a sporty little import, and I guess I just rose to the challenge."

A quick swipe of her tongue across her lips. Did she still have any lipstick on? She *knew* she should have put more on at the last rest stop.

"You can't let other people do the driving in your car, sir."

That was clever. He wasn't only the cutest thing she'd seen since she arrived, he was *smart*, too.

"Now 113km in an 80 should be a three-hundred-dollar fine and six points off your license, but . . ."

Why didn't he look at her?

". . . I'm going to let you off with a warning. This time. If I pull you over again . . ." His voice trailed off.

And he was merciful.

Handing back Harry's paperwork, he finally glanced into the back seat, but his gaze slid over her like she was completely unworthy of being noticed.

Arms folded, brows in, she slid back into her slouch, achieving new lows. What the hell did she care about merciful anyway?

"Thank you, Officer."

"Drive safely, sir. Have a good day, ma'am. Miss."

Her eyes narrowed. "Whatever."

He glanced into the back again, then he smiled at Harry. "Teenagers, eh?"

"Teenagers, eh?" Byleth mocked as the officer returned to his cruiser. "What a jerk."

"Good-looking man, though. Wasn't he, dear?"

"I never noticed. And what are you smiling about?" she demanded as the Porters exchanged an amused glance.

"Nothing."

"Good." Glaring straight ahead, she refused to acknowledge the police car as it passed, repeating, "Jerk. Jerk. Jerk. Jerk," vehemently under her breath.

"Careful, Austin." Scooping him back up onto the seat, Claire wore a worried expression. "Are you all right? You were sound asleep, and then . . ."

"And then I wasn't. Yeah, I know." He got his legs untangled and climbed over to her right thigh, where he could stand and look out the window. "Something we passed woke me up."

"Do you want me to pull over?" Dean asked.

"No." He put a paw on the glass and watched the traffic across the median speeding south. "It's gone now."

TEN

—————✦—————

"**Y**OU ARE *SO* NOT LIKE WHAT I IMAGINED an angel to be. Your hair, your clothes . . ."

"My genitalia," Samuel added a little mournfully.

Diana made a disgusted face and shoved mittened hands deeper into her pockets. "I wouldn't know, and I'd really rather you quit mentioning it."

"Them."

"What*ever.*"

"Why?" For no good reason, he jumped up and smacked the No Parking sign, checking out of the corner of one eye to see if the Keeper was impressed. She didn't seem to be.

"They're just not something people talk about in public."

"Should we go someplace private?"

"You wish."

"For what?"

"Pardon?"

"What do I wish for?"

"Well, if you don't know, I'm not going to tell you."

"But if I knew, you wouldn't have to tell me," he pointed out reasonably as they turned the corner onto Yonge Street. Across the road, a double line of people stood stamping their feet and blowing on their hands. "Those people are cold. Why are they standing there?"

"Best guess, they're waiting to get into the electronics store for the Boxing Day sale."

"Why?"

"What do you mean, why? Because it's a sale." She rolled her eyes. "I thought you had Higher Knowledge."

"I do. The 26th of December is called Boxing Day because in Victorian England that's when the rich boxed up their Christmas leftover for the poor."

"Really?"

"It's one theory. But it still doesn't explain that." He waved a hand at the crowd across the street. "Most of those people are anxious, over half are actually unhappy, and although they'll be saving money, they'd all be better off if they just didn't spend it. A new stereo won't give meaning to their empty, shallow lives."

Diana grabbed the back of his jacket as he stepped off the curb. "Where are you going?"

"To tell them that."

"I'm just guessing here, but I think they know."

He half-turned in her grip. "Really?"

"Uh-huh. It's a human thing; a new stereo will help them *forget* their empty shallow lives."

"Human memory is that bad?"

"Well, duh. Why do you think platform shoes and mini skirts have come back? Because people have forgotten how truly dorky they looked the first time." Diana shuddered. "Me, I've seen my mother's yearbook pictures." She hauled him back up onto the sidewalk. "You hungry?"

"Starving."

"You're not supposed to be." His situation had deteriorated farther than she'd feared. "Come on, I'll buy you . . ." She checked her watch. ". . . lunch and we'll talk."

". . . and that's why you're here." Diana peered over the pile of fast food wrappers in front of the angel. "Are you blushing?"

"You said your sister . . . you know," he mumbled.

"I really think you've got more to worry about than my sister's sex life." Elbows up on the table, she ticked the points off on her fingers. "One, angels are, by definition, messengers of the Lord, but because of the way you came into being, you have no message, thus leaving you with a distinct identity crisis."

"Thus?"

"Don't interrupt. Two, you can't return to the light, so you're stuck here even though you have no reason to be here and no visible means of support. Three, from what I've seen so far, the boy bits seem to be doing all the defining."

"The what?"

She sighed. "Don't make me say it."

"Oh. Them. No, they're not."

"Yeah, they are."

"No."

"Yes. You shouldn't be perpetually hungry. You shouldn't know what a six-liter engine is." Her eyes narrowed. "And you shouldn't be looking at my breasts!"

Ears burning, he locked his gaze on her right eyebrow. "You're a Keeper. You could send me back."

"Only if you want to go." Pushing a desiccated French fry around with a fingertip, she sighed again. This was, after all, why she'd come to Toronto. It had only taken a small prod from St. Patrick for her to realize that an angel designed by committee would need a Keeper's help to go home—her help. "The problem is," she said slowly, "if I send you back, you won't be you anymore. You'd just be light."

"But that's what I am."

Diana shook her head. "That's not all you are. If I send you back, then the you that I'm talking to, the you that's experienced the world, he'll disappear. I'll have killed him."

"Killed me?" When she nodded, he frowned. "That sucks."

"Tell me about it."

"You already know about it."

"Figure of speech, Samuel. I was agreeing with you." She dropped her chin onto her hands. "I don't know what to do, and I really hate that feeling."

"Tell me about it," Samuel muttered, unwrapping a fourth . . . something that seemed to involve chicken ova, a slice of pig in nitrate, and melted orange stuff probably intended to represent a dairy product. He'd eaten the first three too fast to really taste them, which all things considered, had probably been smart. "So, what you do think of the idea that I am the message? That I'm here to help people?"

"How? And don't give me that look," Diana warned him. "I'm not being mean, I'm being realistic. You can't even help yourself."

"I've been managing."

"No. You haven't. Can I think of an example? Hmmm, let's see." She leaned forward. "How about: without me, you'd be covered in pigeons."

"Well, yeah, but . . ."

"And pigeon shit."

His brows drew in. He didn't know they could do that. It was an interesting feeling. "I'm still a superior being, I can figure stuff out."

"How do you know you're a superior being?"

"I just . . . know."

"So does every other male between twelve and twenty," she snorted, folding her arms. "But that doesn't solve their problems either."

Samuel stared at her for a long moment, then he smiled. "I could be insulted, but I know you're only saying that because of your own sexual ambiguity." He took a large bite and chewed slowly. "I mean, you say you're a lesbian, but you've never actually made it with a woman although you did make it with a guy and it wasn't entirely his fault it was such a disaster."

Her lip curled. "If you were to choke right now, I wouldn't save you."

———— ·--·-- ————

They left the highway just north of Huntsville, heading southwest on 518.

"We're close," Claire insisted when Austin pointed out the total lack of anything but Canadian landscape around them.

"Close to what?" he snorted. "The edge of the world?"

"We need to turn right soon. There." She pointed. "Is that a road?"

It was. After another thirteen kilometers of spruce bog and snow, they passed the first house. Then the second. Then a boarded-up business. Then, suddenly, they were in downtown Waverton—all five blocks of it.

"Park in front of the bank."

Braking carefully, Dean peered down at the thick, milky slabs of frozen water. "I don't know, Claire; it looks some icy."

"We'll be okay."

"If you're thinking of using my kitty litter to make it okay, think again," Austin muttered, climbing up onto the top of the seat.

"You mean because I'm only a Keeper with access to an infinite number of possibilities and wouldn't be able to get this truck moving without a bag of dried clay bits designed to absorb cat urine?"

"Essentially . . ." He paused to lick his shoulder. ". . . yes."

Lips pressed into a thin line, Claire reached into the possibilities and slid the truck sideways across the nearly frictionless surface, bringing it to a gentle stop against the slightly higher ice sheet that was the curb.

Dean released the breath he'd been holding and forced the white-knuckled fingers of one hand to let go of the steering wheel long enough to switch off the engine. "You need to warn me when you're after doing something like that," he said, still staring straight ahead as though he intended to keep the truck from ending up at the New Accounts desk by visual aids alone. "Sideways is not a good way."

"Sorry."

He turned to face her then. "Really?"

"No."

"Austin!"

"Just giving him the benefit of my experience. You've never been sorry when you do that sort of thing to me."

"When have I ever . . . ?"

"Plevna. December 12th, 1997."

"How was I supposed to know claws don't provide traction? It was an honest mistake."

"Uh-huh."

Yanking her toque down over her ears, Claire got out of the truck. "He scored the winning goal," she pointed out to Dean as she closed the door.

"How did you hold the stick?" Dean wondered, pulling on his gloves.

Austin's head swiveled slowly around. "I. Didn't."

"Oh." His hindbrain decided it might be safer to back away, making no sudden moves. He caught up to Claire by the corner of the bank.

"Someone set this fire," she said, looking up at the damage. "And that opened the hole." Hugging her own elbows, she shook her head. "There's a lot of nasty coming through for the size. This might take some time to seal up; can you keep me from being disturbed?"

"You got it, Boss."

"You haven't called me that for a while."

Their eyes locked.

"You haven't told me what to do for a while."

"Maybe I should start."

"Maybe you should."

A muffled "Get a room!" from inside the truck redirected their attention to the matter at hand.

"Excuse me, Miss!" Mr. Tannison, the bank manager, hurried toward his damaged building from his temporary office across the street, upstairs over the storefront shared by Martin Eisner, the taxidermist, and Dr. Chow, the dentist. "You can't stay there. Bricks could fall." He forgot about the ice until his front boot surrendered traction and he began to slide. Before he could steady himself on the truck parked in front of the bank, a large hand caught his arm and set him back on his feet.

"It's okay, sir. She's perfectly safe."

"She is?" Something about the young man made him feel like a fool for asking. He considered himself a good judge of character—well, he had to be in his position, didn't he?—and by voice, expression, and bearing, this stranger said, *I will have my withdrawal slip filled out properly before I approach the teller, I would never stand too close at the ATM machine, and your pens are sacred to me.*

"Yes, sir."

"Oh." The blue eyes behind the glasses made him think of contributions to retirement savings plans done monthly rather than left until the last minute. "You're not from around here, are you?"

"No, sir, St. John's. Newfoundland."

"Small world. One of my tellers is from St. John's. Rose Mooran."

"Does she have a brother named Conrad, then? I played Peewee hockey with a Conrad Mooran."

"No, not her brother, that would be her husband."

"Husband? Lord t'undering Jesus."

They spent a while longer discussing hockey and the relative size of the world, then Mr. Tannison patted a muscular arm, flashed a relieved smile, and hurried back across the street.

The clutch of eight-year-olds were a little harder to impress.

When Dean limped back to the truck, Claire was standing by the passenger door looking a little stunned.

"Is it closed?"

She nodded.

"What's wrong?"

When she held up her hand, her fingertips were dusted with black glitter.

"Char?"

"Demon residue."

"Once you're in the city, where are you planning on going, dear?"

Byleth stared out past the Porters' heads at the Toronto skyline, thrusting up into a gray sky like a not particularly attractive pot of gold at the end of a rainbow. "As far away from you as possible," she muttered.

To her surprise, Harry Porter lifted an admonishing finger toward her reflection in the rearview mirror. "That is quite enough of that, young lady. There is no call for you to be so rude. You will apologize to Mrs. Porter this instant."

"As if."

"Fine." At the first break in traffic, he moved into the right-hand lane and began slowing down.

"Harry . . ."

"No, Eva. She apologizes, or she walks the rest of the way."

Demons understood bluffing. Byleth folded her arms and waited.

When the car finally rolled to a stop, Harry put it into park and turned around. "Last chance," he said. "Apologize, or this is as far as we go together."

She tucked her chin into her collar and glowered.

"If that's the way you want it." He unbuckled his seat belt, got out, and opened her door.

When she stared up into his face through the blast of frigid air, she realized he wasn't bluffing. "You actually want me to walk. We're still miles away!"

"We're still kilometers away," Harry corrected. "And I want you to apologize. It's your choice whether or not you walk."

It was cold outside. It was warm inside the car.

"Get back in the car and drive."

He merely stood there. She might as well have tried to command a rock.

"I'll hitchhike, then, and get picked up by a mass murderer, and then how will you feel when they find a broken bleeding body by the side of the road." It wouldn't be her broken, bleeding body, but he didn't need to know that.

Harry shook his head. "Not even mass murderers would stop for you. Not at these speeds. You'll be walking all the way."

"I don't want to walk!"

"Then apologize."

The car rocked as four transports passed, belching diesel fumes. She contemplated kicking Harry into traffic, but Eva would likely fall apart and be totally useless and although she knew how to bring plagues and pestilence, she didn't know how to drive.

"Make up your mind, Byleth."

"Fine." Anything to get her into the city where she could ditch these losers. "I'm s . . ." Her very nature fought with the word. "I'm sorr . . ." She had to form each letter independently, forcing it out past reluctant lips. "I'm sorry. Okay?"

"Eva?"

"Apology accepted, dear."

"Now was that so hard?" Harry asked, smiling at her reflection as he slid back behind the wheel.

"Yeah, it was."

"Don't worry. It'll get easier with time."

She was afraid of that.

"Excuse me." Braced against the movement of the escalator, Samuel reached forward and tapped the heavyset matron on one virgin-wool covered shoulder. "The sign says that if you stand on the right, then people in a hurry can walk up the left."

"There's no space on the right," she pointed out sharply.

"Then you should have waited."

"And maybe you should mind your own business."

"You shouldn't let the fear of being on your own keep you in a bad relationship. Your husband is controlling and manipulative, and just because he doesn't love you anymore, doesn't mean you shouldn't love yourself . . ."

The sound of her palm connecting with his cheek disappeared into the ambient noise. In the fine tradition of mall crawlers everywhere, those standing too close to have missed the exchange either stared fixedly at nothing or isolated themselves from the incident behind a loud and pointless conversation with their nearest companion. As they reached the second level and the heavyset woman bustled off to the left, Diana smoothed the tiny hole closed, grabbed Samuel's arm, and yanked him off to the right.

"What was *that* all about?"

Rubbing at the mark on his cheek, he looked confused. "I was just trying to help, you know, do that message thing."

"And what help is a message telling that woman her husband's a creep who doesn't love her anymore?"

"She knows that. Now she needs to move on."

"And *you* know that because . . . ?"

He shoved his hands in his front pockets and shrugged. "I have Higher Knowledge."

"Which gives you personal information on the life of a perfect stranger but neglects to tell you what a stoplight means?"

"Yes."

She'd never heard such a load of sanctimonious crap. "Just don't do that again, okay?"

"Sure."

"Did you know that with the price of those boots you could feed a Third World child for a year?"

Something in the gold-brown eyes compelled an honest answer. "Yeah, I do."

"So . . . ?" Samuel prompted, smiling encouragingly.

"So why don't you mind your own fucking business, dude?"

"That's the guilt talking."

"Yeah?" A very large hand wound itself into the front of Samuel's jacket. "And in a minute you're gonna feel my fist talking!"

Diana handed the shoebox to the clerk and reached into the possibilities just in time to keep an innocent Bystander from committing mayhem on an angel—as justified as that mayhem may have been. Freeing Samuel's jacket, she shoved him out of the store and started things up again.

"I was just . . ."

"Well, stop it."

"But . . ."

"No. People like to have their moral failings pointed out about as much as they like to have their personal lives discussed in public by strangers." She tightened her grip and dragged him quickly past a couple playing what looked like the Stanley Cup finals of tonsil hockey. When she finally slowed and took a look at him, he seemed strangely restrained. "What?"

"Those two people . . ."

There were thousands of people in the Center, but she had a fairly good idea who he meant. "Yeah? What about them?"

"They had their tongues in each other's mouths."

"I didn't notice."

He snorted, a very unangelic sound. "They looked like they had gerbils in their cheeks."

"Okay." She had to admit she was intrigued by the image. "So?"

"So isn't that unsanitary?"

"Gerbils?"

"Tongues."

"Not really. And don't get any ideas—our relationship is strictly Keeper/Angel."

"I wasn't . . ."

"You were."

"I couldn't *help* it."

He sounded so miserable, Diana found herself patting his shoulder in sympathy. "Come on, we'll duck out at the next doors—a little cold air will clear your head."

"It's not my head."

"Whoa. Didn't I make myself clear? We're *not* discussing other body parts." If the last pat rocked him sideways a little more emphatically than necessary, well, tough.

The sidewalk outside the mall was nearly deserted. There was a small group of people huddled together at the corner of Yonge and Dundas, waiting for the streetcar, and a lone figure hurrying toward them from the other direction in what could only be described as a purposeful manner.

Hair on the back on her neck lifting, Diana stared at the approaching figure, then looked down at two identical snowflakes melting on the back of her hand. "Shit!"

"What's that smell?" Samuel muttered. He checked the bottom of both shoes.

"Forget the smell. Move it!"

She hustled the angel north, hoping that Nalo hadn't seen them. The older Keeper had no more authority over Samuel than she did, but something—the identical flakes that continued to fall, the way every car on the road was suddenly a black Buick, the street busker playing "Flight of the Bumblebee" with his lower lip frozen to his harmonica—*something* was telling her to keep them apart.

At the corner of Yonge and Dundas, Diana felt the possibilities open.

"Hold it right there, young lady!"

Grinding her teeth, she pulled a token out of necessity, shoved Samuel into the line of people climbing onto the eastbound Dundas streetcar, and told him she'd catch up later.

"But . . ."

"Trust me." She pried his fingers out of the down depths of her sleeve and, with one hand on an admirably tight tush, boosted him up the steps. "And try not to piss anyone off!" she added as the door closed. Staring back out at her through the filthy glass, he looked lost and pathetic, but she couldn't shake the feeling he was safer away from the other Keeper.

Wrapping herself in surly teenager, she turned, stepped back up onto the sidewalk, and folded her arms. "Don't call me 'young lady'," she growled, when Nalo closed the last of the distance between them. "I really, really hate it."

"Really? Tough. Now, you want to tell me why you were hauling ass away from me, or do you want me to make some guesses?"

They were alone on the corner—there'd be no help from curious Bystanders. Diana snorted and rolled her eyes. Not a particularly articulate response but useful when stalling.

"Your parents don't know you're here, do they? Don't bother denying it, girl . . ." An inarguable finger cut off incipient protest. ". . . you've got guilt rolling off you like smoke."

Perfect! True, if a tad trite. Diana could have kissed her. She widened her eyes. "You won't tell?"

"None of my business. I don't care if you're here to waste money, I don't care if you're here to see that boy you stuffed on the streetcar—oh, I saw him, don't give me that look—but I *do* care about what you've been up to since you got here."

"But I haven't done anything!"

"You stopped time, Diana."

Oops.

"I was trying to prevent a fight."

Nalo sighed. "Girl, I don't care if you were trying to prevent an Abba reunion. . . ."

"Who?"

"Never mind. The point is, you've been messing with the metaphysical background noise since you got here The whole place is buzzing."

"It wasn't me!"

"No? Then who?"

A black Buick cruised by, and Diana bit her tongue.

"Look, I spent half an hour on the phone with the 102-year-old Keeper monitoring that site in Scarborough who's positive we're heading toward a battle between the dark and the light, and I have better things to do with my time than convince the senile old bird we're not heading for Armageddon. Either tone it down or take it home, but stop screwing up my . . . what's that on your arm?"

Diana brushed away a little snow, taking the angel residue with it, and peered down at her sleeve. "Where?"

The older Keeper shook her head. "Must've been ice crystals." She tucked a cashmere scarf more securely into the collar of her coat. "I think I'd like to keep an eye on you for a while. You can join me for a bit."

Surrender seemed the only option, but she made a token protest regardless. "I can't afford the kind of restaurants you like."

"Honey, we're Keepers. We should be, if nothing else, adaptable."

"You buying?"

"I might be."

"Then I can be adaptable."

Distress bordering on panic pulled Samuel off the streetcar and across the road into a maze of four-story apartment buildings and identical rows of two-story brick town houses. He found the source of the distress crouched miserably at the bottom of a rusty slide and dropped to his knees beside her.

With gentle fingers, he brushed snow off her head.

She turned toward him, looked up into his eyes, and threw herself against his chest. "Lost, lost, lost, lost . . ."

"Shhh, it's all right, Daisy." He had to physically brace himself against the force of her emotions. "Don't worry, I'll help. Do you live in one of these buildings?"

Shivering, she pressed herself harder against him. "Lost . . ."

He could see where she'd entered the playground, but her prints were filling in fast. "Come on." Standing, he tucked two fingers under her red leather collar. "We'll have to hurry."

They weren't quite fast enough. The paw prints had disappeared under fresh snow by the time they got to River Street.

"Now where?"

The Dalmatian looked up at him with such complete trust, Samuel had to swallow a lump in his throat. Dropping to one knee on the sidewalk, he held out his hand. "Give me your paw."

She looked at him for a long moment, looked at his hand, then laid her right front paw against his palm.

He reached into himself for the light.

———

"What was that?"

Diana kept her attention on her stuffed pita. "I didn't do anything."

"Did I even mention you?" Nalo swiveled around, her right hand combing the air. "Something shifted."

"It's not a hole."

"No, it isn't." She sat down again, eyes locked on the younger Keeper. "So I guess it's none of our business."

———

The glowing paw prints led him to a town house in the Oak Street Co-op. As they turned down the walk, Daisy pulled free and raced for the door.

"Home! Home! Home!"

The door opened before she reached it, and a slender young woman rushed out and dropped to her knees throwing her arms around the dog. "You rotten, rotten old thing. How could you put me through that. Where've you been, eh?" Brushing away tears, she stood and held out a hand to Samuel. "Thank you for bringing her home. We just moved to Toronto from New Brunswick, and I think she went out looking for our old neighborhood. She doesn't have her new tags yet." Suddenly hearing her own words, she frowned. "So, without any tags, how did you find us?"

Samuel grinned, unable to resist the dog's happiness. "We followed her prints."

"Her prints, of course." As a gust of wind came around the corner, she smiled out at him from behind a moving curtain of long, curly hair. "You must be half frozen. Would you like to come in and thaw out? Maybe have a hot chocolate, eh?"

He was suddenly very cold. "Yes, please."

"In. In. In. In." Daisy insisted on being between both sets of legs, but they somehow got inside and closed the door.

Her name was Patricia, her husband's name was Bill. As Daisy enthusiastically greeted the latter, Patricia took Samuel's jacket and led him into the living room. Left on his own, he felt a heated gaze on the back of his head. Slowly he turned.

"What is it?" The long-haired apricot-and-white cat turned his head sideways and stared at Samuel with pale blue eyes. "It's awfully bright."

"It's an angel," snorted the seal-point Siamese beside him, staring down the aristocratic arch of her nose. "Or a sort of an angel anyway. Someone seems to have messed up the design."

"What's an angel?"

"It's like a cat, only with two legs, minimal fur, and no tail."

"Oh." Confused but clearly used to taking the Siamese's word for things, he wrapped a plumy apricot tail around his toes. "It almost looks as if it understands us."

"It does. Don't you?"

"Yes."

"Yes?" Patricia repeated, returning with three steaming mugs on a tray. "Oh. I see you've met Pixel and Ilea." Setting the tray on the coffee table, she scooped up the Siamese. "This is really Ilea's house. She only lets us live here because we know how to work the can opener."

That was enough to distract Samuel from the heady scent of the hot chocolate. "Really?"

Rubbing the top of her head under Patricia's chin, Ilea purred. Some questions were too stupid to need answers.

———————

"Turn here."

Dean glanced toward the boarded-up J. Henry and Sons Auto Repair and then back to Claire. "There's a big batch of snow blocking the driveway."

"Park on the side of the road, then, and we'll walk in."

When Austin made no protest, Dean sucked a speculative lungful of air through his teeth and pulled as far off the road as he could. It was one thing to have Claire explain exactly what demon residue meant and another thing entirely when the cat faced a walk over snow in subzero weather without complaint. Things were clearly some serious.

He shut off the engine and reached for his hat. "Is it Hell again?"

"I'd like to think we'd have noticed that," Claire told him, chewing nervously on the thumb of her mitten.

"Well, I'd like to notice about a half a dozen garlic shrimp," Austin pointed out acerbically, "but that doesn't mean I'll get them, and let's face facts, there was a hole to Hell in Kingston for over forty years you Keepers never knew about."

"You didn't know about it either."

"Hey, I'm the cat. I do comfort when needed and color commentary. I don't deal with metaphysical rifts in the fabric of the universe, and I don't fetch. Live with it." His single eye narrowed. "Now let's get on with it before it gets any colder out here."

The snowbank blocking the driveway was about four-and-a-half-feet high but packed hard and easy to climb over. The snow in the parking lot was almost as deep and a lot softer.

"I'd better go first to break a trail," Dean offered. "You can follow me, Austin can follow you. Which way?"

Claire pointed. A line of footprints, strangely unfilled by blowing snow stretched back behind the building. "Angels walk lightly on the world, they don't leave footprints. Demons do. Demons want people to know they've passed by because you can't tempt people who aren't paying attention."

A side door, leading into a small office, was open. Streaks of demon residue crossed the crumpled lock.

"It was in here," Claire said softly, turning in place.

"No shit, Sherlock." Austin kicked snow off first one back foot and then the other. "Its prints lead right to the door.

The Keeper ignored him. "It took something from that hook, from the back of the chair, and from under the desk. Something that's been here for a while given how thick the dust is." Reaching into the possibilities, she filled the empty spaces with spatial memory. The translucent image of a pair of overalls hung from the hooks, a jacket draped over the back of the chair, and a pair of grimy running shoes lay half on top of each other under the desk. "Clothes?"

"Demons don't wear clothes?" Dean asked, unable to resist poking a finger through the overalls as they disappeared.

"Yes, but I've never heard of a demon buying off the rack, let alone . . ." She waved a hand around the room and shuddered. "Granted they tend to be a little too fond of shoulder pads, but this is just not them."

"The footprints keep going back into the woods."

"Then that must be where the hole is, and if you say, 'No shit, Sherlock' to me one more time," she warned the cat before he could speak, "you'll be sorry."

Austin stared up at her, whiskers bristling with affronted inno-cence. "I was merely going to ask if that was where Summons came from, but if you're going to get snappy . . ."

"I'm sorry." Pulling off a mitten, she rubbed at the crease between her eyes. "The thought of a demon wandering around unremarked by the good guys has me a little tense. I'd better lead from now on," she added, walking back to the door. "If there's danger out in those woods, better a Keeper face it than a Bystander."

Although Dean didn't like it, he couldn't disagree and stepped out of her way.

"You *were* going to say 'No shit, Sherlock,' weren't you?" he asked Austin quietly when Claire had moved a few paces ahead.

The cat snorted. "Well, duh."

Claire picked her way carefully to the center of the small clearing, avoiding the worst patches of filthy snow. Squatting, she dragged her right mitt off with her teeth and extended her hand, fingers spread.

"What's all over the snow?" Dean murmured to the cat he held cradled against his chest.

Austin squirmed around to get a better look. "Darkness. When it took form, it flaked."

They watched Claire sift the air for a moment, then stand, frown-ing.

"This hole is tiny and old. It should have closed on its own and as far as passing a demon—it would have been like passing a kidney stone." She shook her head. "I could be days defining it well enough to close it."

"Gee, days spent out in the bush." Austin sighed and laid his head in the crook of Dean's elbow. "Words can't express my elation."

"You needn't get too elated," Claire told him, yanking her mitt back on. "And you needn't get too comfortable either, I'm going to need you."

"For what?"

"You get to play bad cop. Dean, maybe you should go back to the truck."

He took a deep breath and let it out slowly, wreathing his head in vapor. She was using the voice Diana referred to as more-Keeper-than-thou and, in his experience, that was never good. "Why should I go back to the truck?"

"We need answers, and we need them quickly. I'm going to gather up the darkness around the hole, and Austin's going to question it."

"The darkness?"

"It *is* substance; it should be coherent. But this is one of those 'the ends justify the means' situations and that's always tricky for the good guys." Reaching up, she broke a dead branch off an oak tree. "We'll pull more darkness from the hole. I can contain it in a circle, but it's going to want out, and you'll be the only thing it can use to break free."

"You'll be inside the circle?"

"I'm a Keeper. I can deal."

"And Austin?"

"It isn't actually possible to make a cat do something a cat doesn't want to do."

"But we try to keep that quiet," Austin added as he moved from Dean's arms to Claire's. "We learned a long time ago if people can hang onto the absurd hope that someday they'll train us to stop scratching the furniture, they'll keep handing over the salmon treats."

Dean squared his shoulder. "I'm not leaving you if you're going to be in danger."

"I'll be in more danger if you stay. And, you'll be in danger. If you leave . . ."

"I won't be able to help if you need me."

"You're fighting testosterone," Austin murmured into her ear. "Millions of years of evolution that says he has to protect his mate. You can't win."

"His mate?"

"Mate, girlfriend, old lady—all valid evolutionary terms."

"What?"

The cat sighed, his breath painfully loud up under the edge of her toque. "You know, if you watched more *National Geographic* specials and fewer after school specials . . ."

"You watch *National Geographic* to see lions mating!"

"So?"

Without the time to count to ten, Claire counted to three, looked into Dean's eyes, and reluctantly decided Austin was right. She couldn't win. If she convinced Dean to leave her, it would diminish him in his own eyes and, all things considered, further diminishing would not be a good thing.

"Okay. You can stay." His smile made the potential for disaster almost worthwhile. Deep down, she realized how completely asinine that thought was, but she couldn't seem to prevent a warm glow from rising. "Whatever happens," she murmured a moment later, leaning away from his mouth, "don't break the circle."

To Dean's surprise, the darkness gathered into a familiar form. Its legs were froglike and ended in three toes. Its arms, nearly as long as its legs, ended in three fingers and a thumb. Its eyes were small and black, and it appeared to have no teeth. Its fur and/or scales changed color constantly.

Imp.

The last time Dean had seen an imp, he'd been scraping the lumpy mass of its pulverized body out from under a sheet of wallpaper. The last time he'd seen an imp alive, it had been dangling from Austin's mouth.

The tiny piece of physical darkness sat up, looked around, squeaked something that sounded very much like "Oh, fuck," and disappeared under Austin's front paws.

Claire squatted beside the cat. "Tell us everything that went on here, and I'll pop you back through the hole before I close it."

Faint defiant squeaking.

"Wrong answer."

Austin's tail lashed and the squeaking grew louder.

"You're lying," Claire sighed.

Indignant squeaking.

"I know, it's hard for you to tell the truth. But it's hard for Austin to keep his claws sheathed, too. You don't honestly think *they'd* lie to protect you?"

Reluctant acknowledgement. From the intensity of the high-pitched torrent that followed, the imp was clearly spilling more than name, rank, and serial number.

Shifting from foot to foot, Dean tried not to think about how cold he was getting. Maybe he should have gone back to the truck. Maybe he should go now. He'd just go in and tell Claire he'd decided to leave.

Go in?

The toe of his right boot rested less than an inch from the circle Claire'd sketched in the snow with the oak branch. Backing quickly away, he tried and failed to remember moving forward. *". . . it's going to want out, and you'll be the only thing it can use to break free."* But if the darkness could reach outside the circle, did that mean the levels inside with Claire had become dangerously high? Claire was in danger. If he loved her, he had to save her!

If he loved her?

No if. In a world that had become a stranger place than he ever could have imagined, loving Claire was the one thing he was sure of. As he realized that, he realized he was standing back at the edge of the circle. He had to do something to distract himself.

"Wow, this is really . . . tidy." Claire shifted her grip on the cat and turned slowly to look around the clearing. "Really."

Dean finished squaring up a pile of fresh cedar prunings and straightened. "Are you okay?"

"We're fine." Erasing an arc of the circle with the edge of her boot, she stepped clear. "I got enough information to close the hole. I know why it never closed on its own, and I know how the demon came through. But you're not going to like it."

He didn't.

"So you're saying that by making the angel *we* made the demon possible?" When Claire reluctantly nodded, he felt the blood drain out of his face. It was a distinctly unpleasant feeling.

Austin studied him for a moment, then looked up at Claire. "I hope you weren't planning on sex any time soon."

In spite of the cold and the approaching dusk, there were still hundreds of people surging back and forth between the lights at Bloor and Yonge. Most of them, heavily laden with consumer crap they didn't need, were tired, cranky, and desperately in search of one last bargain. Byleth had never seen anything so wonderful.

One hand clutching the dashboard as though she needed to anchor herself to the car, Eva shook her head. "I don't like just leaving you here."

"I'll be fine." She'd have been out of the car at the stoplight except the damned seat belt had jammed. And it would be damned, she see to it personally. "Pull over anywhere."

"We're willing to take you where you're going," Harry told her as he maneuvered the car into a parking place on the south side of Bloor Street, just past Yonge. "Eva's right. I don't like just leaving you."

"I'll. Be. Fine." The stupid bulky coat was in the way. That was the problem. She squirmed around and yanked at the . . . there! A jerk on the handle had the door open. Byleth flung herself toward the world just in time to hear Eva say:

"I'd feel better if you took this money. It's not much but . . ."

Half out of the car, she reached back and grabbed the envelope without slowing her forward momentum.

"I wrote down our phone number. Call us if you need help!" Eva called after her.

That would be a cold day in Hell, Byleth decided shoving the envelope in her jeans—Twelfth Circle excepted, of course.

"That's certainly a generous offer, sweetheart, but I'm afraid you're making it to the wrong guy." He winked and patted her shoulder as he moved away. "Sorry."

Byleth made a mental note not to offer that particular temptation to men wearing eyeliner. Beginning to get cold, she moved into the nearest store and sidled through narrow aisles to a young man examining a portable CD player. "You should steal that, Steven," she murmured.

"Lifted one this morning," he told her absently, responding unconsciously to the dark aura. "Besides, right at this mo, I got so many disks down my pants I can hardly walk."

"That explains why your pants look like they're about to slide right off your skinny ass," she muttered.

"What's your damage?" Projecting tough guy, he shot her a look from under pale brows and folded his arms. "Santa not bring you any prezzies?"

Santa had never brought her any presents—her part of reality never having exactly welcomed the spirit of giving. And frankly, that sucked. In her whole entire life, Santa had never given her anything! Okay, her whole entire life was just under forty-eight hours long and the Porters had given her plenty, but that was so not the point.

The tough guy look vanished. "Oh, man, I'm sorry. I never . . . I mean . . . it's just . . ." Rifling his pockets, he pulled out a Santa Pez dispenser and held it out. "Here."

"What is it?"

Steven folded the head back, forcing out a tiny pink tile. "It's candy," he said when she hesitated.

Break Santa's neck, get a hit of sugar. Byleth crunched reflectively. *I can deal.*

"Take it."

"What's the catch?" Taking the Pez, she shifted her weight to one hip and looked him in the eye. "Did you want to have sex with me or something?"

His face flushed crimson, his ears scarlet. It wasn't a particularly attractive combination. Muttering something inarticulate, he scuttled away as fast as the CDs down his pants and the crowded store allowed.

Byleth was confused. A total stranger had just give her a gift and refused something he wanted in return. Crunching candy, she went looking for store security. Ratting Steven out would realign her world.

        ❖   ❖   ❖

"Hey, there's a . . ."

"I'm dealing with a customer." The harassed looking young women pushed past without really seeing her. "You'll have to talk to someone else."

". . . particular model has a greater range, you'll find . . ."

"That guy over there is shoplifting."

". . . that the battery may need to be recharged more often."

Byleth pushed between the two men. "Did you hear me?"

"In a moment, Miss. Of course our spare batteries are also on sale, so that could easily solve the problem," the salesman continued, passing the cell phone over her head.

"What about those chargers that fit into your cigarette lighter?"

"Hey? Hello?"

"We carry them. I'm not sure whether we have any left."

"Why won't anyone listen to ME!" They were ignoring her. It was like she didn't exist—almost like, like she was actually a teenager! "This is MAKING ME ANGRY!"

"Hey! That's enough of that!" The burly security guard folded her arms over her imitation police blazer and glared down at the demon. "You're going to have to leave now, Miss."

Byleth folded her own arms. "Make me."

It shouldn't have been possible.

"Fine!" she screamed from the sidewalk. "Like I care!"

Reaching into the dark possibilities and activating the store's sprinkler system made her feel a little better.

"Summons?" Diana asked as Nalo paused, head cocked, listening to nothing.

After a moment, the older Keeper nodded. "Close, too," she said, climbing the last few steps and emerging back out onto the corner of Yonge and Dundas. "Probably no farther than Bloor. Did you want to come with me?"

"Love to, but . . ." The sudden realization that it was almost dark cut off a fine sarcastic response. "Holy sh . . ." Nalo's lifted brow cut off the expletive. "I've got to get home!"

And I do have to get home, she reminded herself a few moments later, racing back down the stairs to the bank of pay phones in the subway station. But first she had to find an angel.

A little confused, Patricia held out the phone. "It's for you."

Samuel mimicked the motion he'd just seen Patricia make. "Hello? At the Oak Street Co-op at just up from the corner of River and Dundas Streets, town house four."

"How does it know that?" Pixel wondered.

"It has Higher Knowledge," Ilea informed the younger cat without opening her eyes. "It knows things."

"It didn't know us."

"So? Even Higher Knowledge has an upper limit."

Distracted by the cats' conversation, Samuel had to ask Diana to repeat herself, twice. Finally he nodded and handed back the phone. "My Keeper is going to meet me here."

"If it's all right with you," Ilea prodded.

"What?"

"Ask my soft, smiley can-opener if it's all right with her, you moron."

"Of course it's all right," Patricia told him when he'd relayed the cat's message.

"You're relieved I have a Keeper?"

A polite response was lost in the gold-on-brown eyes. "Oh, yeah."

Climbing up onto the streetcar, Diana felt her gaze pulled to the north. Something was . . . was . . . awareness trembled on the edge of consciousness. . . .

"Hey! Exact change!"

. . . and tumbled into the abyss.

Unrighteous anger kept her warm for a few blocks, but with the setting sun, the temperatures had plummetted. By the time she got to Yonge and Dundas, her teeth were chattering so loudly she almost couldn't hear the security guard kicking her out of the Eaton's Center. He walked away, scratching at a brand new case of head lice, but that was of little consequence when she was still out in the cold.

"You don't look very happy. Maybe I can help."

Byleth turned to find a middle-aged man standing very close. Under the edge of a sheepskin hat, his hair was graying at the temples, his smile was warm and charming, his eyes crinkled at the corners with sincere goodwill, his heart was blacker than hers.

"All right, let's get this straight," she snarled, tossing aside even a pretense of subtlety. "Thinking that I'm lost and alone in the big city, you're about to get all fatherly and offer me a place to crash. Over the next little while you'll addict me to heroin, then put me out on the street to quote, pay you back, unquote. You'll take every cent I make and control me with physical violence." He stepped back. She closed the distance between them. "Did I miss something?"

"I'm not . . ."

"You are so. But that's not the point. The point is you're trying to pull this bullshit on me." Her eyes narrowed and went black from lid to lid. "I've had a really bad day. I mean, like really bad. I'm not even supposed to *have* genitalia!"

"I . . ."

"You can take a walk in traffic, asshole!"

Emergency crews were scraping him out from under the streetcar when she realized she could have handled that better. She couldn't feel her feet, every muscle in her body had clenched tight, she couldn't seem to get her shoulders to come down from around her ears, and her stomach felt like it was lying along her spine. *Stupid, stupid, stupid. Next time wait until he's got you inside the apartment!* A quick examination of the gathered crowd suggested there wouldn't be a next time any time soon. "Isn't that always the way," she muttered miserably, "never a pimp around when you need one."

Manifesting the dark powers left her feeling wrung out and weak—it shouldn't have, but she couldn't manage enough energy to care.

"Hey, you look like you could use a place to stay."

"Well, duh." Turning, she came face-to-face with . . . "Oh, great. A God-pimp."

Leslie/Deter's lip curled. Pretty much all his understanding and patience had been used up earlier in the day when he'd gotten physical with his so-called friends. "Fine. Stay outside and freeze, then."

Since that was beginning to seem highly likely, Byleth grabbed his arm as he started to walk away. "You're supposed to be nicer than that. I'm not, but you're one of the good guys." When he continued to look annoyed, she sighed. "All right, I shouldn't have called you that. I'm so . . . sorry."

Harry Porter had been right. It did get easier. The implications made her knees buckle.

Leslie/Deter caught her, apologizing profusely in turn, and walked her toward the mission, explaining that after the meal they'd be hearing the word of God.

"Which word?"

"What?"

"Where I come from, we get a kick out of hearing the old guy try and say aluminum. . . ."

ELEVEN

 ──────•─◄═◆═►─•──────

THE PHONE WAS RINGING when Nalo got back to her apartment. The strident and slightly superior tone suggested she'd best hurry and pick up, or the next call would happen at a considerably more inconvenient time. So there. Some of the older Keepers had a theory that the entire telephone system had been touched by darkness just before the invention of call waiting and had grown increasingly corrupted ever since.

Kicking off her boots before she hit the carpet, she lifted the receiver and snarled, "I am not interested in changing my long distance service provider, but I will change you into something unpleasant unless you leave me the hell alone."

"Nalo?"

"Oh. Claire." Turning on the table light, she dropped onto the sofa. "Well, wasn't that a waste of a bad mood. What's up?"

On the other end of the line, Claire took a deep breath. "We've got trouble."

"Out there in River City."

There was cognitive pause, then: "What?"

Swinging her feet up onto the coffee table, Nalo sighed. "Never mind. And while I feel for your trouble, it can't possibly top what I've got going on right here."

"There's a demon loose."

"And then again . . ." The older Keeper stared down at the black glitter dusting her fingertips. "I closed a couple of holes it opened today."

"Are you all right?"

"I'm fine. It seems to be starting small—a little vandalism, a little urban renewal . . ."

"Urban renewal?"

"It convinced a pimp to walk under a streetcar. Hard on the driver but no loss to the city. There'll be cascading holes from the witnesses still to track down but, around here at least, it's been a low-key embodiment of darkness."

"That's a relief."

"And a bit of a surprise."

"Yeah, well, there's more."

"You mean the way we can't track it down because there's also an angel walking around big as life and twice as shiny?"

"How did you . . . ?"

"Know that? Well, I'd have to say that a piece of darkness walking around without any of us the wiser was the first clue, but I also ran into your sister today. . . ."

"Why would Diana hide the angel from another Keeper?"

"Why would Diana turn the vacuum cleaner hose into kudzu?" Austin snorted, kneading a pillow into shape. "Why does Diana do anything?"

"Because she's a pain in the ass?"

"That would be my guess," the cat agreed.

"Maybe she's embarrassed about her part in his creation," Dean offered.

"I don't think Diana gets embarrassed."

"Maybe she's taking him for a test drive." When both Claire and Dean turned to stare, Austin shrugged. "Well, pardon me for using a euphemism, but didn't Nalo say that from a block away she thought he was just a guy?"

"Diana wouldn't . . ." Claire's voice trailed off. "Okay, it's possible," she admitted after a moment's thought, "but she says she's a lesbian."

"No, she said she was a lesbian back in November. She could easily be a hemocyanin by now."

"I don't think that's . . ."

"The point is," Austin interrupted, "is that she's seventeen and subject to change without notice. And she's met a young man she can be herself with. Or have you forgotten how seductive that is?"

Claire looked up at Dean, looked past her reflection in his glasses, and sank into the blue of his eyes. "No. I haven't forgotten."

He reached out and stroked the back of his hand over her cheek. "I'm sorry I got you into this."

"We got into this together."

"Still . . ."

"Still need to get hold of Diana," Austin reminded them acerbically.

Claire reluctantly sat back and picked up her cell phone again.

"Yes, okay, I *should* have thought of how I'd get home *before* I went into the closet." Diana held the phone out from her ear, counted to six, then tried again. "Mom . . . Mom! I'm *not* being a smart-ass, I'm agreeing with you. And since there was money for a hotel room, not a bus ticket home, I'm obviously supposed to be here—no harm, no foul. Aren't you the one who always says, nothing happens to a Keeper by chance?" She winced. "Of course I listen to you. Yeah, okay, I didn't listen to that. Or that. Mom . . . Mom. Mother! I have to go now. I'll stay in touch. 'Bye. No. Now. Good-bye."

She hung up, leaned back, closed her eyes, and began rhythmically beating her head against the wall.

"You didn't tell your mother I was with you," Samuel pointed out from the room's other bed.

"No, I didn't."

"A lie of omission is still a lie, and a lie is the destroyer of trust."

"Why don't you just let me deal with that?"

"Banging your head isn't going to do anything but annoy the person in the next room."

She opened her eyes and glared at him. "There isn't anyone in the next room."

"But still . . ."

"Shut up."

"The phone's ringing."

"I'm beginning to think Claire was right about this whole joining the twenty-first century thing." Scooping up the receiver, she closed her eyes again. "Sorry, Mom, but nothing's changed in the last thirty seconds."

"It's not Mom. It's me."

"Oh, joy." Straightening, she mouthed, *It's Claire, so no background noise,* toward Samuel. "How did you get this number?"

"It's your cell phone number."

About to explain that she didn't have her cell phone with her, Diana decided that might be something she'd be better off keeping to herself. "Oh. Yeah."

"Diana, that angel you're hiding is blocking my . . . our, ability to find the demon that came through at the same time, so you've got to stop playing around and send it back."

"It's not an it, Claire, it's a him and . . ." The rest of the sentence suddenly clicked into place. "Did you say demon?"

"Demon?" Samuel scooted to the edge of the bed, eyes wide.

Diana mouthed a stern, *"Shut up!"* at him so she could hear Claire's answer.

"Yes, a demon."

"That's so not good."

"Low-fat cheese is not good, Diana. *This* is bad. I don't know what you're up to with that angel, and I don't want to know . . ."

"Come to think of it, how do you know?"

"Nalo saw you with him and mentioned it when I called her, but that's not important. He's got to go back right now."

"No." Diana shook her head—an unseen emphasis from Claire's point of view but emphasis just the same. "Sending him back would be the same as killing him."

"You can't kill him, there's nothing to kill. He's a being of light."

"He's more than that."

"How can he be more than that? He's already a superior being!"

"Fine. He's less than that, then. He's a person, Claire." Who was attempting to eavesdrop on both sides of the conversation. A vigorously applied elbow solved that distinctly unangelic problem. Flashing him a triumphant smile, as he flopped around gasping for breath, she amended, "Okay, maybe he's not entirely a person, but there's a person *in* there."

"No."

"No, what?"

"No, you are not suggesting that a . . . a penis and a couple of testicles is what makes a man." Claire's tone laid a distinctly weird subtext under the words.

Wishing she had time to translate, Diana sighed impatiently. "No, I'm not suggesting that. But they've given him access to emotions and experiences genderless angels can't have."

"I'm happy for him, but there's a demon loose we can't find until the angel goes—therefore the angel has to go. And if he knew what was at stake, I'm sure he'd agree. Is he there with you right now? Let me talk to him."

"No."

Samuel poked her in the leg. "Your sister wants to talk to me?"

She couldn't lie to him. "Yes."

"So give me the phone."

"Not happening." Scooting out from under his arm, she crossed the room and glared at him from beside the bathroom door, the phone cord stretched taut between them. "One step in this direction and I'll lock myself in."

"Diana!"

"Claire!" Attention jerked back to her sister, she rolled her eyes. "You don't need to yell. It doesn't matter if he agrees with you or not because I'd still have to kill him, and I won't do it."

"For the last time, you wouldn't be killing him!"

"Would."

"Stop being so childish. Listen, I can't get there tonight; the OPP have closed the highway north of Barrie because of the storm. But we'll be leaving *first thing* in the morning. This is serious. Send the angel back. Remember your responsibili . . ."

Diana jabbed at the power off button and pitched the phone across the room. "I do not need her to remind me of my responsibilities," she growled as Samuel rubbed his ear where the phone had clipped him on its way by. "If they knew you, they wouldn't be able to kill you either."

"I don't want to die."

"Good."

He sighed and spread his hands. "But there's a demon in the world, and if returning me to the light would expose the demon . . ."

"You have to say that," Diana interrupted. "And knock off the sacrificial pose, I'm not buying it." She threw herself down on the empty bed.

"Bouncing like that will destroy the mattress and the box spring."

"Who are you getting your Higher Knowledge from, Martha Stewart?"

"Did you know you can create a lovely mailbox cozy out of a piece of felt and only six hundred dollars' worth of handwoven French taffeta ribbon?"

"What?" She squirmed around and stared.

Samuel grinned.

The corners of her mouth beginning to curve, Diana grabbed a pillow and heaved it at him. "Jerk!"

He wasn't sure why he considered that a compliment, but he did. "Diana, you have to send me back. I don't want to go, but I understand why I have to."

Squinting in the sudden glow, Diana sighed. Nothing like self-sacrifice to bring out the angel in a guy. If Claire or any other Keeper met him in this state, they'd send him back without even thinking about it. Easy answer—don't let Claire or any other Keeper meet him.

And how hard could that be? No Summons, no directions—no way to find them.

"Mom? Claire. When you were talking to Diana a few minutes ago, did she happen to mention what hotel she's staying at? Carlton Hotel, room 312. Thanks."

"That looks like room 81Z," Austin pointed out.

"I'd like to see you do better with an eyeliner on a condom wrapper."

"Well, it's nice you found something to use them for."

Dean reached across the cat and picked up the address. "I don't like this."

"But they're the only kind we've got."

"What? No!" Suddenly flustered, he dropped the packet. It bounced off the sniggering cat and rolled under the bed. "I meant, I don't like going to your mother," he explained, dropping to his knees and running his hand beneath the edge of the bedspread. "It seems, I don't know, sneaky."

"No choice." Claire folded her legs up out of his way. "First of all, Diana's confused. Secondly, I've dealt with nothing but angel or demon sites since it happened, which is telling me pretty clearly that this is my responsibility. Third . . ." Reaching out, she grinned and ran her fingers through his hair. ". . . there's just something about a man on his knees."

"Claire . . ."

"What?"

"Found it!" Straightening, he was about to toss the packet onto her lap when he frowned. "This isn't ours . . ."

"Eww."

Still glowing, although beginning to dim, Samuel lay back on the bed, hands under his head, and stared at the ceiling. "You know what I'd like to experience before I . . . go back."

"You're not going back," Diana told him absently. She paced the length of the hotel room one more time, examining and discarding another half-dozen bad ideas. The best she'd been able to come up with so far had involved rather more duct tape than she thought she could get her hands on.

"But still . . ."

"No."

"Pizza."

"What?" Either angels came with euphemisms high school didn't cover—which was highly unlikely—or that wasn't the experience she'd been expecting.

"And loud music."

"Why?"

He shrugged as well as he was able, given his position. "I don't know."

Well, she hadn't come up with any better ideas. "I could handle a pizza."

"I think I just want to eat mine."

"Oh, please, send me back now." Falling backward, Samuel groaned and rubbed both hands over a visibly distended belly. "Why did I do that to myself?"

Compelled to answer truthfully, Diana snorted. "I think you were showing off."

"Showing off what?"

"Beats me."

"I feel awful."

She dropped down onto the other bed. "What did you expect after a large with the works and half of my Hawaiian?"

"I wasn't expecting anything!" A mighty belch delayed part two of the protest. Startled but impressed, he waited until the echoes died down before continuing. "I just thought. . . ."

"Thinking? As if. You were being a guy." She squirmed back toward the pillows, propping them against the wall. "And speaking of, you're starting to smell."

"My olfactory senses have been working since I got here, thank you very much."

"Right. Rephrasing—you stink."

"I stink?"

Eyes rolling, she picked up the TV remote. "Don't take my word for it. Check the pits."

He lifted an arm. "I'm not supposed to smell like this?"

"No."

"Good."

"I'll show you how the shower works in the morning. After that last incident, I don't want you approaching new plumbing on your own."

"I thought I was *supposed* to urinate against the wall."

"Uh-huh." A quick flip through the available channels brought the expected result: there was nothing on.

"What was that?" Samuel heaved himself up onto his elbows. "No, not that. Back. Back. There."

Diana frowned. "It's a documentary on lions."

"What are they doing?"

She adjusted the contrast, but they were still doing it. "They're having sex."

"Kewl."

"You're disgusting."

Vaguely proud of himself, although uncertain of why he should be, he belched again.

Byleth hadn't expected to have so much fun. With a sense of Keepers too close for comfort, she'd planned on a low profile and a road trip in the morning. She'd listened to the praying, she'd eaten the meal, and she hadn't been able to stop a snort of amusement during the preaching.

So they'd asked her if she had a question.

Surrounded by teenagers pulled from the streets, Byleth stood—hands jammed into the pockets of her black jeans, weight resting on one hip, expression sullen—and asked, "If Lloyd leaves London at 6:00 p.m. on a train heading east going 90 kilometers an hour and Tom leaves Toronto at 6:15 p.m. on a train heading west at 110 kilometers an hour, when will they die in a fiery explosion?"

Eyes dark from lid to lid compelled the truth.

"I don't know."

"Why?" She threw the word onto the end of his sentence so quickly momentum kept the ball rolling.

"I never paid attention in math."

"Why?"

"I was fixated on Miss Miller's breasts."

"Why?"

"They were perky. What does this have to do with the text?" Leslie/Deter demanded, fingers white on the edge of the lectern.

"Nothing." The last thing she wanted to do was test the man's faith. That was the sort of inane probing the good guys got up to. "Boxers or briefs?"

"Egyptian leather thong."

Things went downhill from there.

Staring up at the exit sign, Claire listened to Dean breathe and waited for morning. Diana had gone too far this time. She hadn't been Summoned to the angel, or she'd have mentioned it—Summoned Keepers had the final say on any situation. Diana without a Summons meant Diana should be at home studying or whatever it was teenagers did these days. Piercing something maybe.

Claire hadn't been Summoned either, but as an *active* Keeper that only meant that she was already doing what she was supposed to be doing. The angel's physical form blocked any attempt to find the demon. Therefore, she had to return the angel to the light. QED— essentially, Latin for "so there."

Diana's personal opinions on the matter were irrelevant. Even more so than usual.

If functional genitalia defined personhood, then Dean . . .

She chopped off the thought before it could crawl out any further. Functional genitalia didn't define love either, and she loved Dean. In a relatively short time he'd become as essential to her life as breathing. She loved being with him, talking, laughing, traveling, cuddling, touching, kissing, caressing; turning her head, she pressed her face against the warm skin of his shoulder. He smelled so good, she wanted to . . .

Okay, that's it. Get up. Which wasn't, perhaps, the best chastisement under the circumstances. Sliding out from under the covers, she grabbed her robe off the other bed.

"Hey! I was asleep on that!"

"Sorry."

"I should hope so." Disdaining the jump, Austin stalked over the bedside table and curled up between Dean's legs muttering, "Angels, demons, impotence; I see no reason why the cat should suffer."

She woke Dean at five, and they were on the road by six-thirty. They would have been on the road an hour earlier, but when they went to check out, Dean discovered that the sleepy middle-aged woman behind the desk had once lived in St. John's right next door to a guy he'd played hockey with. The permutations took a while to work through.

Although the plows had been busy all night, it was still snowing lightly and the driving was treacherous. When it became apparent that Dean needed to concentrate on the road . . .

You'll find out what Diana's up to when we get there.

Could we deal with what happens after the angel's gone, after the angel's gone, then.

Claire, please shut up."

. . . she amused herself by watching a pair of frost fairies skating along the hydro lines. Matched double axles, a star lift, and a thrown triple salkow later, she popped in a tape of *The Nutcracker*.

"This is different." Austin climbed out from behind the seat and settled in her lap. "You don't usually like classical music."

"I know, but somehow it seemed to fit."

They stopped for breakfast in Huntsville.

"I should get gas," Dean observed as they pulled out of the diner's parking lot.

"I *got* gas," Austin moaned, head and both front paws draped over the edge of the seat. "I should never have eaten those sausages."

Claire folded her arms. "What sausages?"

"Did I say sausages? I meant, uh . . ." The windows rattled as his stomach made a sound between a gurgle and plate tectonics. "All right. I meant sausages; three plump juicy sausages. Slightly over-cooked and containing bits of two items I couldn't identify. The kid in the next booth dropped them on the floor, and I ate them."

"When?"

"When Dean was explaining to the waitress how running the dish-washer at a higher temperature would keep the cutlery from streak-ing."

"Right. Then."

"Yeah, then. When you were studying the menu with such intense concentration."

Pulling up in front of the gas pumps, Dean shot her a quick look. "You were embarrassed?" When she nodded, he grinned. "Why? The waitress didn't mind."

The waitress didn't mind because he'd been smiling up at her and the combination of Dean's smile and accent and shoulders made most women and a goodly number of men between the ages of thirteen and death temporarily lose cognitive functions. He could have told the wait-ress how to get black heel marks off the floor, tomato sauce stains out of her apron, and greasy thumbprints off the napkin dispenser—all of which he'd done in the past—and she wouldn't have minded. In the past he'd never noticed the reactions he provoked, but something in the way he grinned as he got out of the truck suggested that had changed.

"So he's noticing people are noticing." Austin twisted his head around until he could spear Claire with a pale green gaze. "So what?"

She watched Dean clean the windshield, carefully lifting each wiper blade and setting it just as carefully back in place. "So I'm not sure how I feel about it."

"About him noticing that waitress noticed him?" When she nodded, he snorted. "Don't worry about it. She made him French toast. You made him a man."

"But he really *liked* the French toast."

"And once you've dealt with the angel . . ."

"And the demon."

"*And* the demon—he'll really *like* locking me in the bathroom again."

"You think?"

"No. I'm just talking to hear myself." Belly sagging, he heaved himself up onto his feet. "Now open the door. There's a trio of sausages I have to introduce to a snowbank."

"I'd have thought that angels were more the early to bed, early to rise types."

Samuel heaved himself up into something close to a sitting position, blinked at the room in general for a few moments, and then reluctantly swung his legs out of bed. "Why?"

"I dunno. The whole sentiment is just so sanctimonious I figured it had to be one of . . . oh, man!" Diana clapped her hands over her eyes and rocked back in the chair. "Like I needed to see *that* first thing in the morning. I thought you were going to sleep in your underwear."

"This is what was under what I was wearing when you said that."

"Pardon me for not assuming angels would head out commando style." A quick look elicited a low whistle. "You ought to send Mr. Giorno a nice thank you letter."

His eyes widened. "It's doing it again!"

"Well, don't wave it at me!"

Ears burning, Samuel grabbed a pillow off the bed and held it protectively in front of him. "I'm not doing anything. It just . . ." He started to gesture, thought better of it, and resecured the pillow. "It just does that," he finished miserably. "I hate this body."

"Are angels allowed to hate?"

"Are we allowed to walk around with one of these?"

"You have a point."

He sank down onto the edge of the bed, pillow on his lap. "Like I need you to remind me."

Diana could feel the laughter rising. When she tried to hold it back behind her teeth, it escaped out her nose. Any chance she might have had at stopping it after that got blown away by Samuel's affronted glare. Nothing to do but ride it out. After a few minutes, she wiped her eyes, drew in a shaky breath, and managed a fairly coherent, "Sorry."

"Sure. Whatever." He glanced under the pillow. "Anyway, you've taken care of the . . . Would you stop that!"

This time the apology came out in separate syllables as Diana slid off the chair.

Samuel sat and watched her flop about, indignation wrapped around him like a cloak. Finally, he stood and walked into the bathroom, every movement radiating injured dignity. "I'll figure out the shower on my own," he informed her reproachfully, reaching back for the door.

Wondering who he could possibly be reminding her of, Diana waved a weak hand in his general direction and fought to pull herself together. With the door closed, with her anatomically correct angel safely behind it, she staggered to her feet and dropped back into the chair. Her stomach hurt. She hadn't laughed so hard since the time Claire'd coughed half a cheese sandwich through her nose listening to one of Dad's old George Carlin albums.

Claire.

Suddenly it wasn't so funny.

Claire was on her way to Toronto believing she had to send an angel back to the light for the greater good. But, logically, emotionally, rationally, and every other ally Diana could think of, destroying a life couldn't be a part of the greater good.

There had to be another way to find the demon.

"All right . . ." She stood and walked purposefully over to the big mirror on the wall. Hands flat on the dresser, she leaned forward and glared at her reflection. "Let's do something radical for a Keeper. Let's actually think about the situation instead of just reacting to it."

Her reflection looked skeptical.

"Problem: there's a demon in the world, a big ol' walking around piece of darkness. And that's bad. We can't find it because there's also an angel in the world. Which would be good if it wasn't bad. We can't find the demon because of the angel. Because the big chunk of light that's Samuel balances the dark." She glanced over at the bathroom, then back at the mirror. "Except that the dark hasn't really been very dark, has it?"

Her reflection frowned in thoughtful agreement.

"You'd think that a demon would cause more havoc, wouldn't you? All the active Keepers should be scrambling to repair the damage it's caused, and I should have been Summoned to help. But that hasn't happened. Why? Why hasn't the demon caused more havoc?" She was close. She could feel it. "The demon is balancing Samuel. It hasn't caused more havoc because balancing means it's an exact opposite of Samuel."

Following the cord, she dove under the bed for the phone.

In the mirror, her reflection performed a truncated version of Deion Sanders' touchdown dance.

"All right. The demon's a fully functional teenage girl. We still can't find it while your angel is in the world. Yes, that narrows the search but not enough. Diana, I'm sor . . ." Claire let her head fall back against the seat as she powered down her phone. "She hung up on me."

"She's some set on saving that angel," Dean noted, carefully easing the truck around a blind curve.

"I know."

"Is there any chance she could be right?"

"No."

"You're sure?"

Claire sighed. "I'm a Keeper, it's my job to be sure."

Austin stretched out a paw, his claws sinking into Claire's jeans. "Far be it from me to point this out, but you seem to be forgetting something."

"I fed you. Although I don't see why, when you tried to kill yourself with sausages."

The claws sank a little deeper. "You're forgetting that Diana is also a Keeper."

"So?"

"It's as much her job to be sure as it is yours."

"All right, fine. So Claire can't find her, big whoop. That doesn't mean I can't." Euphoria having been shot down, Diana sat cross-legged on the end of the bed, reached into the possibilities, and jabbed seven numbers into the phone. "Local call," she muttered after the first ring. "I'll just deal with the demon before Claire clears Barrie, and she can stuff her . . ."

"Greenstreet Mission. Drop by and hear the word of God."

Diana opened her mouth and closed it again. Finally she managed a strangled, "The what?"

"The word of God." The young man on the other end of the phone sighed deeply. "And, no, it isn't aluminum."

"Okay."

"Can we help?"

"No. That is, sorry, I've got the wrong number." Hanging up considerably more gently than she had the last time, Diana stared across the room at her reflection. Her reflection stared back, equally appalled.

Higher Knowledge had told him that showers were both the cubicle or bath in which one stands under a spray of water and the act of bathing in same. It offered no help at getting the water the right temperature, but after a few false starts—and he would *not* give Diana the pleasure of hearing him scream—he worked it out.

Soaping up gave him the first chance to really examine the body he found himself in. Was he supposed to have hair in so many weird places? Why were his feet so big? If he hadn't actually been born, which he hadn't, why did he have a belly button? And nipples—sure they added visual interest to the male chest but what were they actually for?

"These things really ought to come with owner's manuals," he sighed, reaching down to turn off the water.

The tiny room didn't seem significantly drier.

Shaking drips off the ends of his hair, he stepped out of the tub, slipped on the wet tiles, and suddenly found himself airborne.

Seventy-eight percent of all accidents happen in the bathroom, Higher Knowledge informed him as he landed.

"Samuel? Samuel, how many fingers am I holding up?"

"Why?"

"I have no idea, but it's what they always do in the movies when someone knocks themselves out."

"I'm not out." He blinked and tried to focus on what looked like three fat pink sausages. "I'm in the bathroom."

"No, you're not. I moved you to one of the beds."

"You carried me?"

"As if. I just, you know, poof."

"Oh. Poof. Was that the burst of light?"

The sausages disappeared and the edge of the bed dipped as Diana sat down. "No. I think that was when your head hit the edge of the tub."

"My head . . ." Movement brought smaller bursts of light. Pain. He remembered pain. On the up side, it didn't hurt as much as catching himself in the zipper.

"There's a bump, but angels seem to be pretty tough."

"Yeah, well, soldiers in the army of the Lord and all that." He could feel her concern—her pain for his pain—and he kind of thought he ought to do something about it but he just couldn't seem to muster the enthusiasm.

"Samuel, I don't want to rush you or anything, but could you get over this a little faster. Checkout time is at noon, and I don't have enough money for another day—which clearly means we're not supposed to stay."

We. He felt a vague nostalgia for the time he'd spent on his own. "Maybe it means you're supposed to send me back to the light."

"Maybe you should just stay out of this."

"Sure."

Her eyes narrowed. "What's that supposed to mean?"

"It means my head hurts."

"Oh. Sorry."

The bed rocked as she threw herself off it. Samuel winced. "You want to hear the weird thought I had as I finished showering?"

"I guess."

"That makes me feel more human."

"What does?"

"The shower, I guess. It's the thought I had: That makes me feel more human. And then . . ." He waved a hand in the general direction of his head. ". . . this. Pain."

Diana snorted. "Got news for you, bucko. Pain is the general human condition."

"Then send me back. I don't think I want to be human anymore."

"Well, that's just too . . ." Her voice trailed off into thought. They couldn't find the demon because she was the exact opposite of Samuel. The exact opposite. Throwing herself back onto the bed, she grabbed his shoulders hard enough to dimple the bare skin. "I'm an idiot!"

"Look, I know it's unangelic of me, but I don't really feel up to dealing with your lack of self-esteem right now."

"What?"

"Stop shaking me!"

"Sorry." She pulled her hands away but continued looming over him. "I've just solved the problem. If you don't want to be in a human body, you don't *have* to be."

"I don't?" Pushing back against the pillow accomplished nothing much, but he didn't like the way her eyes were gleaming.

"No, you don't. I helped make you. My, for lack of a better word, power signature is a part of you. That's why I can unmake you, but it should also mean I can transform you."

"Should?"

Ignoring him, she leaped up and spun around, arms outstretched. "You'll still be you but different. The demon copied this body, so without it, we'll be able to find her. It's simple."

"I won't be human?"

The spinning stopped. "No."

"But I'll still be me."

"Yes."

"What will I be?"

"I don't know. I'll undo the human seeming and the light will rearrange. Without Lena and her father to interfere, you'll self-define."

Suddenly serious, she sat down and pushed her hair off her forehead. "I don't want to push you into this, Samuel, but it would solve all our problems."

It took him a moment to figure out her expression. When he realized he was looking at hope, he couldn't stop himself from smiling. Hope was, after all, one of the primary messages of the light. Maybe this was why he was here. "Would my head hurt?"

"Different body. No reason why it should."

"Then let's do it."

Claire and Dean had opened the way for the light, but her crepe-paper snowflake hanging from the ceiling in the gym had held it together. Standing at the foot of the bed, Diana closed her eyes and reached into the possibilities until she could see Samuel lying in front of her. Slowly and carefully, she detached the parameters Lena and her father had placed around him. She took him back to what he had been in the gym, then wrapped the part that was Samuel in the possibilities and pushed him forward.

In the instant between Diana taking him back and shoving him forward again, Samuel thought he heard voices.

"So he's off the duty roster?"

"Let's just say he's on an extended leave of absence."

"Let's just say?" The first voice snorted. "Oh, easy for you, Gabriel. You're not the one who has to fill his post on the Perdition front."

"Bitch, bitch, bitch."

"Hey, there's a war on, you know. Or maybe that's something you guys in the band have forgotten."

And then there was only light, and a question.

If he wasn't an angel, and he wasn't a human, what was he?

Diana blinked away afterimages and stared down at the towel she'd thrown over Samuel's crotch. Whatever he'd become fit under it with room to spare. Fingers crossed, she bent down and flicked it back.

The marmalade tabby sat up and looked around.

"You're a cat."

"Well, duh. Didn't anyone ever tell you that angels were like cats only with . . ." He cocked his head, trying to remember just what it was Ilea had said. ". . . you know, differences."

Staggering back, Diana went to sit down on one of the chairs but, at some time during the proceedings, it had self-defined as a plant stand, and she hit the floor instead. It suddenly became painfully clear who Samuel had reminded her of as he'd made his reproachful way to the bathroom.

Austin.

TWELVE

◆—·—≡◆≡—·—◆

SINCE DEAN HAD POLITELY but vehemently objected to her willing the truck faster, Claire let her head loll back against the headrest and closed her eyes. Extending her will toward Toronto, she slid
past the permanently monitored sites, her passage noted only by the
elderly Keeper at the site in Scarborough.

"Oh, sure, you can go by like a ship in the night, but you never
write, you never call. A lousy birthday card would kill you? The best
forty-two years of my life I give to you and you don't even remember
my birthday. You got a memory like a cantaloupe."

"Excuse me?"

"Why? What did you do?"

Claire moved on into the possibilities a little faster. Keepers who
essentially became the seal that stopped darkness from emerging out
of an unclosable hole, became caricatures of their former selves. She'd
narrowly missed becoming the youngest Keeper to ever hold such a
position and shuddered at the sudden vision of herself at ninety-two
in stretch capri pants and wedges, scarlet lips and crimson fingernails,
badly dyed hair poofed out over way too much purple eye shadow—a
cross between Nancy Reagan and Miss Piggy.

Didn't happen, she reminded herself. *Didn't* . . .

Wait.

Something was happening.

She heard voices . . .

"I'm warning you, Michael, don't touch the horn."

"Or you'll what? Blow me?"

. . . then a sudden flash of light threw her back into her body. She stiffened and moaned. The Summons hit a heartbeat later.

"As much as I'm happy you two are back into it," Austin muttered without opening his eye, "given that we're speeding down a snowy highway with a bunch of lunatics who've forgotten how to drive since the last time the frozen white stuff fell, don't you think Dean ought to keep both hands on the steering wheel?"

"I can feel the demon."

"I thought you were calling it Floyd. Ow!" He turned his head and glared at her. "Don't poke the cat, I'm old."

"So Diana came through, then?" Dean asked, making a mental note to ask about this Floyd guy when the cat wasn't around.

"I knew she would."

Austin snorted. "You thought she was going to destroy the world as we know it, bringing upon us the Last Judgment and roller disco. Not that there's a lot of difference," he added.

Somewhat redundantly in Dean's opinion. "Are we still after heading to Toronto, then?"

Claire checked the Summons. "So far."

They drove in silence for a few moments.

"The angel's gone, then?"

Curious about Dean's tone, Claire turned to face him. "Yes."

"And you can find the demon now?"

"Uh-huh."

"And when you find the demon, you can get rid of it?"

"I'm a Keeper. Of course I can get rid of it."

He glanced toward her and smiled suggestively. "No angel, no demon . . ."

"No problem." Realizing where he was headed, she returned his smile and stroked one finger along the top of his thigh.

"Is it just me," Austin asked, sitting up, "or are we suddenly moving a lot faster?"

The angel had changed.

Feeling suddenly exposed, Byleth ran into the only room in the mission where she'd be left alone—unexpectedly finding three other girls already in there sharing a cigarette.

The dominant member of the trio slid off the sink and turned to face her. "You want something, new girl?"

The part of her that was a seventeen-year-old girl wanted to protest that she'd just come in to use the bathroom and she wasn't looking for trouble. Then the rest of her pushed that part down and stole its lunch money. "I want you to leave."

"What?"

"Leave." Breathing heavily through her nose, barely holding all the parts together, Byleth reached into the darkness. "I want you to leave."

"Yeah? Well, I don't give a half-eaten rat's ass for what you want. I . . . What's that?" Pierced brows drew in and scowled at the dripping bit of flesh hanging from the tail in Byleth's hand.

"It's a half-eaten rat's ass. Take it and go."

Eyes locked on the partial rodent, the other two girls sidled by and out the door. In the complex hierarchy of adolescence, having a rat's ass conveniently on hand clearly trumped a pack of smokes and an attitude.

"What kind of retarded shithole do you come from?" their abandoned leader asked, taking an unconcerned drag. "That is so totally not what I meant. Now, me, I'm going to finish my cigarette and . . ." Her gaze locked on Byleth's nose. "I never saw you light up."

"I didn't."

"But there's smoke . . ."

"Get. Out."

"Hey, you're not the boss of me." Bravado winning over common sense, she flicked her butt toward the sink . . .

"NOW!"

. . . and was out the door before it actually touched the porcelain.

Byleth tossed the rat in the garbage and stared at her reflection. "Why is it so damned foggy in . . . oh." Like thousands before her, she found it a lot harder to stop smoking than to start, but, after an extended struggle, she managed it. Not that it mattered, her cover had been blown. She might as well walk around in a pair of horns, carrying a pitchfork—if that particular look wasn't *so* yesterday's demon. Without equal and opposite coverage by the light, she'd be easy to spot by any Keeper and probably most Cousins. Metaphysical alarms would be screaming, "Demon in the world!" and every Goody Two-shoes in the area not currently helping little old ladies across the street would be zeroing in.

She should have changed with the angel. He was as much tied by the stupid body he was wearing as she was. Therefore, he couldn't have changed on his own. He *so* cheated.

"Oh, yeah, he got a Keeper to change him so they could find me. Fine. You want to find me, Keeper, you'll find me!" A light wisp of smoke drifted out of both nostrils. It felt great. "If I'm going out, I'm going out big. No more just hanging around and irritating people." She spread her arms. "I'll open a hole of darkness so big it'll make the Home Shopping Channel seem like a cable network!"

Her reflection frowned. "It is a cable network."

"Shut up!"

"And you can't open a hole of darkness big enough to cause much trouble because the physicality of the body denies you access to that kind of power."

"I *am* that kind of power."

"Then you'll have to destroy the body. You'll cease to exist. Gone. No more reality than you can find in that stupid television program about those people on the island."

"What do you mean?"

"Read your lips. You'll be absorbed back into the darkness. No more you."

"Oh, like it's such joy to be a teenager." But it was better than being nothing at all, better than being a lesser part of a greater whole— actually it was remarkably similar to being a lesser part of a greater whole. Byleth chewed thoughtfully on the edge of a thumbnail, spitting bits of navy blue polish into the sink. If she could open a big enough hole, cause enough mayhem and destruction, she could maintain her identity even in the darkness where individuality depended on being more of a shit than the next guy—and not always metaphorically.

She'd have to open the hole quickly, before the Keepers found her, so she'd need a spot where at least part of the work had already been done.

"And I know just the place."

Unfortunately, her evil chortle fell flat as her reflection ignored her, concentrating instead on the dorky little flip ruining the right side of her hair.

"One, two, three, *four*. One, two, *three*, four."

"Are you all right down there?"

Samuel stopped counting and glared up at Diana, cream-colored whiskers bristling indignantly. "Why?"

"No reason,"

"I'm fine."

"Okay."

"This four legs walking stuff is a lot harder than it looks, you know."

Diana bit back a snicker as she pushed the elevator call button. "It couldn't possibly be. I think I should carry you," she added as the elevator arrived. "I've set it up so people's attention will slide right off you, but in an enclosed space you'd likely get stepped on."

"Something tells me I didn't think this transformation thing through," Samuel muttered as she scooped him up. Still, it felt surprisingly pleasant to be held. He flicked his tail out into a more comfortable position as the door opened.

A small child stared up at them with widening eyes. "Kitty, Mama!"

"Yes, sweetheart," his mother agreed, as Diana moved past her, "a stuffed kitty."

"Who's she calling stuffed?"

"Kitty talks, Mama!"

"Toy kitties don't talk, sweetheart."

A small hand closed around Samuel's tail and pulled. "Ding dong!"

"OW!"

"Kitties don't ding dong either, sweetheart." Shooting Diana an apologetic smile, she grabbed her son's wrist with one hand and pried his fingers free with the other. A bit of fur came free as well. "And it's not polite to touch things that belong to other people."

"Especially tails!" Hooking his claws in Diana's jacket, Samuel swiveled around until he could stare down at the child, golden eyes narrowed to glimmering slits. "Listen to your mother, Ramji, because someday she'll die and you'll wish you had."

Ramji wrapped his arms around his mother's leg. "Kitty knows my name."

He was still wrapped around her leg when the elevator reached the lobby, and she crossed to the hotel's front door with a resigned shuffle.

"That's a kid who's going to need serious therapy down the road." Diana shifted her grip. "What kind of an angel says something like that?"

"The kind that just got his tail pulled. Besides," Samuel continued after a few quick licks at his shoulder, "it's the truth and one day he'll thank me for it."

"One day he'll spend thousands of dollars being convinced you were a metaphor for toilet training."

"He grabbed my tail!"

"I know. I was there."

"You said people wouldn't be able to see me properly."

"He was a proto-person." She set him down in one of the lobby's over stuffed chairs and stepped back. "I'm going to check out. Stay there."

"Or what?"

"I haven't got time to go into it right now, but why don't you apply that Higher Knowledge thing to the joint concepts of can openers and opposable thumbs." As she walked over to the counter, she considered all the things he could have become and asked the world at large, more in search of sympathy than enlightenment, "Why a cat?"

The world at large offered no answers.

Left to amuse himself, Samuel did a little kneading, claws moving rhythmically in and out of the corduroy cushion covers. Shoulders up, head down, his eyes began to close as he moved in a slow circle. He didn't know what it was, but something about that yielding surface under his front paws created the most incredible feeling. Kneading harder, really putting his back into it, he heard a sudden loud noise and froze.

Two-stroke engine, single spark, gas and oil mix . . . oh, wait, it's me.

Which was when he spotted the other cat.

A marmalade tabby, it had a cream-colored bib and the same color markings around both muzzle and eyes. The darker stripes down tail and legs made it look as if it was wearing footie pajamas—

the effect emphasized by the way the legs were still a bit too long for the body.

Samuel stared at it.

It stared back.

Head cocked to one side, Samuel took a cautious step forward.

It took a cautious step forward.

Hoping he wasn't rushing the introduction, Samuel leaned forward for a good long sniff.

The cinnamon triangle of his nose mashed flat against the mirror.

Leaping back, his back feet scrambled for purchase as he nearly went off the chair, only the barricade of Diana's legs saving him from an embarrassing fall. Blinking rapidly, he leaned against her knees, looked up at her, and said in what he hoped was a convincing tone, "I meant to do that."

"Okay."

"I knew it was a mirror."

"I believe you."

"Right." He took a few quick licks at the edge of a stripe. "So, where do we go from here?"

Diana sighed. "Home."

"But what about the demon?" Samuel demanded. "I'm not blocking it now. We should go after it."

"Yes, we should. But we can't." She dropped down onto the arm of the chair and scowled at her reflection, one hand absently rubbing the cat behind the ears. "I can feel that there's a demon out there, but I still don't know where she is. Which means some other Keeper has it sealed up. And, gee, I wonder which other Keeper?"

"Claire?"

"Good guess."

Samuel could tell Diana was upset, although he wasn't entirely certain why. "You don't know that for sure," he offered.

Diana snorted. "We—me and Claire—were responsible for you, which makes *us* responsible for the demon, which means *we* should have got the Summons, but since *I* didn't, *she* must have."

He frowned, ears saddling. "Then she must be able to handle the demon on her own."

"Well, duh. What?" she demanded of an eavesdropping Bystander, shooting him the look that had made her the terror of intramural field hockey back before the school board decided it might not be the best idea to give hormonally hopped up adolescents weapons and carte blanche to break shins. "You've never seen anyone talk to a stuffed animal before?"

"Actually, no."

Holding his gaze, she reached into the possibilities. "You still haven't." Scooping up Samuel, she stood and headed for the revolving door. Outside, on Carlton Street, she put the cat down on a cleared bit of sidewalk.

"Hey! I'm in bare feet here!"

"You're a cat. That's the only way your feet come."

"Right. I knew that, but . . ."

As the pigeon back-flapped into a landing, Samuel whirled around and leaped. Had he been in the body longer, he would have had to have dealt with the small ethical dilemma of whether or not an angel could actually eat a pigeon he'd killed—not to mention the slightly larger health dilemma of whether or not anyone *should* eat a pigeon born and raised on the streets of Toronto. As it was, he hooked a tail feather, but the rest of the bird got away, dropping a large, white, hysterical opinion of the change on Diana's shoulder as it passed.

"Go on, chicken, fly! There's more where that came from!" He boxed the feather to the ground, flicked it up, and boxed it down again.

"Are you done?"

"One more time." Both front paws finally holding the feather captive, he smiled up at her. "Okay, I'm done. Now what?"

"First, you can stop being so cute."

"Actually, I don't think I can," Samuel admitted after a moment's consideration.

Diana sighed. "Swell. Do me a favor; if I ever talk baby talk to you, claw my tongue out."

"I don't think I can do that either."

"Not surprised." Bending, she picked him up and settled him in the crook of her arm. "Come on, it's the subway to the train station and the first train to London for us."

"That's it?" When she nodded, he looked thoughtful. "So essentially I became a cat in order to go home with you and live a pampered life devoid of responsibility while others take the risks and get the glory?"

"Looks like."

"Kewl."

The Bystander Diana'd adjusted in the hotel lobby never saw anyone speak to a stuffed animal again. Although his wife didn't believe in the disability, his children learned to exploit it early on by muttering constantly into the ears of plush toys when struck with the need to do something like fit a frozen hamburger patty into the DVD player.

"Yes, I have a car." Backed into a literal corner, panic rolling off him like smoke, Leslie/Deter saw no way out. "Why?"

Byleth smiled sweetly and moved a step closer. "Because I need a ride."

"No."

"If you give me a ride, I'll have sex with you." She probably wouldn't, but it seemed to be the best currency this body offered.

He swallowed and ground his shoulder blades into the wall, feet pedaling uselessly against the gray industrial tile on the floor. "No. I took the ch . . . chastity oath."

"The ch . . . chastity oath?" Her breasts flattened over a good portion of his chest. "Okay, if you give me a ride, I *won't* have sex with you."

"Deal!"

Nalo almost never went to Scarborough. As well as old Aunt Jen, it had another Keeper taking care of day-to-day metaphysical maintenance. Unfortunately, old Aunt Jen had taken a dislike to the man, and Nalo found herself in the unenviable position of comforter and confidante.

So here I am, back on the bus. Reaching into the possibilities, she adjusted the heat blasting out of the grille under the window—a minor technical infraction but preferable to dry roasting. *I know what Jen's thinking, calling me out here again. She's thinking she'll leave me that hole when she dies. Well, she can just think again. I don't give a damn about what's supposed to be, I'm not dropping my ass onto a hole in Scarborough for the next fifty years. The moment Jen passes, I'm hauling Diana out here and she can use that power of hers to slap the sucker closed and I don't care if she's got more important things to do because there isn't anything more important than keeping me out of Scar . . .*

Hellfire and damnation.

Her fingers closed around the cord, and she was up out of her seat before the sound of the bell reached the bus driver's ear.

"That's your car?" Pulling off a mitten, Byleth trailed her fingers along the gleaming black hood of the 1973 Firebird. "Who'd have thunk it—a God-pimp with a truly kewl set of wheels. Maybe I *will* have sex with you."

Eyes wide, Leslie/Deter jerked back. "Hey! You promised!"

Taking a deep breath, she leaned in and rubbed against the passenger door. "I know. But that was before I saw this totally demonic car."

"You want a ride or not?"

"Yessss. . . ."

"Then stop humping my car and get in."

The hair lifted on the back of Byleth's neck. She watched a city bus drive by, slow, and pull into a bus stop at the end of the block.

"Byleth?"

"In a minute. I've got to take care of something first."

The back doors of the bus opened.

She had to distract the Keeper or they'd never get away. Grabbing the first bit of darkness that came to hand, she tossed it into the small clump of preteens waiting at the light where it erupted into a sudden slush ball fight of epic proportions. She saw the massive handful of filthy ice and snow launched; she didn't wait to see it land.

"Let's go, Leslie." Dropping into the car, she slammed the door and reached for the seat belt. "Did I mention I was a demon?" she asked as they pulled into traffic.

His laugh carried distinctly nervous overtones. "I almost believe you."

"Really?"

"You're not like other girls. You're not even like the other girls we help off the street. You're not like any girl I've ever met. You're not . . ."

"I get it. Jeez. And thank you." She needed the reassurance as geeky as it might be.

It was getting harder and harder to touch the darkness.

As Nalo stepped off the bus, time slowed. She saw the slush ball approaching, the bits of rock and mud and ice standing out with unnatural clarity against the tiny bit of actual snow holding the thing together. She saw past it to the expression on the kid's face as he realized what was about to happen. She saw past him to a 1973 Firebird pulling away from the curb.

Then time sped up, and she didn't see anything at all for a few minutes.

Staggering forward, she clawed the slush ball from her face, reaching into the possibilities, past the pain and anger and certain knowledge that she was going to need to have her coat dry-cleaned again. Nalo had been a Keeper long enough that it would take more to distract her than a face full of frozen crap and the prospect of a twenty-two-dollar dry-cleaning bill.

But by the time she could see again, the car was gone.

The young man who'd exited the bus behind her, touched her lightly on one shoulder. "You okay, lady?"

"No. I have a sense of foreboding that can only mean darkness has found a way to corrupt the world, bringing down upon us a future of pain and pestilence. And I seem to have a piece of gravel up my nose."

"Bummer."

"Indeed."

Taking her seat on the half-empty subway, Diana did nothing to keep the other passengers from noticing the cat. Given the invisible walls that Toronto subway passengers erected around them in order to avoid interaction with potential crazies, religious lunatics, and lost American tourists, she could have been carrying a platypus on her lap and no one would have said anything. In fact, it very much looked as if an elderly woman in the other end of the car *was* carrying a . . .

"Hey, there's Doug!"

A talking cat, however, attracted a little attention.

"Hair ball," Diana announced, carefully tweaking reality. When everyone accepted the explanation—and no one took it as an instruction—she breathed a sigh of relief. "Keep it down," she muttered into the plush orange fur between Samuel's ears. "Unless you want to end up on late night TV hawking kibble between the psychics and those live girl phone things."

"1–800-U-CALL-ME," Doug added as he sat down beside them, having left a trail of cheap wine fumes the length of the subway car. "How's it going, Samuel?"

"Pretty good. Still haven't figured out the tail, though."

"It'll come. I see you're down to partial genitalia."

Diana closed her teeth on the comment she was about to make and took a closer look.

"Hey!" Samuel spun around and glared at her. "If you don't mind!"

"Sorry." *A self-neutering cat. Just what the world needs.* "And keep your voice down."

"No need, little lady. We're in my cone of silence." Doug stirred the surrounding miasma with expansive gestures, the cuffs of two jackets and three visible sweaters rising up on thin gray wrists.

Breathing shallowly through her mouth, Diana reached into the possibilities. They showed no cone of silence but, on the other hand, street people were ignored so completely by the rest of the city's residents it amounted to the same thing.

"Any particular reason you decided to walk on the furry side, kid?"

"We needed to expose a demon."

"A demon? In the world?"

While Diana rolled her eyes and wondered why it was taking so long to get from College Street to Union Station where they could lose Samuel's fragrant buddy, Samuel explained the whole thing.

"A demon in the world," Doug restated, frowning thoughtfully. "Well, now, that does explain things. And here I was blaming that bottle of aftershave I knocked back this morning. So you exposed a demon, and now you're off after it, right?"

"Wrong," Diana told him—or more precisely told the space next to him. She was finding it hard to focus on his face, but that could have been because of the pale green strand waving from his nose. "We're off home. Someone else is off after the demon."

"Her older sister," Samuel added.

"And you got a few younger sibling issues with that sister of yours, don't you? No need to deny it, it's dripping from your voice. Well, you know what I think?" He leaned conspiratorially forward. "I think that TV dinners go best with a nice Chardonnay."

"What?"

He blinked. "What did I say?" Diana repeated it and he sighed. "Whoa, train of thought got derailed. Toxic spills. Evacuate the women and children." He drew in a deep breath and released it slowly. Samuel flattened on Diana's lap, and it passed harmlessly over his head. "Okay. Let's try that again: I think you should go after that demon yourself. You have to save her."

"I what?"

"Save her. From your sister."

"It doesn't work that way. First of all, we don't interfere. Second, you seem to be a little confused about the good guys and the bad guys. And third, I don't even know why I'm talking to you about this."

"Because he's an angel," Samuel pointed out.

"Yeah, right, and I'm a model for Victoria's Secret."

Doug's eyes widened and he cupped both hands in front of his chest. "Hubba hubba!"

"Okay, that's it." Diana grabbed the cat and stood as the subway pulled into the King Street station. "I'm gone. We can walk from here."

"If the demon is an exact opposite of the young man Samuel was, then isn't she as much of a person?"

Doug's quiet question stopped her at the door. Diana sighed and let it close in her face before returning to her seat which was, not surprisingly, still empty. "Yes, she is."

"And is your sister likely to take that into account?"

"No, she isn't." If not for an angel, then definitely not for a demon. "I think she's taking this whole thing personally. But Claire's being led to her, and I don't know where she is."

"Does she know she's being hunted?"

"She should."

"So, a demon in the body of a teenage girl knows she's being hunted; what would she do?" He leaned forward, eyes narrowed. "You're a teenage girl, think like a demon."

My cover's been blown, I know I'm being hunted, I know I don't stand much of a chance but I've been backed into a corner . . .

As though he were reading her mind, Doug nodded, the green strand bobbing emphatically. "You'll never take me alive, copper."

"If she's got to go," Diana said slowly, "she's going to flip Claire the finger on the way out, leaving behind the biggest possible mess for Claire to clean up."

The constant pound of the Summons changed tone and timbre. Claire shifted under her seat belt and brought both hands up to rub at her temples. There were times when being a Keeper resembled sitting next to the drum kit at a Moby concert. "It's moving east."

Glancing across the cab, Dean made a deductive leap. "The demon?"

Claire nodded.

"We aren't after heading for Toronto, then?"

"It doesn't feel like it."

"Nice to get some good news." He turned his attention back to the highway. "Going *through* Toronto's insanity enough."

"I never noticed any insanity."

"You're not driving." After his first trip through Toronto, Dean had decided that the Montreal reputation for having the worst drivers in Canada was undeserved. Sure, Montreal drivers all drove like maniacs, but at least they drove like maniacs who knew what they were doing. As near as he could figure, Toronto drivers had their heads so far up their collective arse they had to make it up as they went along.

"The biggest possible mess," Diana repeated as the subway pulled into Union Station. "Oh, my God! She's going to Kingston!" Grabbing up Samuel, she ran for the doors, paused, turned, and said, "Are you really an angel?"

Doug smiled. "Can't you tell?"

"No." The first whistle blew and she stepped out onto the platform. She *should* have been able to tell. Behind the closing doors, Doug spread his hands and bowed. Diana could see his lips move, but the roar of the old Red Rocket drowned him out.

He turned and waved as the subway headed north up the University line.

"I wonder what he said," she murmured, hurrying toward the escalators.

"*Lex clavatoris designati rescindenda est.*"

"Good ears."

"I'm a cat."

"Only recently, so you can cut back on the attitude." Diana shifted the cat to her other arm, cut off an elderly Asian man, and raced up the narrow stairs, boots pounding against the metal treads. "And while I agree that the designated hitter rule has got to go, what does that have to do with him being, or not being, an angel?"

Samuel hooked his claws through her jacket. "Don't angels play baseball?"

"The Anaheim Angels. It's just the name of a team—I like so truly doubt there are actual metaphysical players on it."

"You sure?"

"No. And you know what? I don't care."

"*Qui tacet consentit,*" Samuel muttered, as she stepped out onto the tiles and headed for the train station at a fast trot.

"*Fac ut vivas!* And stop showing off, I can't think of anything more annoying than a cat who criticizes in Latin."

"A cat who horks up a hair ball in a hundred-and-forty-dollar-pair of sneakers?"

"*Tres* gross. You win."

Leaning into the turn leading to a well-worn flight of limestone stairs, he smiled. "Of course."

"*That* was cutting back on the attitude?"

"What attitude?"

Taking the stairs two at a time, Diana realized why so many of Claire's conversations with Austin ended in unanswered questions.

"So why is the demon going to Kingston?" Samuel asked as they leveled out and headed across the polished marble floor toward the line for train tickets.

"She's going to reopen a hole to Hell. OW!"

"Sorry." Samuel fought his claws free of jacket, sweater, shirt, and flesh. "Are you serious?"

"No, I'm bleeding!"

"Hey, I said I was sorry, but you can't just mention Hell to an angel and expect no reaction."

"Fair enough." Diana slid in between the velvet ropes and prepared to wait for the first available sales agent. At the moment, all three of them appeared to be on break. "That's one powerful union," she muttered when reaching into the possibilities produced no visible results.

"Hell?" the cat prodded.

"Okay, short version of a long story: My sister and I closed this really old hole to Hell in the basement of a sort of hotel in Kingston before Christmas. Sealed the site, saved the world—yadda, yadda, yadda—but the place will still remember the hole, so reopening it will give the demon the biggest bang for the least buck. If she gets past the Cousin monitoring the site fast enough—and from what Claire told me about the dirty old man, she shouldn't have much trouble if she came fully outfitted—she'll have time to get the hole open before Claire catches up. We may not have to worry about Claire erasing her personhood because the rising darkness will completely overwhelm it."

"Not to mention overwhelm the world with pure unadulterated evil insuring that everyone on it lives short miserable lives of pain and desperation."

"Well, yeah. That, too."

THIRTEEN

——— • ⊠◆⊠ • ———

"**N**OW BOARDING AT GATE RORG, VIA Rail train number gonta sev to Nootival, with stops at Gaplerg, Corbillslag, Pevilg, and Binkstain."

"That's us," Diana declared, scooping the cat up off the bench as the station loudspeakers repeated the announcement in French.

"Hey, watch the whiskers," Samuel protested as she stuffed him into the backpack she'd bought at the station shop, heaved him up onto one shoulder, and hurried toward the gate. He peered out through the open zipper at the back of her ear. "And I thought we were going to Kingston on the train to Montreal."

"That's right: Binkstain on the train to Nootival."

"You're kidding?"

"Just try to look like luggage, would you."

The sudden blip of a police siren woke Austin out of a sound sleep. One moment he was lying between Claire and Dean with a paw thrown over his eyes, the next he was up over the seat back and into the depths of his cat carrier muttering, "You can't prove it was me, anyone could have left that spleen on the carpet."

"You've got to admire his reflexes," Claire allowed, waving one hand through the contrail of cat hair.

"Do I, then?" Dean asked, gearing down and maneuvering the truck carefully to the narrow shoulder winter had left bracketing highway seven. "Sure. Okay, I guess."

Claire shot him a questioning glance, noted the muscle jumping along his jaw, and the distinct "man about to face a firing squad" angle to his profile. "You've never been pulled over before, have you?"

"No." He sighed and laid his forehead on the steering wheel.

It was a vaguely embarrassed no, but whether he was embarrassed because he'd been pulled over now or because he'd never been pulled over before, Claire couldn't tell. Some guys might be bothered by reaching twenty-one without a speeding ticket—or more precisely the story of how they got the ticket—but would they be the same guys who were bothered by un-ironed underwear? "Don't worry, I'll deal with it." She twisted around within the confines of the seat belt. "There's a demon out there; we haven't time to jump through hoops for the OPP."

"No."

This, however, was a definite no. An inarguable no. She watched Dean's chin rise as he rolled down the window and recognized his "taking responsibility" look.

"You don't do the crime," he announced, "if you can't do the time."

"What?"

"It's the theme song from a seventies' cop show."

"You weren't around in the seventies."

"I saw it at my cousin's. In Halifax. On the Seventies' Cop Show Network. He has a satellite dish," Dean added as Claire's brows drew so far in they met over her nose. "Look, it's not important, I just don't want you messing with the cop's head. I broke the law, so I'm after facing the consequences."

"You were doing one hundred ten in an eighty. It's not like you've been out robbing banks or clogging Internet access to I've-got-more-money-than-brains. com." Over the years, Claire had fixed a number of tickets while catching rides with Bystanders. Once, she'd attempted to convince a Michigan State Trooper that ninety-seven miles an hour on I-90 through Detroit was a perfectly reasonable speed. Poking around in his head, she discovered she hadn't been the first—or even the most convincing. "Dean, I'm sorry, but, as a Keeper, I have to say that getting rid of this demon has to be right at the top of our to-do list."

"It is."

"Good."

"Right after this."

"But . . ."

"Keepers police metaphysical crimes, right?" He caught up her hand and stared earnestly at her over her fingertips.

"Essentially, but . . ."

"How can I help you do your job, if I blow off this guy doing his?" Her eyes widened.

"That's *not* what I meant." His glasses steamed up in the heat rising off his face. "It's not. It wasn't. Look, just let me deal with this. And then you can do what you want to make up the time." The sound of heavy footsteps drew closer. "Claire?"

"Okay," she muttered reluctantly. "But make it . . ."

"A quickie," Austin snickered from the depths of the cat carrier.

As he turned toward the looming figure of the OPP constable, Dean shot a glance behind the seat that promised a discussion with the cat in the near future. Claire didn't know why he bothered since Austin usually went to sleep right around the time Dean started talking about mutual respect, but she admired his persistence—futile though it might be. A cat's idea of mutual respect had nothing about it any other species would recognize as mutual.

"License and registration, sir."

The constable's accent was pure Ontario and Claire felt some of the tension leave her shoulders. Maybe it *would* be possible to get back on the road with a minimum of delay.

Dean struggled to get his wallet out of his back pocket, realized he was strapped in, and jammed his seat belt trying to open it. Pounding the release catch with one hand and yanking at the lap belt with the other, he flopped about, making it worse. With the theme song to "C*O*P*S" running through his head, he fought to keep from hyperventilating as he alternately pounded and yanked. He'd watched enough television to know that when the police thought they were being dicked around life got unpleasant for the perp.

"If you'd just relax . . ."

"Not now, Claire." Just relax and it'll happen. Just relax and don't think so much. Just relax and let nature take its course. After two nights of Claire telling him to relax, that word in her voice got him so anxious he wanted to scream at her to shut up.

"I think your lady's trying to say that the tension against the belt is causing the problem."

"Oh." He sagged back against the seat, pressed the release with his thumb, and pulled the belt free. Fully aware of Claire's pointed stare, he got out his license and registration and handed them over.

"Newfoundland, eh?"

"I meant to get my plates switched—and my license," he explained hurriedly, hoping it didn't sound like he was making feeble excuses for breaking the law, "but I wasn't certain I was staying."

The constable bent down and peered at Claire. "I see. You know a Hugh McIssac?" he asked as he straightened.

"Oh, no . . ."

He bent again. "Ma'am?"

Claire reached into the possibilities.

Five minutes later, they were driving east at a careful eighty kilometers an hour having received a stern although truncated warning that had included no references to hockey.

"Is it warm in here, or is it me?" Austin asked, dropping down onto the seat.

Claire gathered him up onto her lap and shot a worried glance at Dean. He looked as though he'd been carved from flesh-colored marble, the only indication of his mood a certain flare to the one nostril she could actually see. *If he doesn't say something before we reach that pine tree, I'll speak first.*

The pine tree passed.

Okay, if he doesn't say something between now and when we reach those blackthorn bushes by the side of the road, I'll explain.

A lunantishee looked out of the bushes as they went by and stuck a long, mocking tongue out at Claire.

Fine, if he won't talk to me by that next crossroad, he can just sit there. There's no reason I should have to say anything. I was right. Because, after all, we're just on our way to catch a demon and that's so less important than a forty-five-minute discussion of a peewee game played back in 1979.

They crossed the crossroad.

Austin sighed. "So," he said, squirming around to face Dean, "who was Hugh McIssac?"

"A guy." Dean's teeth were locked so tightly together the words barely emerged, but innate politeness forced him to answer a direct question.

"A guy you knew back in St. John's?"

"Yes."

"Play hockey with him?"

"No."

Claire felt the burn rush up her cheeks at the clipped negative. *Oops.* There'd be no way to make this up to him. A sound caught somewhere between an apology and a whimper forced its way past her teeth.

Dean glanced at her and sighed.

"Against," he added grudgingly.

"Aha!"

"Oh, nice way to smooth things over," Austin muttered.

"So, if I hadn't stepped in, we *would* have been there another half an hour!"

Dean shook his head. "You don't know that."

"Because this would have been the time you cut the conversation short?"

"Yes!"

Claire folded her arms.

"Well, maybe."

She snorted.

"Okay, probably not. But that's not the point," he told her indignantly, slowing slightly to let a minivan pass. "You said you'd let me deal with it."

"I didn't change any of the police stuff. He had no intention of giving you a ticket."

"I'll never know that for sure, will I?"

"And there's nothing worse than girding your loins for a battle you don't need to fight," Austin interjected, climbing off Claire's lap and stretching out on the seat.

"You girded your loins?" Claire stared across the cat at Dean.

"No."

"No?"

"I don't even know what that means!" He sighed hard enough to momentarily frost the inside of the windshield. "I just wanted to handle it myself."

"You don't trust me?"

"Yes, I trust you. But you're some high-handed at times!"

"I'm a Keeper! And I'll have you know I'm no more high-handed than it takes to do my job. If you'd rather talk hockey than make love . . ."

"What?"

"We find the demon, I banish the demon, we find a private corner; isn't that the plan? Unless you don't want . . . Why are you pulling over? Dean?"

He put the truck into neutral, stepped down the parking brake, and pulled on the hazards. Then he turned to face her, one hand braced on her headrest, the other on the dash. "I want to make love to you. I want to make love to you so badly it's all I can think about. When I'm eating, when I'm driving, when I'm looking at you, when I'm not looking at you, when I'm talking about demons, when I'm talking about hockey—I'm still thinking about making love to you."

"And this is what you're thinking about when you're talking to me?" Austin demanded, rising up into the space between them. When Dean answered in the affirmative, he sighed and dropped back down again. "Well, that's really going to put a damper on future conversations."

Reaching out, Dean stroked the back of his fingers over Claire's cheek. "But I'm only thinking about making love to you because I can't actually make love to you. If I could, I certainly wouldn't be talking about hockey, I'd be . . ."

"Okay, that's enough. The cat does not need to know the details."

Without taking her eyes off Dean, Claire picked Austin up and dropped him behind the seat. Then she snapped off her belt and slid forward. After a moment she sucked Dean's lower lip away from his teeth and, when the suction finally broke, murmured into the swollen flesh, "Shall we find that demon, then?"

Dean's answer was essentially inarticulate.

Austin opted to stay out of the discussion entirely.

"Would you please stop doing that."

"Doing what?"

"Rubbing my car. It's . . ."

"Turning you on?"

". . . distracting me. I keep seeing peripheral movement, I think someone's about to make a lane change, and it's always you. It isn't easy driving this car in this weather in this traffic, and I'd appreciate just a little . . . HEY! YOU WANNA STOP VISUALIZING WORLD PEACE AND START VISUALIZING YOUR TURN SIGNALS! . . . consideration."

Byleth blinked, looked from Leslie/Deter to the SUV that had just drifted across three lanes of fast-moving traffic and back to Leslie/Deter again. "He didn't hear you."

"I know. But it makes me feel better. Helps me drive."

"Oh."

"It's just a way of releasing . . . TRY LEASING A CAR YOU KNOW HOW TO DRIVE, MORON!"

The car in question braked hard, swerved left, then right, then hit a patch of ice, turned a complete three hundred and sixty degrees and settled safely on the shoulder. A half a kilometer of brakes squealed, dozens of steering wheels were cranked, sudden moisture caused two seat warmers to short out, and then it was over.

Byleth smiled. "He heard you that time."

Fingers white around the steering wheel, Leslie/Deter stared wide-eyed out at the surrounding traffic still moving miraculously to the east and beginning to pick up speed. "God saved us all."

"You think?"

"He reached down His hand to keep His children safe."

"No." Byleth frowned and shook her head. "I'd have noticed that."

"You can't deny that was a miracle."

"Hey! I can deny anything I want," she snarled, folding her arms and slumping down in the seat.

They drove in silence for a few minutes, then Leslie/ Deter sighed and squared his shoulders. "You know, you're not as tough as you think you are."

Byleth glared at him past the lock of hair bisecting her face, her expression as much disbelief as anger. "You have no idea how tough I am."

"You think you're bad."

"I *am* bad!"

"You think it's cool to be all dark and dangerous."

"Hello? Hell to Leslie!" One navy-tipped fingernail poked him hard in the shoulder. "I *am* dark and dangerous."

"I know why you do it."

"Oh, please . . ."

"It keeps people from getting close to you. Keeps you from getting hurt."

"*I* don't get hurt. I do the hurting."

"Essentially the same thing."

"If you think that having red hot pokers stuffed up your ass is the same as stuffing those same pokers up someone else's ass, you're dopier than I thought. And that's almost scary." Beginning to wonder why she hadn't considered the implications of being stuck in a car with a God-pimp for three hours, Byleth unhooked her seat belt and twisted around until she faced the driver, her eyes onyx from lid to lid. "Leslie, look at me."

"Not now, Byleth. I'm trying to keep the car on the road."

"I said, *look* at me."

"And I said, not now!" A glance in the rearview mirror showed the front grille of a transport and not much else. "Unless you really want to end this little journey upside down in the ditch."

She thought about that for a moment, her eyes lightening. "Well, no."

"Good." He leaned back, downshifted, pulled into the passing lane, and, engine roaring, shifted back into overdrive. They screamed past traffic and dropped speed only when they'd cleared the clump and had moved back into the right-hand lane.

Byleth closed her mouth with a snap. "That was *so* kewl."

Bright spots of color appeared on pale cheeks. "Thanks."

"Do it again!"

"Sure, next time I have to pass something."

"What? Like a kidney stone? Do it now!"

"No." Glancing over at her, his eyes widened. "Byleth! Do up your seatbelt!"

"Because you'll get a ninety-six-dollar fine and lose three points if the cops pull us over?" she sneered, her hands as far away from the belt as possible while still attached to her body.

"Because you'll get hurt if anything happens."

"Won't your god protect me?"

"It doesn't work like that."

"Tell me about it," she snorted.

He sighed and shook his head. "I've been trying to."

"I want you to know I'm only doing this up because I have to get to Kingston in one piece," Byleth told him as she dragged the shoulder belt down over her jacket, and shoved the clasp together as hard as she could. "I'm sure not doing it because you told me to. And I so totally don't believe you care if I get hurt."

"I do care."

"Why?"

"Damned if I know."

"Probably," she snapped, sinking down into the depths of the bucket seat, knees braced against the dash.

Samuel poked a paw out through the top of the backpack and tapped Diana lightly on the chin. "What's wrong?"

"Summons," she whispered. Although the train was crowded with post-Christmas travelers, they had a double seat to themselves—mostly because of the disgustingly realistic stain the possibilities had provided. She'd draped her jacket strategically, but talking to luggage would still attract Bystander attention.

"Okay." A quick shoulder lick to gather his thoughts and he had a plan. "Here's what we'll do: you deal with the Summons, and I'll go to Kingston and save the demon from your sister."

He looked perfectly serious. Or at least as serious as an orange cat in a green backpack could look.

"And just supposing I was insane enough to agree to that—how?"

"I'll think of something. I'm a cat."

"You're an angel shaped like a cat," Diana reminded him pointedly.

"That's what I meant, I'm an angel."

"Right. Fortunately, the Summons is on the train. I can deal." She stood, left her jacket lying where it fell and, turning reluctantly in place, attempted to pin down the feeling. It wasn't that she minded being Summoned, it was what Keepers did, after all, but since her wallet had been distinctly short of lineage money, and she'd had to spend her Christmas money to buy the train ticket, it didn't seem exactly fair. Either she was saving the demon on her own time, or she was working—which was it to be? "There! Is that the washroom," she added, smiling broadly down at the middle-aged man whose attention had been jerked away from his paper.

He shot her the look those over forty reserved for those under twenty and returned to a review of *Archie and Jughead,* the holiday's breakout movie. Diana hadn't seen it, but she strongly suspected George Clooney had been miscast.

The sound of claws in upholstery brought her shuffle toward the aisle to a sudden stop.

"Where are you going?" she muttered, bending so that her face was millimeters from the angel's, pushing him back under her jacket.

"With you."

"Why? You won't be able to do anything. I won't be long. Just stay here."

Samuel thought about it for a moment. "No."

"Why not?"

He seemed surprised by the question. "I don't want to."

"Fine." Grabbing the straps, Diana swung cat and carrier up onto her shoulder, enjoying the muffled, "Oof!" rather more than she should have.

As it turned out, the accident site *was* in the washroom. Unfortunately, so was someone else. There were four people already waiting in line and judging by their expressions, not to mention the fidgeting, they'd been waiting for a while. Hoping she wasn't too late, that seeping darkness hadn't claimed a victim, Diana reached into the possibilities just far enough for safety—not quite far enough for voyeurism.

She couldn't quite prevent the astounded sputter.

The motherly woman in line in front of her half turned. "Are you all right?"

"Choked on spit. Hate it when that happens."

"I see." Still looking concerned, although her focus had shifted from concern for to concern about, she turned away.

The possibilities had shown two people in the bathroom. They'd already been there longer than they'd intended, and it seemed like they were going to be there for quite a while yet. Darkness had no intention of allowing a quickie, not when a delay would leave everyone involved so frustrated. Few things resembled a lynch mob quite as much as people waiting for a toilet.

As though Diana's thoughts had been her cue, the first person in line, an elderly woman with deep angry lines dragging down the corners of her mouth, stepped forward and banged impatiently on the door.

Which broke the rhythm and looked to delay things even further.

There seemed to be only one logical thing to do.

A few moments later, the couple emerged looking too totally satiated to be embarrassed by the amount of noise the finale had generated. Muttering in disgust, the elderly woman pushed past them, slammed the door, and shot the "occupied" slide home with such force it echoed throughout the car like a gunshot.

Moving Samuel to her other shoulder, Diana followed the line forward, jerking to a stop at the sound of a happy moan from inside the bathroom, closely followed by a muffled "Oh, yes. Yes! YES!" from the cubicle in the next car. Blushing scarlet, she reached back into the possibilities. She'd only intended to bring the original couple to a conjugal conclusion, not everyone who had to relieve themselves between Toronto and Montreal.

Although VIA *was* trying to get more people to ride the train. . . .

Diana caught herself on the edge of the toilet as the train lurched around a corner, barely managing to keep her head from cracking against the outer wall.

"Better wash your hands when you finish," Samuel observed from the sink. "You wouldn't believe what this place is covered with."

"I can guess."

Hooking a paw around a tap, he braced himself as the car rocked from side to side. "No surprise really, I mean, how can a guy aim when he's being flung around the room."

"How about sitting down?"

"Not manly. Don't put your hand there!"

"Eww. You're not helping." She erased the signature a Cousin had left behind and straightened. "It's not a big hole, but it's been here for so long it may take a while to close it down. I'll have to keep coming back—do it a bit at a time."

"You're going to attract attention," he pointed out, climbing into the backpack so she could wash her hands.

"As if. People don't watch other people heading for the bathroom."

"You think she'd try adult diapers or something."

"Yeah. Adult diapers."

Just past Coburg, heading into the bathroom for the seventh and hopefully final trip, Diana leaned down and smiled sweetly at the two young men who'd made their observation about adult diapers in carrying voices. "I'm on my period," she purred for their ears only.

They leaned away from her, appalled.

"Lots of heavy bleeding."

The blond turned green, his gold eyebrow piercing standing out in stark contrast to his new skin tone.

"Clotting even."

The brunet swallowed three times in quick succession and clamped a hand over his mouth.

"Sloughing off big chunks of uterine lining."

They exchanged identical expressions of horror.

"One more word out of either of you," she promised, "and I'll go into detail."

"Was that nice?" Samuel asked, emerging from the backpack as the bathroom door closed. "I mean, they were just being guys."

"Yeah, well, I am not an angel."

He sighed and shook his head. "You're not even a cat."

"Look, it's easy, stop the truck or I ruin the upholstery. Your choice."

Claire rolled her eyes as Dean began looking for a place to pull over. "You went to the bathroom less than fifty kilometers ago."

"And now I have to go again."

"Austin, we're in a hurry!"

"So am I."

Since the truck was now stopped, there didn't seem to be any reason to continue the argument. Opening her door, she watched Austin leap to the ground and disappear behind a young spruce.

After three minutes on the dashboard clock, she opened the door again and called, "Austin? Are you all right?"

"I'm old," his disembodied voice reminded her. "It takes a while."

"Be careful." She closed the door and sighed.

"Worried about him?" Dean asked gently, brushing a few snowflakes off her hair.

"A little."

"Seemed like some sigh for a little worry."

Noting the sudden spray of snow from behind the spruce, Claire glanced over at the clock and sighed again. "I just can't help thinking that there's got to be a more efficient way to fight darkness. There's a demon loose in the world and we're waiting at the side of the road for a cat to pee."

The certain knowledge that they were not going to be eating in his car gave Leslie/Deter the strength to hold his table against all comers. He looked up from two number fours, one supersized, a coffee, and a hot chocolate as Byleth approached, limping slightly, and demanded, "Are you all right?"

Byleth adjusted her jacket, smoothed her hair back into place, and shrugged. "I had to fight through a busload of old ladies to get to a stall."

Above the line of the black turtleneck, Leslie/Deter's pale face blanched paler still and he glanced toward the women's washroom as though he expected to see a blue-haired horde emerge brandishing American-made toaster ovens. "You didn't wait your turn?"

"As if. I'd still be in there." She looked around the rest stop, noting the lineup of elderly men at all three of the fast food outlets. "I know the baby boom is aging, but this is nuts."

"They're on their way home from a holiday trip to Casino Rama."

"You can tell that from looking?"

Byleth could feel him tottering on the edge of a lie, but in the end he shook his head. "No. It said so on their bus."

"Oh. Well, when I unleash Hell, old people will be among the first to go—because they don't run as fast," she explained when he made a strangled, wordless protest. "I mean, even demons with no actual legs can move faster than some old fart using a walker."

"I wish you wouldn't talk like that." He checked to make sure no one had overheard before squaring his shoulders under the black leather trench coat and meeting her . . .

. . . staring past her left ear. "I don't like it."

"Because of the God thing?"

"Yeah. Because of the God thing." His stance softened as he slid her food across the table. "It isn't funny."

She grinned at him over a mouthful of fries. "I wasn't joking."

"Byleth."

"Leslie. You know what I don't get," she continued. "You drive a really cool car, you've got that high-priced sort of Goth meets 'N Sync look going, you're neither boxers or briefs so what is it with you and God? It's like, so geeky. You don't really believe you have a personal relationship with the big kahuna, do you?"

"Yeah, I do."

She put down her burger and took a closer look. He really did. It was . . . unexpected. And disconcerting. Pushing her hair back off her face, she glared at him from under lowered brows. "In my experience, a so-called personal relationship with God mostly involves criticism of lifestyle choices."

"Lifestyle choices?"

Her eyes went onyx. "I'm a demon."

Leslie/Deter's gaze skittered off hers, wandered the room for a moment, then slowly returned. His hands were trembling, but he swallowed and looked deep into the unrelieved black. "You don't have to be," he said.

And he believed that, too.

Byleth shoved her chair back hard enough to scrape the hard rubber legs across the tile floor with a noise that mixed fingernails on blackboards with the scream of a jammed fan belt. Half the people in the room winced, the rest put a hand to their better ear and shouted, "What?"

"Come on." She snatched her diet cola up off the table. "This isn't getting us any closer to Kingston."

Claire began to get fidgety as the main street of Marmora disappeared behind them.

"Are you all right?" Dean asked, reaching out to capture her hand.

"I don't know. Something's nagging."

He eased off on the gas. "Do you want me to stop?"

"Oh, sure," Austin muttered, stepping indignantly across her lap, "but when the cat has to pee, there's no sympathy."

"It's not my bladder, Austin, it's the Summons."

"I knew that."

"Of course you did." Pulling free from Dean's grip, she stroked her fingers along the brilliant white expanse of stomach fur, the familiar motion and answering purr smoothing out her agitation.

"Claire?"

"Right, the Summons. We need to turn south. Now."

Dean looked past her to the snow-covered fields and copses of naked trees passing on the south side of the highway. "Now?"

"Not exactly now. But as soon as you can." Claire drew the Ontario Map Book out of the glove compartment, found highway seven, followed it to Marmora and beyond. "There." Her fingernail tapped an intersection of two red lines. "Turn off on number 62 to Belleville."

"That where we're headed?"

"No, we have to go farther east, but that's where we'll pick up the 401."

"What's east of Belleville?"

Claire ran her finger along the double line. "There's Napanee," she told them, continuing to check the route, "but I don't think that's the . . ."

"Place?" Austin prodded rolling up onto his feet. Head to one side, he looked from Keeper to map and then followed a thin line of gray up to where it spread out against and disappeared against the gray upholstery on the inside of the roof. "What's that smoking under your finger?"

"Kingston." She closed the book with a snap.

"Kingston?" Dean repeated.

Claire met his eyes and nodded.

Austin sat down again. "At the risk of sounding clichéd, I've got a bad feeling about this."

❄   ❄   ❄

"You know what I love about trains? When they stop between stations for stupid reasons, you can't get off."

Curled up in the depths of the open backpack, Samuel yawned. "Why would you love that about trains?"

"I was being sarcastic."

"I knew that."

"Sure you did." Diana glared out the window at the cars moving by on the highway, one empty, snow-covered field away—her left foot tapping against the floor, right fingers splayed out on the window. "I could have walked over there and got another ride by now, but, oh, no, that'd be against the rules. If I'd been Summoned to Kingston, I could fix whatever the stupid problem is, but only attempting to prevent a gross injustice isn't reason enough. This is *so* lame."

"It's important you follow the rules."

She snorted. "That's something I never thought I'd hear a cat say."

"I meant you specifically."

"Oh, ha! I guess angels don't mind wasting time, the time we could be using to get there first and set a trap." Her right foot took over the beat from her left. "This so totally sucks." The weight of a Bystander's regard pulled her head up. The blond young man she'd previously terrorized was standing in the aisle staring down at her. "What?"

"Are you talking to your backpack?" he asked, leaning forward.

Diana closed the flap on the top of the big pocket. "Are *you* operating on more than two brain cells?"

"I just thought you had a . . ." He dropped his voice below the level of the ambient noise. ". . . cat."

"And what if I do?"

Glancing around, as though he were about to hand over state secrets, he shoved a piece of beef jerky toward her, managed half a smile, hurried away. Frowning, she reopened the pack and offered Samuel the jerky.

"Did you let him leave?" he demanded, hooking it out of her fingers.

"I don't think he'll tell anyone."

"That's not the point," he protested. "The point is, there's always more than one piece in a package of beef jerky."

"Maybe I should just go offer myself to him to keep you from starving." Before he could answer, the train lunged about five feet forward, then began picking up speed in a less vertebrae-separating manner. "Finally! If that demon's raised Hell before we get there, I'm sending a nasty letter to the smoking ruins of the VIA Rail head office."

"Oh, yeah, that'll show them."

"So is there some place you want me to drop you off or what?" Leslie/ Deter asked, as the car squealed its way around the tight exit ramp at Division Street. "If you're on your own, we have a mission in Kingston."

"I so don't care. Besides I know exactly where I'm going."

"Might be nice if the driver knew."

"Lower Union Street. Just off King." Byleth wet her lips in anticipation. "Place called the Elysian Fields Guest House."

FOURTEEN

◆━━◆━━◆

"**I**T DOESN'T LOOK LIKE IT'S OPEN."

"That doesn't matter," Byleth said softly, staring up at the three-story Victorian building. The memory of darkness had left a grimy patina over the red bricks—a discoloration any eyes but hers would assume had been left by modern pollution. Well, the yellow-brown stains eating away at old mortar *had* been left by modern pollution, as had the patches of filthy, crumbling paint on the pale green trim, the white streaks from acid rain on the old copper roof, and the rather amazing amount of rust on every exposed piece of iron. She sighed and wondered why darkness even bothered.

"Maybe I should go in with you."

"Maybe you should mind your own friggin' business." She unlocked the seat belt and shoved open the door with the same angry motion, uncertain of just who she was angry at. *I ought to suggest that he put it in gear and then drive into something solid, but why waste such a cool car.* She considered telling him to park by the lake and walk out until he found a break in the ice. Or to jump off the top of a building. Or to take in a Britney Spears concert. Well, she might not be able to touch enough of the darkness to manage that last one, but all the rest were perfectly feasible. Standing on the road, still holding the car door, she examined her options.

Leslie/Deter ducked down far enough to see her face. "Be careful."

"Whatever." No point in wasting diminishing resources on such a loser, not when there was a world of dark potential at her back. Muscles straining, she pulled at the heavy door and was astonished to hear her own voice just as it closed. "Thanks. You know, for the ride."

Gratitude?

Eww.

Spitting wasn't enough to take the taste out of her mouth. This was so the last time she was manifesting in Canada.

Clutching her open coat more tightly around her, Byleth waited until the car disappeared around the corner before turning toward the house. The God-pimp was just the kind of guy who'd hang around to make sure she was all right. "As though he could do anything about it if I wasn't," she sneered, climbing over a ridge of snow and up the nine uneven steps to the porch. There was a door down an equal number of steps in the area, but a teenager breaking into the basement of a guesthouse might be noticed by the neighbors while a customer, even a young customer, approaching the front door would not— knowledge not from the dark end of the possibilities but overheard last night in the mission dorm. If things went her way over the next couple of hours, there were a few other bits of overheard information Byleth looked forward to trying out—although she wasn't entirely certain what a funchi, key caz star boi was.

The door was unlocked.

The old-fashioned brass knob turned silently.

There'd be a Cousin inside. A Cousin who'd have been able to sense her since this morning when that idiot angel had so unexpectedly changed. A Cousin who had to know she was close. Who could be waiting, ready for her, just inside.

I can take a Cousin.

Palms suddenly damp, she hesitated, wondering why she was leaking. She *could* take a Cousin. Couldn't she? At the precise moment she made form out of darkness, she could definitely have taken a Cousin, but for every moment after that, she'd been changing. Or, more precisely, the body had been changing her. Into what? That was the question. Suddenly racked with very undemonic insecurity, she froze.

I don't even know who I am anymore. This was such a stupid idea.

It took a cold wind blowing in from the lake to get her moving again. Freezing was fine as a metaphor, she decided, pushing open the door, but in the real world it sucked big time. So maybe she couldn't beat a prepared Cousin—no matter how pointless the whole stupid thing ended up being, it was infinitely preferable to spending another moment feeling like imps were jabbing icicles into her ears. She got enough of *that* back home.

It wasn't significantly warmer inside the guesthouse.

The lobby and the tiny office behind the long wooden counter were empty of everything except a rather pitiful looking desk and an old rotary dial phone. Either the Cousin whose presence permeated the building had set a trap closer to the memory of Hell, or he hadn't thought her much of a threat.

Byleth's fingers curled into fists and her mood flipped a hundred and eighty degrees, insecurity trumped by insulted pride. *That's just fine,* she snarled silently. *If you want a threat, I'll give you a threat.*

Tossing a disdainful glance at the hunter-green walls—so yesterday's color—she moved quietly down the hall, allowing instinct to guide her. After it guided her to the kitchen, which decidedly had never held a hole to Hell in spite of a rather eldritch pattern of grape jelly spilled on the counter, she started opening doors.

The basement wasn't that difficult to find.

Given the history of the place, Byleth could think of only one reason for the large metal door across from the washer and dryer, although reasons for it to have been painted turquoise escaped her. A few steps closer and she saw that it was ajar.

This, then, was where the Cousin had set his trap.

"Where to?"

Setting the squirming backpack carefully on the floor behind the driver's seat, Diana dropped into the cab and slammed the door. "The Elysian Fields Guest House, Lower Union just off King Street."

"That's downtown, by the waterfront?"

"Last time I checked." Given the building in question, that wasn't entirely a facetious statement.

"The Elysian Fields Guest House?" the cabby repeated thoughtfully, easing his car into the line of traffic leaving the train station's parking lot. "Bet that's a name that doesn't draw a lot of business. Might as well call it the Vestibule of Hell."

Diana smiled grimly at his reflection in the rearview mirror. "It's been considered."

"'Elysian, windless, fortunate abodes // Beyond Heaven's constellated wilderness.' *Prometheus Unbound*, Percy Bysshe Shelley."

"Gee, and I can't imagine why my guidance counselors keep steering me *away* from an English Lit degree."

"I could also do you a great wanking piece from *Henry V*," he told her, changing lanes on Days Road, "but the city's not sanding as much as they used to and last night's snow is a bit packed in."

"I vote you pay attention to the road. You could even speed if you feel up to it."

"In a hurry."

"Definitely."

"Meeting a boy?"

"What happened to paying attention to the road?"

"Just asking." His reflection frowned slightly. "You got a cat back there?"

"No." It came out a little fast, but Diana thought it still sounded sincere. The last thing she wanted to do was mess with a Bystander's mind in a moving vehicle. Okay, not the last thing, but it was definitely in the top ten somewhere between seeing the N'Sync movie and having a root canal. "It's just a backpack."

"You think you could get it to stop sharpening its claws on the back of my seat?"

"If she opens the way . . ."

"It, not she. It's a piece of darkness given physical form, it's not a person."

Ducking back into the right lane to pass a Mazda Miata toddling along at a mere twenty kilometers over the limit, Dean shook his head. "Diana seems some certain there's a person involved."

"Diana also believes that The Cure is the best band in the world."

"They're decent," Dean acknowledged.

Trying not to feel old, Claire stroked a comforting hand down Austin's back, but whether she was comforting him or herself, she couldn't say. "It won't be that easy to reopen the site. There were three Keepers involved in closing it, as well as you and Jacques, and it's not that easy to find a hotel keeper from Newfoundland and the ghost of a French Canadian sailor in downtown Kingston on a Wednesday afternoon during the Christmas holidays."

"On a Saturday night in mid-January?"

"Not impossible."

"Demons have their own connection to darkness," Austin reminded her. "She won't need to reproduce all the factors."

"It," Claire reminded him. "And I know. But all the convolutions should slow it down."

"Should?" Dean wondered.

"Will. Why are *you* slowing down?"

"Exit ramp."

"Right."

"And there's a police cruiser on the shoulder up ahead."

"Let me worry about that." Reaching into the possibilities, Claire reset the radar gun to the Disney Channel. "You just drive."

There was no trap on or around the furnace room door.

Standing at the top of the stairs leading down to the bedrock floor, Byleth wet her lips and stepped forward. One step. Two.

No Cousin. So far, no Keepers.

"Oh, sure, ignore me all you want, but I'm not going away." The slight echo in the room made her sound more petulant than defiant. Definitely the echo . . .

On the bottom step, she paused, suddenly worried she was about to do the wrong thing.

"Wait a minute." The smack, palm to head, was a little harder than it needed to be. "I'm *supposed* to be doing the wrong thing." Stepping off onto the floor, she walked quickly to where the memory was the strongest and, before yet another mood swing could come along, dropped to her knees, placing her hands flat against the stone. The connection was there, but what should have been a rush of power revitalizing every dark molecule of her being was no more than a mere trickle of low-end possibilities it took forehead-furrowing concentration to feel.

WE'RE SORRY, THE NUMBER YOU HAVE DIALED IS NOT IN SERVICE. PLEASE INSCRIBE A PENTAGRAM AND TRY AGAIN.

"Oh, for . . ." Both palms slapped down hard. "I don't need a freaking pentagram, I'm a piece of you!" All the hair on the back of her neck lifted as her anger lent the connection new strength. They were listening down there, no doubt about it; probably arguing about who was going to take the call. "This isn't evil, guys, this is irritating. Do you want to be released into the world or not? I've got better things to do than sit around waiting for you to get your head out of your ass."

HEY! THERE'S NO NEED TO BE INSULTING.

Byleth sat back on her heels. "Got your attention, so apparently there is."

YOU'VE BEEN CORRUPTED BY THE WORLD.

WE HARDLY RECOGNIZED YOU.

Hell sighed. THEY GROW UP SO FAST.

"Look there's a Keeper coming . . ."

WE FEEL ONLY YOU.

BECAUSE THERE'S NO ACTUAL HOLE, IDIOT.

OW.

Didn't miss that, Byleth remembered. "The point you're not listening to is that we don't have much time so like pull it together into one voice, would you, and tell me how to reopen this thing."

In the long pause that followed she had the strangest feeling Hell was about to ask if she was sure, if she really wanted to wrap the world in a shroud of darkness and pain. All the world, including the Porters and that axworthy guy in the music store and Leslie/Deter and his car. Which was ridiculous because Hell as a general rule could care less about the opinions of and/or motivations of those who offered it a chance to release chaos.

She bit her lip almost hard enough to draw blood.

Was she sure?

ALL RIGHT, HERE'S WHAT YOU HAVE TO DO. . . .

Too late anyway.

"It doesn't look like it's open."

"That doesn't matter," Diana told him, handing over the last of her Christmas money. "The guy who runs this place is a Cousin."

"Ah, yes, family, where they always have to take you in. 'A happy family is but an earlier heaven.' John Bowring."

"And this particular family is trying to prevent an earlier Hell." Backpack on her lap, she slid out the door and straightened. "Keep the change."

"'There is a certain relief in change, even though it be from bad to worse.' Washington Irving."

Smiling tightly, Diana slammed the cab door. "Get a life," she advised as he drove off, then she turned and raced up the porch stairs, ignoring Samuel's muffled protests as he banged against the small of her back. Once inside, she dumped him out on the counter and watched incredulously as he raced to the end, flung himself to the floor, charged across the lobby and halfway up the stairs, spun around, returned at an even higher speed, launched himself back onto the counter, across to the desk, to the windowsill, and back to the counter again.

"What was that all about?" Diana demanded, hoping no one had heard.

"I figured out the legs," Samuel told her proudly. Turning around, he caught sight of his tail out of the corner of one eye and pounced.

"This is so not the time," she sighed as he spun about like a furry, orange, and not terribly coordinated dreidel. "The demon is in the building. Can't you feel the dark possibilities opening?"

Head spinning, Byleth struggled unsuccessfully to make sense of the information Hell had just passed through their tenuous link. "Let me guess," she muttered peevishly, wishing she could rub both throbbing temples, "those instructions were translated from the Japanese by someone whose first language was Urdu."

CLOSE.

"They don't make any sense!"

THEY DON'T? After a moment Hell cleared its throat in a vaguely embarrassed sort of way. UM, THAT'S BECAUSE THEY'RE ACTUALLY THE INSTRUCTIONS FOR HOOKING UP THE CABLES BETWEEN A DVD PLAYER AND A DIGITAL TELEVISION.

"Would they make sense if I *had* a DVD player and a digital television?" she snapped.

NOT REALLY, NO. HANG ON, WE'LL TRY AGAIN.

＊　　　＊　　　＊

"That Cousin who's supposed to be here . . ."

"Augustus Smythe."

Samuel's fur felt as though someone had been standing on a nylon carpet stroking him the wrong way and he had to keep fighting the urge to run up the walls. "He's not here."

"You can't smell him?"

"Oh, I can smell him. But he's not here."

"He's probably bleeding in the basement," Diana decided, wincing as the cat dropped to the floor with an emphatic double thud. "The blood of the lineage is the fastest way to open a dark hole."

"At least we know she hasn't got it open yet."

"Actually, we don't know that for sure because my brilliant sister never bothered to remove the dampening field around the furnace room." Leading the way to the basement door, Diana zipped her jacket back up, wondering why it was so cold. "Okay, full stealth mode until we see how far things have got. We don't want to spook her into destroying herself."

"Or the world."

"Yeah, that too."

Having hit every possible red light since they got off the highway, Claire was considerably less than happy as she reached into the possibilities to change the light at Division and Queen. "It's almost as though something was trying to prevent us from reaching the guesthouse in time."

"Gee, I wonder what that could be," Austin said dryly. "Or maybe we just should've left the highway at Sir John A. MacDonald Boulevard like I suggested, thereby missing the downtown traffic."

"Nothing personal," Dean told him, accelerating through the intersection and not even slowing as Claire changed the light at Princess Street, "but it's some hard to take driving suggestions from a cat."

"Why?"

"You don't drive."

NOW GO RIGHT.

"My right or your right?"

YOUR RIGHT.

"There?"

OH, BABY . . .

"Oh, stop it," she muttered, unamused. She'd been pouring all the darkness she had left in her into the stupidly convoluted pattern that sealed the hole, and although she'd thinned it to a thread, it was nearly gone. There might not be enough, even though she could now feel Hell trying to force its way to her from the other side.

"They'll be sorry." It was meant to be a snarl. It sounded more like a whine. "They'll *all* be sorry."

"Who'll be sorry?" Samuel asked, whiskers tickling the edge of Diana's ear.

"Standard teenage riff when attempting to destroy the world," she explained, crouched down and peering around the edge of the furnace room door. "So what happens if you two touch? Do you blow up? Like matter and antimatter?"

"I don't think so."

"You don't know?"

His tail lashed. "Hey, I just got here four days ago. You're the one maintaining metaphysical balances in the world, not me."

"Well, since this is my first angel/demon crossover, you'd better wait here. We're trying to save her, not lose you both."

"What are you going to do?"

"Convince her that there's another way." She straightened, pushed the turquoise door completely open, and stepped over the threshold.

There was no reaction. Not from the demon. Not from Hell.

Must be really concentrating.

One step. Two.

Maybe I should just try and knock her off the site.

Three steps. Four.

Then I sit on her until she listens to me.

Five steps. Six.

Just wish I knew what to say.

Seven.

The black-haired girl kneeling in the center of the bedrock floor, palms pressed against the stone, looked up, onyx eyes locking on Diana's.

Say something, you idiot. Claire can't be far behind you.

"Whassup?"

Byleth stared at the girl on the stairs in disbelief. "Oh, like that is *so* over. Take one more step, Keeper, and I punch right through to Hell." Which was total bluff; she'd gone as far as she could, it was up to the other side now.

WORK TOGETHER, GUYS! TOGETH . . . STOP THAT!

Clearly, she'd have to stall.

"Send me back now, Keeper, and this is the path I'll take. You'll be opening the hole for me."

"Diana."

"What?"

"My name is Diana, after a great-aunt my mother was sucking up to. I think she was angling for this totally ugly soup tureen. Got a 1915 chamber pot instead. Frankly, I didn't see much difference. Old ugly is still ugly." Two quick steps and Diana was standing on the floor, thankful for the thick-soled winter boots that partially blocked the emanations from Hell.

WHAT PART OF TOGETHER DO YOU NOT UNDERSTAND?

"Hardly your real name," Byleth snorted. "You wouldn't give me that kind of power over you."

"Why not?"

"Duh. Because I'm what I am and you're what you . . ." The onyx eyes blinked. "You did. Are you terminally stupid?"

"No. I hate being called *Keeper,* like I'm an earring or something. And you are?"

"Busy."

"Yeah, and rude. Do you have a name or what?"

"Byleth." She hadn't intended to tell but there was power in trust as well. "Not that it matters," she snorted, fully aware that the Keeper had been able to read the thought from her face, "only Demon Princes actually have names, I just borrowed this one."

Diana shrugged. "Seems solidly yours now."

"No way!"

"Way. You must've noticed how the form you're in has changed you. If all you were was darkness, you'd have had this hole open by now and I'd be talking to you with my head up my ass."

"I'm not sure you aren't," Byleth snarled.

"Nice. The point is, you're not just wearing flesh, because of the way you created yourself, you're wearing a fully functional human body, and it's corrupted you the same way it corrupted . . ." She resisted the urge to glance over her shoulder toward the basement and Samuel. "Well, you know who."

"You're the bitch who changed the angel and exposed me!"

"Yeah, yeah, sticks and stones. Now, shut up for a minute and listen; we don't have much time!"

Byleth's lip curled. "Because all Hell is about to break loose."

"Because my sister is right behind me."

"Ooo, another Keeper! I'm *so* scared."

"You should be. It's her seal you can't get through, and she could deal with *you* in a heartbeat."

"It doesn't look like it's open."

"That doesn't matter." Although the sidewalk and the steps had been shoveled, the driveway and parking lot beyond it had not. Dean pulled up as close to the curb as the snowbanks allowed. "I kept a key."

"Dean, boy, well done." The cat beamed at him as Claire shoved open her door. "It's nice to know that even the most over-ethical has a tiny streak of larceny."

"Mr. Smythe asked me to keep it."

Sighing, Austin jumped down to the top of the snowbank. "So much for that bonding moment."

"Byleth, you've become a person, and while you're not Miss Congeniality, you're not significantly different from at least half the kids I go to school with."

"And that's a good thing?"

"Actually, no, it's just a thing and that's what I'm trying to tell you, take away the darkness and there's a person with the same potentials as anyone else, and that person deserves a life. I want to help."

"Yeah, right. You're a Keeper, you're supposed to stop me."

Hands on her hips, Diana exhaled emphatically. "Look, if I was supposed to stop you, I've have done it by now. Stopped you, sealed the site, and gone for mocha latte. I'm not here as a Keeper. I wasn't even Summoned, I paid my own way with, I might add, money that could have been better spent on a new snowboard."

"I should've known you were a boarder." Her eyes narrowed on either side of the strand of hair. "I so don't see the attraction in careening down a hill in a stupid hat."

"I so don't see the attraction in black clothes and bad poetry, so we're even. Come on! You specialize in lies, you must know that I'm telling the truth. Have I touched a possibility since I got here? If you can't sense that, Hell can." Diana gestured toward the floor, keeping the movement as neutral as possible. This would not be the time or place to accidentally trace a sign of power in the air.

Door. Running footsteps. Another door.

Samuel was up on the shelf over the washing machine before the first set of boots appeared on the basement stairs. It was a pure cat reaction and by the time he realized he should have warned Diana, it was too late.

He recognized Claire immediately; not only did she emanate Keeper almost as loudly as Diana did, but there was a distinct physical similarity between the sisters. Beyond that, they shared the intensity that came from knowing they could, singly or collectively, explain British humor. Not to mention save the world. Unfortunately, Claire seemed as intently determined to send him back to the light as she was to send poor, confused Byleth back to the dark, and that made her someone he had to avoid.

Dean, who followed Claire down the stairs only because she held both handrails, refusing to let him by, seemed like the kind of guy who could be depended on to open the door seven or eight times an hour and pass down a sausage or two to keep a cat from starving.

Close on Dean's heels, Austin stopped suddenly and turned, mouth slightly open. His one-eyed gaze swept over Samuel's shelf like a pale green searchlight and kept going as though he'd noticed nothing.

Samuel wasn't fooled. *He knows exactly where I am. What do I do now?*

There was nothing he could do except tuck in his paws and wait, hoping the possibilities would give him a chance to redeem himself.

"All right, so you're here because you *want* to help me stay me. Big whoop. I'm here for the same thing." Under the red sweater, Byleth squared her shoulders, wishing she could stand and stare this Keeper down but unable to lift her hands from the rock until the link was completed. "When I release Hell, I'll gain the kind of notoriety that'll keep me real no matter how things turn out."

Diana sighed. She recognized bravado when she saw it. It was, after all, something she saw every day at school and occasionally in the mirror. Squatting, so that their eyes were level, she looked deep in the black depths and asked quietly, "Are you sure you want to do that?"

Was she sure? Confused, Byleth wondered how Diana's question could sound so much like the question she'd thought she heard back before Hell decided to cooperate. Maybe . . .

Maybe it wasn't too late.

Then the possibilities opened.

Claire entered the furnace room at a run, not having slowed in any significant way since she'd left the truck. She saw the demon kneeling in the center of the floor, hands pressed against the stone and knew what was happening. When the darkness in the demon reached through the pattern sealing the old hole and touched the ultimate darkness on the other side, all Hell would break loose. Which was an expression Claire had grown heartily tired of.

Banishing the demon down its own power stream and sealing the breach behind it would solve the problem nicely. A few minutes spent reinforcing things, and all but one of the embarrassing complications rising out of Dean's first time would be taken care of and the other Keepers could just go back to saving the world instead of hanging about in metaphysical chat rooms speculating about her love life.

Halfway down the stairs, she reached into the possibilities.

Her focus split between the demon and the anticipation of dealing with that one remaining complication, she didn't see Diana until her sister surged up out of a crouch, whirled around, and caught her power, stopping it cold a full three feet from its target.

The room, the house, and a three-block radius grew so quiet no one dared drop so much as a single pin. The point midway between the Keepers began to crackle and hum.

"I can't let you do this, Claire," Diana announced dramatically. "It isn't right."

Claire closed her mouth so forcefully the crack of her molars impacting could be clearly heard. "What are you doing here?"

So much for dramatic announcements. "What's it look like I'm doing, doofus? I'm stopping you."

"From doing my job!"

"From doing the wrong thing!"

"Says who?"

"Says me!"

"Diana, I'm warning you, get out of my way." Claire's voice had begun to hold more fear than anger. The last time Keeper had fought Keeper, the fight had occurred on the exact same spot and it had ended with one Keeper lost to darkness. "I was Summoned to deal with this thing!"

Diana squared her shoulders. "Then deal with the thing part and leave the rest of her alone."

"It's not a her! It's a demon! Stop being so stubborn and look at its eyes!"

"I've looked *into* her eyes, which is more than you've done, and I know what I've seen."

"You've seen what it wanted you to see."

"You are so wrong. I saw what she didn't want me to see. I saw someone who, from the moment she found herself in that body, made excuses to act against what she perceived as her nature. To act like a person. Okay, a kind of bitchy not easy to get to know I wouldn't trust her to watch my backpack, kind of a person but a person. And you have no right to destroy that."

"She's seduced you!"

"What? The lesbian thing and a cute girl in a tight red sweater? Sure, I've noticed, but I no more let every beautiful woman I meet seduce me than you let every beautiful man." Glancing over Claire's shoulder, she smiled up the stairs. "Hey, Dean. And," she switched a burning gaze back to Claire. "You just called her she."

"That's totally irrelevant!" It didn't matter how much power she pulled, her little sister effortlessly pulled more. "Diana, listen to me. So far the dampening field has contained this little rebellion of yours, but once it gets out . . ."

"Little rebellion of mine?" Diana rolled her eyes in disbelief. "Claire, I'm serious about this. *This* is serious."

"And you don't seem to recognize how serious this is." Older sister clearly wasn't working, Claire switched to older Keeper, her voice cold. "You are betraying everything you're supposed to protect!"

"Hey, Earth to stick up her butt, I'm protecting what I'm supposed to protect! I'm protecting a person from darkness. And you."

The air began to buzz and, between the Keepers, grow distinctly brighter.

Just inside the door, Dean had to squint to make out Diana's face and could only just barely see the back of Claire's head. "Claire, she's making a lot of sense. Why not shut this down and listen to her?"

The temperature began to rise.

"She wasn't Summoned, Dean. This goes against everything we are."

Diana stamped her foot against the floor in frustrated emphasis. "Claire! We're not slaves to what we are. We're as free to make choices as anyone, and I know I'm doing the right thing."

The vibration started in the center of the light and worked its way through the room.

"You'll open the hole yourself in a minute!" Claire warned.

"I'm just standing here, you're the one throwing power."

"Hello? Does anyone care what I want?" Byleth demanded.

NO.

"I do." Austin came out from behind Dean's legs and walked slowly down the stairs, the energy in the room fluffing him out to twice his normal size. He brushed against Claire's legs as he passed and looked pointedly at a drift of orange cat hair on Diana's jeans, then sat down just outside the old pentagram's center. "So tell me, besides the latest Cure CD, what do you want?"

"How did you . . . ?"

He smiled at her. "I'm a cat."

"But . . ."

"Let it go," Dean advised from the top of the stairs.

Byleth looked at him, realized he was nothing more than human but, more importantly, nothing less than human, looked at the two Keepers, looked at the cat, and sighed. "All right. Fine. You want to know what I want? I don't know, okay?"

"You don't know?"

"What, are you deaf?"

"Sounds human to me," Austin declared as though that settled it.

"Well?" Diana demanded, spearing her sister with a dark gaze. "We haven't got time for DNA evidence. Which one of us blinks first?"

Claire could feel Dean behind her, even through all the building possibilities. This was more than a Summoning, this was her chance to fix things between them. Balance of good and evil aside, if she didn't banish the demon, they'd be condemned to long nights of playing cards with a cat who cheated.

"Claire, please?"

She had no intention of looking into the demon's eyes, she knew too well how darkness worked, so she looked into her sister's instead and saw Diana honestly believed in what she was doing. It wasn't defiance, it wasn't sibling rivalry on a grand and possibly explosive scale, it was, plain and simple and totally unexpected, an attempt to do the right thing.

But I was Summoned to deal with the demon.

Would it be enough to destroy merely the demonic?

"Maybe," she said softly, "we're both right."

Feeling her eyebrows singe, Diana smiled, relieved. "I can live with that. Byleth?"

Byleth screamed.

LET THE GAMES BEGIN!

"Break her contact!" Claire commanded, gathering up the possibilities as Diana released them.

They had no more than a heartbeat before Hell reached her. "How?"

An orange blur raced past before Claire could answer, slammed into Byleth's chest and, in flash of both black-and-white light, knocked her over backward.

"She's clear!"

AND SO AM . . .

Claire hit it first with all the power that had been building against Diana's block.

NOT YOU TWO AGAIN!

Then Diana slammed the power from the block against it.

WE ARE THE HEART OF DARKNESS; YOU CANNOT PRE-VAIL.

"Can too."

"Diana, don't argue with Hell."

Together, they backed the heart of darkness down the narrow path, denying the possibilities it represented one after the other, until finally they shoved it right back where it had come from . . .

THIS IS REALLY STARTING TO PISS ME OFF.

. . . and sealed the hole tight.

I'LL BE BACK!

AND I'LL BE BEETHOVEN.

SHUT. UP.

OW!

Dropping to her knees beside Byleth, Diana scooped Samuel's limp body into her arms and peered anxiously into golden eyes. "Are you okay?"

He tried to focus on her face. "I, I can't feel my tail."

"Sorry." She shifted her knees.

"Oh, yeah. That's better."

"He's fine." Austin laid a paw on the younger cat's flank. "That was a brave thing you did, kid."

"It was a dangerous thing," Claire corrected, untangling herself from Dean's embrace and coming to stand over them. "Who are you, and where did you come from?"

Diana sighed. "Chill, Claire. His name is Samuel, and he's with me."

A set of claws pressed into the sleeve of her jacket, releasing a puff of down. "I am?"

"Aren't you?"

He rubbed his head against her face. "Yeah, I am."

Claire opened her mouth to demand more information, but the look on Austin's face stopped her. She smiled and shook her head. "Welcome to the family, Samuel." When Diana glanced up, startled, the smile vanished. "You, however, are still in deep trouble."

"I was . . ." About to say right, Diana glanced past Claire to Dean shaking his head warningly and said instead, ". . . wrong. I was wrong to defy an older Keeper in such a way, but there wasn't time to for anything else. I'm not sorry I did it, but I am sorry we had to clash like that." Settling Samuel against her chest, she held up a hand. "Friends?"

"I'm still mad at you."

"I know."

"This is bigger than taking my bra to school for show and tell."

"It wasn't that big a bra."

"Diana."

"I know."

Claire looked down at their clasped hands, unable to remember the actual moment when their fingers had linked. "This is going to take more than an apology."

"Then tell me what it's going to take, oh, older, wiser, shorter Keeper."

"Stop it." The corners of her mouth twitching, she released her sister's hand. "You were right and you know it, and there's no need to be so irritating about it." Before Diana could disagree, she dropped to her knees on Byleth's other side. "Let's just take care of this little problem before she wakes up and puts us through all that . . . indecision again. I won't go so easy on you the next time." But the heavily mascaraed eye pried open was pale gray and the rest of Byleth's body was equally darkness free. "That's strange. Samuel knocking her free of the site so unexpectedly must have dragged the rest of it out of her."

When no one offered any better explanation, Claire sat back on her heels and spread her hands. "So. What do we do with her now?"

"Why don't I carry her to a bed and we all spend some time thinking about it?" Dean asked, stepping forward. "You two don't always have to have instant answers."

"Obviously you haven't read the handbook," Diana snorted.

Claire ignored her with the ease of someone who'd spent seventeen years living with a cat. "That's a good idea, Dean. I'm sure we can come up with something once we've all detached a little."

"I'll be after putting her in my old room, then." He slid his arms under Byleth's shoulders and knees and lifted her easily. "It's closest."

Rising with Byleth's body, Claire reached out and pressed her hand against Dean's cheek. "I'm sorry I didn't keep my promise to banish the demon."

He smiled. "I'm after feeling it's not going to matter."

"You think?"

"I do."

"Yes!"

"Code?" Diana asked, watching her suddenly cheerful sister follow Dean and his burden up the stairs.

Austin shook his head. "You don't want to know."

"Uh, Austin, about Samuel."

"What about him?" He gave her the sort of look that was usually accompanied by small feathers around the mouth.

Suddenly unsure, Diana set the orange cat on his feet and stood. She had a feeling she'd need all the advantage height could give her.

"He knows," Samuel told her before she could decide how to answer. "He knows what I was."

"Will you tell Claire?" Diana asked the older cat, hoping he couldn't sense how anxious she was. "After what we went through with Byleth, if she found out what Samuel was, she wouldn't want him around. She'd be worried it could happen again."

"Hey, it's none of my business how you two crazy kids got together," Austin snickered, starting up the stairs. "And I think Claire's going to have plenty of other things to do for the next little while." Halfway up to the basement, he turned and glared into golden eyes following close behind, looking concerned. "If you so much as insinuate I'm too old to be doing this, I'll notch those virgin ears of yours."

"I wasn't going to."

"You're a terrible liar."

"Sorry."

"So you should be, kid. So you should be."

Claire was waiting for them at the foot of the basement stairs. "Dean's just digging out a blanket. Diana . . ."

"I thought we worked through this?" Diana demanded, folding her arms and lifting her chin defiantly, working the "best defense is a good offense" line. "Look, I know it was your Summoning and I shouldn't have gotten involved, but you've got to admit you were working from your own agenda here and not seeing what was so obvious to me. If I hadn't stopped you, we'd have lost all the potential Byleth represents."

"I'm not arguing." Her tone was so mild Diana braced herself. "I was only going to ask if Mom and Dad knew where you were."

"Mom and Dad?" It took her a moment to realize the implications. "Oh, no. I got so into stopping you and saving Byleth, I forgot to call." Patting her pockets, she remembered she'd left her cell phone behind. "Nuts! I'll have to use the phone in the office."

Kicking aside the cashews, she raced up the stairs two at a time with Samuel at her heels.

Claire and Austin followed a little more sedately.

"You're not going to go on and on to her about this little incident, are you?"

Claire shook her head, smiling contentedly. "No need. I'll let the pros handle it."

Exiting into the first floor hall they heard a desperate, "But, Mom, I meant to call!" and then giggling.

Cat and Keeper exchanged puzzled looks.

Giggling?

Before they had time to investigate, the only other door in the hall swung open to reveal a small Victorian elevator. Dean and Jacques had repaired it in the fall but when, on the inaugural trip, they'd boldly gone where no elevator had gone before, Claire'd declared it off limits until she was able to study it. Unfortunately, she'd been Summoned away before she had the chance.

A short, gnomelike man stepped out, arm in arm with an elderly bottle-redhead of formidable proportions. Matching his and hers lime-green bathing suits under open parkas and a trail of fine white sand suggested they'd just been to the beach. They stopped short at the sight of Claire and Austin.

"Augustus Smythe? Mrs. Abrams? What . . . ? Where . . . ?" Realizing that shock could keep her stuttering questions she didn't want the answers to all afternoon, Claire managed to pull herself together. "Never mind. Not important."

Snorting hard enough to nearly flip his mustache, Augustus Smythe stepped forward. "About time you got here."

"It is?"

"I should think so. We're on a commuter plane to Toronto in two hours and then it's off to sunny Florida."

"Florida?"

"We have a nice little condo in a seniors building only a block from the ocean." Mrs. Abrams wrapped both hands around Augustus Smythe's upper arm and beamed. "You'll have to come down and see us some time, Connie."

"Claire." This was all just a little more than she could cope with right now.

"Don't contradict," Smythe warned her. "It's rude. And what's more," he continued, turning his scowl on his companion, "she can't come see us, she'll be here."

"No." Claire raised both hands. "I'm not . . ."

"You are. You're the new Keeper for this whole region. Check your damned e-mail on occasion, why don't you. There you are, McIssac, I wondered where you'd got to. Figured you wouldn't be far."

"Mr. Smythe? Mrs. Abrams?" Dean's astonished gaze slid off the shelf of lime-green supported bosom exposed in the open parka and wandered around the hall, unsure of where it was safe to alight.

"Hello, dear boy. My, you're looking well."

"Thank you, um, you, too."

She released her grip on Augustus Smythe's arm just long enough to wave at the elevator. "We've been working on our tans."

"No time for chitchat." One hairy-knuckled finger jabbed toward Dean . . . "McIssac here will run the guesthouse." . . . then changed direction to jab at Claire. "You'll take care of the metaphysical from Brockville to Belleville with this as your base. He needs to be more than your love slave, and this area needs a permanent Keeper. Your cat looks like he could use a few less nights sleeping rough, too."

"He's never slept any rougher than a Motel Six," Claire protested.

"It was awful," Austin sighed.

"No doubt."

"Just wait a minute." Her urge to grab Augustus Smythe's arm aborted when he turned to glare. "Keepers my age don't get tied to one place."

"Times are changing. Thanks to modern communications, modern transportation, and spandex, Keepers can get to sites before they grow big enough to be dangerous."

"I've closed dangerous sites!"

"You dead yet? Then don't argue with me. A century ago, you'd have beaten considerable odds to be alive at your age. But now, fewer Keepers die, more Keepers are alive, the lineage can cover more of the world safely and still have what resembles a life. It's basic math. Your sister'll probably spend her first few years closing sites no one's been powerful enough to close until now. If she doesn't blow herself to kingdom come first."

It sounded good. But there had to be a catch. "So eventually the world won't need us."

"Did I say people were getting smarter?" He turned to Mrs. Abrams. "Did you hear me say that people are getting smarter?"

She beamed down at him. "I surely didn't, puddin'."

"There, see? The dumb asses in this world will always need someone to clean up after them. You're just getting a chance to live happily ever after while you do it. We'll get changed and out of your way. Coming, Mags?"

"Coming, puddin'."

"That was surreal," Austin observed as the two turned the corner into the office and then disappeared into Augustus Smythe's apartment.

Strangely uncertain, Claire looked around at the guesthouse—stopped looking around when her gaze got to Dean. "You want to stay, don't you?"

He shrugged. "It's your choice, Boss."

"Our choice."

About to defer, he suddenly shook his head. "Then, yes. I want to stay."

"Because you want to be more than my love slave?"

"I never said that. Just promise me something," he added after a moment, capturing her face in both hands and holding it far enough away from his that he could look into her eyes. "Never call me pud-din'."

Claire shuddered. "I think I can safely promise you that."

"Hey!"

They moved apart again as Diana and Samuel came down the hall.

"Was that who I think that was?"

"Yes."

"With . . . ?"

"Yes."

"Why?"

"They're moving to Florida together, Dean's taking over the guest-house and, if Augustus Smythe is to be trusted, which, of course, he isn't, I'm now covering a specific area . . ." She patted one of the hunter green walls almost fondly. ". . . based around this very build-ing."

Diana's lip curled. "Oh, man, that's such a happy tie-up-all-the-loose-ends ending I think I'm going to hurl."

"Take a number," Austin advised.

Claire ignored them both. "What did Mom say?"

"That I did the right thing and we'll talk about the rest when I get home."

"Well, she actually said," Samuel began and broke off as Diana glared.

"So what do we do with Byleth long term?" she asked, pointedly changing the subject. "She could live here with you, you've got the space. I think you two would make wonderful parents."

Dean blanched. "Uh, better idea." He pulled out a crumpled en-velope. "I found this in her jacket pocket. It's got the address and the phone number for a Mr. and Mrs. Harry Porter and a note that says 'if you ever need us, call.'"

"I don't know," Claire began.

He handed her the envelope. "The 'i' has been dotted with a little heart."

"Oh, yeah. They deserve each other. Although . . ." She sighed, frowning at the little heart. "I still don't like the thought of releasing even an ex-demon into the world."

"She'll be going to high school," Diana reminded her grimly. "Anything demonic she managed to do in the short time she was here, she'll more than pay for."

"Good point." The envelope changed hands again. "She's your project, Diana, you can do the honors."

"Okay, but I'm doing it from the phone in Dean's old apartment, I *so* don't want to run into Mr. and Mrs. Scary Old People again." Pivoting on one heel, she scanned the hall. "Samuel?"

Just as she started to worry, he emerged from the elevator, jaws working.

"Come on, we're going to go ruin Byleth's life. What are you chewing?" she asked as they started down the basement stairs.

"Someone left a piece of calamari in that little room."

"Eww. Don't eat stuff you find on the floor."

"I'm eight inches tall. My options are kind of limited."

As their voices faded, Claire moved back into Dean's arms, slipping her hands under his coat and grinning at his reaction to the temperature of her fingers. "Now that Hell's back out of the picture, you really have to put a furnace in this place."

"I know. Claire, I was wondering . . ."

"Natural gas is probably cheaper."

"Not that . . ."

Her hands dropped lower. "Just as soon as we get rid of everyone."

"No. Well, yes. Wait a minute." He caught hold of her wrists while he was still capable of stopping her. "The angel, is it gone, then?"

She nuzzled his neck. "Not exactly. Diana turned him into a cat."

"Samuel?" Shoulder blades pressed into the wall, he detached enough to look down at Austin.

"Samuel," Austin told him. "But Diana thinks Claire doesn't know, so keep it to yourself."

"Why?"

He shrugged and wrapped his tail around his front paws, managing to somehow look like a small, furry, one-eyed Buddha. "It's an older sister thing. In an effort to keep a small piece of the high ground, Claire needs to know things that Diana doesn't know she knows because Diana is so much more powerful. Keeperwise."

"Okay. But couldn't this whole thing . . ."

"No, he's no more an angel now than that girl's a demon. They canceled each other out when he knocked her away from the hole."

"Did he know that would happen, then?"

"Does it matter?" Claire asked.

"I guess not."

"I wouldn't worry about him," Austin said soothingly. "He's a cat."

"Which means?" Claire demanded from inside the circle of Dean's arms.

"Which means—and do you have to do that in front of me?—that he's still a superior being."

Long Hot Summoning

Back in the summer of 2001, I attended a convention in Toronto called TT15. Or possibly TT2001 . . . it used to be called Toronto Trek and that's how I remember it. Anyway, after my reading, during the question and answer session, I talked about this book which I'd just started writing. I gave a brief synopsis of what it was about and mentioned that it didn't, as yet, have a title. A woman in the back of the room called out, "What about LONG HOT SUMMONING?"

The perfect title.

I don't know who you are, but if you're reading this, this one's for you!

ONE

THROWING HER BACKPACK OVER ONE SHOULDER, Diana raced out the front door and rocked to a halt at the sight of the orange tabby crossing the front lawn. Or more specifically, at the sight of what dangled from the cat's mouth. With one of its disproportionately long arms barely attached and dragging on the grass, and something that looked like intestine wrapped around one bare ankle, the bogey was unquestionably dead. An eyeball bounced gently against its bloody forehead with every step. "Nice catch," she noted, half her attention on the approaching bus. "Where did you find it?"

"Ood 'ile," Sam told her proudly, his voice distorted by the body.

"You know you can't eat it, right?"

Amber eyes narrowed, he let the bogey drop and fixed Diana with an incredulous glare. "Do I look like an idiot?"

"No, but you haven't been a cat for very long . . ." Six months ago, he'd been an angel. Angels didn't concern themselves with the small things that slipped through the possibilities. ". . . and you know how my mother feels about that whole puking on the white wool rug thing."

"Once! I did it once!"

"Yeah, so did I, and she's never let me forget it either." With a scream of abused brake linings, the bus stopped more or less at the end of the driveway. "I don't have time to bury it now, so try to leave it where Mom's not going to trip over it." Turning, she took two steps and turned again, pulled around by the weight of Sam's regard. "Oh, right. Sorry. You are a mighty hunter. Your skill with tooth and claw is amazing. Fast. Deadly. I stand in awe."

"Hey! Sarcasm."

"Not sarcasm," Diana protested hurriedly. There were any number of imaginative places the dead bogey could be left. "But I've got to go. Mr. Watson won't wait forever."

"I'm amazed Mr. Watson stops at all."

"Yeah, well, need provides and all that. Remember, I'll be home early," she added, trotting backward up the path, "just in case there's anything you don't want me to catch you doing."

A presented cat butt made his opinion of that fairly plain.

Mr. Watson looked more nervous than impatient. He nodded a silent reply to Diana's cheerful good morning, closed the door practically on her heels, and jerked the bus into gear. Had Diana not already been reaching into the possibilities, she'd have landed on her ass as he burned rubber trying to outrun half-buried memories. Fully burying them would have messed with his ability to drive, so only the less likely edges had been fuzzed out, leaving him in a perpetual state of nearly remembering things he'd rather not. Which was actually a state fairly common among school bus drivers.

Diana tried not to resent his attitude, but it wasn't easy. This semester alone she'd stopped a black pudding from devouring an eighth grader, saved Chrissy Selwick from a three-headed dog attracted to the aconite in the herbal body mist she'd been given for Christmas— might as well have had "eat me" tattooed on her forehead—and prevented a Gameboy™ from taking over the world. Handheld computer games were more competitive than most people thought.

She'd also stopped Nick Packwood from hanging a second grader out the window by his heels, but since she still wasn't entirely certain the kid hadn't deserved it, she usually left that particular incident off her "reasons Mr. Watson should thank his gods I'm on the bus" list.

Making her way back through the rugrats, Diana noticed without surprise that the last six rows—the rows reserved for the high school students on the route—were nearly empty. On this, the last day of the high school year, only two freshmen had been unable to find alternative transportation.

"My brother was going to give me a ride," said the first as she passed. "But he had to go to work really early."

"Yeah. I was going to ride my bike, but I had, like, an asthma attack," the other explained, holding up his inhaler for corroboration.

Diana ignored them both. First, because a senior acknowledging freshmen would open up all sorts of possibilities she had no desire to deal with. Second, as the youngest, and therefore most powerful Keeper, as one of the Lineage who maintained the mystical balance of the world, as someone who had helped close a hole to Hell and faced down demons, she didn't need to justify her reasons for taking the bus.

Settling into her regular seat, she thanked any gods who might be listening that this would be the last day she'd ever be at the mercy of public education.

Frowning, Diana crossed the main hall toward the stairs, trying to get a fix on the faint wrongness she could feel. It wasn't a full-out accident site; no holes had been opened into the lower ends of the possibilities allowing evil to lap up against closed doors leading to empty classrooms, but something was out of place and, as long as she was in the building, finding it and fixing it was in the job description. Actually, it pretty much was the job description.

As far as Diana was concerned, all high schools needed Keepers. Nothing poked holes in the fabric of reality faster than a few thousand hormonally challenged teenagers all crammed into one ugly cinderblock building. Unattended, that was exactly the sort of situation likely to create the kind of person who developed an operating system that crashed every time someone attempted to download an Amanda Tapping screen saver.

The sudden appearance of a guidance counselor actually emerging from his office and heading straight for her nearly sent Diana running toward the nearest washroom. She didn't want her last day ruined by yet another pointless confrontation. Fortunately, she realized he felt the same way before her feet started moving. *Fuck it. What's the point?* flashed into the thought balloon over his head and he slid past without meeting her gaze.

The thought balloons had appeared back in grade nine when, after half an hour of platitudes, she'd wondered just what exactly he was thinking. An unexpected puberty-propelled power surge had anchored the balloons so firmly she'd never been able to get rid of them and

she'd spent the last four years finding out rather more than she wanted
to about the fantasy lives of middle-aged men.

Pamela Anderson.

And hockey.

Occasionally, Pamela Anderson playing hockey.

Some of the visuals were admittedly interesting.

The wrongness led her up the stairs, through the first cafeteria and
into the second—weirdly, the hangout of both the jocks and the music
geeks—empty now except for a group of girls who'd laid claim to the
far corner by the northwest windows. A flash of aubergine light pulled
her toward them. The senior girls' basketball team, Diana realized as
she drew closer. Probably hanging around in order to *remain* the senior girls' basketball team. Over two thirds of them were graduating,
so once they stepped out the door, they'd be a team no longer.

". . . so I said to him, I'm not putting *that* in my mouth." Tall,
blonde, ponytail—Diana didn't know her name. "First of all, I don't
know where it's been and secondly, this lipstick cost twenty-one dollars."

"And what did he say?" asked one of her listeners.

"Oh, you know guys. He took it so personally. All like, 'you would
if you loved me.'"

"So what did you say?"

"That I loved my lipstick more."

In the midst of the laughter and catcalls that followed her matter-
of-fact pronouncement, Blonde Ponytail looked up and spotted Diana.

"Did you want something?" she asked icily.

"Uh, yeah." Diana leaned a little closer; trying to get a better look
at the heavy bangle Blonde Ponytail wore around her left wrist. "*Please*
tell me where you got your bracelet."

"This? At Erlking's Emporium in the Gardener's Village Mall. I
got it last weekend when I was visiting my father in Kingston."

Great.

Kingston.

Where there used to be a hole to Hell.

Oh, sure. It *could* be coincidence.

"It's silver, you know."

Well, it was silver colored; the broad band embossed with large flowers each centered with a demon's eye topaz. It was quite possibly the ugliest piece of jewelry Diana had ever seen. "No, it isn't. It only looks like silver."

"What? You mean that troll lied to me?"

Troll.

With any luck, that was a colorful exaggeration rather than the mystical version of a Freudian slip.

Diana didn't feel particularly lucky. Stretching out a finger, she lightly touched the edge of one metallic petal.

A much larger flash of aubergine light.

A moment later, Diana found herself pressed face first into one of the cafeteria's orange plastic chairs discovering far more than she wanted to about the olfactory signature of the last person sitting in it. Then she realized she was actually under the chair and heaved it to one side.

"Are you okay?"

"Fine. Just a little bruised." Accepting the offered hand, she pulled herself to her feet. "Static electricity," she explained, trailing power through the basketball team. "I must have completed some kind of circuit."

Several heads, probably the ones who hadn't passed physics, nodded sagely.

The insistent trill of a cell phone broke the tableau.

"Mine," Diana admitted, digging her backpack out from under the table. Eyes widened as she unzipped an outside pocket. After the unfortunate 1-800-TEACHME incident back in the spring of 2001, students were not permitted to use their cell phones while on school property. *Oh, yeah, I'm a rebel,* she thought flipping it open, then added aloud, "It's my mother."

When the team seemed inclined to linger, she threw a little power into, "Everything's cool. You can go now."

"Diana? What just happened?"

"You felt that at home?" She headed back toward the other cafeteria as the girls reclaimed their table, Blonde Ponytail muttering, "What a piece of cheap junk; I'm going to wring that troll's neck."

"Felt it? Yes, I'd say we felt it. Sam's hanging from the top of the living-room curtains and the coffeepot's bringing in radio broadcasts

from 1520—apparently Martin Luther was just excommunicated. I missed part of Suleiman the Magnificent's birth announcement as your father called to say he'd felt it in the next county. Are you all right?"

"I'm fine. I touched a piece of jewelry from the Otherside and there was a bit of a reaction. Don't worry, I covered everything up, and the jewelry's been totally nullified."

"Where . . . ?"

"Was the jewelry?" Diana interrupted. "Around the wrist of a fellow student. How did she lay her hands on a bracelet—and an incredibly ugly bracelet, I might add—that came from the Otherside? She bought it in a store called Erlking's Emporium. Just where exactly is Erlking's Emporium? Kingston."

"Oh, Hell."

"Probably." Leaving the cafeteria, she headed for the main stairs and the front doors. "I figure I just blew a crack through their shielding and that Claire ought to be getting the Summons any minute."

"Claire's not in Kingston right now; she's answering a Summons in Marmora."

"Well, if it's important, I'm sure the id . . . powers-that-be will give it to someone else."

"You're not getting anything?"

"Nope, nothing." There was no one in the main hall. Another fifteen meters and she'd be out the doors and home free.

"Good. And while I have you, I thought we'd agreed you weren't going to wear that T-shirt to school?"

"Sorry, Mom; the school has a 'no cell phone' rule. Gotta go." Flipping the phone closed, Diana paused in front of her reflection in the glass of the trophy case. The writing across her chest—red on black—said, *My sister's boy toy went to Hell and all I got was a lousy T-shirt.* She seemed to be the only one in the family who found it funny.

"Ms. Hansen."

Phone still in her hand, Diana spun around and smiled up at the vice-principal. "It was my mother, Ms. Neal. I had to take the call."

"Yes, I'm sure. But that's not what I wanted to speak with you about. You're an intelligent young woman, Diana, and while your years here have not been without . . . incident . . ."

The pause nearly collapsed under the memory of the whole football team thing. Some changes lingered, even in the minds of the most prosaic Bystander.

"Yes, well, your marks are good," the vice-principal continued after a long moment, "in spite of your frequent absences, and I can't help but feel it's a real shame that you've decided not to go on to college or university."

Diana shuddered. More time spent under academic authority? So not going to happen. "I'm afraid I'm just not the higher education type, Ms. Neal." Sliding sideways, she moved a little closer to the door.

"Job prospects . . ."

"I have a job. Family business. Pays well, chance to travel, making the world a better place and all that." Also demons, dangers, and the possibility of dying young but it still beat pretty much any other profession as far as Diana was concerned. Well, maybe not sitcom star or Hollywood script doctor but everything else. "You might say it's the kind of job I was born to do," she added reassuringly.

From the sudden contentment on Ms. Neal's face, a little too reassuringly.

"It's nice to know that at least one of my students will be leaving the school for a bright and beautiful future," she sighed. "I'll never forget you, Diana."

Diana smiled. "Actually, you'll forget me the moment I step out the door."

"I don't think . . ."

And then the threshold was between them.

Ms. Neal's brow furrowed. She stared at Diana for a long moment, shook her head, and walked away.

Although not by nature a bouncy person, Diana almost skipped down the steps of the school. It was two thirty on Thursday, June the twenty-third, and she was finally free to be what she'd been intended to be from birth. Crossing the threshold for that last time had moved her from reserve to active Keeper status.

At two thirty-one, the Summons hit.

Both hands clamped to her temples, she tried to uncross her eyes. "Okay. I probably should have expected that."

❖   ❖   ❖

"Mom? You home?"

"She's at the Pough house," Sam told her, coming out of the living room. "There was some kind of emergency involving ravens and bad poetry. She said . . ." He paused, stared at Diana for a moment, then rubbed up against her shins. "We've got a Summons!"

"We do." She told him about the bracelet as they pounded upstairs.

"Kingston?" Sam jumped up on the end of the bed. "Shouldn't it be Claire's Summons, then?"

"No. It's mine."

"Yeah, but . . . you know . . . it's just . . ."

"Austin." Diana dumped assorted end-of-year crap out of her backpack and shoved in her laptop, a pair of clean jeans, socks, underwear, and her hiking boots. There were places Otherside where even heavy rubber sandals wouldn't be enough. Actually, there were places where hazmat suits wouldn't be enough, but she planned on staying away from the Girl Guide camp. "You're afraid to go onto his territory."

"I am *not* afraid. But he doesn't like me."

Zippered sweatshirt. Pajama bottoms. Tank tops. "He's old. He doesn't like anyone except Claire."

"He likes you," Sam protested following her into the bathroom.

"He tolerates me because I can operate a can opener." Shampoo. Toothbrush. Toothpaste. Soap. Towel. "Don't worry. We'll be in and out before Claire and Austin even know we're there."

Eyeing the toilet suspiciously—who knew porcelain could be so slippery—Sam jumped up onto the edge of the sink. "You know, a hole big enough to pass physical objects through might be harder to close than you think."

Diana snorted, threw in a couple of rolls of toilet paper just in case, and headed for the kitchen where she packed a box of crackers, a jar of peanut butter, a nearly full bag of chocolate chip cookies, and six tins of cat food.

"Less chicken, more fish," Sam told her.

"Fish gives you cat food breath."

He looked up from licking his butt. "And that's a problem because . . . ?"

"Good point." She made the change, pulled the small litter box and a bag of litter out of the broom closet and packed them as well. "I think that's everything. Now I just need to leave a note for the 'rents."

"Make sure they can see it." A few moments later, his pupils closed down to vertical slits, Sam stared up at the brilliant letters chasing themselves around the refrigerator door. "That seems a little much."

"Well, they'll be able to see it."

"Yeah; from orbit."

"Some cats are never happy." About to pick up the pack, she paused. "You want to get in now? Our first ride'll meet us at the end of the driveway."

"Might as well." He flowed in through the open zipper, and the green nylon sides bulged as he made himself comfortable. "Hey . . ." Folded space distorted his voice. "What's with the rubber tree and the hat stand?"

"They're holding open the possibilities." Zipping up all but the top six inches, Diana swung the pack over her shoulders and headed for the road.

Their first ride took them into Lucan.

Their second, to London.

In London, they got a lift from a trucker carrying steel pipe to Montreal. Diana spent the trip strengthening the cables that held the pipes to the flatbed—a little accident prevention—and Sam horked up a hairball on the artificial lamb's wool seat cover. Which was how they found themselves standing by the side of the road in Napanee, a small town forty minutes east of Kingston.

At Sam's insistence, they stopped for supper at Mom's Restaurant . . .

"No, that's not a cat in my backpack. It's an orange sweater that just happens to enjoy tuna."

. . . where they met someone willing to take them the rest of the way.

Her back to the West Gardener's Mall parking lot, Diana waved as the metallic green Honda merged into Highway Two traffic. "That was fun. I don't think I've ever heard 'It's Raining Men' sung with so much enthusiasm."

"My ears hurt," Sam muttered, jumping out onto the grass.

"I suppose you'd rather have angelic choirs?"

"Are you nuts? All those trumpets—it's like John Philip Sousa does choral music." Carefully aligning his back end, he sprayed the base of a streetlight. "It's all praise God and pass the oom pah pah."

"I'm not even sure I know what that means, but just on principle, please tell me you're kidding."

"Okay, I'm kidding."

She turned to face the mall. "Now say it like you mea . . ." And froze. "Oy, mama. That's not good."

The circles of light that overlapped throughout the parking lot had all been touched with red, creating a sinister—although faintly clichéd—effect. At just past nine, with the mall officially closed, the acres of crimson-tinted asphalt were empty of everything but half a dozen . . .

"Minivans. It's worse than I thought."

He had stood at this door, at this time, every Friday night for the last twenty-one years. There had been other doors in the long years before, but there would be no other doors after. He would make his last stand here. The door was open only to allow late shoppers to exit; he, a human lock, protected the mall from those who would enter after hours.

He watched the girl stride toward him. His lips curled at the sight of bare legs between sandals and shorts. His eyes narrowed in disgust at the way her breasts moved under her T-shirt. He snorted at her backpack and her youth.

Were it up to him, he'd never let her kind into the mall. He knew what they got up to. Talking. Laughing. Standing in groups. Standing in pairs. Pairs tucked away in Bozo's School Bus using lips and hands.

He stiffened as she stopped barely an arm's length away.

"The mall is closed. It will reopen tomorrow at nine a.m."

Pink lips parted. "*Please* move out of my way."

Twenty-one years at this door. "The mall is closed. It will reopen tomorrow at nine a.m."

Dark brows rose and dark eyes tried to meet his, but he stared at the drop of sweat running down her throat to pool against her collarbone and refused to be drawn in.

"Okay, fine. We'll just have to do this the hard way."

"The mall is closed. It will reopen tomorrow at nine a.m."

"Yeah, gramps, I got it the first time."

His eyes burned and he blinked, only a single blink, but when his vision cleared, the girl was gone.

Good. It was good that she was gone. Gone with her shorts and her breasts and all her infinite possibilities.

Diana stopped just the other side of Bozo's School Bus, set her backpack down on the yellow plastic kiddie ride, and waited while Sam climbed out.

"That was creepy," he muttered, licking at a bit of ruffled fur.

"Very. And aren't people that old supposed to be retired or something?"

"Or something," the cat agreed. "Hey." Front paws on the Plexiglas window, Sam peered into the bus. "This thing has seat belts. They don't take it out of the building, do they?"

"Uh, no."

"Then why seat belts?"

"I have no idea. But you know what's really whacked? My bus—the one I rode down potholed dirt roads at a hundred and twenty klicks every morning and afternoon with a whole lot of very small bouncy children—no belts." Swinging her pack back onto her shoulders, she headed for the main concourse. "Stay close and no one will see you."

Sam fell into step by her right ankle. "Considering what that thing smelled like, I can think of one reason for seat belts. This place is huge. How are we going to find the Erlking Emporium?"

"Easy. We find the you-are-here sign. It's probably at the end of this side hall."

It wasn't.

Although the side hall and one of the huge anchor stores spilled out into the main concourse at the same place, there was nothing to help mall patrons find their way through the two-story maze of stores they now faced.

"Maybe someone from the Otherside took it," Sam offered when it became clear they were directionally on their own.

"It's possible." Motioning for Sam to be quiet, Diana froze as a final shopper slipped through the partially barricaded Kitchen Shop storefront, clutching a cheap manual can opener and trailing the ill wishes of the teenage clerk like black smoke behind her as she hurried down the side hall. "She feels like the last one in here. We'd better get moving before that creepy old security guard heads this way."

Sam butted his head reassuringly against her leg. "You can take him."

"Well, yeah. But I'd rather not. Come on. Blonde Ponytail said . . ."

"Who?"

"The jock with the bracelet. I never got her name. She said the store was on the lower level, so let's find some stairs."

Behind reinforced glass or steel bars, the stores themselves were places of shadow.

Unless the bracelet was the only piece of the Otherside they were selling, Diana should have been able to sense the Emporium, her Summons directing her like a child's game of Warm and Cool where the parts of "Warm" and "Cool" were played by "I Can Live With the Headache if I Have to" and "Shoot Me Now." Unfortunately, the Summons was unable to poke through the interference from the back rooms where a hundred part-time teenagers counted up a hundred cash drawers and ninety-seven of them came up short. By the time the cash had to be counted for the third time, the emanation of frustrated pissiness was so strong Diana couldn't have sensed a trio of bears if they were sneaking up beside her.

"Hey, Rodney River has orange polyester bellbottoms on sale for $29.99."

"Is that good?" Sam wondered.

Diana shuddered. "I can't see how." Pleased to see that the escalators had already been turned off—cat on escalator equaled accident waiting to happen—she led the way to the stairs.

Only the emergency lights were lit on the lower level, and the footprint of the mall seemed to have subtly changed.

"There's too many corners down here. And if I can smell the food court, why can't we find it?"

"I don't . . . Someone's coming." Scooping up the cat, Diana backed into a triangular shadow and wrapped the possibilities around them both half a heartbeat before a flashlight beam swept by.

"I know you're here." One shoe dragging *shunk kree* against the fake slate tiles, the elderly security guard emerged from a side hall. Massive black flashlight held out in front of him, he walked bent forward, his head moving constantly from side to side on a neck accordion-pleated with wrinkles.

Diana would have said the motion looked snakelike except that she rather liked snakes.

Shunk kree. Shunk kree. "I will find you; never doubt it. I know you've hidden your lithe bodies away in the shadows."

Sam twisted in Diana's arms until he could stare up at her. His expression saying as clearly as if he'd spoken, "Lithe?" She shrugged.

"Long, loose limbs stacked unseen against the wall." *Shunk kree.*

Who was he looking for? It couldn't be her and Sam—he thought *they* were gone.

The flashlight beam flicked up, caught the pale face of a store mannequin, and stopped moving.

"Can't run now, can you?" He shuffled past so close to her hiding place that Diana could almost count the dark gray hairs growing from his ear. "Can't run with your muscles moving inside the soft skin."

Diana gave him a count of twenty, then prepared to slip out and away. She had a foot actually in the air when cool fingers wrapped around her upper arm and held her in place.

Shunk. The security guard pivoted on one heel, turning suddenly to face back the way he'd come, flashlight beam exposing circles of the lower concourse. "Not too smart for me with your young brains," he muttered, turning again and *shunk kreeing* his way toward the mannequin.

The cool fingers were gone as though they'd never existed. Since Diana was certain she and Sam had been alone in their sanctuary, the logical response seemed to be that they never had. That they'd been a construct of self-preservation. Her own highly developed subconscious holding her back from discovery. On the other hand, logic had very little to do with possibility, so Diana murmured a quiet thanks to the fingers as she left the shadow.

Cat in her arms, staying close to the storefronts, she raced down the concourse toward a side hall they hadn't tried, at least half her attention listening for the *shunk kree* following behind her. After weaving through a locked-down display of hot tubs, she sagged against a pillar, adding its bulk to the space she'd already put between them and the old man.

"Okay," she whispered into the top of Sam's head. "I am officially squicked out. Where did they find that guy? He's like every creepy, clichéd old man rolled into one wrinkly package and wrapped in a security guard's uniform. I mean, I know he's just a Bystander and I handled him at the door, but still . . ."

"Still what?"

"You know, *still*."

"If I knew, I wouldn't have asked," Sam pointed out, squirming to be let down. "And by the way, we've found the food court."

Only six of the seven food kiosks were currently occupied. Directly across from them, a poster on plywood announced the future site of a Darby's Deli. At some point, a local artist had used a black marker to make a few additions to the poster's picture of Darby Dill, creating a remarkably well hung condiment. Tearing her gaze away from the anatomically correct pickle, Diana spotted yet another hall on the far side of the food court, the rectangular opening tucked into the corner between Consumer's Drug Mart and a sporting goods store.

"It's got to be down there."

"Why?"

"Because it isn't anywhere . . . What are you eating?"

Sam swallowed. "Nothing."

As they entered the hall, the tile turned to a rough concrete floor. The bench and its flanking planters of plastic trees, although outwardly no different from other benches and other trees, had a temporary look. Only three stores long, the hall ended in a gray plywood wall stenciled with a large sign that read, "Construction Site: No Entry." The last store before the wall was the Emporium.

Tucked into another convenient shadow, Diana studied the storefront through narrowed eyes. "I can't sense a power signature, so I'm guessing the power surge only went one way."

"If they'd known you were coming, they'd have baked a cake?"

She stared down at the cat. "Something like that, yeah. Who . . . ?"

"Your father."

"Well, do me a favor and don't pick up any more of his speech patterns because that would be too weird."

"Why?"

"Sam, you sleep on my bed. Just don't, okay?"

He shrugged, clearly humoring her. "Okay."

Diana turned her attention back to the store. "They're not being very subtle, are they? If any of the Lineage had ever window-shopped their way down here, the name alone would have given the whole thing away."

"The Lineage is big into window shopping?"

"Not my point."

"Okay. But I think Erlking Emporium has a marketable ring to it."

"Marketable? First of all, you're a cat; marketable for you involves a higher percentage of beef byproducts. Second; do you even know what an Erlking is?"

Sam shot her an insulted amber glare, the tip of his tail flicking back and forth in short, choppy arcs. "According to German legend, it's a malevolent goblin who lures people, especially children, to their destruction."

Which it was. "Sorry. I keep forgetting about that whole used-to-be-an-angel had-higher-knowledge thing."

"Yeah, you do. But I learned that off a PBS special on mythology."

"While I was where?"

"Cleaning the splattered remains of a history essay off your bedroom walls."

"Right." A lapse in concentration and the Riel Rebellion had spilled out of her closet. It had taken her the entire weekend to clean up the mess, and most of it had turned out to be nonrecyclable. "I think I've seen enough. Let's go."

The purely physical lock on the door took only a trickle of power to open.

Sam radiated disapproval as he slipped through into the store. "Breaking and entering."

"Technically, only entering." Locking the door behind them, Diana tried not to sneeze at the overpowering odor of gardenia coming off the display of candles immediately to her left. A quick glance showed that the gardenia had easily overpowered vanilla, cinnamon, bayberry, lilac, belladonna, monkshood, pholiotina, and yohimbe. Unless the Colonial Candle Company was branching out into herbal hallucinogens, at least half the display had clearly been brought over from the Otherside.

Not just the bracelet, then.

Rubbing her nose, she moved cautiously into the store, skirting a locked glass cabinet filled with crystal balls, and ending up nearly treading on Sam's tail as, hissing, he backed away from . . . Diana bent over to take a closer look and had no better idea what animal the pile of stuffed creatures was supposed to represent. In spite of neon fur, they looked remarkably lifelike—given a loose enough definition of both life and like.

"I was just startled," Sam muttered, vigorously washing a front paw.

"If I was closer to the ground, they'd have startled me, too."

"I wasn't afraid."

"I know." She stroked down the raised hair along his back as she straightened. "I think we can safely say the hole's not out here. Let's check out the storeroom."

"It's not back there either."

Not Sam. Not unless Sam's voice had deepened, aged, and moved up near the ceiling.

Diana dropped down behind a rack of resin frogs dressed in historical military uniforms and began to gather power.

"Think about it for a minute, Keeper; if I wasn't on your side, I'd have already sounded the alarm. Why don't you drop the fireworks and come over here so we can talk."

He—whoever he was—had a point. Diana stood, slowly, and looked around. The shadows made it difficult to tell for certain, but she'd have been willing to bet actual cash money that she and Sam were alone in the store. "Where are you?"

"Up in the corner."

The only thing she could see in the corner was the convex circle of a security mirror. Just as she was realizing the reflection seemed a little off, a familiar pair of blue-on-blue eyes appeared. "You've got to be kidding me. They're using a magic mirror for security?"

"Ain't life a bitch," the mirror agreed. "Got pulled out of a well-deserved retirement—quiet hall, nice view out an oriel window—and got stuffed up here by Gaston the Wondertroll."

"So there's a real troll?"

"Large as life, and twice as ugly. Actually, larger than life if we're reflecting accurately."

"Great."

"I wouldn't worry about him, kid; he's just the front man." Faint blue frown lines. "Front troll. Those actually running this segue are keeping their heads tucked well down until it's too late for your lot to stop it."

Good thing she'd touched that bracelet, then. The energy discharged had been enough to crack the shielding and send the Summons. No touching, no Summons, no chance to stop the . . . "Wait a minute. Did you say, *segue*?"

"I did."

"Okay. This is one of those times when I really wish I could swear." She took three quick steps away from the mirror. Three quick steps back. "I should have known there was more to this than a cheesy gift shop selling . . ." A glance down. ". . . fake fairies on sticks."

"Look again."

Under the lacquer and the glitter . . .

"Eww."

"Duck!"

"Where?" Diana didn't even want to think about what these guys could do to a duck. A sudden circle of light hit the back wall of the store and she dropped to the ground. Oh. *Duck.*

The emporium's door rattled as someone shook it, testing the lock. *Now who could that be? Two guesses and the first one doesn't count.* Flat against the carpet to keep the curve of her backpack behind cover, she tried not to think about the dark stain just off the end of her nose.

"Think you can get away with anything. Young bodies, supple, lissome."

Adding that to lithe and limber, there seemed to be a thesaurus specifically for dirty old men.

"You can't hide forever." The circle of light swept across the store and disappeared. Through the glass came a muffled *shunk kree, shunk kree* as the security guard moved away.

Remembering the warning delivered by imaginary fingers, Diana hissed, "Sam, stay down," a heartbeat before the light flashed back through the window. She counted a slow ten after *that* light disappeared before she stood. "Sam?"

He crawled out from behind a box of glow-in-the-dark Silly Putty and shook his fur back into place. "Don't worry about me. I'm way faster than a geriatric rent-a-cop."

"Good. So." Arms folded, she stared up at the mirror. "Let's cut to the chase before we're interrupted again."

"Fine with me, Keeper. Here's the deal: I give you what help I can; in return, you get me out of here when you shut this place down."

"Agreed."

"And you recognize that when the shit hits the fan, I'm breakable and more than just a little exposed."

She nodded. "We'll be careful."

"We? That would be you and the cat?"

"Us, too." Diana took one last look around the store and decided she really didn't need to know just what exactly the weights on the wind chimes were made of. "I think we're going to need a little help."

TWO

———— · ⊠◆⊠ · ————

DROPPING HIS SPRAY BOTTLE of window cleaner onto the old-fashioned wooden counter, Dean McIssac crossed the small office and caught the phone on the second ring. "Elysian Fields Guest House." A small frown of concentration appeared as he flipped open the reservation book, a leather-bound tome with the phases of the moon prominently displayed by each date. "Yes, sir, we still have rooms available for next Wednesday. We can certainly accommodate you and your mother. Sorry? Oh. Your mummy. No, that's fine; many of our guests arrive after dark. We'll hold the rooms until midnight. A dehumidifier? That can be arranged, I understand how mold and mildew could be a problem. No, unfortunately, I can't guarantee the Keeper will be here, but I'm sure you'll find our . . ." His cheeks flushed. "Thank you, sir. I'll see you Wednesday."

"Flushed is a good look on you."

"Claire!" The receiver fell the last six inches into the cradle as Dean flag-jumped the counter and gathered the smiling Keeper into his arms.

"You made good time," he murmured when they finally came up for air.

"I had a good reason."

"One that I should know about?"

Dark brown eyes gleamed suggestively up at him. "Definitely."

His fingers tightened on her shoulders and he began to pull her close again.

"Hel-lo! Crushing the cat here!"

Dean released his hold like he had springs in his fingers, and Claire leaped back, exposing the indignant, black-and-white cat cradled between them. "I'm sorry, Austin. I just got excited about being home."

"Oh, yeah," he muttered as she set him carefully on the counter. "It's home that gets you excited. Tell us another one. No, wait . . ." He turned and glared at her from a single emerald eye. ". . . don't."

"Okay." Her hands free, she slid them up the sculpted muscle of Dean's torso and around the back of his neck, fingers entwined in thick hair. "I can't resist a man in a pink T-shirt."

He shifted his grip to her waist, thumbs working against the damp line of flesh between cropped tank and skirt. "Someone buried a red catnip square in the laundry basket."

"That's right. Blame the cat. The starving cat!" Austin snapped after a moment when it became quite clear he'd been forgotten again. "The old starving cat who just spent three hours in a car listening to sappy tales of dear, departed Muffy—who probably threw herself in front of that truck in an effort to escape the schmaltz with what was left of her dignity. The old starving cat who's going to give you a count of three before he starts making pointed comments about your technique!"

"Austin, there's a package of calf liver in the fridge." Dean slid his hands down to the backs of Claire's thighs and lifted her up onto the counter, hiking her skirt up over her knees. "It's after being yours if you'll disappear for ten minutes."

"Fifteen," Claire growled, licking at the sweat beading Dean's throat. She kicked off her sandals, crossed her ankles behind him, and dragged him closer.

"You guys do know this is a hotel, right? Like, get a room!"

Forehead to forehead, Dean stared deep into Claire's eyes. "You didn't lock the door?"

"Apparently not."

Lip curled in disgust, Diana closed the front door, pointedly locked it, and strode across the lobby toward the long hall that led to the back of the guesthouse. "We've got a bit of shopping-mall-takes-over-the-world situation here, but you guys go right ahead and continue with that whole blatant heterosexuality thing; there's probably time. I'll just make myself a sandwich and feed the cats. Coming, Austin?"

"Finally," he snorted, jumping carefully down off the counter, "someone who has their priorities straight!"

"Are they always like that?" Sam wondered as the older cat fell into step beside him.

"Are you kidding? They've only been apart for three days—you should see them after a week. Spontaneous combustion."

Sam frowned. "Wouldn't that kill them?"

"You'd think."

As the footsteps of the two cats and her sister faded toward the kitchen, Claire sighed. "Well, I'm no longer in the mood. You?"

"Not so much. That was after ending things for me." He lifted her down off the counter and steadied her while she slipped her sandals back on. "Just so I'm clear on this; strangling your sister is not an option, then?"

"If you want to strangle my sister," Claire told him as they left the lobby, "you'll have to wait in line."

"I hope you guys postponed instead of finishing," Diana snorted as they entered the kitchen, "because if that was it, Claire should file a complaint. I mean it's not like I'm an expert on these things," she continued, assaulting a leftover roast with the carving knife, "but someone's getting left a little short. No offense." She grinned up at Dean.

"And yet, I'm offended anyway." Grasping her wrist with one hand, he confiscated the knife with the other and jerked his head toward the dining room table. "You sit. I'll do this."

"I don't know, Dean. I like my sandwiches made slowly and with care."

"And you might want to reconsider further commentary," Claire interjected from the dining room, "since he's eight inches taller than you and holding a knife."

"Please," Diana scoffed, grabbing a bottle of juice from the fridge and coming around the counter that separated the two rooms, "Dean's a pussycat."

"Now, *I'm* offended," Austin muttered.

Sam looked up from his cat food and frowned. "I thought you liked him."

"Yeah. So?"

"I don't understand."

"You're not supposed to," Claire told the younger cat comfortingly. "Let it go and move on." Pulling out one of the antique table's dozen chairs, she folded a leg up onto the red velvet seat and sat, indicating that Diana should do the same.

Diana didn't so much sit as gang up with gravity to assault the furniture.

Claire winced as the chair protested, but hundred-year-old joints and wood glue held. "You said something about a shopping mall taking over the world?"

"I'm amazed you heard me."

"You have a talent for attracting attention. I assume this concerns your first Summons as an active Keeper?"

"Got it in one." Smiling her thanks at Dean for the sandwich, she waited until he sat down and pulled his seat up close behind Claire's before she continued. "It all started this afternoon on what was, thank God, my very last day of school . . ."

When the story arrived at the mall, Claire interrupted.

"You should have called me."

"Chill, uberKeeper. You weren't in Kingston, and until I actually got to the Emporium, all I had was a piece of ugly jewelry. I'd have been further ahead closing down the Home Shopping Network. Unfortunately, once at the Emporium, I discovered we're talking about a little more than a mere accident site—according to the magic mirror they're using for security . . ."

"Magic mirror?" Dean leaned forward, one hand on Claire's shoulder. "Like in the fairy tales?"

"Just like. Well, not exactly like," Diana amended after chewing and swallowing the last mouthful of sandwich. "He's a little pissed about being yanked out of retirement by Gaston the Wondertroll and is willing to do what he can to close the whole thing down."

"Troll?"

She nodded. "They're not just under bridges anymore."

"According to the magic mirror," Claire prompted, poking her sister with a Tahiti Sands-tipped finger.

"Ow."

"Diana . . ."

"Okay, fine. According the mirror, whose name is Jack, it's a segue."

"A segue?" When Diana nodded, her expression making it clear she wasn't kidding around, the older Keeper ran a hand up through her hair. "I have a sudden need for profanity."

"Yeah. That was my reaction. That mall's got to cover at least four acres. Maybe as much as six."

"Segue?" Dean asked, dragging his chair around far enough to see Claire's face.

"A metaphysical overlap intended to displace reality."

He switched his attention to Diana.

She scratched thoughtfully at her left elbow and tried to come up with an explanation he could understand. "You know how the Other-side is neither here nor there? That everyone—good guys, bad guys, the Swiss—can all get in but can only get back out into their own reality, the one they left from? Well, in a segue, someone, or something, matches up a piece of the Otherside to this reality and blends them together until enough of the copy occupies the space of the original whereupon the copy takes over. That puts a piece of the Otherside inside this reality so that anyone can enter it from their reality and exit here. The Erlking Emporium is anchoring the biggest segue I've ever heard of."

"The biggest?"

"Well, you can't count Las Vegas, that's a metaphysical heritage site. All that bad taste in one place put a real strain on reality."

It took Dean about half a heartbeat to decide that was one of those comments he didn't need to understand. "But how did the segue in the mall get so big without you guys noticing?"

"Hell," Austin answered before either Keeper could. He put his front paws up on Claire's knee and she lifted him onto her lap. "They hid a smaller bad inside the noise of the biggest bad. They probably set the anchor last fall while we were closing the hole and after that, it was just a matter of keeping things moving ahead, slow and steady."

"And they are?"

"Your guess is as good as mine. Oh, wait. No it isn't." He paused and licked at the quarter-sized bit of black fur on his front leg. "For simplicity's sake, let's just call them the bad guys."

"But the Otherside isn't necessarily bad."

"Doesn't matter; with a segue *anything* can cross over. Bad, good . . ."

"Hey!" Sam protested, coming out of the kitchen. "This world could use a little more good in it. I ought to know."

Austin sighed. "Yeah, yeah. Light. Angel. Cat. Yadda. We all know the story and you're missing the point. A little good is fine. A lot of good isn't."

"Keepers maintain the balance, Sam. A functional segue could tip it in either direction, and if they're using trolls, well, I'm guessing we're not heading for hugs and cheesecake." Claire rubbed her thumb gently over the velvet fur between Austin's ears. "Shutting them down is a tricky business," she added thoughtfully. "It can't be done from this side; I'll have to cross over and go to the source."

Diana rolled her eyes. "*You'll* have to? Try *we'll* have to. If I can't close something this big on my own, you certainly can't—Basic Folklore 101, the younger sibling is always more powerful. I have the power, you have the experience. United we stand, divided we fall, yadda yadda. So I suggest you get over yourself, drop the whole I'm-the-only-one-who-can-save-the-world crap, and recognize that *we've* got trouble."

"Right here in River City," Sam added.

"Show tunes?" Austin glared down at the orange cat. "You have got to be kidding."

"I have three words for you, Austin." Diana leaned a little closer to Claire's lap and flicked up a finger for each word. "Andrew Lloyd Webber. But that's so not what we're talking about. We need to get back into that mall and close that segue. It's going to take some time, so I suggest we start tonight."

"Ignoring your less than flattering opinion of my character," Claire muttered darkly, "I agree."

"I don't."

"Listen much, Dean? Segue bad. Keepers good. And I don't know where I was going with that, but the sooner we get the sucker closed down the better."

"Not arguing," Dean told the young Keeper calmly. "You said it's going to take some time—that means you'll be there for a while?"

Diana shrugged. "Yeah, but . . ."

"So you can't just rush in all unprepared."

"I guess not."

"You'll have to pack."

Claire twisted around until she could see his face. "We have everything here . . ."

"It'll still take time." He glanced over at the old school clock hanging on the wall in the kitchen. "It's past eleven now. It'll be close to midnight when you're ready to leave. By the time you get to the mall, you've both already been up for what—sixteen, seventeen hours? You'll be facing whoever created this thing when you're tired. You won't be thinking as quickly or as clearly. The bad guys could win before you even get started and then where's the world? Up sh . . . the creek without a paddle." Taking a deep breath, he let it out slowly, holding Claire's gaze with his, lacing the fingers of his right hand through the fingers of her left. "You've got to weigh the delay against going in tired and unprepared. You should sleep tonight and go in tomorrow morning."

Diana opened her mouth to deliver a blistering reply, and snapped it shut again as Austin said, "He's right."

"He's a Bystander!"

"And I'm a cat, so listen up." He climbed from Claire's lap up onto the table, leaving sweaty paw prints on the polished wood. "Going in tired and unprepared is a good way to get our collective butts kicked but, more importantly, going in tonight gives the advantage to the other side."

"You mean the Otherside?" Diana sniped.

"Don't interrupt. Two Keepers and two cats head into an empty mall in the middle of the night and we might as well call first to tell them we're coming. There's no way even the most idiotic, written for television, evil overlord isn't going to notice something like that. The moment we cross over, BAM! And that's if we're lucky. We all know there's a whole lot worse than BAM waiting out there."

"No, we don't." Ears saddled, Sam sat down on Diana's foot. "What's worse than BAM?"

"Splat. Crunch. Grind. Chew." When no one seemed inclined to argue, Austin continued. "We get a good night's sleep and go in tomorrow morning with all the other shoppers, hiding in plain sight. We slip across with no one the wiser, you two close down the segue, and we're home by lunch."

"Lunch?"

Austin snorted. "Okay, it's a metaphorical lunch some days in the future."

"Look, it's my Summons," Diana protested, tumbling Sam off her foot and jerking her chair away from the table. She had a strong suspicion that had come out sounding whinier than she'd intended.

"You came here for help," Claire reminded her. "You were there, in the mall; is there a chance the copy will be matched up before morning?"

"No. But . . ."

"Then I vote we wait. But you're right." She raised the hand not holding Dean's in surrender. "It's your Summons. Only you can make the final decision."

"Don't patronize me."

"Then stop acting so childish. When you got here, you were willing to stop for a sandwich, and now you're set on charging in where angels fear to tread."

"Angels don't fear much," Sam began, caught sight of Austin's expression, and decided he'd rather be under the table.

Diana folded her arms and just managed to stop her lip from curling. Knowing they were right didn't help. "All right, fine. We'll go in the morning."

"Fine."

"Good."

"And now that's settled, I'm going to bed." Austin stepped from the table to Claire's lap to the floor, glaring at Dean on the way by. "These days, if I don't stake my claim early, all the good spots are taken."

"We'll be there in a few minutes," Claire told him, her tone very nearly making the words a warning.

"Oh, joy." He stopped, one paw in the hall, and glanced back over an immaculate black shoulder. "Don't forget to pack the cat food."

"And thus we have the subtitle for my life," Claire sighed, getting to her feet. "When you left to answer this Summons, did you tell Mom and Dad where you were heading?"

"They weren't home. I left them a note."

"You should call before you go to bed."

"Yeah. Right." Picking up her sandwich plate, Diana headed for the kitchen only to be stopped by Dean's outstretched hand.

"I've got it."

"I was just going to put it in the dishwasher. Claire said business was good enough that you guys bought a dishwasher."

"We did."

"So?"

The blue eyes behind the glasses met hers without apology. "I like to load it."

"He has a system," Claire put in.

"Whatever." Diana handed over the plate and watched Dean walk into the kitchen. "He's just a little obsessive," she murmured as Claire moved up beside her.

"A little . . ."

The faded jeans stretched tight as he bent over to set the plate in the lower rack.

". . . but there are compensations."

"Oh, yeah. I can tell you're with him for his mind." Grabbing her backpack, she headed for the hall. "So, in the interest of being rested and prepared, I'm going to grab the key to room one and crash. Come on, Sam."

Eyes still on Dean, Claire waved absently toward her sister. "Call home."

"Bite me."

Accelerating to make the end of the advance green, Dean cranked his truck hard to the left and roared up into the mall's parking lot. Just after nine *a.m.* the temperature had already climbed past thirty degrees C; unusually hot for the end of June. Three adults and two cats didn't leave a lot of room for air flow in the cab and exposed skin would have been covered in a glistening layer of sweat had not the fine patina of cat hair caught—and dimmed—the glisten.

"That's the entrance by the food court," Diana declared, pointing out the open window. "Turn here."

Dean turned.

"If it's the closest entrance to the Emporium, it'll be the most watched and therefore the most likely to be guarded," Claire argued, holding her skirt up off the damp skin of her legs with two fingers. "Turn back onto the roadway and head for the door Diana used last night. We know we can get through that one."

Dean turned.

"We don't know that we can't get through the closer one."

"We don't want to risk setting off an alarm."

"And the longer we spend wandering around the mall, the greater the chance we'll be discovered. Dean, turn here."

Dean turned.

"Charging in on a direct line to the Emporium is a lot more likely to get us noticed. Dean, turn here."

Dean stopped the truck.

Both sisters shot him essentially identical looks of disbelief as they rocked forward against their seat belts.

"You either walk from here," he told them calmly, "or you agree on an entrance."

The cab filled with overlapping protests and no agreement.

Irresistible brown eyes met immovable brown eyes.

"Okay, that's it." Austin flowed up over the back of the seat. "Since two of us are out here sweltering in fur coats . . ."

"I'm okay," Sam interrupted.

"Shut up, kid. . . . sweltering in fur coats," he repeated, "and there's air-conditioning behind whatever door we decide to go through, I'm making an executive decision." He jumped down onto Claire's lap and put his front paws up onto the dash. "What's wrong with those doors? They're closest."

Claire shook her head. "They lead to one of this reality's anchor stores. The way things are skewed, we might not be able to get out."

"Fine. What about the next doors?"

"Same store."

"And the doors after that?"

"That," Diana told him, arms crossed and sitting as slumped as her seat belt and the crowded conditions allowed, "is where I went in last night."

"Then that's where we're going in today."

"But it's my Summons. I should be in charge."

Austin's head swiveled slowly around and caught Diana in an emerald glare.

"Okay," she muttered, wondering whose bright idea it had been that Keepers hang out with cats. "We'll go in there."

"Excellent idea. Claire?"

She decided not to point out that it was where she wanted to go all along. "I agree."

Unable to stop himself from grinning, Dean put the truck into gear. Given the nonfeline connotations, he didn't think he could say the words *pussy whipped* to his true love and her little sister—no matter how accurate the observation.

As they came around the corner of the building, he felt Claire stiffen beside him. "What is it?"

"Minivans."

"They were here last night as well," Diana said grimly.

"You should have told me."

"Why? There's nothing we can do."

"It's just . . ."

"Yeah. I know."

Minivans? In the nine months Dean had known Claire, he'd gone briefly to Hell, driven around northern Ontario after a demon, and discovered that all those clichés about regular sex were pretty much true. He'd also learned that there were some things he was happier not knowing. This seemed like one of them.

"What was wrong with that parking spot?" Claire demanded as he drove past open pavement.

"Nothing. But I can get closer."

"Okay, there's one."

"I see it."

"And you just drove by it."

"I can get a better spot."

"The doors are right there!"

"I see them."

"So *park* already."

Speeding up to cut off a circling red sedan, Dean pulled in between a midnight-blue and a seafoam-green minivan and shut off the engine looking proud of himself. They were four spaces in, straight out from the door.

Claire rolled her eyes. "You are such a *guy*."

He grinned and threw one arm along the seat back behind her, the close quarters allowing his fingers to trail down the damp, bare skin of her arm. "You have a problem with me being a guy."

"Well, not right at this minute . . ."

Unbuckling her seat belt, Diana threw open the door and dropped down onto the pavement. "You guys are terminally embarrassing and . . . I'm sinking."

"What?" Setting Austin on Dean's lap, Claire slid across the seat and peered down at her sister's feet. "That's impossible. It's not *that* hot out."

"Hey, you don't have to take my word for it." Stepping two careful paces back, heavy rubber tread imprinting the asphalt, Diana gestured for Claire to join her.

The low heels on Claire's sandals poked square holes into the pavement. Pulling her skirt against her legs so that she could see her feet, she frowned. "This isn't good. The influence has reached the parking lot."

"Well, duh." Diana swung one arm out in a wide, demonstrative arc. "Minivans?"

"Right. We'd better carry the cats. Dean, can you get the back-packs?"

Even with the extra weight, the pavement remained firm under Dean's work boots.

"That's a relief," Diana noted as she set Sam down on the concrete pad outside the door and began scraping the felted layer of orange cat hair off her arms. "If it's only affecting us, it hasn't spread as far as we thought."

"And I'll be pleased about that in a minute," Claire muttered, glaring down at the tar stuck to her heels.

"I told you those were stupid shoes to wear Otherside."

"No, you didn't."

"Didn't I? I meant to."

"I was after thinking that the whole rubber tree/hat stand thing kept these light." Stepping over Austin, who'd sprawled out on his side in the shade, Dean set both packs on the black metal bench to one side of the door. "What's *in* here?"

"A serious lackage of rubber trees and hat stands." Wondering why Claire seemed to be cat hair free, Diana crossed to her pack and lifted it. "It's against the Rules to access the possibilities once we've crossed over, so stuff like that won't work. Which means we have . . ." She swung it up onto her shoulders. ". . . a few clothes, some preset odds and ends—possibilities having been used to create them but no longer necessary, so hopefully they'll still work. . . ."

"Hopefully?" Dean interrupted with a searching glance at Claire.

"Hopefully," Diana repeated when it became obvious that Claire had nothing reassuring to say. "But mostly we're carrying food and water because it's dangerous to eat or drink on the Otherside."

"Why?"

"Are you kidding? They put sauces on everything so it's all high-cholesterol-let's-slap-the-calories-right-onto-the-hips time."

"The food changes you," Claire interjected, shooting Diana a *stop messing with his head* look. She laced her fingers through Dean's and smiled up at him. "Different foods do different things, and all of it ties you to the Otherside, making it harder to get home. You've heard of Persephone and the pomegranates?"

Dark brows dipped down under the upper edge of his glasses. "Early eighties girl band? Had one hit 'You're Not Seeing My Depression'?"

Diana snorted. "It was, 'You're Not Seeing My Repression.' Although, given the hair, I totally admit they had reason to be depressed."

"How do either of you know what was going on in the early eighties?"

"MuchMusic Classic Videos," Sam told her, sitting down by Austin and wrapping his tail around his toes. "There's, like, two hours of them every Saturday afternoon."

Claire looked from the younger cat to the older.

"Don't look at me," Austin sniffed disdainfully. "If we're not out saving the world, I'm usually napping Saturday afternoons. And speaking of saving the world, I'd just like to point out that we still haven't reached the air-conditioning. Not that I'm complaining or anything. Much."

Hearing impending volume and duration in that final pause, Claire released Dean's hand and reached for her backpack only to find Dean there before her. She turned so he could lift it up onto her shoulders and shivered as he kissed the back of her neck, murmuring, "Be careful." against damp skin.

"I'm always careful."

"What about Sharbot Lake?"

"That wasn't careless, that was just unexpectedly deep." She turned again, facing him now. "Will you be okay?"

He lifted her chin with a finger. "Without you? Probably not."

"Enough with the clichés, already." Thumbs through her pack straps, Diana paced to the edge of the concrete and back making gagging noises. "I've just figured out why Keeper and Bystanders together are such a bad idea. You're boring. And sappy enough to cause insulin shock."

Dean ignored her, his eyes remaining locked on Claire's face. "I'll be waiting here."

"We'll be a couple days; remember?"

"But only on the Otherside." When Claire shook her head, he frowned. "Time runs differently there. You can come out just after you went in. Right?"

"Probably not. Time might run faster or slower in pockets, but in order for the segue to work, they'll have to make time run concurrent on both sides." Hands flat on his chest, she studied his expression. "You knew that, right?"

"And how would I be knowing that if you didn't tell me?"

"I didn't tell you?"

"No." He sighed and pulled her closer. "You'll actually be a couple of days on this side as well?"

"Maybe more. I've set my watch so that we'll know."

"Okay, now we've got that settled," Diana prodded, "just say goodbye already, suck a little face, and let's *go* before the Otherside comes to us."

Dean stared down into Claire's face for a long moment before his mouth finally curved into a worried smile. "Got my heart?"

She laid a hand lightly against her chest. "Right here. Got mine."

He mirrored the motion. "Safe and sound."

"And did I mention, barf! Hey! I said suck a *little* face. You do know she's already had her tonsils out, don't you? So if you're in there looking for them, you're out of luck."

Claire pulled out of Dean's embrace, turned on one heel, smacked Diana lightly on the back of the head, and walked toward the doors— all in one smooth motion. "Someday, as unlikely as it seems, you're going to find someone able to overlook certain personality flaws and I'm going to be there to do the color commentary."

"As if," Diana snorted, waving to Dean and falling into step beside her sister.

"I thought the color commentary was my job?" Sam asked Austin as they followed the Keepers through the doors.

Austin sighed. "There's usually enough to go around."

Once through the inner doors, Keepers and cats both disappeared. Standing with one hand spread out on the outer door, Dean could see his own reflection and little else. It was just a trick of the light, at least that's what he told himself as he walked back to the edge of the concrete and stared out at the heat-silvered sky and the minivans keeping a silent vigil. He felt fidgety, restless—what his grandfather, an outport minister back in Newfoundland, would have called flicy. Hands shoved deep into his pockets, he turned and stared at the mall.

The vertical concrete slabs were almost the same shade as the sky.

Even without knowing what was going on inside, something about the building made his skin crawl. He would have said it was because it looked like a prison except there were two prisons within Kingston's old city limits and both of them were more attractive.

Claire figured they'd be in there for a minimum of two days.

"When do I start worrying?"

"When another Keeper shows up with the Summons," Diana snorted.

"Don't worry," Claire told him, shooting her sister a quelling glance. *"I'll always come back to you."*

Austin rolled his eyes and horked up a hairball.

Not an entirely comforting memory, Dean realized walking back to the bench and sitting down.

"Oh, my God. They've muzaked Alien Ant Farm. It's the second sign of the Apocalypse."

"What was the first?" Claire wondered, shifting her pack straps.

"Orange polyester bellbottoms. On sale."

"How much?"

"You're not serious." A quick glance over at her sister and Diana winced. "You are serious. One of us *has* to be adopted."

"I tried adopting you out for most of your childhood. No one would take you."

With the cats hard on their heels, they stepped out into the main concourse and paused. Four senior citizens sat soaking up the air-conditioning on a bench close by the escalator. There was no one else in sight.

Diana pushed damp and rapidly cooling hair up off her forehead. "So much for that hiding in the crowd theory; there were more people in here last night."

"All right, we're a little early for the crowds. But as far as the Otherside is concerned, we're still just shoppers with a perfectly valid reason to be in here. Nothing for them to worry about."

"And the cats?"

"Given the metaphysical buzz this place has, they'll never notice the trickle of power it'll take to hide the cats . . . provided one of the cats doesn't decide to use a planter as a litter box," she finished glaring at Austin who was digging in the plastic bark chips.

"Old kidneys; give me a break. Besides . . ." One last swipe with a back leg and he jumped up onto the planter's broad rim. ". . . I might have been the first *cat,* but I wasn't the first."

"That's mildly disturbing," Claire admitted, scooping him up into her arms. "Diana, where . . ."

Eyes closed, head swiveling slowly from side to side, Diana waved a silencing hand. "There's something," she murmured, trying to pin it down. "Something close."

"Something? I'm amazed you can sense anything in this."

"Feels like the bracelet. It'd be harder to find if I hadn't already touched . . . There!" Her eyes snapped open and she pointed across the concourse to Heaven Sent Cards and Gifts. "Whatever I'm picking up, is in there."

"Overpriced ceramic angels?" Claire stared at the storefront in dismay. "Lots and lots of overpriced ceramic angels?"

"They're not angels," Sam sniffed, whiskers bristling. "They're cherubs. Useless little twerps in the heavenly scheme of things."

"Well, it's not them." Diana crossed to the store, her soles squeaking faintly against the tile. The moment she stepped onto the dark gray carpet, the feeling strengthened, and she turned to face the cash desk. "It's over there." A quick glance showed Claire and the cats had followed her across the concourse and were standing just off the edge of the carpet. "I'll deal with this while you guys search the rest of the store, just in case. And Sam, do *not* spray those angels."

"Cherubs," he muttered, trying to look as though he hadn't been about to lift his tail.

Claire reached out and poked him lightly with her foot. "Come on. We'll start at the back and work our way forward."

When Diana turned to face the cash desk again, the heavily mascaraed teenager standing behind it was watching her in some confusion.

"Who was she talking to?" she asked, gesturing in the general direction Claire had taken. "If somebody sprays those angels they're, like, going to have to pay for them, you know."

Closing the distance between them, Diana smiled at her. "*Please,* don't worry about it."

"Okay." She nodded slowly, looking slightly stoned and remarkably happy. Looking, as it happened, very much like she was never going to worry about anything ever again.

"Oops." Apparently, her power problems hadn't been solved by moving off reserve status. Reaching out carefully, Diana tweaked things, just a little, and was relieved to see a frown line reappear.

"If you're looking for something, I can't, like, leave the cash desk, so you'll have to find it yourself."

"Not a problem." There were a dozen tubs, boxes, and spinners of impulse kitsch nearly covering the glass counter. If customers actually wanted to buy an item larger than a foot square, they were out of luck. Problem was, in a dozen containers of assorted bits and pieces, the thing she sensed could be . . .

In the tub of magic wands.

"You've got to be kidding me."

The clerk blinked and focused. Lips almost as pale as the surrounding skin twitched. "Kids love these."

"I'm sure." *Especially if they get one that actually works.*

The wands were about eight inches long; a hollow tube of clear Lucite partially filled with a metallic or neon sparkling gel and topped with a plastic star the same color. The fourth one Diana pulled from the tub jerked in her hand, rearranging a display of 'flower of the month' tea cups into a significantly larger porcelain cherub. She was beginning to understand why Sam disliked the things. A quick flick of the wand changed it back.

"What was that?" the clerk demanded, whirling around toward the sound of metal ringing against china.

"Falling halo," Diana told her, continuing to pull wands out of the tub.

"What?"

"Forget about it. Specifically, about *it*," she added hurriedly, heading off inadvertent amnesia.

"Forget about what?"

Nothing like a cliché to measure effectiveness. "Exactly."

The remainder of the wands were no more than they appeared.

"I'll take this one."

"Whatever. That'll be twelve ninety-five. Plus tax."

"Fourteen ninety-four," Diana complained, showing Claire the wand. "For a piece of plastic crap."

Claire stepped aside so that the neon pink star no longer pointed directly at her—she'd seen what had happened to the cups and had no wish to suddenly acquire a useless pair of wings and a winsomely blank expression. "Not a bad price for a working wand, though."

"And the plastic crap was on sale for five dollars," Sam added. "There was a whole box of it at the back of the store."

"From the Otherside?"

"No, I think it was from a Rottweiler."

Should have seen that *coming.* Reaching behind her, Diana slid the wand into a side pocket on her backpack. "Taking this across with us should neutralize it. You're sure there was nothing else?"

"A few Chia Pets left over from Christmas—made on the Otherside, but I checked their bar codes and they were all legally imported."

"Then our work here is done." Diana nodded down the concourse toward the stairs. "Let's go close this sucker down."

"Chia Pets are imported from the Otherside?" Sam asked, as he and Austin fell into step between the Keepers.

"They were part of a whole Free Trade thing that fell apart over softwood lumber."

"That doesn't make any sense."

"And that's what I told them at the time."

"That wasn't what I . . ." A half glance over at the older cat and Sam realized that it didn't really matter what he'd meant. "Okay. Never mind."

There were more shoppers on the lower levels and a dozen senior citizens in the food court, having coffee and complaining about the way the younger generations were dressing.

"I've had it with my granddaughter," one sighed loudly as the Keepers and cats passed her table. "She's constantly borrowing my clothes."

Her companion set down her blueberry bran muffin and smoothed her *Canadian Girls Kick Ass* T-shirt over artificially perky breasts. "I hear you, Elsie. I hear you."

"That was disturbing," Diana muttered as they headed down the last short hall toward the Emporium. "Didn't you find that disturbing?"

Claire shrugged. "Not really, but then I'm not wearing the same shirt as a seventy-year-old."

"Hey, hers was red on white, mine's white on red. Not the same shirt!"

"Okay."

Marvin Travel, The Tailor of Gloucester, The Erlking Emporium . . .

Trying to appear as though they were just resting, they sat down on the bench across from the Emporium and took turns glancing through the open door.

"Is that your troll?" Claire asked.

"Okay, first; not *my* troll. And second, why couldn't he have a part-time teenager covering the weekend shifts like almost every other store in the mall?"

"That could be a part-time teenager."

"Good point."

Given the wide variations in human physiognomy, the troll could pass—provided no one looked too closely and were willing to ignore an unfortunate truth; most humans his color had been dead for a couple of days. A couple of hot days. His head was bald, his goatee had probably come off a real goat, his sunglasses appeared to be Ralph Lauren. He was just over six feet tall and only one short third of that was leg. Huge fists dangled even with his knees.

"At least he dresses well."

"Yeah. Nice tie. I wonder what kind of leather it is."

"Not what," Austin said, jumping up onto the bench. "Who."

"Eww."

"His shoes seem to match."

"Like I said, eww."

"It's your Summons," Claire pointed out. "How do we get past him?"

"We've got someone on the inside, remember?" Diana stood, stretched, and started toward the window. Do-it-Yourself Voodoo Kits were forty percent off. Faking an interest in the display, she slid sideways until she could see herself reflected at the very outside edge of the mirror's curve. Blue-on-blue eyes drifted up from the depths.

"Hey, Boss!"

The troll's head jerked around, taking most of his upper body with it owing to a distinct lack of neck. "Are you insane? What if we'd had customers?"

"Then they'd probably be a little freaked by the way the rubber snakes are moving."

"What, again? I knew I shouldn't have trusted that warty little reject from Santa's workshop." Bitching about the way salesmen took advantage of honest retailers, he stomped out from behind the counter and across the store.

Diana, who'd returned to the bench, grabbed Claire's arm. "Now."

When they reached the store, she tugged her sister lower. "Duck!"

Claire almost pulled out of her grip. "Where?"

"Cute, but we did that one already. Just stay low."

A rubbery squelch and a satisfied, "Let's see how much moving you do with your tail stuffed down your throat," propelled them all through the door to the supply room.

There was no immediate sound of pursuit.

And the one nice thing about trolls, Diana acknowledged, *they don't sneak worth a damn.* "Do you think he saw us?"

"Let's not risk it." Claire took three long strides across the storeroom to the steel door that led to the mall's access corridors. She frowned at the hand-lettered "Staff Only" sign, then yanked the door open. "Come on. We've got to be out there to cross over anyway. This is the safest place to emerge into and in order to emerge, we have to exit."

Diana nodded. "An obvious but valid point. Sam . . ." She slipped through after the cat.

Austin followed her.

Claire followed him, checked to make sure they could get the door open again, and carefully closed it.

They found themselves in a concrete corridor where grimy fluorescent bulbs shed just enough light to illuminate a recurring pattern of stains at the base of the walls. The air smelled of old urine and older French fry grease.

Pivoting to the right, Diana took a step toward the ninety-degree turn only a few meters away. "I've always wondered what it looked like back here."

"Here specifically?" Austin snorted.

"No, you know, in back of the shopping parts of shopping malls."

"You need to get out more."

"And we need to get out of here," Claire reminded them, her hand on the latch. "This is where the troll crosses over; there's so much power residue on and around this door, we'll be able to use it without even causing a blip on their radar."

"Unless we send up a major 'hey look at me' flare because we're going in the opposite direction."

All eyes turned toward the younger cat.

"Sorry. Bit of leftover higher knowledge. It's *possible.* But not very likely," Sam added hurriedly as Austin advanced on him. "I mean, power residue's power residue; right? And besides, what would I know."

"Austin!"

Austin shot a "spoilsport" glare at Claire and suddenly became very interested in cleaning his shoulder, his claws almost totally retracted again.

"It's my Summons." Diana reached out for the latch. "The risk should be mine."

Claire shook her head, blocking Diana's hand. "If one of us is going to send up a flare, I'd rather they knew about me—leaving the more powerful Keeper in reserve."

"That's a good point, but here's a better one. We don't know what we'll face on the other side of this door. I should cross first to make sure we're not stopped before we get started."

"Why don't we cross together. They won't get a good reading from either of us and we'll be ready for whatever we have to face."

"But I get to take it out."

"Be my guest."

On Diana's nod, Claire threw open the door.

The storeroom on the Otherside looked almost exactly like the storeroom they'd left behind. The same metal utility shelves, the same jumble of empty boxes, the same overstock. The only real difference was the light—low, diffuse, and slightly green.

The two Keepers stood weighing the silence for danger.

"Hey." Sam jumped up on a stack of old plastic milk crates. "Where's Austin?"

THREE

ONE MINUTE, he had the tip of an orange tail in his face. The next, he felt the possibilities shift and he was walking alone into the storeroom they'd just left.

The door to the access corridor was closed.

The door to the store was closed.

Austin sat down, wrapped his tail around his front feet, and glared at nothing in particular. The urge to piss on something was intense. Like all cats, he knew when he was being told "No!"; he usually ignored it, but he knew.

He'd just been told in no uncertain terms.

The possibilities would not allow him to cross over.

When the door to the access corridor remained closed, his eye narrowed. Had she been able to, Claire would have returned immediately to find him. She hadn't, so therefore she couldn't. The question now became: why?

Fortunately, there was a way to find out.

Unfortunately, even up on his hind legs, he could just barely stretch to touch the bottom of the latch plate.

Okay, new plan.

Dropping to all fours, he stared at the closed door, a position proven to bring a talking monkey trotting to his assistance.

"Not a problem, ladies, I've got more T-shirt sizes in the back room."

Or possibly a talking whatever the troll claimed as an evolutionary precedent.

As the door opened, Austin slid in behind a crate marked with both a biohazard and a live cargo symbol. Curious, he took a sniff at one of the air holes, but the crate was empty and had been for some time—probably a good thing although he could easily imagine scenarios where it wouldn't be. With the troll's full attention fixed on pulling an XXX large *Astarte Fan Club* out of a shipping carton of T-shirts, he slipped through the doorway and into the Emporium.

A fast right, a dive under a raised display case, a quick creep forward belly to the ground brought him behind a basket of small plastic jewelry boxes. Head cocked, he listened for the straining gears that would indicate someone with a desire to hear music played on pieces of bent tin had wound the key. When he finally found a silent box, he flipped it open. The miniature Republican in a frilly pink tutu remained motionless in front of the mirror.

Austin smacked the tiny politician out of his way and tipped the box back until its mirror reflected only the security mirror up by the ceiling.

Fortunately, cats were masters of refraction.

The direct approach would have taken him right into the troll's line of sight now that the big guy was back at the counter explaining washing instructions to the T-shirt's new owner—apparently, the bloodstains were not supposed to come out.

Blue-on-blue eyes drifted up from the depths of the jewelry box mirror.

"What are you doing here?" the mirror demanded, its usual booming tones more of a low tinkle.

Muzzle so close his breath fogged the glass. "The possibilities wouldn't let me cross."

"Age thing?"

Austin shrugged. "Maybe. Maybe the idiots in charge think two cats would give the good guys an unfair advantage; I don't know. Can you get a message through to my people on the Otherside? I need to know that Claire's all right; she needs to know that I'm safe."

"I can do better than that. I should be able to patch you through, cat to cat. Video only, though, no audio. You want full bandwidth, you'll need a crystal ball."

"Video's fine." If Claire could see him, she'd know he was okay and could concentrate on doing her job. He scanned the store for some-thing visual that would help get his message through and just when it seemed that nothing at all said "Dean," he spotted the rack of ceramic nameplates.

The rules governing tacky gift store purchases clearly stated that no one was to ever find exactly the name they were looking for.

Cats made their own rules.

Utilizing the speed that could hook a fry from unsuspecting fin-gers during the instant it passed between plate and lips, Austin leaped into the air, got a paw under his objective, and was on the floor with it before the troll could look up from making change, the impact with the carpet barely audible over the muttered, "Five and six is thirteen plus eight is twenty."

The name was right although the decoration of two obscenely cute mice eating a giant strawberry didn't exactly say six foot two, obses-sively tidy, Newfie hockey player. Oh, wait, not a giant strawberry—they just had most of the skin off.

Positioning himself by the mirror again, Austin leaned in until his whiskers touched the glass.

"Do it."

"What do you mean, where's Austin?"

Sam rolled his eyes. "I mean, he's not here."

Diana grabbed Claire's wrist as she reached for the door. "Where are you going?"

"Back. He could be hurt."

"He could be anywhere. Just because the possibilities didn't bring him through here doesn't mean they left him in the other mall."

"There's only one way to find out."

"And if he isn't there?"

Pulling free, Claire took a deep breath and looked her sister in the eye. "Then I'll come right back."

After a long moment, Diana nodded.

Claire closed her fingers around the latch, and froze.

Footsteps. Marching footsteps.

Distant, but coming closer.

Hard soles against concrete.

Hard *something* against concrete. Hooves, maybe? Impossible to tell.

The Keepers could feel the floor vibrate against their feet. Sam's tail puffed out to four times its usual sleek diameter.

Diana wound her fingers through Claire's pack straps and hauled her toward the other door. "We've got to get out of here!"

Closer.

A pair of snowflake paperweights vibrated so violently they shattered, spilling out miniature Grendels chewing on the bloody ends of Viking arms.

"We don't know what's out in the store," Claire protested, as Diana yanked the door open.

"It's got to be better than what's out there!"

Sam leaped off the milk crates and raced between their legs.

"Sam thinks it's safe! Move!"

They dove through the door after the cat. Diana slammed it behind them.

The sudden silence was almost overwhelming.

The hair lifting off his spine into an orange Mohawk, Sam moved out into the store. "It's so thick, it's like walking through pudding."

"You should know," Diana muttered, hands flat against the door, straining to hear if they'd been followed.

"That was an *accident.*"

"Maybe the *first* time. I can't hear anything moving in the storeroom." She turned to her sister. "You?"

"Nothing. Wait here. I'll go back for Austin."

"No need."

"Sam!" Claire glared down at the younger cat . . .

. . . who ignored her, his head raised, his eyes locked on the back corner by the ceiling.

The mirror on the Otherside was a sheet of thick, silvered glass, about half a meter wide by a meter long, in an antique wooden frame. It was currently reflecting the store they'd just left. The troll flirted with the two teenage girls standing by the counter, a woman pushed a baby stroller out into the concourse, one of the rubber snakes disappeared under the pile of stuffed toys, and Austin stared down at them from beside a basket of tiny plastic music boxes.

"He's all right." Claire released a breath she hadn't realized she'd been holding. "Thank God."

"You're welcome."

Diana rubbed her hands over the goose bumps texturing her arms. "Uh, Claire, ixnay on the anking-thay odgay while we're erehay. Attracts the wrong kind of attention."

"I know."

"I know you know. You were just relieved to see, you know." She nodded toward the cat in the mirror.

"What's he trying to . . . oh. Dean. He's going to go to Dean."

Eyes narrowed, Diana peered up at the ceramic name plate Austin had pushed out into the aisle. "Are those mice eating a pixie?"

"What? No, they're eating a straw . . . Okay, that's really, really gross."

Then they were staring up at themselves.

"Hey!" Claire folded her arms and stomped one foot—which would have been a more effective protest had the tar residue not temporarily attached her heel to the carpet. She jerked it free, caught hold of a display shelf as her backpack shifted suddenly, threatening to topple her over, and snapped, "What happened?"

The blue-on-blue eyes managed to look slightly sheepish. "Sorry. Lost the signal."

"How?" Diana demanded. "You forgot to disable call waiting?"

"No, it's a hardware problem—those newfangled convex mirrors distort everything. Look, I've got to get back on duty, but don't forget what you promised."

She nodded. "To get you out of here before we shut the place down. I remember."

"You remember now," the mirror acknowledged. "Harder to remember when you're pinned down under enemy fire."

"What enemy fire?" But the eyes were gone and her reflection looked as annoyed as she felt. "What enemy fire?" she repeated in her sister's general direction.

"What difference does it make? Stop thinking about it!"

Diana blanched. The Otherside built substance from the subconscious of its inhabitants and she was suddenly unable to think about anything else. Distraction, distraction . . . "OW!"

Looking smug, Sam removed his claw from her foot.

"So I'm suddenly less convinced that mirror's on our side." Dropping to one knee, she licked her finger and dabbed at the blood. "What do you think, Claire?"

"About what?" She forced her gaze off the mirror. "Sorry. I'm worried about Austin all alone in that mall."

"Austin's older than most of the weekend staff," Diana reminded her. "And it goes without saying he's smarter. I'm totally sure he'll have no problems getting back to where we left Dean."

"We've been here a while. What if Dean's not there?"

His biggest problem was going to be getting out of the Emporium unseen. Capture out in the mall would mean, at most, a few unpleasant hours until he escaped custody. Capture in the store would mean mustard. Trolls put mustard on everything they ate. Usually, to kill the taste. Occasionally, to kill the food. Austin had no intention of dying by condiment.

Concentrating on keeping his tail close, he crept along the floor using every bit of cover an eclectic array of merchandise provided and trying not to notice what he was creeping through. Trolls weren't known for the cleanliness of their carpets and some of the merchandise was eclectic in ways that stained. A little over a meter from the door, he ran out of things to hide behind.

No customers remained to distract the troll.

Even at this distance, the wards around the door stroked energy into his fur. If he read them right, which went without saying, they needed only a single word to close them down and create an impenetrable barrier. Given that he had to cross directly through the troll's line of sight, it would take luck as much as speed to ensure he was on the right side of the barrier when that word was spoken.

Okay. He drew his legs in tight to his body, weight to the back, ready for powerful haunches to launch him forward. *Remember, you're only as old as you feel.*

. . . ready for powerful haunches to launch him forward.

And I feel like I'm going to be eighteen in August.

. . . launch him forward.

Eighteen's old for a cat. If I was a dog, I'd probably be dead. Of course, if I was a dog, I'd want to be dead.

. . . forward.

Oh, crap.

His first leap took him nearly to the threshold. He heard the troll yell "Cat!", then he heard him yell "Endoplasmic reticulum!", saw a flash of aubergine light, smelled the unmistakable odor of burning cat hair, and was in the concourse under the bench, patting out the smoldering end of his tail. Fortunately, his fur was long enough so that no actual damage had been done.

Another flash of aubergine light and an impact that set his whiskers vibrating.

Heart pounding, he turned toward the Emporium.

The troll lay flat on his back just inside the door. Apparently, the wards were set to keep everything in.

"Idiot," he muttered, and washed a triumphant paw.

"Kitty!"

His attention had been so completely on the store that the toddler squatting down and peering under the bench, his diaper nearly touching the tiles, one chubby hand reaching for Austin's head, came as a complete surprise.

"Are you *trying* to give kitty a heart attack," he gasped when he could catch his breath.

"Pretty!"

"Don't touch that!"

"Come on, Brandon." A woman's feet came out from behind a massive stroller. Large hands tucked themselves into the child's armpits and hoisted him out of sight while ducky sandals kicked futilely in protest. "Let's get you home while you're still in a good mood."

Austin inched carefully forward until he could get a good look at young Brandon's destination. The stroller not only had plenty of room for hitchhikers but a large flat canopy. When the back rack was full of bags—which it was—the adult pushing couldn't actually see the seat. He waited while the seat belts were secured, waited while the woman went around to the handle, then, just as the stroller was about to move, he leaped.

"Kitty!"

"No kitties this trip, big fella," the woman corrected, adding with some pique, "and next time we'll stay away from the pet store."

He hadn't been seen and Brandon already had a cover story in place. "Way to go, kid," he murmured into a chubby ear. "Hey! Arm does not go around kitty's neck."

"Kitty soft."

"Yeah? Well, baby smelly." Tucking legs and tail close to his body in an attempt to look as much like a stuffed toy as possible, Austin settled back to enjoy the ride. *If they turn left once they've crossed the food court, I'll have to bail.*

The stroller turned right.

What are the chances, they'll head for the upper level . . . ?

The stroller's front wheels bumped against the escalator.

"You okay in there, Brandon?"

"Okay!" The stroller tipped back and began to rise. "Kitty?"

"I'm good. And do *not* put that in your mouth, it's attached!"

At Sunshine Records, his luck ran out.

"Just going to make a quick stop, kiddo, then we'll head for the parking lot."

With the stroller stopped, someone in the record store would be sure to do that "make faces at the baby" thing that adults found so impossible to resist. After a lifetime of similar faces looming over him, Austin had a strong suspicion the babies weren't as thrilled by it. As they began to turn, he murmured a quick good-bye and jumped clear, racing for a planter and the cover of a plastic shrub.

No hue and cry.

Now to find out exactly where he was.

It looked good. Ten meters of main concourse, then the short side hall to the doors where they'd left Dean. A little exposed until he got to the side hall, but if he remembered correctly—which, of course, he did—once there, he'd have plenty to hide behind.

Play the skulking music, boys.

Checking that no one was looking his way, he jumped down and began moving along the clear Lucite barrier that kept the careless, the stupid, and the carelessly stupid from falling through a hexagonal opening to the lower level.

Clear Lucite barrier?

"Hey!" The shout came from across the concourse. "There's a cat over there! Let's get it!"

Oh, crap.

Wondering how much longer he was going to wait, Dean tried to find a comfortable position on the metal bench and picked up his last remaining section of the Saturday paper. He'd read the comics, the sports pages, the wheels section—which was pretty much the newsprint version of infomercials but about cars so that was okay. He'd read life, and entertainment, and even the report on business. There was nothing left but the actual news.

The front page shared space about equally between a doom-and-gloom prediction of an economic slowdown caused by consumer inability to realize the need for more electronic crap and the continuing disappearance of Kingston's street kids. "Look, the day you can keep track of three hundred and ten cases and not lose a few of the mobile ones, you let me know. Until then, get off my fucking back!" a social worker was quoted as saying. Dean couldn't decide which impressed him more, the social worker for saying it or the paper for actually printing it.

The Children's Aid Society requested that anyone with news contact them at any time, day or night, where any time actually meant between eight and four Monday to Thursday, and eight to noon Fridays because of government cutbacks.

"Okay, now I'm depressed." Folding the section neatly, he piled it with the rest. Claire'd told him that they'd be inside for a couple of days; maybe it was time he went . . .

Paws drumming on glass.

Paws?

Leaping to his feet, he ran for the doors.

Up on his hind legs, his stomach fur a brilliant streak of white, Austin pounded to be let out. As Dean yanked the door open, he fell forward, hit the concrete running, and disappeared into the parking lot before Dean could get a question out.

The trio of teenage boys in hot pursuit made at least one of the questions moot. They rocked to a halt at the edge of the asphalt, stopped as much by the heat as the sudden disappearance of their prey.

"Lose something?" He had four or five years on them and a couple of inches as well as a lot of muscle on the biggest. If it came down to it, Austin was in no real danger.

"You let the cat out, man. We were trying to catch it!"

"Why?"

"Why?" The speaker exchanged a clear but silent *"Dude's an idiot"* with the other two. "'Cause there's not supposed to be cats in the mall."

Dean glanced pointedly out at the parking lot.

"It's not in the mall now 'cause we chased it out of the mall." Eyes narrowed. "It's not your cat."

"I know." Austin considered Dean one of his ambulatory can openers, but that was beside the point.

"If it's anyone's cat, it's our cat. We saw it first."

"I don't want the damned cat, man." One of the other boys hauled up the shorts falling off skinny hips and looked longingly back toward the air-conditioning. "Come on, it's hot out here."

Under the shadow of a scruffy teenage mustache, the first boy's lip curled. "So we just let the cat win?"

The third boy sighed and scratched at the growing damp spot under his arm. "Cats always win. One way or another."

"Oh, yeah, hiding under a parked . . ." Narrowed eyes widened. ". . . minivan." He shifted his gaze across the nearly uniform rows of family vehicles until it returned, eyes wide, to Dean. "You find the cat, man, you can have it. We don't want it." Hands shoved deep into his pockets, he turned on one heel. "Come on."

Does everybody *know about the minivans?* Dean wondered as the three boys slouched back inside the mall. He waited until he heard the doors close, then he waited a few minutes more, just in case. Picking the folded newspaper up off the bench, he walked out to his truck.

As he stepped off the concrete pad and out of the building's shadow, the heat hit him like a warm, wet sponge. By the time he had the driver's door open, his T-shirt was clinging damply to his back.

"Took you long enough," Austin panted, crawling out from under the truck bed.

"Sorry." Scooping the cat up in one hand, Dean dropped him gently on the seat and slid in after him. "What happened, then?"

"The possibilities wouldn't let me through, but the others are fine, so don't sweat it." An emerald eye turned briefly toward Dean. "That was sort of a joke. Is there any water in here?"

After their last visit to the vet, Claire'd begun keeping a bottle of water and a small bowl in the glove compartment. It was tepid, but Austin drank almost all Dean poured.

"Are you okay?"

"Give me a minute." The cat sat up, rubbed a paw over wet whiskers, and sighed. "Ever notice how much a group of teenage boys resembles a dog pack?"

"Uh, no."

"So that was some other guy doing all that alpha male posturing?"

Dean thought back over the encounter and frowned. "I didn't . . ."

"You didn't sniff their butts, but other than that, it was all big dog, little dogs. Don't get me wrong. If it weren't for my whole dogs-are-an-accident-of-nature belief system, I'd have been very impressed." He folded himself into tea cozy position. "Well?"

"Well, what?" Dean asked, still working his way through the dog thing.

"Well, why are we still sitting here? I have some serious napping scheduled for this afternoon and I'd like to get to it."

"We're just going to leave, then?"

Austin sighed. "Yes. I don't like it any more than you but that's the way it is. We leave. They stay. They save the world. We go home and you feed the cat. At least now you also have vital and important duties to perform."

"Right." Dean fished his keys from his pocket and started the engine. "Don't be taking this the wrong way, but I'd be happier if you were with Claire."

"Likewise."

"You know, I'm starting to think this isn't the actual anchor. That it's just the tip of the iceberg."

"Mixed metaphors aside, I think you're right." Claire straightened up from examining a display of remarkably realistic stone garden gnomes. "I also think they're using a basilisk, so keep your eyes peeled."

"That would explain the stone guy with the stone net and the wet stain on his stone trousers," Diana acknowledged, crossing toward her sister. "I was wondering why they'd only stock one of such a guaranteed big seller. Where do you think it is?"

"The basilisk? Hopefully, not here."

"Not the basilisk, the anchor."

"It's got to be close. It's not in the store. It's not in the storeroom . . ."

"It's probably behind the construction barrier," Sam yawned. He closed his mouth to find both Keepers staring at him. "What? It's covered in *danger, keep out, authorized entry only, this means you* signs. It seemed kind of obvious."

After a moment, Diana sighed. "He's right."

"You say that like you're surprised," the cat protested.

"Only because I was," she told him reassuringly as she shoved him off her backpack and heaved it back up onto her shoulders. "Let's get a move on. They've got to know we're here by now."

"If they don't, they will in a moment." Claire nodded toward the door. "It's warded to keep things in."

"Given the basilisk, good. Otherwise, that kind of sucks."

"And it explains why no one's shown up so far. They know they can take their time coming to get us because we're not going anywhere."

"We aren't?"

"Hypothetically. Do you think you could not want those wards there enough to get rid of them?"

"I could just *get* rid of them." As Claire turned toward her, Diana raised both hands. "Except I'd be imposing my will on the Otherside, and that would be breaking the Rules, and so I would never, ever do it because that would make me just like the bad guys."

"Hey!" Sam bumped her in the calf with his head. "What are you talking about?"

"You can influence the Otherside with strong subconscious desires or by consciously wanting or not wanting something badly enough, but you can't just demand it be one thing or the other," Diana explained, bending just enough to stroke the end of his tail through her fingers.

"Even if you're very young and it was sort of an accident, no matter what people say."

"Is this another doesn't-know-her-own-strength story?" the cat wondered.

Claire nodded. "Every door that had ever been used as an access was blown off its hinges."

"Okay, okay, fine. But nobody got hurt, so no harm, no foul." Diana stepped closer to the wards. "You do something once . . ."

"Twice."

"Okay, twice, and all of a sudden you can't be trusted."

"I trust you. I'm the one who asked you to not want the wards, remember?"

"Right." Her brow furrowed. The absolute last thing she wanted was to be stuck in a shadow Emporium with a possible basilisk and her sister telling remember-how-Diana-blew-up-the-sofa stories. The wards flickered. And again. And disappeared to the sound of sirens and a blinding array of flashing lights.

"I think you set off an alarm!" Sam yelled.

"What was your first clue?" Diana shrieked back at him as the three of them ran out the cleared door and into the concourse.

"It was either the sirens or the flashing lights!"

The shadow construction barrier was the same painted gray plywood as the original.

"Unless this is the original and the other one's the shadow."

"Not imortant right now!" Claire had both hands pressed flat against the wood. "We've got to get through this."

"How? There's no door!"

"Then want to get through harder!"

"I am!" Diana scanned the barrier for any kind of a seam, but all she could see were the warning signs and the ubiquitous, *Kilroy was here.* "Oh, sure, but he's not here now. The obnoxious gnome owes me ten bucks."

"What?"

"Nothing!"

Claire smacked the barrier with the palms of both hands, then backed away. "We're going to have to use the access corridor to get behind it!"

"I hate this, but you're right!"

They turned back toward the store, but before they'd taken a single step, the door to the storeroom crashed open and half a dozen misshapen bodies in badly fitting navy blue track suits charged through. Essentially bipedal, they looked like someone had crossed a rhinocerus with a hockey player.

"Great! Not wanting *them* doesn't seem to be working either!"

"What are they?"

"Who cares?" Diana grabbed Claire's hand, yanked her around until she was facing down the concourse, and gave her a shove. "RUN!"

Sam was already almost at the food court.

The Tailor of Gloucester had become The Tailer of Gloucester with a number of samples hanging in the window. Diana would have liked a closer look at the multicolored fog swirling about inside the travel agency, but something slammed into her backpack as she passed the store and she decided that maybe concentrating on running would be the better plan. Fortunately, here on the Otherside, concentrating on running was enough to lend new speed to her feet.

"What are they throwing?" Claire demanded as they began weaving through the tables in the food court.

Something buzzed past Diana's ear with an almost overpowering scent of gardenias, dented one of the metal chairs, and bounced out of sight.

"I think it's scented candles!"

"Oh, that's just great! Those things are deadly!"

"Only in enclosed spaces!"

On the far side of the food court, they followed Sam to the right; the crashing and banging of their pursuers through the tables and chairs drowning out the distant sound of the sirens.

"Where are we going?"

"I don't know!"

"Hey! Up here!"

Both Keepers skidded to a halt and squinting up through the hexagonal opening to the upper level trying to make out the features of the person leaning over the edge.

"Are you a good witch or a bad witch?" the spiky silhouette demanded.

"We're not . . ." Claire began but Diana drove an elbow into her side.

"Good witches!"

"Then haul ass to the stairs! We'll hold them off."

"We're not . . ."

Diana grabbed Claire's hand again. "Close enough. Shut up and follow Sam!"

Something whistled through the air behind them as they pounded up the concourse after the cat. The escalators were insubstantial, but the stairs were much as they'd left them. Except for the piled barricade at the top and the half-dozen teenagers standing behind it.

Sam scrambled up and over but as the Keepers neared the top step, a genuine wood finish laminate armoire was rolled back out of the way. The packs made it a tight fit, but they both squeezed through and collapsed panting to the floor.

Candles pounded the barricade, hitting with enough force to slam through a display counter and into the piled barbeques behind it. The tempered steel rang like a gong but held.

The whistling noise was defined as the teenagers fired ceramic cherubs from heavy duty slingshots.

"Did you want these guys?" Claire murmured.

"I wanted rescue," Diana admitted, "but I don't think either of us had anything to do with this. It's too . . ."

"Clichéd?"

"I was going to say too real, but strangely enough, too clichéd also works."

"They're hitting the things," Sam reported from the top of the barricade. "It's stopping them, but they don't seem to be taking much damage."

"Nah, they never do," explained the teenager next to him, aiming and releasing again. "But if you hit them in the head, the bits of broken ceramic get in their eyes and they totally hate that. Damn! I don't know what you guys did to get 'em so worked up 'cause usually they got a zero attention span."

Another volley. And then another. And then a cheer went up.

"And we win again. The meat-minds'll mill around for a while, then they'll head home." She tossed long, mahogany dreadlocks back behind her shoulders and stared down at Sam. "You talk."

He shrugged. "So do you."

"Good point." Holding her bow across her chest, she turned to face the Keepers. "I'm Kris, Captain of the Guard. Who are you?"

"Too real?" Claire whispered.

Although Kris and the other archers were dressed in combinations of clothes obviously pulled off the rack, there could be no mistaking the pointed ears or the great hair.

Elves.

Except, of course, that elves didn't actually exist.

FOUR

＊ ・ ＝◆彡 ・ ＊

AS THE OTHERS MOVED TO STAND BEHIND KRIS, it became obvious that some ears were less pointed and some hair less blatantly great. Lined up in order, the seven would have looked like time lapse photography—from almost human to full elf.

Claire's eyes widened. "They're Bystanders."

"Maybe once," Diana agreed, watching one of them flick a brilliant red braid wound through with neon tubing back over his shoulder, "but not now. This place is changing them." Feeling like a turtle stuck on its back, she tried to stand, struggling against the weight of the backpack. When Kris grinned and held out a hand, she accepted it gratefully. The elf's grip was warm and dry, surprisingly callused and remarkably strong; Diana found herself lifted effortlessly to her feet.

"You're 'bout right for walkin' on the weird side," Kris observed as Diana reluctantly released her hand, "but your . . . sister?"

Both Keepers nodded. Probably because of the Lineage, the family resemblance had always been strong.

"Well, she's a little old for this sort of thing."

Diana hid a smile as she helped a glowering Claire stand. Since Dean and the seven-year age difference, the whole age thing had become a sensitive point.

"And, no offense," Kris continued, "but you're both too well fed."

"Too well fed for what?" Claire demanded, smoothing her skirt over her thighs.

"For livin' rough."

"That's because we haven't been."

"Totally obvious they didn't fall in off the street," the redhead snorted.

"No, we didn't." Diana agreed, breaking in before Claire's tone got them into trouble. "We came here deliberately."

That got everyone's attention.

A very pale blond with eyes so light only the pupils showed, stepped forward. "You can do that? Come here deliberately?"

"Well, duh." A boy who might have been East Indian jabbed him with the end of his slingshot. "They're here."

"Well, duh, maybe they're lying."

"Yeah? Maybe you're an idiot."

"Yeah, well, you're a . . ."

"Colin. Teemo."

Names held power. Whether Kris had known that before or had discovered it after crossing, she certainly knew it now. The argument stopped cold, both boys looking sheepish at suddenly being the center of attention.

"*We* can cross deliberately," Diana said into the sudden silence. "Not everybody can."

"How?"

"Did we get here?"

"Yeah. That. And why did you come? And who the hell are you?"

Diana exchanged a speaking glance with Claire. If the, well, elves—for lack of a better word—could still swear with impunity, then they were influencing the Otherside on a subconscious level only. However they'd changed, they remained Bystanders, and the Lineage worked very hard at keeping Bystanders unaware of their existence.

"Your Summons," Claire murmured. "Your choice."

"The Rules . . ."

"Diana, there's a sign in that shoe store window advertising ruby slippers for half off. Unless they're trying to attract the Otherside drag queen business, I'd say that the Rules have already been twisted pretty far out of shape."

"O–kay." Claire had been a total Rule follower her entire life. Dean had obviously loosened her up a lot more than Diana had suspected. *Bad, bad mental image. Think about . . .*

Kris folded her arms and glared. Her expression promised violence if she didn't get an answer soon.

Yeah, that works. "My name is Diana. This is Claire. That's Sam. Essentially, we're a sort of wizard called a Keeper."

"We're not wizards," Claire sighed.

"Okay," Diana muttered sotto voice, not the least surprised Claire'd had to stick her two cents in regardless of what she'd said about choices and whose they were. "*You* explain to the *mall elves* exactly what we are in three thousand words or less."

Claire's eyes narrowed, then she sighed again. "Essentially," she told their fascinated audience, "we're wizards. It's our job to make sure that metaphysical balances are kept."

"That the magical stuff between the worlds doesn't go out of whack," Diana clarified as half a dozen pairs of eyes stared at them blankly.

Kris shook her head, dreadlocks bouncing. "You're wizards?"

"*Essentially* wizards," Claire amended reluctantly.

"They're wizards," Sam snorted. "I'm a cat."

"Right." Kris acknowledged him with a quick smile and turned her attention back to the Keepers. "Well, since you're here and since we're here and since our candle throwin' friends with the negative number IQs are here and since this is a fuckin' *shopping mall,* I'm guessin' that the magical stuff between the worlds is way whacked."

"Good guess."

"Yeah, well, we're not stupid."

"Kris." One of the others, a skinny, dark-haired, androgynous kid probably no more than fifteen jumped the barricade. "The meatminds have retreated back past the food court."

"Thanks, DK. All right, the rest of you go back to what you were doing before Jo gave the alarm. Me and Will'll take these guys in to Arthur." She jerked her head down the concourse toward the anchor store at the far end. "Let's go."

Will turned out to be the redhead.

"Actually," Claire announced in a tone that suggested she'd neither forgotten nor forgiven the earlier *too old and too well fed* observation, "we've got to get back to the other end of the mall. We appreciate your assistance, but we have a job to do here."

Kris shrugged. "So do I. And my job says I take new people in to see Arthur."

"Claire . . ."

"Diana?"

She flashed Kris a smile, grabbed Claire's arm, and yanked her close enough to mutter into her ear. "I know that time is a factor, I mean, it is *my* Summons and all, but these guys are a factor, too, because whoever's running this segue isn't going to be able to finish it while they're still here. I mean, we weren't expecting indigenous life."

"They aren't indigenous!"

"Maybe they didn't used to be, but they are now.'"

"All right, fine." Claire pulled her arm free. "But if this thing goes critical while we're talking . . ."

"Then we'll be in the right place because it can't go critical until the forces of darkness attack and destroy this last bastion of the light."

"The forces of darkness are throwing scented candles!"

"Yeah, but they're throwing them really hard. And besides, you know as well as I do how fast things can change on the Otherside." Diana patted Claire's bare shoulder in a comforting sort of way and turned back to Kris. "So, take us to your leader. He *is* your leader, right?"

Claire sighed. "Well, if he isn't, you've just wasted that line."

"He *is* our leader," Kris told them, and this time when she indicated they should start moving, there was very little room for arguing with the gesture.

As the Keepers stepped away from the barricade and Sam jumped down to walk between them, Will fell in on one side, Kris on the other. They were clearly being escorted. Diana decided to think of it as an honor guard.

"So," she prodded after a moment. "This Arthur; what's he like?"

Kris glanced over at her and shrugged. "Not like us."

"Like you are or like you were?"

"What's the diff?"

"You know; the whole ears, thick flowing tresses thing."

"The what?"

Bystanders could lie to Keepers; they just couldn't get away with it. Kris honestly didn't know what Diana was talking about. Apparently their perception of themselves had changed as they had changed. Now why they'd changed the way they had; that was a whole different question without an answer. "Never mind, it's not important. So, how *is* Arthur different from you?"

"He came from outside."

"Outside?" Diana was beginning to have a bad feeling about this.

"Yeah, outside the mall." Kris waved to the tall, slender girl standing guard at the intersection of the main concourse and the short hall leading to one of the outside doors. "We don't know how he got in, 'cause we can't get out, but he understands this place. He keeps us together; he made us strong. We were getting our asses kicked by all sorts of strange shit until he showed up."

"And he made you the captain of his guard?"

"Yeah. He did. You got a problem with that?"

"No. Of course not. You're obviously really good at it and you, you know, you're in charge and um . . ." *Babble much? She's going to think you're an idiot. Get a grip!* Diana took a deep breath and ignored Claire's raised eyebrow. "So, were you the first one who crossed over?"

A muscle jumped in Kris' jaw. "Second."

Something in her tone made Diana remember all the things Austin had listed that were worse than BAM. Splat. Crunch. Grind. Chew. For some reason, especially chew.

They were heading toward the large department store at what had been the west end of the mall. Cosmetic counters had been stacked on their sides to make a solid wall across all but a small section of the store's wide entrance. A nod of Kris's head and Will lounged in the opening.

"Just so you know," Claire said, delivering a speaking look to her sister, "you can't hold us."

Kris shrugged. "Just so's *you* know, I'm not planning on it. But I believe in coverin' my ass, just in case."

"Of what?"

"Whatever." She led Diana, Claire, and Sam into a large open area where the faint, antagonistic scents of a dozen different perfumes lingered, told them to wait, and disappeared between two racks of plus size winter coats.

"You know they might be able to hold us," Diana murmured, with a quick glance at Will's back. "This being the Otherside and all. If there's enough of them wanting us held . . ."

"You were the one who wanted to see their leader. I just think we should go in from a position of strength."

"They had to rescue us from walking cat food throwing scented candles," Sam pointed out, tail lashing as he paced the perimeter. "Oh, yeah, that's a position of strength."

Claire glared at the cat.

Diana punched her lightly on the arm. "Missing Austin?"

Claire shifted her glare up and over. After a moment, she sighed. "Yes. A lot. I hope he's all right."

"Don't worry, he's with Dean. On second thought, worry about Dean."

"Very funny. I'm sure Austin will be a huge help to Dean at the guest house."

"You're delusional. You know that, right?"

Claire smiled tightly. "It helps when you work with cats."

They watched Sam explore nooks and crannies they couldn't see and listened to the distant sound of someone beating a drum kit to death with a couple of guitars and an electronic keyboard.

"So, Arthur," Diana said at last, rubbing her nose and moving away from a particularly strong patch of Phobia™ for Men. "He came in from outside the mall to bring them together and make them strong."

"The name could be a coincidence."

"Oh, please."

Claire sighed as deeply as the weight of her backpack allowed. "They needed a leader; he's what their subconscious created."

Fur between his eyes folded into a darker orange "w," Sam frowned up at them both. "Do you guys know this Arthur?"

"Not *this* Arthur, but he's just the sort of opportunistic archetype who'd show up in this kind of story. And you never just get him, do you?" Her own brow furrowed, Diana folded her arms.

"We should be glad they're not a little younger," Claire reminded her. "Or we might have been dealing with Peter Pan."

"Yeah, but they've turned themselves into elves. Wouldn't Oberon make more sense?"

"I doubt this lot's read much Shakespeare, but you have; you'd honestly rather deal with Oberon?"

Diana considered it for a moment. "Okay, good point. Ass ears; not a great look. But still, that whole Immortal King crap just gets up my nose. Follow me, serve me, love me . . . gag me!"

"Your opinion aside, Arthur is a nice, classic, archetypal answer to a leadership dilemma."

Arthur turned out to be a tall, broad-shouldered, narrow-hipped young man in his late teens with startlingly blue eyes and a wild shock of blue-black hair that kept falling attractively forward over his face in spite of a silver circlet.

"Okay," Claire said slowly as they walked toward him, drawn by the brilliant, perfect white crescent of his smile. "So he's a nice *anime* archetypal answer to a leadership dilemma."

"And we can be grateful they're becoming elves, not Pokémon," Diana added.

Dressed in black and silver—jeans, boots, T-shirt, leather jacket, lots of buckles—and wearing a very large sword across his back, he waited for them in the electronics section of the department store. The sword, at least, should have looked out of place. It didn't.

A burgundy leather sofa and two matching chairs, heavy on the rivets, defined three sides of the space. Under the furniture, was a square of carpet patterned in shades of gray. The fourth side was a massive, rear projection television—its screen a reflective black. The mere lack of accessible electricity wouldn't have been enough to keep the TV off had enough of the mall elves wanted it on but, subconscious desires or not, the programming would have been beyond their control. Diana had seen a TV in one of the bleaker Otherside neighborhoods that showed nothing but reruns of *Three's Company.* Next to the Girl Guide camp, it was as close to actually being in Hell as she ever wanted to get.

There was no sign of Arthur's usual entourage and although the coffee table had smoothed corners, it could in no way be called round.

"When Kris said that a pair of Keepers had crossed over, I thought the news was too good to be true," Arthur announced, moving to meet them as they stepped onto the carpet. "And yet, here you are." He looked so pleased that Diana found herself grinning foolishly in response. A quick glance over at Claire showed she was having much the same reaction.

"Sire? About some us heading out scavenging?"

"Of course." Arthur nodded toward the Keepers. "If you'll excuse me." When he turned his attention to Kris, it seemed almost as though the lights had dimmed.

Oh, great. Diana scowled at her reflection in the television. *That's so* not *good.*

Wait a minute, the lights have *dimmed.*

She glanced up at the ceiling. The huge frosted squares over the fluorescent tubes were becoming distinctly gray. "Claire . . ."

"I see it. I think this store is almost real and the mall in the real world is closing down for the day."

They were right under one of the emergency lights. As the rest of the store filled with shadows, the area defined by the sofa, the chairs, and the television remained, if not bright, at least lit. "But it's barely midafternoon."

"A little past." Claire thrust her wrist and watch into Diana's line of sight. Six fifteen. The second hand swept around the dial almost too fast to see. Six sixteen. Seventeen.

"Give me one good reason why I should feed you anything different than I would if Claire were here?" Dean demanded, lifting Austin off the table and out of his supper.

"Claire's not here."

He thought about that for a moment then cut the cat some cold beef. "Okay. Good reason."

"But time was running one to one when you checked at the Emporium."

Claire nodded toward Arthur, who was still speaking quietly with Kris. "I think he's a time distortion. He's pure Otherside. Whoever's running this segue can't control him."

"Yeah, but they clearly can't control the *elves* either."

"It's June." Austin settled himself in tea cozy position on the coffee table. "Why are they still playing hockey?"

"Because they're not finished."

"You know, the world made a lot more sense when I was young."

Dean twisted the cap off a beer and toasted his reluctant companion. "Oh, yeah, I'll drink to that."

"They had no trouble controlling the elves before Arthur showed up. Kris said they were getting their asses kicked."

"Okay, so these kids get caught in the segue, but it happened over time, so the darkness had to know about it, which means it has to want them here to . . ." Diana glanced around at the department store, complete to the sale banners hanging from the ceiling. ". . . to help define this end of the mall—which is where they'd end up, running from the darkside at the other end. The darkness figures it can remove them easily enough before the segue's complete, but it doesn't count on them banding together and being able to bring in outside help. Darkness underestimates Bystanders, the latest in a continuing series. But it must have realized that Arthur was a threat to its plans—so why hasn't it moved to destroy him and his merry men?"

"Watch it, you're mixing archetypes."

"So? What's the worst that could happen?"

"I can think of a dozen really bad movies that essentially answer your question," Claire told her in a low voice. "And bits from any of them could show up if you're not more careful!"

Diana shuddered and checked out the surrounding shadows. So far, they seemed clear of movie clichés. "Sorry. But I'd still like to know what the darkness is waiting for."

"Maybe it's not waiting. Maybe it's just that the other end of the mall's running a lot slower than this end."

Time was relative, sure, but the Otherside took it to extremes. "Given your vast years of experience, what are the odds that our presence acts like a catalyst for a little localized Armageddon?"

"Pretty good."

"How good?"

Before Claire could answer, Arthur clapped Kris on the shoulder and sent her on her way. Forgetting Armageddon, Diana watched her leave, watched the swing of her hips and the movement of her hair against her back until she disappeared around a corner. Then she stared at the corner as though wanting could make the other girl come back. Actually wanting *could* make her come back. As Kris reappeared, looking confused, Diana forced herself to think of other things.

Like being overrun by the forces of darkness.

On second thought, let's not think too hard about that *either.*

"Come, drop your gear. Sit and we will speak together." Arthur's voice was deep and a little rough. It was a voice that spoke of fairness and trust and responsibility and the kind of values people always said they were looking for but never much liked once they found them.

He sounds just like the kind of guy you'd buy a new operating system from, Diana realized suddenly. *And he sounds a lot older than he looks. Which he is. Thus the immortal part of that whole Immortal King thing. Duh.* Still, losing the backpack seemed like the best idea anyone had had in days. Diana let it slide down her arms, caught it just before it was about to drop, and fell back gratefully onto one end of the sofa.

"Here, let me help." Arthur stepped forward and lifted Claire's pack off her shoulders. He showed no surprise at the weight, merely settling it to one side as Claire thanked him.

Stronger than he looks, Diana noted. *Just another piece of the whole, too good to be true, package.*

He waited until Claire and Sam were sitting before shoving his sword back out of the way and sprawling bonelessly over one of the armchairs. Archetype or not, he still sat like a teenage boy.

A teenage boy with a big honkin' sword.

"Will you take refreshment?" He waved at a stack of juice boxes.

"No, thanks." Diana pulled a bottle of water and Sam's saucer out of a side pocket. "We brought our own. We're not staying," she added, as Arthur began to frown. "And we'd just as soon not have our ears sharpened."

Wrapping himself in his tail, Austin glared up at Dean. "Just so we're both clear on this, no cuddling."

"Maybe you shouldn't be sleeping on Claire's pillow, then." Setting his glasses carefully on the bedside table, Dean reached up and turned off the light. "Suppose I wake up lonely and confused?"

"Lonely, confused, and *lipless* if you come anywhere near me."

"No tongue . . ."

"Because I'll have ripped it out and batted it under the bed!"

"Good night, Austin."

"Eating or drinking while we're on this side, will make it more difficult for us to cross back," Claire explained.

"I could be insulted that you refuse my hospitality, but you are of the Lineage, so I bow instead to your wisdom." Suiting action to the words, he bowed where he sat and then straightened, flipping his hair back out of his face. His revealed expression was serious. "So, Keepers, what *are* you doing here?"

Diana passed the water bottle to Claire and told the story of the bracelet one more time.

"I don't remember your bits of the dialogue being quite so witty the first time I heard this," Sam muttered.

Ignoring him, she told Arthur about the Emporium, the mirror, and the segue.

"That explains a great deal," he said thoughtfully. "Whoever is behind this no doubt allowed my people through in order that their beliefs hasten the reality of the mall, figuring to pick them off when their usefulness was done."

"Yeah, we think so, too." Diana fought the urge to be unreasonably pleased that Arthur agreed with her.

"They can't be happy that I have made them one people, strong and able to defend themselves."

"No, they can't—mostly because these sorts literally can't *be* happy. The best they can manage is triumphant glee."

"In order to complete their plan, they must attack us in force and wipe us from their reality."

He caught on fast. Diana reluctantly admitted she liked that in an archetype. It made for less exposition. "Yes, they must."

"You must close the segue before this happens."

"Duh."

Arthur lifted a single brow. "I'm sorry?"

"We have every intention of closing the segue before anyone is hurt," Claire explained, shooting Diana a look that promised a future lecture on the inappropriate use of the smart-ass response. "Unfortunately, the anchor's hidden somewhere in the construction zone, and when we left the Emporium, we set off an alarm. The dark guards your . . . people call the meat-minds arrived before we could get to it."

"And if that's not enough happy happy," Diana broke in, "we can't seem to influence that end of the mall, so we're going to have to go into the construction zone through the access corridor."

"Darkness has more deadly servants than the meat-minds patrolling the access corridors," Arthur said quietly.

Claire nodded. "We heard some—or one—right after we crossed over."

"Some of them *are* large," Arthur admitted, pensively rubbing a buckle between thumb and forefinger. "Some are smaller but dangerous still. We've barricaded them out of our territory, but I fear they stay away more out of their desire than ours."

"They don't push because, so far, they don't want to, not because they're afraid of you?"

"Of me and my people, yes."

"That's not good." Which, given the situation, was pretty much a gimme. Diana glanced up as the ceiling lights came on, glanced down to note that Claire's watch was still keeping speedy time, and decided not to worry about it. "So, about your people; from what Kris said about living rough, I'm guessing no one's going to miss any of them back home?"

"Until they came here, they had no home." Releasing the buckle, he curled his hand into a fist. "They are the unwanted youth of your world. Rootless and wanting to be elsewhere. With the shadow mall in place, it took only the opening of a door to cross over. Most of them crossed when leaving the public washroom by the food court."

"Oh, yeah, public washrooms," Diana snorted. "Always an adventure. The food court would put them pretty close to the Emporium and a whole bunch of the bad stuff."

"This is why not all of them survived." He studied all three of them for a long moment, his pellucid gaze moving unhurriedly from Keeper to Keeper to cat. "You told them you are wizards," he said at last, the sentence falling between question and accusation.

Diana's tone sharpened in response to the later. "Keepers, wizards—it seemed the simplest explanation since it's essentially true."

"Essentially," Claire muttered under her breath.

"Essentially?" Arthur repeated. "Are you saying then that Merlin was of the lineage?" Full lips twisted up into a half smile.

"Sorry, classified. But speaking of Merlin . . ." Diana leaned left and peered past the television, searching the shadows around the stacks of boxed DVD players. ". . . don't you usually come with a side of fries?"

Azure eyes blinked. "What?"

"Yeah, what?" Sam turned around on her lap, fabric bunching under anchoring claws, and stared up at her. "Even I didn't get that one."

"Extras. Baggage. Bad choices. Betrayal." Diana sighed. "I could go on, but we all know the story. No Lancelot? No Guinevere?"

"Not so far." Arthur looked pleased with himself and remarkably young. "I think I managed to ditch them this time. That whole star-crossed lovers thing—definitely getting tedious."

"Tedious?"

When he nodded, Diana shook her head. "Nice try. But isn't it part of what makes you Arthur?"

"Not in the oldest stories. In the oldest stories, I make one people out of a number of warring tribes and then lead them out to face a common foe. All the sex? You can blame that on the French."

"Actually, we can't; it's a Canadian thing. And," Claire continued in her best *I'm a Keeper and you aren't* voice, "none of that's important. What's important is that we close this segue down before there's an open access into our world and before your people are . . ."

"Crunched?" Sam offered helpfully.

"I was going to say 'attacked', but 'crunched' works. Maybe a little too well . . ." She started to stand. "Which means . . ."

"We're going to need your help."

Dropping back onto the sofa, Claire glared at her sister. "What?"

Diana shifted around to meet Claire's glare. The protest had been expected, an argument had been prepared. "These guys know every accessible inch of this mall. Plus, they know the safest way into the access corridors, what to expect when we're there, and how to avoid it."

"They're Bystanders!"

"So's Dean."

"I *knew* you were going to bring him up."

"Who's Dean?" Arthur asked.

"Something you can't blame on the French," Sam snickered.

Arthur looked confused, but both women ignored the feline non sequitur with practiced ease.

"Dean has nothing to do with this, Diana." Eyes narrowed, Claire punctuated her protest with a stabbing finger. "I agreed to exchange information, but I draw the line at bringing Bystanders any further into our business."

"First, it's my Summons, so it's my line. Second, this is totally their business. This is their world now, they've changed too much to go home, and they have a right to defend themselves. Their best defense . . ." She spread both hands. ". . . and I'm willing to bet that it's their only defense—is helping us to close this thing down before the bad guys make their move. Considering how complete things look—time shifts or no time shifts—that move can't be too far off."

"My scouts have reported more activity in enemy territory," Arthur allowed.

Diana jerked around to stare at him. "You have *scouts?*"

"Not the scary kind," he reassured her. "No shorts, no apples."

"Good."

"Where were you?" Austin demanded as Dean closed the front door.

"Where I told you I was going, playing ball with some friends. Just like I do every Sunday afternoon." Tossing his glove onto the counter, he headed for the kitchen. "The answering machine was on, and you were asleep."

"Well, I woke up and I was hungry."

"I left you a bowl of dry." Something crunched underfoot and Dean noticed the kibble spread evenly over the floor. "Which you obviously found. You think you could have caudled things up any more?"

"This is a big place," Austin reminded him. "But before you start looking, how about feeding me."

Head to one side, hair falling attractively, Arthur studied the Keepers. "If we have battle coming—which I'd be a fool to deny—why should I split my strength by helping you?"

"When we remove the anchor and close the segue," Diana told him, peeling her bare thighs one at a time off the leather and scooting to the edge of the sofa, "we'll be able to influence the other end of the mall. Our influence could save your butts."

"Even though our influence would be *totally* subconscious," Claire added.

Diana waved off the warning. "And besides, you said it yourself, it's part of your original raisin of the day—you make one people out of a number of warring tribes and then you lead them out to face a common foe."

"Raisin of the day?"

"I assume she means *raison d'etre*."

"Hey, I'm trying to keep the French out of it. We don't need Arthur's baggage finally making it through customs."

Arthur glanced around uneasily. "Could that happen?"

"Keepers. Otherside." Diana shrugged. "Anything could happen."

A siren shrieked out on the concourse.

In the heartbeat of silence that followed, Claire and Sam turned to stare at Diana.

"What? I didn't do it!"

On his feet and running full out between one moment and the next, Arthur charged past them, clearing Electronics in three long strides and disappearing between the racks of winter coats.

"You know that question about us being a catalyst?" Claire snarled, swinging her pack up onto one shoulder. "This answer it?"

"Unfortunately!" Grabbing her own pack in both hands, Diana pounded after Arthur, Claire behind her, Sam taking the high road over the furniture to end up leading the way.

Chaos filled the concourse. Meat-minds, some wearing a fine dusting of ceramic cherub, lumbered after the more limber mall elves. Arthur leaped forward, shouting orders and using his sword like a baton to direct a reorganized defense. Claire and Diana rocked to a halt in the entrance to the store.

Sam skidded out into the battle, claws scrabbling for purchase against the slick tile floor. When a massive foot slammed down in his path, he let his slide close the distance, bumping up against an enormous instep, sinking claws deep into gnarled flesh. Finally able to control his momentum, he pushed off and raced back to Diana's side.

"You okay?"

Ears saddled, he looked as though he was trying to back away from his own feet. "Word of advice, don't stick your claws in those things!"

The meat-mind ignored him, pounding off after the tiny female elf in the PVC corset.

"I thought those things got easily discouraged?" Diana protested.

Claire pointed to a tall, slender figure in black armor. The red plume on his helm bobbed over the battle. "Meet their motivation."

The figure turned to meet Arthur's charge.

"A dark elf?"

"Given what the kids are turning into, it almost makes sense." On one knee beside her pack, Claire rummaged out her bag of prepared possibilities.

"It looks like the barricade at the stairs is intact," Diana told her, yanking a bulging belt pouch out from under the half a dozen cans of cat food in her pack. "They must have come through another way."

"The access corridors?"

"No. Arthur said they're guarded. Someone would've given the alarm."

A pair of charging meat-minds crashed to the floor for no apparent reason. A pepper grinder in one hand, Claire glared at Diana.

"Totally subconscious, I swear; they just look *really* clumsy!" Here and now, she wasn't going to risk feedback. It was one thing to break a Rule with only her own life hanging in the balance, it was another entirely to risk Claire and Sam and a group of teenagers she'd only just met. With a powerful enemy on site, any power she released would, at the very least, be sucked up and used against them. Definitely embarrassing. Probably fatal.

One of the meat-minds stepped on its own hand as the two she'd dropped scrambled to their feet. It bellowed in pain and swung what looked like a plastic tote bag at its companion, knocking it down again. One of the mall elves darted in, wielding an aluminum baseball bat, and it stayed down.

"You've got to like the kid's enthusiasm."

"I don't have to like anything about this," Claire snapped. "I'm going to try and take a few of those things out. You find out where they're coming from and close the door!" Waving the pepper shaker, she plunged into the fight.

"How is seasoning going to help?" Sam demanded as Diana buckled the belt pouch around her waist.

"Peppercorns are seeds." She stuffed the wand into a pocket, just in case. "Seeds carry certain distinct possibilities." A running dive took her past a meat-mind's outstretched arms. "Claire has hers rigged for sleep," she grunted, sliding into one of the plastic wood planters.

"But why pepper?" Sam jumped up onto the planter's edge.

"Except for the Minute Rice, it was the only seed Dean had in the kitchen and Minute Rice comes with that unfortunate time restriction." Scrambling to her feet, she joined the cat and took a moment to study the battle. The clash of blade against blade and the distinctly less musical clash of aluminum against meat, echoed under the twenty-foot ceilings. From her vantage point, she could see that the meat-minds in the main concourse were fighting in a random pattern, but by the entrance to the short hall—the one leading to the entrance where Claire'd left Dean way back when—they all faced one way. Into the concourse. Even the bulky body stretched flat at Kris' feet and being efficiently bludgeoned pointed in the same direction.

Then, between one swing and the next, a meaty hand snaked out and closed around a slender ankle.

Kris' next swing went wide.

Then the meat-mind was on its feet and Kris was swinging, dreadlocks sweeping back and forth across the floor.

Darting into the melee, Claire pounded one of the meat-minds on the shoulder—given the location, it was probably a shoulder. When it turned, she ground fresh pepper into its face. It looked affronted, then blinked onyx eyes, scrunched up its nose, and sneezed, covering Claire in a dripping patina of snot before falling backward to the floor.

Teemo, his orange-and-yellow Hawaiian shirt clutched in bratwurst-sized fingers, went down with it. "Is it dead?" he panted, bracing red hightops against the meat-mind's stained sweat suit and yanking himself free.

"No," Claire spat, scrubbing at her face with the hem of her skirt. "Asleep."

"Bummer." Switching to a two-handed grip, he set about changing that.

Given her sudden, desperate need for a shower, Claire wasn't at all surprised when the sprinklers went off.

"Geez, these guys are clumsy," Diana muttered, as she ran. "Clumsy, clumsy, clumsy." But it was hard to hold the thought when the only thing she could see was Kris dangling by one foot. Her mouth might be saying clumsy, but her brain kept insisting, *don't stop her.*

Closely followed by: *Would you stop whaling on it! You're just pissing it off!*

Closely followed by: *I guess that answers the 'do they or don't they' genitalia question.* as Kris' flailing bat impacted between the creature's legs with no effect.

Its knees were significantly more sensitive.

Howling in pain, it whipped Kris twice around its head then threw her toward the concourse.

Diana rocked to a halt, spun around as Kris sailed by, yanked open her pouch, and broke a lime-green feather in half.

The mall elf floated gently to the floor as the sprinklers came on.

A tote bag whistled past Diana's head fast enough to part her hair, the letters on the bag a red-on-white blur. Heart pounding, she raced past the furious meat-mind while it struggled to recover its balance, the force of the swing having nearly tipped it over.

"Diana! Over here!" Sam paced in front of the optical shop, tail lashing marmalade lines in the air. "Something's happening!"

Inside the store, a multicolored fog had begun to swirl.

A familiar multicolored fog.

Diana skidded to a stop by Sam's side. "The travel agency?" All of a sudden, the whole attack made a horrible kind of sense. The red plume on the dark elf's helm, the tote bags. The darkside had chartered a trip into the mall elves' territory. "Who's coming *up* with this stuff!" she snarled, reaching back into her pouch.

"Hurry!"

As the fog grew thicker, a familiar trio of shapes began to take form.

"Not this time, bologna for brains."

As the three meat-minds charged toward the door, Diana dropped to her knees and slammed a key down on the threshold. Slamming into the barrier with enough force to vibrate glass all the way to the exit, they bounced back into the fog and disappeared. It was probably imagination that provided the crash of impact at the travel agency, one level down and a quarter of a kilometer away.

"You sure that'll hold them?" Sam demanded, looking dubious as he checked out the key.

"Hey, when I lock a door, it stays locked." She rocked back on her heels and stood. "Why aren't you wet?"

"Why should I be?"

"The sprinklers . . ."

He stared up at her, amber eyes challenging.

". . . never mind."

A quick run back to the end of the hall.

Out on the concourse, about two thirds of the meat-minds were down, those parts of their faces not being covered by the impact of baseball bats, covered in fresh ground pepper. Claire sat slumped against the art supply store, cradling one arm. Scattered, brightly colored heaps marked fallen elves, Kris and Colin weaving among them pulling downed comrades to safety.

Wet blades glistening, Arthur and the dark elf fought on.

As Diana stepped forward, Arthur danced sideways to avoid a lunge and tripped over a discarded tote bag.

He began to fall. His sword rose to block a descending blow, but the angle was wrong and everyone could see it.

The Immortal King was about to die.

A simple "no" could prevent disaster.

Diana could feel the word rising.

But that "no" could provide the enemy with power enough to complete the segue.

She had nothing in her pouch, nothing that might . . .

The wand. The wand belonged on the Otherside.

Yanking it from her pocket, Diana pointed the pink star at the dark elf, tried very hard not to think of how stupid this had to look, and opened herself up to extreme possibilities.

The sudden spray of pink power froze him in place, his dark sword no more than a centimeter from Arthur's throat. Glistening lines raced over his armor, connected the water droplets, and flared into a rose-white light too bright to look at.

When the light finally faded and everyone had blinked away the aftereffects, the dark elf was gone.

The few meat-minds still standing threw themselves over the barrier to the lower level, landing five meters down with a disconcerting splat.

"Wicked."

Diana turned to see Kris smiling at her admiringly.

"And thanks for that, you know, feather thing."

Diana would have liked to have spent a moment basking in Kris' admiration, but the wand dropped from numb fingers and a heartbeat later she followed it to the floor, not entirely certain if she wanted to puke or pass out. Unable to decide, she did both.

Dean brushed his palm over a depleted spray of lime-green feathers and sighed. "Austin, what happened to my feather duster?"

"Don't look at me."

"I thought you knew everything."

"I do." Rolling over, he exposed his other flank to the square of sunlight. "I just don't want you to look at me."

FIVE

❖

"IT'S BEEN THREE DAYS."

"Four," Austin corrected morosely from his place on the counter. "They left Saturday, it's now Tuesday."

"They left at nine-thirty Saturday morning. It's only eight forty-five." Dean expertly worked the broom into a corner of the office, capturing an elusive clump of cat hair. "Technically, it hasn't been four days."

"You're amazingly anal about a lot of things, aren't you?"

"If I'm going to do something, I'm after being accurate."

Austin sighed and dropped his chin down onto his front paws. "You missed a spot."

Dean bent to push the broom under the desk. He knew he was displacing his anxiety, but even the hand-waxed shine on the old hard-wood floor seemed less, well, shiny than it had. "I miss Claire."

"I miss her more," the cat muttered.

"I'm not arguing." Mostly because he'd finally learned there was no point in arguing with a cat but also because, in this particular instance, there really wasn't anything to argue about. Austin probably did miss Claire more than he did. The two of them had been through a lot together over the last seventeen years. In fact, given what the three of them had been through over the last nine months, Dean was willing to bet that "been through a lot" didn't even begin to start covering the highlights of the previous sixteen years.

Straightening, he glanced over at the counter. "I bet you've got a lot of great memories."

"Great memories, good memories, and a few 'holy crap I can't believe we survived that' memories," Austin agreed. "But don't get your hopes up, broom boy; I'm not sharing stories of what a cute little Keeper Claire was. Nothing against you personally, it's just not something cats do."

"Why not?"

One black ear flicked disdainfully. "Hey, I don't write the rules."

"You don't even follow the rules," Dean pointed out, frowning down at a set of parallel scratches gouged out by the desk chair. "Before Claire went in, she said they could be in there for a couple of days. We're already past that estimate."

"True. But they could still come out yesterday."

That was enough to pull Dean's complete attention from the floor. "What?"

"Time on the Otherside runs differently: four days here isn't necessarily four days there, so they could come out at any time."

"What?"

Austin sighed and sat up. "If they can come out any time," he reiterated slowly and distinctly, "then as long as they don't come out before they left, they can come out yesterday."

"But we've already lived yesterday and part of today without them."

"Doesn't matter, we won't know that we did. This particular reality will simply disappear, a new reality with Claire and Diana and that orange thing replacing it and becoming the only reality."

"Really?"

"Nah. I'm just messing with your head." He looked significantly more cheerful than he had for days. "Once time's been used, it's done. Nobody wants time with turned-over corners and pencil scribbles in the margins."

"Do cats get senile?" Dean asked the room at large. When the room didn't answer, which around the guest house wasn't always a given, he knelt to whisk the pile of dirt and cat hair—mostly cat hair—onto a dustpan. Still on his knees, he heard the outside door open and half a dozen people tromp in. Without wiping their feet. Wondering why Newfoundlanders seemed to be the only people in Canada who grasped the concept of not tracking dirt inside, he called, "I'll be right there." He spilled the dustpan into the garbage and stood.

A young woman waited in the lobby, half leaning on the counter and stroking Austin. Tied back off her face with a ribbon, her shoulder-length hair was so black the highlights were blue. Her skin was very pale, her fingers amazingly so against Austin's fur, and her lips were a dark red . . . red as blood. Dean looked out the window and once he was certain the sun hadn't set early and no unscheduled total eclipse had darkened the sky, he exhaled a breath he hadn't realized he was holding. The continuing presence of daylight came as a distinct relief. He had nothing against vampires in general, but they always drew groupies and those guys just weirded him right out.

He smiled what Claire called his innkeeper smile. "Can I help you?"

"We were wondering if you had rooms available."

We? Dean leaned forward and found himself staring down at seven muscular men in shorts and tank tops. The largest of them barely cracked four feet tall. "Uh, we only have six rooms and they're all doubles . . ."

She waved off his protest. "Not a problem. Four rooms are fine; we're not made of money, so we're used to sharing. It's just we've been on the road all night and we'd like to catch some sleep before the game."

"Game?"

"Yeah, we're basketball players," one of the men announced belligerently, weight forward on the balls of his feet as though daring Dean to make something of it.

"Okay."

"They're the Southern Ontario Midget Basketball champs," the young woman announced proudly. "I'm their manager, Aurora King."

Dean shook her hand. "Pleased to meet you."

"We have an exhibition game this evening at the community center." Leaning toward him, she dropped her voice and added, "If you can knock a little off your room rates, I'm sure I can score you some tickets."

To a midget basketball game. *Were people even allowed to say midget anymore?* Dean wondered. Although all things considered, he had to assume Ms. King would know the politically correct . . . label? Word? Description? Realizing she was waiting for his answer, he shrugged. "Uh, sure."

"Come on, come on, enough of the chitchat," yawned a member of the team. "I'm so tired I'm going to sack out right here."

"Low blood sugar," snorted the young man standing beside him.

"Premed," Aurora murmured as Dean pushed the registry toward her. "He diagnoses everything. Drives us nuts." Her voice rose back to more generally audible levels. "You guys work out who's sleeping where and with who."

A strangled cough drew everyone's attention to a redhead blushing almost the exact same shade as his hair.

"Lord fucking save us, the new guy's shy," muttered the first player who'd spoken.

Teasing the new guy kept everyone amused while Dean finished the paperwork and reached for the keys. "I'd just like to point out that there's no smoking in the rooms."

The entire team turned to stare at a diminutive blond.

He pushed short dreadlocks back off his face and shrugged. "Hey, man, I'm cool. No mellow the day of a game. I know the rules."

"Strangely enough," Aurora laughed as Dean's eyebrows rose, "he's one of the best guards we ever had."

"That's because I control my own space, Dude."

After a short tussle over the keys and a little more teasing of the new guy, they started up the stairs. Six steps up, one of them sneezed violently. "I think I'm allergic to the damned cat."

"Well, he won't be in the damned room," Aurora mocked, slipping her arm around the shoulders of the last man standing in the lobby. He wrapped his arm around her waist and they walked in lockstep up to the second floor.

"I'm guessing that one's happy," Austin murmured as they heard the fourth door close.

Dean removed his glasses and polished them against the hem of his T-shirt. "I'm not going there."

"Probably wise."

Struggling up through a pounding headache and the kind of nausea that made even breathing seem like a bad idea, Diana opened her eyes. The ceiling—a long, long way up—didn't look familiar. Where was she? Mattress and pillow under her. Blanket over. She was obviously in a bed. In her underwear. So she'd been here for a while.

Her head flopped to the left and she could see a row of beds stretching off across a . . . store?

To the right, baby and toddler pajamas were twenty percent off.

Okay. Got it now. Otherside. Mall. Meat-minds. Mall elves. Battle. Wand. Ow.

The two nearest beds were also occupied. She identified Colin by his pale hair but didn't know who the second wounded elf was.

Raising her head, she could see another row of beds facing the first. Since all the beds were made—bedding, aisle fifteen—she assumed the elves were using it as a dormitory slash infirmary.

"Hey. You're awake."

"Claire!" A strong hand behind her back helped her sit. The world tilted. "Bucket!"

A bucket appeared with an efficiency that suggested this was not the first time.

Legs crossed, Diana grasped the turquoise plastic sides firmly and bent over.

"I can't believe you've still got that much in your stomach," Claire murmured worriedly when Diana finally sat up.

"I don't. We're on the Otherside, remember?" Diana gratefully took the offered water, poured some into her mouth, rinsed, and spat. "I could be channeling it from anywhere. Why is everything on an angle?"

"I'm guessing that when you sat up, the world tilted. It's been happening every time you vomit, but don't worry, it settles down."

"I hurl and the earth moves?"

"I know, just what you need, more ego reinforcement." Eyes averted from the contents, Claire set the bucket into the lower cupboard of the bedside table and closed the door.

Diana thought about that for a moment and shuddered. "Uh, Claire . . ."

"Do you want to deal with it?"

"Well, no, but . . ."

"Well, I don't want to deal with it either and that means we don't have to. Next time it comes out of the cupboard, it'll be a new bucket. Okay, once it was a new cauldron because a couple of the kids were hanging around, but, mostly, it's a bucket."

"Cauldron?"

"We're wizards."

"Right. Don't cauldrons go with witches?"

"I suspect the kids were a little confused by that wand trick." Arms folded, brow furrowed, Claire walked almost all the way to Baby and Toddler Pajamas, returned, and reluctantly continued. "And they were also impressed."

"I get the impression you're less impressed," Diana sighed.

"When you used the wand to destroy the dark elf, it didn't pull power from the possibilities, it pulled it from you."

"No sh . . . kidding, Sherlock." Throwing back the covers, Diana cautiously swung her legs out over the side of the bed. The world wobbled a bit but went no farther off center. "That certainly explains why I feel like I've been puked up and left to dry on the sidewalk. Do you think the wand was a trap?"

"No, I think it was thrown together for the tourist trade with no real thought. It'd have little effect on a Bystander and a Bystander would have less effect on it, but a Keeper . . ."

". . . it sucks dry."

"It's why you collapsed."

"Yeah, I got that." She glanced around for her clothes, saw them folded neatly on the end of the opposite bed, and sent a pleading look toward Claire.

"Are you sure you're well enough?"

"My head's pounding, but I don't actually want or enjoy the feeling of my brain being ground between bricks, so I should be better soon." It wasn't until Claire picked up her shorts and T-shirt with her left hand that Diana realized her right arm was held tight against her chest. "You okay?"

Claire followed her gaze, flexed the fingers, and nodded. "I took a hit from one of those tote bags when the dark elf realized what I was doing with the pepper. It's almost healed."

"How long was I out?"

"About four hours." Three words. A whole lot of feelings.

Diana reached out and touched her sister lightly on the shoulder. "I'm okay."

"I know."

"And if I wasn't okay, it wouldn't have been your fault."

"I know."

"I'm an active Keeper now, and I'm my own responsibility."

"I *know*."

"Okay, that last one sounded like you actually believed it." Diana would have grinned, but it hurt to move the muscles of her face. "So give me a hug and let me get dressed. Since we seem to be stuck with him, I'd just as soon not appear before the Immortal King in my underpants and a sports bra."

"You saved his life, he wouldn't mind." Claire pulled her into a fiery one-armed hug. "And you haven't seen what his elves consider party wear," she added, as they separated. Scrubbing away a tear, she nodded toward Diana's clothes. "Although we do have the dignity of the Lineage to uphold."

"Right. Dignity." Carefully, she pulled her shorts up over her hips. "So. Four hours. Big delay in our plans to close the segue. That's not good."

"No. The darkside may have lost the battle, but it won time, and it has to be pleased about that."

"What about Colin and the other kid?"

"Colin took a tote bag to the forehead while he was dragging Alanyse to safety and Stewart got pounded against a wall." Claire walked around to the end of the next bed and lightly laid a hand on the blanket covering Colin's foot. "They'll both be okay, though."

"How do you figure?" Diana demanded, emerging from the T-shirt with teeth clenched. Dragging the reinforced neck over her head had done nothing to help the brick-grinding-brain problem.

"Arthur's convinced them that they can't die. As long as they believe that, everything heals."

"Nice if he could have convinced them they couldn't get hurt." A quick, careful search found her sandals under the edge of the bed.

"I think that's beyond even his powers of persuasion. These kids came off the street and before that from places even less pleasant. They *know* they can get hurt."

"Good point. Hey, where's Sam?"

"Sam's fine. He's out by the fire."

That pulled Diana's attention off her fight with a buckle. "Fire?"

"They have one every night. Here, let me get that before you vomit again." Claire hiked up her skirt and knelt by Diana's feet. "I don't know how it started, but it's become symbolic, so now it's self sustaining."

"Like the one at the Girl Guide camp?"

The older Keeper shuddered. "Different archetype, so let's hope not."

"I'm starving."

"Hardly surprising, we missed lunch and it's past time for supper. Come on, our packs are by the fire."

"My pouch? The wand?"

"I put them away. You won't be using the wand again, of course, but I thought it was safer in your pack than out where one of the kids might get to it."

Diana didn't see why if it would have little effect on a Bystander, but since her pack was still the best place for it, she didn't argue. Nor did she argue about that *of course*. It was an older sister thing and could safely be ignored. As things stood right now, she had no intention of using the wand again but, as her grade twelve sociology teacher used to say, change is the only constant. And the road to Hell was paved with good intentions. Dean had probably given them a polish on his way by.

The fire burned in a circular pit in the open area just inside the doors. There'd been no pit or even a sign of one earlier, but consistency frequently took a beating on the Otherside. They appeared to be burning charcoal briquettes, fake fireplace logs, and remaindered novelizations of *Everybody Loves Raymond*. Apparently, everybody didn't.

The party clothes Claire had mentioned seemed heavy on the high-heeled boots, leather, and lingerie. Had she ever thought about it, Diana would have said that a run of the mill, middle-class shopping mall wasn't likely to carry PVC corsets—and she'd have been wrong. Gilded by the light from the leaping flames, it looked like the elves were about to break into a coed version of "Lady Marmalade."

Arthur sat on the only chair in the circle of cushions. Although missing legs put it low enough to the ground that he had to cross his own legs in front of him, it still put him head and shoulders above everyone else. The fire reflected off his silver circlet and off the hilt of the sword thrusting up over his shoulder. He was gnawing on a drumstick and looking suitably barbaric until Diana noticed the red-and-white-striped bucket at his feet. The elves had apparently dared the food court.

A quick search spotted Sam perched on the lap of the tall, slender girl that Kris had signaled during their original walk down the concourse.

"He's telling Kith everything that's happened on *Buffy* since she crossed over," Kris said suddenly by Diana's shoulder. Diana tried not to shiver at the warm breath laving her neck. "Your cat watches too much TV."

"Tell me about it. He hogs the remote, too."

Sam's ears flicked back at the sound of her voice, and an orange blur launched itself into the air. The background noise grew richer with the sound of Kith swearing in at least two languages as Diana's arms filled with cat.

"You made me worry!" Amber eyes glared accusations at her.

"Sorry."

"Don't do it again!"

"Okay."

"Now put me down!"

"Sure." She kissed him behind one ear and stroked two fingers back over his head as she set him on the floor. Spinning around, he gave the side of her palm a couple of quick licks and then bit down—not quite drawing blood.

The moment his mouth was empty, he glared up at her. "I meant it when I said don't do it again."

"I know."

He butted against her leg, hard enough to leave the imprint of his head as a purple-and-green bruise. Tail straight up in the air, a fuzzy orange exclamation mark, he stalked back around the fire.

"He's gonna have to make with the apologizing. Kith loves her leather pants."

"Cats don't apologize," Claire said, from Diana's other side, her voice the voice of experience. "He'll convince her the whole thing was her fault."

"Yeah, but he . . ."

Diana cut the protest short. "It doesn't matter."

"If you say so." Kris' fingers were warm in the crook of her elbow. "Come on, himself wants to thank you."

"What for?"

"Duh. Saving his ass and nearly killing yourself doing it." Her grip tightened. "I'm with the cat on that bit. Don't do it again!"

"Look, if another situation comes up . . ." The dark glare from the guard captain was very nearly more heated than Sam's. *Ohmygod, she cares!* Nearly breathless, Diana maintained just enough self-control to shove her free hand into her pocket and cross her fingers. "Okay. Not doing it again."

"Good. Because I'll kick your ass if you do."

Arthur tossed a bone onto the fire as they approached and rose fluidly up onto his feet, wiping greasy fingers on his jeans.

Immortal King. Teenage boy. Mixed messages, Diana sighed silently, *that's what's wrong with the world.* And while they weren't strictly in the world, it was a universal kind of observation. Well, maybe not the Immortal King, teenage boy part but the rest of it.

A hush fell over the assembled mall elves. Arthur touched his right fist to his chest and inclined his head in a regal salute. "My heart rejoices to see you well again, Keeper. I thank you for your timely intervention. I very much regret you were injured for my sake."

His words carried the weight of ritual. Diana felt her cheeks begin to heat and sternly told herself to get a grip. Keepers didn't do liege lord stuff—totally independent contractors. *She* didn't do liege lord stuff. The blood rising into her cheeks ignored her. Nothing to do but blame the color on the fire and make the best of things. "Hey, no big." Her shrug was as nonchalant as the circumstances and the lingering effects of her headache allowed. "I knew the job was dangerous when I took it."

"Then I thank you for your willingness to do the job." His gesture included Claire in his gratitude. "We all thank you."

On cue, the elves began to whoop, then one of them flipped on a boom box and the first track off The Melvin's *Hostile Ambient Take-over* ripped through the remaining silent spaces.

"Oh, yeah, that's appealing. If they really wanted to thank us, they could find something that sounded like music," Claire muttered.

Diana snorted. "Too old to appreciate the good stuff?"

"I'll let you know when I hear some."

"People who only listen to the CBC have no grounds for criticism."

"I'm sure you're both hungry," Arthur interjected smoothly, his voice sliding through the ambient noise. One hand indicated the bucket of chicken. "I'd be honored if you'd join me."

"We'd be pleased to eat with you," Claire said while Diana swallowed an inconvenient mouthful of saliva cased by the rising scent of eleven different herbs and spices deep fried to an extra crispy goodness. "But as we mentioned before, we can only eat the food we brought with us."

"I understand." He sank down into his chair—a gold brocade wingback; the legs having very likely gone to fuel an earlier fire—and waved the two Keepers into the space on his right, empty but for two cushions, their packs, and a saucer.

"Sam couldn't wait." Claire kicked off her sandals, crossed her ankles, and descended gracefully. "I fed him while you were out."

Diana dropped and sprawled, one hand digging in her pack for food before her butt hit the cushion. "I figured. I also figured a full stomach was the only thing keeping his fuzzy head out of the chicken."

"It's not actually chicken." Both Keepers turned to stare at the cat. Backlit by the fire, his fur looked more red than orange. "I'm not even sure it's some kind of bird."

As one, the Keepers turned to stare at Arthur who shrugged and pulled out a wing that was just a little too large and folded one too many times. "It *tastes* like chicken."

"What doesn't?" Diana muttered, biting into her tuna salad sandwich. Chewed. Swallowed. Scraped her tongue against her teeth. "Oops. My bad."

Claire flicked a coral-colored fingernail through her chicken-flavored carrot sticks and sighed. "Try to be more careful." She offered one to Sam who turned up his nose at it.

"I don't care what it tastes like," he sneered, "it's still a carrot."

On the other side of the fire, bodies leaped and twirled, flames burnishing hair, and skin, and jewelry. The more *elfin* the dancer, the wilder the dance although even Jo, whose ears had barely begun to point, moved with both grace and abandon to the pounding music. It wasn't the kind of dancing Diana was used to, that was for sure.

"Your face wears an interesting expression. What are you thinking?"

Her attention drawn back across the fire, Diana glanced up to find both Arthur and Kris watching her. The guard captain had settled a little forward of the Immortal King's left hand in order to see around the edge of his chair. "Interesting?" she asked, trying to figure it out from the inside. There were, after all, a limited number of ways two eyes, a nose, and a mouth could combine.

"Speculative."

"Okay." It seemed to have something to do with eyebrows. "I was just thinking how much these guys would have livened up one of my high school dances. You know, the kind where the DJ's playing a dance mix from when *he* was in school so the music's all at least three years old and almost no one's dancing and the jocks stand with the jocks and the geeks stand with the geeks and someone always shows up drunk and pukes in the hall and half the kids who think they're taking ecstasy are really taking baby aspirin and actually . . ." She frowned. ". . . so are the other half because that's why the 'rents force me to attend these things in the first place and the one guy who's out on the dance floor grooving to the beat is being made fun of by the other guys. The air is heavy with angst and hormones and there's enough hair spray in the girl's can to open a new hole in the ozone layer."

"It sounds . . ."

"Like major suckage," Kris supplied when Arthur seemed stuck for a word.

He nodded. "Indeed. And you think my people could help?"

Diana took another look. Feet planted, Will undulated hips and arms and scarlet braid in time to the music. "They sure couldn't hurt."

"But in your world, my people would have no reason to dance."

Street kids, CSA kids . . .

"Sure they would." She answered Arthur, but her eyes locked on

Kris. "Dance to escape. Dance to forget. Dance to lose yourself in the way your body works; it's the one thing in your life a bunch of over-worked bureaucrats can't control."

Kris made a sound somewhere between a snort and a sigh. Not exactly agreeing but not dismissing the observation out of hand.

Arthur glanced from one to the other and then back at the danc-ers, nodding thoughtfully. "Here, they dance to celebrate their victory over the dark forces."

"It's only a temporary victory," Claire reminded him grimly. "The dark forces will be back and they won't stop until you're all destroyed."

"Way to be a downer," Diana grunted, fishing a nectarine from her pack.

"Ignoring the problem won't make it go away," the older Keeper insisted.

"Jeez, Claire. Hair shirt much? They're not ignoring the problem, they're recharging so they can continue to fight."

"Well, we don't have that luxury. We have to deal with this segue and in order to do that, we have to know what's happening at the other end of the mall."

"And in order to do *that*, we'll need their help. The food court's at the other end of the mall," Diana continued before Claire could voice one of her usual "Keepers do it alone, yadda yadda" protests, "so they obviously know a way to get in and out again." She wiped nectarine juice off her chin and glanced at Kris, who nodded.

"We do."

Her gaze shifted from Kris to the King. "So we need to set up some kind of a recon mission. I suggest that Kris and I wander down for a quick look. She takes care of the navigating and any necessary bad-ass whupping, and I handle the metaphysical stuff."

Sapphire eyes narrowed in confusion as Arthur leaned forward, arms braced across his thighs. "Bad-ass whupping?"

"She means, sire, that I can smack any meat-minds we run across," Kris explained, grinning broadly. "But don't ask me why she's talking like that."

"Don't ask me either," Diana muttered weakly. She could only as-sume that the thought of spending time alone with Kris skulking through a dark mall had cut the circuit between her brain and her mouth. Claire was looking less than pleased with the suggestion and Sam . . . Sam was buried so deep in her backpack that only his butt and his tail showed. Grateful for the distraction, Diana tossed the nectarine pit into the fire, turned, and hauled him clear.

"Hey! I was just checking to see if you packed my hairball medicine!"

"You don't have hairball medicine." She pulled out a second tuna sandwich. The wrapping had been holed and a fair bit of the tuna excavated. "You have your own food!"

"Yeah? So?" He licked down a bit of ruffled fur. "You going to eat that? I mean, since it's kind of covered in cat spit . . ."

Diana sighed and handed over the sandwich.

"You shouldn't let him get away with that kind of behavior."

As Sam retreated to the edge of the firelight, she turned a pointed look on her sister. "Like you're the expert. Austin totally runs your life."

"Austin and I have an understanding."

"Yeah, that he runs your life."

"A reconnaissance mission has merit," Arthur announced suddenly. From his tone, Diana assumed he'd done some thinking about it while she'd been dealing with Sam. "But are either of you well enough to go? Both of you were injured in the recent battle; perhaps two of my scouts . . ."

"No." Claire was using her don't-even-bother-arguing-with-me voice. "It has to be one of us. Your people can't see what we need to know."

"And I'm fine," Diana broke in. "Headache's mostly gone, I had a nice nap, I have two working arms . . . it has to be me."

Claire nodded agreement. "You're right."

"And Claire obviously got hit on the head and we never noticed."

Arthur turned an anxious expression on the older Keeper, but she waved him off. "Diana's just trying to be funny."

"Now is not the time."

Apparently a sense of humor was not a requirement to be an Immortal King. "Sorry." The apology slipped out before Diana remembered that Keepers never apologized.

Still suitably serious, Arthur nodded. "Then, as you request, Kris will accompany you. She has been into enemy territory many times and is therefore your best chance to not only get in but get out again."

"Out again, that's the tricky part," Kris muttered.

"When should this . . ." He stumbled a bit over the shortened word. ". . . recon mission take place?"

Claire held out her good arm. The hands of her watch continued to spin wildly. "As soon as possible."

Kris rose fluidly to her feet. "I'm good." She raked a critical gaze over Diana's clothes as the younger Keeper stood. "You'll have to change. Dark colors, nothing to catch the light."

"I brought jeans."

She gestured back into the store, her rings glittering in the firelight. "We'll find you something better."

"You should have been there last night, Austin, those guys kicked tall ass!" Dean stepped back from hanging a signed picture of the team on the wall of the office and turned to grin at the cat. "You missed a great game."

"I also missed being smuggled into the arena in a gym bag," Austin muttered without lifting his head from his front paws. "Pass."

Before Dean could answer, the phone rang.

"If it's three bears," the cat announced as Dean's hand closed around the receiver, "tell them we're full. That one only ever ends well for the bears."

Black leggings, black tank, black zip-up sweatshirt, black socks, black canvas fanny pack, black leather driving gloves—Diana wore her own hightops and drew the line at using a black lipstick as camouflage paint. The line stayed drawn for about fifteen seconds.

"So you're not as pale as your sister . . ." Finished wrapping the last of her dreadlocks up into one long tail, Kris reached for the tube. ". . . you'll still show up in the shadows."

"I'm a Keeper . . ."

"And I know what I'm doing. Hold still."

"I'm sorry, Sam, but you can't come."

His eyes narrowed, flaying Diana with amber scythes. "You're ditching me so you can be *alone* with your new *friend*, aren't you?"

"No!" She dropped to one knee and beckoned him closer. "Look, I'm really worried about Claire. She's not used to being without Austin. I mean, one of those meat-minds actually hit her with his little concrete bag thing. How weird is that? Claire never gets hurt. I'm afraid of what might happen to her if there's no cat around at all."

Sam snorted. "What a load of crap."

"Fine; I need someone here who can remind Claire that she's not always right, that this was my Summoning. I'd rather you were with me, but I don't want her screwing things up from this end."

He thought about it for a moment. "Okay, that one I'll buy. Be careful."

"You, too. Remember, she gets cranky when she's crossed."

"Please, if Austin can handle her, how hard can it be?"

They took the first set of stairs down to the lower level, past a pair of elves standing guard who might have been fifteen in the outside world but here were becoming ageless.

"It's sort of neutral territory between these stairs and the next ones," Kris murmured as they descended toward the lower concourse. "The meat-minds never go much farther than the stairs they chased you and your sister up, but that doesn't mean there isn't some nasty shit hanging around. There're a few storefronts you don't want to get too close to."

"In a way that's a good thing."

"Yeah? I doubt you'll think that when the pieces start rolling out of the Body Shop."

Pieces. Body Shop. Evil was remarkably literal-minded at times.

"You smell something like a seaweed emulsion," Kris continued, "you haul ass. You hear me?"

"What's a seaweed emulsion smell like?"

"Dead fish and seagull shit."

"Okay." Diana took a vigorous sniff but could only smell the perfume/plastic mix of the lipstick smeared all over her face. And maybe, just maybe something warm and spicy and slightly intoxicating rising off Kris which she was going to work very hard at not thinking about until they were safely back in King Arthur's Court.

King Arthur's Court. A legless armchair at a metaphorical fire.

Somehow, and she had no idea how, that wasn't as lame as it should have been.

Two more steps. "Looking at the bright side, continuing weirdness means there's still some time before the segue. The more normal this place is, the closer the bad guys are to success."

"Yeah, well, if it's all the same to you, I'm gonna worry about what's going down *before* the muzak starts play . . . Fuck." She spat the profanity between clenched teeth.

"What?"

They were standing at the west end of the lower concourse. Behind them, what should have been another entrance to the department store the elves had claimed was, instead, a solid wall of glass. Diana could barely make out the barricade beyond it. To their right, a Mr. Jockstrap. Sporting goods. She tried to remember if the original mall held a store by that name but couldn't. In a world with Condom Shack franchises, she supposed it was possible. The lights were low, the only sound the bass beat of a fast hip-hop track pulsing down from the upper level. Nothing looked particularly dangerous.

"It's night."

"Okay."

"He's here at night."

"Who?"

"Some old security dude."

Diana felt a chill run down her spine and really hoped it was a gust from the air-conditioning. "Walks with a limp? Kind of weaves his head from side to side like a snapping turtle? Mutters things like lithe and lissome?"

"I never seen a snapping turtle, but that sounds like the guy."

"But he's not in this mall, he's in the other mall. The real mall."

"Yeah? Well, he gets around. Don't let him catch you in his flashlight beam. He nails you with that and you're gone."

"Gone?"

"Gone." Kris rolled her eyes impatiently. "Speak English much? Gone. Not here. Now come on, we got some distance to cover."

They stayed to the darker shadows of the kiosks and the potted trees; Kris leading, Diana half a pace behind doing her best to mimic the other girl's economical movements. Their path led down the center of the concourse until they neared the second set of stairs when Kris began to veer left. She tucked into the rectangular shadow of the last storefront before a side corridor and motioned for Diana to join her.

"Shoe stores are safe," she whispered in answer to Diana's silent question, her mouth close to the Keeper's ear. "What's gonna come out? They watch these stairs," she continued, softening her esses. "It's why we couldn't use them. We have to get to that hall up there. Where the sign for the security office is."

The sign was across the side corridor and four storefronts farther east.

"We used to come down through the store at the end there . . ." A quick jerk of Kris' head, the motion felt rather than seen they were so close together, indicated the corridor. ". . . another big one, like ours, but lately it's been locked at night. Good thing we didn't fuckin' risk it."

"Because it's night."

The elfin captain patted Diana lightly on one cheek. "Can't put nothing past you Keepers."

Diana felt her face heat up under its mask of lipstick. The store locked at night could only mean reality had found another foothold, but she decided not to mention that at the risk of being thought obvious as well as dense. She watched as Kris dropped to her belly and inched forward toward the corridor along the angle of floor and wall. Was she supposed to follow?

Apparently not.

Just as she began to seriously consider dropping to her knees, Kris began to back up. Feet under her, into a crouch, standing . . . warm breath against Diana's ear. She clenched her hands to keep from shivering.

"It's clear. Move fast, don't make any noise, and try to look as little like a person as you can."

"What?"

"If they see you, you want to leave some doubt about what they're seeing."

That made sense. Although "look as little like a person as you can" didn't. Not in any useful sort of a way.

"All right. Let's . . ."

shunk kree, shunk kree

Kris slammed back against her as a line of light split the concourse.

He was coming from the west. From the same direction they had. He'd been behind them the whole time.

shunk kree, shunk kree

Unable to use the possibilities, even in the minimal way she had in the original mall, Diana was left feeling like she imagined Bystanders must feel all the time. Helpless. Angry. Vaguely pathetic. How did they manage? Kris' back pressed hard against her, warm and comfortingly solid. It helped. The cold glass and dark store behind her didn't.

Shoe store, she reminded herself as the light swept through the shadows under the stairs. *What could possibly come out of a shoe store.*

Actually, she could think of a few things.

None of them good.

All of them the *last* thing she should be thinking about right now.

shunk kree, shunk kree

She was listening so hard to the sound of the security guard shuffling down the concourse that she didn't hear the music start inside the shoe store. By the time she noticed, it had already reached the chorus.

These boots are made for walking . . .

And over the faint, tinny music, another sound. Heels. Rhythmically hitting cheap carpet.

Diana winced. *That can't possibly be good.*

SIX

————· ⚎◆⚎ ·————

CLAIRE WATCHED DIANA follow Kris past the guard and almost instantly disappear into the shadows of the concourse. She should have been visible longer, even dressed like a department store ninja, but this was the Otherside and the usual rules of perspective and perception didn't always apply. Their farewells had been short . . .

"Remember you're only gathering information."

"My Summons, Claire."

"Just be careful!"

"Well, duh."

. . . and now all she could do was wait. And gather what information she could from talking to Arthur's scouts. And help secure this end of the mall against another attack. And find an exit that could show her what was happening outside because there might be something there she could use. And check the lock Diana had set during the battle. And lock any of the other storefronts the elves didn't actually use; the damage had sounded extensive, but the travel agency could be up and running again at any time.

But mostly, wait.

For her little sister to return safely from enemy territory.

Claire envied the other Keepers—*all* the other Keepers—who had no siblings and would never know how it felt allowing the person who'd taken their first steps with chubby fingers wrapped around yours to walk blithely into danger when every instinct screamed, *"Stay here where it's safe. I'll do it,"* no matter who logic declared was the better choice for the job.

If something happened?

She had a brief, horrid vision of explaining the situation to their parents. Infinitely worse than trying to explain how she'd only turned her head for an instant and two-year-old Diana had eaten the entire tube of yellow poster paint.

And vomited it up on the white wool rug.

So nothing *would* happen. Nothing bad. This was the Otherside; all she had to do was hold tight to that belief.

Holding tight, she returned to the fire and sank down on her cushion beside Arthur's empty chair. First, she'd talk to the elves who'd raided the food court earlier in the evening. They'd have the most recent information about that end of the mall. Arthur would know who they were.

As though her thoughts had called him, he appeared, walking around the fire with the loose-limbed self-confidence of a young man who'd never been called geek, who'd never had a girl turn him down for a date, who was captain of both the football team and the debating club . . . Claire shook her head and rewound the thought. He was walking with the confidence of a young man wearing a huge, mythical sword strapped to his back. A huge, mythical sword he knew how to use.

"I have sent word to Bounce and Daniel that you wish to speak to them." Arthur sank into his chair and flipped his hair back off his face. "They'll be here shortly."

"Are they out scavenging again?"

"No. They're taking advantage of the darkness to . . ." He finished the sentence with an incomprehensible gesture.

"To?" Was he blushing? He was. The Immortal King had turned an uncomfortable looking shade of deep crimson. Suddenly, Claire got it. "Oh. To . . ." She repeated the gesture. "They're being safe, right? I mean, these kids didn't come from the best of backgrounds and you have no idea of what I'm talking about, do you?"

"They're in no danger."

"Okay." Probably best to leave it at that. Feeling, well, old in the face of Arthur's embarrassment, Claire searched for a less loaded topic. "So, the darkness—I'm a little surprised it's lasted this long. Time's been moving fairly quickly up until now."

"The darkness last as long as the fire does."

Were it not for the implications of that statement, his relief would have been amusing. Claire glanced down at her watch. The second hand lay motionless over the two. "Great." Once Diana reached the area controlled by the dark forces, she'd be moving in a totally different time. *At* a totally different time? Prepositions just weren't set up for this sort of thing.

According to her watch, Dean and Austin weren't moving at all. On the bright side, that should keep them out of trouble.

Austin poked Dean's rigid arm with a paw and snorted. Walking around the phone, he took a closer look at the watch on the wrist below the hand holding the receiver. Stopped.

"Fortunately," he said, trotting to the end of the counter and leaping carefully down, "time waits for no cat."

And with any luck, the fridge door would be open.

The weight of a constant regard between her shoulder blades spun Claire around. "What?"

Sam blinked. "Nothing."

"Well, stop it."

The weight didn't change. She turned again. "What did I say?"

"Weren't you listening either?"

"Did Diana tell you to watch me?"

"Why would she do that?"

"Are you watching me?"

He licked his shoulder. "I don't know what you're talking about."

"A cat may look at a king," Arthur observed, grinning.

"Yes . . ." Claire shifted emphatically on the cushion, feeling a bit like a butterfly on a pin. ". . . but he's not looking at *you.*"

shunk kree, shunk kree

You can't see me. You can't see m . . . us. You can't see us.

Diana repeated the mantra silently, hoping it would be enough. She could make it enough. The smallest act of will would slide that flashlight beam right on by. But the smallest act of will would break the Rules, strengthen the bad guys, and get her in major shit with Claire and the rest of the lineage.

So all she had was hope.

Hope, and Kris' warm body pressed tightly against her as they squeezed into the darkest part of the shadow.

Okay. The situation wasn't *all* bad.

The glass behind her shivered at a sudden impact, but the beam never wavered and the step/drag of the old man's approach didn't change. How had he not heard that?

"I know you're here. Soft, round flesh not to be touched."

shunk kree, shunk kree

Maybe he hadn't actually crossed over. Maybe he couldn't hear the music and the boots banging against the glass because he was walking the borderland between the world and the Otherside.

"Pliant, flexible, heated limbs. Can't hide forever. I will find you. Oh, yes."

Maybe he was a freakin' fruitcake and not the good kind of fruitcake either. No icing. The kind of dried fruit that either broke fillings or curled tongues. Cake dense enough to pound nails with . . .

And I'm so totally babbling.

She'd faced demons, disasters, and Hell itself with more composure. What was it about this guy?

For that matter, what *was* this guy?

The circle of light swept up the underside of the staircase, then flicked across the concourse to illuminate the window of a gift shop where a line of porcelain dolls sat with their eyes squeezed shut. Hard to tell for sure at such a distance, but they looked much the way Diana felt. The old man couldn't possibly be seeing the Otherside contents of the stores or he'd have surely reacted to the rude gesture being made by a well-dressed teddy bear propped up behind the dolls. First teddy bear Diana'd ever seen with articulated fingers.

If he followed the path of the light, if he kept it pointed in the same direction, he'd be heading away from them, down one of the short arms that turned the lower concourse into a weird kind of enclosed "y." He'd be heading into territory controlled by the dark side. Diana wondered how *they* coped, if his light had any effect or if his overlap only included the elves.

Did it include Keepers?

Something about the way the hair lifted on the back of her neck suggested it did.

Standing motionless, listening, he kept his flashlight beam trained on the gift shop window. Let them think the useless pieces of pretty debris held his attention. Let them grow complacent and move. Or better yet, let them grow afraid as they waited. Let their muscles tense and their limbs begin to tremble. Let breath catch in their throats and their hearts flutter as they tried to make no sound he would be able to hear.

Let them finally break from cover, unable to stand still any longer.

He would have them then.

Not sneering, not laughing. Hard/soft bodies caught and held.

They had no business being in the mall after closing.

They had no business being so young.

There.

He rocked his weight back on one heel, spun to the left, and whipped the light across the concourse.

Diana stifled a gasp as Kris jerked back against her—although whether she was gasping at the sudden increased contact or at the flashlight beam that swept the tiles inches from the toes of Kris' Doc Martens, she couldn't say for sure.

shunk kree, shunk kree

You can't see us . . .

The old man came closer. The puddle of light spread until Kris was standing with her heels together and her toes splayed almost a hundred and eighty degrees apart. Feeling her begin to totter, Diana slipped an arm around the guard captain's waist. They were pressed so closely together their hearts began to beat to a single rhythm. Why that rhythm seemed to be reggae when the boots were still banging an old Nancy Sinatra hit on the other side of the window, Diana had no idea.

Then, finally, the light began to move on down the mall; east, the way they had to go. But better to have the ancient nutbar in front of them than behind.

shunk kree, shunk kree

As he passed, his head slowly turned, and he peered into their rectangle of shadow. His eyes narrowed. His grip shifted on the flashlight.

You can't see us . . .

And he passed on by.

They listened to his footsteps fade. They took their first breath in unison. Then their second. Then Kris murmured, "He's gone, Keeper. You got reasons for hanging on that I should know?"

"No." Because, *you feel so good* wasn't really a reason Diana wanted to get into right now. She dropped her arm and tried not to feel bereft as Kris stepped away. "What should we do about the boots?"

"Do?"

"They could come right through the window."

"It's summer, there aren't a lot of them and even if they break the glass, the security cage'll keep them in." She reached back and wrapped her hand around Diana's wrist. "Come on."

The feel of cool fingers on the skin between sleeve and glove was familiar.

"That was you, Friday night. You held Sam and me in the shadow so we didn't get caught in the beam when the security guard flashed back the way he'd come."

"Yeah. That was me. Now do me a favor and never use the word *flash* in the same sentence as that scary old dude again." Her lip curled, showing a crescent of teeth. "Bad image frying the wetware."

Diana caught the image and shuddered. "Eww."

"Big time."

"But how did you . . ." She looked down at Kris' hand, still around her wrist, and then up at the other girl's face. "We weren't even in the same reality."

Kris shrugged. "Reality's what you make it."

"True enough. You got reasons for hanging on I should know about?"

"No."

It was a familiar sounding *no*. Diana grinned as she followed Kris back out onto the concourse. *Hey, Sam, I think she likes me.*

It wasn't difficult to imagine Sam's response.

"And what am I, chopped liver?"

"No, I mean she likes *me."*

"So what are you going to do about it?"

What *was* she going to do about it? And should she even do anything? And when? Actually, that last question was a no brainer.

Not now.

"Remember, stay low, move fast, and try not to look like a person. We're in the bad guys' fuckin' territory." Kris dropped into a crouch and scuttled across the side corridor, one arm crooked over her head.

She looked exactly like a person in a crouch with her arm over her head, but Diana figured she knew what she was doing, so she folded herself into a mirror image of the position and scuttled after. Shadows spilled out of the far end of the corridor, but they came with no accompanying feeling of being watched—a faint feeling of looking ridiculous but that passed as she reached the storefronts on the opposite side and straightened.

Tucked up tightly against the wall, Kris moved steadily toward the short hallway leading to the security office.

Security office?

Oh, great. What's wrong with this picture?

Grabbing the back of Kris' waistband, Diana dragged her to a stop. "What if *he's* in the security office?" she hissed.

"What if he is? We still gotta go that way. It's the only safe way to the food court."

About to ask what definition of "safe" Kris was using, Diana jumped almost into the guard captain's arms as a thick, purple tentacle slapped the glass beside her. "I didn't do that!"

"Of course you didn't." The *dumbass* was silent but clearly implied. "It's the pet store."

"Right. And that's . . . ?"

"Beats the fuck out of me, but it's not a squid."

"What happened to the puppies and kittens?"

"I'm guessing it ate them."

"Of course it did."

They reached the hall without further incident. Narrow and lit by every third bank of fluorescents in the dropped ceiling, it went back about thirty feet, ending in a cross corridor. Diana could just barely make out two signs on the back wall. The first read: Elevator to Rooftop Parking and included a red arrow pointing left. The second: Baby Change Room; arrow to the right. What the babies changed into was anyone's guess. The closed door to the security office was about a third of the way up the hall, on the right. That far again was a small water fountain.

No *shunk kree*. No advancing armies of darkness.

The only sound was the hum of the lights.

Like it would kill them to learn the words? Diana wondered as Kris began moving faster and she hurried to catch up.

Both walls were covered in crayon portraits that shifted. A great many of them seemed to be of a dark silhouette, horned and cloaked and possessing glowing red eyes. None of them were particularly good.

Although the eyes seem to be following Kris, Diana realized. *Are following Kris,* she amended as a pair of crimson orbs plopped out of a portrait and rolled almost to the mall elf's heels. An emphatic poke turned Kris around as a pointing finger directed her gaze to the problem.

Kris rolled her own eyes and took a quick step back.

A sound like bubble wrap being popped.

A bit of waxy residue on the floor.

A quick glance at the rest of the portraits showed them all pointedly looking in different directions. Whatever dark power controlled them, it wasn't strong enough to overcome basic self-preservation.

Passing the security office, Diana worked at remembering trig formulas and other useless bits of high school math rather than merely trying not to think about the old man opening the door. In this situation, getting caught up in the old "try not to think of a purple hippopotamus" problem could have disastrous results.

At the water fountain, Kris indicated she needed a boost.

Diana dropped to one knee, let Kris use the other as a step, and watched amazed as, standing on the edge of the fountain, she reached up and shoved one of the big ceiling tiles off the framework. Were the elves keeping supplies inside the dropped ceiling?

Kris braced her hands and smoothly boosted herself up and out of sight.

Okay, that's not poss . . . Biting the thought off before Kris crashed through acoustic fibers and aluminum strapping that couldn't possibly hold her weight, Diana sat in the fountain, drew her feet up next to her butt and, pushing against the side walls of the alcove, stood. Apparently, she was supposed to follow. *No matter how imposs . . .* She bit that thought off, too, and concentrated instead on doing the mother of all chin ups. Sneaker treads gouging at the wall, she managed to hook first one elbow behind a cross brace and then the other. A little involuntary grunting later, her upper body collapsed across the dusty inner side of the ceiling. Strong hands pulled her farther in and dropped the open tile back into place.

For no good reason, there was enough light to see a path worn through the dust. It headed off to the right on a strong diagonal. Southeast, Diana figured after a moment. Directly toward the food court. They were going to reach the food court by traveling inside a dropped ceiling—something it looked as though the elves did all the time.

Even though it couldn't be d . . .

It could be done.

It had been done.

A lot.

Hold that thought, Diana told herself as she crawled after Kris. *Don't even consider thinking about how stu . . .*

Fortunately, crawling after Kris provided its own distraction.

Her knees were raw and the lump on her forehead where she'd cracked it on a pipe was throbbing when the path stopped at the edge of a concrete block wall. Kris motioned for silence. Diana tried to ache more quietly.

Another tile was lifted carefully aside and, after a moment, Kris dropped down out of sight. Her head reappeared almost instantly and then one arm, beckoning Diana forward.

They weren't in the food court.

They were standing on the sinks in the women's washroom.

Together, they replaced the tile and one at a time, jumped down.

"This is the way you always go?' Diana asked quietly.

Kris nodded and pulled her bound dreads back with one hand, bending to drink from the taps. "Meat-minds have never caught on," she said proudly when she finished drinking. "It's like they can't wrap their tiny fucking brains around the idea."

That's because acoustic tiles and aluminum strapping could barely hold the weight of a full-grown mouse and certainly couldn't hold a couple of full-grown elves. Or even mostly grown elves. Definitely not an elf and a size twelve Keeper. People, or in this case, elves, who believed that a dropped ceiling provided a secret highway between distant destinations got their information from bad movies and worse television. The meat-minds, who watched neither, knew that no one could travel by way of dropped ceilings. No wonder they couldn't wrap their tiny brains around the idea.

Believing seven impossible things before breakfast was pretty much standard operating procedure on the Otherside, but even in a place where reality depended on definition, some things were apparently too much.

Diana said none of this aloud. Had no intention of ever mentioning it.

The certainty of the mall elves that it *could* be done because they'd seen a hundred heroes and an equal number of villains do it, had created the passage. She had no intention of messing with that certainty. Certainly not while they still needed it to get home.

Only the full toilet paper dispensers in every stall and the lack of graffiti scratched into the pale green paint suggested this wasn't the actual women's washroom in the actual mall—another indication of how close the segue was to completion.

Kris opened the door just wide enough for the two of them to slip through. Moving quietly from shadow to shadow, they peered out into the deserted food court.

Diana's nose twitched at the smell of freshly brewed coffee. She must have made a noise because Kris grinned and murmured, "Starbucks."

"You mean an Otherside corruption of Starbucks."

"Is that what I said? I mean an actual Starbucks."

"Man . . ." Diana shook her head in reluctant admiration. "Those guys are moving in everywhere."

Claire yawned, rubbed her eyes, and realized that the lights had come back on in the department store. The fire had gone out. She checked her watch; the second hand was revolving at significantly better than normal speed. Time had become relative again. When she glanced up, the fire pit was gone and one of the mall elves, a dark-haired petite girl who looked capable of precision kneecapping, was sweeping up the ashes. Jo, Claire remembered after a moment.

"You done with us, Keeper?"

Daniel was lounging back against the few remaining cushions, one long, denim-clad leg draped over Bounce's lap. The other boy had his eyes closed, a glistening line of drool running from the corner of his mouth and down the side of his chin. They hadn't been able to tell her much; only that the food in the food court was a lot less weird than it had been and as the food got more *normal,* the meat-minds patrolled more frequently.

"And at certain times of the day, there's like a bazillion old people hanging around."

"Are they eating?"

"Listen, much?" Daniel had snorted. *"I said they were hanging around. Kind of dropped down from the ceiling like big old wrinkly spiders."*

"Are they dangerous?"

"Nah, just a big fat pain to get around."

"Keeper?"

"Thanks, guys. I'm done." A little sleep would be nice, Claire thought as she watched Daniel rouse his friend and the two of them disappeared into the depths of the store, but she couldn't risk it. The first year she was on active duty, a Keeper had fallen asleep on the Otherside; fallen asleep and dreamed. He'd woken up at his old high school . . . naked. Fixing the resultant fallout had definitely been one for the history books. Chapter seven. Right after the Riel Rebellion. Some nice black-and-white pictures, too. They'd pulled all the copies from circulation, but Claire knew a couple members of the Lineage who'd kept personal copies, allegedly for research purposes.

Arthur touched her lightly on the shoulder as someone carried away his chair. "I must attend to the business of the realm. If you require me . . ."

"I should be guarding you." Claire stood and smoothed down her skirt. "They could send an assassin." It would cost them a lot, single travelers always paid a premium, but she didn't doubt for a moment that if they could pay, the darkside wouldn't hesitate. Kill Arthur; destroy the united defiance raised against them.

"They would kill the Immortal King?"

"Don't get too attached to the label," she told him acerbically. "Just because you never stay dead doesn't change the fact that you die and kingdoms fall every time you're removed from the equation."

"I have doubled the guards on all points leading to this level and I will be careful. But if you have nothing better to do than to act as my nursemaid . . ." He bowed slightly, hair falling into his face and swept up as he straightened. ". . . then I will be honored by your company. Although I had thought you wanted to take a look outside."

"I do."

He smiled and waited. He had a way of waiting that reminded her of Austin.

"All right, I'll go have a look out the nearest doors, but I want you surrounded at all times by your best."

"My very best went with your sister."

"Fine, your second best, then, until I get back. I'll be as quick as I can. Sam, you coming?"

"Nope. Not even breathing hard."

Claire stopped, and the orange cat bumped into the back of her calves. "What?"

"It's just something Diana says."

"Why am I not surprised?"

"If you actually want me to answer that, I'm going to need more information," Sam pointed out as they began walking again.

The key locking the optical shop not only continued to hold but couldn't be moved. Claire pushed against it with one finger, then with her entire hand, then sat back on her heels with a satisfied nod.

"So, what's it worth to you to have me *not* tell Diana you were checking up on her work?"

She turned her head just enough to spear the orange cat with a disdainful gaze. "What's it worth to you for me *not* to tell Diana you tried to blackmail me?"

Amber eyes blinked. "You're assuming she'd care?"

"Good point."

On the 'better safe than sorry' principle, she locked the rest of the stores along the short corridor. Once they defeated the darkside, she'd unlock them and give the elves access to the entire mall but, for now, the last thing they needed was a horde of meat-minds charging out from behind a rack of cheap silver accessories.

The doors at the end of the corridor—the doors they entered the mall through way back whenever—were unlocked. Claire wasn't sure why. They could have been open because it was now business hours in the real mall or they could have been open because she wanted them to be. She had to be more careful about her desires before they set up a beacon the darkside could use to . . . to . . . she honestly couldn't say what the darkside would do, but it went without saying that it wouldn't be good.

"Sam, you wait in here."

"Why?"

"Because going through a door on the Otherside can be dangerous; you don't always end up on the other side of the door and I don't want to explain to Diana that I lost her cat."

"Her cat?" Sam snorted. "I am a free agent in the universe."

"Not until you can open your own cans of cat food, you aren't." Without waiting for a reply, she pressed down on the bar latch, and pushed. Her mind carefully blank, she stepped over the threshold. And then again—press, push, blank, step—for the outside door.

She was still on the Otherside. A half turn. She was outside the copy of the mall. All things considered, it wasn't a bad copy. Some of the edges in the middle where neither the elves nor the darkside held complete control were a little fuzzy, but, even so, it would pass.

The concrete pad was exactly as she remembered it: black metal bench, newspaper box. The headline GFDHK SCGH TPR! was different—most newspapers used at least a couple of vowels—but the hockey scores seemed current. That probably wasn't relevant. Or no more relevant than the appalling reality of hockey in June. The only things missing were Dean and Austin and they were safe in the guest house.

She didn't remember it smelling so bad.

Although the edges of the parking lot faded into mist—intent on their segue, the darkside hadn't bothered to anchor the mall on the Otherside—the lot itself was glossy black, the yellow lines gleaming.

And steaming. And bubbling. Claire jumped back as an ebony bubble swelled to iridescence then burst almost at the edge of the concrete. The parking lot was a very *very* large tar pit. She had no idea how the yellow lines stayed in place, but at least that explained the smell.

On the bright side, there'd be no attacks coming in through this door.

As she turned, she noticed something she'd missed before. A sign and a ramp. There was parking on the roof.

Frowning, she remembered there were skylights over the hexagonal cuts through the floor. Designed to send light down into the lower level, Claire had a sudden image of dangling . . .

Not ninjas. Think old people, dangling old people. Images that were already real.

Trouble was, she remembered looking up and seeing handrails around the skylight.

There had to be a way up to the parking on the roof.

Where?

"Greetings, I am Professor Jack Daniels . . ."

Far too polite to say what he really thought, Dean peered across the desk at the balding man in the tweed jacket and said, "I'm sorry?"

"Jack Daniels . . ."

"Is a kind of whiskey."

"Oh." He sighed, looked down at his hands, and up again. "Bad choice?"

"Not a good one," Dean allowed. "Besides, you gave me your real name when you called." He spun the registration book around and pointed. "Dr. Hiram Rebik."

"Right." Another glance down at his hands. "I'm uh . . . I mean, just so you know, I'm not a medical doctor. I have a doctorate in archaeology."

"Yeah? I've seen *Raiders of the Lost Ark* more than twenty times."

"Have you?"

"Maybe thirty even, it's some good. I'm Dean McIssac."

A small self-conscious smile. "Pleased to meet you."

"You wanted a room for you and your mummy."

"Yes."

"I've had the dehumidifier running in room two all day."

"Thank you."

"Did you want help carrying him . . . or her," Dean corrected hurriedly, "inside?"

"No, thank you. I'm parked in the back. I assume there's a back door?"

"Yes, of course." Coming out from behind the counter, he indicated that Dr. Rebik should follow, and led the way down the hall.

"You have an elevator," Dr. Rebik observed as they passed. "Late Victorian?"

"Sometimes." Slipping back the deadbolt, Dean opened the door out into the narrow passageway that separated the guest house from the building to the north. "I hope there's enough room."

"Plenty."

As Dr. Rebik hurried out to the parking lot, Austin appeared to wind around Dean's feet. "I wonder why he wanted to use the back door."

"Well, it's a mummy. There's got to be, you know, a sarcophagus or something."

"You think that skinny little guy could carry a sarcophagus on his own?"

"No."

"Then . . . ?"

Dean shrugged. "You're the expert, you tell me."

Two sets of footsteps approached down the passage; one slow and steady, the other shuffling along, feet never leaving the ground.

"Okay, that's . . . weird."

"I'm just guessing here," Austin muttered, backing up to cover both possible lines of escape, "but I think the phrase you're looking for is: Oh, my God! The mummy! It's alive! Alive being a relative term," the cat added thoughtfully.

"You're not helping."

"Oh. Was I supposed to be?"

Before Dean could answer, Dr. Rebik appeared in the doorway carefully supporting a slender figure wearing a floor-length, hooded cloak. *Where would you buy something like that, then?* he wondered stepping out of the way.

"Mr. McIssac, this is Meryat. She was Chief Wife to Rekhmire, Grand Vizier to Ramses the Great."

"Ma'am."

"Meryat . . ."

And that was the only word Dean recognized. Made sense; why would an ancient Egyptian speak modern English? On the other hand, why would a modern archaeologist speak ancient Egyptian? Still, that was a moot point given that there was a mummy shuffling toward the dining room. Was she hungry? What would he feed a reanimated corpse?

"Uh, Dr. Rebik, just so we're clear, the guest house has a few rules. No bloodsucking, no soul sucking, no dark magic in the room, anything that detaches while you're here leaves with you . . ." They'd added that one after a trio of zombie folk musicians had left part of the base player in the bathtub. ". . . and all long distance calls must be either collect or on your calling card. We've been stuck with the bill a few times," he expanded when Dr. Rebik looked confused. "As long as you're in the dining room, will you be wanting anything to eat, then?"

"Nothing for me, thank you, Mr. McIssac. Meryat . . ." Again a soft string of words in a foreign tongue.

This time, there was an answer.

Meryat's voice was husky—a whiskey voice, his grandfather would have called it—and a small hand wrapped in strips of yellowing linen emerged from the depths of the cloak to close gently over Dr. Rebik's. He held it as though it might break—which for all Dean knew, it might—and smiled into the shadows of the hood.

"Meryat thanks you for your consideration, Mr. McIssac, but she only wants to rest a moment before she attempts a flight of stairs. She's not very strong yet."

"Okay. Sure. Uh, when you said mummy on the phone, I was assuming it . . ."

The hood turned toward Dean.

"Sorry. . . . *she'd* have her own place to sleep. Our rooms only have one bed."

"That's fine." Another smile into the shadows. They were definitely holding hands.

It was kind of sweet. Creepy, but sweet.

SEVEN

————⚡————

DEAN LIFTED AUSTIN'S CHIN out of his eye socket, and sat up in bed scrubbing at the cooling cat drool running down beside his nose. Something . . .

Pounding. Distant pounding. At the front door.

Groping for his glasses, he pushed the arms more or less over his ears and peered down at the clock. Six twelve *a.m.* Almost a full hour before the alarm.

More pounding.

"Why don't you just ignore it?" Austin grumbled from the pillow. "Make them come back later."

Wishing he could curl up and wrap *his* tail over *his* nose, Dean swung bare feet out onto the floor. "That would be rude." His jeans were folded neatly over the back of an old wooden chair. He stared at them stupidly for a moment, then shook them out and raised his right foot. "Besides, it could be important."

More pounding.

About to shimmy the faded denim up over his hips, his brain finally caught up to his body.

"It could be Claire!"

"Don't be ridiculous, she has a key," Austin reminded him as he tucked in and zipped up just a little too fast to be safe.

"Then it could be someone with news from Claire!" More pounding as he ran from the bedroom and across the living room, exploding out into the office. Hoping the scream of hinges hadn't woken up either of their guests—Claire referred to them as eldritch hinges; multiple cans of WD-40 had no effect—he threw himself to his knees and slid under the drop leaf at the end of the counter, a black-and-white blur barely seen in the corner of one eye. By the time he reached the door, Austin was there waiting for him.

"I thought I was being ridiculous?" he panted, fumbling with the lock.

"If it's news about Claire, you'll need me to be here."

"Why?"

Austin snorted. "Because I'm the cat."

"*The* cat?" Twist back the deadbolt.

"The only one talking to you."

He wrapped his hand around the doorknob, turned, and yanked.

The man standing on the porch was a little shorter than Dean's six feet. His hair and eyebrows had been sun-bleached to the color of straw. Sunburn lent a painful-looking ruddiness to his complexion, and the end of his nose was peeling. Bulky muscle making him appear stocky, he wore a tan short-sleeved shirt with the top three buttons undone, matching shorts—with all buttons safely fastened—and hiking boots. A number of leather pouches hung from his broad leather belt and both his arms were covered in an interesting patchwork of scars.

"All right, where is it?"

Not Australian in spite of appearances; the accent was Canadian heartland.

"Where is what, then?"

"The mummy!" His pause carried the expectation of a musical emphasis, as though his life came with its own soundtrack that only he could hear. "I know it's here," he continued when Dean didn't immediately respond. "I tracked Dr. Rebik's car to your parking lot!

That didn't sound good. Unwilling to give the benefit of the doubt to someone who banged on doors at six in the morning, Dean barely covered a yawn and decided to play dumb. "Why?"

"Because I'm hunting the mummy!"

"Why?" Maybe if he kept repeating himself, he'd get an answer.

"It's a mummy!"

Okay. New track. "So what's Dr. Rebik's mother done to you, then?"

"Not mother. Mummy!" Veins bulging on his neck, mouth open to continue his protest, he paused and glanced down. "Is that cat laughing?"

Dean shoved Austin with the side of one bare foot. "Hairball."

"Right. Look, my name's Lance Benedict . . ."

This time both men looked down.

"Really *big* hairball." Dean shot Austin a warning frown.

"Right." Lance's broad smile showed perfect teeth. "Anyway, I realize this must all seem extraordinary to you, an ordinary kind of a guy, living an ordinary kind of life . . ."

Dean bent down and turned Austin around to face the kitchen. "You should be having a drink of water to take care of that hairball." One hand against the cat's back legs, he shoved. If looks could maim, he'd have collapsed bleeding on the hardwood.

The angle of his tail promising later retribution, Austin stalked off down the hall.

When Dean straightened, Lance sighed. "Everything will make perfect sense the moment I explain it!"

Sighing and exclaiming simultaneously *was* quite the trick, Dean had to admit.

"Evil is afoot!"

"It's not in Dr. Rebik's car, then?"

"Not on foot! Afoot!" Another, more dramatic sigh. "Can I come in? Your neighbors must not discover the darkness that hides in the forgotten corners of their little worlds!"

Curtains twitched in a second-floor window across the street and Dean realized he was standing in the doorway wearing only his jeans and his glasses. Professor Marnara had been slipping salacious haiku in the mailbox for a couple of months now and she really didn't need more inspiration. "Yeah. Sure. Come in." He stepped back and closed the door firmly behind the mummy hunter. "All right, then, explain."

"You're Irish, aren't you? I can tell from your accent; it's a skill I have! County Cork, by way of Dublin."

"Newfoundland. Harbor Street, St. John's, by way of Herring Neck."

"Right. Sixteenth-century Irish derivative. Corrupted, of course."

Dean's lip curled. Good manners only extended so far. "The explanation?"

"Right." Lance leaned forward and lowered his voice. "Dr. Rebik has been vilely kidnapped by a woman who died almost five thousand years ago! Late one night in his lab, the unfortunate doctor broke the spell confining her wretched, evil form to her sarcophagus. She rose and took over his mind, feeding off his life force to reduce the gruesome effects of centuries of decay. When I discovered what she'd done, I fought valiantly to stop her, but her control over Dr. Rebik was so strong he attacked me and left me for dead!"

"And you got messed up in this because . . . ?"

"Because I'm Dr. Rebik's grad student and I intend to save him! I am quite possibly the only person now alive who knows how to stop the foul fiend!" His hands curled into fists as he rocked forward on the balls of his feet. "Just tell me what room that pustulant monstrosity is in!"

"Meryat?"

"That's her!"

Mummies. Doctors. Grad students. Dean weighed what he knew and came to a decision. "Third floor. Room six. You should take the elevator, it'll be faster." He led Lance to the brass gates, folded them open, and waved the other man inside. "Just pull that lever over to the three. I'll wait in the lobby in case she makes a run for the front door."

"Good man!" Legs braced, back straight, Lance yanked the lever toward him. The elevator began to rise.

"Was that nice?" Austin asked as the dial showed the elevator just passing the second floor.

Dean shrugged. "Before he left, Augustus Smythe fixed it so that the third floor always opens to the beach. We haven't seen a giant not-quite-squid in months and the fire sand is all posted. There's food and water in the cabana. Lance'll do some exploring, he'll get a bit more sunburn, maybe he'll go swimming. He's safer there than back out on the street."

"So it *was* nice." Austin looked disgusted. "Just when I think you're acquiring a personality that doesn't involve cleaning products, Claire, or hockey. I suppose I should be moderately encouraged that you actually lied to the man."

"And I should be concerned that you're having a worse influence on me than Hell ever did."

"Flattery will get you nowhere, but don't stop." He ran to catch up as Dean started back down the hall. "What are you going to do now?"

"Put a shirt on and wake Dr. Rebik. I'm after hearing his side of the story."

Lance stood ankle-deep in white sand, staring at the brilliant blue sky, and the turquoise breakers. A breeze off the distant dunes caressed his cheek with the scent of warmed sweet grass. This had to be another one of the mummy's evil spells—a way to turn this world into the ancient world she'd lost. Which hadn't included an ocean or a sign that read *Please return your towels to the guest house,* but that had to be only because she wasn't yet at full strength.

He still had time to stop her.

But first, he had to find Dr. Rebik. Or what was left
of the man.

He pulled his cell phone from its belt pouch and punched in Dr. Rebik's number. His mentor hadn't answered any of his previous calls, but there was always the chance that the resurrected she-demon had left her captive alone for a moment or that—as he was now so close— he'd hear the ringing of the doctor's phone.

"We're sorry; this number can not be completed as dialed. You must dial bleri or syk before the number. Please hang up and try again."

Bleri or syk? Brows drawn in to meet over his nose, Lance stared down at the keypad. His phone didn't come with a bleri or syk. Damn! It was the whole pizza number debacle all over again. No bleri, no syk, no eleven . . . he should never have been seduced by that "Friday the Thirteenth Free" calling plan.

No matter.

Tucking the phone back into its pouch, he pulled a bandanna from another and tied it around his neck. Although Dr. Rebik could be anywhere in this mystical world of dark magic, the cheery looking blue-and-white cabana perched just above the high tide mark seemed the logical place to start.

"Lance is . . ."

Meryat offered two words from within the shadows of her hood.

"No, he's not an idiot." Dr. Rebik smiled and stroked the back of her hand with one finger. "He's just under the impression that archaeology should be an adventure, like it is in the movies and on television. Mystic relics. Cursed idols. Dark magics. The return of ancient gods, wrathful and virtually omnipotent. He has a problem differentiating between fact and fiction."

"And yet . . ." Dean set a mug of coffee in front of the doctor and dropped into a chair across from him, cradling his own mug with both hands. ". . . you *are* traveling with a resurrected mummy there."

"Yes, well, there's always an exception that proves the rule."

"He said you broke the seal keeping Meryat in her sarcophagus."

"I did. Good coffee. Blue Mountain?"

"Organic Mexican."

"Ah." Another swallow and a happy sigh. His face puffy and deep purple bags under both eyes, the archaeologist looked as thrilled to be up at six thirty as Dean felt. "My Meryat was once the wife of Rekhmire, Grand Vizier to Ramses the Great. *One* of Ramses' Grand Viziers at any rate. He had four that we know of during the many years of his rule. She used to give the most magnificent parties—we've found records of them in a number of writings of that era—and at one of them she inadvertently insulted a High Priest by . . ."

Another word from within the hood.

Dr. Rebik cleared his throat, his ears red. "Yes. Well, there's no need to go into the specifics. The point is, the priest was insulted and, in a fit of pique, had her poisoned. Then he cursed her ka so that Anubis could not find it, confining it and her to the sarcophagus until a string of peculiar conditions were met that allowed the lock to be opened and Meryat to rise again."

"Peculiar conditions?"

"Learned man. Eyes the color of rotting reeds. That sort of thing."

"A learned man with greenish-brown eyes doesn't seem that peculiar."

"Three nipples . . ."

"Ah." Cheeks burning, Dean paid a great deal of attention to his next swallow of coffee. "Lance says Meryat took over your mind."

The doctor smiled into the shadows as desiccated fingers with blackened tips closed around his hand. "Meryat took over my heart.

How could I not love a woman who'd suffered so bravely for so long? I know what you're thinking, she's not at her best physically, but every day she's in the world she gains back a little more of her beauty."

"She's not sucking the energy out of people, is she?"

"People give off energy merely by existing. She absorbs that."

"Lance said that when you left the lab, you left him for dead."

That drew his attention back to Dean. "I pushed him into a supply closet," he explained dryly, "and locked the door. Lance tends to exaggerate."

"Yeah." Dean decided he'd best keep both the foul fiend and pustulant monster comments to himself. "Does he exclaim everything he says, then?"

"Almost everything, yes. I'm amazed you managed to send him away. He's remarkably tenacious."

"I didn't so much send him away as send him on a wild goose chase. He still thinks he's after you."

"I'm glad he isn't. Well done and thank you." As Dr. Rebik drained his mug, Meryat asked a question, her words running together like liquid and music combined. "Meryat wonders if *you* wonder how we found this place. This sanctuary."

Dean shrugged, trying to look as though having the guest house called a sanctuary didn't please him as much as it did. "You'd be amazed at the people who find this place."

"In our case, it came about when Meryat's ka managed to gain a small amount of freedom even before I opened the sarcophagus. Still trapped, it couldn't touch the real world, but it could touch what she calls the possibilities. They told her of the Keepers and specifically of the Keeper who works from this inn. We were hoping you'd help us. Until she fully regains her physical form, Meryat is helpless and prey to every media influenced, addle-pated adventurer we meet."

"Meet a lot?"

"You'd be surprised."

Dean considered the hole to Hell that had once heated the guest house. "Not really, no."

"So will you?"

"Will I what?"

"Help us."

"Me? I'm not the Keeper."

Meryat's hand which had been reaching toward him, exposing more of a wrapped arm than he really wanted to see, withdrew.

"You're not?"

"No. The Keeper's my, uh, girlfriend and she's away on business right now. But I'm expecting her back any time," he added as Dr. Rebik's face fell and Meryat's hooded head sagged forward. "The room's available as long as you need it."

"So we'll wait."

Meryat asked another question.

"No, my love, I can't think of a place we'd be safer. And now, if you don't mind, Meryat needs to lie down. As yet she can manage only an hour or two on her feet a day."

Dean stood as they did and managed to keep from flinching when Meryat's fingertips touched the bare skin of his forearm for an instant as they passed. He took a long, comforting swallow of coffee and when he heard the door close on the second floor, said, "You were some quiet."

Austin, who'd been lying on the windowsill, lifted his head from his front paws. "Something Dr. Rebik said isn't right."

"Yeah, three nipples. That's just *wrong*."

"Hey, I've got six!"

"My point exactly; nipples should come in even numbers."

Austin shot him a suspicious look but let it go. "Something else . . ."

"Last night he had to translate for her; this morning, she understood what we were saying."

The emerald eye blinked once in surprise. "You're not as dumb as you look. But that wasn't it."

"You think Dr. Rebik was lying?" Dean asked as he gathered up the doctor's empty mug and headed for the dishwasher.

"No, but I think there's stuff he's not telling us."

"He said he's sparing Meryat's feelings. You can't blame him for that."

"Why not?" Austin's tail carved a series of short jerky arcs through the air. "I wish Claire was here."

"Me, too."

❖   ❖   ❖

"Elderly ninja assassins?"

"I didn't say that."

"Well, you kind of implied it."

"Sam . . ."

His ears bridled as he leaped to the top of Bozo's School Bus and turned to glare. "You did. You said there were handrails around the skylights and, if the way to the roof was in the wrong area, we could expect an attempt on Arthur's life. Then you said, *'but not ninjas'* and you've been mumbling about dangling old people ever since. So: elderly ninja assassins."

"Okay, you win." Claire scooped him off the ride and continued out into the main concourse with him tucked indignantly under one arm. "Just stop repeating it so I can stop thinking about it!"

"It's not the worst thing you could be thinking about," Sam muttered. "I mean if anything's got to drop down from the roof, el . . ." He squeaked as she tightened her grip. ". . . *that* would at least be easy to beat. Right?"

"Wrong. The Otherside deals with subconscious imagery, it takes what you think you're thinking about and warps it."

"So if I was thinking about a nice, juicy, unattended salmon?"

"Nothing would happen. When I say it takes what you're thinking, I don't mean you specifically. Cats live in the now, there's nothing in your thoughts the Otherside can use."

"Fine. If *you* thought about a nice, juicy salmon?"

"We'd probably get grizzlies."

Back feet braced against her hip, he squirmed around until he could stare up at her. "You're kidding?"

"Or a rain of frozen peas. Maybe even big, green, frozen grizzlies."

"Why would the Otherside want anything to do with what's in your head?" he demanded as Claire set him down. "Things aren't weird enough around here without your two cents' worth?"

"Apparently not."

"Hey, what if you thought about big, green, frozen grizzlies?"

"You wouldn't get salmon." She stroked a hand down his back. "Wait here." Kith and Teemo glanced around as she approached the barricade and then returned to staring down the stairs into the lower level. As far as Claire could tell, it looked like the lower level of the

West Gardner's Mall. No eldritch mists. No skulking shadows. No shambling hulks of darkside muscle.

Nothing out of the ordinary.

That wasn't good.

"Any sign of Diana and Kris?"

"Nada." Teemo scratched in through the ripped armpit of his now sleeveless Spider-man T-shirt—looking less like the semimythical creature he was becoming and more like the fifteen-year-old he'd been. "There was some crap-ass music playing, but it stopped a while ago. Don't worry about your blood, Keeper, Kris'll keep her safe. She's one sneaky bi . . . Ow!" He shot a pained glance over his shoulder at Kith. "I wasn't gonna say bitch!" he protested. "I was gonna say . . . uh . . ."

Kith raised a remarkably sardonic eyebrow.

"Never mind what I was gonna say. I wasn't talkin' to you nohow." He turned his back on the other elf with such exaggerated indignation, he reminded Claire of Austin. "Kris'll keep your sister safe," he repeated. "Arthur already said that if we see any shit happening, we should let you know."

"Thank you." She didn't recognize the elf on guard at the hexagonal opening until she got close enough to see the features under the lime-green hair. "Daniel?"

"Hey, Keeper."

She'd only walked down to the end of the small corridor, been outside for a minute, two at the most. Three on the absolute outside. How had he had time to . . . ? "What did you do to your hair?"

He pulled a strand forward, looked at it, looked at her like she was asking a trick question. "Uh, dyed it. Wicked look, right?"

The second hand on her watch zipped around from the eight to the two, then slowed.

She hated time distortions.

"Right. It's very . . . green." And *not* something she was responsible for. "Listen, I was wondering, do you know where the access to the roof is?"

"The roof?"

Claire leaned back and pointed up. "There's got to be an access. There's parking and there's handrails."

"Okay." Daniel squinted into the gray light currently substituting for actual sky. "I never seen any stairs, but there's an elevator down by the security office. I seen the sign on food court runs."

"Where's the security office?"

Leaning over the Lucite barrier, he pointed down the left side of the lower level. "It's not too far past the bottom of the stairs 'cept you go along the other hall."

"It's on the darkside?"

"Arthur says it's sort of territory we both claim, but yeah."

"Do you know if it works?"

"The security office?"

"The elevator."

"No friggin' idea, Keeper."

"Okay . . ." This was very bad. "They could come through the skylight. You'll have to watch up as well as down."

"Through the skylight?" Daniel repeated, glancing up again.

"Yes."

"That kinda sucks."

"Yes. It does." Pivoting on one heel, Claire headed for the department store and nearly tripped over Sam.

"I've been thinking."

"Good. Think and walk; I have to warn Arthur."

"That's what I've been thinking about. Assassinating the Immortal King makes sense—cut the head off the snake and the snake dies."

"What do snakes have to do with anything?"

"Sorry, angel leftover. We . . . they . . . use snake analogies a lot. You know, *up there*. Occupational hazard." He jumped up onto the edge of a planter and hooked all five claws on one front paw into Claire's skirt, dragging her to a halt. "If I was the darkside, and if this whole segue thing meant enough to me, I'd drop an assassin in during the battle when no one would notice. If the dark elf wins, the assassin helps the meat-minds pick off the mall elves. If the dark elf loses, then it finds a place to lay low until it gets its chance. Bada bing, bada boom."

She pulled her skirt free. "Another leftover angel thing?"

"No, I've been watching *The Sopranos* with your dad. Look, it makes sense for the darkside to kill Arthur, but it doesn't make any sense for them to drop an assassin in now after the battle when all the elves are on full alert."

Claire looked back at Teemo and Kith on the barricade. At Daniel. Were there more shadows on the upper concourse than there had been?

It was definitely too quiet.

"You're right," she said. And started to run.

Sam jumped down and raced after her. "At the risk of sounding last millennia; duh."

Sunlight streamed down through the skylight into the food court, bright enough to wash away the light spilling from the bulbs over each table. Bright enough to wash away the shadows.

Kris frowned. "There's never been sunlight before."

"It's probably coming through from the real world. This end of the mall's almost totally matched up. We haven't got much time."

"Is this the sort of stuff you and your sister need to know?"

"No. This is the sort of stuff we pretty much already knew. We have to go deeper in. We need to see *who* more than what." Diana dunked her face into a filled sink, trying to rinse away the soap she'd used to remove the lipstick camouflage. *Man, that stuff could remove freckles!* When she surfaced, Kris was waiting with a paper towel. "Thanks." The towel was only marginally less destructive than the soap, and they were both an exact match for supplies in women's washrooms worldwide. Diana made a mental note to check the supplier when they got home. This could be a foothold situation that the Lineage had missed for years. And the toilet paper was definitely Hellish.

"So," Kris grunted, leaning against a stall and watching Diana in the mirror, "what now?"

"Now, unless we open the door and there's a power-of-darkness coffee klatch happening close enough for us to eavesdrop on, we need to get to the Emporium. It's as close to the anchor as we've ever come." She tossed the damp paper in the wastebasket and turned to face a skeptical mall elf.

"It's where you two came through. They'll be guarding it."

"You've taken me as far as we agreed. You don't have to go on."

"Like I'm supposed to go back to the other wizard and tell her I ditched her kid sister just when things got tough? Fuck you."

"Okay. I mean, you're right," Diana corrected herself hurriedly, hoping the flush she could feel would be taken as the result of strenuous exfoliation. "Then if it's just meat-minds on guard, we'll go around them. If it's something else, then *that* could tell us what I need to know. I wish I'd been able to get a look under that dark elf's helm."

"Before you slagged him?"

"Not much point after." She glanced toward the washroom door. "There's not going to be a lot of cover out there."

"No shit. You'd think they'd leave all that sunshine for the end. Doesn't evil usually prefer darkness and all?"

"Common mistake. Evil doesn't care. The thing you've got to remember about evil," she murmured, falling into step just behind the other girl's left shoulder as they headed for the door, "is that it's an unapologetic opportunist. It'll move in wherever there's an opening."

The smell of fresh coffee wafted up the short hall.

The black clothes made them stand out against the pale green tiles like . . .

. . . *like licorice in mints, like cow patties in the grass, like Goths in a flower shop, like the wipeout from the wand caused permanent brain damage. What's up with Analogies R Us?*

Diana forced herself to pay attention just as Kris said, "I don't see anyone . . . anything. Let's go."

They turned left, away from the food court, staying close to the lockers and then ducking low to cross the open front of the sporting goods store. Diana thought she saw a rack of torture implements as they passed—which was actually encouraging because she was fairly certain such stores didn't usually stock thumb screws in with their free weights in the real world. *Although it certainly explained that whole no pain, no gain thing.* Vaguely human shapes moved around in the big drugstore across the hall and she could only hope they were part of a darkside patrol. Customers, even faint images of customers, would be bad. Not that a darkside patrol would be exactly good. . . .

Kris' grip on her arm dragged her attention back to their more immediate concern—the length of corridor they had to cover unseen in order to get to the Emporium. The two planters and four benches provided the only cover. But, on the bright side, the corridor was empty except for those two planters and four benches.

Nothing ventured . . . Diana shrugged free, dashed forward, dropped as she passed the first planter, slid the last five feet to the bench, and rolled under it at the last instant.

"What do you think you're doing," Kris growled into her ear a moment later.

Diana turned and tried not to think about the confined conditions pressing them cheek to cheek. "I was thinking that the Emporium wasn't going to get any closer and the longer we waited the more risk of someone coming through the food court and spotting us." So not the time to say something like *"You smell incredible."*

"Next time, warn a person!"

"I thought you might protest . . ."

"Yeah. Good call."

". . . and we didn't have time."

The lights were off in the travel agency and a handwritten sign taped to the cracked window said only, "Closed for Renovations." A poster advertising London at $549, Berlin at $629, and Gehenna at $666 was the only other visible indication that the store had ever been used. Either she'd really done some serious damage when she smacked the travelers back or they were too close to segue for any more tours to be booked. The Tailer of Gloucester still had bits off animal butts hanging in the window, so hopefully it was the former not the later.

Hopefully and *animal bits;* not the sort of things that usually showed up in the same thought.

"Next bench," she murmured against Kris' skin. "You've got to go first."

Kris' reply was essentially unintelligible although the sarcasm came through loud and clear. Out from under the bench, she pushed herself up into a sprinter's start, and disappeared from Diana's line of sight.

Diana followed half a heartbeat behind, put a little too much push on the final slide, and would have gone right past the bench had strong hands not grabbed a double handful of clothes and yanked her sideways. Her face impacted at the join of shoulder and neck, her nose connecting painfully with Kris' collarbone.

"Is this the place?"

Blinking away tears, she lifted her head as far as the bench allowed. In the short time since they'd crossed over, the Emporium had come to look almost identical to the store in the original mall. "This is it."

The corridor was still empty. But then, why wouldn't it be? Why would the darkness bother running patrols this deep inside their own territory? They were a lot safer here than they'd been out in the lower concourse.

"I'm going to take a closer look."

"We're going inside?"

"We have to. We haven't actually learned anything yet."

"I've learned that you got no sense of self-preservation. I'm not going in there."

"Good. You keep watch." She was out from under the bench on her hands and knees before Kris could stop her, then quickly crawled across to the window for a careful glance inside. The window display was pretty much as she remembered it and so was the stock beyond. In the back corner . . . She shuffled forward just far enough to get a better angle. In spite of other changes, the mirror remained the Otherside edition, thick silvered glass in an antique wooden frame. She couldn't see any indication of Jack but figured he was probably watching the other store.

Dropping back below the window ledge, Diana crawled to the edge of the open door and, lying down, peered around the corner. No troll. Not even the shadowy suggestion of customers. Better still, no wards keeping people from entering—although the exit wards were still in place and would need to be dealt with later.

She flashed a quick thumbs-up back at Kris—who did *not* look happy—and slipped over the threshold into the store. The fairies on a stick had been marked down and the frogs in military uniforms had been joined by newts in science fiction costumes.

Who buys this stuff? she wondered crawling toward the back. The newts were a little weirder than even she could cope with. Skirting the rubber snakes, she sat back on her heels and peered up at the mirror. "Pssst, Jack!"

The blue-on-blue eyes appeared almost instantly. "Where the hell have you been?"

"At the other end of the mall."

"Doing what?"

"Getting caught in time distortions and fighting off a pack of traveling meat-minds. It's not like I forgot you or anything; this is the first time I've been able to get back."

"They know you're here."

"Here, here? Like here and now? Or just in the mall here?"

Faint blue frown lines appeared as he worked that out. "In the mall."

"Well, gee, that alarm we set off probably had something to do with that."

"You th . . . Who's that?"

Diana jumped as Kris' hand came down on her shoulder. "You're talking to a mirror?"

"You're turning into an elf?"

"Yeah. Okay. Fine. Your point."

"I thought you weren't coming in?"

"You were taking too long."

"Hey!"

Both girls looked up.

"You want to save that? This is not a place you should be hanging around."

Diana nodded. "You're right. We've got to go farther in."

Jack's eyes widened. "Are you nuts?"

"Exactly what I keep asking," Kris muttered. "But she's not answering me."

"Look, both of you, we're on a scouting mission, trying to find out who or what we're dealing with darksidewise, and so far, we have found out nothing. There's nobody around. Nobody lurking. Nobody skulking. Nada. I keep going until I get a look at something. No farther . . ." She raised her hands as both Jack and Kris began to protest. ". . . so I don't cut off my escape route. Unless . . ." Locking eyes with Jack. ". . . you've got new information for me."

"About who's behind this?"

"Well, yeah."

"No. He's never come out this far, but I have heard a compelling kind of voice coming out of the storeroom, so he could have been there."

"A compelling kind of voice?" Diana repeated. "What does that mean?"

"A voice that compels. A voice belonging to the kind of guy who could put all this . . ." His eyes rolled around the mirror. ". . . in motion."

"If not *the* big cheese; one of?"

"That'd be my guess."

"Okay, I'll check the storeroom for residual energy."

"Be careful. If you access the possibilities, they'll know exactly where you are."

"Really?" She frowned at the mirror. "I never would have remembered something so crucial to my own survival."

"Well, excuse me for being concerned."

"Sorry. It's a polarity thing. They're bad, I'm good. Opposites attract. Good can, therefore, track evil, no accessing of the possibilities necessary." Turning to Kris she nodded at the storeroom door. "You coming with?"

"Not so fast." The mall elf held up a cautioning hand. "Good can track evil?"

"Yeah."

"Then evil can track good. Can track you."

"Only if they know I've been there. But unless they walk in *while* I'm there, why would they know that?"

"You make it sound so easy," Kris snorted. "And we both know it isn't."

"Well, yeah. But why make it harder than it has to be? You don't have to come . . ."

"Right. Again with the ditching as things get tough; not going to happen."

"Good."

"Yeah, good."

Still on her hands and knees, Diana headed for the storeroom, not entirely certain if anything had actually been resolved.

The storeroom seemed empty of anything relevant although it was difficult to tell with all the basilisk sculpture stacked along the walls. She walked to one end then zigzagged her way back. Nothing. No sign of major evil. No minor evil. Not even a hint of metaphysical PMS.

"Where is everyone?" she demanded, yanking at the locked drawers of the filing cabinet. "This is nuts!"

Kris snorted, leaned back against the door, and folded her arms. "Stress much? Look you've got to get a bit more relaxed."

"No. I've got to get farther in."

"Yeah." The mall elf sighed. "I knew you'd say that."

Abandoning the files, Diana crossed to stand in front of Kris, her eyes narrowed. "You don't have to . . ."

". . . come with, I knew you'd say that, too." She straightened, then leaned slightly forward, capturing Diana's gaze with hers and holding it. "Now, what am *I* going to say?"

Hopefully not "get your hands off me you lezzy pervert." Their faces were so close together, their breath mingled.

Diana moved just a little bit closer.

As first kisses went, it was kind of a nonevent, but no noses ended up out of alignment, no teeth got cracked, and Kris seemed, if not enthusiastic, at least receptive. Diana would have considered it a promissory kiss except she knew the danger in foreshadowing.

"You're thinking," she said quietly, "that you'd rather be with me than waiting here in the storeroom all alone."

Kris nodded, her expression confusingly noncommittal. "Close enough."

Reminding herself that closing the segue and saving the world had to remain at the top of her to-do list, that she and Kris were now literally from two different worlds, that she was an idiot, Diana stepped back, turned, and cracked open the door to the access corridor. Her line of sight was limited, but she couldn't hear anyone—or anything—hanging about. When Kris moved up close behind her, a crystal shot glass in the B cup of her slingshot, she opened the door the rest of the way.

The access corridor was just as she remembered it, an empty concrete tunnel; although a little darker and a little smellier and the stains seemed to be from something a lot less pleasant than merely urine.

Going left would take them back into the mall. Right would take them behind the construction barrier.

Which was where they needed to go.

Touching Kris lightly on the arm, Diana pointed to the right. The mall elf nodded and moved out in front, silently indicating it was the best place for the person with the missile weapon to be. Given that the alternative would be the perfect setup for a shot glass in the back of the head, Diana decided not to argue.

Moving silently, they slipped along the wall and around the corner. Unfortunately, the meat-minds were waiting just as silently.

The shot glass thudded into the middle of an approaching body without slowing it down.

"Run!"

It wasn't meat-minds behind them, cutting them off. Meat-minds didn't move that quickly or look that dangerous.

Hanging from the taloned grip of her captor, Diana shot a glance at Kris who had finally worn herself out and was dangling quietly. Nothing they'd been able to do had had any effect on the grip of the long legged, multijointed, vaguely buglike bad guys, so she'd stopped struggling early on and tried to memorize the path they'd taken down past the construction barrier and into this ornate and, frankly, overdone throne room. Walls of etched gold, a floor of polished marble, the heads of various creatures displayed on wooden plaques, torches— who used torches in the twenty-first century?

Her nose was bleeding again. All she could do was let it drip.

Claws skittering against gleaming black stone, the two bug things carried them toward the massive jeweled throne and the silver-haired man who sat on it, one elegantly clad leg crossed over the other. He smiled, showing very white teeth as they were dropped unceremoniously to the floor, and then leaned forward with pale hands spread in a mock welcoming gesture.

"I knew you would come to me eventually, Keeper."

Diana blinked, took a second to make sure Kris was moving, and sat up to find cold, corpse-gray eyes staring down at her with triumphant familiarity.

"Right," she said, wiping her nose on her sleeve. "Who are you?"

EIGHT

"YOU ASK WHO I AM?" The silver-haired man with the corpse-colored eyes leaned forward. "I am your worst nightmare."

"My worst nightmare?" Diana repeated. She hauled herself up onto her feet, hoping Kris realized that, as much as she wanted to spend the next ten minutes doing nothing but reassuring herself that the other girl was okay, duty called. "Dude, you've never been to high school. You've never had that 'sitting down to a final exam and realizing you never actually went to the class' dream, have you? Or had your bladder haul up the 'I really have to pee, but the only toilet I can find is in the middle of the main hall and classes are changing' scenario. Or done the 'scenes from the most boring Canadian short stories ever written start coming to life in freshman English.' Oh, wait . . ." She frowned, wiping her bloody nose on her sleeve. ". . . that last one actually happened. But the point is . . ." Arms folded, she met the eyes of the man on the throne. ". . . you are so not my worst nightma . . ."

The front pincers of her buglike captor smacked her behind the knees, and she went down hard.

Ow. Ow. And OW! Marble floors didn't get softer with repeated impact. Hissing with pain as she propped herself up on a bruised elbow, she gave the enemy her best "get over yourself" expression. Six months with Sam had made it pretty effective. "If it means that much to you, you can be a bad dream and work your way up."

He smiled almost pleasantly. "I recognize bravado when I hear it, Keeper. Brave words from a little girl in way over her head."

Diana sighed. "Look, seriously, I really don't know who you are.

If you want me . . . us," she corrected as, beside her, Kris struggled to her knees, "to cower in terror, it would work a lot better if we knew to whom we were cowering. So, if you could, *please* tell us your name."

"Please?" His snort was elegant, aristocratic, and dismissive. "Did you honestly think so simple a magic would work on me?"

"Can't blame me for trying."

"I could kill you for trying," he pointed out reasonably. "And if you do not know my name, I am not so foolish I will give you the power of it."

"Okay, but head bad guy? Nasty number one? So not terrifying."

"Not," Kris agreed, and Diana flashed her a pleased smile for being willing to play. If they could get the guy's name, if they could find out *anything* about him, she might be able to do something. Given that she wasn't allowed to access the possibilities, she wasn't sure what, but something. She was fairly sure her subconscious agreed his ass needed serious kicking. Unfortunately, at the moment, her subconscious was busy having mild hysterics about the giant bugs.

"If you want terrifying, Keeper, I'm willing to oblige, but, for now, there are only two things you need to know." Sitting back, he flicked a pale finger into the air. "The first is that you live now only because I have not ordered your death. The second . . ." A second finger joined the first. ". . . is that you have failed. You have not shut down the segue, and the darkness will gain entry through it to your world."

"Okay, one . . ." Diana flicked the second finger on her right hand back at him. ". . . I haven't failed yet, *and* I'm not the only one fighting you."

"If you speak of your sister, we can defeat her as easily as we have defeated you. More easily, I suspect, as you have by far the greater power. It was your Summons; you were your world's best hope, and here you are. If you speak of your little friend . . ." He inclined his head graciously toward Kris and then jerked it back a lot less gracefully as she spat a mouthful of blood almost into his lap. ". . . her companions, or the Immortal King, they are even now being dealt with. The Immortal King will die and after, as always happens, the fellowship of those he leads will not survive his death. That is, after all, in the Rules."

"What's he talking about?" Kris demanded.

Diana touched her lightly on the arm. "I'll tell you later."

"You may not have a later."

"Up yours."

A brilliant and speculative smile. "Perhaps."

Was he hitting on her? He was hitting on her. Eww.

"But for now, let's have a look at the weapons you brought to the battle."

"What weapons?" Diana demanded. "Your bugs totally trashed Kris' slingshot and dumped her quiver back in the access corridor when they grabbed us."

He shook his head and pointed at . . .

She couldn't stop herself from looking down.

. . . her belt pouch. So much for subterfuge. Still, in order to take it off her, he'd have to come close enough to grab. It was possible that direct physical contact could work in her favor—darkside and lightside canceling each other out until only the more powerful remained. While willing to admit that finesse was not her strong point, Diana was fairly sure that in a contest involving raw potential, she'd be the last one standing.

Unfortunately, it seemed that she wasn't the only one who thought so.

The bug shoved one of its smaller serrated legs between the strap and her waist. A quick sawing motion and it caught the belt pouch in its pincer as it fell. A quick twist scattered bits of the pouch and her defensive possibilities over the base of the dais.

"A few keys. Some seeds. Thread. A watch face. All primed and ready to be used. Such a shame if these fell into the wrong hands, Keeper." He laughed at the wand which looked even more pink and plastic than usual against the black marble. "Oh, wait; you also brought a toy sent out to spread discord amongst the great unskilled." He shook his head. "You thought you could defeat me with this?"

Since it seemed to be a rhetorical question, Diana settled for glaring. He would have felt the power discharge when she defeated the dark elf, but he clearly didn't realize the wand had directed it. That might give them an advantage later. If they had a later . . .

Frowning, he looked down at the last item, a white, paper-wrapped cylinder that had bounced away from the rest. "And what," he demanded, "is this?"

"You don't want to know."

Kris snickered.

"On the contrary." A gesture brought a meat-mind out from where it had been lurking, the torches throwing its shadow around the room as it moved. Another gesture had it bend and pick the paper cylinder off the floor. "Do you tell me, or do I have my minion use it against you?"

Diana sighed. "It's a tampon."

The meat-mind blinked, looked down at what it was holding, and dropped it, shaking its fingers free of any contamination.

"Oh, please. It's not like it's been used."

"Guys," Kris snorted.

"Really."

"Perhaps," snarled the man on the throne, his lip curled in disdain, "you'll find the situation less amusing after a little torture."

"With a tampon?"

The disdain became confusion. "What?"

"You're going to torture us with a *tampon*?"

Became distaste. "Stop saying that!"

"Saying what?" Diana asked. "Tampon?"

"Feminine hygiene product?" Kris offered.

"Maxi pad?"

"Cramps."

"Bloating."

"Clotting."

"Yeah, I hate it when that happens."

He stared at them for a long moment, eyes wide and disbelieving. "Nice girls do not talk about those kinds of things!"

"But torture, that's okay?"

"Double standards of the patriarchy," Kris growled.

His grip tightened on the arms of the throne to the point where already pale knuckles whitened. "Get them out of here!"

Diana yanked at the chains securing her wrist cuffs to the wall and sighed. "I hate to say it, but the nameless nasty was right; this is already less amusing."

"Are they really going to torture us?" Kris panted, hanging limp and exhausted. It was fairly clear they wouldn't be able to kick, twist, or thrash their way to freedom.

"Probably." If she only had the wand. It was times like this, chained to a wall by the nameless evil who planned to use a shopping mall to take over the world, that a few hours of unconsciousness followed by a little puking started to look good. "First they'll leave us here to think about it for a while."

"You know what? I'm thinking about it. And you know what I'm thinking? I'm thinking I don't want to be tortured!"

"Who does?"

Kris found the strength for another yank at the chains. "So do something!"

"Like what?" Diana demanded, sagging back against the rough rock. "If I reach into the possibilities to free us, I break one of the big Rules. If I break a big Rule, that opens the way for them to break a big Rule and you really don't want that to happen."

"Hey! Read my lips, I really don't want to be tortured either!"

"So *you* do something!"

"You're the freakin' wizard!" Kris slapped her chains against the wall for emphasis.

"It's Keeper! Now stop yelling at me and let *me* think! Just because you couldn't come up with something useful doesn't mean I can't!"

Their breathing sounded unnaturally loud in the silence that followed.

Finally, Diana sighed. "Sorry. It's just . . ."

"Yeah. I know."

She turned to see Kris frightened and battered but almost smiling at her.

"You're supposed to be saving the world, not just hangin' around here with me."

"For what it's worth, I'm glad you're here. Not, here . . . here." Diana winced as Kris' eyebrows rose. "I mean, I'm glad I'm not alone."

"For what it's worth, I'd rather you were."

Diana sighed again as Kris returned to yanking the chain. This was not going well on a number of levels; personal, professional, and probably a few other "p" words she'd come up with later. If they had a later.

They'd been chained in an alcove hacked out of the limestone walls not far from the throne room. Chained and abandoned; they hadn't seen meat-minds or bugs since.

"How long do you think we've been here?"

Diana twisted her wrist until she could see her watch. "About six minutes."

"Seems longer."

"Yeah."

The torches across from their alcove flickered although the air was still. In the distance, something screamed.

"So, about those Rules."

When Diana turned, Kris' expression announced *I'm not fuckin' scared* as loudly as if she was shouting the words. The profanity was particularly obvious. "You want me to tell you about them *now*?"

Her upper lip curled. "You going somewhere?"

"Well, no." Maybe defining a few metaphysical parameters was just the kind of distraction they needed. Maybe not, but it was all she had. Kris didn't seem like the type to be interested in "the cute things my cat's done lately" or what Ms. Harris and the graduating president of the chess club had been doing with two tubes of acrylic paint and a number three sable in the art supply closet on the last day of school. Which had only been. . . ? Diana counted back. She'd traveled to Kingston on Friday; the same day school'd ended. They'd crossed over into the Otherside mall on Saturday. Was it still Saturday and, if so, which Saturday? That whole "time was relative" thing made her want to hurl—although in this instance the urge to hurl likely had more to do with the bug leg—arm? limb?—that had impacted with her stomach. Bruises were rising even . . .

"Hey!" Part summons, part protest, it yanked her wandering attention back to the alcove.

"Right. The Rules. The uh, the Rules impose order on the chaos of metaphysics. Magic," she amended catching sight of bravado becoming impatience. "Right here and now, the biggest Rule to remember is that the Otherside is neutral ground, so neither good nor evil can control it."

"Why would evil give a shit?"

"'Because when you break the Rules, you sow the seeds of your own destruction. That's also in the Rules.'"

Kris snorted. "I think I read it in a fortune cookie."

"Could have." The lineage liked to spread the platitudes around.

"Although I'm sure it would be all awe inspiring or something if we weren't chained to a fuckin' wall."

Diana thought about it for a moment, squinting up at the flakes of rust raining off the eyebolt as she yanked her chain against it. "Probably not," she admitted.

"So what about that whole 'bad guys gotta gloat' thing?"

"Just basic psychology according to my mother. What's the point of being an evil genius if there's no one to tell?"

"No point, I guess."

They hung in silence for a few minutes, then Kris muttered, "That dude on the throne, he didn't seem like the genius type."

"He didn't seem like much of anything," Diana agreed. As far as a meeting of good and evil was concerned, it was kind of a nonevent. "The bugs were cool, in an *oh, gross, get it off me, get it off me* kind of way, but he was bland. Boring. Disappointing, even."

"Except that, you know, he won."

"Yeah. Except for that."

Off to the left of their alcove, claws skittered against stone, evoking an interlude of panicked struggles to be free. After a while, when the claws came no closer, both girls relaxed.

"It's the fuckin' waiting," Kris snarled, kicking at the wall with the heel of her cross trainers. "Why didn't they just whack us and get it over with?"

"I think they need us for something."

"What? Getting their rocks off while we get peeled?"

Diana considered that for a moment. "No," she decided at last, "that's too direct for the Otherside." The first time she'd crossed over, Claire had tried to make her understand that the shortest distance between two points was usually the long way around. Then she'd added that Diana was never, ever to think about the Smurf village again. Their mother had been furious about all the blue gunk on their shoes. "Plans on this side are always a lot twistier."

"Okay, so if you breaking a Rule lets them break a Rule, then maybe they're putting you in a spot where you gotta break a Rule to get free. You know, so they can break a Rule."

Diana turned to stare at the other girl. "That's brilliant."

"Don't sound so fuckin' surprised," Kris snorted. Her eyes widened. "Wait; you mean I'm right?"

"Probably."

"Wicked."

"Although it's insulting that they think I'd break the Rules just to escape torture and death."

"'Cause that's not a good reason?"

"No."

'Keepers could lie to Bystanders without breaking a sweat. To balance that, they could speak the kind of Truth that went straight to the heart.

Kris stared at her for a long moment. Then nodded. "Right." And another long moment. "Okay. So, *now* how long have we been here?"

"Since the last time, about another eight minutes. Fourteen minutes all together."

"Seems like longer."

"Yeah."

"Looking on the bright side, it's a lot cooler down here."

"Cooler than what?"

"Than it is back home."

"Your home?"

"Yeah."

"I wouldn't know."

"Right."

One of the torches sputtered, almost went out, then began to burn steadily once again. They could hear nothing but their own hearts beating. Smell nothing but themselves and each other.

"What's your mother like?" Kris threw the question out like a challenge.

"What?"

"Your mother. You said she was into that psychological shit. What's she like?"

Diana shrugged as well as her position allowed. "She's a Cousin."

"Your mother's your cousin? That's got a whole unexpected squick thing goin'."

"Not my cousin. A Cousin. It's kind of an auxiliary Keeper. Less powerful."

"You're more powerful than your old lady?"

"I'm more powerful than the entire lineage. All the Cousins. All the Keepers."

"And how's that workin' for you?" Kris snickered.

Bugs. Chains. Torture. "Not real well."

"You look like her?"

"Not really, Claire and I both look like our dad which is kind of funny in a way because Claire's so little and he's n . . ."

"He's what?"

Diana chewed on her lip. She almost had it. "You've been fighting the darkside in this mall for a while now, right?"

"Yeah."

"Have you seen any women, human-looking women, fighting on their side?"

"No. Sexist bastards. They think a sister can't be evil enough? They never met my Nana, that's for sure."

"Do they ever take any of the elves prisoners?"

"No."

"So if they're going to chain something up, they'd be chaining up their own guys."

Kris glanced up at the chains, then back at Diana. "Okay, but why would they do that?"

"They're evil."

"Right."

"And all of their guys are a lot bigger than we are."

"Yeah."

"And these manacles are two solid halves of iron. Not adjustable. In order to hold their guys, they've got to be a certain size." Diana folded her thumb in against her palm and slid her right hand free. "They're too big to hold us." Sliding out her left hand, she beckoned to Kris. "Come on."

"But . . ."

"I'm out, aren't I?"

Frowning, Kris worked at her lower lip with her teeth and slowly slipped both hands free. "So how come they *were* holding us?"

"Because we believed they would." It was *twistier* than that, but not really by much.

"If that's a Rule, it's a fuckin' stupid Rule."

"So not arguing here."

They stepped out of the alcove together, but as Diana began to turn right, Kris' fingers closed around her arm, dragging her to the left with a terse, "Come on."

Diana dug in her heels. "No. We need to go the other way."

"Delusional much? We need to get back and warn the others." Her grip tightened. "That guy, he said they were being dealt with."

"Except that we don't know how time's running in that end of the mall. They might've been dealt with days ago."

In the barely adequate light from the torches, Kris' eyes looked completely black with no differentiation between iris and pupil. "Then it might not have happened yet." She gave Diana's arm an impatient shake. "We need to get back and help them! I'm Arthur's captain. I need to be there."

If anyone could understand the pull of responsibility, it was a Keeper. Still . . . "There's nothing you can do. You . . . we, have to trust that Claire handled it. Can handle it. Will handle it." She wanted to sound comforting but suspected she sounded as though she were trying to convince herself. "Besides, she has Sam with her."

"And what's he supposed to do?"

"Probably nothing, but that's not the point. The point is I have to go on. The anchor's that way and unless we at least get a look at it, we don't know any more than we did when we left."

Kris shook her head. "We know there's an old white guy in charge—big surprise—and he's got bugs."

"But that tells us nothing."

"It tells me I should be hauling my ass—and yours—out of here."

"No. You can haul your own—I can't make you come with me—but I'm going farther in." Diana pulled her arm free and half turned; enough to make her choice of direction obvious but not enough to turn her back on the other girl.

"It would help if I knew . . ." Kris drew her lower lip in between her teeth; the most vulnerable move Diana had seen her make. "It would help if I knew if he was still alive."

"Look, whatever the processed cheese spread of evil out there is planning, it definitely hasn't gone down because if Arthur was dead, *things* would be happening."

"*Things?*"

"*Things*. Bad things."

Kris' gesture covered the alcove, the chains, and the general dungeonlike tone of the décor. "Worse than this?"

"Much. Season finale of Buffy kind of worse."

"Which season?"

"Does it matter?"

"I guess not."

Right or left, the passage looked identical; equally grim, equally foreboding.

"Look at the bright side," Diana offered after a moment, "When they discover that we've escaped, they'll never think of searching for us deeper in their territory. They'll assume we headed out."

"That's because they're not as stupid as they look and we are." She drew in a deep breath, slowly releasing both it and Diana's arm. "Fine. Let's get going, then. Standing around 'looking at the bright side . . .'"

She had the most sarcastic air quotes Diana had ever seen.

". . . is exactly the sort of shit that calls wandering mons . . . Where are you going?"

"Farther in."

"Fine." A none too gentle shove pushed Diana up against the wall and out of the way. "I'm the one with the pointy ears. I'm out in front."

"And that's connected how?"

"Ears. Elf. Never get lost. Unless you don't *want* to eventually find your way out?"

"We may have to go all the way in to get out."

Kris shot her a look, equal parts irritation and exasperation, as she pushed by. "Man, I am so not envying your cat if this is the shit he has to put up with."

Sam raced past and disappeared behind the winter coats as Claire slowed to avoid trampling the elf on guard at the entrance between the cosmetic counters. It seemed as though he might try to stop her but clearly thought better of it as he got a closer look at her face.

"Shit, Keeper . . ."

"Arthur!" She spat out the name. "Where is he?"

"Large Appliances."

"And that's where?"

"Straight to Children's Shoes, hang a right, then a left at Women's Accessories and straight to the back. You want I should sound the alarm?"

"No." The alarm would only warn the assassin she was coming. Hopping on first one foot then the other, she slipped her sandals off—bare feet would make a lot less noise—then, hiking her skirt up above her knees, lengthened her stride.

Children's Shoes, Women's Accessories . . . The floor was cold, and the air smelled like overheated Teflon, like someone had left a nonstick frying pan on the stove and not realized the burner was still hot. As she ran, Claire hoped the smell was seeping through from the other mall. She didn't like the implications if it wasn't.

She could hear voices up ahead.

Arthur asked a question about fabric softener.

One of the elves snickered.

A cat screamed.

Sam.

Heart racing, she tried to remind herself that cats screamed as much for effect as affect and were as likely to scream in rage as in pain. It didn't help. Death of the Immortal King, successful segue, end of the world aside, if Sam got hurt, Diana was going to kill her.

Large Appliances. Buy the washer; get one hundred dollars off the ticketed price of the dryer.

Sam crouched on top of a washing machine, tail lashing, fur straight up along his spine, ears clamped tight to his skull. He didn't look injured. He didn't sound injured. He sounded like a cross between a rabid raccoon and a civil defense siren.

Arthur had his sword out.

Facing them both was . . . at first Claire thought it was the shadow of the assassin, then it moved, an almost fluid flow from one shape to another, and she realized it *was* shadow and it *was* the assassin.

The shadow feinted right; Arthur moved with it, keeping his blade between them.

The shadow rose up ten, fifteen feet, stretched into a thin line, then whipped forward. Arthur dove out of the way, one hand reaching out to the mall elf beside him and dragging her behind a free-standing dishwasher.

Claire pulled a length of white thread from her belt pouch, tied two quick knots, and threw it into the darkness.

It froze, shivered once, shifted shape, and turned toward the Keeper, the thread anchoring it in place. Given the power pulling against it, the thread wouldn't hold long.

Shrieking a challenge, Sam launched himself off the washing machine.

It arched just enough of itself out of the way.

Rising up on one knee, Arthur swung. Missed. Leaped to his feet. Swung. Missed. Nearly had his head taken off by a sudden side shot. Got his sword around in time to cut off a piece eight inches long by about three inches in diameter. It hit the floor, flattened, and shimmied its way almost too fast to follow back into its dark bulk.

Claire winced. *That's not good.*

The thread was beginning to give.

Light could defeat it. Shadows disappeared in the light.

Unfortunately, the closest thing to a light source was in the refrigerator beside her and it went off when the door closed.

. . . door . . .

It could work. If she could get it to chase her. If the shelves hadn't been put into the refrigerator. If she hit the back of the fridge with time enough to set a second path.

An ice cream scoop flew through the center of the shadow, whistled past her arm close enough for her to feel the breeze, and clattered off white enamel. The good news; the cavalry had arrived. The bad news; it was half a dozen mall elves with slingshots and bats. *They couldn't have brought flashlights?*

"Careful!" Arthur's voice rising above the sudden babble.

And a voice out of the babble. "Fuck! What is this thing?"

"An assassin!" Claire snapped. "It's here to kill Arthur, but it'll just as happily take any of you. Don't let it touch you; it'll suck your life out through any exposed skin!" If she'd thought—suspected even—that they'd be fighting shadow, she'd have brought along some lotion with an SPF of at least 30. Rummaging in the belt pouch, she pulled out her compact. "Get back! All of you. You, too, Arthur. In fact, you especially."

He shook blue-black hair off his face. "Your spell will not hold it for much longer, wizard. I would rather be facing it and ready to fight when it breaks free than running away with my back exposed."

"Fine." He had a point. "Then *back* away, but give me some room to work and try to remember that you must stay alive."

"What are you planning, Keeper?"

Switching the compact from hand to hand, she wiped her palms against her skirt. "I'm going to get it to chase me into this refrigerator."

"Are you totally *mental*?"

A good question. Exactly what Diana would have asked were she around. Claire spent a moment believing her little sister was up to whatever she might have to face, then flashed the assembled mall elves a confident smile. Belief and confidence both for the benefit of the Otherside. "Trust me. Just don't close the door until I find my way out."

"Of the refrigerator?"

"Yes."

The shadow swayed left, the elves shifted right, and Claire felt a cold wet nose bump up against her shins. "I'm going with you."

"No, Sam, you have to watch out for Arthur and the elves while I'm gone."

Amber eyes narrowed. "You can't tell me what to do!"

The shadow rose up, then snapped flat. Arthur swung his sword like a nine iron and sliced a piece off as it tried for his ankles.

"I'm not." Too many years with Austin for her to even attempt it. "I'm just telling you what the right thing is and hoping that you'll do it."

"But what . . ."

No time for extended arguing. "You attacked the shadow, didn't you? Kept it from sneaking up on Arthur from behind?"

"Yeah but . . ."

One of the knots released. Held at only one point, the shadow lashed out at the elves, fell short, and gathered itself up for another attack.

"You kept him alive. We need him alive."

"Fine, but . . ."

Claire took that as an agreement and shoved Sam aside with one leg just as the second knot gave way. Snapping open the compact, she caught Arthur's reflection in the mirror and wrapped the seeming around her. This wasn't exactly what this had been intended for, but . . .

. . . close only counts with horseshoes and hand grenades.

Which wasn't at all reassuring.

"Hey! Tall, dark, and two-dimensional! Over here!"

A choice between two targets.

But only one of them with a blade sharp and shiny.

Claire threw herself sideways as the shadow attacked, yanked open the refrigerator door, stepped up onto the top of the double crispers, and dove inside. Substance began to distort. Caught her. Then, as an icy touch stroked the bottom of one bare foot, caught the shadow. She jerked her foot away, tumbling through the unformed reality. Allowing the path to take her where it would, she concentrated on splitting it off behind her, on sending the shadow to its ultimate defeat.

Nothing definite. Not *exactly* imposing her will— Her subconscious was in full agreement with her conscious when it came to destroying that thing.

For an instant, she smelled woodsmoke and burning marshmallows and heard high, girlish voices singing rounds. Then smells, sounds, and shadow were gone.

Another slow tumble and there was water all around her.

She dropped the compact and began kicking for the surface.

"How much longer until the Keeper emerges?"

Sam's ears flattened, but his gaze remained locked on the half-open refrigerator door. "I don't know."

Arthur crouched down beside the cat, stretched out a hand to stroke him, and thought better of it. "I think that she is safe. I think that she has defeated the shadow. I think that even now, she makes her way back to us." When Sam's only response was his tail tip, jerking back and forth, he sighed and straightened. "I will leave you, then, to your vigil. I think that the Keeper will be pleased to see you here when she returns."

As the footsteps of the Immortal King faded into Women's Accessories, Sam sighed. "*I think that Austin's going to kill me.*"

Head up, Austin remained motionless on Claire's pillow sifting the night for what had awakened him.

Dean? No. One arm stretched up over his head, bare chest rising and falling in the slow rhythm of sleep, Dean hadn't moved for hours.

Something outside? No. He could hear the occasional car going by on King Street, two raccoons up a tree arguing about whose turn it was to dump the garbage but nothing unusual. Nothing to lift the fur along his back.

He glanced toward the wardrobe, Claire's preferred entrance to the Otherside. The door was closed. Even if there was trouble, nothing could seep through.

But something *had* wakened him. Something *had* lifted the fur along his back. Therefore, something was wrong.

He stood, stretched, walked over Dean's stomach to the edge of the bed, and jumped cautiously to the floor. Over the last year or so, the floor had developed a nasty habit of being farther away than it should be.

The bedroom door was open. Whiskers testing the air with every step, Austin crossed the living room, the light spilling in around the edges of the blind just barely sufficient. Except for Dean's unfortunate taste in artwork—who really believed dogs had enough imagination to play poker—and Claire's equally unfortunate inability to say no to him, everything seemed fine.

The door between the living room and the office was closed, but it had been years since Austin had allowed that to stop him.

With no blind on the front window, the office was lighter than the living room. And empty.

The elevator?

No.

The basement?

Not this time.

The kitchen?

He was too unsettled to be hungry.

Only one place left. Only one room occupied.

Usually, Austin preferred to stay away from the guests but tonight, he'd make an exception. Slowly and silently he slipped up the stairs, along the hall. Another closed door.

There were two bodies in the bed, the perpetually nervous scent of Dr. Rebik as distinctive as the dust and desiccation scent of his companion. His tail lashing from side to side, he crept closer, unable to shake the feeling that something was wrong but willing to believe it could be prejudice on his part. He'd half expected Meryat to have been up and *walking*, arms outstretched, a bit of musty linen trailing off one heel. The whole concept of the undead annoyed him. Nine lives and it's over, that was his motto.

A tray on the small table by the bed held two empty mugs and a plate covered in muffin crumbs. Under the table, crumpled up against the table leg, was a dead mouse.

Okay, not so much wrong as embarrassing.

The mice had come to his aid after his . . . *meeting* with the Keeper who'd been interred in room seven and when he and Claire had returned to the inn just after Christmas, they'd come to an understanding. He would see to it that they were left in peace and, in return, they would be circumspect in their foraging, stop shitting behind the microwave, and never again wear orange waistcoats with blue breeches. Mice had appalling color sense and *The Complete Tales of Beatrix Potter* that had been left in the attic had only black-and-white illustrations.

This particular mouse looked to have died of old age.

Austin looked from the body up to the top of the table and shook his head. A mouse that age had no business even attempting such a climb. *Stupid little bugger's heart probably gave out on him,* he thought as he sank his teeth through the tail of the brocade frock coat.

He carried the tiny corpse over to the dresser and set it gently on the floor. A strong smack with his right paw and it slid out of sight. When he heard it whack lightly against the baseboard, he nodded in satisfaction and left the room. The mice had an exit under there; now they could retrieve the body without the possibility of a guest being subjected to the sight of a tiny funeral cortege.

Nothing looked more asinine than a mouse in a black top hat and crepe.

He was halfway down the stairs when, between one heartbeat and the next, he felt something pass.

Something old.

And hungry.

And gone so fast he might have imagined it.

Except that he was a cat and cats knew . . .

Dean!

Heart pounding, he raced back to the bedroom and bounded onto the bed.

"Ow! That was my arm!"

"Yeah, whatever." He freed his claws from the surface layer of skin and walked up Dean's chest until he could stare into his face. Blue eyes blinked myopically back at him.

"What?"

"You're okay?"

"I'm bleeding and I'm after being awake when I'd rather not be, but yeah." His voice softened, and one hand stroked gently along Austin's spine. "What's wrong, then?"

"Nothing. Why should anything be wrong?"

"I just thought . . ."

"Well, don't." A purposeful climb over an inconvenient shoulder and onto Claire's pillow. Snuggling down, he glared at Dean, now gazing at him with concern. "I thought you were sleeping?"

"I was."

"So sleep."

"All right. But we'll talk about this in the morning."

"Not so smart to warn me," Austin muttered. Not one of his best comebacks but he was shaken. He watched Dean until he went back to sleep. Watched him sleep. Could see nothing wrong.

He'd been so sure on the stairs.

So sure.

He thought about the mouse lying dead under the table and sighed.

Maybe he was just getting old.

NINE

———•—◄◙►—•———

A PALE AND SLIGHTLY MURKY GREEN, the water had never been treated by chemicals or filtered through anything but a fish bladder. As Claire's head broke the surface and she sucked in a welcome lungful of air, a light caress trailed down the inside of one leg.

Oh it's fresh *water. Great.*

Pushing her dripping hair out of her face with a quick swipe of one hand, she began treading water and trying to figure out exactly where she was. A combination of sunshine and a gentle swell threw reflected light up into her eyes, making her squint.

Outside.

Far enough beyond the segue for there to be actual weather—not the neither/nor sort of sky that had been draped over the mall—but still on the Otherside.

She'd been lucky. With both her conscious and subconscious preoccupied in sending the shadow assassin to a place where it would be no threat, she could have ended up anywhere. Stepping through a door on the Otherside with no clear idea of a destination could have resulted in a visit to any number of unpleasant places, not only on the Otherside but in the real world as well.

She could have ended up on the south side of Chicago.

Vancouver's Downtown Eastside.

The West Bank.

The north of Afghanistan.

At a second-run theater screening of *Attack of the Clones*.

Claire shuddered.

A little water was a small price to pay.

She was wet and her batik silk skirt might never recover but she was safe. Arthur was safe. She had defeated the shadow. All that remained was to find her way back to the mall, which shouldn't—wouldn't—be a problem for a Keeper of her abilities.

The Otherside was no place for false modesty.

Or actual modesty.

Kicking harder lifted her head above the swells. Unfortunately, it didn't change what she could see—water and sunlight. She turned slowly. Water and sunlight. Water and sunlight. Water and sunlight and . . . something. It might have been fog. It might have been land, lying low along the horizon. She sank down until her chin settled just under the water, rested for a moment, then took another look.

Something.

Exactly what I need, she amended silently and started to swim, the water lapping at her in a vaguely lascivious way.

Years of practice kept her from thinking about all the many things that could go wrong before she made it back to the mall. Plenty of things were likely to go wrong without her help.

"No, you cannot go after Diana. I forbid it."

"You forbid it?" Sam's ears flattened as he glared up at Arthur. "News flash; you're not the boss of me!" Tail lashing from side to side, he stalked toward the door.

Only to find himself lifted off the floor by strong hands tucked into his armpits.

Folding himself almost in half, he got a back paw between his fur and an unprotected palm, got a claw out, and raked it downward.

Anyone else would have hollered and dropped him. Screamed and thrown him aside. Cursed and pitched him. All possible reactions and all a variation on a theme resulting in his freedom. Arthur jerked a little at the sudden pain but held on, and Sam realized he'd continue to hold on even if his hands were ripped to bloody shreds. For a moment, he considered testing that conclusion, then the moment passed and he found himself dangling helplessly.

"I'll put you down if you give me your word you'll remain in the store."

"And if I don't," Sam sneered.

"Then I'm afraid I'll have to put you somewhere secure until you give me your word or until one of the Keepers returns. They both wished you to remain here and I will not risk their wrath."

"And my wrath?" He had a feeling his look of disdain would have been more successful had Arthur not been holding him so he could see only the back of his head.

"Your wrath, I'm afraid, I will have to risk."

He flexed his claws. "Big mistake, bub."

"Do I have your word?"

"No." He needed to be free. He couldn't be bound to the store by his word when either Diana or Claire might need him. *Austin* would never allow himself to be held. Too late, he realized Austin would have lied—given his word, and then broken it with a perfectly clear conscience. He could almost hear the older cat's voice as the door to the pet crate closed behind him.

"What part of 'cats make their own rules' did you not understand, kibble-for-brains?"

"I changed my mind. You want my word, you've got it!"

Arthur shook his head. "Too convenient a conversion, I fear, but we'll speak again later."

"I saved you from that shadow! You owe me."

"I do."

"And this is how you repay me?"

"The two are not connected."

Sam watched the Immortal King head out of Pet Supplies and searched for a sufficiently scathing last word. Unfortunately, nothing came to him. One paw braced on a crossbar, he rose up on his hind legs and studied the latch. It could only be opened from the outside.

"Hey, little furry dude. What're you in for?"

Sighing, he dropped back down to all fours and glanced mournfully up at Stewart. "I wouldn't promise Arthur I'd stay in the store."

"Oh, for crying out loud; what part of 'lying' did you not understand?"

Oops.

"Couldn't lie to him, eh? Yeah, I know how it is. He's the kind of guy you can't lie to because this little voice in your head just kind of chimes in and says he deserves the truth."

"The little voice in *my* head keeps calling me kibble-for-brains."

"Harsh."

"Yeah, but cats are supposed to be good at lying. And they're supposed to only think of themselves, but I can't stop worrying about Diana. And Claire. And you guys."

"Us guys? Hey, we're fine."

Sam swept an amber gaze up one side of the mall elf and down the other, getting full mileage from the disdainful expression Arthur hadn't seen. "No, you're not. The only person I'm not worried about is Dean, and that's because he's got Austin with him and Austin knows what he's doing. He can keep bad things from happening. I can't." The stripes on his forehead folded back into a worried frown. "I just haven't been a cat long enough."

"Yeah?" Stewart picked up a tiny purple mouse on a scarlet string, looked at it thoughtfully for a moment, then began attaching it to a braid. "What were you before you were a cat?"

"An angel."

"An angel? A real angel? No shit?"

"Not until I got a body, then it came as a bit of a surprise."

"Okay." Reaching into a birdcage, the mall elf pulled out a tiny mirror. "Why do you suppose birds want to look at themselves?"

"I have no idea."

"Are they just, like, really vain? Or do they think the mirror's some kind of, I don't know, magic window to another bird?"

Mirror's some kind of magic window.

Magic mirror.

Sam padded over to Stewart's side of the crate. "Can I have that?"

"The mirror?" He finished checking the position of the purple mouse, flipped the narrow braid back over his shoulder, and shrugged. "Sure."

That was easy.

"Can you unlatch the crate?"

"Sorry, little furry dude, not unless Arthur says it's okay."

Oh, well. Worth a try.

Back in the Emporium, Austin had used a mirror to talk to the magic mirror and then used the magic mirror to connect to him. Well, technically, Claire; but the basics were the same. If he could use the budgie mirror to contact the magic mirror, then he could find out where Claire was and if Diana was okay. Sam ran through that one more time, just to be certain it made sense, then had Stewart hook the mirror over the crossbar. Ignoring the dangling bell and bits of fake feather, he stared at his reflection.

His reflection stared back.

Apparently, there was a trick to it.

He leaned closer until his breath fogged the glass. Leaned a little closer until there was less than a cat-hair's width between his nose and the mirror. He was *not* in the mood for tricks. "HEY!"

Blue-on-blue eyes snapped up out of nowhere. "I'm not deaf! Or I wasn't," Jack added petulantly as Sam jumped back. His eyes slid from one side of the mirror to the other, then widened. "Okay, this is new. Hold it!"

Sam froze, one paw in the air.

"Don't move your reflection off the glass. It's all that's holding me here. Not that it *should* be holding me here. Or that I should be here at all." The eyes narrowed speculatively. "Who knows, maybe our earlier connection left some residue or something. So what do you want?"

"Information."

"Yeah? Well, I'm a mirror—not a database."

"Information on Claire and Diana."

"You lost *both* Keepers?"

Sam really didn't like the way that sounded. "You know something."

"Not about Claire, I haven't seen her since you guys crossed over, but . . ."

Jack's pause suggested all sorts of horrible possibilities. "But what?" Sam demanded, surging back toward the mirror.

"Diana was in the store; her and some elfin cutie. They stopped and talked, I told them what I knew, and they went into the back room. I don't know how to break this to you, kid, but from the buzz I picked up later, they got caught."

"By the bad guys?"

Blue-on-blue eyes rolled. "No, by the Publishers' Clearing House prize patrol. Of course by the bad guys!"

"And?"

"Sorry, kid. That's all I know."

"Okay." Sam stepped away from the mirror, and the eyes disappeared. Tail whipping from side to side, he caught Stewart in an amber gaze and growled, "Get Arthur."

Dean knew he was dreaming because, although he had once played hockey in his underwear, he'd never had so much trouble covering the ice. It had to have been five or six kilometers between the goals and by the time he crossed the blue line, he could barely put one skate in front of the other. With all his remaining strength, he drew back his stick, set up for a slap shot, and stared in amazement as the blue light around the puck turned white and sparkly and, for no good reason that he could determine, it ascended, becoming a higher being.

"Hey, McIssac!"

He looked down at Austin, wondering how he could actually blow a whistle without lips.

"What have I told you about keeping your stick on the ice?"

It took him a moment to remember how his mouth worked. "Nothing."

"Fine. If that's the way you're going to be about it, get up and feed me."

"What?"

"I said, get up and feed me!"

A sudden sharp pain on his chin jerked his eyes open in time to see Austin pull back his paw, claws still extended.

"What's a cat got to do to get some breakfast around here?"

Rubbing his chin with his left hand, Dean reached for his glasses with his right. "That'll do it." The sheet felt like it weighed a hundred pounds and after he swung his legs out of bed, it took him a moment to remember what he was supposed to do next.

"Are you all right?"

"Just some tired." He squinted toward the bedside table. "Is that the time, then?"

"Let's see . . ." Austin walked across the pillows. "Numbers on a clock; yes, I'd have to say that was the time."

"It's seven thirty. I slept through the alarm." He never slept through the alarm. *Had* never slept through the alarm. Ever. It bordered on irresponsible. Two tries to stand up, but once he was actually on his feet, his head seemed a little clearer. Washing, shaving, dressing, refolding perfect hospital corners; by the time he set Austin's saucer of cat food on the floor, he'd shaken off the sluggishness and was feeling more like himself.

Moving the fridge out from the wall and vacuuming the cooling coils banished the last of it.

It had probably been nothing more than a reaction to the uncomfortably warm temperature in the bedroom. He hated sleeping with a fan on and the air outside was so still and hot, an open window made little difference.

"Good morning."

A pleasant soprano voice but not one Dean recognized unless Dr. Rebik had woken up in even worse shape than he had. He finished shouldering the fridge back against the wall, turned, and was surprised to see Meryat's shrouded form standing alone at the end of the counter dividing kitchen and dining room.

"It is a . . . beautiful day."

It was already 29 degrees C, the sun so bright on the front of the guest house he'd nearly been blinded stepping into the office. Still, for someone used to the weather in Egypt it probably felt like home.

"You're speaking English."

Although he still couldn't see her face, the tilt of her hood looked confused. "England?"

"No, Canada."

"But . . . English?"

"Canadians speak English. Except for those of us who speak French. We have two official languages, see, and we have people who speak both. And a Prime Minister who speaks neither. Sorry, that was kind of a joke," he added hastily as he felt her confusion level rise. Taking a step toward her, he tried to explain. "He's after having this accent that's uh . . ."

Her hand rose toward his chest.

His voice trailed off and he froze, trying to decide which would be ruder, backing away or shuddering at her touch.

Fingertips, a little less black than they had been, stopped just above his T-shirt. Close enough that he could feel body heat filling the space.

"You are . . . strong."

"Strong?" Then he remembered she'd seen him move the fridge and blushed. "Well, yeah, I guess. Thank you."

"Strong is . . . good."

There was a note in her voice that deepened the color of his ears. Nine months ago, he wouldn't have even realized she was hitting on him, but since Claire . . .

"Your Keeper . . . will return . . . soon?"

"I hope so."

She was smiling. He *knew* she was smiling. He just wished he knew what to do about it.

"Meryat?"

Her hand fell, but the heat lingered. She turned toward Dr. Rebik and murmured something in her own language. When he shook his head, she repeated it. Or something so close to it Dean couldn't tell the difference.

The archeologist sighed and motioned toward the dining room, allowing Meryat to precede him. "Would a little breakfast be possible, Mr. McIssac?"

"Sure."

"I'll have what I had yesterday, and Meryat would like to know if there's any chance of chopped dates and honey on a flatbread."

Why didn't she ask him herself?

"Sorry, no, but I could do up some grape jelly on Melba toast."

Dr. Rebik glanced down at his companion then back at Dean, and shrugged wearily. "Close enough."

"I don't trust her. You're too tired to get up this morning, and suddenly she's able to complain about the food."

"It's not what she's used to."

Austin sighed and walked over to stand on the dishwasher where he could look Dean in the face. "You're missing the point. You're tired.

She's got new skills. She's a mummy. Mummies are known for sucking the life force out of the people they come in contact with."

"We're not in a cheesy horror movie here," Dean protested as he straightened.

Austin merely stared.

"No matter what it seems like most of the time," Dean amended. "And besides, you said you checked on her and she didn't leave her bed. She'd have a little trouble sucking my life force from the second floor."

"You don't know that."

"Why are you so suspicious?"

"Why aren't you?"

"Austin, I can't be after accusing her of something without proof. It doesn't do any harm to think the best of people."

"Yeah, tell that to your dried and desiccated corpse," the cat muttered. Jumping carefully down, he followed Dean out into the hall. "Now, where are you going?"

"Up to the third floor." He hauled back the elevator door. "I can't just leave Lance at the beach indefinitely. You want to come, then?"

"No . . . yes."

"You're thinking he'll be an ally in this sudden antimummy thing of yours, aren't you?"

Austin wrapped his tail around his toes and snorted. "I don't know what you're talking about."

By concentrating on what a pleasant swim she was having, Claire managed to have pretty much exactly that. Granted, the water had a tendency to throw in a grope or two when she was least expecting it, but she was a strong swimmer and, bottom line, it made what could have been a tedious hour a little more interesting.

When she could hear the breakers folding against the shore, she stopped and had another look, checking out potential landing sites. The white sand beach stretched in a shallow arc for six or seven kilometers rising up from the water in a series of staggered dunes, sand giving way to grasses, to low ground covers, to aspens, and a good distance inland to the darker blur of a mature forest.

The blue-and-white–striped cabana, flags flapping, sides billowing in the gentle breeze, looked ridiculously out of place.

Blue-and-white–striped cabana?

Claire lost her stroke, got smacked in the face by a wave, choked, coughed and started swimming with everything she had left. Assumptions, conscious or subconscious, were no longer relevant. She *knew* what lived here.

The first time they'd used the elevator, the first time they'd stepped out on this beach, had nearly been their last. While she and Dean had been wading, taking a bit of a break from the extended responsibilities their lives had become bogged down in, a giant not-a-squid had heaved itself up through the surf, attacked, and almost crawled—squelched? flopped?—back into the elevator with them. It had moved terrifyingly fast even on land, out of its natural habitat.

Did an unnatural creature have *a natural habitat,* Claire wondered, sucking in a lungful of damp air and then burying her face again for another dozen strokes. *Or would it be an unnatural habitat?*

Not that it mattered. It was fast on land. In the water . . .

The gentle touches had become motivating rather than interesting, each bringing with it the image of a tentacle tip rising from the depths.

Or the shallows.

The waves were stronger this close to shore and gritty with sand scooped up from the bottom. Claire crested a breaker, let it carry her forward, tumbled out of it, rolled once, got her feet under her, planted them firmly, and pushed off. It wasn't quite body surfing, but it was faster than swimming.

Still not as fast as the not-a-squid.

Would you just shut up!

Subconscious, conscious; she neither knew nor cared.

During the brief time Augustus Smythe had been back in charge of the guest house, he'd killed three. In the first two months they were back, she and Dean had taken out two more. They hadn't seen one since.

Which didn't mean anything, really.

What part of shut up are you having trouble understanding?

The next time her feet touched bottom, she was standing in water only thigh-deep and it was faster to run. Her skirt, which had been floating free and in no way impeding her kick, had decided to buy into the general sense of urgency by wrapping around her legs. Wet silk had the tensile strength of 80s hair spray and, unable to get the knots untied, she finally hoisted it to waist level and made it ashore.

Well aware that collapsing at the edge of wet sand, sinking down, gasping for breath, and giving thanks for her survival would have been the proper dramatic gesture, Claire kept moving until she got to the cabana. A dramatic gesture on the Otherside tended to call an appreciative audience. She did *not* need to deal with any more weirdness right now.

Throwing back the flap, she stared down at the large blond Bystander lying on one of the air mattresses, his left arm tucked up behind his head, his right curved around an inflatable shark. Even in the dim light filtering through the canvas, all his exposed skin was a deep, painful red; Claire'd seen rarer steaks.

His eyes were a brilliant blue.

Eyes?

"Nice underwear!"

Dropping her skirt, she wondered why she'd expected him to be Australian. "Who are you?"

"Lance Benedict!" Tossing the shark aside, he bounded to his feet. "You escaped from her, didn't you?"

"Who?"

"Meryat!"

"No." She stepped inside and let the flap fall. "How did you get here?"

"The same way you did, I imagine!"

"Do us both a favor and don't imagine anything." Technically, Bystanders couldn't affect the Otherside, but in all the times she'd taken the elevator to the beach, Claire had never realized it was on the Otherside so . . . wait. Could there be more than one Otherside? Would that not depend on how many sides reality started with? And did that not depend on an agreed upon definition of reality?

My head hurts.

"Did she throw you from her dahabeeyah?"

"Her what?" With any luck, there was some variety of painkiller in the first aid kit.

"Her boat. You're wet! Did she throw you from her boat?"

"Who is *she?*"

"Meryat, the reanimated undead! I'm the only one who knows how to stop her!"

Claire looked down at the two aspirins in her hand and realized they were going to be insufficient. *"Please,* tell me everything from the beginning."

"In the beginning, only the ocean existed, and on this ocean appeared an egg from which was born the sun-god, Atum. He had four children, Geb and Shu, Tefnut and Nut. Planting their feet on Geb . . ."

"Lance."

"Yeah?"

"Skip ahead."

Okay. There was a 3,000-year-old mummy and the archaeologist who'd freed her from her cursed existence in the guest house with Dean and Austin. Given the type of clientele the guest house attracted, this was in no way surprising. A pair of Shriners and their wives, yes. Reanimated Egyptian noblewomen, no.

But Lance believed that Meryat was dangerous, that she would suck dry the lives she came into contact with until she regained her former power, that she would then use that power to take over the world. He also believed that Dr. Rebik was under some kind of mind control that kept him from seeing Meryat as she really was and that the beach was her initial attempt to bury the world under the sands of ancient Egypt.

Just because he was wrong about that last point, did that automatically make him wrong about the rest?

Claire glanced across the cabana at Lance; currently making entries in a PDA he'd pulled from a belt pouch. She wanted to believe he'd spent way, way too much time in the sun, but the fact was that here *he* was.

Dean obviously hadn't believed Lance's story, or he wouldn't have sent him on his little elevator ride. As Dean gave pretty much everyone he met the benefit of the doubt, he had to have doubted Lance more than Meryat and Dr. Rebik.

Conclusion; Dean and Austin were in no danger. Lance was

merely a Bystander who'd applied a Saturday Afternoon Movie explanation to his first contact with the metaphysical.

And he'd spent way, way too much time in the sun.

Since they knew they were being hunted, she couldn't come up with a reason for the mummy and Dr. Rebik to stay at the guest house for more than one night. As soon as they were safely away, Dean would be up to retrieve Indiana Lance from his sandcastle of delusion.

Although the thought of seeing Dean made her heart beat faster, and she missed Austin with an almost physical ache, she had to get back to the mall. She'd left an eighteen-month-old cat guarding an Immortal King, her little sister was out scouting the darkside, and, if not stopped, the post-segue owners would not be exaggerating when they advertised the "sale to end all sales."

If this was the Otherside, then she could lift the stack of extra towels and find a pen and piece of paper tucked beneath them. Holding that image in her mind, she lifted the towels. Three tiny bones, a catnip square, and what looked like the spleen of a small animal. Either Austin had found something to hunt on their last visit, or he was casting auguries again. Either way, she didn't want to know.

Claire let the towels drop and turned to Lance who was stowing his PDA in its pouch. "I don't suppose you have a pen and some paper? I need to leave a note."

"Better!" He crossed the cabana in two long strides, holding out a small black book and a pencil. "When you're on a dig at Karnak, you need a writing implement you can fix with a knife!"

"Do you have a knife?"

"I have a pencil sharpener."

"Okay."

She'd entered by water; she'd have to exit by water. Unfortunately, that meant a sudden and total immersion with no thoughts of vicious not-a-squids waiting for her below the surface.

"Where are you going?" Kicking out a fine spray of sand, Lance hurried to catch up.

"To the headlands."

"Great idea! The high ground will give us a chance to see where

Meryat's hiding. She's sneaky, but there's got to be a palace around here somewhere."

Claire sighed. He was consistently delusional at least.

Eventually—after embalming, ancient Egyptian magic, and the tracking of the risen undead had been thoroughly explained—the soft sand gave way to pebbles and then to the ridge that jutted out into the water. She winced as a sharp rock dug into the bottoms of her feet.

"I bet you wish you had shoes on!"

Actually, she was trying very hard not to wish he'd fall and break his neck.

The rock smoothed out on the top of the ridge and she was able to move quickly out to the end. They were twenty, maybe twenty-five feet above the water.

"Long walk back," Lance observed, one hand shading his eyes as he gazed toward the distant cabana.

"Not necessarily."

"The sun hasn't moved!"

"It never does."

"I don't see Meryat's palace."

"As Diana would say, 'Quel surprise. Not.'"

"Who's Diana?"

"My sister." Who needed her. In the mall. Not standing here trying to see past reflections to what might be lurking below the surface. Fortunately, she didn't need to convince herself that there was nothing there, only that it didn't matter. She wasn't jumping into water; she was using the change, the line between air and water like a door. "Go back to the cabana and wait for Dean."

"I think I should keep searching for Meryat."

"Whatever." This Bystander, at least, was not her responsibility. Stepping back half a dozen paces, she ran for the edge of the rock and jumped, folding her knees tightly against her chest, arms holding them in place in order to cross the line as *simultaneously* as possible.

Just before she hit the water, she heard:

"Cannonball!"

"Lance!" Dean moved a little farther away from the propped-open door of the elevator and yelled again. "LANCE!"

"Maybe Meryat ate him."

"Not funny, Austin."

"Not joking."

"He's not answering and I don't see . . . Austin!"

"I know, I know." Austin stepped off the path and began digging a new hole. "Just because this place looks like the world's biggest litter box doesn't mean I should yadda yadda." After checking depth, he stepped forward, positioned himself, and glared up at Dean. "Do you *mind?*"

"Sorry." Ears red, Dean headed for the cabana. "I'll be after checking if Lance is inside."

"Yeah, you be after doing that, then."

There were a suspicious number of footprints around the cabana's flap. A large bootprint—Dean dropped to one knee and measured it against his hand—probably belonging to Lance, and a small bare print that appeared to have come up from the water.

"Hey, Claire's been here."

"Claire?" Heel, toes, instep; still anonymous to him. "How can you tell?"

"I'm a cat." Flopping down, Austin rolled over on his back, sunlight gleaming on the white fur of his stomach as he rubbed his shoulders into the compacted sand. "And I'm generally a lot closer to the ground than you are."

Hard to argue with. Leaping to his feet, Dean grabbed for the canvas. "Claire!"

"She's not here, hormone-boy. Look there, the same footprints heading out. She's been and gone."

"How long ago?"

"About thirty-one minutes. She was walking quickly, carrying a ham sandwich, and humming *The 1812 Overture.*"

"You can tell all that from her footprints?"

"No, you idiot, I can't. But I'd be just as likely to know the last two as the first." Shaking his head, the cat slid through the break in the canvas.

Because he couldn't think of anything better to do, Dean followed. "Still no Lance." But there *was* a note on the beer cooler. *"Just passing through. Still working on the mall. I agree with your assessment of*

Lance. Austin, you're eating the geriatric cat food and that's final. Love you both. Claire." He folded his hand around the paper.

"Are you going to do something sappy, like hold the note up to your heart?"

"No." Not now he wasn't. "Do you think she took Lance with her?"

Wrapping his tail around his toes, Austin looked thoughtful. "They definitely headed off together, and she said she trusted your assessment of him."

"Well, after hearing Lance's story, it wouldn't be hard for Claire to figure out that I sent him up here to get him safely out of the way."

"So maybe she took him with her because this place is no longer safe."

Dean's brows drew in and he studied the cat. "Facetious comment?"

"Experienced guess."

Fair enough. "And if this place is no longer safe . . ."

". . . we should go." Austin finished, jumping down and running for the cabana's flap.

Dean caught up to him halfway back to the elevator. "Did you know there was a back way into this beach?"

"Sure."

"You lying to me?"

"You'll never know."

"It's like a fucking maze down here. What do they need all these tunnels for?"

"Nothing. It's what *we* expected to find." Specifically, it was what she'd expected to find, unable to shake the feeling that they couldn't just go straight to the anchor—way too easy. About to suggest they stop wandering and start coming up with some sort of a plan, she snapped her mouth closed as Kris raised a silencing hand.

Voices.

Angry voices.

Not very far away but bouncing off the rock.

Head cocked, ears fanned out away from her skull, Kris slowly turned in place. Barely resisting the urge to make beeping sounds, Diana waited. After a long moment, Kris pointed to the left. "That way."

"I guess Chekhov was right."

"What does *Star Trek* have to do with this?"

"Not *that* Chekhov. The Russian writer—we studied him last year in English."

"You studied a Russian in English?"

"Yeah. Go figure. He said that you never hang elf ears on the wall in act one, unless you're going to use them in act three."

"You're not making any fucking sense. You know, that, right?"

The tunnels to the left slanted away on a slight downward angle—just enough to be noticeable. Heading down toward evil . . . it was annoyingly clinchéd and beginning to make Diana just a little nervous. She'd cop to the maze but not the slope, she just didn't do symbolism that blatant. Which meant something that did was in control of this part of the Otherside.

The voices grew louder, and Kris pointed to an inverted, triangular-shaped fissure in the rock.

And this is why I get the big bucks, Diana reminded herself, kicking the toe of one sneaker into the bottom of the crack and heaving herself up into the passage. It took her a moment to figure out how to tuck herself inside, but she finally started inching sideways toward the distant argument. Rocks jutting out from the sides of the fissure scraped across her stomach, laying out what she was sure would be a fascinating pattern of bruises, and there were one or two places where she was positive she lost chunks of her ass. *Memo to self: lay off the ice cream and thank God I don't have much in the way of breasts.*

She didn't expect Kris to climb in after her but couldn't do much about it since she'd reached a spot without enough room to turn her head.

Stretch out left arm, stretch out left leg, anchor both, and shimmy sideways.

And then she ran out of fissure.

Dipping her left shoulder, Diana forced herself close enough to the outside edge to get a look around.

They were in a crack about twenty feet up the wall of a huge circular chamber.

The generic nasty from the throne room was standing just off center.

In the center, in the exact center, was a hole. Not a metaphysical hole, an actual round hole. Like a well.

Before she could follow that new information through to any kind of a logical conclusion, a piece of shadow fell screaming from the ceiling. Shuddering, she had to admit it had reason to scream. Reasons. Reasons that started with the baby doll pajamas, worked through the lopsided braids, and finished at the residue of melted marshmallow, chocolate, and graham cracker crumbs.

No Name Nasty didn't seem to have much sympathy for it.

"I don't care how many boxes of cookies you have to sell! You're pathetic. You were sent to assassinate the Immortal King . . ."

Diana felt Kris' gasp by her right ear and managed to wrap a hand around the other girl's arm. Now was not the time.

". . . and you failed!"

There. It failed. Good news.

"YOU HAVE BOTH FAILED."

Diana stiffened. "Oh, Hell."

"I thought you weren't supposed to swear," Kris muttered.

"I wasn't."

TEN

———◆———

BACKING OUT OF THE FISSURE scraped and bruised a number of interesting new places, but given what she now knew, Diana found the pain a whole lot easier to ignore. *There's was nothing like finding yourself right back at a potential apocalypse to put a bruised boob in perspective.*

"FEE, FI, FOE, FEEPER . . ."

That didn't sound good. She poked Kris, trying to get her to move a little faster. Kris flashed her a one-finger answer.

"Feeper? What's a feeper?" The guy from the throne room, now positively identified as a Shadowlord, had become a lot harder to hear.

"IF I COULD FINISH!"

"Sorry."

"NOT YET, YOU AREN'T. BUT YOU WILL BE."

With any luck, the punishing of the unnamed Shadowlord would distract . . .

"AS I WAS SAYING; FEE, FI, FOE, FEEPER, I SMELL THE BLOOD OF A NEARBY KEEPER!"

. . . or not.

Kris dropped down into the corridor.

"We have a Keeper in chains . . ." the Shadowlord began.

"NO, YOU DON'T."

"Yes, we . . ."

"NO."

"But . . ."

"YOU'RE AN IDIOT."

Diana stumbled as she landed, cracked her knee against the stone floor, and told herself to ignore it. "Come on." Grabbing Kris' hand, she dragged the mall elf into a run. "We've got to get out of here."

"Haven't I been saying that?"

"Yeah, but now I'm saying it." First, up the slope. Then, when the floor leveled out, she'd follow the signature of her scattered stuff back to the throne room. After that, a fast run through the construction site and into the access corridor. Granted, the last time she'd covered that particular bit of the escape route, she was being dragged by a giant bug, but she was fairly sure she remembered the pattern of water seepage on the ceiling.

As they turned the first corner, Kris leaned in close and said, in an urgent whisper. "Who was that talking?"

"I told you."

"You said; oh, hell."

"Close." A short pause at the second corner to make sure the way was clear. "I said, oh, Hell."

"And the diff?"

"Capital letter."

"So that was really. . . ?"

"Yeah." At the third corner, the floor leveled out. Diana reached out, feeling for possibilities out of place. Not surprisingly, it wasn't hard to pick up the signature of Keeper-designed weapons over the general hum of evil.

"But Hell's a place. Places don't talk."

"It's not so much a place as it's a metaphor."

"Whatever. Just so's you know, I don't believe in Hell."

"Just so *you* know, that doesn't matter.

"It isn't real!"

Diana sighed. "Six months ago, you were freezing your ass off, trying to survive on the streets during a Canadian winter. Now, you're an elf, living in an evolving shopping mall, having been made the Captain of the Guard for an allegorical king. All things considered, I think you should be a little more open-minded about the parameters of reality."

"All things considered, I think I have the right to be fucking terrified!"

On a list of bad times for a second kiss, a kiss intended to fall between attraction and relationship, standing in a torchlit tunnel, deep in territory controlled by the dark side of a segue that could allow Hell itself into the world, ranked up there near the top—above "during the funeral of one of the participants" but definitely below "in the holding cell at a maximum security prison."

Figuring that there wasn't likely to be a right time any time soon, Diana closed her eyes and leaned in. After a moment—a long moment of soft lips and gentle pressure and just a little tongue—she pulled back and murmured, "Still terrified?"

"Yeah."

"Oh . . ."

"But if you were trying to distract me, I gotta say it was a better idea than more stupid stories about your cat."

"Hey, that's Claire! I don't tell stupid stories abo . . ."

The third kiss involved a little more tongue and strong fingers cupped around the nape of her neck. Diana's left hand buried itself in the warm mass of mahogany dreads and her right spread out to touch as much of a narrow waist as possible.

"I'm not sayin' this is anything more than a reaction to that whole Hell thing."

Still close enough that Kris' voice was a soft warmth against her face, Diana murmured, "I'm not asking it to *be* more than a reaction to that whole Hell thing."

"I'm not sayin' that it isn't either."

"Okay."

"I thought we had to get out of here?"

"We do."

"You can beat this thing, right?"

"Sure."

Kris' eyes widened and she stepped back, breaking the heat between them. "You don't know, do you?"

"Look, I'm the most powerful Keeper in the lineage right now, and Claire's already closed this thing down once. Anything's possible, so all we have to do is find the right possibility. Which we won't find standing here." Taking a deep breath, she added a little more distance between them. "Let's go."

By the time they reached the alcove where they'd been chained, they could hear the distant sound of pursuit behind them.

"I guess it's stopped arguing," Diana muttered as they began running faster.

"You mean they've stopped arguing."

"No. The guy from the throne room is a Shadowlord, as much a shadow of Hell as the assassin; just bit more formed, is all."

"Hell was arguing with itself?"

"It's a thing it does. It doesn't get out much."

"And that's good, right?"

Diana shot a quick, disbelieving glance at the elf. "Generally speaking, yeah." They took a small flight of stairs two steps at a time. "This also explains why the Shadowlord thought I should know him and why he lacks a name. Bits of Hell don't get names until they've really distinguished themselves in some truly disgusting way."

"So Jerry Springer's pretty much a gimme?"

"Pretty much, yeah."

They were running between walls of dressed stone now. Walls that had been built rather than carved out of the bedrock. They were very close to the throne room.

"Good thing . . . the torches are still . . . lit," Kris panted.

"Yeah. They're lit . . . because I expect them to . . . be. We need them . . . to get out of here."

"Wouldn't Hell . . . know that?"

"Probably. But I don't . . . think it has direct influence . . . this far out yet."

Between the time her right foot rose and she brought it under her body, ready to stretch it out front once again, the torches went out.

"Of course, I could be wrong."

The bedroom was dark when Austin woke. The day just passed had grown overcast, although no cooler, and that overcast had lasted into the night, blocking starlight and moonlight and, very nearly, streetlight. Eye open the merest slit, he could see Dean's darker-on-dark silhouette on the other pillow and not much else, but he knew they weren't alone. Something stood beside the bed.

Something satisfied . . .

He sprang without warning, over Dean and off the edge of the bed. So positive that his claws would connect with linen bandages, he was taken completely by surprise when he hit the floor.

And was blinded an instant later.

"Austin?" One hand on the switch for the bedside lamp, Dean blinked down at the cat. "What's the matter, then?"

"She was here. Just a second ago."

"Who was?"

"Who do you think?"

"Meryat?"

"Give the man a rubber mouse." He stalked stiff-legged out into the sitting room. "She's gone."

"I didn't hear the door . . ."

"Neither did I."

"So how did she leave without opening and closing the door? She couldn't go through it—she's touched me, you know. She's solid. And slow. You've seen how she walks."

"Maybe she's just pretending to be slow."

"I think I'd know if she was faking it."

Austin snorted. "You'd be surprised." He padded back to the bedroom and stared up at Dean. "I don't know how she's doing it, but she's been sucking your life force!"

"You sound like Lance."

"Yeah?" Hooking his claws into the edge of the mattress, he rappelled his way up the side of the bed and stood on Dean's thighs. "You look exhausted. Explain that!"

Dean squinted at the clock. "It's three forty-seven *a.m.*"

"You were sleeping; you should be rested."

"I should still be *sleeping.*" Settling back against his pillow, he gently stroked the spot behind Austin's left ear with his thumb. "Has it occurred to you that maybe you're having mummy nightmares because you're a cat and cats have this whole Egyptian connection going?"

Eye narrowed, Austin glared. "You know nothing about that."

"Not true. When I had the new strut put in the truck, there were *National Geographics* in the waiting room and I read this article on cats in ancient Egypt."

"How old was the magazine?"

"Some old, but they were talking about 1,500 BC; does it matter?"

"I am not having nightmares. I am not imagining things. And I did not tell you to stop doing that."

"Sorry." Dean started stroking again as Austin stretched out.

"I will get to the bottom of this," he vowed, sweeping his tail across Dean's legs.

"Sure you wi . . . OW! Lord t'undering Jesus, cat! I'm attached to those!"

"Then maybe you should consider where my claws are before you make another patronizing observation." Having leaped safely away from any physical retaliation, Austin curled up into a tight ball on Claire's pillow and closed his eye. "Turn out the light, would you. It's the middle of the night."

"Where are we?"

"Based on the cannons, the parapets, and that big guardhouse," Claire hissed, grabbing a handful of Lance's wet shirt and dragging him down behind the buttress, "I'd say we were in a fort."

"Which fort?"

"I don't know." They were still on the Otherside, although which Otherside she wasn't entirely certain—a concept she'd take the time to find disturbing the moment she was no longer personally responsible for an idiot Bystander. Motioning for him to follow, she murmured, "Stay close," and led the way along the inside curve of the outer wall. When she paused in the triangular shadow of a small lean-to, he tucked up tight behind her. She reached back and shoved hard enough to break the contact between them. "Not *that* close."

He inched in again. "What are we doing here?"

"You yelled cannonball as you hit the water and that influenced the path."

"This is Meryat's doing, isn't it?"

"No." Claire measured the distance between their hiding place and the guardhouse and decided a sprint across open ground with a Bystander in tow was just too dangerous—no matter how much she would dearly love to lose said Bystander. They hadn't seen any actual guards, but that didn't mean there *weren't* any actual guards.

"But . . ."

"Would you *please* shut up."

"But why is it dark?"

"It's night." She didn't know why the magic word wasn't working—whether it was her, or him, or a combination of them both—but only an urgent need to return to the mall kept her from trying out a few more words. Any delays at this point would only serve the segue.

"It wasn't night at the beach."

Any delays at this point . . . "No, it wasn't." She'd be willing to detour and take him back to the beach, but that didn't seem to be possible. That path had closed behind them. And taking him back to the real world would take far too long. Time she—and the world—didn't have.

"This is Meryat's . . ."

"No, it isn't. Shut up."

On the other side of the lean-to, the wall curved out to the left. Wet skirt clinging to her legs, she crept forward, stumbled as Lance grabbed hold of the fabric, and managed to regain her balance without doing anything Lance would regret for the rest of his very short life. She followed the wall into a shallow alcove and began running her hands over the stone.

Lance crowded in with her. "What are you looking for?"

"A door."

"Why?"

"So we can go through it."

"And then we'll be on the other side of it!"

"Yes . . . no." She didn't know what the alcove was for, but it wasn't an access to anything. "Didn't I tell you to shut up?"

"Yes!"

Turning brought them almost nose to chest. Claire glared up at the oblivious grad student. "How many times am I going to have to say shut up before you actually do it?"

Lance looked thoughtful. "I don't know."

"So you used this budgie mirror to contact a magic mirror in the Emporium . . ." Frowning at his reflection, Arthur turned the tiny mirror between long fingers. ". . . which is both the store nearest to the darkness anchoring the segue and the place where you and the Keepers crossed through to this side."

Sam hooked his claws on the crossbar of the crate and stared at Arthur—who'd crouched just out of paw reach, his sword point on the floor, pommel jutting up at a sharp angle over his left shoulder. "Yes."

"And this mirror said it saw Diana and Kris pass through the store?"

"Yes."

"But that it later heard gossip suggesting they had been captured?"

"Recap much? Get on with it!"

"And this . . . story isn't merely a ploy intended to secure your release so that you can run off after Diana?"

"No." In all the time he'd been a cat, he'd never realized just how satisfying a good tail lashing could be. If he moved it any faster, he was afraid it might come off his butt. "Would I do something like that?"

Arthur straightened, reached back, and adjusted his sword. "As I understand cats, yes, you would."

"But I'm not!"

"And you heard this conversation with the mirror?" Arthur asked, flipping his hair back off his face as he turned to Stewart.

The mall elf froze in mid squeak of a rubber fire hydrant. "No words, sire, 'cause the mirror's real small and it was down by him, not up with me, but I heard the talking."

"Hey!" Sam drew the attention of both the Immortal King and the elf back to the crate. "You know I suck at lying. If I was any good at it, would I be in here?"

"You have a point," Arthur acknowledged after a moment's consideration.

"I have a whole lot of points," Sam muttered, "and I know where they'll hurt the most."

Sapphire-blue eyes narrowed. "What was that?"

"Nothing. Look, it's real simple. The bad guys have Diana. We have to rescue her."

"We?"

"I'm smart enough to know when I need help. You can't just leave her there! And what about Kris. You can't leave her! You're supposed to be this great leader, but isn't abandoning your people a bad thing?"

"Yes." Arthur bent and opened the crate.

"Finally." Sam raced out and up onto a stack of dog food, reclaiming the high ground. "What convinced you?"

"With one Keeper taken and the other gone, the darkside will want to close the segue as soon as possible, before the light has a chance to send other wizards. In order to succeed, they must remove us. They will, therefore, be massing to attack. I have always preferred to attack on my terms, not the enemy's."

"I didn't say any of that."

"I know."

"But Diana . . ."

"Will be freed when we defeat the darkside."

Sam opened his mouth to ask what would happen if they didn't defeat the darkside, but he closed it again when he realized he already knew the answer. And he didn't like it much.

"What a lovely cat."

Dean glanced down in time to see Austin pointedly cross to the other side of the dining room—as far from Meryat as he could get and still be contained within the same four walls.

"I don't think he likes me."

"Foolish kitty," Dr. Rebik murmured, bringing the blackened tips of the mummy's fingers to his lips.

Trying not to shudder, Dean developed a sudden interest in cleaning nothing off a spotless floor. He was doing his best to be open-minded about this—he was involved with an older woman himself—but he just couldn't get past the reanimated corpse part of the relationship. When he straightened, all ancient digits were back within the masking folds of Meryat's cloak and Dr. Rebik was finishing his oatmeal.

"As Meryat would like to remain here until your Keeper returns," the archaeologist began, setting his spoon aside, "I was wondering, Mr. McIssac, if you could do me a favor."

Ignoring Austin's warning twitch, Dean nodded. "I'd be happy to."

"It's just I don't have a lot of clothes with me and, were I to go out to a coin laundry, I'd have a choice of either not washing my trousers or not wearing them while they washed. And they do need washing."

From what he could see of the cream-colored chinos, that was an unfortunately accurate observation. "I'd be happy to do a load for you. Put everything you want washed in one of the pillowcases and set it out in the hall."

"Thank you, Mr. McIssac." He set both palms against the tabletop and pushed himself to his feet, then tucked a hand under Meryat's elbow to help her stand.

"Yes, Mr. McIssac." The morning light illuminated the depths of her hood as she turned and Dean got an unwelcome education in what bits rotted away even in a very dry climate. The dark eyes looked out of place amidst the lack of cartilage and fat. "Thank you."

He assumed she was smiling although the words "rictus grin" couldn't help but come to mind. "You're welcome."

"You know, *I* was wondering something myself."

All three heads rotated toward the cat, the new angle throwing Meryat's face back into shadow.

"Why is it that you want to see the Keeper?" Austin continued, suddenly sitting at the end of the long table. Dr. Rebik looked startled, a ripple traveled the length of Meryat's cloak, and Dean tried to pretend that he didn't usually let the cat sit with the breakfast dishes. Not that "let the cat" was in any way pertinent to cats in general and this cat in particular. "She's on assignment. You could have quite the wait."

"I am willing to wait." Meryat folded her hands into her sleeves. "I am hoping she will be able to give me back all I have lost."

"You seem to be doing fine without her."

"But so, so slowly. I look forward to the day when I can . . ."

"Rule the world?"

"Go out in public."

Shooting a "now see what you've done" look at Austin and another at Dean, Dr. Rebik slipped his arm around Meryat's bowed shoulders and led her from the room. During their slow shuffle down the hall and up the stairs, Dean loaded the dishwasher, swept the dining room floor, polished the table, and did his best to ignore the expression on Austin's face.

The distant sound of a door closing on the second floor brought the cat to his feet. "Convinced? It's going too slowly and she needs to suck the life out of Claire to finish rebuilding herself."

"I thought you said she was after sucking the life out of me."

"Yeah, but *slowly*. She doesn't want to spook Claire the moment she gets in the door. Trust me, Claire'll notice if you're a desiccated corpse propped up in the corner, but a couple of missing years'll slip on by."

"That's reassuring."

"Yeah, well she's not going to be too happy that another woman's su . . ."

His ears scarlet, Dean clamped a hand over the cat's muzzle. "There was no one in the bedroom last night and you said Meryat was asleep when you heard something moving around the night before. Drop it. You're imagining things. You're some worried about Claire and it's stressing you out. Giving you nightmares."

He removed his hand.

Austin shook his whiskers back into place. "Cats don't have nightmares," he hissed. "Cats have premonitions of disaster, and I'm having one now. Gag me again, and you'll lose the hand."

"Stop touching me!"

"Sorry. It's just this is a little . . ." Lance waved a hand at the milling herd of purple hippopotamuses. ". . . weird."

"Yes, it is. But it's only weird because you seem to be incapable of doing what you're asked."

"You told me to think about nothing."

Claire slapped a hippo on the rump and moved it out of her way. "These aren't nothing."

"I tried to think about nothing, but that made me think of how difficult it was to think about nothing and that made me think about that whole 'don't think of a purple hippopotamus' thing."

"You know, I figured that out without the explanation."

"How?"

She exchanged an exasperated look with a lavender cow. "It wasn't hard. We're in a herd of purple hippopotamuses. Who usually live in water. And aren't purple."

"I don't see any doors."

"Shut up and keep walking." On the one hand, they were definitely back in the right Otherside so if nothing else, the last path took them closer to the mall. On the other hand, there was nothing like walking through a herd of herbivores in bare feet to put a person in a really, really bad mood.

"Where did you guys find armor in a department store?"

"Sporting Goods." Will flipped his braid out from under the edge of his shoulder pads. "There's enough hockey gear in there to outfit the entire NHL."

"In June."

The elf shrugged. "End of season sale?"

"Okay. That makes as much sense as anything else around here." Sam tucked his tail carefully out of the way as more and more elves wearing hockey equipment returned to the area by the fire pit. "Now correct me if I'm wrong, which I'm not, but didn't you guys used to be twenty-first-century street kids?"

"Yeah. So?"

"So how do you even know what armor is?"

"It's all in the book, man." Reaching behind him, he pulled out a familiar orange-and-blue book.

"*The Dumb-ass Guide to Elvish Armor,*" Sam read, squinting a little in the uncertain light.

"Kris found a bunch of these in the bookstore back in the day. You know, while we were still getting stomped by the bad guys. She used *The Dumb-ass Guide to Not Getting Your Butts Kicked* to start bringing us into one group. Then, when Arthur showed up, she checked him out against *The Dumb-ass Guide to Leadership.* Lately, we've been using *The Dumb-ass Guide to Living in a Magical Freakin' Shopping Mall* as a kind of Bible."

"Really?"

"Nah, I just like saying dumb-ass. We figured out the whole living in a shopping mall thing on our own."

"What's the skateboard for?"

"Sort of our version of cavalry." He flipped the board up on end. "Makes us a lot faster than the meat-minds, more mobile. And it comes straight out of *The Dumb-ass Guide to Making the Most of the Skills You Got Handy.*"

Orange stripes folded into a "w" between Sam's ears. "Really?"

Will grinned. "Man, you are one gullible cat."

❖   ❖   ❖

"Ow! Try walking on your own feet, why don't you!"

"Sorry." Adjusting her grip on Kris' arm, Diana continued moving them as quickly as possible along the wall. As long as she didn't lose the signature of her stuff, they were fine. Well, maybe *fine* was stretching it a bit.

"I don't see how you can be so freakin' calm about this!" Kris ground out through what were clearly clenched teeth. "Fact, I don't *see*! I can't see! We got shadows from Hell coming after us—really from Hell, not just from some bad-ass place people are calling Hell—and we can't see squat because it's pitch-black down here!"

"That's one of the reasons I'm calm."

"What is?"

"Shadows are impotent in total darkness. They lose all definition, all ability to act. In order to actually do anything to us, they'll have to turn the lights back on. If I can see them, I can fight them."

"'Cause you're the most powerful Keeper in the world."

"Yeah."

The mall elf snorted. "Like I'm so impressed."

"Look, you've got every right to be scared, but don't take it out on me just because I'm the only one here."

The only sound for a few long moments: the pounding of their hearts, the whisper of their breathing, the shuffle of shoes against a stone floor, the soft hiss of fingertips against a stone wall.

"Sorry."

"It's okay. I understand."

"I still shouldn't have said it."

"I'm not arguing."

"So what's the other reason?"

"What?"

"You said that shadows what can't get it up is *one* of the reasons you're calm. What's the other reason?"

Diana worked "shadows what can't get it up" back to impotent and grinned. "Just that I've been training for this my whole life."

"This?"

"Yeah."

"Your whole life?"

"Uh-huh."

"Damn. You must've gone to one bitch of a nursery school."

"Fine. Not my *whole* life." Her right fingers ran out of wall. She braced her knee and reached around the corner. "Doorway."

Kris leaned close enough to breathe a question into her ear. "Throne room?"

"With any luck."

"Oh, yeah. And our luck has been so good."

Reaching back, Diana stroked two fingers down the other girl's cheek. "I'm not complaining."

"Man, you are one cheap date."

But she traced a smile before she took her fingers away. The silence on the other side of the doorway felt bigger, like it was filling more space. She counted thirty heartbeats, then sighed in relief. "I don't hear anything. If we follow the wall around, we'll eventually trip over the dais. Once I have my stuff, we'll make a run for the access corridors. If we can get into the Emporium, I think we'll be safe."

"You think?"

"Jack said the big boss has never come out into the store." Careful not to lose contact with the stone, she moved them through the doorway and along the wall of the room.

"Always a first time."

"Here's a thought. Why don't you say something positive?"

"Positive?"

"Yeah, like not negative." Diana rolled her eyes as the pause lengthened. Three steps. Four. Five . . .

"If memory serves, you got a wicked ass in those pants."

Ears burning, she stumbled, recovered, and mumbled "Thank you."

"So, about that training," Kris prodded, sounding much happier. "Any actual experience?"

"I was with Claire when she closed Hell down the last time, I helped integrate a demon into a small town in northern Ontario, and I . . ."

"Hawaiian pizza!"

"That wasn't me. And besides, what's wrong with . . ."

"No! I can smell Hawaiian pizza!"

All at once, so could Diana. Spinning around, she scooped Kris' feet out from under her and followed the mall elf to the floor.

Which was when the lights came on . . .

. . . and the Shadowlord smacked a large club against the wall right through the space they'd just vacated.

From her position half sprawled over Kris, Diana could see all four bugs and half a dozen meat-minds waiting motionless in front of the dais. Nearly motionless. One of the meat-minds was chewing in a decidedly guilty way.

Three guesses about what he's eating, and the first two don't count. Diana was fairly certain there were stranger things than feeling grateful to ham and pineapple in tomato sauce, but right at the moment she couldn't think of any.

Grateful wasn't even close to what the Shadowlord seemed to be feeling.

Pivoting away from the wall, he heaved his club at the chewing meat-mind and screamed, "I don't care what your union says about lunch breaks!"

"Union?" Kris asked as the gnarled wood smacked meat-mind skull and the two girls scrambled to their feet.

"Otherworld Pan-dimensional Service Employees Union."

"You're fucking kidding me."

"Yes. Run!"

"I'm glad to see you're taking me seriously."

Dean dropped the pillowcase into the washing machine. "How's that?"

"I just saw you go through Dr. Rebik's pockets."

"And how is that taking you seriously?" he asked, reaching for the laundry detergent.

Austin jumped onto the dryer, walked over, and peered into the tub. "You're looking for clues."

"I'm looking for tissues."

"To send away for forensic testing?"

"To keep from filling the washing machine with little bits of wet tissue." He closed the lid, checked that the water temperature was on cold/cold, and started the timer. "I know I'll be after regretting this, but what kind of clues did you think I'd find? If Meryat's the bad guy . . . girl . . ."

"Corpse."

Given the look he'd got at her face, that was hard to argue with. ". . . then isn't Dr. Rebik the victim?"

"So?"

"So what kind of clues would he have in his pockets?"

"An amulet controlling his free will. A note written in a moment of clear-headedness begging for rescue. And maybe he's not a victim at all; maybe he's helping her in return for a slice of the world domination pie."

"Maybe I should never have taped that *Scooby Doo* marathon for you."

"He's a dog," Austin snorted, jumping down and following Dean up the basement stairs. "He's not going to notice anything he didn't sniff off someone's butt. *I'm* telling you there was something in the bedroom last night and probably the night before!"

"Okay, let's say there was." Dean bent and lifted the cat up onto the kitchen counter, sanitary issues losing out over the inconvenience of holding a conversation with someone six feet closer to the floor. "But just because you sensed something, that doesn't mean it was Meryat. It's not like this place hasn't had *visitors* before. Ghosts, imps," he added when Austin merely scowled at him.

"I knew what you meant; I just think you're an idiot." Sitting down, he swept his tail regally around in front of his paws. "I talked to the mice."

After a moment spent trying to match up the end of that declaration to the beginning, Dean surrendered. "Okay."

"The mice," Austin told him in a tone that suggested *idiot* was actually a little high on the scale, "said that the dead mouse I found in room two was just a kid; six months old, prime of his little rodent life."

"And?"

"Oh, for the love of kibble, would you at least try to connect the dots!" Leaping to his feet, he paced to the end of the counter and back again, his tail covering twice the horizontal distance. "That mouse had his life sucked out right next to the mummy!"

"So you're saying that sucking the life out of that mouse gave

Meryat—who can barely walk at the best of times—enough energy to get downstairs and then back upstairs again moving so fast that you couldn't see her? Some mouse."

"You're forgetting her visit to you. The mouse only had to get her downstairs."

"And you don't think I'd notice if a reanimated Egyptian mummy was su . . ." Cheeks flushed, he suddenly decided there'd been a little too much use of the verb *to suck* in recent conversations. ". . . absorbing my energy?"

"You spent six months not noticing a hole to Hell," Austin muttered, "I'm not sure you'd notice if a reanimated Egyptian mummy was doing the Macarena."

"Hey! I'd notice. Nobody does the Macarena anymore."

"Oh, give her a break! She's been dead for three thousand years, it takes a while to catch up."

"If we're talking three thousand years," Dean snapped, "she'd be doing the hustle!"

The silence that followed was so complete, the distant sound of skateboarders in a neighbor's pool came clearly though the open dining room windows.

"Dude, what's with the water?"

After another long moment during which it became clear that neither skateboards nor skateboarders could float, Dean managed to find his voice.

"Did I just make a disco reference?"

Austin nodded.

"Lord t'underin' Jesus."

Austin nodded again. "If that's not a sign there's evil energies about, I don't know what is."

"Granted. But that still doesn't mean it's Meryat."

"Why are you so resistant to the obvious?"

"Maybe I just like the thought of people being in love without any sucking going on!"

Oh, yeah. Definitely too much use of the verb *to suck*. He kind of wished he'd remembered that.

But all Austin said was, "I wish Claire was here."

ELEVEN

— ·— ◆ —· —

CLAIRE CLOSED HER FINGERS just a little too tightly around Lance's arm. They were standing at one end of a massive hall—although massive didn't really do the place justice—on a pair of circles made of the only red tiles visible in a blue-and-gold mosaic floor. Just to be on the safe side, she looked up and breathed a sigh of relief. So far, no falling anvils. Behind them was a set of what looked like fifty-foot-high, solid gold doors. In front of them, a double line of huge pillars disappeared into the darkness above. If they were supporting a roof, Claire couldn't see it. The walls behind the pillars appeared to be covered in tiny black dots although, given how far away they were, it was entirely possible they were covered in huge black dots. Light levels were comfortably bright in spite of no visible light source—which was hardly surprising as ambient light was the one thing pretty much every reality took a crack at. If she'd been in one cave with phosphorescent fungus, she'd been in fifty.

"So. Where are we?" she asked, a little surprised by how calm she sounded. They were no longer on the Otherside—either Otherside—that much and that much alone she was sure of. Well, that and how much she'd like to kick Lance.

"I don't know!"

Not exactly a surprise.

"What were you thinking when we went through the door?" Maybe calm wasn't exactly the right word. *Tight* was closer.

"That if I didn't get it right this time, you were going to give me hell."

"This isn't Hell."

"How can you be so sure?" Lance demanded, turning to stare down at her with wide eyes.

"It's my job to be sure."

"Of Hell?"

"Of what isn't Hell." While he was thinking about that, she turned to face the doors. Doors were doors. Fifty feet high and solid gold, two feet high at the end of a rabbit hole—it didn't matter. If she could get them open and fit through over the threshold, she could use them. In this particular instance, getting them open might be tricky since the doorknobs were a good twenty feet above her head.

A quick glance around determined the area was unfortunately empty of a small table holding a bottle and a note that said, *Drink me*.

"Incoming!"

Does he have to sound so cheerful about it? Claire turned again and watched as two figures approached from the far end of the hall. Of course, since she couldn't see the far end of the hall that was an assumption only. Wherever they'd come from, they were moving fast.

Very fast.

Impossibly fast.

One moment they were barely visible in the distance. The next, they were standing barely two meters away.

On the left stood a cat-headed woman, barely covered from neck to ankles in a sheer linen shift. Her fur was pale brown with darker fur outlining golden eyes, lighter fur around the mouth, and two large pointed ears; both pierced, with a small gold ring in each.

On the right, a jackal-headed man, naked to the waist, wearing a pleated linen skirt held in place by a wide leather belt. Two small metal disks, stamped with hieroglyphs, hung from the front of the belt.

Do not go there, Claire warned herself. *It doesn't matter what it looks like, just do not go there.*

"I know where we are," Lance offered helpfully.

"So do I." When PhD candidates in Egyptology thought about Hell, they didn't think about Dante. Granted, neither did Keepers, but that was mostly because they preferred not thinking about hell at all and they sure as . . . heck . . . had no intention of handing it helpful definitions.

"They aren't dead," Anubis growled.

Bast shot him a disdainful golden glare. "And once again I marvel at your grasp of the obvious."

"If they aren't dead, why are they here?"

"Since they aren't dead, why don't we ask *them*? Or maybe you could fill in the details with a little butt sniffing."

His eyes narrowed. "It doesn't work that way."

Claire bit her lip to keep from laughing. Apparently jackals were just as clueless about sarcasm as dogs. She'd seen Austin reduce Rottweilers to twitching bundles of confusion with only a few barbed comments about their bathroom habits. Of course, the chances were good Anubis didn't drink out of the toilet.

As though thoughts of Austin had pulled her attention, Bast turned the full force of her golden gaze on Claire. "You're a Keeper, but this isn't one of the realities you Keep. Why are you here?"

Lesson number one in dealing with gods: don't lie to them. "I'm trying to return to a *situation* on the Otherside, but circumstances have landed me with a Bystander and his thoughts keep turning the paths."

And the corollary to lesson one: keep it simple.

The cat goddess glanced over at Lance. "He holds his thoughts strongly?"

"Oh, yeah. Once he gets something into his head you can't shift it."

And right on cue:

"*I* know why we're here. This is Meryat's work! She's trying to stop me from stopping her by sending me to the Hall of Osiris!"

"Lance . . ."

"No! It all makes perfect sense!" He gripped her shoulder with one hand and waved the other around the Hall. "She's trying to cheat the afterlife by sending me . . . us . . . in her place."

"When the ka is strong enough . . ." Bast began.

"This ka has been bound between life and death for three thousand years," Lance interrupted. He ignored Claire's elbow in his ribs—interrupting gods was never a smart action in her experience—and continued. "As soon as it was freed, it sucked the life out of Dr. Rebik."

Anubis shrugged. "It happens."

"It does?"

"Sure. Not as much as it used to, though."

"But that's not what happened this time," Claire insisted. "I don't know about Dr. Rebik and the life-sucking part . . ." Although, given that Meryat was staying at the guest house, she really hoped Dean was right and Lance's lunatic theories were just that. Lunatic. She *had* to get back to the mall and Diana, so she'd have to trust Austin to keep Dean safe. ". . . but I do know exactly why we're here." She pointed at Lance. "Bystander. Path. Idiot."

Bast nodded, gold ring swinging as she flicked her ear. "I believe you. After three thousand years, this Meryat would have to absorb a truly powerful ka, the ka of a Keeper, say, in order to have enough strength to rip the veil between the world of the living and the world of the dead."

The pieces began to fall together. If Meryat would be that strong after absorbing the ka of a Keeper . . . "She's waiting for me to return to the guest house. Dean's safe enough until I get back, and then she'll take him in order to take me."

"I can stop her."

Claire turned to glare at Lance. "You're not there. And unless you get a grip on your thought processes, you may never be there!"

"That's not our concern," Bast pointed out a little sharply.

Right. Don't ignore the cat goddess . . .

"No, it's not your concern, and I apologize for taking up your time. If you can point us to a door, we'll be on our way."

Anubis pointed over Claire's shoulder.

Right. "A smaller door?"

"That's the only door in the Hall of Osiris and only Osiris himself can open it. If you were dead, we'd take you before Osiris to be judged, but since you're not dead . . ." His muzzle wrinkled as he tried to work it out.

Bast sighed. "Dead or alive, it doesn't matter; in order to leave the Hall, they have to be taken before Osiris."

"But we're only supposed to escort the dead. We could kill them," he added, looking hopeful. At least Claire thought it was hopeful; she wasn't too good at reading jackal physiognomy.

"Or we could just escort them to Osiris and let him work it out."

"I'd be honored to meet the Lord Osiris!" Lance declared, striding half a dozen quick steps forward and five back. "He'd appreciate my plan for dealing with Meryat! I could show him my thesis! No, wait." He bounced up and down on the balls of his feet. "I don't have my thesis with me!"

"Does he exclaim everything he says?" Bast asked Claire her ears slightly saddled.

"Pretty much."

"We could just kill *him* if you like. No bother."

Without Lance, the next door would take her back to the mall. The door after that, back to Dean. "Thank you for the offer." And she meant that sincerely. "It's tempting, but Lance knows how to deal with Meryat and besides—that whole Keeper thing—I'm not allowed to have even the most irritating Bystander put down."

"Pity."

"Sometimes."

It was a long walk to the other end of the Hall. The tiles were cool underfoot and it would have been a pleasant journey but for the heavy scent of embalming spices in the air and the sound of distant lamentation that started up the moment they'd both left the squares of red tile. At that, the lamentations were preferable to Lance's running commentary on the Egyptian afterlife.

When Bast's ears flattened against her skull, Claire grabbed Lance by his much less indicative ear and yanked his head down beside hers. "I've come to realize that telling you to shut up doesn't work, so instead I want you to remember everything you've ever heard about the dangers of pissing off gods." Not to mention cats. "Remember that the gods are invariably described as cruel and capricious and remember that everything you've ever learned about them is true."

"But a lot of the information contradicts . . ."

"Doesn't matter."

"But . . ."

"It's *all* true."

"Even . . ."

"*All* of it."

He straightened rubbing his ear. "So you're saying I should shut up?"

"Yes."

"Okay."

For a while, Lance and Anubis walked on ahead, circled around, walked with them for a few paces, walked on ahead, and Claire finally realized what Lance reminded her of. A half-grown, golden retriever puppy.

"His heart's in the right place," Bast murmured.

Claire waited.

The cat goddess didn't disappoint.

"That'll make it a lot easier to remove."

About the time they began to see their destination at the far end of the Hall—although it was still little more than a big golden wall with some smaller unidentifiable things in front of it—Lance returned to walk by her side, allowing the two gods to lead them the rest of the way into Osiris' presence.

"When we arrive," Bast announced as it became obvious that one of the distant objects was a huge throne, "I'll do the talking."

Anubis turned his head far enough for Claire to see a flash of teeth. "Why?"

"Because you've been known to leave out important bits of information about the deceased, and it would be unfortunate if that happened this time."

"Unfortunate?"

"Very."

"Why? Dead's dead."

"These two are alive."

"Oh, yeah . . ."

"They're not how I imagined gods," Lance said almost quietly.

Claire shrugged. She didn't want to get into it.

"I mean, they look like gods," Lance continued, clearly not picking up the subtext, "but they don't sound like gods. First of all, they use contractions."

That was unexpected enough to get Claire's attention. "What?"

"Contractions. You know; don't instead of do not. Or we're instead of we are. Or . . ."

"I know what a contraction is."

"They use them."

"So?"

He exhaled explosively. "So who ever heard of a god using contractions? It just isn't godlike."

Claire'd heard of gods who took their own names in vain three words out of seven, but she decided not to mention that to Lance. "What's second?" When he looked confused—well, more confused than usual—she expanded the question. "You said *'first of all,'* so there must be at least a second."

"Right!"

And the exclamations were back.

"It's the two of them, the way they interact. They're like *Ruff and Ready!*"

"Who?"

"You know; the cartoon!" Waving his hands from side to side, sketching out the beat, Lance sang, "They're Ruff and Ready. Always Ruff and Ready. They sometimes have their little spats, even fight like d . . ."

Up onto her toes, she got her hand over his mouth just in time. Anubis was showing rather a lot of teeth, and Bast's ears were flat against her skull while the triangle of fur that touched the top of her spine had lifted. Lesson . . . actually, Claire'd lost track at this point, but it had to be around lesson seven or eight in dealing with gods. Do not *ever* compare them to cartoon animals.

"Please . . ." No power, just a heartfelt plea. ". . . ignore him. He's just a Bystander."

"He is . . ."

". . . annoying." Anubis finished, the word emerging as one, long growl.

"I know. But we'll be gone soon and—gross!" She snatched her hand away and wiped it on her skirt. "You licked me!"

Lance grinned down at her. "It worked."

"How'd she taste?"

Bast and Claire turned as one toward the jackal-headed god.

"How did she taste?" Bast demanded.

Anubis shrugged. "I'm just curious."

"Pretty good," Lance allowed thoughtfully. "A little salty."

His muzzle wrinkled as Anubis took a step toward her, and Claire was ninety percent sure she was about to be licked again. *Oh that's just great. I am so not a dog person.*

Bast's hand on his arm yanked him to a halt. "The Lord Osiris is waiting."

Sure enough, there was now a figure sitting on the distant throne.

Sighing deeply, Anubis began walking again. "You never let me have any fun."

"Oh, yeah? Who throws all those damned balls for you?"

Instead of growing larger, the throne grew smaller as they approached until it, and the male figure sitting upon it, were only slightly bigger than the human norm. Osiris wore a pleated linen skirt similar to Anubis' but with a cloth-of-gold overskirt. Gold sandals laced up around muscular calves, and a huge gold-and-obsidian collar rested on broad shoulders over impressive pecs. In spite of the traditional stick-on beard, the god of the underworld was a piece, no question about it, although Claire was fairly sure she'd seen the same outfit while closing an accident site at the Pyramid Club in Las Vegas.

Before either of their guides could speak, Lance pulled his PDA from its belt pouch, hit a quick sequence of keys, and read, in what Claire assumed was ancient Egyptian, "Praise be unto thee, O Osiris, lord of eternity, Un-nefer, Heru-Khuti, whose forms are manifold and whose attributes are majestic. It's a hymn to Osiris from the Book of the Dead," he added, sotto voce in English. "I've got the whole thing in here! Had to get extra memory! It goes on for a bit."

"I think you hit the high points."

"You understood that?"

"It's a Keeper thing." One golden-shod foot had begun to tap. "I'll explain later. Why don't we let Bast speak now?"

"Why do you need *me*?" Bast wondered pointedly. "You seem to be doing so *well* on your *own*."

Seventeen years with Austin had given Claire seventeen years of practice groveling, and a cat goddess was by no means as picky an audience as an actual cat—particularly one who'd accidentally been shut outside in the rain. Austin had made her pay, and pay, and pay for days, but by the time Bast turned to Osiris, she was almost purring.

Claire tuned out the story of their arrival in the Hall and worried about Dean instead. It was her fault he was in danger, her fault he might get his life sucked out by a reanimated Egyptian mummy. Women who went away on business and only worried about the man they left behind compulsively gambling away their savings or getting involved with the floozy at the coffee shop had no idea how good they had it. At least they had better-than-average odds that the man they loved wouldn't end up as bait in a deadly plot that involved power sucking and world domination. Well, better than average odds everywhere but New York and LA.

"It has been a long time since the living came to my Hall," Osiris said thoughtfully as Bast finished. His voice reminded Claire of that velvet glove/iron fist combination and while he was speaking, she couldn't take her eyes off him. "You are not on the Otherside, Keeper. You could reach into the possibilities here. Why haven't you?"

"This is your domain, Lord Osiris. To breach your parameters would be at best very stupid and at worst, incredibly rude."

He frowned. "Don't you mean that the other way around?"

"No. It's a Canadian thing," she added when he continued to look confused. "Lord Osiris, all we want to do is to leave. I'm in the middle of trying to stop a shopping mall from taking over the world, and Lance here . . ."

"Isis embraceth thee in peace and she driveth away the fiends from the mouth of thy paths."

"Not now, Lance."

"If not now, when?" he asked.

Clarie admitted he had a point. Unfortunately, she had no idea how long they'd been traveling as her watch had stopped working between the beach and the hippos and she couldn't risk squandering the time. "Probably never. Sorry. Lord Osiris, if you could point us toward a door . . ."

"Unfortunately, there is only one door out of my Hall and to go through it, you must be judged."

"But we're not dead."

"I would so have remembered to tell him that," Anubis muttered.

"Living or dead, it doesn't matter," Osiris pointed out. "Judgment is the only way out. One at a time, your hearts will be weighed against a single feather. If your heart is lighter than the feather, you will be declared *maa kheru* and the door will be opened. If it is heavier, then you stand condemned and will be devoured . . ." He gestured toward a triangle of deep shadow to the left of his throne. ". . . by the Eater of the Dead."

"But we're not dead," Claire repeated, enunciating carefully.

NOT A PROBLEM. I'LL FIGURE SOMETHING OUT.

"Claire?" Lance grabbed her shoulder and shook her hard enough to rattle her teeth. "Your mouth is open."

She closed it. Opened it. Closed it again. "What are you doing here?" she demanded at last.

DARKNESS. CONDEMNED SOULS. I GET AROUND. Obviously."

I KNOW SOMETHING YOU DON'T.

Claire snorted. Only a rookie would fall for that.

IT'S ABOUT YOUR LITTLE SISTER.

Her toes were at the edge of the shadow before she was even aware of moving. "You stay away from my sister!"

OH, I'M SO SCARED. MAKE ME.

About to reach into the possibilities, Osiris' voice snapped her back into reason. "You two know each other?"

"We've met." Walking carefully, deliberately, back to Lance's side, Claire turned on one bare heel and glared at the shadow. "Last couple of times it happened, I kicked metaphorical ass."

YOU KNOW WHAT THEY SAY, THIRD TIME LUCKY.

"Really? You know what else they say?" She folded the fingers of her right hand into an "L" and tapped it against her forehead. "Loser. Loser. Loser."

"Keeper!" The Lord of Judgment's voice had picked a tone somewhere between Darth Vader and her mother. "Stop taunting the Eater of the Dead."

"Sorry."

YOU WILL BE.

"And that's enough out of you as well." Osiris stepped down off the throne, his size changing from gigantic to merely tall. "Anubis, bring out the scales."

Claire didn't exactly catch where Anubis brought the scales out from. It appeared between one heartbeat and the next, the onyx center post exactly as tall as Osiris, the onyx arms, the same measure. Shallow golden bowls hung at the end of golden chains.

"Thou turnest thy face upon Amentet and thou makest the earth to shine as with refined copper."

"Lance, what are you doing?"

He lifted his eyes from the small screen. "Sucking up!"

This had to be the most sensible thing he'd said since the beach. "Carry on."

"Those who have lain down, rise up to see thee, they breathe the air and they look upon girls, girls, girls. You wanna see girls? We got the best at www.ohmama.com. Wait a minute, that last bit's something else I downloaded!"

"I guessed."

"How'd it get into this file?"

"Shut up, Lance."

"But I have more!"

It was always hard to tell with anthropomorphic personifications of gods, but the expression on Osiris' face was making Claire just a little nervous. "No, really, Lance, shut up."

Maybe she'd finally reached the magic number. Maybe he was trying for a satellite uplink. Whatever the reason, he actually stopped talking.

"Bast. The feather."

Bast pulled a white feather from the air and laid it in one of the shallow bowls.

"This feather is from the Sacred Ibis." Osiris shot Bast a look as he spoke. Claire knew that look although the accompanying dialogue had gone *This feather is from Mrs. Griffon's canary!* "Who will go first to judgment?"

"I will!"

When Osiris turned his dark gaze on her, Claire realized she must have made some small sound of protest. But did it really matter which of them went first? This wasn't something she could protect a Bystander from and, who knew, maybe enthusiasm would count for something. Still . . . "If he passes and I don't, do I have your word you'll send him home? To *his* home," she added hastily. Rule whatever—be specific.

"You have my word," Osiris answered solemnly.

"Good enough."

Anubis beckoned Lance forward.

"This is amazing! I mean you can read about this sort of thing and study it, but to actually be a part of . . ."

The jackal-headed god's hand sank into Lance's chest and emerged clutching his beating heart.

". . . ow! You know, I thought this would be a little more meta-phorical!"

Osiris shrugged. "I weigh your heart against a feather. Seems fairly straightforward to me. Anubis . . ."

Lance's heart landed in one of the shallow bowls with a moist thud as Osiris laid the feather in the other. The scales began to shift.

"Wait a minute! That's my . . ." Pale blue eyes rolled up so only the whites showed.

Claire danced back as Lance hit the floor. "You know, up until now, he'd been taking this whole experience annoyingly well."

"He's not the first fainter we've had," Osiris said matter-of-factly as he watched the bowl holding Lance's heart begin to rise. "He'll be fine once he gets his heart back. I'm getting the impression he doesn't worry about much," he added as the feather continued to drop. "He treats his life as a series of grand adventures; this one merely a little more grand than usual. Besides, I can feel a place where his ka was brushed by a dark ka. As long as that shadow remains, he'll be . . ."

"Distracted?"

"Focused."

Well, that explained the Meryat obsession. "Does the shadow affect . . ." She waved a hand toward the scales . . .

. . . which had stilled with Lance's heart holding steady a good six inches above the feather.

"Not in the least. I judge this man to be *maa kheru*. He is free to go. Anubis."

Anubis, who'd been licking his fingers, leaped forward, retrieved Lance's heart, squatted down, and pushed it carefully back into his body.

"Bast . . ."

Caught between bracing herself and trying to relax, Claire missed Bast's hand plunging into her chest, but she certainly felt it coming out. Ow! was a bit of an understatement. The cat-headed goddess frowned slightly as she crossed to the scale and Claire began to have a bad feeling about how this was going to turn out.

Of course her heart was heavy. She was a Keeper. She was responsible for the metaphysical protection of a good chunk of southeastern Ontario and upstate New York. And then there was the guest house and Diana, and being away from the segue, and dragging Lance around the Otherworlds, and not even knowing there were Other-*worlds* until she found herself plunged into the middle of them. Or maybe it. And she'd left Dean alone to face a reanimated mummy. Sure, Austin was with him, but he wasn't supposed to be, and what had she been thinking dragging a seventeen-year-old cat into an evil shopping mall anyway?

"Well. This is . . . interesting." All three gods were staring at the scales. The bowl holding the feather was brushing the floor. The bowl holding her heart was an arm's length above Osiris' head.

"Is this happening because I'm a Keeper?" Claire hazarded.

"No. This is happening because this isn't your heart."

She glanced down at her chest and up at the bowl. "Pardon?"

"It appears you have given your heart to another. This heart is his."

Dean stared down into Claire's face for a long moment before his mouth finally curved into a worried smile. "Got my heart?"

She laid a hand lightly against her chest. "Right here. Got mine."

He mirrored the motion. "Safe and sound."

"A most unusual young man."

He'd lived next to a hole to Hell for six months and it hadn't even convinced him to drop his underwear on the floor.

"He is, yes."

The Lord of Death dragged Dean's heart down to where Bast could reach it. "You realize you're getting off on a technicality."

"Yes, I do." The return was painless. It was a pity Lance was still out; Claire had a feeling things couldn't get much more metaphorical than this.

HEY! THIS ISN'T FAIR!

Osiris shot an exasperated look toward the shadow. "Death seldom is."

SHE CHEATED!

"No one cheats death in the end."

WHAT, I'M SUPPOSED TO EAT PLATITUDES NOW?

"If you like."

And you can choke on them, Claire thought as Lance's eyelids started to flutter. Dropping to one knee beside him, she shook his shoulder. "Come on, big guy. We're leaving."

"Going home?"

"Not right away. I've got some shopping to do first."

"I like shopping."

"Great. Hold that thought."

It took Anubis and Bast helping to get him to his feet. He swayed slightly and blinked at Anubis. "Hey, who's a good OW!"

Violence against Bystanders was permitted only in circumstances where it saved said Bystander, or Bystanders, from a greater violence. Claire figured calling Anubis a "good doggie" was definitely in the greater violence category.

"You pinched me!"

"Yes, I did."

"Okay, then. How did we do?" he asked, rubbing one cheek.

"Neither of you were found wanting," Osiris answered. He stepped forward, and Claire wasn't surprised to find the three of them suddenly standing in front of the huge golden doors. Only now the doors were a standard height.

"Hey! We grew!"

Okay. That worked, too.

"Dr. Rebik?" The cleaned and ironed chinos hanging over his arm, Dean knocked on the door to room two. "Dr. Rebik, your pants are ready."

"Maybe they're having a nooner."

Dean turned to stare at Austin in disbelief.

The cat shrugged. "Why not? They're young and in love . . . oh, wait, my mistake, he's having his life sucked out and she's a reanimated corpse."

"And it's twenty after ten." He knocked again.

"I find it disturbing that you're more concerned with the time than the corpse."

"I find it disturbing that you know what a nooner is." About to knock a third time, he lowered his hand as the door opened and Dr. Rebik slipped out into the hall. Dean caught a quick glimpse of Meryat lying on the bed, wrapped arms crossed over her breast, then Dr. Rebik pulled the door closed.

One hand clutching the waistband of a pair of borrowed sweatpants, he stared up at Dean through bloodshot eyes as if unsure of who he was speaking to. "Yes?"

Dean held out the chinos.

"Ah. Yes." Comprehension dawned slowly. "You were washing them for me." His hand trembled slightly as he reclaimed his clothing.

"You all right, Dr. Rebik? You're looking some poorly."

"Some poorly?" The archaeologist managed a tired smile. "It's the waiting. It's hard on Meryat."

"Looks like it's hard on you."

"We are as one in this."

"Okay. Sure." Frowning slightly, Dean watched as Dr. Rebik slipped back into his room. Meryat hadn't moved. If he didn't know better, he'd have to say she looked dead. As he stepped away from the door, he noticed a worn, brown leather wallet lying on the floor.

The way those sweatpants had been sagging, it had probably fallen from a pocket.

Dean bent, scooped it up, and lifted his hand to knock again.

Austin cleared his throat.

Don't look at the cat. Just give it back.

As subtlety didn't seem to be working, Austin sank a claw into Dean's ankle just above his work boot.

"Son of . . ." He danced down the hall, collapsing against the wall by room one. "What'd you do that for, then?"

"Aren't you the least bit curious?"

"About what? Tetanus?"

"About what's in his wallet."

"An amulet controlling his will? A note asking us to save him?"

Austin speared him with a pointed gaze. "You didn't used to be this sarcastic."

"I didn't used to live with you!"

"Maybe he dropped it on purpose, did you think of that? Maybe it's a cry for help."

"You're reaching."

"You're opening it."

And he was. He didn't know what he expected to find, but he found he couldn't give the wallet back unexamined. It *had* fallen some conveniently. "I can't believe I'm after doing this."

"I can't believe it's taking you so long."

Credit cards. Health card. Driver's license . . . His eyes widened. If forced to guess, he'd have said Dr. Rebik was in his mid to late sixties.

According to his driver's license, he was thirty-eight.

And he looked worse than his picture.

"I was right."

"I know."

"You were wrong."

"Yeah. I got that."

"There's a song, you know. When I'm right and you're wrong."

Dean stopped pacing long enough to glare at the cat. "Don't sing it."

Austin sat down on the dining room table, stuck a foot in the air, and began washing his butt.

"Very subtle." The dining room was exactly fourteen paces long. Provided he shortened the last step. "What do we do now?"

"You mean now that you admit I'm right?"

"Yes!"

"Well, we have to stop her. She's sucking your life force out and what's to say she won't get tired of waiting for Claire and start sucking harder."

"Lance said he knew how to stop her."

"Which would be relevant if Lance wasn't off with Claire."

"Can we use the elevator on her?"

Austin sat up and shook his head. "It's a little obvious. I suspect she'd sense it. What are you doing?"

Dean paused in the middle of crumpling up a sheet of newspaper. "I'm going to clean the windows. It's what I do when I need to think."

The two huge windows in the dining room were already spotless, but he sprayed them with a vinegar-and-water solution and began to rub.

"That's a very annoying noise."

"Sorry."

"You're not going to stop, are you?"

"No."

When the paper was wet, he tossed it into the garbage and reached for another sheet. As he pulled it off the early edition, Austin's paw snaked out and smacked it back down.

"There's our answer!"

Dean scanned the headlines and frowned. "The waterfront renewal project?"

"No. The life-sized stone statue found at the mall!"

"*The* mall?"

"The very one! And you know what a life-sized stone statue means."

"Bad garden art?"

"Basilisk! We go to the mall. We capture it. We turn Meryat to stone!"

"Claire . . ."

"You want Claire coming home to find Meryat waiting for her."

No. He didn't. "How do we capture a basilisk without turning to stone ourselves?

Austin stared up at him in disbelief. "Do I have to think of *everything?*"

TWELVE

WHILE KEEPERS SPENT pretty much their entire lives fighting to keep the world safe, they didn't usually get involved in *actual* fighting of the hand-to-hand, teeth-to-arm, knees-to-groin variety. And no matter how many Saturday afternoons got wasted watching badly dubbed kung fu movies, it didn't help.

Diana realized this about ten seconds into the fight. She couldn't reach the possibilities, she'd lost her prepared defenses, and she had no idea how to disable her opponents with a shopping cart. Not that there was a shopping cart handy.

Running, while the intelligent response, had got them exactly seven paces closer to the throne before two of the giant bugs—moving in that creepy, skittery, *fast* way that giant bugs had laid claim to since the old black-and-white movie days—had cut them off. Diving out of the way of a flailing forearm, or foreleg, or sixleg or whatever it was called on a bug, Diana smacked her head against the floor and, just for an instant, heard the voice of Ms. McBride, her last biology teacher.

"*. . . size to mass ratio . . .*"

Yeah. That was helpful.

Fortunately, her belief that the meat-minds were too clumsy to simultaneously walk and breathe made them an avoidable threat for the most part. The bugs were the problem. Just as the bugs had been the problem in the access corridor.

"*Diana, are you listening?*"

Apparently not.

She caught a quick glimpse of Kris going up and over a meat-mind, her black hightops digging into knees, thighs, hips, chest, and shoulders like they were part of her own personal jungle gym. As the mall elf leaped clear, the pursuing bug knocked the meat-mind ass over tip and got itself tangled in the sudden barricade of flailing arms and legs. Diana wasted a moment imagining what Kris could do with a shopping cart, then, at the last possible instant, dropped flat and slid under a descending carapace.

And let's hear it for polished marble floors! she noted as her slide put her considerably closer to the wand. She could see it, lying all pink and plastic on the steps of the throne, but she couldn't . . . quite . . . reach . . .

The bug's leg caught her a glancing blow, skidding her a couple of meters in the wrong direction.

"This will *be on the final exam."*

What will?

She'd written her final biology exam only ten days ago. *You'd think I'd remember more of it.* Which was either a scathing indictment of the public school system, or she should start worrying about her short-term memory.

Curved, swordlike mandibles cut through the back of her sweater and hoisted her onto her feet.

Mandibles. Maxillae. Labium or lower lip.

Her final exam'd had an entire section on bugs. Class Insecta. A useless spewing of information she assumed she'd never need again—her present situation having been unanticipated at the time. Evidently, a little shortsighted of her.

Insects. Nearly a million known species.

Every kind of land environment supports a flourishing insect population.

"So, Ms. McBride, if bugs are so great, how come they aren't taking over the world like in them old movies?"

Diana smiled and mentally thanked Daryl Mills. The bug holding her shuddered as its exoskeleton cracked in a dozen places with a sound like cheap wineglasses hitting a concrete floor. She jumped clear as it collapsed under its own weight. Most of a sperm whale's weight was supported by water. Elephants had evolved massive bones and muscles to deal with their bulk. Size/mass ratio.

Giant bugs were impossible.

So there.

The sound of breaking glass filled the throne room and pieces of chitin buzzed around like shrapnel. The Shadowlord shrieked like a hockey mom after a bad call.

Three steps and she'd be at the dais. Up two stairs and she'd have the wand. One moment after that, it would all be over but the fat lady singing. Whatever that meant.

Three steps and . . .

Something caught her between the shoulder blades and she went down, hard.

Epicuticle, she thought muzzily as it bounced and landed about two centimeters from her nose. *This isn't* . . .

A booted foot pressed hard against the back of her neck.

. . . good.

She swung out as a hand in her hair dragged her up onto her knees but only succeeded in overbalancing and nearly scalping herself. Blinking away memories of grade school ponytails so tight she looked like Mr. Spock's kid sister, Diana screamed "RUN!" over the Shadowlord's ultimatum that Kris surrender.

"What did you listen to him for?" she demanded a moment later as two meat-minds dropped Kris beside her.

The mall elf got shakily to her knees. "Like I was going to leave you here alone?"

How romantic. *Well, since you asked, not very.* "You could have gone for help!"

"As if. It's wall to friggin' wall of meat-minds out there. Couldn't get past them."

Okay. Even less romantic.

"So I remembered something I was told, way back," Kris continued. "If you're going to lose anyway, surrender *before* they kick your ass—not after."

"Arthur?"

"My mom."

"Smart lady."

"That time."

"Are you two finished catching up?" the Shadowlord snarled.

"So, 'rents still together?" Diana asked, shuffling around so that she was facing the other girl.

The mall elf stared at her for a moment, then disbelief disappeared behind a gleeful smile as she caught on. When it seems like there's no options left, there's *always* the option of being a pain in the ass. "Nah, my dad split about six years ago. I'm guessin' you've got the whole happy suburban family thing going down?"

"Oh, yeah. We're a walking, talking WASP cliché except for that whole Keeper, Cousin, cat thing."

"Silence!" At some point the Shadowlord had retrieved his club, and he was stroking it as he loomed over them.

"You know if you think that looks threatening . . ." Diana nodded toward the club. ". . . you're so wrong. It's screaming, 'hey, girls, look at my big substitute . . .'"

She'd been a little worried she might provoke him into actually using the club, but, fortunately, he went with the personal touch. The backhand lifted her off her knees and threw her back over the steps of the dais. Moving around to face Kris had placed her at exactly the right angle—no brainer to figure he'd lash out—and she grabbed the wand as she sprawled over it, stuffing it down into the front of her pants.

Diana'd seen the same stunt on a television show once. On a seventeen-inch screen it hadn't looked as painful as it really was. Bells and whistles were still going off inside her skull as a pair of meat-minds hauled her onto her feet and dragged her back before the Shadowlord.

"Foolish little girl. I should kill you where you stand."

"Not actually standing here . . . Ow!" The dangling she could cope with, but the shaking was a bit over the top. "Besides, you can't kill me or you'd have already done it. And do you know why you can't kill me?" For the same reason she hadn't used the wand the moment her fingers closed around it. "Because you're not the Big Bad." She was not wasting their one chance on a flunky. "Killing me would release all sorts of energy down here. Energy you can't control. That's why you didn't kill me . . . us," she corrected, glancing over at Kris. ". . . before. That's why you can't kill me now."

"I can't, but that from where I came, can."

Diana blinked. Even her eyelashes hurt. "What?"

"I speak of the Pit. The Darkness. The . . ."

"Yeah. Okay. I get it. You can't. Hell can. It may have split you off, and given you a personality—of sorts—but it still keeps you under its thumb."

"That's not . . ."

"Hey, denial; not just a river in Egypt. Face it, Hell's just using you. In fact, there really isn't a *you* at all. You don't have a name, you don't have an identity; you're just an itty-bitty part of a greater whole. Hell doesn't trust you with any *real* power." As the last words left her mouth, Diana knew she'd made a mistake. The Shadowlord had been frowning as he listened to her, clearly not liking what she had to say—possibly not liking it enough to challenge Hell and cause a distraction, allowing her to seal the hole and shut down the segue thus saving the world—but at *trust,* he smiled.

"Of course, Hell doesn't trust me," he said calmly. "Hell is me. And I am Hell."

"A little-bitty part . . ."

"Enough. Your blatant attempt to drive a wedge between me and my origin might have worked were we in the sort of fairy tale where the good guys always win, but we're . . ."

"In the subbasement of an imaginary shopping mall," Diana finished as dryly as her current position allowed. *Oh, great, I'm starting to sound like Claire.*

He stepped forward and pressed the end of his club under Diana's chin, forcing her head back. "What part of 'enough' are you having difficulty understanding?"

"Well, duh; the part where I do anything you say."

"Then perhaps you should consider this . . ." Had he been breathing, his breath would have caressed her cheek. As it was, she felt a faint frisson of fear spread out from the closest point between them, as though his proximity caused an involuntary physical reaction. ". . . I can't kill you, but I can bludgeon you senseless."

"Right. Enough; adverb. To put an end to an action." Clearly she'd been paying more attention in English than biology, and she really *really* wished he'd back away. "As in enough taunting the Shadowlord. I should stop it. I can do that."

"Good."

✿   ✿   ✿

"Is there any particular reason you asked the three-thousand-year-old, reanimated Egyptian mummy that's been sucking out your life force if there was anything we could get her while we're at the mall?"

"I was just being polite," Dean protested as he turned off Sir John A. MacDonald Boulevard and onto Highway 33.

"She's sucking out your life force," Austin repeated, enunciating each word with caustic clarity.

"And that's a reason to be rude, then?"

"Some people might think so."

"Some people might be after jumping in the harbor; that doesn't mean I'm going to do it."

"So, just out of curiosity . . ." He hooked his claws in the seat as the truck maneuvered around another corner. ". . . what would be grounds for rudeness in your book?"

Dean's brow creased above the upper edge of his glasses as he thought about it.

After a few moments, Austin sighed. "Never mind."

There'd been discussion about Austin remaining at the guest house to keep an eye on things, but in the end they'd decided it was too great a risk. Without Dean there to snack on, there was always the chance that Meryat would turn to the cat and the cat didn't have life force to spare.

"Although it's entirely possible she can't feed from me."

"Why?" Before Austin could answer, Dean had raised a hand, cutting him off. *"Because you're a cat."*

"Does there need to be another reason?"

"Is there ever another reason?"

The guest house had proven it could take care of itself.

The mall parking lot was about half full. Fully three quarters of the parked vehicles were minivans, which was disturbing mostly because Dean didn't know how disturbed he should be. Or why. Just to be on the safe side, he parked next to a white sedan with Ohio plates.

"I'd feel better about this if I could go in there with you," Austin muttered as Dean pulled an empty hockey bag out from behind the seats. "Do you remember the plan?"

"Find a spot by the food court, place the bag on its side with the zipper open, place the dish of cold Red River cereal in the bag, close the bag while the basilisk is eating, only look at it with this piece of mirror." Dean held up the sideview mirror that had broken off the truck on his first drive to Ontario a year and a half ago. The support had snapped, but the glass was fine, so he'd hung on to it. "You're sure it'll come to the cereal, then?"

"It's got to be hungry, and that stuff's close enough to chicken feed it'll never know the difference."

"I can't believe we're . . ."

". . . utilizing local resources to disable a metaphysical threat."

Dean stared at the cat.

Austin stared back.

"Well, when you put it like that," Dean said at last. He opened the door and stepped down onto the asphalt. "Try to stay out of sight. The windows are open and you've got lots of water, but I don't want some good Samaritan calling the cops on me because they think you're suffering."

"Nobody understands my pain."

"You can say that again," Dean sighed as he closed the door.

The parking lot felt soft underfoot. It wasn't the heat, even though it was hot enough to paint his T-shirt to his body, and bright enough to light it up like Signal Hill; it was as if the asphalt *itself* was rising around each boot and trying to drag him down. Not exactly what had happened to Claire and Diana the morning he'd dropped them off since they'd left visible footprints in the tar and he had no actual evidence that this was going on anywhere but in his head. No footprints. No smell of melted tar. Just a feeling. Accompanied by the certainty that things on the Otherside had gotten worse instead of better.

Things always get worse before *they get better,* he told himself and didn't find it very reassuring. He wanted to help. He couldn't help. All he could do was make sure that when Claire came home, she wouldn't be facing a life-sucking reanimated mummy. Given the condition of the parking lot, it didn't seem like enough.

He found himself walking with an exaggerated, high-stepping gait. And he wasn't the only one. Across the lot, two kids, one around three, the other no more than five, were walking the exact same way. The funny thing was, their mother—Dean assumed it was their mother although she could have been a babysitter—didn't seem to notice. Her feet were dragging with the unmistakable exhaustion of someone who'd just spent the morning with two preschoolers in a shopping mall.

Were children more open to the extraordinary?

He flushed as he realized the mother—or babysitter—was aware of his attention. Flushed darker when he realized she was staring at his . . . uh, jeans . . . and smiling in a way that was making him distinctly nervous. Picking up his pace, he made it to the concrete in time to turn and see all three of them pile into a later model station wagon.

Not a minivan.

Which was good; right?

Feeling vaguely nostalgic for the days when he knew what the hell was going on, he went into the mall.

The air-conditioning hit him like a dive into the North Atlantic, and the sweat dribbling down the sides of his neck dried so fast it left goose bumps behind. A trio of fourteen-year-old girls burst into high-pitched giggling as he stepped back and held open the door for them, the giggling punctuated by "Oh. My. God." at frequent intervals as they passed. Dean had the uncomfortable feeling they were referring to the rip in the right leg of his jeans. Maybe he shouldn't have worn them out in public, but after years of being washed and ironed, they were so thin that they were the coolest pair he owned in spite of how tightly they fit.

He'd parked by the food court entrance, having a strong suspicion that a man carrying a basilisk in a hockey bag was going to need to cover as short a distance as possible inside the mall.

By the time he reached the edge of the seating area, he remembered what he hated about these kind of places. He'd seen dead cod with more personality.

Actually, in this kind of weather, dead cod had personality to spare.

Only the fact that the forces of evil were using this mall as part of their attempt to take over the world made it any different than a hundred malls just like it. Although not a lot different.

Austin had been certain the basilisk would be hanging around the food court.

Dean studied the area carefully, walked over to the ubiquitous Chinese Take-Out, and bought an egg roll and a coffee. He couldn't just sit down at a table in the food court without food, taking up space he had no real right to; that would be rude. Tray in one hand, hockey bag in the other, he made his way through a sudden crowd of teenagers toward the more thickly filled of the two planters—the perfect basilisk hiding place.

The good news: the table closest to the planter was empty.

The bad news: either a chicken-lizard combo smelled like the shallows after one of the big boats had just flushed her bilges on a hot day or the basilisk wasn't the only thing the planter was hiding.

It certainly explained why the statue they'd found had been holding a trowel and a bucket.

He wasted a moment wondering why they'd positioned plastic plants under a skylight, then reached into his bag and took the top off the container of cooked cereal. With the open bag carefully braced between his feet, he set the mirror in his lap, and opened his coffee.

As he took his first sip, he heard his grandfather's voice, *"Fer the love of God, bai, you don't go buying coffee from a Chinese Take-Out! That's why the good laird gave us Timmy Horton's!"*

Dean put the lid back on his cardboard cup, forcing himself to swallow.

His grandfather had been a very wise man.

The egg roll probably would have tasted better if his sense of smell hadn't gone numb. On the other hand, had his sense of smell still been functioning, he wouldn't have been able to eat the egg roll, so he supposed it evened out.

How long was he supposed to be waiting, then?

"Dean McIssac? Christ on crutches, it is you!"

The young woman who dropped into the other seat had a blaze of red hair over startlingly black eyebrows and breasts that threatened to spill out over the top of her . . . Actually, Dean had no idea of what she was wearing. He remembered the breasts. When he wasn't playing hockey, dreams of those breasts had pretty much got him through his last year of high school. And occasionally when he *was* playing hockey, which was how he'd dislocated his shoulder. Unfortunately, she'd been dating the same guy since grade nine and no one else stood a chance. She'd been the perfect, safe, unattainable fantasy. "Sherri Murphy. What're you doing so far from home?"

"Working. Same as. Got a job out at the nylon plant." Sherri grinned across the table at him. "Damn, it's some good to see a familiar face. You here alone?"

"Yeah . . ."

Her grin sharpened.

Dean wondered why he'd never noticed the predatory curve to it before. No wait; he knew why. "Uh, Jeff . . ."

She shrugged, and he missed the first few words. ". . . boat with his dad. Like you can support a family fishing these days." Her gaze turned frankly speculative. "What about you?"

"Me?"

"You got a girl?"

"A girl . . . yes." Floundering without knowing how he'd gotten caught up by the surf, he clung to the thought of Claire. "She's around here somewhere." Which, if *somewhere* was stretched about as far as it could go, was the absolute truth.

Head cocked to one side, Sherri studied his face. "You know, word was, Dean McIssac couldn't lie to save his life." The tip of her tongue traced a moist line over her lower lip.

Something warm and soft brushed up against Dean's ankle, and he felt his cheeks begin to burn. "Listen, there's a, uh, bar down in Portsmouth Village, the, uh . . ." The pressure against his leg increased, moving softly up and down his calf. ". . . Ship to Shore. Bunch of us from home are there most Saturdays."

"Talking about when you're going back east?" Her voice had picked up a wistful tone.

"Yeah. That, too. The owner has a load of Black 'Arse trucked up from home about once a month."

"Beer and nostalgia, hard to resist."

The lightest touch against the inside of his knee. Dean's whole body twitched although, crammed into the seat as he was, he couldn't jump back. He was amazed she'd found enough room to maneuver under these tiny tables.

"I'm not remembering you as being this jumpy." Smiling like she knew a secret, she stood. "Saturdays, eh? Maybe I'll be stopping by, then. I'd like to meet the girl who finally got you."

More than a little confused, he watched her walk away.

Got me wha . . .

A gentle caress against his other leg.

Sherri had disappeared into the drugstore.

How did she . . . ?

Oh.

Ears on fire, he glanced down at the mirror in his lap. The chicken half of the basilisk was in his hockey bag eating Red River cereal. The lizard part, a long, prehensile, bright green scaly tail, was rubbing up and down his leg.

She must think I'm a total idiot.

Leaning forward, both hands under the table, he gently shoved the tail into the bag.

Claire could never find out about this.

A warm beak investigated his fingers. He pushed it back down toward the cereal.

Austin could never find out about this.

Holding the zipper clear of stray feathers, he quickly closed it.

The squawk was remarkably loud. Half a dozen heads turned toward him.

"Just caught my basilisk in the zipper," he explained, threw the bag over his shoulder and hurried for the door, his ears so hot he was sure they were leaving a thermal trail behind them.

Dean listened to the flat, definitive click in disbelief and then turned the key again, just in case. Another click followed by a silence so complete he could hear feathers being rearranged in the hockey bag now tucked behind the seats. "I don't believe this. The battery's dead."

"You were gone for a long time; I got bored." Austin licked his shoulder. "I was listening to the radio."

"But I have the keys, and you couldn't use a key if you had one." Click. Nothing. "How did you even turn the electrical system on?"

"It's a cat thing."

He laid his head against the steering wheel and jerked it back almost immediately as the black plastic branded the arc of its upper curve into his skin. "You're telling me cats can hot wire cars, then?"

"Don't be ridiculous," Austin snapped. "This is a truck."

"Right." Because that was all the explanation he was ever going to get. *Okay.* He got out of the truck and stared across the parking lot, watching the heated air rise up off the asphalt and shimmer like a curtain between worlds. If only it was that easy. Kevin had borrowed his jumper cables back in March and never returned them. He'd be smacking the buddy upside the head for that come Saturday, but it wasn't going to do him any good now. *A basilisk, a talking cat, and a dead battery walk into a bar . . .* Turning his back on the minivans, he banged his head against the hood of truck.

"You look like you're having a bad day. Is there something I can do to help?"

She was about his age, her name was Mary, she was up from the States for a music festival, and she had, not only a set of jumper cables, but a set long enough to reach from her battery to his. "My brother bought them for me," she told him tossing a waist-length braid back over her shoulder as she efficiently hooked the two vehicles together. "There, try it now."

The truck turned over on the first attempt. Dean hit the parking brake, put it in neutral, and got out to help Mary coil her cables.

"Is that your cat?" she asked as Austin put his paws up on the dashboard and peered out at them.

"Not exactly."

"Ah." She nodded wisely. "Your girlfriend's cat. You have the look of a man in over his head."

As she bent to put the cables in the trunk, Dean was horrified to see the hockey bag rise up from behind the seats and attempt to take flight. He gestured wildly at Austin, who made a rude gesture in return just as the bag slid forward, hit the seat, and knocked Austin's feet out from under him. On the bright side, bag and cat were out of sight by the time Mary turned. Dean thanked her in a hurry, shook her hand, yanked his feet out of the tar, and dove back into the truck.

The bag was on the floor on the passenger side. Austin was on the bag, smacking random bits of covered basilisk. "I'm getting too old for this kind of . . ." A fast right, quickly followed by a left hook, quelled an incipient uprising. ". . . shit."

"If you hadn't run down my battery, we'd be home by now!"

"Oh, so it's *my* fault you had to be rescued by a girl?"

"Yeah. It is. Your fault." He glanced up, noticed Mary frowning at him, waved, put the truck in gear, and started for home. In over his head. That pretty much summed up his life of late.

He needed Claire back in the worst way.

Sam knew he was supposed to be calm, cool, and collected—although he had no idea of just what he was supposed to collect. He knew that he, as a cat, should be an example of self-confident serenity to the horde of mall elves, armed and armored from sporting goods, who were about to go into battle against the forces of evil.

Sporting goods aside, this wasn't going to be battle by Disney.

He had a feeling that even as an angel, he'd sucked at serenity. Unfortunately, since that whole Soldier of the Lord thing would come in handy right about now, the more time he spent in fur, the less he remembered about his life BC. Before cat.

Back and forth across the top of the shelves that defined the open court around the fire pit. He couldn't stop pacing.

The unmistakable of sound of a two-fingered whistle echoed through the enclosed space, instantly silencing the babble of conversation. A dozen heads of exotic hair turned toward the sound.

"Dudes! Listen up." Red braid swinging across the broad shoulders of his hockey pads, Will nodded toward Arthur, who stood beside him on a chair pulled away from a kitchen set in home furnishings. "Our fearless leader's got something to say!"

The Immortal King looked out at the crowd, his blue eyes sweeping from face to face, refusing to be hurried. Under his black leather jacket, he was wearing an umpire's padded breastplate. In his left hand, he held a pair of heavy leather gauntlets from gardening supplies. In his right, he held Excalibur.

It was so quiet Sam could hear only the faint creak of plastic padding. It was almost as though the mall elves were holding their breath, waiting for their leader to speak.

The ringing crash of the aluminum bat bouncing loudly across the tiles spun everyone around. They watched in unison until the bat finally hissed to a stop under Kith's raised boot. Then they all looked at Sam.

He hadn't even noticed the bat before he knocked it off the shelf.

Ignoring the pounding of his heart, and pretty sure he'd just lost

the first of the alleged nine lives, he sat down and wrapped his tail
pointedly around his front paws. Given the overwhelming, all encompassing level of noise, he didn't think he could pull off the classic "I
meant to do that" expression, so he settled for the slightly less difficult
"What?" aimed directly at Arthur. Unable to help themselves, the
elves turned again, searching for what he was staring at.

Poets knew that cats looked at kings because poets were no more
immune than anyone else when it came to discovering what cats were
staring at.

Arthur sighed. "You called me here," he said after a moment, "to
make you one people. To stop the bickering that made you easy prey
for the darkside. To teach you how to hold the line against the darkside
and say, this far you shall go and no farther. This I have done. You are
one people. You act as one against the darkside. You hold the line. But
it is no longer enough. The darkside has taken one of us and one of the
Keepers who came to set us free. We cannot just hold the line while
Kris and Diana are in the hands of our enemies. It is time we take the
fight to them!"

"Fight! Fight! Fight! Fight!"

Caught up in the rhetoric, it took Sam a moment to realize why
the response made him so edgy. He'd seen much the same thing on a
grade-school playground while waiting for Diana to close an accident
site under the slide.

Tossing back his hair with one hand, lifting Excalibur above his
head with the other, Arthur yelled out, "Who is with me?"

All the hair lifted along Sam's spine and in the second between the
question and the answer, he shouted, "Wait!"

"Ow! Where are we?"

"In a refrigerator." Bent nearly double, Claire reached for the
door, hoping it was still open. "I'd have told you to duck, but I didn't
want to end up on an extended visit to Donald, Daisy, or Howard."

"So, Meryat's not in here?"

"No. Meryat's not in here." There was focused and then there was
obsessive. Lance had crossed the line some time ago. "Hands off!"

"Sorry! There's not much room!"

"Well, it's a *refrigerator*," she muttered, flicking the edge of the egg tray and trying to remember if it was on the door in this particular model. They had more than the actual room available but not by much.

"Would this be a good time to tell you that I'm a little claustrophobic?"

"No." Okay. That was the butter thingy. Had to be the door. Both hands against it, Claire pushed.

"We need to get out now."

"I'm working on . . . Hey!" Those were hands where they had no business being. Not that Lance seemed to notice as he began to throw himself against the sides of the fridge. "Careful! You're going to . . ."

Too late.

The fridge went over, the door flew open, and Claire spilled out into Large Appliances wrapped up in a panicking grad student. She slapped him purely for medicinal reasons.

Rolling free, she found herself staring up at a pair of worried amber eyes, cinnamon nose nearly touching hers. No mistaking the tuna breath. "Sam! Ow!" Half a heartbeat later, she had an armful of marmalade cat and a row of bleeding puncture marks along her collarbone. "Oh, baby-cat, you have no idea how glad I am to see *you*."

The ecstatic purring stopped. Sam squirmed free and backed up until all four feet were each applying approximately ten pounds of pressure to Claire's chest. "Baby-cat?"

"Term of endearment."

"*Baby*-cat!"

"I'm sorry. I was caught up in the moment. It will *never* happen again."

Whiskers bristling, Sam stared at her with such intensity, her eyes started to water. "See that it doesn't," he snorted at last and walked away muttering, "Baby-cat? I'd like to see what'd happen if she tried that on Austin. He'd remove her spleen . . ."

Claire smiled and sat up. It was good to be back.

"What's with the elves in hockey gear?" Lance demanded, bouncing up onto his feet, panic forgotten.

Actually, that was a good question.

White, plastic shoulder pads gleaming under the store's florescent lights, the mall elves pushed their way between the washers and dryers and surrounded the open area in front of the toppled fridge. Whatever they'd been doing, it had certainly got them worked up; Claire'd never seen them so excited. They were in constant movement, all talking at once. Half a dozen hands reached down to lift her to her feet.

"Thank you, okay, that's great, I'm fine, yes it's good to be back . . . Hey!" An elf she didn't recognize backed away, hands in the air. Sure, he *could* have just been smoothing down the back of her skirt and she *could* have just spent a couple of hours with the gods of ancient Egypt. *Oh, wait . . .*

"They're happy to see you!" Lance pointed out, accurately but unnecessarily.

"He's not Australian?" Stewart asked, shooting a disbelieving glance up at the taller blond.

"Not so that you'd notice."

"Weird." He handed over her sandals. "You left these here."

Claire thanked him, bent to slip them on, and straightened as the surrounding babble rose in volume.

Lance's fingers closed over her shoulder. "Meryat!"

She sighed. "Arthur." And stepped forward to meet the Immortal King.

He clasped her wrist in a warrior-to-warrior move Claire'd only ever seen performed in old movies. It was moderately reassuring that he hadn't changed enough from his basic parameters to greet her with a high five. "I am truly glad to see you back, Keeper."

"I'm truly glad to be back." She glanced at his chest. "Decided to have a sports day while I was gone?"

"We are armored for battle."

"Battle? The darkside is attacking?"

"No." Blue-black hair fell over his eyes as he shook his head. "We take the fight to them."

It seemed like she'd managed to find the mall just in time. "No, we don't . . ."

"Your sister, the Keeper Diana, and Kris, my captain, have been captured."

"Yes, we do. How do you know this?"

"A budgie mirror gave the news to Sam."

"Okay, then." That was just ludicrous enough to be a reliable source. She waved toward the various bits of surrounding padding. "Can I assume you were about to leave?"

"We were."

"Just let me get my stuff . . ."

"Claire?"

Right. Lance. Her own personal albatross. Except that an actual albatross would be significantly less annoying. Still . . . Bystander. Keeper. Responsible. Yadda. "Lance . . ." She reached back, got a good grip on his sleeve and dragged him forward. ". . . this is Arthur. He's in charge of the elves."

"*The* Arthur?"

"Yes."

Lance frowned. "I would have thought Oberon . . ."

"Apparently not."

"He's younger than I imagined him being."

"That's because you *didn't* imagine him." She gestured toward the kids. "They did. Arthur, this is Lance. He's a very confused grad student looking for his professor and a reanimated mummy."

Arthur stared up at the large, blond man and his pale cheeks paled further. "Lance?"

"Yes."

"Du Lac?"

"Benedict."

The Immortal King released the breath he'd been holding. "Thank God."

YOU'RE WELCOME.

THIRTEEN

"**Y**OU LOCKED SAM IN A CRATE?"

"With both you and your sister missing, I felt responsible for his safety. I asked him to give me his word that he'd remain here, in the store. He wouldn't." Arthur glanced over at Claire, his expression somewhere between concerned and defiant. "I thought I was doing the right thing."

"You were," Claire told him reassuringly. "But that's not actually relevant. If I were you, I'd check your bedding before getting into it and your shoes before putting them on."

A quiet voice murmured "Ooo, shoes . . ." from around ankle height but when Claire looked down, Sam was nowhere to seen.

"Sorry."

Arthur waved it off. "It's all right . . ."

He was lying, but she appreciated the effort.

". . . we have greater troubles now facing us than possible retribution by one annoyed cat."

And if Arthur was very lucky, Sam hadn't heard that. "So you've armed your people and are about to . . . ?"

"Meet the enemy head on, rescue your sister and my captain, and end this once and for all."

"That's the plan?"

"No, those are our objectives. How we achieve those objectives—that's the plan. Once we have drawn the enemy into battle, Teemo and Kith will take the scout's route in behind their lines and effect the rescue."

"And ending this once and for all?"

"I will be leading my people. Once I am on the darkside, I do not doubt their leader will personally try to kill me. We will meet in battle and in single combat decide the fate of this mall."

Claire stopped walking and turned to stare at Arthur. "I beg your pardon?" She could almost hear Diana asking him if his baseball equipment was cutting off the oxygen supply to his brain.

"I have been in these situations before, Keeper. This is what always happens."

"Yes, and you *lose*."

His smile was almost condescending. "There is no Mordred in this reality."

"Okay, first of all, you don't know that. We don't know who or what is pulling the strings on the darkside. That's what Diana and Kris were supposed to find out instead of getting themselves captured and possibly tortured, and it's all very well for you, but what on earth am I supposed to tell my mother if I come back without her?"

Arthur blinked, glanced back at Lance, who shrugged and finally offered, "Tell her that Diana gave her life in the service of the greater good."

"Uh-huh." Claire chewed a bit of nail polish off her right thumb. "And on a pure Keeper/Cousin level that might work but I'm talking about my little sister and my *mother*." She spat a bit of Midnight Coral out with the last word, then sighed. "I'll be going with Teemo and Kith. If Kris and Diana have been taken by the enemy, there isn't a chance of getting them back without my help."

"Then your help is gratefully accepted."

"Good." They began walking again, skirting the edge of Giftware and cutting through Leather Goods. Given what the elves considered party clothes, Claire wasn't surprised that particular section had been emptied out. "Where was I? Rhetorical question," she added quickly as Lance made an *I know, I know!* kind of noise. "The whole Mordred thing is irrelevant. You're the archetypal symbol for one side, and if you face the archetypal symbol for the other side—we can call it Big Bird if we want to, but it won't make a difference—you'll die. This is the Otherside. I am a Keeper. I believe this, so it *will* happen. If it makes you feel any better, you can blame Mrs. Saint-Germaine and grade eleven English."

"But . . ."

"No."

"If I . . ."

"No."

"It isn't . . ."

"What part of 'no' are you having trouble understanding? You *must not* face the leader of the darkside in combat." Claire ran both hands up through her hair and sighed again. "All at once, I understand exactly how Yoda felt."

"Who?"

"Not important."

Arthur looked as though he was about to protest, then clearly thought better of it. "Okay."

"I'm going to go get changed."

"Petite Sportswear is against the far right-hand wall."

"Thank you. Lance . . ." A half turn to find him smiling down at her. She had a sudden vision of him let loose in the mall and shuddered. ". . . you'd better stay with me."

"Sure! Hang on a minute!"

Since she didn't have a hope of moving him, she folded her arms and waited as he stepped forward, his pale blue eyes locking onto Arthur's azure ones.

"You're the actual Arthur?" he asked.

"I'm a version of the archetypal Arthur."

"Cool! Can I ask you something?"

"Yes."

"What the hell are you doing here?"

The broad brow under the silver band wrinkled. "I am making a fractured people one. I am a leader where there is need."

"But here? In a shopping mall?"

"Yes."

"With elves?"

"Yes."

Lance frowned. "I'm confused."

"You're not the only one." Claire patted him reassuringly on a sunburned forearm. "Come on . . ."

❖   ❖   ❖

Black stretch pants, black tank, black hood, black running shoes, black belt pouch . . . Claire had no idea if the real-world store carried the same selection, but on the Otherside this was clearly the place for one stop skulking. She either looked like she was going to a very casual funeral or about to fill her evening with a little B&E—she couldn't decide. Maybe both; B&E at a casual funeral . . .

Stop it. Do not think of funerals. You'll get Diana back.

Her hands were shaking as she dropped to tie her laces. "Is this really necessary? Ninja dressing didn't keep Kris and Diana from being captured."

"I totally doubt it was the clothes that got them snagged," Kith snorted, tying off the end of her braid with a black elastic. "You walk the walk, you wear the cloth."

"Excuse me?"

"You gotta dress like you do."

"Yeah. Okay." Communication between seventeen and twenty-seven occasionally took place in two distinct languages. Buckling on the belt pouch, she hurried out of the dressing room in time to smack a piece of chocolate away from Lance's mouth.

"Hey!"

"If you ever want to go back, you can't eat or drink *anything* on this side that you didn't bring with you."

"But I'm hungry!"

Actually, so was she. "I've got food in my pack. Come on."

Her pack was with Diana's, just inside the front door. Claire dragged Lance through the milling crowd of mall elves, tossed him a power bar and a bottle of water, and began filling her belt pouch with preset possibilities.

"I'd send you back to Kingston if I could," she told him, tucking a folded piece of paper behind three glass marbles, "but with the darkside influencing the paths, I can't guarantee where you'd end up."

"I'm willing to take that chance in order to stop Meryat!"

"Since you're the only one who *can* stop Meryat and since she's with Dean, I'm not. We rescue Kris and Diana, we stop the darkside, we stop its influence, I send you to the guest house, you stop Meryat, and . . ."

"We all live happily ever after!"

"Sure. Why not." The small plastic packet of cayenne pepper got slid very carefully up against the flat side of the pouch. "But for now, you'll have to stay here in the store where you'll be safe."

"I'm not afraid to fight!"

"Good. If the store gets attacked, you'll have to." Fortunately, with Arthur out in the mall, there'd be no chance of that. Claire unzipped an outside pocket on Diana's pack, reached into it, and froze as her fingers closed around air. "The wand. Diana took the wand."

"That's bad?"

"When she used it against a minion, it nearly killed her. If she uses it against the darkside . . ."

"But I thought she was captured?"

"So?" It took all of Claire's strength to push that single syllable out against the certain knowledge that her little sister was as good as dead.

"So if it's that powerful, then she didn't get to use it before she was captured. After, well, they'll have taken it away from her so she *can't* use it. Right?"

Claire actually felt time start up again. "Right." For the first time since the beach, she looked at Lance with something other than pique. Like he was something other than an unwanted responsibility. "Thank you."

His cheeks flushed under the sunburn.

"So what's the holdup?" Sam jumped up onto the top of Claire's pack. "Why aren't we moving out?"

She zipped the belt pouch closed. "We?"

Amber eyes narrowed, and his tail traced one long, slow arc from side to side.

"You're right." Claire raised both hands in surrender, ignoring Lance's questioning glance. Some arguments didn't require actual dialogue. "But you're not coming with me because I need you go with Arthur. If he's challenged to single combat, he'll forget everything I've told him about why he shouldn't and leap forward to do what he considers the only honorable thing."

"I want . . ."

"Sam, there has to be someone there to tell him when he's being an idiot and that's one of the things cats do best."

"But Diana . . ."

"Needs my full attention. I can't be worrying about what Arthur's going to do if I'm to have a chance of saving her."

Sam's ears saddled. "You're that sure he'll answer a challenge?"

"I am. It's one of the benefits of working with an archetype." As Arthur climbed up onto the chair, she frowned thoughtfully and added, "Actually, it's pretty much the only benefit."

Arthur stared out at his assembled elves, raised his sword, opened his mouth, and closed it again.

The moment had long passed.

He jerked his head toward the mall. "Let's go."

"So, we're winning, right? And this is part of your plan?"

Diana glanced over at Kris as the surrounding meat-minds shoved them along familiar corridors. "This?"

"Yeah. This." Her gesture took in the meat-minds and the back of the Shadowlord walking up ahead. "You know, being captured and taken back to that . . . hole. 'Cause that's where you want to be, right?"

"Kris, that hole is essentially an entrance to Hell."

"So, as a plan, it sucks. But it *is* a plan, right?"

Since the other girl so clearly needed to hear a specific answer, Diana smiled and lowered her voice. "Yeah, it's a plan. It's not much of one now, but it will be by the time we get there."

"Wicked."

Actually, yes, it being Hell and all, but Diana figured Kris *didn't* need to hear that right now. Closing Hell down in the real world had been difficult enough, closing it on the Otherside without access to the possibilities would be almost impossible. Rules would probably have to be broken. *Hey, it's not like I haven't broken rules before.*

Although not big ones.

Not on purpose anyway.

And intent counted.

I'm intending to save the world. That ought to count for something.

Destroying the bugs had been easy—once she'd plugged the small memory leak—as easy as tripping up the meat-minds by noticing how clumsy they looked. but Hell hadn't given either the bug or the meat-minds substance. People preferred their world to have form and function and by giving darkness definition, they gave it a physical presence. The mall elves had created their own monsters. Giant bugs, skittering around inside the walls, and big, slow-moving guys with short hair, beady eyes, heavy guts and hands that were too big for their bodies.

The mall elves had been street kids before they found their way through to the Otherside.

The meat-minds were broad stereotypes of bad cops.

Maybe we should throw coffee and donuts at them. Answer one bad stereotype with another.

"You just had an idea."

"What?"

Kris dug her elbow into Diana's side with unconcealed glee. "You grinned. And your eyes were gleaming. You just had an idea. Hey, you! Piece of Hell Guy!" She raised her voice. "My girl's gonna kick your Metamucil ass!"

He turned, his expression so affronted Diana couldn't stop herself from laughing. "My what?"

"I think you meant metaphysical," she murmured into an elven ear.

"Metaphysical, metamorphosis, metronome, *The Metropolis Daily Planet!*" Kris snorted. "The *point* is the ass kicking."

His lip curled. "The point is that you are my prisoners, and I know a great many ways to make you scream."

Remember the meaning of enough, Diana pleaded silently with Kris. *If you push him too far . . .* She'd only get one chance to use the wand and the last thing she wanted to do was weigh the life of one beautiful, funny, interested girl against the world.

And, for a change, it really *was* the last thing she wanted to do.

When neither Keeper nor elf responded, he nodded, turned, and the whole procession began moving again.

About five minutes of shoving later, Kris sighed. "I should've said it'd take more than an old white guy to make me scream. Wrong color. Wrong gender. Wrong wang."

"Yeah, you always think of the good lines when it's too late."

"Truth."

"Wang?"

"You know." She pumped her hand at her crotch.

"Ah. Wang."

By the time they reached the cavern, the wand had slid out from under her waistband and started down her right leg. It would have slid farther, but one of the points got caught on the leg elastic of her underwear. Diana half expected Hell to say, *Is that a wand in your pocket or are you just happy to see me,* but the pit remained silent as they were marched toward it.

She'd only get one chance.

One.

As the meat-minds released them, the Shadowlord stepped back and wrapped long pale fingers around their upper arms, dragging them to the edge.

Diana could feel Hell watching her. She was going to need a diversion. Meanwhile, there was no point in cowering. "So . . ." Given the way the hair was raising off the back of her neck in reaction to Hell's attention, bored was a bit more than she could manage but—thank God for being seventeen—insolent was no problem. ". . . what are you going to do with us?"

WHAT DO YOU THINK?

"Don't tell me. Not the virgin sacrifice again."

APPARENTLY NOT.

Hell sounded put out about her moral failings? "Oh, ha ha."

THANK YOU. I'VE ALWAYS PRIDED MYSELF ON MY SENSE OF HUMOR.

"That explains a whole lot about Comedy Central."

HEY, DON'T BLAME JON STEWART ON ME. I DON'T EVEN GET CABLE.

"Well, it's *Hell.*"

AND YET YOUR LOT ALWAYS SEEM SO SURPRISED WHEN I TRY TO EXPAND MY HORIZONS.

"You're trying to take over the world for cable?"

NOT *JUST* CABLE. YOU MAKE IT SOUND SO PETTY.

"Sorry."

NO, YOU'RE NOT.

Diana sighed. "You're right. I'm not sorry." She tried to yank her arm free without success and sighed again. "Could we get on with it?"

IT?

"The part where you gloat about what you're going to do to us."

YOU'RE IN A HURRY?

"I just thought we should get it out of the way." She leaned forward far enough to catch Kris' eye around the Shadowlord's black-clad body. "It's in the Rules."

"Gloating?"

"Yeah."

"I always wondered. And the giant snow-cone machine?"

Diana grinned. She was so definitely in love. "That's optional."

YOU'RE BAIT!

That's what she'd been half afraid of. But this was not the place to let fear show. "Sorry?"

YOUR SISTER WILL COME FOR YOU AND THE IMMORTAL KING WILL COME FOR HER. UNPREPARED TO FACE ME, THEY WILL BE DESTROYED.

There was her diversion.

While Hell's attention was on the destruction of Arthur and Claire, she'd take her one shot with the wand and pour everything she had into closing the hole.

And it would take everything, too.

As plans went, it sucked—worst case scenario left the ground littered with bodies—but at least now she *had* a plan.

"I'm after having second thoughts about this plan. That is one pissed-off basilisk!"

Austin smacked at another bit of rolling canvas. "You're surprised? You don't go zipping mythological creatures into hockey bags and expect them to be pleased about it." He dug his claws into the upholstery as Dean turned the truck into the guest house driveway. "Later, when we've got the time, remind me to tell you about what happened when Claire stuffed a pixie into her purse."

"Messy?"

"In a manner of speaking." The truck rocked forward and back, the jerky stop giving Austin some indication of the state of Dean's mind. He didn't really *care* about the state of Dean's mind, but he had a pretty good idea of what was going on up there. "You're wondering if you can go through with this."

"Yeah."

"You're concerned because, sure she's an evil, life-sucking mummy, but is that any reason to turn her to stone."

"Yeah."

"And you're thinking that a life-sized statue of a reanimated corpse is not only going to destroy the ambiance of the guest house but will probably gouge the hell out of the hardwood floors when you try to move it."

"I'm *not* thinking ambiance!"

Austin took a swipe at the immaculate white fur on his shoulder. "Too many syllables for you?"

"I'm thinking . . ."

As the pause extended, he looked up to see Dean clutching the sides of the steering wheel, his head bowed and resting against the top curve. "Stop."

"Stop what?"

"Stop thinking." He stood, stretched, smacked the hockey bag again, and put his paw on Dean's thigh. "Look, you're just a Bystander and you should never have had to deal with anything stranger than laundry instructions. That said—although I'll call you a liar if you ever repeat this—you're dealing with it admirably. Just *keep* dealing with it and you'll be fine."

"I don't look like a man who's in over his head . . . OW!"

Austin retracted his claws and muttered, "You look like a man with blood on his jeans and a basilisk in a hockey bag. Get over yourself and let's get on with this. I'm hot, I'm hungry, and I'm missing Oprah."

The guest house was cool and quiet as Dean pushed open the back door. With the curtains pulled across the dining room's big windows, the sun hadn't had a chance to heat things up. And that was good because the air outside was rapidly approaching dry roast. He wasn't so sure about the shadows, though; they made the place look mysterious, spooky even and, all things considered, that wasn't exactly reassuring.

Grunting as a tail or a foot or a wing or *something* caught him in the stomach, he heaved the hockey bag up onto the dining room table. Then grabbed it as the basilisk's struggles sent it skittering across the highly polished surface. Okay, maybe he had gone a little overboard with the wax.

"Dean."

Heart in his throat, he whirled around. "Jaysus, Dr. Rebik, don't be sneaking up on me like that!"

The old man managed half a smile. "Sorry."

Old man.

They'd been gone for—Dean glanced down at his watch—just over two and a half hours. In that time, Dr. Rebik had aged a good thirty years. Actually, a *bad* thirty years.

He blinked rheumy eyes. "What's in the bag?"

"You know, word was, Dean McIssac couldn't lie to save his life."

"Well, it's uh . . ."

"Personal," Austin snapped. "Just a little cat business Dean's helping me out with." He stalked past the professor, tossing an imperious, "Let's *go*, Dean," back over one shoulder.

Dean shrugged apologetically, picked up the bag, and started to follow, his eyes flicking back and forth from one shadow to another. If Dr. Rebik was here, the obvious question became, where was Meryat?

Right on cue, she stepped out of the shadows, blocking his way. He could push past her, even though she looked significantly less dead than she had, he was still twice her size. But that would be rude. Clutching the handles of the hockey bag in suddenly sweaty hands, he stopped.

"You seem distracted, Mr. McIssac." She smiled. Her lips went almost all the way around her mouth. "Were you looking for me?"

"What's he looking for?"

"Us." Teemo squirmed a little farther into the shadows, only stopping when Kith squeaked a protest. "Well, not like totally us. But, you know, *us*."

Claire frowned and peered out past the elves at the elderly security guard. "He's not even in this reality."

"Doesn't matter. He's got this kind of . . ."

"Teenager sense," Kith finished. "It's like he hates us, and that helps him find us."

"Really?" She could feel her eyes narrowing all on their own.

"Yeah. Really. He's the freakiest thing in here, and that's saying something."

But exactly *what* it was saying, Claire wasn't certain. Had the old man been changed as the mall changed? Over the years, had he allowed his job to define him until he became his job and the job became his definition of reality? Was there darkness enough in him that the darkside had been able to hire him to work the segue as well as the original mall?

Using *hire* in the broadest sense of the word.

"Fuck, he's coming this way!"

He was. Then he paused and turned and stared into the shadows where Arthur's army was hiding.

Trying to hide.

There were too many of them for the nooks and crannies of the concourse to hold, so they stood and silently watched the old man approach. As the beam of light swept up, three of the skateboarders sped out from under the stairs.

Drawing his fire.

As she watched them cut the concourse into wild patterns, staying inches ahead of the light, she realized, for the first time, that the good guys might stand a chance. This was their mall now and although they were going to take on the darkside with skateboards and baseball bats, they believed they could do it. On the Otherside, belief was everything.

Two of the boarders went over the beam. The third went under.

Now, *she* believed they could do it.

Given who she was and where they were, that might be enough.

And it might not, but the point is they're farther ahead than they were . . . oh no.

Someone zigged when he should have zagged. Golden hair blazed out under the edge of the helmet as the light caught one of the elves, holding him in place six inches off the end of the metal bench. Stewart. Half a heartbeat later, both Stewart and the old man were gone.

"Where . . . ?"

"We think he'll go back to the other mall." Kith sounded very young as she stepped out of the shadows. "But we don't know for sure."

Across the concourse, Arthur's army began to move out.

Claire looked for Sam but couldn't see him in the crowd. She did see Jo raise her bat to the place Stewart disappeared. From the look on her face, the security guard should thank any gods willing to listen that he *wasn't* in this reality and that Jo could never cross back.

But I can.

Claire added another note to her mental to-do list—after *rescue Diana* and *save the world* but before *pick up dry cleaning*.

"Come on." A hand on skinny shoulders got her escort's attention. "Let's do this."

IT BEGINS.

The declaration jerked Diana up out of her slump, spilling Kris' head off her shoulder. "What does?"

WHAT DO YOU THINK? *IT!*

"Right." It. The battle. Her diversion. She shuffled around toward Kris, using the motion to cover an attempt to move the wand a little farther up her leg. "You okay?"

"Oh, yeah, fuckin' great. I wasn't asleep."

"Okay."

"I was just . . . you know."

Looking for an excuse to cuddle. Diana grinned. "Okay."

Kris flipped her dreads back off her face and sighed. "You have to sound so smug?"

"Pretty much, yeah." Keeping her back against the wall of the cavern, she got to her feet and held a hand down to the elf.

"So this where all Hell breaks loose?"

Someone had to say it, Diana reminded herself. It wasn't exactly a Rule. Some things didn't have to be. "Not yet."

With any luck, not ever.

Leaning out around the quartet of meat-minds left to guard them, she watched as the Shadowlord came into the cavern—not walking, *striding,* and being pretty da . . . darned obvious about it, too. Over the whole black-on-black wardrobe, he was wearing greaves, vambraces, and a polished breastplate. Also in black. He pulled his sword—not black, Diana was happy to note, although it wasn't like he hadn't already beat the theme to death—and knelt by the edge of the pit.

"Is it time?"

IT IS. ARE YOU READY?

"I am."

"Who writes their dialogue," Kris muttered as the Shadowlord stood, his blade lifted in salute.

Diana had a witty comeback ready, but it slipped off her tongue. The Shadowlord's hair, definitely blond on all other occasions, was looking more than just a little red. It might have been reflected light from the pit, but she had a horrible feeling he was about to earn a name.

Given who he'll be fighting, three guesses as to what name and the first two don't count.

Sam trotted along at Arthur's heels, vaguely aware that this wasn't the first time he'd gone to war—Angels being soldiers of the Lord and all that. He just wished he could remember more of his life before he became a cat. Well, he remembered the few days he'd been essentially a human teenage male, but since that had mostly involved being confused, hungry, and obsessed with genitalia, it wasn't a lot of help.

He would rather have been with Claire, rescuing Diana. He would rather have been *with* Diana right from the start, but no one ever listened to him.

This made his ability to stop Arthur from doing a little one-on-one whacking with the Big Bad just a little suspect. The access to higher knowledge he retained in this form was no help at all.

So.

What would Austin do?

"The trick in getting them to listen is making sure you've got their attention before you start."

"But how?"

Austin stretched out a front leg and flexed the paw. His claws sank a quarter inch into the sofa cushion. "Use your imagination, kid. That's what it's there for."

Well, if a cat could look at a king, he supposed it was only a small step from there to leaving scars. Feeling more confident, he began memorizing the places Arthur's padding didn't quite cover. Just in case things got unpleasant.

❊   ❊   ❊

"Did you have a pleasant time at the shopping mall, Dean?" Meryat's voice was low and musical, her movements graceful, even considering she was still more than half corpse.

Dr. Rebik stared at her in open-mouthed fascination.

Dean stared in horror.

Austin seemed to have disappeared.

"You seem to have done some shopping," she continued, her eyes following the movements of the hockey bag. "Is it another kitty?" Her arm whipped forward with snakelike speed and one finger poked the canvas. The answering squawk was more indignant than pained. "No, not a kitty. If I didn't know better, I'd say you'd bought yourself a chicken."

Dean really didn't like the way she'd emphasized *If I didn't know better* . . . His grip tightened around the straps of the bag, the wrapped canvas growing damp under his fingers.

"Why don't you show me?"

Okay. He thrust the bag toward her. Austin's plan had involved getting Dr. Rebik out of their room, leaving the bag outside the door for her to find, assuming she'd go after the life force of whatever was in it. She'd drag it inside, and open it, never suspecting a Bystander capable of delivering a mythological creature capable of turning her to stone. The threat of life sucking would be over and the basilisk would be safely contained until Claire came home.

Still, as long as he closed his eyes and got Dr. Rebik to close his eyes *and* assumed that Austin was somewhere safe, this should do as plan B. Given that the basilisk had been hiding out in a shopping mall with minimal statuary happening, it clearly preferred hiding over stoning. Stoneage. Turning people to stone.

Meryat pushed the bag back toward him. "You open it."

That would make things a little trickier.

Meryat was a foot shorter than he was, slim, and not entirely alive. If he shoved her out of his way, could she stop him? If he shoved her into the wall, was she still brittle enough to break?

"You can't, you know."

Dean swallowed and found his voice. "I can't what, then?"

"Just charge past me." His eyes widened and she smiled. "No, I'm not reading your mind; I'm reading your face. Everything you're thinking, everything you're feeling is right out there."

"You don't ever hit someone smaller than you."

"What about Brad Mackenzie? He's smaller than me, but he's plays for St. Pat's, and if I don't hit him, we'll . . ."

His grandfather sighed. "All right, fine. You don't ever hit someone smaller than you unless they're wearing hockey skates."

From the way Meryat was smiling, that had shown on his face, too. He was some screwed because he'd never get her into hockey skates.

"Every hero needs a fatal flaw. Now, for the last time, Dean, open the bag."

"And what if I'm after saying no?"

"Then I'll suck my darling Dr. Rebik dry, right in front of you." A gesture brought the archeologist around to her side. She slid a slender arm through his and smiled. "Your choice."

Dean set the hockey bag down on the kitchen counter and began fumbling with the zipper. "She's killing you, you know!"

Dr. Rebik matched Meryat's smile. "I die of love."

"Yeah, right . . ." The bit of basilisk he'd caught back in the food court was jamming the zipper closed. If he kept his eyes shut . . .

Would Claire be able to fix him if he was turned to stone?

If she couldn't, would she put him out in the garden?

Would pigeons shit on his head?

It'd be sea gulls back home, so he supposed pigeons would be an improvement.

"Are you stalling, Dean?"

Dr. Rebik moaned low in his throat and a patch of hair fell out, slid down the curve of his head and off his bowed shoulder to the floor.

"I'm going as fast as I can!" he cried, yanking at the zipper and fighting the urge to go for the whisk broom and dustpan. "It's stuck!"

"I see. We'll just have to . . ."

Out in the office, the phone rang.

"Where are you going?"

"I'm after answering . . ."

"No."

"But this is a business," Dean protested indignantly. "You can't be letting the phone ring!"

"I can and I will."

Four rings. Five. Six.

The machine should have picked up on five. As it didn't . . . "Look, it's Claire's mum. As long as there's someone here, it won't stop ringing."

Meryat frowned thoughtfully. "Is the Keeper's mother also a Keeper?"

"No!"

Seven rings. Eight.

The frown lines deepened with a faint crinkling sound. "Then how does she know there's someone here?"

"Claire's her daughter!" Which was the absolute truth. Maybe not the whole truth but the truth, so with any luck at all, that whole lousy lying thing wouldn't come into it.

Nine rings. Ten. Eleven. Twelve.

"This grows very annoying. Go!" A fingernail flew off with the expansive force of her gesture. "Answer it!"

Dean took two grateful steps toward the office.

"Mr. McIssac, aren't you forgetting something?"

Biting back a curse, he returned for the hockey bag.

Thirteen rings. Fourteen. Fifteen.

Closely followed by Meryat and Dr. Rebik—too closely followed as far as Dean was concerned—he set the bag on the desk and reached for the phone.

Sixteen.

"Elysian Fields Guest House."

"Dean, it's Martha Hansen. I've got this terrible feeling that the girls are in trouble. Not that the girls being in trouble is ever a good feeling, but this is remarkably strong considering that they're still on the Otherside and I'm worried. You haven't heard from them, have you? That's not why you were so long answering?"

"Uh, no, it's not." He had no idea what, if anything a Cousin could do over the phone, but this was his one chance to get help. "You just called at a bad time. There's . . ."

". . . no need for further explanations," Meryat said as Dr. Rebik's shaking finger came down on the disconnect. "The noise has been stopped, and we have business to conclude." She glanced around the office, and her eyes narrowed. "Although this is not the best place; we could be interrupted, and that has already happened once too often."

Dean suddenly realized she wasn't talking about the phone. "Lance."

"Yes. When my binding came undone, he was partially caught by my counterspell. It seems to have unbalanced him."

"He's not Australian," Dr. Rebik announced calmly.

Meryat rolled her eyes. "He might as well be. Now then, I think we'll take this someplace more private." Her gaze traveled slowly down the length of Dean's body and he shuddered. Before Claire and he had . . created an angel, he'd never noticed that sort of thing. After, he realized—to his intense embarrassment—it had happened a lot. "Let's go to your bedroom."

Suddenly, being a statue didn't look like such a bad future.

He only hoped Claire remembered to dust him.

Claire stifled a sneeze against her shoulder unable to believe the amount of dust in the dropped ceiling. She stopped herself from wondering where it came from before the Otherside provided an answer, and concentrated on crawling after Teemo's narrow backside.

Fortunately, Diana had already taken this route, so she didn't need to worry about securing its reality.

The drop down into the bathroom was a little farther than she was comfortable with. One foot slid off the edge of the soap dispenser and into the sink, but Kith steadied her as she landed, averting disaster with a steady grip above both knees.

The room smelled of cleaners and disinfectants, and all at once she missed Dean so badly it was like a physical ache. In fact, it wasn't *like* a physical ache at all. It was a physical ache. Austin would do what he could, but a reanimated mummy was a just a little beyond what snark and sympathy could hope to deal with.

She had to defeat the darkside and return to them before it was too late. Or get Lance to them if that was all she could manage.

Save the world.

Save Diana.

Save Dean.

At least this time, there'd be no nasty surprises in the final inning.

And that was an unprovoked sports metaphor. Even her subconscious missed Dean. At one time, she'd thought maintaining a relationship would be a distraction. It wasn't, it was a goal. Something she could use as incentive to charge right through the worst the possibilities could offer.

Memo to self, she sighed, following Kith and Teemo out into the hall, *watch a little less Oprah with the cat.*

They were almost to the food court when a rumble of thunder flattened them back against the wall, Teemo raising an unnecessary finger to his lips.

No. Not thunder. Meat-minds. A whole herd of them pounding purposefully past the food court in ranks that were more or less even. Claire thought very hard about saving the world; thinking about how clumsy they looked would only set up a chain reaction of vaudevillian proportions and give away their position.

Bringing up the rear between four meat-minds more defined than the rest was a vaguely familiar warrior dressed and armored all in black. His skin was milk pale and his hair a deep red. Really red. Blood red. Bad fantasy cliché red.

That couldn't be good. Claire sent a silent plea that Sam remembered what he had to do.

On the bright side, if their leader had taken the field, both Diana and the segue would be minimally guarded. Pulling Kith and Teemo closer, she whispered, "From here, I go on alone."

"No way, Keeper. Arthur . . ."

". . . is going to need you. You saw the size of the army he's facing; pull some weapons from that sporting goods store, and attack from the rear. Remember, as soon as I shut down the segue, the meat-minds will fall apart, so you don't have to win so much as you have to not lose."

"What?"

Okay. That hadn't made a lot of sense to her either. "Look, I usually work alone. I clearly suck at motivational speaking. Just be careful." She put a hand on each of their shoulders, squeezed lightly, then turned and raced down the hall toward the Emporium.

They hadn't come through the store. The plywood construction barricade was gone; in its place was a dark tunnel leading down under the mall.

Only one meat-mind on guard.

He saw her, turned, and, because she believed he would, tripped over his own feet.

Getting past him was as easy as dropping a marble on his head.

The passage ended in what was obviously a throne room. Kicking through bits of shattered chitin, Claire approached the dais where she found, amid the broken insect bits, a tampon lying crushed and forgotten.

Diana.

She paused and quickly checked her memory of the charging meat-mind army. Well, the odds were very good it was Diana's anyway.

A few scorch marks against the polished stone showed where preset possibilities had been destroyed. None of them looked large enough or scorched enough to have been the wand.

Then there was a chance Diana still had it.

Definitely a good news/bad news scenario.

Only one exit from the throne room. A stone corridor leading even farther down. The moment she stepped into it, Claire felt a familiar pull.

Running as quietly as she could under the flickering torches, Claire hurried toward it. This wasn't her Summoning. She shouldn't be feeling a pull, familiar or otherwise.

It was possible that she was sensing Diana's presence by the segue.

But she didn't think so.

FOURTEEN

DIANA COULD FEEL THE POWER FLUCTUATIONS. They filled the cavern, rippling from side to side, up and down, raising all the hair on her body. Not exactly a pleasant feeling. They were strong enough that she suspected she could see them if she just unfocused her eyes the right way.

The good news was they weren't all coming from the pit.

Most, but not all.

Some of them were coming from her.

Some from outside the cavern.

She felt it the moment the armies joined. Felt it as the weight of Hell's attention grew lighter. Soon.

Only one small problem.

She stood, stretched, and beckoned for Kris to join her. "There's a few thing I'd like to do before we die."

Which was the absolute truth and always the best way to deal with Hell. No point playing in its court.

I'M SURE THERE ARE, Hell snarked as Kris put her hand in Diana's and allowed herself to be pulled to her feet. BUT YOU CAN'T DESTROY ME, AND IF YOU TRY, I WILL MAKE YOU VERY VERY SORRY. I NEED YOU ALIVE AS BAIT, BUT I DO NOT NEED YOU UNHARMED.

Hands on Kris' hips, Diana snorted in the general direction of the pit. "It's not always about you, dude."

The kiss had a touch of desperation about it—the odds were extremely good this would be one of their last, after all—and things heated up a little past the point where brain cells started to fry. Somehow, Diana managed to keep a small fraction of her mind on something other than the way Kris' lips felt under hers and got them turned around until the mall elf's body was between hers and the pit. Chewing along her jaw, Diana sucked the lobe of a pointed ear into her mouth and murmured, "Slide your hand down the back of my pants!"

And let's hear it for enthusiasm.

"Farther . . . oh, yeah . . . no . . . down the leg." Diana squelched a sudden desire to giggle at what sounded like bad porn dialogue. "The other leg."

As Kris' fingers touched the top of the wand, she stiffened, suddenly realizing what this was about. From the way she began to pull back, she wasn't entirely happy about it either.

Diana tightened her grip and yanked their bodies into even closer contact. Licking her way around the inner curve of Kris' ear, she sighed, "If I survive this, I promise I'll make it up to you."

Kris' answer was an emphatic wriggle.

Probably trying to get a better grip on the wand.

Probably . . .

She could feel the wand begin to move up her thigh, toward her waistband and couldn't resist. "Oh, yes! Yes! That's it!"

OH, FOR . . . GET A ROOM!

Staying close to Arthur wasn't easy. The Immortal King moved through the battle with archetypal skills and the flexibility of a teenager. Sam did the best he could, and if he took a few detours to avoid being pounded into marmalade-colored kitty paste, well, he figured he was entitled. Squashed flat was not a good defensive position.

The trick was to see the pattern of the battle and then become a part of it.

The trouble was that his part of the pattern took him across the concourse at the same time Arthur's brought him face-to-face with the tall redhead in the so cliché black armor. Who was very definitely not a meat-mind. And who looked vaguely familiar.

The hair rose along Sam's spine.

He leaped a fallen elf and darted between two massive legs. He had to get to Arthur before . . .

"What say you? Your sword against mine. Let us leave the young and the stupid out of what we both know is our battle." The redhead's voice filled a lull in the fighting; everyone froze for a heartbeat, then dark and light turned to face the middle of the concourse.

Sam raced up and over a planter and found himself peddling air as Will grabbed him and clutched him tight against his hockey jersey.

"Put me down!"

"Shhh, it's a challenge."

"I know it's a challenge! I have to . . ."

"You have to wait," Will said, cutting him off. "When a challenge has been made, everything stops until it's been answered."

The mall elf didn't add that it was a Rule, but then, he didn't have to. Sam could feel the Rule holding elves and meat-minds both in place. Fortunately, he was neither.

"Put me down, or I'll add a few new piercings to your nose."

"What?"

A claw hooked into the inside of Will's left nostril.

"Right."

And Sam was back on the floor.

"So, do you accept my challenge?"

Arthur's back was to him. Sam had no way of knowing what his answer would be, but something in the redhead's pale eyes suggested he was about to get the response he desired. Too far away to stop Arthur from speaking, Sam did the only thing he could. "I accept!"

Everyone blinked in unison.

The redhead recovered first. "I was not speaking to you, cat."

"Should've been more specific, then." Sam walked out into the open space between the two, sat down, and washed his shoulder.

Arthur shook himself and took his eyes off the redhead for the first time since the battle had brought them face to face. "Sam, you can't . . ."

"And I won't!" the redhead snorted.

"I can and you will." Sam stood and stretched, butt in the air. "The challenge has been made and answered. You can deal with him . . ." A jerk of his head toward Arthur. ". . . later, but the Rules say you have to deal with me first."

"The Rules . . ."

"You break them, we get to break them. Up to you, crud for brains, but you know who's here and you know what she's able to do if you give her the chance."

The redhead frowned and suddenly squatted, peering into Sam's face. "I get the feeling we have fought before, you and I. A long time ago, before all . . ." His gesture managed to encompass the elves, the meat-minds, the mall, Arthur, and their own bodies. ". . . this."

"Well, at least one of us has come up in the world," Sam snorted. "We gonna fight, or were you planning on talking me to death."

"When I kill you," the redhead purred, straightening, "I will have my name. I will use the subsequent death of the Immortal King to gain the kind of power that will cause whole kingdoms to tremble before me!"

"Subsequent death? You pick up that word-of-the-day toilet paper at the Emporium?"

"No, at the stationery shop."

"Ah."

"Sam." Arthur stepped forward, Excalibur a gleaming silver line across his body. "I can't let you do this."

"You have no choice," the redhead snarled, shifted his weight, and swung.

Sam leaped left. Then right. Then left. Then up and over another planter.

"Damn it, cat! Hold still!"

"You think I'm going to hold still because *you* want me to?" Sam ricocheted off a meat-mind and folded back on himself. "You're not only evil," he snorted, raking his claws across the redhead's wrist as he rocketed by, "you're not too bright. . . ."

"You, turn on the lights." As Dr. Rebik stretched a palsied hand toward the switch, Meryat sat down on the edge of the bed. "You, put the bag on the floor and open it."

"I don't think," Dean began, searching for a protest that would carry some weight.

"Good. You're not supposed to think. You're supposed to do as I say." She smiled and brushed dry, brittle hair back off her face with fingertips that were still a little black. "So what did I say?"

"Put the bag on the floor."

"Do it." Her hand closed around Dr. Rebik's arm. "Or have you forgotten the consequences? He dies, and it's all your fault."

There had to be a way out of this. There had to be. Unfortunately, Dean had no idea of what it was. Coming up with a last minute solution wasn't in his job description. Run the guesthouse. No problem. Anchor Claire in the real world. Got it covered. Get a high enough gloss on the dining room table that he could stop nagging about coasters. Almost there. He even did windows. Pull a brilliant plan out of nowhere just as things were about to land in the crapper—not likely.

Where was Austin? The wardrobe door was open about six inches. Was he inside? Waiting for the perfect moment?

Dean set the writhing bag on the floor.

Meryat smiled. He really wished she'd stop doing that—although all things considered, her teeth were remarkably good. "Open it."

Austin needed to hurry it up. They were rapidly running out of perfect moments.

Dean dropped to one knee—the last thing he wanted was to be bending over the bag as the basilisk emerged—closed his eyes, and yanked the zipper open.

The scream of an enraged cat filled all the empty spaces in the room. Adrenaline surged through Dean's body demanding flight or fight and getting neither. He jerked his eyes open in time to see a scaled tail disappear into the wardrobe.

Austin leaped from chair, to dresser, to the top of the wardrobe and sat there looking smug. "The half with the brain is a chicken," he said.

"You do realize that a basilisk would have no effect on me," Meryat murmured conversationally.

"Obviously not," Austin purred in much the same tone.

"But since there's one available, I was thinking that turning Dean here to stone would reverberate through their bond and bring the Keeper racing back believing she was about to face a basilisk."

"Whereas sucking Dean dry would bring her back prepared to face you."

"Exactly. While she's dealing with the lesser threat, I will . . ."

". . . suck her dry and regain youth, beauty, and power in one fell swoop."

"What a smart kitty you are. I think the Keeper might miss *you* more. Get down from there."

"Or you'll what?" Austin snorted. "Suck Dean dry? You're going to do that anyway. Kill Dr. Rebik? Talk to someone who cares."

"I see cats haven't changed much in three thousand years."

He looked seriously affronted. "Why should we?"

"Excellent point. All right, if you won't cooperate, I suppose I'll have to return to my original plan. Dean, get the creature out of the wardrobe. Try to pick an attractive pose; you'll be holding it for very long time."

Turned to stone, he'd have a chance at being turned back when Claire kicked mummy butt. With his life sucked out . . . Dean glanced back at Dr. Rebik who seemed to have fallen asleep propped up against the wall. He stood and headed for the wardrobe where he found seventeen pairs of shoes, a crumpled pile of Claire's clothes . . .

"What are you doing?" Meryat demanded.

"Hanging things up."

"Well, stop it!"

. . . but no basilisk.

The wardrobe was Claire's usual access to the Otherside. He'd used it himself once, following the path Claire had laid down. But this time, Claire'd crossed over in the mall, so no path. No escape for him. Apparently, basilisks were mythological enough to make their own way over. Dean pressed his hand flat against the back wall, the wood rough and reassuring under his palm. *That's it, Lassie* . . . Collies. Basilisks. Whatever. . . . *bring back help.*

Oh, Hel . . . p. Claire stood at the entrance to a huge circular cavern and stared at the pit in the middle of it. No wonder the power fluctuations seemed so familiar. *Been there. Done that. Should've got the T-shirt.*

Not a segue, a hole. A hole capped only by an incomplete segue. The moment the segue was finished, Hell itself would have unlimited access to four acres of suburban Kingston. Which was *not* a redundant observation, no matter how much Claire hated the suburbs.

The problem was: how did she close a hole to Hell without access to the possibilities? Marbles and spices were not going to be enough.

The wand.

If Diana still had it, it was their only chance.

If.

Belief in this instance would accomplish nothing, but as it would do no harm, Claire decided to believe, with all her heart, that Diana had the wand.

She leaned a little farther around the edge of the cavern entrance and finally spotted her sister by the side wall. Not injured. Not even confined. Her hands were wrapped around various bits of Kris and Kris' hand were . . . actually, Claire couldn't see what Kris' hands were doing, but the result seemed to be a fair bit of wiggling. Neither of them seemed too upset by their captivity.

TEENAGERS, Hell sighed. If the pit had eyes, they'd have been rolling.

The groping had to be part of Diana's plan.

Forcing Hell to underestimate her.

Lulling Hell into a false sense of security.

Convincing Hell there would be no attack.

Of course, there was always the possibility that Hell was right and, when faced with their imminent death, the two girls had decided to get in one last . . .

No.

At the very least, they were creating a distraction. She'd have never gotten this close unchallenged had the darkside been paying attention.

Time to return the favor.

The cayenne pepper in one hand, a marble in the other, Claire sprinted for the edge of the pit.

She made it about two thirds of the way.

One of the wand's points had snagged on the inside of Diana's black stretch pants and wriggling didn't seem to be freeing it.

"Harder!" she growled, her mouth against Kris' ear.

"I don't want to hurt you!"

"I can take it!"

OKAY, UNDER THE CIRCUMSTANCES, I HAVE TO SAY THAT THIS IS INAPPROPRIATE BEHA . . . AH!

Between one heartbeat and the next, Diana felt the power fluctuations stop and the cavern fill with a grid of dark bands. She saw Claire snatched up into the air and held writhing. She heard Hell begin to laugh.

Then the wand ripped free.

She met Claire's eyes.

Said a silent good-bye.

And shoved Kris out of the way.

With its pink star pointed toward the pit, the wand bucked in Diana's hand like a living thing, fighting to find the possibilities through the power of Hell.

Hell's first attack slammed her to her knees. The pain of impact almost broke her concentration, but four years of enforced PE lent her strength. If she could work through the pain of field hockey, she could work through this.

Had to work through this.

She touched the edges of the possibilities.

Not enough.

Hell's second attack slid shadows through her mind.

THEY WILL PAY FOR EVERY MOMENT YOU FIGHT ME!

Images of Claire, of Kris, of her parents, of Sam broken and bleeding.

With Hell's attention split, Claire managed to open her hand although she broke a finger doing it. The marble rolled from her palm, fell too slowly to the stone, and shattered.

Brilliant white light burned the shadows away.

It only lasted for an instant.

It lasted just long enough.

Free of the darkness, Diana touched the possibilities and threw herself open to them. No fear. No doubt. No regrets.

This had been her Summoning not because she was closest but because she was youngest and most powerful.

All that she was.

The end of the wand erupted. Streams of pink luminescence sizzled and danced their way down into the pit.

NO!

Diana reluctantly admitted to a brief moment of sympathy—it *was* disturbingly pink.

Then the pink began to mute as lines of gray snaked up from the pit, twisting and spiraling around the light toward the wand. Toward her hand. Toward her heart.

HA! NOT GOOD ENOUGH.

Blood in her mouth. The taste of iron. Her vision began to blur.

"Get . . . stuffed."

Her Summoning because she was youngest and nothing but possibilities.

All that she would be.

Bubble gum pink. Barbie pink.

The scent of brimstone disappeared. The flickering red light against the cavern's roof began to brighten.

The pit began to fill with glittering, gleaming, shimmering, incandescent pink.

Diana could no longer tell where her hand stopped and the wand began. At the edge of her vision, she saw Claire fall, missed her impact with the floor, but saw the remaining shadows given form. Had to trust her sister would stop them. At this point, she could no more stop the flow of possibilities than Hell could.

She didn't realize she was moving until her toes stubbed hard against the edge of the pit.

IF I GO, YOU GO WITH ME!

Well, duh.

All she was, all she would be, given to save the world. How hard was that to understand? It was, after all, what Keepers *did*. Evil had a distinct tendency to keep missing the obvious.

She wasn't so much falling forward as moving through the wand.

And then . . .

. . . falling back.

She saw Kris poised on the edge of the pit, the wand raised in a defiant fist.

Saw her totter.

Saw her fall.

Pink light filled the cavern.

When Diana could see again, the pit was closed.

Someone, she thought it might be her, threw themselves forward, pounded bloody fists against solid rock, and screamed "No!"

There were Rules to follow, after all.

The problem was, Sam couldn't just run. The Rules said he had to engage in battle or he wasn't actually answering the challenge. The problem was, although he had *more* pointy bits, he was fighting a Shadowlord with a great big sword.

He zigged.

The Shadowlord zagged.

A great big sword *and* opposable thumbs.

Dangling by the scruff of his neck, Sam struggled to fold himself in half and get a claw into the hand holding him. Shrieking defiance, he felt the sword begin to descend.

Flash of silver.

He felt the impact reverberate through fingers buried painfully deep in his fur. Hissed and spat as he was thrown aside.

Twisting in the air, he landed on his feet. Tail lashing, singing his challenge, he spun around.

"Let it go, Sam. I am permitted to intervene at the last instant in order to save the life of my champion." Arthur stared over his blade at the Shadowlord. "Let's get it on." When his opponent looked confused, he sighed and translated. "It's our fight now."

Not quite human teeth flashed in a brilliant smile. "I have always killed you."

"Yeah, yeah. That was then."

"Fear me."

"Bite me."

Sam had to admit the dialogue was less than archetypal. Maybe, hopefully, *possibly* that would be enough.

Or not.

As swords clashed overhead, hilt caught on hilt, body slammed against body. Eight inches from the floor, his angle unique, Sam saw the Shadowlord pull the dagger from his belt. Saw a black-clad elbow pull back. Slam forward.

My bad.

His failure.

I'm sorry. I'm sorry. I'm sorry.

Then the world turned pink.

Really, really, *really* pink.

When he could see again, the Shadowlord had vanished and Arthur was standing with Excalibur over his head, hips canted back, staring down at a hole in his chest protector.

The circle of mall elves seemed frozen in place as Sam crept forward. "Are you . . . ? Did he . . . ?"

Holding his position, moving only his left arm, Arthur slid a finger into the rent.

Pulled it out again.

The tip was red.

A strangled cry from a dozen throats.

"No, no, it's okay." Excalibur's point clanged against the tiles, as Arthur relaxed. "He barely pricked me."

They were all still too close to the edge for cheers.

Then someone sighed, "Close one, dude."

In the joyful chaos that followed, Sam lifted his tail and sprayed the place where the Shadowlord had been standing.

"Enough of this!" Meryat rose from the edge of the bed and locked Dean in place with a pointed finger. "These games no longer amuse me. I will take your life *now* and face your Keeper stronger because of it!"

"Not so fast." Austin crouched at the edge of the wardrobe and stared down at the mummy/Dean tableau. "If I'm not mistaken, which I'm not, so don't go there, the Rules state you, as the villain of the piece, have to brag about how you defeated us before you administer the coup de grace. That's the finishing stroke," he added for Dean's benefit.

Dean's expression suggested he didn't appreciate the translation.

"The point is," Meryat sneered, the missing piece of her lip adding further scorn to her expression, "you have *been* defeated. What difference will bragging about it make?"

Austin shrugged. "Well, I personally could care less, but if you break the Rules, we get to break the Rules."

"You? What can you do?"

He licked his shoulder at her.

"Fine! I've waited three thousand years; I can wait a few more minutes."

FIFTEEN

—•— ⚔ —•—

"**C**OME ON, DIANA, you've got to run. This whole place is coming down!"

Diana twisted free of Claire's grip and headed back toward the center of the cavern. "We've got to get her out!"

"We can't." Claire hooked her fingers into the waistband of Diana's pants and yanked her to a stop. "You know as well as I do that there's a hundred ways to go to Hell—hand baskets, good intentions—but we can't use any of them if we've been crushed under a pile of . . ." She threw herself sideways, taking Diana with her as a piece of the cavern ceiling crashed down. ". . . rock."

Considering where they were, the light bulb wasn't entirely unexpected. Claire batted it out of the way with her good hand as Diana surged up onto her feet.

"We'll go after her!"

"Yes, but . . ."

"But nothing." Diana's hand closed around her wrist and yanked her up. "Let's move!"

It seemed that their presence alone had been maintaining what little stability the cavern still had. As they crossed the threshold, the rest of the ceiling crashed down. Coughing and choking in the billowing clouds of faintly pink stone dust, they ran faster, the tunnels collapsing behind them.

Which is certainly better than in front of us, Claire acknowledged as they raced toward the throne room . . .

. . . only to find the entrance blocked.

"Is there another way out?" Mouth close to Diana's ear, she still had to shout to be heard over the roar of falling rock.

"This is the only one *I* know!"

"Oh that's just great!" One-handedly fighting the zipper on the belt pouch open, she found Diana there before her. "What are you doing?"

"If we don't get out, we can't save Kris. So we're getting out!" Snatching out the folded piece of paper, Diana knelt and stuffed it between two of the rocks that blocked the door.

"Diana, that won't work! Rocks can't read!"

"I'll read it for them." Yanking Claire out of the way, she pointed back toward the oncoming destruction and yelled, "Move!"

The paper released the possibilities it held.

The rocks moved.

They moved as though they knew full well they'd be pounded to sand if they didn't.

The black marble floor had cracked and buckled and the wall behind the throne had canted inward at an impossible angle, but structural integrity was being maintained. Provided the definition of both structural and integrity was less than precise.

And then, lungs burning, they were running on concrete, not stone.

Almost out . . .

They missed the turn that would have taken them through the construction zone and found themselves in the access corridors instead.

The troll was waiting at the back door of the Emporium.

Before Claire could stop her, Diana grabbed him by the tie and shoved her face up into his, snarling, "Your choice, Gaston! The Otherside's a big place. You can lose yourself in it, or you can deal with me."

His eyes widened, showing pale yellow all around the gray. "But . . ."

"Billy goats *but* as you very well know. I'm counting to three. One . . ."

On two, he chose to leave the tie in her hand and pound farther up the access corridor into the mall.

Diana dropped the piece of pale leather and swiped her hand

against her thigh, moisture drawing darker lines through the pale pink dust. "Eww."

"Definitely," Claire agreed, using the moment to catch her breath. Not the way she'd have handled it, but since it worked . . . "What are you doing?"

"This is where we came in. This is the best place to cross back!"

Bad hand cradled against her chest, she stepped between her sister and the steel door. "We're not done."

"The Summoning ended when that hole closed; *I'm* done!" Dark brows drew in, their challenge plain. "And *I'm* going after Kris!"

Claire had her choice of half a dozen good arguments. She used the only one that would work. "What about Sam? He's still in the mall. I left him guarding Arthur."

"*You* left him," Diana snapped. "You go . . . you . . ." She blinked. Swallowed. Scrubbed her hand across suddenly wet eyes. "Sorry. I just . . ."

"I know."

"You *can't* know."

"Dean . . ."

"Didn't go to Hell for *you*! I'm sorry." She scrubbed at her eyes again. "But he didn't."

"I know," Claire said again, because it was pretty much the only thing Diana was willing to hear at the moment. She jerked open the steel door with her good hand. "Let's go get Sa—" A crack opened suddenly in the concrete floor. Somewhere, not very far away, a steel reinforcing rod snapped with an almost musical twang. "Not good!" Shoving Diana into the storeroom, she slammed the door shut with her shoulder and locked it.

It sounded like someone was playing a steel guitar in the access corridor. Playing it badly.

"How far do you think the destruction will come?" Diana demanded as they charged through shards of broken garden gnomes toward the store.

"It's already come farther than I thought it would."

"Great."

"Not really. I was wondering, last time you used the wand, it knocked you flat. This time . . ."

"I think Kris' sacrifice caused a backlash. I got—I don't know—refilled. I'm feeling . . ." Diana flashed half a pain-filled grin and straight-armed the door out into the Emporium. ". . . in the pink."

Claire managed a nearly identical smile. "We'll get her back."

"I know." Easily clearing the fallen T-shirt rack, Diana lengthened her stride and raced for the concourse. One foot out the door, she stopped, turned, and ran back.

"Where are you going?" Claire figured she had grounds for sounding shrill. From behind them, one small room away, came the unmistakable sound of a steel door buckling.

"Promises to keep." Dragging a wooden crate of resin frogs under the antique mirror, she climbed up, and slapped the glass. "Jack! Hey! Time to go."

The blue-on-blue eyes popped into view so fast they came accompanied by a faint *boing*. "The whole place is falling apart!" Jack also sounded a little shrill, Claire noted. "What did you do?"

A green glass ball fell from a shelf and shattered. Something hissed and scuttled away.

"We won. Sort of."

"How do you *sort of* win?"

"I don't want to get into that right now."

"Yeah, but . . ."

A muscle jumped in Diana's jaw. "I said, I *don't* want to get into it." She ducked her head behind the edge of the frame. "Is this all that's holding you on?"

"How should I know?" Shrill had given way to slightly panicked. "I don't have eyes in the back of my glass."

"Fair point. Claire . . ."

No time to argue. Claire reached up, noted somewhat absently that much of her left hand seemed to be purple, and grabbed the lower edge of the carved and gilded wood. "I've got it."

Jack was a lot heavier than he looked. They dragged him past the writhing box of rubber snakes, past the toppling display of scented candles, and reached the concourse just as the windows started to shatter. As the first triangular piece of glass whistled past, Claire spun him around, his back to the store, and pushed Diana down behind him.

"Claire, we haven't time . . . !"

"To get cut to ribbons? You're right."

"Hey!" Jack's eyes were as wide as Claire'd seen them. "Get me farther away! I'm breakable here!"

Barely enough room for them both but barely was better than the alternative. "Calm down. You've got a wooden backing."

"Calm down? That's glass breaking! Lots and lots of breaking glass! Do you know how that makes me feel?"

"Do I care?" Claire snapped. As Jack's eyes fled to the far corner, two tiny blue pinpricks deep in the glass, she sighed. "I'm sorry. I do care. We've just had a . . . bad time."

"Sort of winning?"

"Yeah."

Sort of . . . Diana lifted her head out of the shelter of her arms and stared into the mirror. She didn't look any different. She should have looked different. Wasn't that the sort of thing that changed a person?

It took her a moment to realize that the mall was totally silent. No more crashing. No more breaking. No more dying. Apparently, this was as far as it went. "Claire?" She almost didn't recognize her voice. She sounded about seven. "Why did she do it?"

Carefully brushing aside broken glass, Claire sat down cross-legged on the floor. It wasn't quite a collapse. "I don't know. I guess she didn't want you to die."

"Yeah, but it's part of the whole 'saving the world' thing. It's in my job description. Our job description."

"And it seems that saving you was in hers."

"I didn't want her to."

"She didn't ask you." Claire reached out and wiped away a tear with her thumb. "We'll get her back."

"Because you promised?"

"Because it's part of our job description."

"Right." Diana dragged her sleeve under her nose, leaving a smear of darker pink across one cheek. "Time to sit around and sob about things later! Let's get Sam and . . ." She paused, half standing, and cocked her head. "Is there a reason you're flipping me the finger?"

Swelling had moved the second finger on her left hand out from the rest. "It's broken."

"It's *what*?"

"Broken."

"Why didn't you tell me?"

"When?"

"Before!"

"During our copious amounts of spare time? While we were running for our lives, saving Jack, or trying not to be julienned?"

"Yeah, then."

"Sorry, next time. Don't touch it!" She leaned back away from Diana's questing fingers. "I'll fix it as soon as we cross back."

"Does it hurt?" Jack wondered, coming out to the front of the glass.

Did it hurt? There were a number of things Keepers weren't permitted to say to Bystanders. But since Jack was a metaphysical construct . . .

"Diana!"

Claire closed her mouth, words unsaid, watched Sam race toward them, and sighed. Probably for the best.

". . . and then, he just vanished!"

"You accepted a challenge from the Shadowlord?"

Sam squirmed around in Diana's arms. "For the three hundredth time, I'm fine."

"You could have been killed."

"For the five hundredth time, I wasn't!"

Continuing to ignore the post-fight metaphysical analysis going on around her, Diana buried her face in Sam's fur and held on tight.

"Ow, that was a rib."

"Sorry." She loosened her hold just a little and drew in a deep breath of warm cat. He smelled like safety and comfort. Okay, scraping the clump of shed cat hair off her soft palate wasn't exactly comfortable, but still . . . She didn't know what she would have done if she'd lost him, too.

Too.

Right.

As they reached the stairs, the whole procession moving at the snail-like pace of the most seriously wounded elves, she tucked Sam back under one arm and grabbed Claire's sleeve. "Let's go."

"Diana, you have no idea how much I wish we could. While you were gone, I found out that Dean is in danger of . . ."

"Overfeeding the cat? Stepping on a hairball? Austin's with him, how much danger can he be in?"

They were facing off at the bottom of the stairs, Arthur's army breaking into two streams around them. The two elves carrying Jack set him down and leaned on the top of his frame.

"There's a three-thousand-year-old life-sucking mummy staying at the guest house."

"A three-thousand-year-old life-sucking mummy?"

"Say that three thousand times fast," Sam muttered."

"No." Diana absently stroked a marmalade shoulder and frowned at her sister. "Since when?"

"Impossible to tell with the time distortions."

"How did you . . ."

"Claire!"

Claire nodded toward the sunburned blond starting down through the climbing elves, her pack in one hand and Diana's in the other, declaiming apologies with every step. "He told me."

"Who's he?"

"Lance."

"A lot?"

Arthur stopped beside them and visibly shuddered. "Fortunately, no."

"While you were gone," Claire explained, "I went on a little tour of the Othersides and . . ."

"The Otherside's what?"

"The Othersides plural. Long story."

"Then skip it. You found him . . . ?"

"At our beach."

"The one in the guest house?"

"Yes. Longer story."

"Skip it, too."

"He's not Australian," Sam announced as Lance reached the lower concourse and set the packs down.

Diana looked confused. "Why would he be?"

The cat shrugged as well as his current position allowed. "I have no idea."

"He's a Bystander. Wait." She raised a hand cutting off Lance and Claire together. "I don't care why he's here, but as he obviously can't stay, we've got even more reason to leave immediately. He's got to go back, Dean's in danger, Kris is in *Hell*—three strikes, let's motor!"

Without the time to count to ten, Claire counted to three. "Believe me, Diana, I *want* to, but the injured elves are our responsibility."

"No, they aren't." Diana nodded toward the Immortal King. "They're his responsibility. We did our bit. The hole's closed. The segue's been disrupted, and without an anchor the two malls will continue to drift farther and farther apart. Street kids looking for a place to belong will have to look somewhere else—not necessarily a good thing but a thing. *Our* work here is done."

Claire sighed, cradling her left hand in her right. The pain in her broken finger—which was now hurting up her arm, across her shoulders and into her right ear for reasons she wasn't entirely clear on—made it difficult to concentrate, but Arthur *was* alive, Hell *had been* defeated, and the world *had been* saved from a shopping mall where midnight madness sales meant exactly that. However, while Diana had a point, she'd missed one as well. "Diana, Kris . . ."

"*Now,* Claire! Or are you tired of Dean already?"

Even the ambient noise of bells in elvish hair quieted. Lance opened his mouth. Arthur shook his head. He closed it again.

There were also a number of things Keepers didn't say to other Keepers. Claire made a mental note to say most of them to her younger sister at a later time. "I'm going to allow for the stress you're under," she said quietly. "Pick a door." Any door would take them back to the access corridor in the actual mall. The point of departure remained the point of return regardless. "Let's go home."

"Fine!" Pivoting on one heel, shifting Sam's weight against her hip, ignoring the little voice that told her she'd gone too far, Diana scanned the lower concourse stores. "There, that kid's store, the Rainbow Wardrobe. Nothing bad should come out of it."

"How responsible of you."

"Don't patronize me!"

"Fine." Claire turned toward Arthur. "The mall is no longer a segue, so we can come and go the same way we can from any other place on the Otherside. I'll be back to check on things."

The Immortal King glanced at Diana, his blue eyes sympathetic, then turned his gaze back to her. Less sympathy, more understanding, Claire noticed. "When?"

Her watch appeared to be keeping time to a rhumba beat. "Unfortunately, I have no idea."

"Claire! Now, or I'm going without you!"

Under no circumstances was Claire allowing Diana back into the world unsupervised. Even standing right beside her, it would be hard enough to keep her from making a foolish attempt to rescue Kris the moment she could manipulate the possibilities—on the other side of reality, it would be impossible. Claire picked up her pack, wrapped her good hand around Lance's arm, and hurried to join Diana at the store.

When the door flew open on its own, they stepped back together. Jumped back together. Fortunately, Lance was in hiking boots.

A sound spilled out first—like a terrified chicken being chased by a snake.

Dropping her grip on Lance, Claire shoved her hand into her belt pouch. She hadn't closed the zipper after the throne room and for one, heart-stopping moment she thought it was empty. Then her fingers closed around a peppercorn. Enough? It had to be. Releasing the contained possibilities, she yelled, "Everyone close your eyes!" as something squawked and exploded out into the lower concourse.

A moment.

Two.

Cats hunted by sound. "Sam?"

"I don't hear it."

"I can't open my eyes!"

She signed and opened hers. "Yes, you can, Lance."

"Oh, this is just great . . ." Diana would have thrown up her hands had she been willing to put Sam down. ". . . Hell's gone, and this place makes even less sense. I don't see the connection between a basilisk and a children's st . . ."

"So you're saying that while your body stayed in the room, your ka moved around sipping off bits of Dean's life and spying on us?"

Austin's voice ghosted out the open door.

"That's exactly what I'm saying. I knew everything you had planned from the instant you planned it."

"Meryat!"

Claire and Diana together grabbed Lance as he surged forward.

"Wardrobe-to-wardrobe connection?" Diana asked, brow furrowed, curiosity momentarily flattening the peaks of other emotions.

"Seems like."

"I think that fulfills my part in this foolishness, cat. I have explained, I have gloated, now I will have what I want."

The sound of a struggle.

"A valiant attempt, Dean. But you are mine."

"I don't think so, bitch!"

Diana's eyes widened as her head snapped around toward her sister. "Claire!"

"Lance . . ." Claire yanked him free of Diana's grip, her fingers dimpling his arm. Yanked him around to face her. ". . . can you stop Meryat?"

He pulled a roll of ancient linen out of his right front pocket with his free hand. "Yes!"

"Then go!"

Diana grabbed too late as Lance raced for the storefront, so she grabbed her sister's shoulder instead. "Claire, that isn't where he came in. There's no way to be sure he'll come out in your bedroom! Not without . . ." Her voice trailed off at the look on Claire's face.

Claire reached into the possibilities and set Lance's feet on a single path.

Rules broke.

Dean's hair had begun to gray.

Since it seemed to be his only remaining option, Austin launched himself from the top of the wardrobe, screaming a challenge.

Meryat swatted him aside. Lost a little flesh tone in the use of power but quickly gained it back as Dean seemed to shrink in on himself.

"Hold hard, you ancient and perfidious evil!"

Her attention lifted off Dean. "What?"

Austin muzzily wondered much the same from where he sprawled against the headboard. When *he* was a kitten, perfidious and evil meant the same thing.

Bounding out of the wardrobe, Lance twirled a line of linen across the room.

Meryat stared at him in disbelief for a heartbeat, then laughed and raised a hand. "Foolish b . . . OW!"

As the linen looped around her neck, Dean slid off the edge of the bed. It had taken everything he had left to overcome the years of training that Meryat had called his tragic flaw but, in the end, he'd managed a solid kick in the ankle. Now his back hurt, he had an intense craving for prune juice, and he couldn't actually hear what Lance was shouting. Wasn't entirely sure it was English. *That's the trouble with kids today, talk a language all their own. It's all the fault of that MT . . . Whoa.* Suddenly, he felt a lot better.

Meryat wasn't looking too good.

A finger dropped off and shattered to dust against the floor.

Lance wrapped another loop of linen around her body and kept shouting.

Another finger fell. The rest of her followed about seven syllables later.

Dean covered his mouth and nose as a fine particulate rose and settled.

"Dr. Rebik!"

The archaeologist now looked only five or six years older than his driver's license picture. Which wasn't exactly good, but he inarguably looked better than he had been.

"Lance!"

In turn, Lance no longer looked like he'd taken too many hits from a croc.

Although he still looked Australian.

As the professor and his grad student caught up, Dean stood and leaned over the bed. "You all right?"

Austin checked extremities, sneered in the general direction of the reunion, and reluctantly admitted he was fine.

"Good. I'll be after getting the vacuum, then."

❖   ❖   ❖

The sheer enormity of what her sister—her older, responsible sister—had done shouldered its way past loss and grief. Diana felt as though she was thinking clearly for the first time since Kris' sacrifice. And Claire *so* didn't want to know what she was thinking. She'd been hurt before, upset, now she was angry. "I can't *believe* you did that!"

"Believe it!"

When Rules were broken, there were consequences.

Claire slammed the door closed, counted to ten, and yanked it open. They stepped through together.

They stepped from the lower concourse into a children's clothing store.

"You've permanently warped it," Diana snapped as she tightened her hold on Sam and they ran for the next storefront.

"I had to save Dean!"

"Sure you did!" Because Claire could do what Claire wanted and too bad if anyone or what anyone else needed to do got in her way.

Jeans store.

Fabric store.

They ran past the watching elves and tried the other side of the concourse.

The doors opened only to their singular, prosaic destination.

They couldn't cross back over.

When Rules were broken, there were consequences.

Squirming free, Sam jumped up onto the edge of a planter and looked from Claire to Diana. "So, we're stuck here?"

"Looks like!" Diana's lip curled. "Because Ms. I Always Have to Have My Own Way had to save Dean at the expense of everyone else!"

"I was not going to let him die!"

Less than an arm's length between them now. Voices raised and getting louder. The mall elves started studying the tiles, the light fixtures, the cat.

"Did you even *once* think of me?" Diana snarled.

Claire snorted. "Do *you* ever think of anything but yourself?"

Sam dropped back onto the floor.

"Oh, fine talk from someone who goes on and on about sacrifice to the greater good and who just condemned my . . . condemned *Kris* to save her boyfriend!"

The shrieks of pain sounded pretty much simultaneously. In the silence that followed, Sam returned to the planter.

Claire rubbed at the blood on her ankle, looked up to see Diana doing the same, realized the tears were not from the cat scratches and reached out. "Oh, Kitten, I'm sorry."

Things got a little damp and mushy for the next few minutes, embraces awkward because of the packs but determined.

"Well done," Arthur murmured by Sam's shoulder. "I had begun to think I should intervene."

"That would have worked, too," Sam admitted. "But you probably wouldn't have liked the result."

"Oh?"

"Common enemy."

"But you . . ."

"Are a cat."

"Right."

Caught up in the circle of Claire's arm, Diana sniffled and raised her head. "You haven't called me Kitten in years."

"You started hitting me when I did it."

"Oh, yeah."

"And then you filled my bed with butterscotch pudding."

"Technically, I turned your sheets to pudding, but I can see why you stopped."

They separated slowly, wiped tears, and mirrored watery smiles.

"Rough day."

"Yeah."

"Diana, Kris . . ."

"I know. We'll save her. And I've figured out how to get us home."

"Diana, I'm not a teenager."

Diana straightened her pack straps, then bent down and scooped Sam off the floor. "Look, it's after hours, you're with a teenager and a cat, and we've got a mirror we definitely didn't pay for—it's covered."

Shunk kree. Shunk kree.

"That certainly sounds like it's covered," Claire admitted. She closed her good hand around the edge of Jack's frame. "Jack, are you sure?"

"I just want out of the mall. The guesthouse sounds fabulous and . . . Hello! Fingerprints on my glass!"

"Sorry."

Shunk kree. Shunk kree.

Sam tucked his head up under Diana's chin. "What's taking him so long?"

They were alone on the lower concourse, Arthur and the elves back in the department store in an effort to minimize time distortions. Good-byes had been perfunctory at best.

"I'll be back with Kris as soon as I find her. Now go away, or this will never work!"

Claire thought she could smell the fire, could definitely hear the music. Actually, now that the mall was nothing more than a place on the Otherside, they could probably hear the music at the Girl Guide camp. The mall elves were great kids, but she could see why Jack didn't want to stay

Shunk kree. Shunk kree.

The circle of light swept across the concourse.

Swept back.

His eyes widened as he stared at the two girls and the cat. Twenty-one years he'd been patrolling this darkness, finding the hidden ones, dragging them out to face the consequences. Girls. Boys. Young bodies. Lithe bodies. Hard bodies. All their possibilities caught and held.

They thought they were better than him. They laughed. Here, in the darkness, he made sure they stopped laughing.

Not the first time he'd caught two at once.

Not even the first cat.

The first pair with a cat. And a mirror?

Caught himself, he stared at his reflection and almost saw something stare back.

"That was unpleasant." Although she hadn't actually touched the old man, Claire wiped her fingers against her thigh as they hurried toward the nearest exit, Jack riding the possibilities behind them.

"Yeah, lots of waxy build up in there. How much did you wipe?"

"His memory of us."

"And that whole 'geeks that hunt the night' thing?"

"Couldn't touch it. It was tracked in too deep."

"That's almost . . . sad."

"Might be for the best, though; Arthur will have an easier time with the elves if they continue to face a common enemy."

"That's an interesting definition of 'for the best.'"

"Remind me to check at Children's Aid tomorrow and find out where they're holding Stewart."

"You'll send him back?"

"Of course I will. If he wants to go."

"Can't see why he would," Diana snorted. "I mean, reality's just so much more meaningful than a life you've made for yourself." Barely slowing, she popped the lock on the exit's inside door and held it open. "How's your finger," she asked as Sam raced through their legs and off the concourse.

Claire flicked it at her sister. "Good as new."

Grinning, Diana flipped a finger back as Claire dealt with the outside door. "Sam, she'd be a little faster if you weren't quite so underfoot."

"I just want to get out of here."

"I hear you." Bending, she picked him up again and rested her chin between his ears. "I'm totally web shopping from now on."

Jack glanced up at the security mirror as he passed between the doors. "Is that what I looked like on this side?"

"Pretty much, yeah."

He frowned. "Did that curvature make me look fat?"

The heat outside the mall hit them like a wet sponge.

"Oh, man, I so didn't miss this." Diana waved the hand not holding Sam between their black-on-black outfits. "And we're so not dressed for it."

"Not a problem. First, it's the middle of the night. Second, if anyone does say anything, we'll tell them we're from Toronto."

"Works. Now . . ." Deep in Diana's pack, her cell phone began to ring, the sound remarkably loud in the empty parking lot. She touched the possibilities. "That's Mom."

Claire winced. When Rules were broken, there were consequences. "I don't suppose . . ."

The ringing stopped. "Battery must've gone dead."

"Thanks."

"De nada."

"It'll be something when your mother catches up to you," Sam muttered.

Diana ignored him. "So, like I was saying; now what?"

"Home."

"The guest house?"

"Yes, because . . ."

"Because the residual power signature in the furnace room will lead us right to Kris! And you have to check on Dean and Austin," she added hurriedly as Claire's brows drew in. "I understand. But you know; two birds, one stone. Let's move!"

Claire reached into the possibilities and called a cab.

Chin resting on one hand, Dean covered a yawn with the other and watched Austin eat a sausage he wasn't supposed to have. After everything they'd been through, it was reassuringly norm . . . "Austin?"

Both ears were up. His head turned suddenly toward the front door. A heartbeat later the rest of his body followed.

With a shriek of wood against wood and a crash as his chair hit the floor and bounced, Dean followed.

Claire stepped out of the taxi and braced herself as a black-and-white streak flew down the front stairs of the guest house and into her arms. She winced as claws sank deep into both shoulders but only murmured reassurances into the top of a velvet head. After a moment, Austin calmed enough to pin her in an emerald gaze.

"Never go away for that long again!"

"I missed you, too."

"We could have been killed!"

"I'm sorry."

"If you hadn't sent Lance back . . ."

"I know."

"I had everything under control."

"Of course."

"If that's Dean I hear pounding toward you, put me down before I get crushed."

It was, so she did.

Sitting on the sidewalk, Austin finished smoothing rumpled fur and looked up to see Sam watching him, head cocked to one side. "I'll make her pay later," he said.

The younger cat nodded. "I never doubted you."

"I assume there's a story behind the whole 'dressed like they're heading out to do some second-story work'?"

"Yes."

"Well, skip it."

Diana wrestled Jack out of the back seat—bending half a dozen or so possibilities in the process—and shoved him toward the guest house as the cab roared off, the cabby remembering only the twenty percent tip. The possibilities were cheaper, but their mother had called twice more on the ride home. Once on the cabby's cell phone. Once using a phone booth near the intersection where they were waiting for the light.

Sooner or later, one of them would have to answer.

Claire would have to answer, Diana corrected glancing over at her sister and Dean. About to suggest Claire leave tonsillectomies to the medical profession, another phone rang. Actually, not another phone. Her phone. In her pack. Mom had clearly found a way around the dead battery.

At this point, the fastest route to Kris might be to answer it. While *she* hadn't broken any Rules, at this point in the proceedings, she was likely to catch just as much Hell. Leaning Jack carefully against the porch railing, Diana slipped off her pack and began to search for her cell. Finding it at last under a tunaless tuna sandwich, her thumb was poised over the connect button when the sound of squealing tires drew all eyes to the street.

A minivan pulled up in front of the guest house and stopped on a dime. With a tinkle of nine cents' change hitting the pavement, the side door opened and a familiar body exploded out onto the sidewalk.

"Freakin' OW!"

"Kris!" Diana raced forward as the van roared away. Throwing herself to her knees, she gathered the crumpled body of the elf up into her arms. "Kris say something!"

Kris blinked, and looked around. "This is Hell?"

"No, this is Kingston!"

She was still holding the wand, now flaccid and more puce than pink. "I was falling and this is where I landed."

"You were in a minivan."

"No. I think I'd remember that. Cavern. Falling. Pink stuff. Here."

Diana twisted around to stare at Claire.

"I kept trying to tell you." She leaned back against Dean's chest and wrapped herself in the safety of his arms. "Rule one . . ."

"The possibilities are not to be used to bring in HBO?" Diana asked, unable to see the relevance.

"Okay, rule two. Hell can't hold a willing sacrifice. It couldn't hold Kris any more than it could hold Dean."

"And you tried to tell me that?"

"A couple of times."

Diana's heart felt like it was beating normally for the first time in days. "Next time, try harder."

"You guys want to keep it quiet out there!" The voice drifted down from one of the surrounding windows, open because of the heat. "It's three in the morning and some of us are trying to sleep!"

"You want to sleep?" Claire reached into the possibilities.

"Then sleep." Diana added her two cents' worth as she helped Kris to her feet.

From where Diana had dropped it at the base of the steps, the phone began ringing again. She looked at Claire. Claire took a step forward, turned, and looked at Dean. Who took two steps sideways and brought his work boot down as hard as he could. Sam batted the pieces down into the area by the basement door.

"Might as well be hung for a sheep as a lamb," Claire said with satisfaction.

"I could go for some lamb," Austin murmured as he followed Sam up the stairs.

"I don't know about lamb," Diana sighed as she led Kris into the guest house, "but I could eat."

Claire waved Jack in ahead of them—time for introductions when there was less chance of being overheard—and laid her head on Dean's shoulder as he slipped an arm around her waist. They climbed the stairs together. "Where's Lance?"

"He and Dr. Rebik are . . . Uh . . . Sleeping."

A half turn, and she could see his ears were pink. "Sleeping?"

"Probably. By now."

"What?"

His eyebrows made an appearance above the upper edge of his glasses.

"Oh. Happy endings all around, then."

"Well, Dr. Rebik definitely lost a few years and Lance—actually, since I wasn't after knowing him before, I don't want to assume . . ."

"Happy endings," Claire repeated, leaving no room for postgame analysis.

"Yeah."

"Good. I want to hear everything that happened while I was gone, but for right now, there's just one thing I have to know."

He kissed the top of her head as they stepped over the threshold. "What's that?"

"What were you doing with a basilisk in the bedroom?"

The door closed on his answer.

From King Street came the faint sound of a minivan being pulled over by the police.

And for the first time in days, a cool breeze blew in off the lake.